AGENT PROVOCATEUR

A FLIGHT OF FANCY

JEFFERY LEE SATTERFIELD

authorHOUSE®

AuthorHouse™
1663 Liberty Drive
Bloomington, IN 47403
www.authorhouse.com
Phone: 1-800-839-8640

© 2010 Jeffery Lee Satterfield. All rights reserved.

No part of this book may be reproduced, stored in a retrieval system, or transmitted by any means without the written permission of the author.

First published by AuthorHouse   3/12/2010

ISBN: 978-1-4490-9776-9 (e)
ISBN: 978-1-4490-9775-2 (sc)
ISBN: 978-1-4490-9774-5 (hc)

Library of Congress Control Number: 2010903177

Printed in the United States of America
Bloomington, Indiana

This book is printed on acid-free paper.

AIR SHIP THAT SAILS
California Invention Makes a Long Trip at Night
... About 1 o'clock last Monday morning the inhabitants of Sacramento, who were astir at that hour, claim to have seen an airship passing rapidly over the city. Some merely said they saw a bright light, while others went so far as to say they saw a cigar-shaped flying machine ... The residents of Oakland also say they saw the same sight.
— *Washington Post*, November 23, 1896

SCIENTIFIC NOTES AND NEWS
There is, it appears, in San Francisco, an incorporated Atlantic and Pacific Aerial Navigation Co., which proposes to build a large airship and has, at all events, purchased from the Pittsburg Reduction Company a quantity of aluminium.
— *Science* (New Series). v. V, no. 110 (February 5, 1897)

TOPICS OF THE TIMES
That mysterious airship which some months ago disturbed the minds – or dreams – of people living in the far West has appeared again, this time at Omaha. The vessel ... seems to be making its way eastward by easy flights ... One Omaha observer says: "We thought at first it was a balloon, but if there is such a thing as an airship, I believe now that this was one ..."
— *New York Times*, March 19, 1897

LIVE TOPICS OF TODAY
Recently there has been much perturbation among the credulous people of Missouri and Kansas in regard to an alleged airship that has been seen plowing through the ether for several evenings ... Some will have it that the machine is one sent out by the British government, filled with spies ... Others say that it is the device of a Kansas City inventor who is trying out the contrivance before selling it to a syndicate for several billions of dollars, and one skeptical individual suggested that it might be a lantern on the tail of a kite, but he was instantly suppressed and barely escaped a coat of tar and feathers for his temerity.
— *Chicago Tribune*, April 1, 1897

SAW STARS INSTEAD OF AIRSHIP
Thomas B. Fluke climbed on the roof of 1515 Chestnut Street early Wednesday morning to see the airship. He lost his balance and fell to the ground. He had a rib fractured and one of his ankles sprained. He was put in plaster of paris and went home.
— *St. Louis Post Dispatch*, April 14, 1897

TOPICS OF THE TIMES
Airship stories are now coming in from Irondequoit, a town close to Rochester, and not far enough from New York to enable one to believe that the metropolis will much longer be spared the epidemic which has worked such havoc in the West . . .
— *New York Times*, April 19, 1897

EDISON SCOFFS AT THE AIRSHIP
Says that it is all a fake and that at best such machines are only toys.
"I have no doubt that airships will be successfully constructed in the near future, but there has been too much talk about this supposed airship out west . . . It is absolutely absurd to imagine that a man would construct a successful airship and keep the matter secret . . . When an airship is made it . . . will be a mechanical contrivance, which will be raised by means of a very powerful motor, which much be made of a very light weight. At present no one has discovered such a motor, but we never know what will happen. We may wake up tomorrow morning and hear of some invention . . . Their success may come."
— Thomas Edison, quoted in the *Chicago Tribune*, April 20, 1897

WIRELESS TELEGRAPHY
. . . Very recently Mr. Tesla has announced that he has completed his wireless telegraph to such an extent as to permit of telegraphy through the earth for a distance of 20 miles or more, and his experiments satisfy him of the feasibility of wireless telegraphy on a much more extended scale . . . While Mr. Tesla has been wrestling with this great problem . . . Mr. Marconi, a young Anglo-Italian, has been working on the same line in England . . .
— *Scentific American*, June 19, 1897, v. LXXVI, no. 25

We'll daily pray, we'll nightly pray
On Bended knees most fervently,
That the time may come, with pipe an' drum,
We'll welcome hame fair ALBANIE

Robert Burns, "The Bonnie Lass of Albanie"

PROLOGUE:
June 21, 1897
Just Before Midnight

"Okay, Strangways. Toss out the shovel."

Herron Strangways hurled the shovel from the grave he had just dug for himself at gunpoint.

The man motioned with his pistol. "You next. Out of the hole."

The second murderer demanded, "Why git 'im out once he's in it?"

"He might duck down when I shoot, dunce. Let's make it easy on *us* and not waste more than one shot. Get up here, Strangways."

Herron hadn't thought to dig steps for walking up out of a grave. Squirming over the rim of the pit, he toyed briefly with the idea of diving for the shovel, knocking the first man's pistol away with it, and braining the other fellow.

Unfortunately, the men were standing too far apart. Only one actually had a gun trained on him, but both men were armed. Herron might take one of them to the grave with him, but the other would kill him just as dead. Besides, he'd thrown the shovel too far away.

"Kneel on the ground with your head over the hole. It'll be cleaner."

Reaching into his inner coat pocket, the second murderer stepped toward Herron. "Let me do 'im Jake."

"You had the first go yesterday – and your performance was less than adequate. I get first crack today."

"That wasn't fair. I didn't get a clear shot at 'im."

"You get first shot next time. We agreed on the strict rotation."

The second man drew a greasy deck of playing cards from his dungarees. "Cut you for him."

The man with the gun rolled his eyes. "Just stand by and apply the *coup de grace*. I doubt we'll need it. I've potted smaller birds with one bullet."

"Hey!" said Herron, "Don't I get a blindfold and a cigarette?"

"This is not a firing squad, Mister Strangways. It is an execution."

"Yeah," echoed the other man, snorting a chuckle through his nose, "where do you think you are, a firing squad or sumpin'?"

"You've wasted enough of our time. Besides, I do not smoke, so I have no cigarettes on me. And my friend has none ready-made. Just try to relax. Stare into the pit and it'll all be over before you can say Jack Robinson."

"And I'll do the cootie-grah," said the other.

As Herron knelt and extended his head over the hole that would be his home for the rest of eternity, he realized the man with the twisted moustache had been right about one thing – if only one.

No cavalry was riding to rescue him at the last moment. Neither Jessup, nor the Major, nor that Inspector Chubb who had been trying to get him jugged for the last two days, could help. No one on earth knew where he was except the men who had brought him here expressly to kill him.

After three days of almost constant movement, Herron felt he deserved a good, long rest. He was just about to be put to one.

His only hope was that *she* would get through with the key to the whole mess.

Not that it'll do me any good. And the "key" to the whole mess hadn't made sense, even when they cracked the code. Herron was literally and figuratively going to his grave in the dark.

As he heard the large pistol being cocked, Herron decided—yes, on the whole, this was a particularly rotten Monday.

And the week-end had not been much fun, either.

Saturday, June 19, 1897

CHAPTER I

When Herron Strangways saw a man struck and killed by a locomotive, he thought it made the perfect end to a perfectly beastly day.

More importantly, it appeared to end his prospects of wangling an introduction to the pretty young lady standing nearby.

Tall – she came up to Herron's shoulder and he was six feet and a bit. Slender – in the right places (the brown cloak she wore to ward away soot made it impossible for him to accurately triangulate her contours). Golden-brown hair – the color of perfectly prepared toast – piled on her head and pinned under a straw hat cocked over one eye.

Might there come a time, he wondered, studying the her hair through his monocle, when he'd gaze down and see it spread out on a pillow?

A surreptitious glance from her almond-shaped eyes (green, he thought, but the light was confoundedly dim) confirmed that she noticed him notice her.

She flashed a devastating smile at him – then proceeded to ignore him in that calculated way of a woman who'd like to know a man better.

From the moment he set eyes on her, Herron tried to connive a scheme to introduce himself, using whatever means lay at hand.

The closest means appeared to be an old fossil in a Bath chair.

The young lady had pushed the woman in the Bath chair through the crowd. Parking the chair near the front of the platform and braking it, she stood before it like a sentry; so Herron deduced a connection between the two ladies.

They made a startling contrast.

The doyen was all wrinkles and liver spots. Her frowning lips rendered her countenance faintly amphibian. She worsened her appearance with a small, black bonnet wreathed with silk bows and topped by four black, knife-like feathers stabbing up like the plumes of a horse pulling a hearse.

The older lady's frame was petite. Her black dress, trimmed with deep violet, was so bulky she seemed to be bombazine clear through. Clearly a woman who valued jewelry by its size, she dotted her mourning clothes with gaudy brooches.

Every stone the old lady wore appeared genuine.

Her colors and jewelry suggested she was in half-mourning, that final furlong of grief when the bereaved is thundering down the straight toward the finish line.

The woman's grief, as grief, was inconsequential to Herron. Since he did not recognize the lady, he was unable to use commiseration as a tactic to finagle an introduction to her protégé (i.e., *"My dear Mrs. So-and-so, I knew your husband/sister/son/poodle so very well"*). He had gained much success with ladies of all ages through the clever manipulation of mourning.

He could not simply stare at unknown ladies of any age in a public place. Women had set the police to dog him home on less provocation.

Fixing his soft, brown eyes on neither lady, in his peripheral vision Herron caught the older lady fiddling with a tawdry parasol on a shortish bamboo pole.

Considering that a family of four in the East End of London might have lived comfortably for years off the proceeds from her jewelry, the parasol was chintzy. And its handle was loose. She twisted it this way and that; then, finally, she brought it to her eye and peered down it, as if she were about to call, *"Land Ho!"*

Herron pocketed this information for later use. She might have been a short-sighted lady too proud to wear glasses. Myopia might help him ingratiate himself with a grande dame by imposture.

Then again, the most likely explanation of her behavior was that she had a few shingles loose in the attic.

In either case, Herron felt life was too short to waste eyeballing wizened ladies.

And life was certainly too short to let a treasure like the younger lady slip from view-halloo without his concocting some scheme, however drastic, to trail her. He felt like an astronomer who had just spotted a new planet. He could not let her swim out of view without marking her place in the heavens.

Herron was a very good swimmer; had they been on a pier rather than in an enclosed Underground railway station, he might have shoved her into the sea just to leap in and rescue her from drowning.

Nudging through the hordes on the platform, Herron sidled casually closer to the two ladies, keeping the younger lady in sight while pretending not to notice her. He acted like he was being pressed inexorably toward her, against his will, by the force of the crowd.

After creeping stealthily through the undergrowth, he sprang to his full height immediately downwind of her with both his hands before him on the ivory knob of his stick. He stood so close, they looked like they were about to sing a duet.

For her part, she stood demurely swinging her reticule behind her. After the first exchange of glances, for all the notice she took of him he might have been nothing more than a sudden lamppost.

Having stolen within range of his quarry, Herron considered his options.

His preferred method at this jucture was to bait ladies into speaking first to him – but how? That often took time, and time was precious. The train was due any moment and might, by some miracle, be on schedule.

He aimed his monocle down the track, as if peering for an ersatz incoming train or two. Edging next to her, then looking away, camouflaged his motives, making it appear the purest coincidence they were standing side-by-side.

This momentary respite helped him marshal his thoughts.

Perhaps he could slip a clandestine calling-card into her reticule . . . ?

No. He rejected that approach. Underground train stations were foul-smelling holes filled with the noxious fumes of enclosed locomotives and the hardy British workman. Yet, he was close enough to her to get a whiff of her fragrance. Any young lady who wore that scent, with it almost imperceptible suggestion of gardenias, was far too refined for such a blatant invitation.

That single, sly glance, that coy flash of smile, suggested she was a woman who would be irked at being taken for granted. Finding an unsolicited calling-card in her reticule, she might rip it to shreds and dance on its remains. Though she might, upon reflection, desperately sift through the rubbish to piece the card together again, her anger might not cool until the dustmen had emptied the bins.

It's these wretched days we live in, Herron sighed, bitterly. Even in this technologically advanced year of 1897, one did not speak directly to a female to whom one had not been introduced, unless she was a streetwalker.

That's why *the game* was necessary.

Oh, the direct approach had reaped benefits, and with ladies of good name, both the married and the un-. But Herron's vast experience suggested that was the wrong approach for *her*.

He recognized her fighting spirit. Whether for the sake of propriety, or simply because she enjoyed *the game* as much as he, she would make him battle for dear life over every inch of ground. She struck him as the sort of woman who played *the game* well, and by her own, peculiar set of rules.

Rules were vital, and to survive *the game* one had to locate the boundary markers quickly. Once the rules were set, Herron rigidly observed them – calling anything "fair" that was not explicitly spelled out beforehand as out-of-bounds.

No "Hoyle" existed for this game. It had infinite variations, and each game had its own etiquette. It might be fast and exciting, like roulette. It might be slow and methodical, like chess. A few times, Herron gambled everything at once, as if risking his entire fortune on a single throw of the dice.

Always the gentleman, Herron yielded right of way for the ladies to establish their unique "house rules." Then he proceeded to outmaneuver them, even when they changed rules in mid-play – as so many of them did.

He had once played *the game*, by a woman's fluctuating rules, for more than a year before his own hand was strong enough for him to call her bluff.

He won. And, he liked to think, so had she.

That year had not been a drought, otherwise. No juggler worthy of the name keeps only one ball in the air at a time.

The women established the rules of play, but the first serve was up to Herron.

His first move was always an exchange of glances. Herron had batted his brown eyes across the train station at her. By returning his serve with a wily smile, she showed she knew what she was doing.

More importantly, she knew what *he* was doing.

They were off.

After her counter-gambit, she acted so completely oblivious to him, Herron realized he was in the presence of a worthy opponent. Well, the more prowess the other player displayed defending the goal, the better he liked it.

And from what he could discern in this poor lighting, she was worth keeping the game alive for a record stretch. Her poise was self-assured; her expression, ethereally calm.

He knew her type. He had played their games often. If accosted by a strange man in a public place, even if her eyes were saying *come in unto me*, she would return such a withering come-back Herron might have to limp home in a crouch.

Their sort, with their pleasantly smiling poker faces, played their little games beautifully. It was harder gauging their rules, however; and just at the showdown, they invariably produced Aces they'd hidden in their petticoats.

He relished that sort of game. It was no fun to win too easily.

After all, *the game* was played on both sides for the same stakes. Whether he won on her terms on or his made no difference to Herron. He often cheated and let the woman win. They both won, in the end, and it was often a more exciting finish to hole out when the woman thought she had won the match her way.

When Herron played *the game*, he perceived no degrees of victory. Whether he divested a woman of her all clothing or only got them half-off made no difference to him. A mere kiss on the lips was as substantial an achievement as a view of her bedchamber. Even if he got no farther, he thrilled at a surreptitious touch of fingers as she passed a plate of sandwiches at tea.

Not getting past the first volley of eyeballs, however, was failure. The challenger was proving her mettle with every tick of the clock. If the train slid alongside the platform before he got the ball rolling on *the game*, she would believe he was an unworthy of her. He was determined not to let that happen.

Sneaking a glance at the doyen over his off-side shoulder, Herron decided she might take so much as a "Hello" as tantamount to a sexual assault. She looked like the type who would carry a police whistle, and might be just dotty enough to use it. He could sense watchful eyes glaring out from their folds.

The old lady was a course hazard. Herron didn't want to get the younger lady in trouble of any kind, or himself, so he had to negotiate over or around her. Whatever his plans for meeting the young lady he first had to leap her as the first obstacles. She turned what might have been a dash into a steeplechase.

Maintaining the pretense that he had merely blundered up beside the younger lady by accident in the crush, he drubbed his brains for any way to manufacture an introduction acceptable to the umpire.

If he only recognized the doyen! He could let the ladies go their way tonight without any further notice on his part (leaving the young lady wondering—always good gamesmanship).

The moment they were out of sight, Herron would begin hacking a path, however torturous, through friends in common until he arrived on their doorstep with a letter of introduction.

But both ladies were utter strangers to him. The elder lady must be *somebody*, and he silently cursed himself for not being a devotee of the Society pages. He had an aunt well up in the Society tree; but she disapproved of his lifestyle and she would be no help at all in helping him track his game.

He dared not look directly at the young lady again. He had absorbed her thoroughly, in his excellent memory. He'd made his first move. She had answered it positively – but unhelpfully. He was amazed at how well she had played so far. Ever since that initial meeting of eyes and her first, encouraging, smile, she had acted like he wasn't even there. *Cagy minx.*

The next move was entirely his. And his next step must be carefully chosen.

Before proceeding, therefore, Herron paused to make a few deductions.

While gliding through the thicket of people, Herron had marked nothing of mourning about the young lady – not so much as a black arm-band or a black bow on her high-topped button-shoes.

From that, he deduced she probably was *not* the older woman's daughter. In fact, she probably did not even know the deceased.

Her youthful ebullience and pleasant smile also indicated she was a post-bereavement acquisition. Anyone who had been with *that* dowager lady for long would wear a careworn, defeated appearance. Her perfectly-poised shoulders would slump and her graceful neck would crane under a weight of vexation.

Herron mentally flipped through a variety of plausible relationships between the two ladies.

Since she was pushing the old lady about in a Bath chair, she might be a poor –with luck, extremely *distant* – relation, working for the old lady for a promise of a mention in the will.

She might be a ward, held against her volition in the old woman's clutches by legal bonds – a Cinderella with a fashion allowance.

In the rosiest scenario, she was an unrelated paid companion, wheeling the doyen around in public and reading to her in private from thick romantic novels with extremely fine print.

Of course, it didn't matter a hang to Herron whether she was the old lady's daughter or her merest hireling. He did not care if she was rich or poor. Herron was totally republican in his sentiment. He was above class-distinctions.

All women – whether they were the daughters of the blue-bloods or the lowest scullions in service, whatever their coloring or pigmentation, whatever their height or weight – were equal in the eyes of Herron Strangways, so long as they were pretty and over the age of consent.

Chancing one quick, sidelong glance at the younger of the duo, he perceived it was more than her sprightly good looks that drew such a sharp distinction between her and her charge. Her whole attitude was spring to the dowager's winter. Her smile beamed into that cavernous Underground station like a shaft of fresh sunlight after rain. She seemed to have no guile in her.

She must practice that sincerity in her mirror for hours a day!

Well, if she was Cinderella, she did have a good couturier.

Beneath her cape she was dressed simply but tastefully in earthy hues. A sprightly fawn dress reached from her wasp waist to her button-shoes. Her cream-colored blouse puffed out at the shoulders, and around her throat was a brown, ribbon string tie. Over her blouse she wore a short, bolero-cut coat; fawn, like her skirt, with a gold decorative border.

The coat was cut so short, it would not pull together in front. And for good reason. Between the blouse and the coat, a russet, feminine waistcoat bound her delectable breasts as tight as sausages.

Herron wanted to play Abe Lincoln; like the great Republican president, he wanted to free them from their bondage.

He slapped himself back. *Look no farther ahead than the next step.*

She was dressed beautifully, but Herron disapproved of her hat. It was a tasteful boater-type straw hat, embellished only by a long red-white-and-blue ribbon. That was satisfactory, so far as it went.

Once, after a night of merrymaking, Herron had been terrified by a woman's hat fitted with an enormous swooping bird. Ever since, he was gratified by restraint in female *chapeaux*.

But this hat's brim, angled at a fetching slant over one eye and an ear, shadowed the beauty on that side of her face in this lighting.

Herron *assumed* her beauty was symmetrical; but he learned the arts of female legerdemain through ten years of ceaseless study. He knew how women plucked out, propped up and painted over. A single corset might mask untold horrors.

He did not blame the women – those were all legitimate course hazards. But after what he had witnessed, the hat roused his suspicions.

For all he could tell, the hat might disguise a huge, purple birthmark.

He factored the birthmark into his calculations. Its possibility did not unduly distress him – the most successful endgames invariably occurred in the dark.

But lots of daylight remained between now and then, and he knew from hard experience how difficult it was to forever dodge round a woman to keep her best profile toward him.

With fawn gloves buttoned up her wrists beneath the tight sleeves of her blouse, and her long neck sheathed in a high collar, her only visible flesh was the appetizing morsel not shaded by her hat.

Herron thought she was the most beautiful woman he'd ever seen, recently. And that was saying a lot.

2

Tomorrow, Sunday, was the very day of Queen Victoria's Diamond Jubilee. That Gracious Lady had been on her throne for sixty years. And millions of tourists had flocked to London to celebrate with her.

For weeks, beautiful women from all nations had surged around Herron in the streets, at the theaters and restaurants, on the 'buses and in the trains.

Dusky Indian maidens with darkly luminous eyes; robust Canadians; ivory-skinned Orientals whose sable hair appeared as soft as the silks they came wrapped in; Irish colleens with richly freckled cheeks on rosy complexions, like fresh strawberries—

—and, best and worst of all, Americans and Australians who, for some unfathomable reason, claimed to share a common language with the English.

Admittedly, American and Australian women were gorgeous. Herron had a deep and heart-felt appreciation for every one of them. Americans especially.

The American melting-pot fused every variety of humanity and spewed forth a plethora of female pulchritude. A recent tour of America left Herron dazzled that so many women from one country could be so diverse, yet all so lovely.

But their accents could stop him with the force of a bullet.

He could bear, often without a shiver, the long, southern-American vowels.

New England women were to be kissed quickly and often because one can't kiss and talk simultaneously (though many American women tried).

Mid-westerners were as flat in tone as their plains. Oh, midwestern women usually compensated for flat voices by other intriguing elevations, but their intonations had choked many promising young games in their cradles.

As for Australians . . . their language was shocking. Beautiful—ye gods! And delightful down under. Herron never regretted playing an Australian woman's game, win, lose or draw. But God alone knew what they were talking about. He never comprehended a blind word they were chewing. Herron liked to kiss Australian women with tongues, to keep them from speaking in them.

For weeks, women from all over an Empire the sun never set on had swarmed like bees around Herron's hive in London. If he noticed the international smorgasbord of beauty, he might have believed he was in "paradise enow" as the Persian expressed it. "A bottle of Chateau Lafite Rothschild '75, a Camembert, and a million thous beside me in the municipal parks."

For he genuinely loved women and actually preferred their company to that of men. To Herron, each woman was as individual as a snowflake, while men were as alike to him as snowfalls.

Some men with Herron's satyric proclivities sought only their personal gratification. They cared for, what they callously termed, their "conquests" no more than a turkey they might have been stuffing. Their interest was not personal so much as gynecological.

Starting his lengthy tour of America, Herron found New York harbor a fascinating port of entry; and he had enjoyed every moment he spent in it. Yet beyond the waterfront lay a vast continent worth a thorough exploration. He felt the same way about women. He liked to forge deep into their interiors. Each was special. Whatever transpired, Herron felt enriched by every individual woman who shimmered through his life.

Even when *the game* ended by their checkmating him. When that happened, he felt more sorrow for her loss than his. After all, he knew other women he could turn to for solace—but there was only one Herron Strangways.

Yet, with so many souls in London these past few weeks, singling out individual females was like choosing one particularly fragrant flower from a field of millions. Not one notable new face had glimmered through his monocle in a fortnight. The flavor of his favorite dish had died from his tongue. He was so inundated with beauty he no longer noticed it.

Rather than viewing the bounty of visitors as a way to sharpen his gaming skills by learning new rules of play from women of various cultures, Herron resented every last one of them. As a lifelong Londoner, born within the sound of Big Ben, he regarded them as poachers on his private preserve.

And he was sick to death of the Diamond Jubilee. For months it had been "Jubilee this" and "Jubilee that." He had been surrounded by Jubilee plates, Jubilee books, Jubilee tea towels, Jubilee handkerchiefs – and even more grisly "commemorative" rubbish. And so much of it bearing the Queen's pudgy image (except the hankies, which were Union Jacks—too bad, for Herron would dearly have loved blowing his nose on Her Majesty).

He knew all the Jubilee folderol intimately. His chain of stores, *Strangways' Emporia*, had shoveled it in. And it was selling briskly. Herron could not look the gruesome merchandise in the eye, but he felt no twinge of conscience about trafficking in it. Someone wanted his tacky commemorative wares, he wanted their cash. So long as he gave value for money and it was an exchange that left both parties satisfied, Herron didn't care what his stores sold.

He only hoped he was sloughing most of it off to Americans and Australians and Canadians and Indians, so he'd never have to set eyes on it again.

After months of build-up to the Jubilee, the crushing and crowing and merchandising had become indigestible.

For the last week Herron had considered seeking asylum as a refugee abroad until the Jubilee blew safely over. Dropping all his engagements, he would leave this London bursting its seams with gorged human flesh and make a tour of the continent. Judging by the number of people in London, he assumed every other European country was empty and he could rattle around the continent as solitary as a pea in a whistle.

Then – in, of all places, a murky, smoky Underground train station – Herron discovered the positive side of a surplus population. Had it not been for the overcrowding on the platform, he might never have been jostled close enough to notice this young lady – in this lighting, under that hat.

And Herron was more than a trifle peeved that she had waited until practically the last moment to emerge from hiding. Some of the worst weeks of his life might have been numbered among his best.

But he could raise that point with her later. His immediate quandary: how to keep from losing her. It was vital that he make contact immediately.

The woman in the Bath chair looked thoroughly, not to say offensively, British; but, for all he knew, she had arrived from any port in eleven million square miles of Empire, and she would leave London – with her companion in tow – after Tuesday's Diamond Jubilee Procession.

And this was Saturday! Scouring a supersaturated London for a half-glimpsed face in three days was inconceivable. Even if they stayed on for next Sunday's naval review at Spithead, the extra days would hardly make a difference.

This staggeringly lovely young lady might leave London forever in three days, returning to Hong Kong, Pondicherry, Sydney, Vancouver or Zanzibar. Beautiful names for beautiful places where beautiful females might go to earth and never be seen again. Even if he picked up her scent later. Unlike chess, a satisfactory game of this nature could not be played by mail.

Daring another sidelong glance—her features struck him as deucedly familiar. *Yet he neither knew nor recognized her.* Had he ever seen her before?

He never forgot a single face of any woman with whom he had played *the game*. He did this to keep cherished memories—and also for his own protection. Because of his good nature, he remained friends with nearly all the women he had played with. Remaining friends was good policy. And it was possible since he preferred the sort of women who knew the score going in. He liked females whose parents or guardians had told them *all about men*, meaning things which applied only to a few like Herron Strangways. They played with him instead of against him, and always for the same goal. Oh, Herron was broad-minded enough to take under his wing a few who had a lot to learn. And he had taught them well. The green ones were often the most fun once they started to ripen.

And Herron rigidly refused to play with the sort of woman who, when a romance ended, served herself a swig of Prussic acid or a drop of hemp. Suicide sounded romantic to certain unhinged females who read too much Shakespeare; but inquests were invariably dreary affairs, and Herron meant to avoid them.

All his women were alive, and nearly all were pals.

Nevertheless, on certain occasions he dived into alleys and squatted behind dustbins when he saw familiar faces approaching. A few ladies never accepted the end of a romance, and whenever they met Herron they tried to unearth and revivify its rotting corpse. He ducked round corners when he saw them coming.

So, he remembered all of their faces. And most of their other parts, as well.

And he was *virtually* certain he had never enjoyed the company of this woman, who was so preternaturally lovely she sparkled as a singularly bright jewel in a long, black-velvet counter.

Or was it her dreary setting? Were the dingy surroundings of an Underground station required for the comparative beauty of this half-glimpsed face?

No. On occasion, the women he'd played the game with "seemed like a good idea at the time." Not this time. He was in the presence of an enchantress, and his heart yearned for her enchantment.

He *knew* he had never been introduced to this woman. If he had ever set eyes on her before, there might never have been another game. He could never have topped perfection. Win or lose, he'd have retired his lance from the field.

Yet . . . her face was confoundedly familiar. If only he could remember *where* or *when* she had crossed his path, he might use that as an entrée into her society.

For her part, she offered no hint of recognition. After that first smile, she paid him no more mind than she paid the columns supporting the roof.

Clever, he thought, admiringly. *She's the best*. If he could only nail an introduction, he thought he might just have the ride of his life.

3

Introduction, he scolded himself. *Think, Herrie.*

Thrusting his suspicion of *deja vu* to the back of his mind, Herron hastily mapped out a plan of campaign directed at the dowager. Despite a rising gorge, Herron had to chat up the frog-fossil first.

Wheedling an introduction might prove easy enough. Bath chairs, with two big wheels behind and one small wheel in front steered by a tiller by the occupant, were clumsy contraptions. For all her femininity, the young lady undoubtedly possessed strong shoulders and arms to push it along; but when trains puffed into stations and passengers boarded, men's arms were needed to load invalids.

Herron would step in amongst the porters to assist the ladies, pretending he was simply doing his Good Samaritan routine. Like a knight of old, he'd be helping a lady in distress. (He doubted the knights would approve. He wouldn't be helping the lady, but the dragon.)

From a knight, Herron would transform himself into a magician. Holding the older lady spellbound with one hand, with the other he would spin out his conjuring trick of seducing the younger.

He never considered failure. Herron's greatest initial advantages – which he realized all too well – were good looks and his charm. Whatever "white" lies he used to worm his way into a woman's affections, he was rigorously honest with himself. He never underestimated his winsome appeal for ladies of all ages.

Including staid older ladies with faces like topographic maps of Tibet.

Herron had a position to uphold as the proprietor of one of the largest privately-owned firms in the Empire, so he dressed conservatively: frock coat; dark suit set off by a silver watch-chain and jeweled fob; high, silk hat; pearl-grey gloves; stick with genuine ivory knob; monocle.

His funereal attire appealed to any mothers, aunts, and guardians shallow enough to believe that clothes made the man. A mother looking out for her daughter's morals would be inclined to trust a man dressed like Herron Strangways. This rang even more true with old ladies whose wards or paid companions were less dear than daughters.

And "trust" . . . meant *leverage.*

It was simple for a good-looking, noticably wealthy, appropriately-dressed young man to talk his way around dowager ladies.

Once he had contrived to meet the elder lady by assisting her onto her train, he would become her earnest disciple. He understood that women of her type doted on ears. Believing they had a hoard of good advice, they liked nothing better than being listened at by young people.

And they were so easily gulled into believing handsome young men were interested in *them*. They all fancied they had been the belles of Society in the dark ages at the beginning of the old Queen's reign, and nothing in Heaven or Earth could persuade them that sixty years had dulled their allure. Even ladies who could barely walk penciled Herron Strangways in on their dance cards.

Yes, Herron concluded, the best way to wedge his foot into the door of this *menage* was by shoving it in through the old lady.

They were *simpatico*. Timeworn beldams and conceited young *boulevardiers* like Herron had one favorite topic of conversation in common: themselves.

Possessing a lazy man's infinite patience, Herron was skilled at listening to elder ladies while make sly eyes at daughters, wards and paid companions.

The doyen might accept Herron on his looks alone—but Herron was too meticulous to leave anything to chance. He had to establish a tangible connection between them.

Didn't we meet at So-and-so's garden party?

That was usually a safe bet. Females of the fossil's geologic age never recalled everyone they had been introduced to, especially at garden parties. Herron would subtly imprint a memory of himself on her mind's eye.

If she said, *I've never been to a garden party at So-and-so's; she hasn't a garden, that I'm aware of,*

Herron would counter by snapping his fingers and responding, *No, not So-and-so . . . I mean . . . oh, what was the name?*

She would prompt, *Thus-and-so?*

Herron would take the bait. *Thus-and-so! Of course, how stupid of me.*

And the dowager would complacently conclude, *Thus-and-so is So-and-so's sister*, or cousin, or—

In an inbred aristocracy, the greasy chain of kinship could stretch *ad infinitum*. Whatever name Herron mentioned, a Society dame of so many years would find (or invent) a relationship to someone she knew intimately.

Herron would then apologize abjectly for his confusion.

Oh, please don't fret about it, the ancient one would reply, in a confidential tone. *I sometimes confuse things myself.*

Tickled at the evidence of her superior memory, she and Herron would become fast friends. (Herron firmly believed that women of all ages became fast friends with a man whenever they were convinced they had the upper hand. It was a always good ploy to let them have the illusion of an upper hand first thing off the starting block.)

Next, Herron would up the ante by producing his calling-card.

Herron Strangways.

Playing her hand close to the vest, she would venture, *Are you related to Strangways' Emporium?*

That's when he would play his high card. *I am Strangways' Emporia. Plural, for we are Legion.*

Oh, she would say, impressed by a new aura from the glow of his wealth, *but you're so young. I was buying things there when I was just a wee mite of a girl.*

Throttling back the urge to say *That must have been a long time ago, indeed,* Herron would explain that his grandfather had been the first Strangways' Emporia, but Herron now ran the show.

(Actually, Herron took little interest in the day-to-day running of the business. His Emporia were managed by a dour Scot aptly named Grouse, who was as scrupulously honest as he was irritable. Herron had been carefully drilled in business and economics by his father as well as any military on parade. He was taught economics with a razor strop applied to the seat of learning. He could have run the firm successfully. He simply preferred not to, when there were so many fun things to do for a young man in the spring-time of life – which he believed ought to last until he was at least sixty-three.)

This exchange would establish that Herron, while technically of the *hoi-polloi*, was richer than most of the nobility – and therefore receivable in any home.

Eleazer Strangways, Herron's father, firmly believed the Queen had been on the point of bestowing a knighthood on him for his economic services to the Crown. Then, he had inconsiderately dropped dead before the honor arrived. The business fell into Herron's lap, but not the honor.

A pity, Herron thought. *"Sir Herron" would look good on my calling-cards.*

It was unlikely he'd ever receive the *Sir* by anything he did with his own, two mitts (he had no interest in playing *the game* with the Queen). Herron considered adding his *per annum* to the card, but decided that might be overreaching. Though that was all Society women cared about. The better ones, anyway.

In Herron's profoundly confident mind, by the time they swapped calling-cards the connection between himself and the dowager was a *fait accompli*.

From that point forward, Herron would pretend to be interested in *her*, to listen to *her*, to give *her* his undivided attention.

After their exchange of eyes on the platform, the younger lady would stew in jealousy that this tall, rich, handsome, *eligible* young man was giving all his attention to a woman old enough to be dead.

By long trial and error, Herron knew just how long to keep a stewing woman on the boil. While the fossil droned on with her interminable reminiscences, he'd slowly reward the younger lady with meaningful glances, until they were making love with their eyes.

If he went too far and the elder lady caused an *eyeballus interruptus* by reproving him for inattention to *her*, Herron was capable of charming his way out of trouble. He had done it before and would do it again.

By the time the train puffed into whatever station they were bound for, the she would have invited Herron to tea.

Tea bored Herron. He never had afternoon teas at home; he sauntered out to his Club for a more spirited refreshment. But he attended every tea he was invited to in houses where lovely young females were stabled and groomed, whether they were daughters, domestics or wives.

From tea onward, *the game* might take any number of diverting directions.

If the young lady was the elder's relative, Herron would use their tea party as a springboard to further ingratiate himself until he won the run of the dowager's household—and her family.

If his luck stayed with him, the young lady would have a sister. If they were both smitten with him, so much the better. Herron loved angling sisters off each other in bank shots.

I shall not let my love for you come between the affection of sisters was one of his favorite ploys. He would say that to each sister in turn, in private, and she would have a good cry on his shirtfront. Each sister would adore his selflessness. And she would hate her sister for depriving her of this fine man's love.

The jealousy of sisters always accelerated games. And a pinch of sibling rivalry always increased the heat during endgames. In the worst case . . . she would have a *brother*.

At Cambridge, Herron had tested his fists at amateur boxing. And from a boy he had been trained with swords and firearms. He might survive a fair fight.

But he had once been clobbered from behind with a cricket bat wielded by a peevish brother with no sense of fair play, and it had nearly caved in his skull. He saw double for a month and no amount of drinking would put it right.

Determined not to allow another brother to have a crack at him, he never turned his back on any of them. This was a drag on love-making, when it was preferable to face woman he went to woo.

If this present young lady was a paid companion or some other domestic, so much the better. Herron wouldn't have to mop up any more tea. He would use the first tea to furtively arrange an assignation on her afternoon off.

Fortunately, she was not a governess. He knew that at a glance. Governesses were inundated in a sea of small children, usually in sailor suits, always dragging their heels and yelling "No!"

Governesses spoiled Herron's batting average. This was not because they necessarily had more moral fibre to resist his manifold temptations. It's just that Herron was never in top form when children were obstacles in the fairway.

Aere paid companion could venture out – ostensibly to walk the dog – and make a surreptitious jaunt to his place, tying the dog in the foyer.

A governess could not simply shackle children in foyers while she and Herron charged for the bedroom.

And all Herron's wealth could not buy the silence of tots. He'd tried. The little savages who had no conception of the value of money tattled; and the little savages who knew the value of money held them up for further extortion.

4

Herron worked all this out in his mind within the course of half a minute. He considered every contingency except failure.

In reality, Herron's schemes did not all run like clockwork. On rare occasions, victory of any sort eluded him.

Even in mid-victory, he had tasted defeat. He had sweated out unpleasant confrontations with indignant parents, guardians and husbands. He had been forced to make rapid getaways out rear windows or down back stairs in *deshabille* – never good in parky weather.

Yet Herron remained an optimist. He did not even worry that a woman with this young lady's sangfroid might possess that bane of the modern Victorian female, *morals*.

Once he had a scheme, like the Bath chair stratagem, Herron was invariably speedy in effecting its operation and never allowed the possibility of failure to color his plans.

Today, however, he was slow launching his onslaught due to a Skye terrier.

5

At first glance, the dark lump of fur slung over the dowager's arm might have been a muff with a tongue.

When he had been creeping to the front of the platform, in the scant light of the station Herron's eyes had gradually picked out the moist, tell-tale black dot of a doggy snoot poking through the undergrowth.

The surest method of ingratiating himself with older ladies was to make passionate love to their doggies. By focusing his attention on the pooch,

Herron had time to cast his spell before the train sidled up to the platform—even though its distant whistle was alerting him to its imminent arrival.

I'm sorry, I know we haven't been introduced. My card. Card first, always, in that situation. Get the money question answered fast. *I was standing over there, thinking, what a marvelous animal. I'm something of a dog-fancier and I've rarely seen such a fine slice of canine. What's the little chappie's soubriquet?*

When it came time to load the lady, Herron would take charge of the dog, carrying it like it was made of glass, leaving the heavy lifting to the porters.

And so on, until the happy ending.

But the last Skye terrier Herron met had mistaken fingers for food. When the bleeding stopped, Herron discovered the gnashing of teeth had barely punctured his skin; but Herron had a low threshold for being eaten. He had no intention of becoming this beast's afternoon snack.

Young women reacted so differently to blood, too. In some, it aroused a maternal instinct. Others merely laughed. A few swooned. Some absolutely refused to let Herron's near them with his blood staining everything.

Herron had a way of manipulating all of these situations to his advantage.

In fact, he began to think a nice, hard bite might be the quickest way to finesse an introduction. And – it would force the young lady to show her hand. If she laughed or was squeamish, or became maternal or stand-offish, he'd instantly identify facets of her character that sometimes took weeks or months to isolate.

Yet, being bit *hurt*. It was difficult for him to deliberately stick a finger between those pearly whites the dog was already champing in his direction.

So he vacillated about the terrier until he heard the train steaming into the station. For the first time in living memory – *dash it* – a train he wanted ran according to the timetable.

No time for worming into the old lady's heart through her dog. Plan Bath Chair was in effect.

Then this lummox elbowed between Herron and the girl.

"Steady on, my good man—!" Herron started.

Even while Herron was upbraiding him, the man pitched himself headlong off the platform, into the path of the train.

6

Then came screams, and a ripple of general panic.

Half the crowd was retreating to keep from seeing the macabre spectacle; the other half was pressing forward for a better view. Those in front, like Herron, were nearly additional victims pushed into the slowing train.

The young woman beside Herron did not scream, though she clapped her hands over her face at the initial crunch of flesh and bone.

Herron was furious. If he had only overcome his qualms and paid the appropriate attention to that hairy son-of-a-(or daughter—who could tell with all that fur). Anyway, if he'd shown due care and attention to the mutt he might already have charmed his way into the company of those ladies well enough to let the younger one hide her face in his shoulder.

Horror would prove an effective bond between them. And so handy! It would have spared Herron a tedious train journey chatting up the toad-lady. He'd merely have produced his card – promising, merely out of the goodness of his heart, to call on the ladies at the first convenient moment – to make sure the dowager was coping, of course.

. . . And, oh yes, that young lady who was with you. Since I am here. I may as well inquire about her, too.

Herron sighed. His careful plans blown all to perdition by one inconsiderate oaf who had chosen a singularly inconvenient moment for suicide.

The perfect end to a perfectly beastly day.

That was another misjudgment on his part. His day was far from over.

CHAPTER II

The train rolled the man's body on, littering the track with bits of him all the way along. Herron saw it no more. *Good riddance.*

Desperately using his ivory-knobbed stick as a crowbar, Herron freed himself from the press of people. He wondered if he could salvage anything from the disaster by kindly asking if the lady in mourning needed *anything*—

—but the young lady had quickly recovered her presence of mind and was already wheeling the Bath chair away.

In an *Open, Sesame* moment, the horde parted for them out of respect.

Herron tried to pursue, but the crowd snapped shut, nearly clamping him in its jaws. He realized how the Egyptians must have felt at the Red Sea.

Poetry was not Herron's strong suit, but he recalled a lines by Robert Burns,

> *The best laid schemes o' mice an' men*
> *Gang aft agley,*
> *An' lea'e us nought but grief an' pain,*
> *For promis'd joy!*

Herron's schemes had ganged about as agley as possible. And the promise of joy had just wheeled her charge out of his life, probably forever.

Policemen began prodding the people along, taking statements from everyone.

Out of deference to her age, her mourning and her invalid status, the woman in the Bath chair was allowed to the front of the queue (with her companion).

Herron, at the forefront of the platform, was at the end of the line.

I'll never meet her, now, he sighed. *All because of a blasted hank of hair swanking about under the decent name of "dog," and a man who couldn't hang himself in the privacy of his own home like a considerate Englishman.*

Herron had long suspected suicides were egotists who took swan dives off bridges and public buildings just to get their names in the papers. Now he had been discomfited by just such an exhibitionist. He'd have kicked a nearby post in a fit of pique, if he hadn't feared scuffing his patent leather shoes.

Herron glared critically through his monocle at the queue waiting to give statements. A heightened police presence prowled London for the Jubilee. For weeks policemen had been squirming underfoot wherever Herron had trodden. Now there were far too few policemen to handle the present crisis. *Typical.*

"Pardon me, sir."

Turning, Herron was confronted by a man in a long, dark coat. Herron was slower to notice details about men. Tall, chunky, balding, toothbrush moustache. He was the living embodiment of those police inspectors who were invariably outfoxed by cunning private detectives in magazine stories.

"Did you see the accident, sir?"

"I saw a man fall in front of a train, if that's what you mean."

"'Fall,' sir?"

"Just look at him! What's left of him. Don't read too much into the 'fall.' Even if he jumped, he'd have fallen, Inspector—?"

"Call me Stoker."

Herron nodded. He looked like the type to be descended from those who made their living by the shovel, consigning coal to furnaces.

"Were you close to the man, sir?" Stoker asked.

"We had not been introduced."

"I mean, in proximity. When he fell."

"Close as I am to you. Closer. He nearly carried me with him. And a young lady, to boot!"

"You were next to him when he physically left the platform?"

"A shade too jolly close."

"You are a vital witness, sir. Please accompany me for special treatment."

"What—now? Can't I come 'round in the morning, Inspector Stoker?"

Herron cast another glance at the Bath chair. The old lady was talking volubly to a harried policeman, who was writing as fast as he could to keep up with her. She would be leaving soon, taking the girl with her.

In a flash, Herron devised a brilliant new scheme. *They* would be through soon, but it would be some time before the trains could run again. Since he was resigned to being in the back of the queue anyway, Herron would have time to ingratiate himself with the old lady. He'd even chat up the pooch! He'd laugh when the brute nibbled him to the bone. What was a finger, more or less, with such a prize at stake!

Yes, a sound new plan – but one requiring Herron's bodily presence in the station. "I'd prefer to wait and give my evidence here, if I may."

"It would be most helpful if you would give us any assistance you can while the facts are fresh in your mind."

"Well, yes, I suppose so." Herron's voice was prickly. He opted to go with the law willingly, before they produced the manacles. He had an vague idea that material witnesses might be treated the same as perpetrators, and he had no desire to be frog-marched out of the station. Since the young lady was out of his life forever, Herron was willing to do anything that expedited the process of getting him home to his cold, lonely bed.

"Thank you, sir. Please, do come with me. We won't detain you long."

At the barrier, Stoker stepped up to the guard – and a policeman waiting with him – for a word or two in private. After the word, the policeman saluted him.

Stoker then hustled Herron outside the station and into a waiting brougham.

When Stoker opened the carriage door, Herron perceived another man, also in a long, dark coat, sitting inside and facing forward.

The second man had no moustache, but he looked like he hadn't been able to locate his razor that morning. He was a youngish man of athletic build, prematurely lined. His hair was light, as were his gimlet eyes.

As he nudged Herron into the brougham, facing forward between them, Stoker called the man "Sergeant Hawkins" – and they laughed.

Sergeant Hawkins appeared to have only the most rudimentary notions of personal hygiene; and he had slicked his hair with a disgusting pomade.

"Rather a tight fit," Herron remarked, pointedly, hoping one of the two would take the hint and move to the other seat, facing the rear.

They didn't take the hint. Before Herron could elaborate on just how uncomfortable they all must be, Stoker hammered on the top of the carriage with the his stick and the driver whipped up his horses.

As they began moving, Stoker and Hawkins yanked shades down over all the windows, including the one in front.

"Anyway," Herron started, "I was standing on the platform, don't y'know—"

"Not here, sir. When we reach the office."

"Stoker . . . Where have I heard that name?"

No reply. Not even an *I'll ask the questions, sir.*

Herron fell silent and put the ivory knob of his stick to his mouth, brooding on what might have been. Fortunately, he had no inkling of what was coming.

CHAPTER III

The carriage rattled through the streets, sometimes over cobbles, sometimes over asphalt, but always very fast. Herron wondered how the driver maintained their speed. The streets were jammed with vehicles at the best of times; these days, with London so much more crowded than usual, it was worse than ever.

The speed did not bother Herron *per se*. He wanted to get through this as soon as possible – so long as they didn't barge into anything. All the joy had passed from his life; but he wanted to endure the drawn-out process of drowning his sorrows. He didn't want his sorrows to end all at once in a smash.

Herron tried to recall the young lady's soft, gardenia fragrance; but the memory, growing fainter with every mile, could not compete with the Sergeant's pungent aroma.

The men proved untalkative, to him and to one another. And since Herron had nothing to say to them, their journey was conducted in silence.

As was his habit when he was bored by a long carriage ride, Herron closed his eyes and began unconsciously counting turns – which the driver seemed to make at every intersection.

After about three quarters of an hour, the brougham drew to a halt. The driver hopped off his perch and trotted away. Herron heard the squeal of rusty hinges. Then the driver returned and opened the door of the brougham.

Herron heard the dings, sirens and horns of river traffic, he inhaled the muddy stench of dirty old Father Thames. As Stoker and Hawkins hustled him from the cab into the building, however, he was unable to see the neighborhood.

Inside, as none of the gas jets in the building were burning, they clattered upstairs in the dark. Herron assumed everyone had gone home. It was nearly the solstice, so sunset was quite late. No doubt workers in this musty-smelling office building had long since fled into the long, warm Saturday evening.

One floor up, Stoker and Hawkins stopped at a closed office near the stairway. Stoker fumbled with a handful of keys before opening the door. Herron did not hear a key turn in the lock, but he was too haunted by his loss for that salient point to register immediately.

The door frame was thin, but Stoker and his assistant managed to step inside with Herron sandwiched between them.

The room contained a single desk, just visible in silhouette in the faint light oozing through a grimy window. Stoker turned no gas on, so the desk remained in shadows. He banged his knee rounding it.

Groping his way into his chair with an string of invective, Stoker struck a match to a paraffin oil lamp on the desk.

"You'd think Scotland Yard would have gas laid on," Herron joked.

The two men exchanged brief glances, then pivoted their eyes back to Herron.

Stoker said, "What makes you think we're Scotland Yard, sir?"

"Oh, aren't you?" He glanced uneasily from one man to the other. "I knew this wasn't *New* Scotland Yard, don't you know, but I thought . . . that is, I *thought* . . . uh . . . Who are you?"

Stoker cocked his head toward Herron and peered at him from the corner of his eye. "Young man, are you a patriot?"

"Oh, ra-ther, don't you know."

Patriotism was all the fashion this year. However much he hated it, in deference to the Queen's Diamond Jubilee Herron wore a red, white and blue ribbon in his buttonhole rather than a flower. Despite the Union Jack ribbon in his buttonhole, Herron had never really considered patriotism one way or another. His country *was*, and he accepted it on those terms.

Herron had no personal politics worthy of the name. He was chameleon enough for his colors to match the politics of any woman he happened to be with. If he was in the company of two women with opposing political viewpoints, Herron remained silent and let them cat-fight it out.

He failed to see any obvious connection between his patriotism and a feckless ninny trying his luck at the "standing broad jump in front of trains" event for the next Olympiad . . . But to make these two men happy, Herron became a patriot.

He gave his buttonhole ribbon a significant tap as evidence of his stern regard for England and Empire.

"We serve Her Majesty in a . . . less public capacity than Scotland Yard."

"Ah-ha." Though Herron was in the dark, literally as well as figuratively, a glimmer of light flashed through his cranium. He leaned confidentially forward on his stick. "Hush-hush stuff, eh, what?"

The men smiled at each other, as if sharing a private joke.

Stoker extracted a note pad and a pencil from his breast pocket. "If you'll tell us about the events of this evening, we'll pass your information on to the Yard at our earliest convenience. The man who fell in front of the train was one of our agents. Your information will be vital both for us . . . and for Her Majesty."

"Oh, I say, really?"

"Do sit down, Mister–?"

"Strangways. Herron Strangways." Folding himself into the only other chair, he slipped one of his calling-cards from its case. Laying the card on the desktop, Herron slid it into the halo of light beneath the lamp like he was playing boats.

Stoker referred to the card on the desk, though he did not touch it. "Strangways! Are you related to the Emporium?"

"Emporia. Yes, I am." No need waste his clever "legion" line on the police.

"We do appreciate the cooperation of a man of your standing in the community. We need to clear up the matter of this accident."

Herron burst out:

"'*Accidents*
In Jubilee Week
Personal accidents
Street accidents
Carriage accidents
Accidents from stands and structures
Accidents through crowds
Accidents in excursions
Accidents at the reviews – naval and military
Accidents everywhere
Accidents of all kinds
Covered by the policy of the–'"

(He balled a fist to his mouth and blew a fanfare not unlike a raspberry)

"'–*Accidents Insurance Company Limited!*
£1,000,000 paid in claims
Write for prospects.'"

When he finished, the two men were gaping at him. Herron hadn't meant to be loud but his voice had reverberated through the otherwise silent building. "Sorry," he apologized. "Read that in the paper. Insurance Company advertisement. I'd call this an 'accident through crowds' but I think the poor fellow's prospects are dim for collecting his million pounds, what?"

"Mister Strangways, if you would *please* tell us everything you recall, as accurately as possible—and as quickly."

"Righty-o. Let me marshal my thoughts."

"And, Mister Strangways?"

"Hum?"

"Do take your stick out of your mouth."

Herron laid it aside. "I was on my way from of the Hemlock Club—"

"The which?"

"Hemlock Club. Saint James. I woke this morning with a bit of a head—"

"A *head*?" echoed Hawkins, his words betraying a flat, American accent.

"He means he had a hang-over," Stoker explained with some asperity. "This isn't the *French* Revolution, Hawkins."

Hawkins bitterly remarked, "You and your history, Jake!"

"Please continue with your story, sir," Stoker said apologetically, poising his pen above his notebook.

"Righty-o. Last night I met up with a fellow I was at school with. Old Geeble. He's just back from—some godawful spot, anyway, don't you know. To represent his regiment in the Jubilee Parade on Tuesday. We suffered all the way from grammar school to 'Varsity together, so naturally I poured on more oil than usual. He kept shouting, 'The Queen, God bless her!' and what's a fellow to do?"

In a low tone, with a naughty smile, Herron whispered,

"I thought about slipping a 'damn' into the shouts to see if anybody noticed, but I'm not the one to start a donnybrook, especially when it's my donny they're brooking. I'm a drinker, not a fighter."

Suddenly realizing this admission hardly squared with his declaration of patriotism, he hastily added,

"Just a joke, don't you know. I had thought about going to see Sarah Bernhardt at the Adelphi, but her play got a stinker review in the *Times*, so

I stayed at the Club and met old Geeble and—Well, one thing and another, I was on the delicate side this morning. Merridew, my man, felt my pulse throughout this morning to see if anyone was home. I finally resurrected about noonish."

"This is all very well, Mister Strangways—"

"I sneered at some breakfast, then Merridew wrapped me in cotton and I took an airing through the park hoping that would clear the bean. The park was full up on a Saturday, so I found my steps wending to the Club again, more or less on their own. There, I nestled down in a chair in one of the quieter rooms. One of the chaps with a bit of medical training – he'd have made a doctor if it hadn't been for all the cutting-up they do in medical school – suggested a drop of lubrication was all the machinery needed, so—well, one thing and another, I had only just staggered from the Club when—"

"I am unacquainted with that organization, sir," said Stoker, looking over his notes directly beneath the lamp. "What sort of association is this Hemlock Club?"

"An ordinary gentleman's club. I belong to several, but this one is chock full of chaps I was at school with. I'm one of the charter members. It's not one of your older clubs, all stodgy with history and the ever-present niff of all the cigars smoked since Queen Anne's day. We like to give it an air of *diablerie*, don't you know, and deck it out like the old Hellfire clubs. If you know what I mean?"

"Yes sir. The eighteenth century is my speciality."

"Oh?" Herron wasn't aware secret agents had historical specialities.

"Do you . . . dress the part?"

"All those powdered wigs and lace frippery? Good God, no. We have waiters in red velveteen coats and white knee-breeches and lace-fronted shirts and pig-tailed wigs—if it's your 'speciality' you must know what I mean?"

"I have made a study of the middle of the eighteenth century, sir."

"Then you know what fools we'd all look if actual members dressed that way."

"I'm beginning to form a mental picture of an organization of high-spirited young gentlemen with more money than sense, who posture theirselves on the shady side just so little old ladies will avert their eyes as they pass your doors." "In a nutshell. But you could take your mother there. Honor bright."

"But not, I warrant, my sister."

"All gentleman. A few years back we caught a fellow cheating in cards—"

Herron's voice dropped and his manner showed so much agitation his monocle tumbled from his eye. Reeling it up and screwing it back in place, he continued,

"—'pon my soul, absolutely *cheating*. Think of the damage that can do to a club's reputation. We formed a hollow square and clipped off the blighter's tie and bashed a hole through his topper and shoved the brim down 'round his neck and drummed him right out. I helped carry him. Threw him over the steps into the gutter. Chap that proposed him for membership submitted his resignation, too, and bally right. Sound chap, but gullible. You needn't write that down."

"I promise you I won't." Stoker and the other man exchanged querulous glances. "Sir—"

"Didn't know the blackguard, myself – the card-sharp, that is. Didn't black-ball him. Went on the recommendation of chaps I trusted. Just goes to show you. Played with him a time or two and wondered where he got his diabolical luck. I'm a good player, counting cards and so forth. I can remember what each chap played several games running—"

"Mister Strangways!" snapped Stoker, sharply. If he'd had more hair he'd have clutched at it. "If you would *please* stick to the facts?"

"Righty-o. About what?"

Stoker's voice quivered as he said, "The incident at the station."

"Righty-o. As I was saying, I didn't want to dive into the deep end two nights running – not as young as I was – so I took no more than a medicinal gargle. It didn't totally alleviate the discomfort, but my outlook on life was rosier. I decided I'd spend a quiet evening at home. Have Merridew make up a chop, don't you know, and maybe read a bit – I'm starting a real shocker – and then early to bed and late to rise. I didn't feel like walking, and the thoroughfares are so crowded these days cabs are slow. So I ventured into the Underground and slithered to the front of the platform. And all of a sudden this rather haggard bird did a springbok between us, out onto the tracks, and caught a locomotive in the small of his back."

"Us?"

"Pardon?"

"You said he pushed 'between us . . .' Who was with you?"

"No one. I referred to a rather nice young lady standing nearby." He didn't like mentioning her. Only a bounder discussed ladies openly. Also, since she had passed from his life forever, Herron preferred not to dwell on his her. "I just noticed her, don't you know."

"You don't know her name or how we might contact her?"

"Sorry. Wish to God I did."

"You did not know the deceased? No. Ever see him before?"

"Oh, yes."

Stoker sat forward. Hawkins, who had remained standing due to the dearth of chairs, snaked a hand inside his coat pocket.

"I saw him pacing the platform earlier."

The two men exhaled simultaneously. Their postures relaxed. Hawkins withdrew his hand from his coat and leaned back against the wall with crossed arms.

"Describe this man, if you can . . . Mister . . . ah . . . Strangways."

"Just what I said. A haggard bird."

"A . . . *haggard bird*?" snarled the American.

"Well, you know what 'haggard' is. Or, maybe not." He peered at the dimly-lit Hawkins. *You'd know if you glanced in a mirror once in a while.* "Looked like he hadn't slept regularly for a year or two. Seemed to be in a hurry to get someplace. Eyes darting around. Like one of those chaps pursued by the Furies."

Herron was rather proud of this bit of imagery – but then, these men, historians though they professed to be, might not possess the full fruits of a classical education. He added,

"If you know what I mean by 'Furies.' Three spirity female things that chase you around and drive you right out of your tree. With a rather beaky nose – oh, I'm talking about the 'haggard bird' again, not the Furies; I don't know what their noses looked like. When I saw him looking so haggard and beaky, I thought, 'My, that's a haggard bird.' Then he caught a breath of a passing scent, like spring blowing over a winter wasteland, and I realized there were finer things in life than haggard birds. I spied a young lady with this fossil in a Bath chair—"

Stoker glared up. "I beg your pardon, sir?" Meaning, *Stay on topic.*

Herron did not read between the lines. "Bath chair," he repeated, enunciating the words clearly so there would be no misunderstanding. "The older lady might have been excavated from an Egyptian tomb. I saw a face like it in a glass case once, on a trip to the Museum as a boy. I wanted to see it in more detail but my governess refused to linger. She merely sniffed at it and said humans beings should be properly buried and not pickled—"

"The station, Mister Strangways, please!"

"I wormed through the crowd until I was standing beside the young lady. No sooner was I next to her than I felt a shove and this haggard bird flew between us and took a header off the platform. Might have taken her with him. Or me. Dashed inconsiderate."

"Did he . . . say anything to you?"

"The haggard bird? Not much time for famous last words."

"Think very carefully. Did he say anything at all?"

Having read detective stories, Herron realized they asked the same questions over and over, listening for new meanings in slight shades of difference in the wording of answers. So he wasn't surprised when Stoker pressed this point.

What annoyed Herron was Hawkins, who had remained in the shadows until now, stepping uncomfortably close behind his chair.

"Had he seemed to *want* to speak to you? Or to get your attention before rushing past you?"

"No. My attention by that time was wholly occupied by the young lady—"

"Yes, yes. Mister Strangways, Her Majesty is not interested in your sex life."

"I should hope not!"

"Did you actually *see* him fall?"

"Oh, yes, I saw him *fall*. Then I saw him bound merrily away at the point of the train. What I did not see was what happened before he fell."

"You did not see what caused the fall?"

Herron shook his head.

"And he did not speak to you at all?"

"Not a peep."

"So only you and the young lady were standing beside the man when he fell?"

"Or was pushed."

Another sharp glance between Stoker and Hawkins. Hawkins pulled himself to his full height, the fingers of his right hand twitching. Stoker gave him a signal with his hand that seemed to mean, *Not now*.

"Why did you say that, sir?"

"What? Oh, 'pushed'? I was just finishing the thought. It sounds like an expression one might read in the papers. '—fell or was pushed.'"

"Do you think he might have been pushed?"

"I can only say he rushed between us like his bally trousers were on fire."

"And that's all you know?"

Herron nodded.

Stoker closed his notebook. He hadn't made a mark in it for some time. "Thank you for your cooperation, Mister Strangways."

"Is that all?"

"If you will tell us where you live, in case we have further questions—?"

Herron provided his address, and that of his Club.

Thinking he had time to relax, Herron brought forth his cigarette case, opened it, and offered one to Stoker (who declined). He pointedly did not offer one to Hawkins. *Take that*.

Screwing a cigarette into his holder, Herron lit it with a match.

He'd barely shaken the match out when the men grabbed an arm each. A thread of smoke was still rising from the fallen match when the men bundled Herron outside between them.

In moments, they had clattered downstairs and were outside in the closed brougham, pressing Herron between them.

The two men proved no more talkative on the return journey. Falling into counting the turns, Herron discovered they took a different route back.

The brougham drew to a hasty stop before the Underground station. When Stoker emerged, Herron, who had been packed in tight, practically sprang out.

Without a word of thanks – or even acknowledgment – Stoker disappeared again into the brougham and banged the roof with his stick. The driver whipped up his horses and the carriage rattled away into the rising fog of evening before Stoker had even closed the door.

Herron watched them go with a raised eyebrow. "Odd people," he muttered. But he supposed it took odd people to do that cloak and dagger stuff.

Entering the station, Herron saw the queue of witnesses had gone – and with them the old lady, the Bath chair, the terrier, and the most beautiful young lady Herron had ever seen, recently.

Weary of trains, Herron returned to the street and hailed a cab. He just wanted to get home and wrap himself around a generous helping of brandy.

Sunday, June 20, 1897

CHAPTER IV

"Mister Strangways? Sir?"

Herron creaked open an eyelid. "Merridew?" he rasped.

Merridew was Herron's valet and domestic factotum. "Tea or coffee, sir?"

Herron pressed the heels of his hands to his temples to keep them from exploding outward, "Give me a moment to decide which head to put on."

"Very good, sir."

"*You* may think so—!"

Herron uttered a strangled cry as Merridew flung open the curtains over the bedroom window, which faced east over the street in the front of the house.

While lighting the room, Merridew hummed a hymn, "Sunshine in My Soul."

> "*O there's sunshine, blessèd sunshine,*
> *When the peaceful, happy moments roll;*
> *When Jesus shows His smiling face,*
> *There is sunshine in the soul–*"

In the first weeks after hiring Merridew, Herron had spoken quite harshly to him about humming hymns at unpropitious moments.

Merridew tried to comply – but his humming was altogether unconscious.

They had been together several years, now, and these days Herron only upbraided Merridew when his head was peculiarly fragile. He wanted to apply a few words of censure – but first, he needed a hot beverage.

That reminded him—"What did you say again, Merridew?"

"Tea, sir, or coffee?"

"I thought that's what it sounded like. You have them both ready?"

"Yes, sir."

Herron squinted at the window. "The sun looks all wrong."

"It's before time, sir. There's a man come to see you." His voice dropped warningly. "From the police."

Merridew had brought in a silver salver bearing a plain visiting-card. He'd left it on the bureau until Herron unglued his eyes.

Wiping his eyes and straining to focus them on the card (for none of his senses were at their most acute at this time of the day) Herron read:

Inspector Broughton Chubb

"Never heard of the blighter. Where did you stow him?"

"In the library, sir."

"I suppose it's about the accident."

"Sir?"

"Oh . . . some johnnie tried to stop a train by throwing himself across the tracks. Train won on points. Most unpleasant. I had to talk to one lot of people about it last night and this morning I've got another aggregation queuing up at my door – before breakfast! Persecution, that's what it is. Oh, well, that clenches it! There's only one thing to do in this situation. Coffee. Black."

"Yes, sir." Merridew withdrew for the coffee and tea pots he'd left in the corridor.

While Merridew was gone, Herron clenched his eyes, to keep the blaze in his head from forcing them out from their sockets.

2

Reaching home after his interview with Stoker, Herron had brooded over the events of the day. Not the accident, of course. That was inconsequential. He had done his civic duty and paid the price for it.

But he could not squeeze that young lady out of his head. As an antidote, he had taken an liberal dose of his best brandy.

Though he was accustomed to larger applications, the brandy had an unfortunate reaction with what had been prescribed for him at the Club.

After taking his medication, Herron had tried to read the "shocker" he'd mentioned to Stoker; but the words went wobbly on him, so he shelved it and went straight up to bed, leaving a trail of discarded clothing all the way – except for his frock coat, which he had hung up on the hall tree in the foyer.

Actually, the brandy initially had a beneficial effect. Oiling down between the sheets, Herron dropped off easier than he had anticipated.

Now, Herron faced one intractable law of nature: the easier he went to sleep at beddy-byes, the harder it was to locate the edge of the bed come morning.

Mix in policemen swarming in his library before breakfast, and Herron knew he was on the verge of another beastly day.

Merridew brought in a tray containing a simple breakfast of toast, butter and marmalade. He always anticipated what Herron would appreciate for breakfast by the way he shed his outer skin.

When Herron did not spend a lonely night, he might return any time between midnight and noon. On those occasions, he folded all his clothes neatly over an armchair in his bed chamber, and his mood on rising was chipper. Merridew prepared a hearty breakfast and Herron ate well.

When, however, Herron cluttered the fairway with clothes as he tottered upstairs, Merridew prepared the sort of breakfast he'd offer a recovering, but still weak, convalescent.

Eating was not one of Herron's favorite morning-after activities, but he needed to fortify himself against this onslaught from the constabulary.

The silver tray's little legs fit snugly over Herron's slender waist. Once it was in place, Merridew placed a heavier tray with cups, saucers, and large pot of hot black coffee on the bedside table and served what Herron required.

Merridew handed down a plate of toast and a butter dish. "Shall I pour, sir?"

Herron signaled the affirmative, moving his head to the minimum.

Propping the Inspector's card at a slant in one corner of the breakfast tray, Herron studied it while lathering a slab of toast with butter.

The card adamantly said nothing except the Inspector's cold, fishy name.

"This Chubb – is he still on the premises, Merridew? No chance he got tired of waiting and filed his way out the window?"

"He is still in the library, sir. I heard him talking to his assistant."

"What's he doing?"

"Pacing. Perusing the bookshelves. Giving everything a good look-see."

"I hate to have him snooping. You can't tell him to take an egg and beat it?"

"No, sir."

"Well, let him wait. I didn't invite him here. I don't keep open house for the *gendarmes* on Sunday mornings. At least I haven't have anything to hide down there." He glanced sheepishly up over his toast. "Have I, Merridew?"

"Not just now, sir."

"Good. Newspaper, Merridew?"

"Yesterday's *Evening Star*. You had not read it."

"I peeked at it before I left the Club – and I wish by all that's holy (if anything) I never had left the Club. I'll take the paper. There was far too much hubbub in the Club to absorb what I was reading." Herron wiggled his hands into a couple of gloves he kept on the bedside table, to keep ink from smearing on his fingers, before accepting the paper from Merridew. "Everyone is so excited about this Jubilee. Personally," he snapped the paper open, "it bores me to tears."

Herron did not bother screwing in his eyeglass. He had perfect vision, until it was blurred with drink. His clear-glass monocle was an affectation he never wore in the privacy of his bedchamber.

"Best paper in London," Herron muttered, skimming through the contents. "Though our papers here are never so interesting as the ones in America. Remember when we were over there? Hand me that leather lettercase in the escritoire. Thank you. Looky here."

He removed an article cut from page six of the New York *Tribune* for November 9, 1896, entitled "Signals from the Planet Mars":

> "... about four years ago a small but intensely brilliant spot was seen for a few hours on Mars, whereupon some one offered the sensational suggestion that maybe the light was intended as a signal to dwellers on our globe. Well-informed astronomers knew that such spots had been seen before, and they interpreted the phenomenon as a reflection from a snow-capped highland..."

The article detailed how an English geographer-cum-anthropologist believed the signals were an attempt to contact Earth and they should, out of common courtesy, be answered as quickly as possible. The good doctor suggested, "*that some mad millionaire, or billionaire, living on Mars, provided an enormous mirror, or heliograph, from which long and short flashes could be sent...*"

"Just imagine, Merridew, a Martian billionaire inventor building some sort of – oh, I suppose it's a parabolic mirror, like they have in light houses – on Mars, desperately trying to contact us with light pulses in a Martian Morse code."

"Yes, sir?"

"All true – it was in the newspaper. I like all this scientific stuff, don't you know." Folding the clipping, he filed it into his letter-case. "Mad Martian billionaire. I wonder, do they use pounds on Mars, or dollars?"

"It may depend, sir, on whether Martians have ten fingers or twelve."

"Very shrewd, Merridew. What do you think of all that?"

"I'm no astronomer, sir."

"It's a free country. Everyone is entitled to an opinion, however uninformed."

"In that case, sir, with your permission, I can't think why, if there are men on Mars, they wish to contact us."

"Maybe through their telescopes they've gauged the efficiency of our canals."

"Canals, sir?"

"Don't you know anything about Mars?"

"No, sir. Making sense of Earth is challenging enough. I try to tackle only one planet at a time."

"I've looked into it," he said, with the air of a man who had believed himself an expert by dint of having perused a solitary book on a subject. "Apparently you can't sling a stone on Mars without it splashing down in a canal. All good science, Merridew. These Martians have an older planet than ours and they have done – oh, dreadful things to it. So they irrigate their crops and water themselves by melting the polar caps, and that balances them out nicely. They've dug these huge canals to bring water from their poles. Their urban centers are all where their canals intersect. Of course, this scientific chap who wrote the book said we must not think of Martians as being 'real life in trousers.'"

Merridew pursed his lips. "That sounds rather dissolute, sir."

"Y'know, if I had it to do all over again, I'd be one of these scientific inventor johnnies. Like what's-his-name—Edison, don't you know, always inventing things. Sounds loads of fun. Too, since our return to London I've missed all those articles on the airship mystery."

"The . . . what, sir?"

"Didn't you glance at any American papers while we were there?"

"No, sir. An airship is, I take it, a flying contraption?"

"Yes. Like a balloon, only it's not just a bag of wind you puff up. It has a skeleton inside."

This did not clarify the matter sufficiently for Merridew, who wondered if they were used as flying sarcophagi.

"Not a real skeleton. A frame, don't y'know. They're elongated, like a good cigar, and they need a rigid internal structure to maintain their shapes."

"Like a corset, sir?"

"No, a corset sucks in. Anyway, while balloons get blown about willy-nilly and have to go up and down until they find a breeze going their way, airships have engines powerful enough to push them through the ether, regardless of wind."

"I see, sir. And why was this airship a mystery?"

"Well, no one has built a successful airship yet. Officially. But every so often when we were in America, the newspapers would run a piece about some yahoo in a rural district who saw strange lights or a 'cigar-shaped' balloon-like vehicle up in the air – apparently powered and guided. Whoever owns the skies may own the country. Think of invaders raining bombs down on cities, with no way to stop them. They can fly too high for backwoods American riflemen to shoot down."

"Maybe someone has built an airship or two for his own amusement."

"That chap Edison didn't seem to think so. He had some very harsh words, as I recall. And here is another article from the – I think the *New York Times*. Dated—blast it, wait a minute, I folded it and the date's in a crease. Here we go. April 22, this year. It starts out, 'Possibly, even probably, there is no airship sailing about the western skies, but none the less people believe in it.'"

"Did you believe in it, sir?"

"Oh, ra-ther!"

"Why?"

"Well, why not?"

"Very good, sir. May I take the tray, sir?"

"I'm still working on that toast. Leading scientists and inventors don't think anyone has built an airship on the sly for joyrides. There's too much difficulty in building one just for pleasure outings."

"What is the difficulty, sir?" "As I understand it, anyone can build the frame. What they lack is the means of propulsion. Wind's pretty stiff up there in the clouds, they say. I read somewhere that the problem with constructing effective airships is what they call the—" He clenched his eyes to concentrate better – always a challenge with a morning head. "—I have it! The 'power-weight ratio of the engine.'"

"What does that mean, sir?"

"I haven't the foggiest. There was always some story in the American papers that some scientist working on his own invented an airship and flew it all over the American west. A great many persons in remote areas claimed to have seen it. That's what I find most curious, Merridew. It's always some yokel, isn't it, who sees it? It never flies over anyone of education or breeding. Never an urbane city chap who shows the least glimmer of intelligence."

"Like you, sir?"

"Exactly. Why don't they fly this airship to the centers of learning . . . or, on the opposite end of the intellectual spectrum, to Washington? If I invented an airship, I'd land it at Chapel Court at the old College, just to show 'em."

He gave the newspaper a vicious shake as he picked it up again.

"Not that they would care. They'd just ask me to conjugate some Greek noun."

"One conjugates verbs, sir," Merridew gently pointed out.

"There! That's the very sort of narrow-minded pedantry I was up against. I'll conjugate a noun if I want to. It's a free country."

"Well, all that is in America, sir. I suppose there's no danger of our seeing an airship here any time soon."

"No, worse luck. I'd like to. I wish I had one now. I'd take off in it instead of spending a pleasant Sunday morning in company with Inspector Chubby."

Finishing his toast and coffee, Herron lifted his paper and let Merridew remove his tray, including his cup. He hated to see the cup go – he could have downed the whole pot just then. But he could not keep the police waiting indefinitely.

Besides, the sooner he saw these blighters and got them out of his house, the sooner he could start his own day. Herron was ready to face the day, even if he was not quite ready to face Inspector Chubb.

"Over here in England," said Herron, rising and preparing to dress with Merridew's able assistance, "for the last few months all I've see in the papers are Diamond Jubilee articles – people advertising to rent shop windows and upper rooms for other people to view this parade they're having Tuesday. I wish I had gotten out of town, Merridew. I hate parades."

"As I understand it, sir, there was that ruckus over the suicide of that diamond magnate last week."

"Yes—that word again, *diamond*. There must be some connection. And suicide. It all ties together. This haggard bird who killed himself at the station last night probably had holdings in South Africa and foresaw a crash coming in the diamond market after they fished that diamond chap from the sea."

While Herron had been eating, Merridew had been laying out his clothes. First, Herron sat in a chair while Merridew shaved him. Then Merridew helped him dress. Last night, Herron had been in evening clothes. He had a simple dark suit and tie today. Merridew laid out his ruby stick-pin.

As Merridew four-in-handed the necktie, Herron recalled a joke he'd heard about Bible-thumpers like Merridew.

The vicissitudes of employing a Bible-thumper included having hymns (and even Scripture) presented to him with the breakfast bacon – at a time of day when a man like Herron most wanted privacy, without even God peering in on him.

Yet Herron learned to live with hymns being hummed – or even sung in a cheery voice at times when he was in a delicate state – rather than sacking Merridew on the spot, and running the risks of hiring a new man.

Merridew was efficient. He fulfilled his duties scrupulously and cheerfully. He never complained about his wages. He always knew the right clothes to wear for every occasion and he was a master with an iron (Herron had briefly employed a valet who stubbornly pressed his trousers with the creases in the sides).

And Herron had known employees, both at his home and at the Emporia, who *had not* taken Scripture to heart – especially the part about "Thou shalt not steal."

Merridew was also a superb cook of simple fare, which saved Herron from hiring a chef. (If he wanted exotic cuisine, he dined out. At home, he preferred the wholesome, if prosaic bacon and eggs or bangers and mash.)

Merridew was the envy of some of his pals at the Hemlock, who knew him only from his good domestic works and not his personal proclivities. If those fellows ever learned Herron employed a valet who spent his evenings off going to chapel, he'd be laughed right out of the Club.

Taken for all-in-all, Merridew was the best 'man' Herron ever had.

To keep Merridew on, therefore (and to keep him from being poached away by some of the lads at the Club) Herron upped Merridew's salary often. And he tried to keep him in a good mood. That included telling him jokes from time to time that he thought Merridew might appreciate. Even at the Hemlock they occasionally managed to repeat jokes that were funny despite being clean.

"I say, you're a hymn-singing chap, Merridew. I heard a good one at the Club the other day. It's about one of those progressive American johnnies who are always trying to prohibit good, honest drink. He was holding one of his Temperance lectures and he said, 'If I had my way, I'd take all the booze in this town – and dump it in the river. Why, I'd take all the booze in this county – and dump it in the river. Why, I'd take all the booze in this state – and dump it in the river. Now, take your song-books—we'll stand and sing old number eighty-eight, 'Shall We Gather at the River.'"

Herron tittered, to signal the end of the joke.

Merridew quietly finished with the tie and nipped around behind to adjust the rear of Herron's accoutrements.

Herron was a trifle disappointed that his anecdote wasn't received with chortles of laughter; but he had known Merridew to be slow to grasp the gist of jokes before. He supposed the man's mind was too occupied right now in straightening his waistcoat. Once he was back in his cozy kitchen, the point would strike Merridew over the head like a coal shovel; and he would collapse in laughter, straining for breath like his lungs were filling with fluid.

Still, Herron did not like having his jokes not laughed at, and his tone was sprinkled with frost when he asked,

"Do you think the eyeglass would be appropriate, Merridew?"

"Not for the police, sir."

"As you say. Buttonhole?"

"The red-white-and-blue ribbon will make an acceptable impression."

Just to show how put out he was with visitors at this ungodly hour, Herron descended the stairs topped by a gaudy, tasseled smoking-cap, with his purple dressing-gown thrown carelessly over his shirt and waistcoat.

He slipped noiselessly to the library. The door was slightly ajar, and Herron peered through the crack while squeezing a cigarette into his longest holder.

When Herron called the room in his ground floor back his "library" he implied only that he did most of his reading there.

The library had a sparce row or two of books on shelves, but the bulk of the reading matter consisted of back numbers of the *Evening Star* (editor, Mister Strap) – which was almost as sensational as the American papers of Hearst and Pulitzer – and stacks of magazines that carried fictional stories.

Several recent *Pearsons* magazines lay open to an on-going serial that had caught Herron's interest. It was all about an invasion from Mars.

Herron kept his cigarette unlit while he deduced which of the two men in the library was Broughton Chubb. He settled on a short, pudgy man frayed at the edges of his brown suit.

Chubb had wearied of pacing and had just started to take a seat. The moment his hindquarters touched the chair, Herron flung open the door and swaggered in.

The Inspector sprang to his feet, gripping his brown bowler hat chest-high in both hands and twisting it slowly counter-clockwise.

At close quarters, Broughton Chubb struck Herron as a deferential man with clean-shaven jowls. His hair was neatly parted in the center, leaving greying brown forelocks swinging away in wings.

"Inspector! I'm sorry to have kept you. Please, do sit down." Despite years of training in posture, Herron flopped his long, slim frame bonelessly onto the cushions of a chair.

He lit his cigarette with a match, which he shook out and tossed in an arc into a standing cigarette tray made to resemble a budding lotus.

"Good morning, sir. Broughton Chubb. Scotland Yard. POTTLE!" He held his arm straight out to his side and a second man slapped a walking-stick into his open palm. "This is Pottle," Chubb said, drawing in the stick, "my assistant."

Herron gave the Inspector's assistant a nod. He was a gaunt chap who might be improved by a good wash and brush-up.

After a perfunctory nod to Pottle, Herron focused on Chubb what attention he could manage at this hour of the day.

The Inspector carried the stick to a window brushed a curtain aside, letting in a modicum of motey light.

When he showed Chubb and his assistant in, Merridew had lit a small coal fire to knock off the morning chill. He also turned the gas on, low.

Herron, in deference to his morning eyes, did not raise the gas, and Chubb was forced to examine the stick in what light seeped through a west window in the early morning.

Since the window faced away from the morning sun, the room wore a funereally indistinct aspect even when Chubb stood shrouded in the open curtains.

Holding Herron's stick at arm's length in his right hand, Chubb examined an inscription scrolling around a silver band just beneath the ivory knob.

"You are Mister . . ." He seemed to have difficulty reading the inscription in that light. He moved it away from his eyes, then drew it closer, until he found the best focus, ". . . Strange-ways?"

"*Strang*-ways." Herron drew a case from his dressing gown, extracted one of his cards, and offered it out to Chubb.

The Inspector did not move. He pointed to Pottle, who took the card and carried it across to Chubb. The Inspector held the card out at arm's length in his left hand, comparing it to the scroll-work on the stick.

This done, the Inspector gave a satisfied nod. He was already slipping the card into his watch-pocket when he said, "May I keep this, sir?"

Herron waved a languid hand. "I have 'em pressed down and overflowing."

"And this is your stick? It seems to be a presentation from your Club."

"It's unique. There are seven of them in existence, presented to the charter members of the Hemlock."

"It's unique . . . but there are seven of 'em?"

"Our names vary on the scrollwork. Did you read the entire inscription?"

"It's in a foreign tongue, sir."

"Latin."

"I don't know it even to look at. I lack the benefits of a classical education."

"I lack the benefits myself, though I had the education. My Latin is rusty but I know what the inscription says, if you would like a rough translation?"

"Maybe later, sir. I understand, Mister Strangways, that you were at the Underground station last night when that unfortunate gentleman met his end?"

"Standing right there."

"Did you see the accident, sir?"

"Saw him fall. Nothing before that." Herron realized his interview with Stoker had been a good dress rehearsal. He'd gotten his lines down pat.

"Did you know it's a serious matter to witness a fatal accident and depart the premises without leaving a statement?"

That was an unexpected question. Herron assumed Stoker had gotten his statement to Scotland Yard by now. Stoker must be a late sleeper. *Lucky dog.*

Herron was about to say he couldn't see why it was any skin off his nose, but then he decided not to be belligerent. Chubb could still slap the handcuffs on a witness and haul him down to the station. The last thing Herron wanted was to be taken down to a station, especially handcuffed.

"It was all hush-hush," Herron laid his cigarette hand to his forehead, as if to massage the sluggish machinery to quicker action, "but I didn't suppose it was going to prove secret from your lot."

"What was 'hush-hush,' sir?"

"The man was, who took my statement."

"You've given no statement, sir."

Herron waggled a finger. "Oh-ho-ho, yes, I did; just not to your lot."

"My . . . lot, sir?"

"They said they'd pass the gist of it along to the police. Haven't got it yet? That's government efficiency for you. What I pay rates and taxes for, I can't imagine. All poured down a rat-hole." He gave an unpersuasive little laugh – that died on his lips when saw Chubb was smiling no more than Merridew had after the hymn-joke.

"To whom did you give this alleged statement?"

"Oh. Ah. What was the chap's name? Stoker. Inspector Stoker."

Chubb gave him a curious glances. "Are you sure you have the name right? I know every inspector at the Yard—"

"That's right. He isn't one of your lot."

"Isn't he, sir? What do you mean my . . . *lot*?"

"He made a point of telling me it was not Scotland Yard. Not a policeman by a strict construction of the Act. But he questioned me closely. Wrote everything down. That should satisfy you."

Chubb looked bewildered. "I don't understand, sir."

"I'll speak up."

"I can hear you perfectly, sir. It's the words what ain't makin' any sense. The constable at the station said that, while he was questioning the witnesses, a man matching your description—"

Chubb pointed to Pottle, who drew a little book from his inside breast pocket and handed it over. Chubb flipped it open and read aloud,

"—who had been at the tail end of the queue, departed the premises and never returned." He snapped the book shut like an exclamation point.

"I did return, in point of fact, but then decided not to go in."

"You returned . . . from where?"

"From talking with Stoker." "Who is Stoker?"

"Ah, now there's a question."

"Yes, sir. There is. Who is Stoker? Description?"

"Tallish—"

"Your height, sir?"

"Not quite. Not an overabundance of hair. Not bald as such, but I think he combs it over. Trim little moustache. Authoritative manner, presumably ex-military. Bulging a bit toward the center-line. I took him for one of your lot, but he said he was working for Her Majesty in a 'private capacity.'"

Chubb scratched his head. "I'm afraid I don't understand—"

"A bobby at the station knew him."

"Did he?"

"Yes. They talked. At the barrier. Just before we left. Stoker spoke to a constable, who saluted him—"

Chubb opened the little book again. He looked like he wished he hadn't snapped it shut, since he had to thumb the book twice over to find the place.

"That was a man introducing himself as one 'Colonel Philgrave.' He said had just returned from overseas. He claimed, according to the officer at the barrier, neither he nor his companion witnessed the incident, but his – tall, sandy-haired companion with an ivory-knobbed stick – was violently ill. They would return to after he had gotten his companion some air. The policeman had ben in the army, and he snapped a salute out of habit. Philgrave never gave a statement, either. Inquiries at the War Office produced no Colonel with such a name in London."

He handed the little book to Pottle, who took out a pencil, licked the point, and poised it over a blank page.

Herron shook his head. "Philgrave? What a ghastly name. Can't be the same chap. Must be two of them the policeman saluted. Man I left with was definitely Stoker. His friend called him 'Jake.'"

Chubb told Pottle to write down 'Jacob Stoker' and then turned back to Herron with as serious a look on his suety face could maintain. "The officers taking information specifically asked for witnesses to remain in the station."

"Yes, I heard them bawl something to that effect. But Stoker wanted to question me in a private capacity."

Bewildered was hardly sufficient to describe Chubb's aspect. "You keep repeating, 'a private capacity.' What does that mean, *a private capacity*?"

"Well, away from *hoi-polloi*."

"And he took you from the train station as well as the oy-polloy?"

"He and his associate."

"Ah. And what associate would that be, sir?"

"Oh, he wasn't so forthcoming, but his name was Hawkins. Just Hawkins. I'm sorry—Sergeant."

"Inspector," Chubb corrected, stiffly, jealous of his title.

"No, no. Hawkins was a Sergeant."

"Hawkins, Sergeant. No known Christian name." He reiterated this information firmly, so Pottle would take it down *not* as Herron offered it but as Chubb rephrased it. "Where did you go off to with these gentleman?" "I don't know. Some office building. It smelled micey and the gas seemed to have been shut off for the night. Good job it's near the longest day of the year or I'd have frozen solid. They wouldn't have found my remains till thaw. Chilly enough as it was, being on the river. All I told Stoker was that I was on the spot, but had eyes for other things when the chap fell. I saw him fall, but that's the size of it. So now you know all. That should satisfy you."

Chubb's manner was far from satisfied. "No one seems to have seen much, or even been close to the accident, except an elderly lady and her paid companion."

Herron smiled. *Paid companion.* The two loveliest words in the English language. They meant the two ladies were probably were not blood kin; and that sweet, almond-eyed lass would not wither away to resemble the terrier-woman in another century or so.

So the police knew who she was! Chubb may very well have her name written down in that very book! And her address! But Herron wasn't likely to get her name and address from Chubb. The police frowned on playing matchmaker.

He was weighing the possibility of offering a substantial bribe for the name, when Chubb said,

"These ladies, the younger one and her elderly companion, both said a tall young gentleman with sandy hair, wearing evening dress and an eyeglass, stood close to them. The younger lady said the man had a stick with an ivory knob. This matches the description of the man who left with Colonel Philgrave."

"Hmm? Oh . . . righty-o. I don't know how I could have mistaken the name 'Philgrave' for 'Stoker,' but that fellow standing by the ladies was me. My monocle is upstairs, should you wish to examine it." He was a flustered at Merridew for advising him not to wear it.

Leaving the window, Chubb extended the walking-stick to Herron with the ivory knob foremost. "Is this stick yours, sir?"

Herron was not allowed to touch it, but he aimed a weary cigarette at the inscription. "It does have my name on it, Inspector."

This proved how stupid the police were: they have his name on a stick, they read it aloud, and then ask if it's his. No wonder private detectives always ran rings around the police inspectors in magazine stories.

"And, in case you didn't know, Inspector, Queen Anne is dead."

So far, Herron could have conducted this interview in bed. As soon as he washed his hands of these oafs, he would repair upstairs and sleep Sunday out.

Because of Herron's Sabbatical necessities (such as coffee and clothes), Merridew typically attended evening, rather than morning, services. When he crawled back between the silk sheets to hibernate until Monday, Herron decided he'd tell Merridew take the morning off as well, so he could indulge himself in an all-day orgy of church-mongering.

Chubb pointed to Pottle, so he would make a careful note of Herron's answer. "You positively identify that stick as your own?"

"It's mine. I realized I didn't have it when I got home, and supposed I must have left it in the cab. I was going to send Merridew to the cab company to institute inquiries. I must really have left it in Stoker's office. I know – I laid it aside when he told me to take it out of my mouth and then I forgot all about it. I don't understand why Stoker sent you my stick and not my statement."

"The walking-stick was found abandoned in the Underground station."

"I didn't return to the station. Did I tell you that already? I don't recall."

Neither Chubb nor Pottle answered.

"Well, I did go back, just to look in. Then I was out again. But I did have my stick when I was talking to Stoker, and I remember now that I did not have it later. I'd have missed the stick if I had walked home – I twirl it a bit, don't you know – but I went from the building to a brougham to a cab—"

"Where is this office in relation to the Underground station, sir?"

"Took us forever to get there. I think I'll tell Merridew an eternity in Hell isn't the worst thing in the world. Try an cab-ride with your nostrils full of that slick, malodorous goo Hawkins used to set his hair in a permanent state of disarray."

"This stick was discovered at the station and turned in by a gentleman—" he pointed to Pottle, who handed him the notebook. Chubb flipped through it, found the place, and read, "—who left no name."

"What did he look like?"

This time, the Inspector had kept a chubby finger at the right place. He read,

"Non-de-script."

Snapping the book shut again, he handed it to Pottle.

"Thank you for returning my stick, Inspector. I'm not sentimental, but it's a bother getting a new one. They needn't have lobbed it out here by the police. I'd have been happy to have sent Merridew 'round to fetch it."

He reached for it, but Chubb pulled the stick out of Herron's reach.

"You can't have that back just yet, sir. Evidence."

"Evidence? Of what?"

"We haven't quite worked that out, sir."

Herron knew nothing about the law, but he did not doubt there were all sorts of hidden regulations that allowed the police to seize one's sticks and hold them for questioning. "I trust you will to return it if you don't find a crime to pin on it?"

"Yes, sir." The inspector tucked the stick under his arm. He reached his other arm behind him, and Pottle handed him the notebook. Chubb began thumbing it casually. "I've been looking into your record, sir."

"My . . . what, now?"

"You are Herron Strangways, only son of Eleazor Strangways?"

"So he assured me. Knowing his proclivities, I'm absolutely certain that I am. I got everything in the will, anyway, and that's what matters."

"Oriental imports, tea, objects-dee-art . . . Very good business, I'm informed."

"We get by. And we're always branching out into new fields."

"Good public school . . . sent down from Cambridge . . ."

"Let's say, rather, I took an exeat and never found my way back."

"No doubt your father endowed something. Wonderful, what money can buy."

"It was all a misunderstanding, Inspector, over a simple prank. I did think the authorities might have evinced a sense of humor."

"Member of the Hemlock Club. Rather rum organization, I am given to understand, but never any trouble, I think."

"Oh, there may be a deal of good-natured hazing going on from time to time, but we just like the mystique—"

"You have been before the magistrates before. Drunk and disorderly—"

"I was *not* disorderly."

"Stealing government property; to wit: the truncheon of p.c. Johnson in the vicinity of—"

Herron drew the line at that. Firmly, "I did not steal it. I took it."

The distinction escaped Chubb, and he said so.

"Well, he left it lying there. What else was a chap to do? It was a gift of the gods. Finder's keepers—that's the law."

"Stealing a potted plant from a high-class dining establishment—" Chubb raised his eyes from the book. "A potted plant?"

"I was afraid you might get around to that. I confess, I did swipe the plant, though 'stealing' has rather a negative connotation. I'd been dining rather high with some friends and a lady of quality in our party expressed a strong desire to have a plant just like it for her front room. What was a gentleman to do? Refuse a lady her simple request?"

"If it violated the law—yes." He muttered under his breath about the plant not being the only thing that was potted.

"I was tiddly. Oh, yes; I admit it, I was tiddly. You can't slap me in irons for it. I paid my debt to society. Hefty fine. There's a word for being tried for the same crime twice, don't you know. Can't recall it at the moment."

"Drunk in charge of a hansom cab—" Chubb was a blase little man, but this caused even him to raise an eyebrow or two. "A hansom cab, sir?"

"Yes. I borrowed it, don't you know."

"*Borrowed?*"

"And I don't mean stole-borrowed. Gave the driver twenty guineas for the privilege. Wager with a chap. Didn't know there were rules about not being a bit squiffy. I thought I handled the contraption pretty well—"

"The hansom cab driver lost his position."

"Good thing, too. You don't want the public thoroughfares choked with cabbies who rent their vehicles to every drunken hooligan who happens along."

Chubb continued flipping, but did no further reading. "There's nothing *serious* against you, sir. Just a number of pranks that went wrong."

Herron smiled. "Good thing you haven't listed the ones that went right."

Chubb shot him a warning glance. Herron volunteered no further information.

"You are a high-spirited young gentleman. And it does seem that all these 'pranks' were performed when you were *dining high.*"

Herron gave a gesture of resignation with his hands, as if to say, *What is a young man to do?* "The best laid schemes of mice and men go wrong when they're soused. How mice enter into it—"

He frowned. That saying reminded him of his loss the night before.

He was in the selfsame room as that young lady's name and whereabouts – but he doubted Chubb would take the bribe. *What's the world coming to?* he thought, sadly, *When money can't buy everything?*

"Fortunately, none of these pranks have resulted in a death before."

"No one has ever died from a stolen potted plant."

"They have been run over by drunken cabbies."

Herron gave a sympathetic flick of his ashes into the tray. His cigarette had nearly burnt out. He drew another from his case and lit it from the remains of the first. He didn't usually smoke so heavily first thing in the morning—

—but the conversation had taken on an atmosphere that made him wary, and when he was wary he smoked.

He was no worrier. No school-fellow or Club mate had ever accused Herron Strangways of showing anxiety, no matter what feat they dared him to do.

But Chubb's words made him uneasy. He couldn't quite put his finger on it.

Then it came to him. It was that word *before*. As in *None of these pranks have resulted in a death before.* Whatever could he mean by that? On the face of it, that was true enough. The only death that had ever resulted from Herron's pranks was his college career. So why did Chubb employ that particular phraseology?

Herron was about to ask – but Chubb seemed almost to have lost interest in the interview. He sauntered over to a bookcase and perused Herron's books while talking in an off-hand manner.

"Were you 'dining well' yesterday, sir? That is, in the drinks line. If you pardon my asking."

"I had a spot at the Club."

"A spot?"

"Say, a dollop. A couple. Hair of the dog." That reminded him of the pooch that stood in the way of that wonderful woman, that Everest of women he would have given ten years off his life to mount.

"'A couple' . . . meaning two?"

"A couple usually means two."

"I've heard 'a couple' used to mean 'a few.'"

"So have I. Quite improper."

"You've never used the term 'a couple' in that sense?"

"Why, yes, if you put it like that, I suppose I have. One can't always speak immaculate grammar in ordinary conversation, Inspector."

"When you said 'a couple' just now, did you mean 'two' exactly?"

"I . . . I didn't keep a running tally on my shirt-cuff—"

"But, to make a long story short, you were feeling more cheerful when you arrived in the Underground station?"

"I may have been a trifle merry—"

"Yes, sir?"

"—but the spirits weren't exactly stratospheric. I was thinking of what a dreary hole London has been this past fortnight. I considered going abroad, maybe even to Africa to pot a lion or two. Then I saw this girl—"

"Why did you leave the station so quickly after the accident, sir?"

"I was dead last in the queue. Stoker said he would take my information."

"Oh, yes. *Stoker*. And *Stoker* identified himself as an arm of the police?"

"He identified himself specifically *not* of the police, arm, leg, or—"

"You called him 'Inspector.'"

"And I might call 'a few' 'a couple.' He never identified himself as such."

"And despite this Stoker never identifying himself as being of the police, you accompanied him out of the station to give important eyewitness evidence to the accident in a 'private capacity' rather than to the proper authorities."

Yes, definitely, Herron thought, *I needed that second cigarette.*

He wondered if he dared to make a trip to the sideboard?

No. Under the circumstances, with the Inspector rabbiting on about his drinking just like his old auntie, Herron decided it might not be wise to start swilling at this time of the morning.

Herron brooding over the insidious tenor this conversation had taken. "You know, Inspector, it does sound rum when you put it in quite those words."

"Yes, sir. That's exactly how I thought it sounded." He stepped over to one of the few rows of books in the library. "I notice you push all your books even with the rear of the shelf."

Herron was puzzled by this a grotesque *non sequitur*. "I beg your pardon?"

"Some people who own books like to keep the spines in line. If they have a longer book next to a shorter book, the shorter book is not pushed all the way back on the shelf, so the spines will make an even row."

"Uh . . ." Herron had never considered it. He wondered why Chubb cared. "When I finish a book I shove it back on the shelf. After that, it's on its own."

"This book, here between two longer books, is all the way in the back." Chubb wiggled it out. "Do you normally push your books all the way to the back?"

"I've no idea. Does it matter?"

"Only because, in the dim light, I almost didn't see this."

Chubb held up a book in yellow cloth, with reddish lettering almost the color of fresh blood.

"Have you read this, sir? Looks brand new."

Herron recognized the book's unattractive mustard color. "I opened it last night but didn't make much headway. Chap loaned it to me, said I might like it. Bought it when it came out not long ago. Told me he started it one morning and was too afraid to put it down and read it all night. Gobbled it up in a day. Said he was afraid to have it in the house any longer. Haven't had time to read it, yet."

"No, sir. I can see you live a busy life."

Herron wondered why this had become a literary symposium. "Have you read it, Inspector?"

"Not much time for reading in police work. Just as, for you, there's not much time for a good book between *pranks*. It takes time to borrow hansom cabs."

Herron started to take issue with the man's tone—

"Do you know who wrote the book, sir?"

"No. I never pay attention to authors."

Chubb handed the book to Herron. Herron read, from the cover:

Dracula

The author had the name *Stoker*.

Chubb opened the book to pages 18-19. "Please start reading—" he ran a stubby finger with a dirty and badly-trimmed nail down the lines of print, "— here. Where the Darcula fellow says, 'I have dined already, and I do not sup.'"

Herron read the next line aloud: "*I handed to him the sealed letter which Mister Hawkins had entrusted to me . . .*"

Herron lowered the book. "Quite a coincidence," he muttered, subdued.

"I would not have known it, except that I've heard it's a rip-snortin' tale, sir, and skimmed through it and noticed the name. In my line of work, we do take notice of names." He took the book from Herron's numb fingers. "How far have you read in this book, sir?"

"Not too far. I . . . I really can't recall. It didn't grip my attention and all I did was turn the pages. It seemed to be all travelogue and recipes. I can't imagine what held my friend so spellbound."

Herron regretted giving the Inspector the time to examine his shelves.

The Inspector motioned for his assistant. With Pottle peering over his shoulder, Chubb plucked a playing card out and held it up as if it were part of a conjuring trick. "I noticed this, too. Is it a place-marker?"

"Yes."

"You put this card in here, to mark how far you had read?"

"Righty-o."

"Do you always use playing cards?"

"Old packs. Might as well make 'em feel useful in their old age."

"And you use these old playing cards to mark the place you have read to, so you can easily flip back to it?"

"Why else?"

"Make a note, Pottle. The card marks page twenty-two. Is that how far you have read in this book, sir?"

"I can't really . . . I wasn't giving it my undivided attention."

"The playing card on page twenty-two is the three of diamonds. Does that have any significance, sir, or do you choose cards at random?"

"I skim 'em off the top of the pack."

"Random. Note that, Pottle. Random three of diamonds marking page twenty-two, and he admitted he put it there on the night of nineteen June."

Chubb's voice was as deferential as ever and his tone was not in the least accusatory. Yet Herron did not like the trend of his conversation.

Instead of slipping the novel back into the bookcase, Chubb returned the playing card to its place at page twenty-two and handed the book to Pottle, who shoved it into a deep pocket in his macintosh.

"The book isn't mine," Herron reminded him.

"It will be returned, with the stick, when we've sorted this matter out."

"Ah. I-I'm sorry, I haven't offered you any breakfast."

"Like Count Darcula, I have eaten, sir. Hours ago. Early risers, we."

"Ah. Do you mind if I go another round with the coffee?"

"If you don't mind, sir, we'd prefer you to accompany us. Perhaps when we take you out into the air you'll remember where you went when you left the Underground station."

"I know where I went, blast it!" Herron cleared his throat and calmed down. "I went with Stoker. I don't know if he plucked his name out of modern literature, or if it's just coincidence. But Stoker and Hawkins took me—"

He paused. Where had they taken him?

"—where to, sir?"

"To a building."

"Can you take us to this building?"

"No. Yes, by jove, I think I can. Do you have transportation? Then drive me to the Underground station." Herron darted for the door.

Chubb put a finger to his nose and then pointed after Herron. "Pottle! Don't let him out of sight!"

On the way out, Herron slipped out of his dressing-gown and smoking-cap and donned the topper and frock-coat on the hall-tree in the foyer.

Outside, Herron saw that Chubb and his assistant were accompanied by two largish, blue-uniformed constables. Their eyes gleamed in happy expectation that the young man might just try to make a break for it.

CHAPTER V

On the way to the Underground station, Herron explained to Chubb,

"Carriage rides always bored me. I like go be different places, but I despise traveling. So I played a game when I was little – counting the turns, remembering which directions we took. If I went a route frequently, I'd try to guess where I was, then open my eyes and peep out the window to see whether I was right. And I listened for sounds, like church bells, to help me along. It became second nature to me. I have a good memory for these things. Too bad it didn't count as a subject to take the place of Greek, what? Greek was always Greek to me."

He tittered, to show it was a witticism. Chubb remained implacably unsmiling.

When the carriage paused outside the doors of the Underground station, Herron stuck his head out the window to make sure they were facing the right way.

"Under starters orders—"

He took out a cigarette, tapped it on his case, lit it, and closed his eyes.

"And . . . they're off!"

Chubb called for the driver to start.

And as Chubb announced the approach of each intersection, Herron said, "Left," "Right" or "Straight on." He had counted it all in his head the night before, but now, to be on the safe side, he counted each turn on his fingers.

Finally, after a roundabout journey, he said, "That's it. Stop—here!"

Slanting over Chubb, Herron opened the carriage window and leaned his head out just as they drew up before a stately old office building.

Pottle kept a tight grip on the tail of Herron's coat, just in case this was Herron's ploy to slip out the window and leg it.

The atmosphere was still thick with the river's pungent, muddy smell. Sunday morning meant less river traffic than Saturday night; but Herron recognized the plash of the Thames and the little dinging and creaking of ships. A foghorn bayed off in an unseen distance.

The building confronting Herron, as he hopped out of the carriage and led Chubb, Pottle and the policemen briskly up the walk, looked old and slightly stooped. It was clearly abandoned – the front door was boarded up.

A sign cocked to one side in front of the structure advised them that the building had been condemned and was dangerous for trespassers. The sign also offered the assurance that new housing would soon be erected on that spot.

Herron gaped up the building's sagging facade. "This can't be it."

"Perhaps you counted your turns wrong, sir?"

"No." Shaking off Pottle, Herron ran to the door. The nails were loose, and he easily tore the boards from the front. Herron was certain these boards had been pried off before and hastily tacked back.

Even with the boards torn away, the front door hardly opened. When Herron finally gave a tug sharp enough to open it, it squealed almost off its hinges.

"Do you recall that sound from yesterday, sir?"

"Yes. I heard it from the carriage. This door was open when I reached it."

"Who opened it?"

"The brougham driver. We sat in the carriage some few minutes while he hopped down and scuttled off."

"You saw him?"

"No, Stoker pulled all the shades. I felt the brougham shake and I heard the driver's fading steps. He tore the boards off the doors, then squealed the door open. Let's go in." Herron darted inside while Chubb was still advising him that it was private property.

As he skidded to a stop in the large, vacant ground floor foyer, Herron said, "I do recall this distinctively musty aroma! I was here!"

Though Herron rarely showed any inclination to exercise before noon, he charged up a nearby staircase two steps at a time.

Chubb, Pottle and two burly constables puffed up behind him.

Herron recalled Stoker's office being the first door up the stairs; but when he threw the door open, dashed in, and looked around – he was confronted with an empty room. No chairs, desks or paraffin oil lamps.

Rushing out, Herron collided with Chubb in the doorway.

Since the building was only days from demolition, none of the doors were locked. For the first time, Herron comprehended the awful significance of not having heard Stoker's key turn in the lock the night before. Stoker had merely rattled his keys to make it sound like he was opening a private office.

Herron panted down the corridor. Opening each door in turn, he poked his head in, glanced around, slammed the door and shot down to the next. The police had struggled to catch Herron on the stairs, but they were on his heels on the flat.

All the rooms were dusty and cobwebby. When he opened a few doors, furry creatures scurried into dark corners. Most were mice. Some were larger than he thought mice should be, but he saw none of them distinctly.

Some rooms had scattered sticks of furniture – chairs, tables . . . abandoned, to be destroyed and carted away as rubbish along with the rest of the building. But he recognized nothing in this firetrap.

When they reached the end of the corridor and Herron burst in the final door, his body language proclaimed defeat. He saw a chair and a desk . . . but no lamp, and no signs of recent habitation.

Chubb stepped up to Herron's shoulder. "If you would come with us, sir, we'd appreciate taking your statement. At the Yard, this time." Herron was subdued. "Lead on, Macduff."

"That's Chubb, sir."

As Chubb turned to go, Herron's eyes hopelessly scanned the room once more.

In the grainy light seeping through the grimy window, he sighted a pasteboard card face-down on the floor. He picked it up, calling, "Inspector!"

Chubb had left the room. He peered around the door frame. "Sir?"

"There must have been another stairway."

"Yes, sir. On this side."

"I ran up the wrong stairs. It's this room! I was interrogated by Stoker here." Pacing to the Inspector with a spring in his step, Herron handed him the card. "Proof positive of my story!"

Chubb studied the front of the card, flipped it over to see if anything was printed on the back, then examined the front again.

He drew the card Herron had given him from his waistcoat pocket and, holding them at arm's length, he compared the two.

"This is *your* card, sir."

"Yes. I have a case full of them."

"Do you have that case with you now?"

"I do. And I gave that card to Stoker last night."

"Yes, sir?" Chubb held the cards up so Herron could see them side-by-side. "They are identical. Was there a special mark on the one you gave this Stoker?" "No. They're all alike. Can't think why he would just toss it down and leave it. I'm glad he did. It proves my story."

"Yes, sir?"

"You don't seem too ruddy impressed."

"This is your card, sir."

"Of course it is." *How dense this chap is!* he thought. *My name's on it.*

"Yes, sir. The two cards, as you said, are identical. This card might have . . . ah . . . *fallen* from your case just now."

Herron lost any respect, if any, he ever had for the Inspector's intelligence. "Now, how can one card have fallen from a closed case in an inside coat pocket?"

"Yes, sir."

"Yes sir—what?"

"Yes sir, it is difficult to imagine one card falling from a closed case in an inside coat pocket. And your case is par-tick-lar-ly well made. I noticed it earlier. If it is impossible for one card to slip from a closed case in a breast coat pocket – which I have not yet determined – you must have taken the card out yourself."

"I just told you I did. I gave it to Stoker."

Herron studied the floor. If it hadn't been so dusty he might have dropped on his hands and knees and studied the floor like magazine detectives. Looking around from a standing position, his sharp eyes caught another piece of evidence. He snatched it up. "Here! Inspector. More proof."

Chubb stared at it blankly. "It's a burnt matchstick, sir."

"Correct, inspector. Got it in one. A burnt match. *My* match."

"Does it have your name on it, sir?"

"Don't be daft. Do you think I have my matches inscribed?"

Taking the partially-burned matchstick, Chubb laid it carefully on the desk. "Please take out another match, sir, and lay it next to that one."

When Herron had done as instructed, Chubb took a matchbox from his own pocket and shook it before Herron's face. Extracting a match, he laid it on the desk flanking the burnt match on the other side.

Except that the match Herron picked up from the floor had burnt down, it, the match Herron laid beside it, and the match Chubb had taken from his own pocket, were exactly the same.

"There's only one reason anyone buys a match, sir." The Inspector struck his match with his thumb and held it up, burning, before Herron's eyes. "To burn 'em. It would be foolish to inscribe an object you mean to destroy."

"Yes! My very point. You put your foot in that one, Inspector." Herron spoke triumphantly, but for some reason he did not feel triumphant.

"And so," said Chubb, "that match cannot be connected to you absolutely."

Forgetting the match while he was talking, Chubb let it burn down to his skin. He threw it down with a yip and shoved his fingers in his mouth. Herron obligingly ground it out with the toe of his shoe, raising an odor of singed dust.

The Inspector sneezed and blew his nose on his sleeve. "*Geshundteit.*"

"Thank you, sir. I'm allergic to dust."

"There's a mark in the dust on that desk." Herron's words sounded hollow. "Where I slid the card along to Stoker."

"You might have done it just now. Or a cat might have done it."

"What cat?"

"Any cat. London's full of strays. They get into buildings like this."

"You can't prove there was a cat in here."

"No sir. It did not leave a calling-card." Chubb folded the burnt match Herron had found, and the card, into a handkerchief and tucked them safely into his breast pocket. Taking Herron by the arm, Chubb began leading him out.

Herron tried not to brush against the Inspector's coat-sleeve.

As he and Herron descended the stairs, Chubb said,

"I'm not one of them story-book detectives who do things methodically, sir. They gather clues one-by-one like they was stringin' so many beads. In real life I ain't one blasted bit sure that what I'm gatherin' at any given moment is a clue or not. I pick up as much as I can, then sort through it, like I was piecin' together a puzzle. Only, I don't know what picture the puzzle is going to make. I'm never sure, 'til I'm done, if there's a piece missin'. Or I may have several puzzles dumped together, and until the picture starts to form I can't tell which pieces go with which. Sometimes a full picture never emerges . . . but in most cases you can piece together enough to nab your man. It may take weeks, months, or even years, for an image to pop out at you. Only when there's a confession do I know right away which pieces fit the puzzle and which don't. And even then – some confessions are out-and-out lies."

"People lie about having committed crimes?"

"You wouldn't believe half of what we hear on the force."

"What if your man doesn't confess?"

"Then we fall back on what we call 'circumstantial evidence.'"

"You'll have a man dancing on a gibbet on circumstantial evidence?"

"I don't hang men, sir. I don't worry about the outcome of a case. I got enough to do figgerin' out which clues might fit on my string. I sift clues and build a case based on 'em. It's the jury decides if the evidence is up to snuff, the judge that passes sentence, and the hangman that gives 'em the drop. We all play out little parts."

"I'd rather have the hard evidence of a confession or a witness."

"Hard evidence is nice, but when you got circumstances . . . you got a pattern. Most men are like trains, sir."

"Are they, really?" Herron was impatient to get away from here, and it showed in his voice.

"They lay their tracks and run on 'em, even if they don't notice 'em. Without knowin' it, they fall into patterns that may be as intricate as a lace antimacassar. You'd be surprised, with just a little workin' out, the number of crimes where we found a criminal bloke's laid out his own little pattern for all the world to see."

"In this case—?"

"Here, sir, we got a circumstance. A man at a train station falls in front of a train. Yessir, that's a definite circumstance."

Herron agreed that was a circumstance.

"As things stand, we don't know if the man ran in front of the train, if he fell in front of the train, or if he was *pushed* in front of the train. As you were a witness, we would appreciate any assistance you could give us with our enquiries."

"I'll be happy to go make my statement. Oh, there was a young lady standing beside me. Do you have her name?"

"We do, sir."

"May I know it? I may want to . . . ah . . . compare notes with her."

"I'd rather you didn't. We want your story to be yours and her story to be hers. Let's keep her "hush-hush" and we'll extend you the same confidentiality. If you will please accompany us to the Yard? We'll have a nice little chat and a cuppa and you can tell us the whole story, from start to finish, again. And again. And again. I'll be mother."

CHAPTER VI

Though he was neither bullied nor threatened, harassed nor touched, Herron spent a tense few hours with Chubb and his associates.

The Inspector simply asked him the same questions over and over and over . . . in exactly the same, calm tone. It was respectful questioning, but unremitting.

Herron had never noticed before how the same sound, even a human voice, heard repeatedly, could rub a man's nerves raw.

Herron wondered what Chubb was getting at with all this repetition. It seemed a harsh punishment for someone who simply had neglected to provide a name and address at the scene of an accident. Chubb had all that information, now. What was the purpose of all this questioning?

Just when Herron felt about to melt in that little, hot room, he was released.

"I'm glad you don't like to travel, sir," said Chubb. "I'd appreciate it if you nailed yourself to London – where we can find you if we have more questions."

You could do with more, Herron thought. *I'm jolly tired of the few you have.*

"I would not choose today, sir, as the best time to go shootin' lions. Are you a good shot, by the way?"

"Pretty fair."

"You could hit a close target?"

"Yes."

"It's just as well for you the man wasn't shot, then."

2

New Scotland Yard was convenient to Herron's row, and he really wanted to go home to bed – and remain there until all this confusion was over. But he needed to brood on what today's activities meant. Walking always helped grease his mental machinery.

The interrogation left Herron with a peculiar nagging in the back of his mind. He could not isolate what caused that vague foreboding.

That penny had not yet dropped.

When he needed to think, Herron liked a long stroll along the Embankment, a road and walkway strung along the north side of the dirty, grey Thames River. And the Embankment was extremely handy to Scotland Yard.

He opted against it. This Sunday afternoon the Embankment, like everywhere else, was far too crowded.

Piccadilly was another one of his favorite haunts; but he knew how full of human flesh it must be, the Sunday before the Procession.

Remaining between Piccadilly and the Embankment was bad enough, so far as crowds went, but it was where he lived most of his life.

It was well into the afternoon and Herron hadn't eaten a morsel since his early breakfast of a single slice of buttered toast.

In his rush to leave with Chubb, Herron had not grabbed much cash and he neglected to bring his cheque book.

He first considered dining at the Club, where he could get a substantial meal, with wine and cheese and a crusted port to follow, on his excellent credit. He had walked practically up to the Hemlock when he remembered that in the Club he was likely to be spotted by someone who would feel free to sit down and start a conversation. Herron was in no mood for chitchat.

He really wanted wine more than food; but Herron never offended his palate with any vintage what he had in his pockets at that moment could buy.

Turning his steps from the Club, he went east onto Pall Mall and fell unconsciously into following the route of Tuesday's Procession.

His pearl-gloved hands felt naked without his stick. When he was in a meditative mood, he ran his stick along the iron bars of every railing he passed. He thought Chubb mean for not returning it. Why impound to an innocent stick?

Rapt in his meditations, he kept bumping into people. At the best of times, London was the most populated and cosmopolitan city in the world. It was more congested than ever today, two days before the Diamond Jubilee Procession.

At every collision, he tipped his hat with muttered apologies; but he never looked in their faces. He wanted no distractions, and if he looked up and saw an attractive female face he would be distracted. He did not even want to see another woman, until he found *her* again. Herron raised his eyes to no one, even the few times he heard someone call his name.

The streets along the Procession route were already closed to vehicles, and they ran thick with pedestrians. Four-and-a-half million souls lived in London, and millions more were visiting, and they all seemed to be promenading out in the streets this Sunday afternoon.

The streets looked even more crowded for being festooned.

In places, they were garlanded across, like it was Christmas. This Christmassy feeling was exasperated by the red drapery hanging from nearly all the buildings and windows. Rather than *Peace on Earth* or *Good Will Toward Men*, buildings had banners stretched along their fronts proclaiming GOD SAVE THE QUEEN. Here and there, upper windows were adorned with "V" and "R" (*Victoria Regina*).

And all the buildings along the route – even the Hemlock Club – had grandstands cobbled together in front of them, for those who could get tickets from the Lord Chamberlain.

So many grandstands stood in front of so many public buildings, a piece in one of Herron's favorite papers, the *Daily Mail*, said it looked as though someone had boarded up the Law Courts and the Houses of Parliament. "They are," the writer added facetiously, "changing all London from building into furniture."

Everyone with a window overlooking the parade route had pocketed a little money from customers wanting to rent them for the hours of the Procession.

A few patient souls were even now, on Sunday afternoon, choosing places where they intended to stand, sit and sleep *until Tuesday morning*.

It was just as well traffic was already blocked off along the parade route; Herron did not even bother looking up when he crossed streets. On an ordinary day he would have been run down, and more than once, as he threaded through Trafalgar Square to the Strand, and Fleet Street.

He was finally brought up short against a barricade. Looking up, he was immensely surprised to find himself staring straight at Queen Anne herself.

Protected in her iron fence, the newish statue of Queen Anne stood in the west front of Saint Paul's Cathedral, hovering over Herron like a chubby angel and aiming her scepter down at him like a dueling foil.

Behind Queen Anne rose the massive western façade of Saint Paul's, 177 feet wide, which dwarfed all the surrounding buildings, even the highest grandstand.

All the streets to the Cathedral were blocked off, even the barriers blocking off the streets were gaudily mantled in red cloth.

The Cathedral itself was less decorated than the rest of the Procession route. A splash of red cloth shone here, a few floral arrangements sprung up there.

Saint Paul's was a doorway to a world beyond worlds, the house of a God Who ruled the immeasurable area of the universe and beyond. Victoria was Queen of an eleven million square mile patch of that cosmos. The churchmen at the ceremony on Tuesday might give thanks for Victoria's sixty years, but the austerity of decorations at the Cathedral was a reminder which of the two was greater, God or Victoria. Sixty years was nothing compared to eternity.

Though considered the masterpiece of architect Christopher Wren, Herron thought it resembled a heavy, rectangular marbled cake offered to him after a large meal. The Cathedral was so huge it required two flights of steps merely to enter it – ten from the street; then a plateau where once could catch one's breath; then a further fourteen up to the western porch and the massive front doors.

The Cathedral's west front had two porches. The lower supported the upper with six paired sets of gigantic Corinthian columns.

The upper portico was crowned with a triangular pediment containing a bas-relief of the conversion of Saul on the road to Damascus. At the apex of the triangle stood a statue of Saint Paul himself. Apostolic statues ran around the edge of the roof; but Paul had pride of place above the west front, since was the patron saint of the City of London.

Flanking the west front were two stubby bell towers, tapering up to 212 feet, 6 inches. The southern tower had a four-sided clock with gold Roman numerals.

From Herron's perspective, the famous dome of Saint Paul's Cathedral rose from behind the statue of Saint Paul.

At the base of the dome was the 'Stone Gallery' – 173 feet above the ground and about seventy feet up from the roof. The Stone Gallery, with its high balustrade, circled the base of the massive dome.

The ribbed dome, curving up to 278 feet above the ground, was a dingy leaden color and had always looked, to Herron, like a grey soft-boiled egg in a fancy cup. On top of the dome was a lantern, surmounted by a ball and a cross. The top of the cross rose to 365 feet above the pavement. From this vantage point, Herron could not see the Golden Gallery around the lantern, but he saw the Cross.

The Cathedral was set slightly askew from the street coming up Ludgate Hill. Some architectural critics fumed that it should have formed a more organic unity with its surroundings; but the Cathedral's makers wanted it to stand on its own, a type of the City of God in a very literal city of man in the city of London.

Herron didn't care for it the Cathedral . . . but he was no architectural critic. Others seemed to approve of it, so what did he care? It was a part of London he'd seen all his life. Though he never attended religious services, he was so familiar with the massive Cathedral, he no longer noticed it. If not for the barricade, Herron might have strolled right by it without seeing it.

Finishing touches were still going up on the west churchyard, where Tuesday morning's main ceremony would be held.

The Thanksgiving ceremony would take place out-of-doors (chancy, given the changeable London weather). But then, the Queen was seventy-eight. She couldn't be expected to hop spryly out of her carriage and trot up the steps into the Cathedral on her pudgy little legs. The Queen herself would remain seated in her carriage, which would be drawn up to the west front steps, which were already carpeted in red.

The front steps were blocked off, except for a narrow opening up the middle. Important, officiating Anglican clergymen would perform their ceremony in that open space. Non-conformist clergy would range to either side of them in the blocked-off areas.

Just like the rest of the parade route, the west front of the Cathedral had grandstands to the north and south of the west front, and on the upper portico. These were for very special dignitaries who could afford the purchase price of the special blue ticket.

Looking beyond the western churchyard, Herron thought of Tennyson. *Grandstands to the left of him, grandstands to the right of him.*

A colossal grandstand stood across the street to his left, on the north side of the western church yard, stretching all the way to Goodman's Dentists (single tooth two shillings and sixpence, and with a five year's warranty). An entire warehouse had been bought and destroyed specifically for its construction. That grandstand had four tiered levels, and the front of the top story bore a banner with the legend:

IN EVERY HEART ONE PRAYER: GOD SAVE VICTORIA

Across the street to Herron's right, south of the Cathedral's west churchyard, stood a dreary, grey-brick warehouse. Its owners kept the warehouse and had rented every single window to spectators. Its gloomy exterior was moderately improved by bunting and *GOD SAVE THE QUEEN* signs.

The streets where the parade would come and go would be open; every other street leading here would be closed, and jammed with spectators on all sides.

Thousands of souls would be clumped together in this small area.

Since it was the Sabbath Day, no one was actually working behind the barricades. But from inside the Cathedral, Herron heard the choristers and choir boys practicing the Jubilee Hymn – music by Arthur S. Sullivan (erstwhile collaborator with William Gilbert) with words by William, Bishop of Wakefield:

> *"Oh Royal heart, with wide embrace*
> *For all her children yearning!*
> *Oh happy realm, such mother-grace*
> *With loyal love returning!*
> *Where England's flag flies wide unfurl'd,*
> *All tyrant wrongs repelling;*
> *God make the world a better world*
> *For man's brief earthly dwelling!"*

Herron shivered. He knew the Jubilee hymn would prove a grim affair.

The hymn had more to go; but the roast beef wasn't all it should have been, and Herron hadn't the stomach to swallow this hymn on top of it.

He began retracing his steps. He was far from home; and after the past twenty-odd hours or so, he desired nothing more than to go to bed – alone.

3

Merridew was probably still at chapel, so at least when he got home Herron would have the place to himself. He had never been a lad for solitude, but today he looked forward to it.

Herron almost envied Merridew, in a way. Merridew was a man who didn't keep his pious face in a box until Sunday, but lived every day as if he were about to go to chapel. He was not a proud man; he knew all the hymns by heart, but he held up his hymn-book when he sang in his loud, cracked voice, so as not to show off. Merridew was a man with a simple faith: man was born without godliness; God had become a man, and was crucified and died, then Resurrected by his own power, to extend godliness to man as a free gift. God would live inside him for this life and then man would find life everlasting.

For Herron, nothing came free. Everything had a catch. Even salvation (perhaps, especially salvation) had to have a price.

Herron had a latchkey tucked into the inside lining of his topper. When he reached his terrace house, he let himself in. Setting his hat upside down on the hall-tree in the foyer, he unbuttoned, stripped off, and tossed his gloves into it.

Without turning up the gas, he slumped wearily up the stairs to his bedroom. His bedroom faced over the front of the house, into the street. The sun was on the west side of the terrace so the bedroom, like the front hall, was in shadow.

Herron did not leave a trail of clothes behind him. It was far too early to go to bed. He wanted to go to bed, but the last thing he wanted was to turn in now, then be wide awake at three a.m.

It was still a long time before sunset. When he entered his bedroom, where the curtains were still open, there remained just enough light for him to see, seated in his private armchair, a largish, fleshy-faced man with grizzled brown sideboards, dressed as a butcher, complete with apron and rolled up sleeves and a yellowed, straw boater hat set back on the crown of his head revealing his high noggin.

CHAPTER VII

"What are you doing in my bedroom?"

"A better question, matey, would be, what are *you* doing in yer bedroom?" His lips curved into a wry smile. "I thought you'd be kippin' in quod."

"I'm sorry . . . I miscued on that one."

"In-bloomin'-carcerated, mate."

"I assisted the police with their inquiries. That's all."

"All my eye and Betty Martin."

"Oh, my God! This is all I need!"

"Chubb must be a-lettin' you pay out yer own rope to top yourself."

"What are you blathering about? Speak English, man."

"Yer gallows, mate. 'e's 'oping you'll string 'em yourself. Good man, Chubb, so I've 'eard. 'As 'is own little ways o' doing things. If 'e were a buy-the-booker you'd be jugged. But 'e's left yer on yer tod 'oping you'll scarper."

"Scarper?"

"Do a bunk. Then 'e'll 'ook you, reel yer in and grill yer."

"I don't have anything to run from."

"Don't yer?"

"Why am I even talking to you? Get out of here or I'll call the police."

"I would not recommend it, Mister Strangways, or you will 'snuff it, mate.'"

Flinging back his apron, the butcher revealed a stubby but serviceable revolver. It was a conveniently portable gun whose barrel could not have been more than two inches and a half. It seemed to be pointed carelessly in Herron's general direction, but he handled his firearm with such professional ease Herron believed he was just liable to bulls-eye whatever he shot at.

"How do you know my name?" Herron demanded.

"I'm in your house."

"Righty-o."

The stranger's smile faded. The chipper voice became stern. "Sit down."

"I prefer to stand."

"On the bed. Hands in your pockets. Feet up."

Herron sat upright against the headboard in the large fourposter. Since he wasn't given time to remove his spats and shoes, he stretched his legs out at a slant with his feet off the bed, crossed at his ankles. With his hands in his frock coat pockets, his elbows jutted uncomfortably straight out to either side.

"I noticed you're pronouncing your 'H's and you've dropped the rhyming slang – or whatever that palaver was. I think you made it up. Who are you?"

"The name's Jessup."

"We all have our cross to bear."

"You have nerve. I like that. It may help you survive."

"Survive what?"

"You witnessed an incident at the Underground station last night?"

"Yes. Everyone in London has questioned me about it. I suppose it is your turn. Don't take long, there's a queue at the door."

"Don't ladle the sauce on too thick, Cokey. You can't tell me anything I don't know. I was there. I saw it all."

"Good. Since you know everything, go away." "But I do have one question: did that man say anything to you in passing?"

"We hadn't been introduced. All I know it, the final score was: Train, one; Haggard Birds, nil."

"That 'haggard bird' went to meet someone on that train."

"How do you know?"

"Three guesses."

"You?"

Jessup gave the best bow he could while seated. "Good shot."

"If you went to meet him, you must know who he was and what he had to say."

"'We hadn't been introduced.'" Jessup did not imitate Herron's voice, but he had precisely captured the music of the young man's speech.

"How did you mean to recognize each other?"

"By signs."

"Oh. Masons?"

One corner of Jessup's mouth scythed into a smile. "We belonged to the same 'fraternal organization.' We arrived at that station at different times by different roads. We were to board the train in different coaches separated by a coach in between. At a certain prearranged tick of the clock we were to rise from our respective seats and make our way casually through the middle coach. Squeezing casually by each other, I would politely ask him for a cigarette."

"Heavy smoker?"

"Not at all. This cigarette was one he rolled himself – with a few words written in pencil on the inside of the paper."

"Clever. Say, if you didn't know each other, how did you know it was him? London's so packed right now anyone might have been knocked off that platform. It was almost me that 'fell or was pushed.'"

"I knew him because I saw who killed him."

"Killed? Pushed?"

"Shot."

While it was Herron's ironclad policy never to argue with a man aiming a gun at him, he challenged this statement, "He was not shot."

"Do be quiet, Mister Strangways, there's a good little tycoon. He didn't give you a cigarette by any chance?"

"I prefer my own brand. Old Dominion. I buy them ready-made to my specifications. Sometimes I ask them sprinkle the tobacco with cloves. By the way, I saw the haggard bird. I didn't see you."

"I didn't look as I do now. And you were too engrossed watching the twist to notice if a rhino had stomped up behind you."

"Twist?"

"Female."

"Why twist—? Never mind! I don't want to know. No more slang, please! Here, if your story is true, and I see no reason to think it is, perhaps 'they' got so close to him he had to smoke his wonderful cigarette."

"'They?'"

"Isn't there always a they?"

Jessup did not deny it. Neither did he confirm it. "If he knew his number was up, he may have smoked the evidence, then said a word or two to a stranger before dying. That's a hazardous game. When you whisper to a stranger all of a sudden, they're bound to hear it wrong. But if the information is vital, in dire straits any extreme is worth trying."

"Well, he didn't speak to me, or give me a cigarette, cigar, or pipe. So, that concluded . . . get out of my house."

"You know, Mister Strangways, right now we each possess something extremely valuable to both of us."

"Oh?"

"You own a house. I own a gun."

"Your set. Another volley?"

"Besides, if I leave your house on your terms, you'll never see me again."

"That's a bad thing?"

"It is for you."

Herron demurred. "Listen, I'm in trouble for leaving that Underground station without a note from teacher. Did you 'scarper' after the accident? If so, just prepare for an English sort of Spanish Inquisition."

"I did not leave. I was a loiterer watching the police examine the body. They emptied his pockets. No cigarettes. No papers. No identification."

"Curious."

"Not really. He was a professional. He would not have carried more than one cigarette. More than one might have risked confusion, unless he marked the right one. And marking it would have been a dead giveaway to anyone with an eagle eye out for secret messages. He was killed to keep from passing that information on, Mister Strangways. That information was not found on his body. We must know if it was taken off him or if he secreted it someplace. Or if, as you suggest, he had to smoke it before the train hit him."

"Some do-gooders insist cigarettes have a deleterious effect on one's health."

"Do you take anything seriously?"

"My neck."

"It's never been in more jeopardy."

"Why?"

"I don't know Chubb personally. I've heard he's a good man. A bit odd in his methods, but sound as a pound. He's looked into your record? Yes. So have I."

"You're not a policeman?"

"I have contacts on the force. You are a lively young man."

"I bore easily. Like now, for instance."

"Young men bore easily who don't have to earn their own spending money."

"I've got you pegged, now! You're a ruddy socialist!"

Jessup chuckled. "Chubb has you written down in his little book as a lad always up to some mischief."

"Not always."

"When you're suffering from *ennui*? Notably, when you've bent the elbows?"

"Just the one elbow. I'm not yet a double-fisted drinker. I have one steadfast rule: never drink between drinks. That's only asking for trouble."

"You are a cool cucumber. It'll be a shame to lose you."

"It won't be, to lose you."

"Chubb has examined you, as have I. We've reached similar conclusions. You're a man who stays bored because he has no work—"

"Work!" The four-letter word offended Herron's delicate sensibilities.

"—so you liven things up by the occasional prank or practical joke. Let's review the circumstances."

Herron sighed. *Circumstances* again.

"Here's a hypothetical situation. A young man – not unlike yourself – let's call him 'Man A' sees an incident like the one you witnessed yesterday. He leaves the station and tells the police he left in the company of two men."

"Man B and Man C?"

"They cannot be identified, so we can't call them anything. He says these two men took him to an abandoned building for questioning, then let him go."

"Well?"

"Man A tells the coppers he left his expensive stick in that abandoned building. But Man A's stick was handed in by a kindly soul *at the station*. It has Man A's name on it, so there's no confusion as to its owner. It's one of a presentation set to the charter members of the man's club, but having his name on it makes it unique. It's the only stick like it in the world."

"I think that's what 'unique' means. I thought I left it behind after my *tete-a-tete* with Stoker."

"You did. I saw you take it out with you. You did not return to the station. Your stick did. I saw the Good Samaritan who handed it in as found."

"Did you recognize him? Maybe he can help us."

"Tall. Prematurely lined, like a withered apple. Light hair."

"That must have been Stoker's man Friday, Saturday. You described him well. And Chubb wrote down that tommyrot about his being 'nondescript.'"

"I'm trained to observe. And to remember. Remembering is a large part of a game where writing is deadly."

"I told them my address. Why did Hawkins turn the stick in at the station rather than bringing it here or to the Club, where he might have gotten a reward?"

"Nature did not give you that head solely for a hat-rack, Mister Strangways. Please use it. May we continue? This man we were talking about – no, not the one who turned in the stick, the one who left the Underground station, Man A – takes the police on a wild goose chase to an abandoned building where he says he gave a full statement to those two men, who specifically identified themselves as not being policemen. At the building he finds no evidence he was ever there, though he does try to fob off one of his own calling-cards – which he might have taken from his case at any time – and one burnt match, indistinguishable from millions of other matches, burnt and unburnt, over greater London." "You do have good sources."

"Unimpeachable."

"I've run 'round that mulberry bush all day with Chubb."

"You haven't run round this, I wager: What the police require are suspects. One good suspect might be a man known for his outrageous practical jokes, who can provide no verifiable – or even half-way sensible – account of his doings after an accident that led to a death."

"So I'm a prankster. I have a few laughs."

"It might be a funny rag to steal a potted plant. It is not funny to drive a cab intoxicated. Man A, who had been oiling the tongue all day, might think it 'a great wheeze' in an extremely crowded Underground platform to put his hand between another man's shoulder-blades – man B, let's call him – and give him a light shove before an incoming train. He means to push man B only just enough to give him a good scare, and have a good laugh at his expense and buy him a drink if he gets offended. But if Man A has already bought himself a drink or few, his push might be harder than he intended – and can't hold Man B back."

Jessup paused.

The penny *finally* dropped. Herron croaked, "Go on."

"Man B falls and is mangled by the train. Seeing his prank murdered a man, Mister Oily-Tongue runs out and takes shelter at home, where he's found the next day looking like something the cat dragged in, chewed up and spit out."

"In the same wrinkled suit, too." Most of the time, Herron's lazy mind was a slow coach; but he could whip up the horses when an occasion demanded. At this crossroads of his life, he required thinking at the gallop. Herron realized what had been nagging him all day about Chubb's behavior. "I wasn't 'assisting' the police with any blasted inquiries. I'm a suspect!"

"No."

"I'm not a suspect?"

"Not 'a' suspect. *The* suspect."

CHAPTER VIII

"Or, perhaps," Jessup continued, "Chubb is clever enough to actually know how the man died. I doubt it—but it cannot be discounted until we know."

"You say he was shot. Even a man with Chubb's pedestrian intelligence can see a whacking great bullet hole in a body."

"If you say so. Either way, whether Chubb realizes how the man died or not, since you were right beside him, you could have done the deed with little effort."

"I was too close to shoot him! At the clip he barreled past me, I'd never have gotten a gun out of my pocket in time. Besides, he did not die of gunshot."

"I only said he was shot. I did not say that's necessarily what killed him."

Herron yawned, "By jingo, you caught me out. I poisoned the bullet first." More seriously, "Looky here, are the police trying to frame me for murder?"

"Nothing could be further from Chubb's methods, I'm sure. Besides, he won't need to frame you, with all the circumstantial evidence shaping up in your image."

"What about the evidence *for* me?"

"What evidence? A planted pasteboard card? That is a flimsy attempt to buttress an untenable alibi. You stick at the station, when it should have been miles away in an abandoned building *is* evidence. It's a flagrant contradiction that blows your house down. That stick means your alibi is a yarn concocted by an insufficient intelligence that got sent down from Cambridge."

"I took an exeat."

"With your stick as hard evidence, your insistence in standing by an improbable alibi adopts a more sinister interpretation."

"Oh." Herron tugged his collar. No wonder Jessup said Herron's neck was in jeopardy. He could almost feel the noose tightening. He loosened his tie.

"Chubb is, by all appearances, one of the good 'uns. If there's a stick-shaped hole in the case against you, he won't see you strung up for it."

"Is someone else trying to frame me, then?"

"If so, I'm sure it's nothing personal."

"I tend to take rather personally being hanged for a murder I didn't commit. Am I being framed or not?"

"Probably not at first. You were taken by these two men and questioned merely to find out if you had any connection with the deceased."

"They were keen to know if he has aught to say. And how he died."

"They know how he died. You were closest to him at the end; they wanted to know if *you* had seen how he died. They probably did not intend to frame you."

"I'm not as certain as you are."

"Oh, that's a lot of unnecessary bother. I'm sure they only meant to kill you."

A shiver ran through Herron's body.

"If you had seen anything, or if you knew anything, or if the haggard bird had told you anything, I'm certain they would have killed you."

"Ignorance *is* bliss."

"And you obligingly gave them your address, so they can always find you if they want to do you later."

2

"So if they didn't want to frame me before – why are they doing it now?"

"I have a theory. It's only a theory, but I try to put myself in their place. Bodies are difficult to dispose of at the best of times. And your body is special."

"Thank you."

"It wasn't a compliment. If they nabbed me, Mister Strangways, they might kill me with impunity. I don't exist, officially. Even people with an official existence usually pose few problems, where killing goes. You saw the multitudes in the streets today? Millions of people more than usual are in London."

"By the looks of them, some of them are more than unusual."

"Shh. A scattered few of the men and women who came to London in the past fortnight will never go home again. No one will ever find a trace of them. Some will meet with foul play. There are men and women who will kill for pennies. Others will vanish of their own accord. They'll start new lives under new names. Or, because of unhappy love affairs or debts or general boredom such as yours, they'll make a hole in the river and won't be identified when they wash ashore. People disappear every day, Mister Strangways."

"Yes, I've seen it in the papers."

"Most of them are missed only by a small, glum circle, who keep forlorn candles burning vainly in their windows. You're different. You own an important business, even if you never do a stroke of work at it. If the owner of Strangways' Emporium disappears—"

"Emporia. We are legion."

"Even better. They're in every major city in England. Strangways' Emporia employ thousands of workers. And the man who hands out their wages has vanished. A story like that might not be splashed all over the front pages in the week of the Queen's Diamond Jubilee—But! You have friends in Parliament?" "Both Houses. One must have contacts. A few lads I went to school with are back-benchers in the Commons – there's one I expect will be Prime Minster one day, and he's just fool enough to want it – and another close pal has already taken his title and sits in the Lords, when he feels like it."

"When he's sober, more like. Questions will be asked in Parliament: 'What happened to Strangways?'" Jessup stroked his chin. "Interesting, is it not?"

"'Interesting' is not the word springing to my mind."

"I mean, it's easy to kill. It's difficult to dispose of a body. Bodies are lumpy and strangely-shaped dead weights to hauled secretly through the streets. They must be disposed of with care, especially if they belong to notable people."

"You sound like you know that from first-hand experience."

"Bingo. But you were in an abandoned building earmarked for demolition in a few days. Who's going to find you there? Why didn't they dust you off?"

Herron shrugged.

"I said some men will kill for pennies. You're worth more than that—but they did not kidnap you and hold you for ransom. They These people have a much bigger score in mind. They want no one standing in their way. Lying, perhaps. They meant to kill you if you knew anything. But you presented complications."

"I'm gratified to hear it."

"Even if they do nose out your body and identify you before the building is razed, think about the *cause celebre*. 'Who murdered Strangways!' It'll be worse than Jack the Ripper. Your friends in Parliament will insist the police find the killers. And the papers will have a field day."

"I don't follow you."

"The most probable reason didn't kill you is that *to keep them from immediate scrutiny*. The police are investigating this 'accident.' If they do it right, it will appear less accidental the deeper they investigate. Their investigations will become more rigorous the moment they learn how the man was shot—"

"But he wasn't shot! I know a gunshot when I don't hear one."

"Their investigations may make the police might intrude into byways certain people do not wish them to travel. So they provided the police with misleading evidence pointing to you, to waste their time. Which suggests," Jessup mused, to himself, "time is precious to them."

"But I'm innocent!"

"Innocence is a very difficult thing to prove. And it may not have to be proved. This obliging Mister Stoker of yours did not kill you last night. The police are treating this as a homicide, and you are at the center of a murder investigation. Or manslaughter."

"'Manslaughter' actually sounds worse than 'murder.'"

"They'll hang you either way. And that takes time. I don't believe they will try to frame you any further."

"Good."

"It's quicker to end the police investigation by letting them find you with a bullet lodged in your skull and your blood spattering a neatly-written confession in your own hand, or a reasonable facsimile. Even without the confession, they'll think they were correct in their suspicions. You were guilty of manslaughter at least and you killed yourself rather than go through the indignity of arrest and trial. End of case, end of investigation. Everyone is happy."

"Except for me! I just won't shoot myself."

"No. But it's incredibly easy to shoot a man in the temple and wrap his dead fingers around the grip of a pistol."

That had the ring of first-hand experience, too. A cold finger seemed to trace Herron's spine.

"Of course, they may knock you around a bit first, to find out what you know."

"The police certainly won't believe I beat myself up!"

"No. But Stoker and his pals can chuck you out the window. Sailing you out this window and letting you bounce across the pavement a few times will cover any bleedings and contusions."

"But . . . but . . . but . . ."

"Please desist with the motor carriage impression."

Herron emitted one more *but* before sputtering out, "I don't know anything!"

"Having met you, I'm persuaded of that. But 'they' must entertain doubts, and it's always better to err on the safe side. You see, they're afraid of you."

"That makes us even!"

"You may be the harmless nincompoop look—"

"I say—!"

"—but even so, they may fear you *saw* more last night than you understood. I think they'll just kill you and have done with it. And if time is as precious to them as I think, the sooner, the better."

"Not by forced suicide. I just won't let them catch me alone in the house."

Jessup clicked his tongue. "These people who want you dead may prefer to kill you on the street. In these crowds, it won't be difficult. Trains run every day. And cabs. And omnibuses. Lots of people on the streets. Any passer-by can give you a shove into the traffic."

"I stuck to the closed streets."

"This street outside your house isn't closed. But – you bumped into lots of people? One of them might casually have inserted a stiletto between your ribs and been off before you noticed you were bleeding."

"How would 'they' find me in this jumble of human bodies?"

"Humans are like trains. They run on their rails."

"Chubb said much the same thing. Both of you are neglecting to understand that I am not a creature of habit. I follow wherever the skirts lead me."

"It must be interesting when you're in Scotland," smiled Jessup.

"You can joke!"

"Yes, I can. You either laugh at your mortality or you fear it. And if I can laugh at mine, it's all the easier for me to laugh at yours. When I saw that man take you away last night, I thought you were either in on the plot . . . or you were a goner. When I learned they took you to an abandoned building, I knew they probably took you there specifically to murder you."

"It would hardly have looked like suicide."

"No, they'd not have bothered with that. When they had you alone and unwatched, they'd have made you kneel and then they'd put a bullet in the back of your head, using a larger caliber pistol than mine. They didn't do that. And they did not molest you on the streets this afternoon.

"So when you walked in I asked: why are you in your bedroom? Why doesn't Chubb have you tucked up in a nice, comfy cell? Better yet, why haven't those men from last night killed you? I would have."

That was not a comforting thought for Herron, who was unable yet to sort his enemies from his allies (if any).

"They should have killed you on the off-chance." Jessup pondered this. "They might have left you in the abandoned building with little fear. Or, if they wanted it to look like suicide, it was only a short distance to the river—"

"The river!"

"They might just have thumped you on the head and thrown you in without wasting a bullet. Water, you see, has a most remarkable attribute."

"What's that?"

"It washes things. Your body might have floated down the river a hundred miles or more, or you might snagged on something here in town. Either way, there would be no sign of what happened to you."

"Wouldn't my being found in the river be suggestive of murder?"

"Explain."

"Well, I'm rich. I'm handsome. I have a nice house and a wide circle of friends. I enjoy life. Suicide is most unlikely.""Oh, really? You enjoy life because you live high and drink too much and chase too many women—"

"I do not *chase*."

"So you're all honey, and flies are drawn to you more than vinegar. But you're too dumb to realize you do what you do because you are bored. Bored young men chuck themselves in rivers every day, or blow out what little brains they have."

"My friends would never believe I killed myself."

Jessup had an even better answer for that. "Stoker and his pals could force you to drink a lot of liquor before throwing you in the river."

"I don't drink with just anyone."

"If they held a bottle to your lips and turned it up you would drink or drown. Either way, you drown. Would anyone in your wide circle of friends ever question whether you might be so sozzled, you lost your footing near the river? If they got you pie-eyed enough, two feet of mud would do to drown you in."

"Do . . . do you mind if I smoke?""Why ask me? It's your house. I thought you'd need one long before this."

Herron had been fingering a stump of a cigarette in his coat pocket. In his agitation he didn't remember that he carried all his cigarettes in a case and never clung to dog-ends. He only knew he needed a taste of tobacco worse than he ever had in his life, and he had a cigarette in his hand.

Shoving it between his lips, Herron reached to the bedside table for a match. The stubby cigarette wobbled up and down as he said,

"I thought you came here to help me!"

"No, Mister Strangways. Just the opposite."

Herron lit the cigarette, cupping his hands over it. "What did you come for?"

"I told you. I came for a cigarette."

With his first puff, Herron spat out the smoke, wheezing. "This isn't my brand. It tastes like someone's old carpet!"

"Give it here!" Jessup demanded, aiming his pistol straight out at the bridge of Herron's nose.

CHAPTER IX

Herron flicked the glowing cigarette at him.

Dropping his gun in his apron, Jessup juggled the cigarette for a moment, then caught it safely. Clapping out the flame, he swiftly unrolled it.

"My message!"

"I say, you're sprinkling that foul mess all over my carpet. Do you fellows always use the cheapest tobacco you can find?"

"Best thing to put in a cigarette when you intend to dump out the contents and read the wrapping. Besides, I think most of it spilled out into your pocket."

Herron felt around the corners of his pocket. Whoever ripped the cigarette in half had given the end a twist, but it had leaked abominably.

Jessup frowned at the paper.

"Bad news from home?" asked Herron, not sympathetically.

Rising from his chair, Jessup handed Herron the small slip of paper. Then he took his seat again, aiming the gun at Herron again. "Read."

The cigarette paper was burned dark at the torn end, so none of the raggedly torn edged remained. Herron read the writing hurriedly scrawled on the inside.

hip he read.

Below that, *chine*.

Then, *GAM*.

"Oh, hieroglyphics."

Below that, Herron made out the eye-chart letters *rt yjr esyrt*.

Finally, in the lower right-hand corner leaned a drawing like a square dancing on *pointe*. And, on the burned right-hand side, a double *i*. "So, your friend's message was, *Hip-chine-gam-rt yjr esyrt-ii*-square. Not a phrase I use every day. A code? Or cipher? I never knew the difference."

Jessup was doubtful. "Codes and ciphers are handy, but what one man can create, another can break . . . and if your 'they' find the man they're after with a code or cipher in his pocket it'll go badly for him."

"I'd think random words jotted on the inside of a cigarette paper would look jolly odd whether they're in cipher or not."

"All you need is a plausible excuse for having words on a cigarette paper. You can say you're a writer and your cigarette papers were all you had handy when inspiration struck you. You made a few random notes, then forgot and rolled tobacco in them."

"He's a rum writer if he uses words like *chine* and *yrt*."

"It's torn in two. And," Jessup added with some asperity, "slightly burnt. Where on earth could the second half be!"

"How did this half find its way into my pocket?"

"Men in our line are often dips."

"They what, now?"

"Skilled pickpockets. I am a 'dip,' myself. A pick-pocket can place an object in your pocket as smoothly as he can remove it."

"So if the haggard bird ran true to form, presumably the other half of the message was slipped into the pocket of another patron of the railway. How did your late friend intend to recover it?"

"He didn't. If he survived, he had the information here." Jessup rapped his temple with the knuckles of his left hand. "The important thing was to get rid of the information so that it wasn't found *on him*, dead or alive. He disposed of it randomly, in the pockets of strangers who could never be traced. Then he could plausibly say he never had it. It's a good thing for you, Mister Strangways, they did not search you last night and find that paper on you, or you would be dead."

"They'd have taken me for the person he was going to meet?"

"Without a doubt."

"Just half?"

"It might have been going to two operatives who would meet again later."

"But it's rubbish."

"It means something to them. Enough to kill you for it."

"So your pal was trying to get me killed!"

"If you had happened onto that half a cigarette anyplace else, without my telling you about it, what would you have done?"

"Probably smoked it, until I tasted it. Then I'd have cast it away."

"Where it would have burned itself up, or been crushed under the toe of your shoe until nothing recognizable remained."

"Ah, but what if I wasn't a smoker?"

"A man who does not smoke, finding half a cigarette in his pocket, would toss it away. If he's on a train, he'd toss it out the window. All the queen's horses and all the queen's men could not locate half a cigarette along the lines. In many areas, the Underground actually runs above ground. If he threw it out of the train above ground, the first rain would have obliterated the paper and the writing."

"And given our weather that could be just about any time now. Like it says in the Bible, *'the rain it raineth every day.'*"

Jessup looked genuinely troubled. His voice trembled when he said,

"This has suddenly become more dangerous than I could ever have imagined."

"More dangerous than it was a minute ago?"

"Affairs have taken a decided turn for the worse."

"Did you get that from that message?"

"Mister Strangways, it's better you do not know why things are suddenly worse. It'll only make you nervous."

"I thought the adage was, What I don't know can't hurt me."

"At least," Jessup corrected, "what you don't know can't hurt you any *more*, since they're already gunning for you."

"How did I become involved in this, anyway?"

"By deciding to take a train rather than a cab, or walking an easy distance from your Club. We are all accountable for our decisions."

"Making a wrong decision doesn't usually get you hanged."

"Mister Strangways, Chubb isn't exactly sizing your neck for a noose, but all the circumstantial evidence is pointing your way. He's sniffing up the right tree. Your haggard bird was definitely murdered."

"You're sure?"

"Cold-blooded and premeditated. I saw it done. So far, you are the only person Chubb sees in the water. He's keeping you simmering, to watch what you do with your freedom. Today, you had a meal and slunk home. Fine. Chubb is a patient man and will give you all the time in the world. However, if a witness comes forward who says he saw you push the man, you're for it. Chubb will swoop down on you and carry you off to gaol and you'll never come out."

"There can't be witnesses who saw something that didn't happen."

"People kill for money, Mister Strangways. They'll lie for it even faster."

"Who would perjure themselves so blithely?"

"A man, say, who turned your stick in at the station when he found it in an abandoned building half-way across town."

"Oh." "By definition, Mister Strangways, lawless people break laws. And those men who took you last night are lawless."

"Surely, you'll help me wiggle off Chubb's hook! Will you come with me to see the Inspector this instant and tell him the truth?"

"No."

"Tomorrow?"

"No. Chubb has his job to do, I have mine. Anyway, what if I came with you on a leash and parroted your story? You are very rich."

"You keep harping on that one note."

"You might easily have found me on the street and paid for my testimony. Chubb would, quite rightly, demand to know more about me than I am willing to share. Chubb would want details I cannot divulge for the security of the nation."

"The nation, now? I'm hounded by the police for the good of the nation?"

"Even if I were so poor an operative as to tell Chubb the truth, he'd write it down somewhere and it would get back to your Stoker and his associates. Then they would know how close we are to foiling them."

"Could you tell Chubb it's hush-hush?"

"A good man like Chubb won't want high diplomatic secrets leaking out. But Chubb is thorough. He would insist upon facts I won't give him. The only way my tale will be plausible is if my superiors contact Chubb through channels to verify my *bona fides*. And I assure you, neither the government nor my organization will do any such a thing. Nor should they. After all, even in the highest levels of government, there are those who take the pay of the other side."

"What other side?"

"Any other side. Espionage is not a two-way street. It's a lousy circus."

"But you know the man was murdered, dash it! And you know I didn't do it."

"I've given you all the protection I can."

"What protection!"

"I've put you on your guard by telling you . . . you're a loose end, son."

"Loose end?"

"A dangling thread that needs tying up. It would suit Stoker's people and Chubb's alike to tie you neatly up." He mimed winding a rope into a noose and slipping it over his neck, then he jerked his arm up. His eyes bulged, his tongue protruded, his head lolled to one side, and his upper torso swayed in his chair like a hanged man. "But I don't think Stoker's lads have time for all that."

"Why should I trust you, anyway? You've been holding me at gunpoint, and I don't usually consider that a sign of wholesome camaraderie. Just what are you?"

CHAPTER X

"How did your Stoker identify himself?"

"He served Her Majesty in 'a private capacity.' Hush-hush stuff."

"There are many organizations . . . unofficial, unsanctioned . . . working for Her Majesty in private capacities, all over the Empire. Most of the work is routine, but it can be *extremely* perilous. I belong to one of these organizations. Our employees live and die obscurely in the shadows – men and women both – so lazy young pups like you may sleep late. And when you roll out of bed you may saunter to your clubs to drink without fear. Every breath of free air you take must be watered to thrive, like a plant. But your freedom must be watered with blood."

"Balderdash. Freedom is the right of every Englishman." He added, with an note of triumph, as if clenching his argument, "I read that in the *Times*."

"Have you read Thomas Hobbes?"

"Good heavens, no."

"He writes *'where there is no security and men live in constant fear the life of man is solitary, poor, nasty, brutish and short.'* Anarchy has a passing resemblance to freedom, but anarchy breeds fear and fear is the very antithesis of freedom. When there are no laws and all men can do just what they want, most men cower in fear from the few. To alleviate fear, humans gather into groups and form societies with governments that provide for their common defense. Freedom is found in *Society*, and its ever-changing kaleidoscope of cute little social norms and rules. The protectors of society – the military, the police, the people like me –*are* freedom, because we buy Society and its little rules with our blood. It is from blood-bought society freedom derives; when society collapses, anarchy follows."

"A little anarchy is a good thing," Herron smiled.

"Total anarchy is barbarity. In anarchy, only might is right. Freedom does not exist to man in his natural state. Freedom lies in security, and security is guaranteed only through organized society. And the security of that society must constantly be paid for in blood, by those who are willing to shed it. And where the culture is most civilized, as it is here in England, the security is most brittle."

"In what way?"

"In primitive cultures, when there is a clear breach of security, everyone grabs a club and takes a whack at it until it stops writhing. Here, we often lull ourselves into the delusion that all our fighting is relegated to the military and the police. 'Civilized' societies may even be so far removed from reality they limit or forbid personal ownership of weapons as if to force their citizens away from self-protection. Certainly, self-satisfied drones like you no longer sense the necessity to defend yourselves. Do you even keep a gun in your house?"

"Why? I go on country shoots, but you don't shoot things in town."

"*You* don't shoot things in town. That doesn't mean you won't be shot in town, or that, for your own, personal safety, you might need to shoot back at someone in town. No, why keep a gun on the premises to protect yourself? You pay 'protection money' in taxes, don't you? But the police and the military work in the *light*. Society is maintained against more insidious enemies by the perpetual warfare in the shadows. Oh, the men and women who work, live – and die – for the maintenance of freedom do realize it will be squandered on the likes of you. I may be forced to die for you one day. And a sad day it will be."

Not as sad as my dying for you, Herron thought.

"I may have to die for you, but that does not mean I have to risk losing my cover to protect you in this instance."

"But . . . they know about you already. If you were at the Underground station last night, you must have given evidence. They'll have your statement."

"I lied."

"To a policeman? Your organization doesn't sound particularly law-abiding."

"It's a paradox, Mister Strangways. Occasionally, to protect and defend Her Majesty's laws, deeds must be done that those laws would not countenance."

"I don't know if I trust you. Stoker never pulled a gun on me."

"He will. Chubb is not your primary worry. Chubb will move slowly and deliberately. One feels pity for him."

"I don't."

"He has circumstantial evidence suggesting that the owner of Strangways' Emporia may have killed a man. On the one hand, if he can bring you to trial on proper evidence and punish you for your misdeeds, his fame will be worldwide. Everyone hates a rich man. On the other hand . . . if he goes ahead with this *cause celebre* and the evidence doesn't stand up in court, he'll look an awful ass the world over. His superiors won't appreciate Chubb making Scotland Yard look as foolish in reality as it already does in detective fiction. Chubb has to walk cannily, to find good grounds for putting you up before a jury. That will take time. Chubb has it. Time, however, is one commodity Stoker's boys don't seem to have. They mean to act, and soon. If Stoker's higher-ups feel threatened by you, they will come for you. And they will get you."

"You're just trying to scare me."

"Is it working?"

"Yes!"

"It snaps you out of your *ennui*."

"If what you say is true . . . I'm in a real facer. I'm squeezed between the police on one side and a shadowy, criminal force on the other."

"That describes your position tidily, with a nice little bow on top."

"What do I do?"

"I run on fewer rails than most men, but even I will reach my terminus one day. And I'm a professional. You don't stand a chance. Get out of the country."

"But the police—!"

"—work in the light. Do not fear the light. Fear the darkness."

"Chubb told me not to leave town."

"If you run, Chubb will swear out a warrant for your arrest for the murder of the haggard bird. But there are places where British warrants have no power. Charter a private yacht out of the country and go to them. You're rich enough."

"But you said Chubb *wants* me to scarper."

"I suspect he's operating on the erroneous notion that innocent men don't run. If you try to run, Chubb *may* arrest you and put you in gaol. If you stay in town, Stoker and his associates *will* kill you. Your pick. Flip a coin if you like."

"I have an aunt who always said she'd see me hanged one day. I'll not be hanged – just to spite her."

"Don't worry. The law won't hang you."

"Good!"

"If Chubb arrests you tonight, you're a dead man before dawn."

"Stoker's people can't get me in prison!"

"Can't they?"

"C-can they?"

"It'll be shooting a sitting bird. And their sort have no scruple about shooting a sitting bird. We have people working in Scotland Yard. So does Stoker's."

"How do you know?"

"They're fools if they don't. If you go to gaol you're only in storage where they can get at you any time."

"How will they dispose of the body in a cell?"

"A man in your position – a rich young wastrel, his life wrecked and all his money of no use – hangs himself in his cell rather than going through the indignity of being hanged by the state. Nothing unusual in that. But, once again, like the gun to the head and the blood-spattered suicide note, it won't be suicide. It'll be Stoker's lads stringing you up."

"Then I'll stay out of prison."

"How will you do that, other than by running away?"

"It must be easy enough to stay out of prison. Every year people manage it in their thousands. You simply obey the law." "I admire the pertinacity with which you depend on the thin veneer of civilization. There's no difficulty getting you in prison, if that's where Stoker's boys want you. Here's the scenario: A policeman passes. A woman screams. She tells the policeman you've touched her inappropriately. A man 'who happens to be passing' at that moment backs up her story. Who would believe *you*? But that's a lot of trouble. I don't see Stoker and his lads sending you to your grave on a roundabout route when the direct approach is less chancy."

"So – what do I do?"

"Run for it."

"I can't see that I'm any freer if I run."

"No. You've just made a larger prison for yourself. You'll be like a hunted rabbit every day of your life. You'll scrutinize every face you pass on the street, wondering if it's a face belonging to the 'Friends of Stoker.'"

"Then I have no chance!"

"Oh, I wouldn't say that . . . "

"Have I?"

". . . a slim one, but a chance."

"Tell me, please!"

"You'll be like a spider dangling by one thread over the mouth of Hell."

"Just tell me, without the lurid descriptions of the arachnid afterlife."

"You must find out what that message in that cigarette means."

"You don't know what it means?" "*Hip* and *chine* and *gam* in capitals and *rt yjr esyrt*? It's impure nonsense!"

"You can't decode it?"

"If it truly is a code . . . no. It's not a large enough sample. I can't begin to guess what it means without the other half of the cigarette. Even supposing the *ii* is Roman numerals – is it a date? And is it the date they mean to strike? What date is it? The Queen's Procession is on Tuesday the twenty-second."

"That's *x-x-i-i*!"

"And on the twenty-seventh, there is the naval review at Spithead, where Stoker and his friends might sabotage every ship in the navy. This '*hip*' could be part of *ship*, but why singular? Why sabotage only one ship in a review? Twenty-seven is *x-x-v-i-i*. Still, it's likely. The Procession is well-nigh impregnable—"

"I wish more women were."

"This is serious, Mister Strangways."

"And I'm not? And that little bit of paper has put my life at stake?"

"Your country is at stake."

"Deuce take it! Countries come and go; but when I go, I'm gone for good."

"Your country depends on," Jessup adopted a Texas accent, "bafflin' them desperados, lassoin' the varmints and corrallin' 'em up." In a normal voice, he continued, "Your neck depends upon it, too."

"Anyone else's?"

"Do you care?"

"No."

"I'll put it in terms you understand. To save that one neck in the world you care about, we must find the other half of that message and find what it means."

"'We'? You mean, *we* as opposed to *they*?"

"I mean 'we' – you and me."

"Me! Or is it I?"

"We're all accountable for our decisions. You made the decision to take the train last night, and now you must accept the consequences."

"For this?" Herron adamantly crossed his arms. "I'm not paid by your organization and I don't want to do anything with consequences."

"Don't take that attitude. You will help me."

"At gunpoint?"

"Of your own volition. Your safety depends on this. You will receive more calls from Chubb. And from your newfound friends of last night."

"Stoker . . . Is that his real name?"

"Like 'Jessup' – it serves."

"Is he behind it?"

"Behind *what*?"

Herron rolled his eyes. "Behind whatever is going on?"

"We don't know what's going on. There's been a lot of chatter in recent weeks among the opposition. We've received all sorts of reports—"

"Have *we*?"

"'We' as opposed to 'they.' Something is going to happen, probably soon. That 'haggard bird' was in deep cover in the enemy camp. He blew his cover by running. No one does that until it's critical. We must know what he lost his life trying to tell us, and we must know soon. We need to know what it is, where it's to be done, when it's to be done, how it's to be done, and who is behind it. You must recover the message and, if possible discover what it all means. Even if you can't discover the meaning . . . get it back to me as soon as may be."

"I've never decoded or deciphered a message in my life. I had enough trouble with Greek at school and it's a genuine language. As far as who is behind it – why can't Stoker be behind it?"

"Do you play cards? Good. Think of Stoker as a number card. Perhaps not even a high number card. He's certainly not a face card in his organization."

"Then we're not playing baccarat."

Jessup returned to his Texas accent. "Nawssir, this is what the Americans call 'good ol' down-an'-dirty poker.'"

"You seem to understand Stoker."

"Yes. I don't know who he is and I don't know his cause. But I do know him, because we do the same sort of job. He has people above him, he has people below. He does the bidding of the people above, and the people below do his. Like the fellow in the Bible, he says go and they goeth. He's a numbered card. Somewhere out there is a face card. A king, a queen, a jack."

"An ace, if they're high."

"One day this face card will order Stoker to pay a call on you."

"And what happens to me?"

"Bang. You're dead."

"What if I find the face card?"

"That's far too dangerous. If you go into that lair, you'll never come out alive. You do your job, I'll do mine. It's a big machine and you're a very small part."

"What is my 'part,' precisely?"

"I'll spell it out as simply as possible: you must recover the other half of the message. Try to work out what it says – and then what it means. *Something* is going to happen, Mister Strangways. We must stop it. *We* opposed to *they*."

"And all this is conducive to my safety?"

"There are larger issues than one man's life."

"Not if it's mine!"

"*All flesh is as grass*, they say."

"Well, I want my grass to grow as old as possible. If the haggard bird ran true to form, he probably slipped the other half in someone else's pocket. How do I find one pocket among millions?"

"There weren't millions of pockets on that platform. Every person on that platform had to show a ticket at the barrier. And every person there – except you and me and Stoker – gave a statement."

"That leaves dozens. It'll take days to interview them all."

"My organization has that list of names. Pilfered from the police. They're working on that. We merely want to utilize your peculiar skills. Let's see if I recall . . . You were on the right-hand side of my late associate when he pushed through, and a young lady was on his left."

"Yes indeedy."

"She and you were near the edge of the platform, but not hazardously so. Yet when he pushed between you I thought you were all three going over!"

"So did I. You're thinking that if the haggard bird gave one half of the thing to me, he may have given the young lady the other half!"

"Possibly." Jessup didn't sound altogether sanguine about the prospect.

"I suppose there were plenty of people on that platform," Herron guessed, though he only had eyes for one. "Is it likely she has it?"

"The people on that platform were packed thick as pilchards. You said yourself, you can't visit all of them. Neither can we, without help. You, with your well-honed skills, might be able to charm your way into her company enough to locate the other half of that paper *if she has it*. If you find it, whether you can or can't make out what it means, bring it to me. But first: find her."

"I've been wondering how to do that a night and a day. I don't know her name. I barely recall her looks. Very pretty, yes, but her image has smeared by now with any number of other pretty faces I've seen in an active life. Exquisitely beautiful women stand out for only a moment. They're like the flame when you first strike a match. It's the ones with the slight flaws whose beauty remains burning in the mind's eye. You can remember a girl with a mole on the cheek, or a bend in her nose, or a freckle or two on the—""Don't worry about her nose, but your neck. *Find her*. Or, as our American cousins say, skedaddle, and keep skedaddling all your – very short – life."

"But . . . London's the largest city in the world, and the population, in case you haven't noticed, has risen dramatically. I never heard her speak a word. She might be an American, or an Australian, or even a Russian . . . I need assistance."

"I'll help you – only because our directions lie on the same lines. I'll look over the list of persons who made statements and get the names and addresses of all the likely young ladies. You may have to visit more than one."

"I'll tell you how she looked like to the best of my ability—"

"I was there. However retentive your memory is mine is better-honed."

"How do I contact you?"

"You don't."

On that note, Jessup rose and backed to the window.

"You're not leaving?" This wasn't sarcasm on Herron's part. A panic gripped his heart like a clenched fist at the thought of being left alone.

If an ongoing war in the shadows did exist, Herron had inadvertently thrown back a curtain and caught a glimpse of it in the half-light. And he had become involved—in what? He needed more answers.

"You've been begging me to go, Mister Strangways. Sometimes getting what you wished for blights your life. We're both disappointed. I came for the information on the cigarette – and it's no earthly use to me. I'll find you when I can with the names and addresses of possible ladies."

As he stepped out the window, the man calling himself Jessup tossed the revolver lightly toward Herron, who caught it gingerly, making sure his fingers were well away from the trigger.

"You might need that. You know how to use it?"

"The end with the hole points out."

"Without the sarcasm."

"Yes."

"Good?"

Herron shrugged. He was an indifferent marksman. If he was ever challenged to a duel – which was a possibility, given his predilections – he'd choose swords.

"When it comes time to use that little pea-shooter," Jessup concluded, vanishing out the window, "fire first and ask questions later. If you're wrong, don't worry about the consequences."

"No?" asked Herron, his spirits rising fractionally.

"The police are measuring you for murder. They can't hang you twice."

With that, he was gone.

It had grown late during their talk. Herron had not turned up the gas in his bedroom. He bounded out of bed to the window in the dark, hoping to see outside; but the gas street lamp outside his house had not yet been lit.

Outside his window stretched a rounded ledge just wide enough to for a man's shoe, standing sideways. All the houses in this terrace were joined, but Herron lived on the end of the row, so the ledge elbowed out at the corner and wrapped around the far end of his house.

The front faced the street, to the east. Immediately below Herron's window yawned a wide area between the house and the iron railings along the front of the house. The wide area was a sunken, with steps leading down to the basement, allowing the morning light in the basement windows and Merridew's quarters.

Jessup was nowhere to be seen as Herron looked right, left, and down. He wasn't on the ledge, he was not down in the area, and he could not have leapt over the spiked iron palings in the fence from this window.

Then, on a hunch, Herron looked up.

The frayed end of a rope was just disappearing over the guttering.

Already on the roof, this Jessup might descend anywhere along the terrace and disappear. Herron hadn't a chance of catching him.

Leaving the window open, he stepped over to the wall by the door. Turning the gas up incrementally, he stood beneath the jet and opened the revolver.

The chambers were empty. Poker-playing Jessup had bluffed him.

2

The noise of the city was constant, especially with his window open over the dusky street. With the Diamond Jubilee Procession two days away, the streets were never still, day or night.

Despite the noise, Herron heard footfalls on the front steps, which were below his open bedroom window, about fifteen or twenty feet to the left.

Herron couldn't remember if he locked the door when he came in. Gun in hand, he leaned out the bedroom window.

He was too late to catch a glimpse of anyone; but, leaning out the window, he heard the opening and closing of the front door.

Whoever it was, they were in the house.

Just as Jessup had bluffed him, Herron intended to put up a bluff of his own.

Stealing from his room, he crept down the corridor in a crouch and peered through the banister.

At the end of the corridor, a narrow stairway went in one flight straight down the wall and finished just a pace or two from an archway opening to a small foyer inside the front door.

Peering through the banister at the top of the stairs, Herron perceived a shadowy figure shuffling in the dark foyer near the hall-tree.

CHAPTER XI

Squatting with his knees against the banister, Herron extended the pistol down through the rails, hoping, in the dim light, whoever was below would see the weapon and nothing else.

"Who's there?"

"Mister Strangways?"

"Merridew!"

In retrospect, he felt he should have supposed that few hired murderers stealthily entered the home of their quarry while loudly humming "Rock of Ages."

"Step up here, Merridew, please."

"Yes, sir. Just a tick."

As Herron rose from his squat and watched his valet mount the stairs with a noticable limp from his old war wound, he realized with a sinking heart that Merridew, *valet par excellence* though he was, lacked a scrapper's build and might not be handy if it came to rough stuff.

Nevertheless, Merridew was another living soul in the otherwise dead house and Herron welcomed his presence.

"I'm sorry I'm late, sir. We were so lifted up at chapel we sang three more hymns before benediction."

"Never mind."

"Yes, sir. What do you require?"

"You were in the service, I believe?"

"Yes, sir. Afghan border. Invalided out."

"Leg injury, was it?"

"And shoulder."

"Both?" Herron knew Merridew limped sometimes, as on those narrow stairs, and he rubbed his shoulder in chilly weather; since he never saw Merridew doing both simultaneously, he never suspected two wounds.

"Yes, sir. One Jezail flintlock bullet passed through my leg and shoulder."

"One bullet? Can't be."

"T'was, sir. So I was told. I was not very lucid immediately following the incident. The Jezail flintlocks have long barrels, sir, and high caliber. They told me that one was rifled."

"It must have been held at a peculiar angle to shoot you through the shoulder and the haunches. I wish I'd listened more closely to your service stories. I'm glad you're here now. I can use the level head of an old campaigner. You see, Merridew, we are under siege. Don't look at me that way, I promise you, for once I am earnestly sober—and all the worse for it."

Merridew was impressed by his employer's demeanor. Herron Strangways drank too much for Merridew's T-totalling taste, but Herron never grew paranoid in his cups, or called Merridew up in the middle of the night to swat invisible spiders or deal with creatures lurking under the bed. Herron was generally a cheerful young man who hated earnestness, and drink increased that mood exponentially. Tonight his voice carried an impressively grave undertone.

Awed, he listened while Herron concisely explained the position of affairs.

"And for some reason," he concluded, "I have a lot of people climbing my tree. I have this sick feeling that any occupants of our little nest are liable to be equally in danger. Including you. We don't know if this so-called Jessup is telling the truth, but it's altogether probable we're in as much danger from the law as—dammit, as whoever is out there. Do you understand?"

"Yes, sir. I have grasped the gist."

"Stout fellow. Now, I need a to go out and find a young lady—"Merridew never upbraided his employer for his amorous escapades, but he couldn't help a sad shake of his head at Herron's present incontinence.

"No, its not what you think – this time, anyway. You do believe me?"

"Should I not?"

"If anyone had spun such a tale I'd say they were talking through their hat. Somehow, I must escape the old homestead, oil my way into this young lady's company without a proper introduction, and frisk 'round her for half a cigarette. I would welcome any suggestions from a military mind."

"I will consider the matter, sir."

"Thank you."

"I was not an officer, though. They're the ones who do the thinking."

"I understand. I'll hole up at the Hemlock tonight. Everyone knows my clubs, so tomorrow I had best discover some other cozy nook. We'll both pack a few things and meet at the back door in fifteen minutes. Pack light."

"Yes sir. I'll go to the cellar and bring up your bag."

"One good-sized carpet bag will carry all I need."

"Yes, sir."

"Have you read *Around the World in Eighty Days*?"

"No, sir."

"Too bad. Neither have I. And it looks just like what we're bound for. Thank you, Merridew. One more thing." Herron exhibited Jessup's pistol. "Do we have any ammunition to fit this? It's a gun of some sort."

Merridew studied the pistol with his trained eye. "Webley .45 caliber 'Bulldog' double-action revolver."

"'Double-action?'"

"The trigger both cocks the weapon and releases it. And rotates the cylinder."

"That's three actions. Don't these gun people have more than two fingers?"

"No, sir."

"They don't? Did they shoot the others off?"

"I mean, we have no ammunition to fit this weapon."

"Buy some, then. All you can. Are any stores that sell ammunition open at this time on a pleasant Sunday evening?"

"I will procure some as soon as humanly possible. And perhaps another weapon or two."

"Stout fellow." Herron went to a drawer in a side-table where he kept money to tip tradesmen. It was mostly banknotes of low denomination (he hated fiddling with change). Finding a ten-pound note in the bunch, he handed it over to Merridew for the purchase of ammunition. He let Merridew keep the pistol so he wouldn't forget its make.

"Did you lock the front door, Merridew?"

"Yes, sir."

"Good."

Dismissing Merridew, Herron returned to his bedroom. He did not turn the gas up. Leaning against the wall, he brushed the curtains back from the wall and peered around the frame.

Dusk had not quite fallen, but the gas street-lamp had been lit while Herron was speaking to Merridew.

Amongst all the people passing on the streets, one man stood still, alone, just on the verge of the light. Herron could not see his face, but by the direction his hat pointed, eyes were turned up to this bedroom window.

Herron wondered if he was the police – or the not-police.

Or . . . Herron did not like to consider it . . . was there a joker in the deck who had yet to be dealt?

2

Normally, Merridew would pack for Herron. He understood far better than his employer what he would require for any journey. But Merridew had to dig out the luggage as well as pack his own effects, so Herron was left to fend for himself.

Herron picked the clothes from his wardrobe he was certain he couldn't do without. By the time he turned around to assess it, he had piled enough garments on his bed to require a steamer trunk rather than a carpet bag.

He was clawing through them when, through the open window, he heard a knock at the front door – actually, the hammering of a fist on the wood of the door rather than using the knocker.

Since he was unable to see his front step from the bedroom window, Herron slipped into the corridor again and drooped over the banister. He could just see the lower half of the front door through the archway leading into the foyer.

No, it wasn't knocking—someone was trying to *kick* the front door in!

"MERRIDEW!"

Just at that moment, the front door swung back, nearly off its hinges.

So much for locks! thought Herron, darting back into his bedroom.

Nevertheless, he locked the door behind him – and shoved the bed against it.

Herron had spent much of his life around beds, sleeping or otherwise, but bedstead-shoving was new to him. The bed had an extremely heavy four-posted frame, but Herron was no weakling. His own frame was slender, but he had acquired a certain amount of raw strength from swimming, rowing, and other exercises typical of the well-rounded British education.

An added dash of adrenaline made Herron Strangways the world's champion bedstead-shover. The shoving didn't not do the hardwood floor of his bedroom any good; but he preferred scuffed floors to a shiny new wooden coffin.

By the time the bed was jammed cockeyed against the door, Herron heard heavy feet clumping along the corridor. He doubted the feet belonged to the police. They tried to open doors with warrants before resorting to their boots.

He spun around the center of the bedroom looking for a way out. Except for the door, he had only one exit – the way Jessup had gone.

A muffled voice seeped in from the corridor.

"Check in there, Hawkins; I'll go this way."

"Okey-doke, Jake!" Hawkins tried the knob. When the door didn't budge, he began pounding his shoulder against it. The heavy bedstead did not give.

Herron tried another bluff. "I've got a gun on you!"

The pounding ceased.

That stopped 'em cold, Herron thought proudly.

A moment later, bullets splintered through the upper door panel. They were wide, catching all parts of the room. Hawkins may have given Herron credit for being too intelligent to stand in a direct line with the door.

It caused him to miss altogether. Had Hawkins centered his shots straight ahead, he'd have plugged Herron repeatedly.

Herron threw himself face-down on the Turkey carpet before Hawkins finally sent two shots straight through the door. They whistled over Herron's head. One of them shattered the upper window pane.

During the silence while Hawkins reloaded, Herron slithered on his belly to the window. He was no longer worried about what to pack.

His bedroom was one story above street level; but the window was directly above the area where steps led down to the cellar and Merridew's quarters. As he eased out the window, he was two stories above solid brick.

Herron briefly considered a spring for the pavement. He might have been sufficiently agile to leap out far enough to clear the cellar area . . . but the spiked iron railing along the front of the house dissuaded him.

The rounded ledge was confoundedly narrower than it looked. Herron's feet were splayed out to either side and bent almost at right angles to his legs as he scraped along the front of the house toward the corner.

Pressing his body face-flat against the wall, he groped the brick facade for loose mortar and indentations. He'd been good at crawling along narrow places in school, but he'd gained weight and height since he was ten. This was no fun for someone just over six feet and more than eleven stone in weight.

Sidling along the ledge, he heard the bed squealing across the wood floor as Hawkins pushed his way inside, roaring and snuffling like an angry bull.

Just as Herron reached the corner of the house, someone leaned a head out his bedroom window and shouted at him in an American accent.

Since it took all Herron's faculties to maneuver where the ledge elbowed around the corner (where he discovered a drainpipe on the far side that he had not factored into his calculations), he did not answer. Hawkins could shoot Herron just as easily whether or not he had his full attention.

He heard the first shot just as he swung around by the iron drainpipe. The bullet struck the corner, spraying out flecks of brick. One fragment nicked Herron's cheek, leaving a line of blood. He was lucky he hadn't lost an eye.

Considering the weight of the bedstead, Herron supposed it had taken both of them to push the door open. That's why no one was firing at him from this side of the house at the moment.

Herron guessed Stoker soon be in the end room. That door was always kept locked; but they'd gotten through the front door without difficulty. With Stoker station in the window of the end-room window and Hawkins in the bedroom, Herron would be caught in a nasty crossfire.

Without a rope, Herron couldn't climb up. This side of the house was only one story above the pavement and it did not have an iron railing, but he balked at leaping. One story was story, and pavement was pavement, after all. And he dared not lean away from the wall far enough to see what lay below to break his fall . . . or his legs.

Pressing his cheek against the cool bricks, Herron wondered, *Now, what?*

CHAPTER XII

The drainpipe stretched down the corner all the way to the ground, where it emptied toward a gutter.

For all his monkeyshines, Herron had never shinnied down a drainpipe. This seemed an auspicious moment to learn how.

It had held up when he swung round on it; but when he put all his weight on it to climb down, the corroded upper part of the pipe broke loose from the house and swung violently down.

Herron felt his stomach rising. But he knew it wouldn't rise long. In moments it and all his insides would be buttered out on the pavement.

Herron didn't strike the pavement. For days, visitors to London had been murdering the sleep of legitimate inhabitants by marching up and down the streets day and night. Even at dusk, Herron came down into someone's arms.

Gunfire was rare in this part of town. So was the sight of men on ledges. London being crammed with visitors in for the Jubilee who roamed the streets at all hours, it was easy for a crowd to accumulate at any hour.

Herron never thought he'd be grateful for the overcrowding until his fall was cushioned by three or four portly souls below who had come to see what all the commotion was about.

Then he was caught in the vortex of a surging crowd. Hands groped him, trying to hold him. They didn't know him, but they connected him to the gunfire and they wanted to keep him for the police.

Though Herron had never won a bout when he tried amateur boxing in college, he was still better at fisticuffs than the average portly man on the street. With fists flying, he broke through the crowd – and collided with a large, blue mass.

The crowd had opened a crack, and a policeman had stepped through just in time to impede Herron's escape.

"Now, now, what's all this 'ere?"

Hands pushed Herron toward the policeman.

"Officer," Herron shouted, "there's been murder done."

"Oh, yes, sir? Whereabouts?"

"Up there!" He pointed to his bedroom. "Two men with guns are in that house! Hurry, we might still catch them! I barely escaped with my life!"

Blowing his whistle, the policeman ran for Herron's kicked-in front door.

"I'll go for reinforcements!" Herron called over his shoulder, dashing away down the street. He didn't know what sort of figure he struck running, but he didn't have time to worry about appearances.

He started to leap into the first cab he found waiting for a fare – then he thought that was just where Stoker might plant an agent. He also passed the second cab, and the third.

Seeing a man he knew alighting from the forth hansom, he swung himself into that cab even before his acquaintance was thoroughly disgorged. He pounded the roof, and when the driver opened the little door there Herron handed up ten pounds and told him to drive.

"Where to?"

"Who cares! Go!" He sank back out of sight as the cab rattled off.

A few minutes later, he gave the driver the address of the Hemlock Club. The cab couldn't enter that street – it was officially closed until after Tuesday's Procession – but Herron preferred approaching the Club at a stealthy walk. Given the current forecast, one never knew who might be waiting there to greet him.

2

Edgar, the Hemlock Club's doorman, was mountainous. Though only a few years Herron's senior, he had already retired from one career. He had spent his youth eking out an uncertain living as a bare-knuckle boxer, and his former vocation was written all over his face.

Edgar's nose deviated more than once from the straight. One of his ears resembled a cauliflower. Other incontrovertible indications proclaimed that here was a man who knew how to use his fists (if not quite so well as his opponents).

In the years following his retirement from the ring, he had bulked up considerably – around the midriff. He filled out his red greatcoat of office, with its large buttons and gold epaulettes, in every direction.

Though he had gained in tonnage, Edgar never lost his pugilistic gifts. He wasn't good enough to be champion, but he was more than capable of barring ordinary folk from admission to the Club.

The members of the Hemlock Club – as Stoker, Chubb and Jessup in turn grasped – were high-spirited young gentlemen. They dabbled in pranks that occasionally led to unfortunate results.

The police had entrée, if necessary, of course; but Edgar's bulging arms, his fists the size of cantaloupes, and his menacing demeanor dissuaded all others from pursuing members once they'd burrowed to earth within the Club.

Edgar was pacing before the doors with his hands behind him when Herron Strangways loped into view.

Herron bounded up the front steps two at a time and seized Edgar by the lapels.

Rather than approaching the Club at an inconspicuous walk, as he had planned, Herron leapt from the cab and sprinted all the way down the closed street, his tensed back expecting to receive a hot bullet at any moment.

At the top of the steps, when he grasped Edgar's coat . . . he had to catch his breath and swallow a few times before speaking.

"Yes, sir?" asked Edgar, stolidly accepting this behavior in stride. During his tenure as doorman, he had seen worse.

" . . . Edgar . . . "

"You're bleedin', Mister Strangways, sir."

Herron put a hand to his abdomen, as if he'd been able to come this far with his bowels stringing out from a large-caliber bullet-hole.

"No, sir – your cheek."

Like a conjurer preparing to perform a trick, Herron whipped out a silk handkerchief and, with Edgar's guidance, dabbed it over the wound he had received from a shard of brick.

"Oh, Edgar, if anyone asks for me – you never seen me." Since his money would be no use to him when he was dredged from the river, Herron slipped Edgar a handsome gratuity. "You're not even sure you recognize my name."

"Yes, sir, Mister Strangways, sir." Edgar saluted sharply.

"Unless, of course, it's Merridew, my man. Do you know him?"

"Only by sight, sir."

"That's a good enough way to know him." Edgar's tip left a gaping hole in Herron's finances, but he looked on it as an investment rather than an expenditure.

Edgar opened the door and Herron stepped gingerly inside.

Ensconced in his Club, Herron felt relieved for the first time since waking that morning. He also had elbow-room to worry about Merridew, last seen descending into the cellar to retrieve bags. He hoped Merridew had been able to sneak out while the gunmen were upstairs blasting away upstairs.

Whatever Merridew's fate, Herron felt like an explorer who, having finally wrenched himself free of quicksand by vines, looks back to see the hat of his bosom companion floating camly on the surface. He felt sorrow for his friend, but his grief was offset by the joy of knowing his own hat wasn't floating beside it.

3

The young men of the Hemlock Club kept irregular hours even on days when without a Jubilee. Many of them were nocturnal creatures who cringed away from the daylight. Others lived abroad – serving in the army or the diplomatic corps, say – and made the Club their G.H.Q. when in London. Even after a leisurely ocean voyage, a man who served for years in Kuala Lumpor did not immediately function on Greenwich time.

So, though it was past dark on one of the longest days of the year, the Hemlock was a hive of activity. The billiard room was packed to capacity. The bar was awash in young gentlemen. The dining room had nary a spare table, despite repeated announcements that the kitchen had closed.

Herron, usually at the epicenter of any devilry going, avoided all eye contact. He tried to find a bed for the night, but every room was stuffed full to maximum capacity with smoking, drinking and gaming, ranging from high-stakes poker to tossing cards into a hat

"Because of the Jubilee, you know, Mister Strangways," apologized a *maitre d'* in a red swallowtail coat and white gloves and white, tailed wig – in case Herron might be hearing the word *Jubilee* for the first time. "I fear we're already sleeping two gentlemen to a bed. There's nary a cot left in the place."

"Even for ready money?"

"I've taken all the ready-money customers. They're even kippin' in the baths. Unless you want to treble up with some of the gentlemen?"

Herron declined. He might shared beds with females for the sake of convenience, but he invariably *slept* alone.

Herron's first thought was to saunter into the bar, to lubricate his jangled nerves. Deciding a clear head was preferable under existing climate conditions, he sauntered into the billiard room instead.

The billiard room was chock-full of friends and acquaintances to every degree, from men he had shouldered all through school with (grammar, public and 'Varsity) to one man he referred to merely as "side-whiskers" because he never recalled hearing the fellow's name.

It was difficult maintaining a low profile in his own stomping ground. Several members greeted him warmly. One offered him a cigar, which he gratefully accepted. Even on the lam, Herron saw no reason not to enjoy his pleasures.

He neither initiated conversations nor encouraged them. One never knew what might tumble out. Though surrounded by friends, some of them life-long, Herron was disinclined to take anyone into his confidence. And this was not simply because most of the men in that room, whom Herron assessed with a critical eye, were less than useless to him in his present predicament.

After his talk with Jessup, Herron simply did not know whom to trust. He didn't even trust his oldest friends. Why, he didn't even trust Jessup!

So far as he knew, every man bent over a billiard table might be a soldier in the shadow war. They wore no uniforms, they waved no banners, their backs weren't slung with shields blazoned with their coats of arms. Shadow warriors.

Not only could he not tell who might be on which side in this war, Herron could not even guess how many sides there were.

He certainly was not satisfied as to which side of the war he'd blundered in on. Stoker and Jessup both had invoked Her Majesty's name. Which of them was lying? Both of them? Whom should he trust? Neither?

Jessup threatened him with a gun (empty, as it turned out, but he didn't know that during the threat). Herron was convinced that was Stoker's voice he'd heard outside his bedroom door. He and Hawkins had shot at him, and missed.

Missed . . . deliberately?

Spying a roomy leather chair, still warm from a previous occupant, Herron dived into it and stretched out his legs. To keep from being bothered, he acted like he'd already tied on too many too tightly, and closed his eyes.

Monday, June 21, 1897

CHAPTER XIII

When Herron opened his eyes, the billiard room was dark. Even the latest stragglers had departed. The only illumination came from a low-burning blue and white flame of gas from the corridor, just across from the open double-doors.

Trying to rise from his chair, Herron found his legs stiff from being stretched at an unusual angle for hours. His hands, which had been hanging over the sides of the chair, were quite bloodless and dead.

He felt the blood rushing into his hands as he moved them. As the frozen stiffness retreated, the pins and needles started.

Winding through the tables, Herron left the billiard room. Going to richly wood-paneled the library, he shouldered up against the wall beside the great bow window overlooking the street from its eyrie above the front steps, slipped a finger behind an edge of drapery that had been drawn for the night, and peeled it ever so slightly aside.

On a clear day he might have seen morning twilight; but a heavy fog had rolled off the river. If anyone was waiting for him out there, Herron couldn't see them.

"Mister Strangways!"

Herron jumped and turned to see a hulking shape silhouetted in the doorway.

The outline was unmistakable. Edgar was not wearing his greatcoat, or even his collar. In rolled-up shirt sleeves and bulging waistcoat. Without his coat and cap Herron thought the doorman looked practically nude.

"Yes, Edgar?"

Being unfamiliar with the finer points of the English language, Edgar accented every syllable of longer words, to make sure he hit the right one. "Pardon my arskin', but is you in some sort of pinch?"

The young men of the Hemlock often fell into difficulties. Edgar was forever being asked – and heavily tipped – to shepherd tailors, book makers, jilted fiancés, distraught lovers, and men with horsewhips away from the premises.

Yet, however dire their straits, Edgar had never told one of "his" gentleman he was bleeding, and watched while that gentleman's hands went automatically down like his guts needed buttoning up.

He rarely came within these precincts, but he supposed seldom were they up before dawn peeping skittishly out of windows. Herron Strangways probably saw dawn only when he was staggering home at the tail end of night.

Of all "his" gentlemen, Edgar was fondest of ten who were exorbitant tippers. Herron Strangways was a fountain from whom money flowed like water even when he was sober. Therefore, Edgar loved him with a dogged devotion.

He wished he had a son like Herron. Rich.

The normally easygoing Herron Strangways was the image of a man pursued by the Furies – or (to Edgar's mind, which was tranquilly uncluttered with classical allusions) by creditors, bookies' collectors, rozzers, wronged ladies and irate husbands, all rolled into one.

Actually, none of this was Edgar's business. He shouldn't have been in the library at all. He might have lost his position if his superiors found him there, especially if they learned he was prying into a member's personal affairs.

But Edgar would not see one of the club's best tippers go down for the third time, and Herron was beginning to look like he was going down for the fourth.

Strangways' Emporia were undoubtedly solvent. Their proprietor had no need to hide out from unpaid bills, Edgar believed a female lay at the root of the young man's troubles. Though if he'd ever heard the expression *cherchez la femme* he'd have answered *gesundheit*, Edgar was looking for the woman in the case.

Or, maybe a clowder of angry females ready to claw Herron limb from limb.

From Edgar's standpoint, a man with Herron Strangways' upbringing was hampered from the full freedom of self-expression. It was one of the rules of this unjust world that a gentleman could not strike a member of the opposing gender, whatever the provocation.

Young Strangways hadn't the option of crumpling a woman with his dukes so long as men endured what Edgar considered the social injustice of having one law for the goose and another for the gander.

Edgar had grown up in a different *milieu*. In his old neighborhood, a solid punch up the bracket was considered most efficacious method of dealing with any threat. He didn't like to hit women, but in his time he had leveled two.

One of them had backed Edgar into a corner and was taking swings at him with a coal shovel. She was his lover.

The other had leapt on Edgar's back in the middle of a bare-knuckle bout he was winning (one of the few) while referring his opponent her "old man." When he shook the woman off he knocked her down for the count, but her "old man" had clobbered Edgar with a stool while his back was turned. That was when Edgar decided to retire from the ring.

If young Mister Strangways' problem was a case of the *femmes*, Edgar felt equipped to deal with it.

On top of that, Edgar never wanted to take money for nothing – which was why his face was so battered. During his prizefighting days he never threw in the towel or took a dive. So long as he could stand on his own power he took his pummeling until the referees terminated his matches out of sheer pity.

This morning, Edgar felt obliged to work off the more than generous tip Herron forked over the night before.

For his part, Herron knew the doorman had been a pugilist in circles not frequented by the Marquis of Queensbury, but he had never seen Edgar without the cherry-red greatcoat. Studying Edgar's silhouetted frame, he marveled at the man's arms. He wondered how Edgar squeezed them into ordinary shirt sleeves.

Even with his pot-belly, Herron realized he wouldn't want to aggravate such a doorman, then accidentally meet up with him on dark night behind a warehouse.

Herron wouldn't mind accepting a man of Edgar's physique as an ally, but he was reluctant to take him fully into his confidence. This wasn't snobbery. It was the question of whether Edgar, with all the blows to the head he had received in his career, retained the necessary acuity to comprehend the situation.

More importantly, however impressive Edgar might appear, Herron had never known a mere muscle to stop a bullet.

He decided to tell Edgar only so much, and no more.

"'Pinch,' Edgar, is a dashed good way of expressing it."

Edgar mistook Herron's reticence as a ploy to swap information, the way players alternated moves in draughts. It was Edgar's ante.

"Mister Strangways, there was bluebottles buzzing 'round here yesterday, asking questions about you."

"The police, you mean? What did they ask?"

"What sort of gentleman you are . . . that sort of thing."

"Did they talk to you?"

"Yes, sir."

"What did you tell them?"

"The truth."

"Damn. You mean, like the time I buttered the stairs."

"That was exactly the sort of thing about which they was inquirin.'"

"You did right. Honesty is always the best policy when you're found out."

"Yessir. I keep to one hard and fast rule, Mister Strangways, to wit: never try to bamboozle the bluebottles. I do what I can to help our gentlemen, but I draw the line at getting jugged for aid-and-abet."

"Would you do me one favor, Edgar?"

"So long as it ain't aid-and-abet."

"It is a delicate task."

"I will handle it with kid gloves on, sir.""Good. Are you off duty?"

"Yes, sir."

"Do you know where I live? No?" Herron told him and gave him cab fare. "What time are you on duty again?"

"Noonish."

"If my man Merridew is in, ask how he's doing. He may have met with an accident. Oh, and please tell a waiter to bring me a pot of tea." He offered Edgar another substantial gratuity, which was promptly accepted.

Herron's finances were ebbing too quickly, but he had a lot of work ahead. He might need allies, and that pump needed priming.

Pocketing the money in his waistcoat, Edgar withdrew with a bow, backing away as if Herron were royalty.

Returning to the window, Herron pushed the curtains wide. The fog was lighter than it had been. He glanced at his pocket watch. A quarter til five on Monday morning. Dawn was breaking on the longest day of the year – and one of the longest of Herron's life.

Throwing back the curtains, he slipped into a chair tucked in the shadows, so he could see down into the street, but no one outside could see up to him.

Everything beneath the window was indistinct. Ghostly figures drifted by, but Herron was unable to discern who they were or whether any of them were watching the Club. Unless someone actually pressed his nose against the glass and rapped on the pane, Herron wouldn't recognize him.

The bow window of the library was one place where the front of the Hemlock Club wasn't cluttered with grandstands. The charter members – including Herron – planned to stand together in that window Tuesday morning to toast the Queen with a fine port while she whizzed by in her chariot. Herron hated parades and the Jubilee, but he liked gatherings – especially when drink was involved.

Eventually tiring of fog-watching, Herron closed the curtains and nosed around in the dark until he found some pink-colored sporting papers. He leaned against the wall by the door and tried to read by the gas in the corridor.

With his own future so uncertain, however, Herron was unable to care much about which horses were in condition to win upcoming races.

2

A waiter arrived bearing a shining silver tea service. When he entered the reading-room, he looked scornfully around with his nostrils high, as if the darkness had been a bad smell.

Herron motioning to a small side table by the window.

The waiters at the Hemlock Club dressed in eighteenth-century style. The original conception of their uniform was designed by a member who based it on a portrait that had frightened him as a child.

The man in the portrait wore a red velvet coat and waistcoat, a frilled white shirtfront with lace at his wrists, and a cravat wound around his neck like he was being garroted. Mercifully, the painting had not shown the man's nether regions; but the member who presented the original design thought that gear would look good with white satin knee-breeches, white stockings and buckle shoes.

This sparked a fiery debate among the charter-members, who thought this garb might prove too hard on the eyes of members waking up from rocky nights.

Herron himself opposed the get-up on the grounds that it was cruel and unusual punishment to inflict on members who were a bit blurry of a morning.

Those opposed were voted down. The waiters were stuck with it.

The cherry-red coats were cut short in the front and tailed long in the back. Waiters also wore white cotton gloves and white wool wigs (unpowdered, since powder got everywhere). The wigs had dainty pig-tails in the back.

In this outlandish costume they waited on well-heeled young gentlemen of the scientific nineteenth century, clad in basic black morning coats and top hats.

Confronting a waiter face-to-face at sunrise, Herron realized he had been correct in his original diagnosis. The waiter gave a distinct sensation of formication when viewed in the clammy light of dawn.

Careful of his finances for the first time in his life, when the waiter set the silver tray down on the side table, Herron slipped him a smaller-than-usual gratuity. He promised more in the future as the waiter bowed out.

If I have future, he added as a silent afterthought.

Lifting a silver lid covering a plate, Herron rejoiced to see that Edgar had gone beyond the call of duty. Perhaps by threatening the kitchen staff, he had provided Herron with a tidy breakfast of toast, butter, eggs (sunny side up) and even a kippered herring grilled reddish brown. Just the sort of repast a man needed to get his heart started in the morning.

Fish was not one of Herron's favorite foods of a morning; but it was supposed to be brain food, and he needed an active brain today of all days.

Sliding a comfortable chair beside the small side table, Herron poured himself a cup of tea, spread the sporting paper over his lap, and nestled in for a pleasant morning's siege.

CHAPTER XIV

Eventually, the Monday morning newspapers trickled in. They mentioned Saturday night's accident, but carried no hint of its being murder.

On page 17 of the *Times*, Herron found a drawing of the route Tuesday's Diamond Jubilee Procession would take. It was no surprise – the *Times* had detailed the Procession route on June 11. Herron studied the route, idly killing time by ticking off on his fingers all the places on the map he had never been.

For instance, he had never set foot in the National Gallery. He'd heard there were some nice pictures there, but he'd just never found the time for them. Besides, the pictures that were so critically were usually disappointing. Once, when a woman in Paris had led him into the Louvre, he was appalled at how plain Mona Lisa was. After all he'd heard of the lady, he supposed she was a stunner. Instead, she was a sluttish, yellowed woman who didn't even have eyebrows.

The pictures Herron hung in his own home were borrowed from the painting department at Strangways'. Most of them were pre-Raphaelite: women in boneless poses, lightly draped in faux-Grecian gossamer (Mona Lisa was covered in some dark horse-blanket). When Herron tired of those pictures, he simply returned them and took new ones.

Buckingham Palace! He'd never been there, though he'd been told the changing of the Guard was worth a glance. He hated acting like a tourist in his own home town, though. He decided he'd go to Buckingham Palace only when he received an invitation. He was surprised he hadn't been invited yet – his father had been, a time or two.

Then Herron saw the route went by the Courts of Justice, and he whisked the paper aside. He did not want to think about Justice while he was eating. He had to choose between being shot by the shadow warriors, or enduring the ignominy of being hanged publicly by the state after a fair trial—

But you won't be hanged by the state, he reminded himself. *Chubb might be sizing your collar for a noose, but If you're arrested you might as well paint a target on your chest.*

If Jessup had been truthful. Herron wondered how far to trust a housebreaker.

Jessup said he would contact Herron today – but how? He certainly wasn't a member of the Hemlock, and Herron had no plans to budge from the Club until he'd arranged, through channels, for a private yacht out of the country.

Forget trying to find a lady he didn't know for half-a-cigarette! Those had been real bullets whizzing around him. His country might need Herron Strangways, but Herron did not need his country if it put him in the line of fire.Completing his breakfast, Herron went to the billiard room to while away the morning. He was trying to relax by practicing a few angle shots when a waiter arrived and whispered,

"Pardon me, Mister Strangways. Your man Merridew is below—"

Waiters at the Hemlock were taught to walk soundlessly. When a whispered voice seeped suddenly over his shoulder, Herron miscued. The white ball flew across the room and ricocheted off another table.

Herron and the waiter hit the floor flat, their arms over their heads.

When the ball bounced to a stop, Herrons head and the waiter's rose slowly over the billiard table to see if the coast was clear.

While they were still on their knees, Herron whispered,

"Is he all right?"

"He was injured in the upper arm. The injury is not serious, I am given to understand, sir. A flesh wound only."

"And?" Herron sensed more was coming.

"Edgar told me he did not get in your house. Bluebottles buzzing everywhere."

"Asking for me?"

"The owner of the house, since there was a disturbance there."

I own the house, Herron thought. *It's me they're after and they know it.*

"And there is also the gentleman asking for you."

Herron cocked a suspicious eye at the waiter. "Gentleman?"

"Not a member. He's asking for you in the foyer. He only just arrived."

"Describe him."

"An officer, sir. Dignified. Clipped pencil moustache. Looks like he might have come from the frontier."

"He didn't call himself Colonel Philgrave, by any chance? Or a Jessup"

"No, sir. A Major Hobbes."

"Tall? Fleshy?"

"Medium height and ramrod straight. He said you would recognize his name."

"Hobbes?" Herron drew perplexed eyebrows together. "Hobbes? Hobbes!"

Herron dashed for the door . . . then stopped, spun on his heel and said, as casually as he could,

"Please go ask my man Merridew if he brought my pistol with him."

"Pistol, sir. Yes, sir."

"And if he has, bring it to me."

The waiter inclined his head and left. The young gentlemen of the Hemlock Club were known to make peculiar requests, and the waiters were trained not to ratchet up eyebrows at any of them. He just prayed silently that young Strangways wasn't given to indoor target practice.

Herron continued angling billiard balls over one of the tables – always facing the door and holding the stick so he could easily flip it over to use as a club if necessary – until the waiter returned with a silver salver. Lifting the cover, he revealed the "bulldog" revolver, extended for Herron's approval.

A box of cartridges standing sentry beside the firearm. *Good old Merridew!* he thought. Even wounded, he managed to scrounge the necessities of life.

Herron took the pistol and cartridge box and laid another tip in their place. Breaking open the pistol, he discovered Merridew had thoughtfully filled all the chambers with shiny, new cartridges.

"Now," he said, snapping the pistol together and gliding it in his side coat pocket, "take me to this Major Hobbes."

With one hand in his pocket, clutching the pistol's grip, Herron trailed the waiter into the foyer.

2

By this time, the Club was astir. Early risers had begun louging in the library even before Herron left it. No one had entered into the billiard room. The clack of billiard balls is one of the happiest noises for a man, second only to the sharp strike of a ball off a bat; but to a man with a morning head, the constant clack of balls can sound like the first exchange of fire in a major war.

The waiter led Herron a circuitous path to the foyer, through the early birds making either for the dining hall or the bar for their breakfasts.

In the foyer, Herron was confronted by a distinguished gentleman with an officious little pencil moustache – and Herron's own monocle screwed in one eye!

Jessup had been in bedroom and had access to his monocle. So had Hawkins. And, according to Edgar, so had the police. Was this Jessup, or one of the friends of Stoker, or a police agent – or yet another player?

The Major wore the uniform of the New South Wales Lancers, brown khaki with red collar, cuffs and piping, and white metal buttons. Tucked under his arm was a slouch hat, with the brim turned up on one side and plumed with a fancy cock's feather. A bandolier slanted up across his front. That part of the uniform blouse not hidden by the bandolier was dotted with medals.

Hobbes shot out a hand and grasped Herron's like a python. "Herrie, me buck! Here I be, as per prearrangement. How are you, old lad!" Herron did not recall anything about this man, but the Major gave him a weird sense of *deja vu*.

"I have information pursuant to our recent chat, Herrie, m'lad."

Herron squinted more closely. Though he saw no part of the Major he recognized, he was almost certain this was Jessup playing at disguises.

His voice had changed. A few hours ago he had been a faux-cockney butcher with an accent that would fool anyone not actually born within the sound of the bells of Saint Mary-le-Bow; and then he spoke like a gentleman who had been at one of the minor public schools.

Now, Jessup was the image of a cavalry officer. The butcher's lumpy middle-aged spread had miraculously evaporated overnight into the broad shoulders, slim waist, and tucked-in elbows of a horseman. The wan, indoor coloring with a slightly ruddy nose had become a skin apparently burnt bronze by the tropical sun.

Lithe and brown, Hobbes looked like he had just ridden at a gallop all the way from New South Wales. He even had a line of untanned white skin just below his hairline, like a colonial military man who never removed his hat out of doors.

"Have you eaten, Herron, old horse?"

"A smell of breakfast."

"Then let's have a light, early luncheon. Tally-ho for the dining room."

Herron started to sign him in as a guest – but the pen in his hand hovered over the register. He'd forgotten the Major's surname.

"Don't forget the 'e' in 'Hobbes,' Herrie, old horse. That's right. Hobbes, Maj. Do hurry. I could eat a b'ar, as the Americans say. Though it's been my experience that once you start tucking into b'ar you find you weren't really as hungry as you thought."

The Hemlock was not a Club where guests were treated like a member's dogs. So long as they gambled on the up-and-up, the more the merrier.

The maitre d' advised them they ought not be sitting lunch for another hour. Upon receiving a sizeable gratuity, he added that the dining room contained only a few lounging late breakfasters, so Mister Strangways and his friend the Major were free to take a table and study the menu *du jour*, should they wish.

"That's fine. Lead on." To the Major, Herron said, "They've hired musicians to play a meal-time during the Jubilee, and we might as well get there before they make their first assault. Unless you want to dine in a private suite? There might be one available now."

"No, no," Hobbes assured him with a smile. "The last time I was in a private suite with you you managed to steal my bags and I had to poke my way home in my drawers. Most embarrassing."

Herron had never been alone with this man before – unless he was Jessup – and he had never de-bagged a fellow male since his school days (though he had played a prank or two of that nature on women).

The Major asked to be seated in the middle of the hall, and he snagged the seat facing the door.

Herron ordered wine, to be served immediately.

When the Hemlock was established, its charter members laid in some excellent vintages. Herron decided that if it was his time to go, a bottle he'd had his eye on for ages would be going with him.

When the Maitre d' and left them with menus, Herron asked,

"Wouldn't a private suite have been preferable for an intimate conversation?"

Holding his menu at a low angle, Hobbes mumbled over it. The sound carried straight up the slant of the pasteboard V.

"Worst place in the world. Best place is a rowboat in the middle of a lake. Then the middle of a flat field. We don't have a lake or a field at our disposal, so we'll post ourselves here. Acoustics are always poor in restaurants and dining halls. And we don't want to do anything to draw attention to us. Listen up: you must be out of here as soon as humanly possible."

"Why?"

In a tone he might have used to ask Herron about the tenderness of the châteaubriand, the Major replied, "If I can find you here, so may others. You sent that hulking doorman to inquire at your house. Very foolish. You might as well have sent them a telegram alerting them to your whereabouts. Fortunately, it probably didn't hurt you. I'm sure, like me, 'they' already had assumed you were squirreled away in here. You have a flair for the obvious."

"We were packing to go abroad when they burst in."

"We?"

"My man, Merridew. I was almost—""Never mind what was almost. Look to your future, such as it is. If you stay here you'll be dead before suppertime."

"Surely they can't get into the Hemlock? We have a strict code."

"I'm not a member and I'm sitting down to luncheon with you. If I had come expressly to kill you, I'd be chatting with a dead man at this moment. I'd rise and stroll casually out the door; and when the waiter returned, he'd find your carcase sitting upright in the chair."

Herron shivered. "I'll just stay away from people. If anyone asks for me I'll say I'm not receiving."

The Major shook his head. "There are grandstands outside the front of this building for the Procession tomorrow. I suppose they're not for members?"

"No. Whomever can buy tickets."

"The government wants no accidents during this celebration, bucko. Inspectors are swarming over every grandstand along the route of the Procession. If the others can't get through the front door as easily as I did—what?"

"What what?"

"They don work-clothes, shove a few nails between their lips, tote a hammer, and they are workers. Or, sticking a pencil behind their ear and carrying a slide-rule and kicking at the struts – *voila!* – they become inspectors. It won't be difficult to crawl beneath a grandstand and jimmy open a window. If you're still in this building at nightfall it's because you're laid out for the Undertakers."

"At least then I might be able to get a bed. No!—In these crowds, they'd probably lay me out on a billiard tables. And I'd be fined for obstructing play."

A waiter arrived with the wine, and they were silent.

The waiter offered the bottle for Herron's approval. As he examined the label Herron felt the bottle, to make sure it had the correct temperature. When he gave a curt nod, the waiter uncorked the bottle and presented him the cork.

Normally, this was all a lot of fun. Herron loved showing off his wine knowledge. He had gotten many a morning head in the line of duty learning about wines the hard way. Today, he gave the cork a cursory glance, then chafed while the waiter poured a sample into his glass. For show, Herron nosed the wine and sipped it, when he wanted to swill it down in one gulp.

The wine ceremony finished, the waiter poured a decent serving into Herron's glass. The moment the waiter's back was turned, Herron upturned the bottle over his glass until it was brimming.

He feared he was not going to do justice to this marvelous fruit of the vine.

The Major sniffed his own glass, then tasted just enough to wet his tongue. "Superb. I always say a meal should be selected to complement the wine, rather than the wine selected to suit the meal."

"What's with that voice?"

"It's my voice."

"It's not the voice you used last night."

"I changed the shape of my mouth. It's not so much the voice that's important, but the *embouchure*."

"The what, now?"

"The shape of the mouth. The human voice is a musical instrument of great power and beauty. Why ruin it with phony voices? Phony voices sound phony. Ask any American from the southern states how many creditable 'southern' accents he has heard on the New York stage. I'm no actor. 'Acting' fools nobody but fools. To be convincing in a part, one must live it."

"You used an accent last night."

"A private performance. In most cases, I prefer to use my own voice. You don't have to make up false voices if you only know how to use your mouth properly. Extend the jaw, you see, and you have a very different voice from your own . . . bring the jaw in . . . and hey, presto, you sound completely different. If you use your own voice there's never any confusion about what you were supposed to sound like – so long as you are rigorous about altering your outward appearance. No one expects the grubby chimney sweep they meet today is the plump, high-stakes gambler they met in Monte yesterday or the balding man they meet tomorrow who has the harried appearance of a clerk."

"So you've just popped by to tell me I can't hole up here."

"That should be apparent even to you."

"Earthquakes in India, cyclones in Paris, now this. It's the End Times! Lookie, what about these 'your people' you boasted about? Why can't they pry me loose from this? Can't they at least tell Scotland Yard to ease up?"

The Major's voice seemed on the edge of a chuckle, but it carried a very firm undertone. He blew on the monocle and polished it on his sleeve.

"*My* people do not work in an official capacity. However well an operative is trained – far better than the best Inspector – he might be working as an office boy in Scotland Yard. Or hauling out the waste-paper. Can you imagine a young fellow who's come in to empty the dustbins sidling up to the Superintendent and whispering from the corner of his mouth, 'Her Majesty's Government wants you to ease up on Strangways.'"

"I see what you mean."

"Besides," the Major said, with a glowing smile, "my people aren't in the least concerned about your situation."

"What!"

This loud exclamation drew a few eyes from late lounging breakfasters.

All at once, the Major began laughing. "So what happens is, the knight is no further than a mile from home, and his best friend gallops up shouting, 'You've given me the wrong key to your wife's chastity belt!'"

And he fell back in the chair laughing, while Herron looked bewildered.

"Just think about it," said the Major, reassuringly. "It'll come to you. You always have been slow on the uptake, Herrie. Then there was the one—"

And his voice faded to a mumble, as if he was reciting a joke that he dared not tell too loudly. Instead, he was saying, "You must control your outbursts."

"Were you telling a joke?"

"I was covering up for your blunder. You drew attention to us."

"Can I hear the rest of it? It sounded good."

"This is no time for joking."

"It's no joke when you said your people didn't care what happened to me."

"I didn't say that, precisely."

"They do care?"

"No. Why should we? You don't know anything, so you present no threat to national security even if you are captured and tortured."

"Tor—tor—?"

"You're the perfect diversion from Her Majesty's genuine operatives."

"Oh, I'm a diversion, am I?"

"Haven't you used human beings as diversions for otherwise tedious hours?"

"I always sent them flowers afterward."

"Very gracious. We'll send you flowers, too. In memory."

Herron pursed his lips. He didn't appreciate gallows humor when his feet were on the trap about to be sprung. "Also, only when they were willing."

"If they played 'the game.'"

"Yes."

"And the woman knew what she was getting into."

"I never took any of them one step farther than she was willing to go."

"But you could drip words like honey to lead her on."

"I only did whatever was fair."

"Playing by 'the rules.' There are no rules in life, m'boy. Only Society has rules. You have ventured beyond Society. You're in a zone where rules no longer apply. All societies delude themselves that their rules *are* life. Yet Society is just another game – a bigger game than chess, perhaps, played on a larger board. But at least, with chess, you know it's a game and that the rules did not just happen in an unnatural act spontaneous generation. Well, when you're playing chess, it's not 'done' for a man to stomp up and give the board a kick. You can imagine it happening, but you don't usually play a chess match overshadowed by that fear. If it does happen, where is your game? Gone. Unrecoverable.

"Societies, with their petty civilities, don't realize the same thing can happen to them. They can be quite psychotic in attempting to apply their little rules to people who do not observe them. Trying to apply their arbitrary rules of societal civility to someone who is trying to rip their society right out from under them is rather like your facing the man who's going to kick your chess board and threatening him with your queen."

Herron didn't know how to respond to this. He merely sat opening and closing his mouth like a fish.

"Herrie, m'lad, I have you pegged as the sort of man who is always thought of himself as a stake driven into the ground, that the world revolves around. It'll do you good to see the earth, for once, without Herron Strangways as its axis."

"I'll be a six feet closer to the center of the earth if I can't get out of this."

"Your loss will be mourned; but I can't say it won't be welcomed in a few quarters. You see, by your death the enemy will think it has achieved a victory—but it will be Pyrrhic. That will delight some of my colleagues."

"Your people aren't very nice, are they?" "We're up against people who aren't very nice. Pray my people who aren't very nice worm to the top of the dung-heap. We, at least, know you're innocent. If things turn our way, we may be able to send word to Scotland Yard – through channels. It might look like political pressure was being applied on your behalf. If the press got wind of it, it would be a storm you'd have to weather alone."

"Just so long as either the police *or* the non-police let me alone. It's being a shuttlecock between them that's wearing my nerves."

"You look calm enough."

Herron shrugged. For all that, he felt calm enough. In fact, even during the dullest moments of today's siege, he hadn't been bored for an instant. This sudden absence of *ennui* had an oddly soothing effect on his system. "Are your 'people' any closer to tying up the other end?"

"We're working on it. Not for you, of course, but for the general welfare."

"I appreciate your solicitude," Herron said, meaning it to sting.

"You must continue to survive however you can. If 'they' catch you, nothing you can say will persuade them you aren't lying. The only way to stay alive is to keep one step ahead of them."

"Is that possible?"

"Offhand . . . I'd say 'No.' You're an amateur at best. They've gotten to too many *professionals* they wanted to eliminate."

"'Gotten to' meaning *bang*?"

"Ye, verily."

"Like the haggard bird." Herron leaned over the table, seeming to warn the Major as well as inform him, "I have your gun in my pocket."

Staring down into his glass while he swirled the wine around, the Major, as if commenting on its coloring or bouquet, said, "I've known many a dead man who had two beautiful pistols in holster-belts. Leave it in your pocket – unless you are prepared to shoot another human being with it. The deader, the better. Can you kill a man, Mister Strangways?'"

The Major swished a sip of wine, then murmured,

"Or . . . a woman?"

"They wouldn't use a female, surely!" Herron hissed, appalled.

"Some of the best assassins I've ever known are women. You're a susceptible man. How many times has a woman lured you into a situation where she could kill you at any moment, and you haven't go so much as a sock on to throttle her with? I've known professional operatives neatly stabbed to death with a hatpin."

"I won't let myself be lured."

This time, The Major's smile seemed genuine. "As much as you think you know about women, you're still innocent. I'd wager fully half the women you thought you enticed into some level of seduction actually baited you; but they knew the fish would be easier to reel in if they let it think it was reeling them."

Herron gave a careless shrug. "I'm broadminded about that. If I can make a woman happy by giving her an hour's pleasure, or two, it's worth the sacrifice."

The Major's eye twinkled behind his monocle. "By God!—I wish I could help you more. I truly am sorry. You deserve to come out of this alive. However, if 'they' send a female assassin, she might as well bring a lily for your hand."

"I just wanted you to know I had it. And you're not getting it back."

"It's not mine – I 'borrowed' it. Anyrate, it doesn't matter. This is not Tombstone, Arizona and you are no Wyatt Earp. What are you going to do, lad, challenge them to a show-down in Piccadilly Circus at high noon?"

"You needn't adopt that tone."

"It goes with the upholstery. Somehow, whenever I put on this sort of kit, I come over all jocose."

"So your 'people' won't help me beat them?"

"We are *trying* to beat them, Mister Strangways. But we must weigh the life of one innocent man in the balance against the life of the whole community."

"You *are* a ruddy socialist."

"I'm here to help you. If I didn't want to help you I wouldn't be jeopardizing myself this way. I've bent every rule to assist you this far." "Oh, so you do have rules?"

"Of a sort. 'Rules of Survival.' They are not written down in a handbook. You learn them by not dying in one mission after the other. I'll bend a rule again to tell you this for nothing: your options are strictly limited."

"I managed to grasp that without your assistance."

"Well, how was to judge your perspicacity?"

"Do me one favor."

"Anything, dear boy."

"Next time you visit me – don't wear *that* disguise."

The Major gave a wry smile. "It does affect one's attitude, eh, what, what?"

"I may be safer behind bars."

"Never allow yourself to think so. If you step into a cell you're dead."

"I'm as good as a prisoner here."

"'As good as' isn't 'is.' If you go to gaol you'll think you're safe, hedged 'round with thick walls and burly policemen. But as we have operatives in the force – and so do they."

"Can't 'they' see I'm exactly what I seem to be?"

"They live in a world where nothing is what it seems to be. It makes them confuse perception and reality. To people who live in a world of deception, perception *is* reality. Scott wrote, *Oh, what a tangled web we weave when first we practice to deceive.* They're tangled in their own net of deceit."

"And they're afraid me?"

"Don't take it personally. They are only afraid that you know too much. Of course, they don't know you as well as I . . ."

"Know too much about . . . what?"

"I wish I knew."

"They're not afraid of me per se, only that I might put a spoke in their wheel."

"Fanatics are unafraid of death. They only fear being stopped."

"What sort of people die so blithely?"

"There are all sorts of people who are willing to die for one cause or another."

"I'm not one of them. The only thing I care that much for is myself, and dying for me sort of defeats the purpose."

"Men and women risk their lives daily for something higher than themselves. A deity, a country. An ideal, perhaps. We lost our North American colonies because Americans were willing to die for an ideal of 'freedom' – and we were unwilling to die for the maintenance of onerous colonial taxation. There are others, Mister Strangways, who risk dying for something *lower* than themselves."

"What are you prattling on about?" "Money. Filthy lucre." The Major evinced surprise at himself. "It's amazing how a disguise affects your language. I never used that term before. Such a *cliché*. You might think, 'You can't pay someone enough to die for you: he wouldn't be able to spend it.' But no one actually believes they're going to die. Oh, they might have an abstract knowledge of it – we all do. But we rarely dwell on it. Think of the turn of, not this coming twentieth century that is already at our throats, but of the twenty-first. January 1, 2001 *anno domini*."

Herron smiled faintly. "My birthday. I'll turn one hundred and thirty-one."

"Happy birthday."

"I sincerely hope I see it. Though I'll settle for tomorrow."

"Millions of souls are milling around London today, but on that day, every man jack of us – except, perhaps, the very smallest tykes – will be dead and buried and mostly forgotten. Two millennia and a half ago, Homer said, *Men come and go as leaves year by year. Even as are the generations of leaves – the leaves that the wind scattereth on the earth – such are those likewise of men.*"

"And literate, with it," groused Herron.

"Yet most people can not imagine themselves in a coffin."

"I've been able to, lately. Quite vividly."

"From 1897 to 2001 is not long compared to the age of the earth. One hundred and four years. I've known men and women who lived that long. Yet in that five score years and four, death will have scoured away our entire modern nineteenth century society and replaced it with totally new faces. They will believe they are the up-to-date ones while we, *their* history, are relegated to being quaint, the same way we think of our own ancestors who wore powdered wigs, like your waiters."

"They aren't powdered. Powder gets into everything—"

"The generation of 2001 will think no one ever laughed before, or loved before – or hurt, or wept, before they happened along. They'll think they discovered copulation, though the extremely large number of people one meets everywhere should suggest it's been going on all the time, right under their noses."

"Spare me your thruppenny philosophy—"

"Some persons living this very day – young people as well as old – will not see tonight's sunset; but very few of them rose from bed this morning imagining they've seen their last ever sunrise."

Herron frowned. The fog obscured what may have been his last sunrise. While the Major was talking, Herron had another glass of wine.

"No one, except the ill and the suicides, starts the day off planning to be a corpse by evening. But it will happen to every one of us, rich and poor, fit and sick. *Golden lads and lassies must, as chimney-sweepers come to dust.*"

"Somebody said that, didn't they?"

"Oh, yes."

"Did they have a point?"

"Just this: everyone dies, Mister Strangways. You will die of . . . well, something . . . sooner or later. With all the monkeyshines you get up to, I'll wager it's sooner. But whether you die today or at one hundred and thirty-one, your generation will yield to the next, just as the last generation yielded to ours – and so on back to Eden. And so on ahead, so long as there is life on the planet. But our civilization, and the freedom it offers, *must* continue from generation to generation. If one innocent man's life is shattered and shortened by a few years, it is a small price for millions of others to live in freedom from fear."

"I don't happen to like that philosophy."

"Only because you're the one. Have you heard, it is better that one man die for the people than the whole nation perish." The Major spoke with a twinkle in his eye he probably meant to be reassuring.

But Herron felt in his gut he was going to regret that twinkle. He lost what little appetite he had. He laid the menu aside and brimmed his wineglass again.

"You intimated last night my situation was worse than you had supposed."

"Yes."

"And you only found it out at that moment?"

"The moment I said it. I put one and one together and came up with an answer that made me sick. Yes. It's extremely perilous for you. And for civilization."

CHAPTER XV

"Oh, come! *Civilization* this time, is it? First it's me, and then it's my Queen, and then it's my country, and now it's bloody civilization?"

"I'm being as honest as I can be with you, Mister Strangways."

"Was the wording of that sentence designed to make me trust you? And what do you mean, my problem is perilous for civilization?"

"Do you know what is going on in the world, Mister Strangways? Do you fully comprehend the present European situation?"

"Certainly not."

"You don't know about the Triple Entente, or the Franco-Russian Alliance?"

"I've seen mention of them in the papers but haven't a clue what they are."

"The Triple Alliance started as a double alliance between the German Kaiser and the Austrian Emperor. Then Italy signed up. Their coalition frightened the Tsar of Russia into a diplomatic alliance with France, so that they would come to each other's mutual defense in case France is attacked by Germany, or Germany and Italy; or if Russia is attacked by Germany, in concert or not, with Austria."

"Huh?"

"Germany, Austria and Russia are huge empires with many satellite countries. The upshot of those two alliances – Germany and Austria, Russia and France – is that virtually every country in Europe has joined one of two teams."

"Like cricketers?"

"Yes. And some of them can't wait to play a match. Great Britain, the most powerful nation in Europe, stands aloof. Because of our rather splendid isolationism, we balance the scales as an honest broker, to ensure one power does not outweigh another. There must always be one, strong nation who holds the balances, without a thumb on the scales. The only other way to keep peace between nations is to see which can shoot more of the others."

"Has Britain any preferences between these Alliances?"

"We are fish, Mister Strangways. Britain keeps to the water – in our gunboats. If a general war erupts between the powers, let the Russian Empire, the German Empire, the Ottoman Empire and the Austrian Empire duke it out. We want no part of it. However . . . that might prove impossible. If the war becomes too big the British won't simply sit on the net and watch the volley."

"What could start a general European war?"

"My biggest fear is that France will attack Germany to regain control of Alsace-Loraine. If that happens, under their treaty Austria would be required to mobilize against Russia—"

"Why?"

"Because of diplomacy. Diplomacy has laid a bomb under Europe, and thanks to diplomats it won't take much to light the fuse. I believe in peace through strength: have an arsenal ready to use in case of attack *and let the world know it*. Our gunboats in this Sunday's naval review, for instance, is a show of our power. *If you show the world all the armaments you have, you're less likely to use them.* So, the more, the merrier, and everyone is safer. It's countries who hide their weapons who intend to use them – or, more precisely, use them *first*. To be an honest broker, have a large stockpile of very powerful weapons ready – and *sit on them*. The world will hate you – they always do hate whoever happens to have the highest tree-house, where Britain is, now – but *you will have peace*. Show them your strength – and your intent to use it if attacked – and dast the whole world to climb the tree and kick you out of your tree-house. Most likely, they dassn't."

Herron already had too much wine in his system to give this much thought.

"Unless," said the Major, ominously, "they are fanatics. Who simply want to kick a sand-castle for no better reason than to see a child cry."

"What's that got to do with European diplomacy?"

"I said have a stockpile of useful weapons, like our gunboats; let the world know they're there; and sit on them. All these blasted *Empires*, however, have foxy diplomats who have out-foxed themselves with the asinine idea of keeping the peace by threatening actual mobilization! In other words, if one empire's army moves one way, another empire's army is set to move another."

"A chess match."

"A bloody dangerous one, with all Europe as the board. A powerful arsenal is a safe thing to sit on. Once armies are actually deploying, on the other hand, any trigger-happy fool may start a war."

"And you think France will kick off the ball?"

"My thoughts have drifted to Bosnia-Herzegovina."

"You made that up."

"Glance at a globe once in a while. It's in Eastern Europe. It hasn't been long since it shook off the shackles of the Ottoman Empire, and it's the focus of those who want to create an independent Serbian state – which Russia wants. However, due to diplomacy, Bosnia-Herzegovina is now under the Austrian sphere of influence. The Austrians have not yet officially annexed it. If there is an incident in . . . oh, Belgrade, say; or Sarajevo . . . Then Austria mobilizes to formally annex Bosnia-Herzegovina. I can see the Serbs appealing to Russia, which sees itself as a protector of Serbian ethnic nationality. Russia will issue an ultimatum for Austrian withdrawal, mobilizing all the while to counter Austria. When the time for the ultimatum passes, if Austria does not halt its mobilization into Bosnia Herzegovina – Germany, required by diplomatic treaty to defend Austria from Russian mobilization, will attack France, probably through Belgium."

"That doesn't make any sense."

"That's diplomacy. The dunderheads don't understand that diplomacy is a *tactic* in international relations. They've gone and made it a policy."

"That scenario is ridiculous. And it has nothing to do with me."

"I hope you're right, because if it does – the Kaiser will be in Paris before the shooting even starts good. Unless Britain came to the aid of France."

"Will we?"

"Cross fingers—no! Even France doesn't like France, the way it keeps overthrowing its own government. Mister Strangways, I do what I do to avoid war. If it ever does come to an out-and-out shooting-war between Germany and Britain over our Gallic neighbor—"

His eyes almost became misty, gazing into an unpleasant future.

"—I can see us pounding mercilessly against each other in the fields of France and Flanders until we're bled dry. Because of the pride of diplomats! I hope Britain has sense enough to sit tight and watch from the sidelines. Then when the smoke clears, we can sort out the blackened remains and try to restructure a decent Europe from the bones."

"That's all well and bad, but what in everloving *hell* do I have to do with it?"

"Britain cannot remain neutral if there is an attack on a representative of a major power in London during the Jubilee."

"And there are plenty of 'em in town, according to the papers."

"Yep. The Kaiser's mother will be in the parade tomorrow, *riding in an open carriage*. The Crown Prince of the Austrian Empire, Archduke Franz Ferdinand – who is in favor of Serbian nationalism – will also be in the Procession. Many other royal representatives are on British soil. What if one of them—falls in front of a train? The results could be unpleasant."

"So what?"

"I told you – we've heard chatter. Something is going to happen. We don't know what, or where, or when, or whom it involves. It may happen here in London, but we can't nail that down with any certainty. Yet that 'haggard bird' of yours would not have broken his cover unless his message was of supreme importance. It's the most important written message that has ever been passed, and you got only half of it. And that was gibberish."

"I still don't believe that war you described is possible. Aren't the Crowned Bonces of Europe more or less related to each other?"

"Emperors and Tsars and Kaisers don't have as much power as they – or we, or the Queen – like to think. This is the nineteenth century! Even tyrants are at the mercy of their bureaucracies (perhaps tyrants more than others, since tyrants keep tidy records). And their diplomats are typically self-righteous busybodies who devise clever little schemes like the one I outlined. One incident might start mobilizations that will leave millions dead on blood-soaked battlefields."

"That's a shame. But right now, there's only one person's blood I care about. Mine. I aim to keep it within my personal epidermis. If I can avert a general war, that's a welcome by-product. But my skin come first."

The waiter appeared and announced that they were serving luncheon.

For his "dinner" as he called it, the Major ordered kidneys on rice with whatever greens were current, coffee – and a whiskey, neat.

When Pooh-Bah, the Lord High Everything Else in Gilbert and Sullivan's *The Mikado*, was informed he would be boiled in oil after luncheon, he replied, *I don't want any lunch*. Neither did Herron. He considered ordering another bottle of wine. He no longer cared for a clear head. The way the Major talked, he was doomed anyway. All of Europe was doomed, the way the Major talked. Herron thought he might as well go out in the cheerful frame of mind one buys by the bottle.

They maintained a silence until the kidneys arrived. Then, as if he were hammering nails in Herron's coffin, the Major continued,

"Once again, Herrie, let me assure you that if you are murdered in their custody, Scotland Yard will go red in the face – and that's all. They want a murderer. You are wiggling on their line. If it's reported you were killed in police custody – *if* it's reported, since the papers have only so much space – by God, the Spanish Inquisition didn't ban nearly so much printable material as the modern newspaper editor does in the interest of 'space' – the public will not be unduly distressed to find itself one murderer fewer. If you want to live, you must remain free. And while you are free, you may as well try locating that woman and seeing if she has the other half of that cigarette."

"You keep saying I'm no professional, and then adding that it's up to me to find and crack that message. Is it your organization's policy to recruit amateurs?"

"This is right up your street: baiting a young lady to get something out of her."

"If I poke my head out the front door, someone may blaze away at it."

"The thought dismays you? Join the army. That will cure you."

"I'm a conscientious objector. I have a conscientious objection to being shot at. It's an antipathy that's been growing, lately. Are you in the army, now?"

"Joined up today, when I stole the uniform. I'll be discharged by night."

"Isn't wearing a uniform you're not entitled to criminal offense? And all those flashy medals?"

"When I leave, I will march straight into a rag-and-bone shop, try on a few rags, and slump out into the street with new old togs. I will not pay for the clothes I wear out, but these will be more than a fair swap. If I am stopped before I can change, since I have no papers I'll say I'm attending a Jubilee costume ball."

"At this time of the morning?"

"I just came from one, then. After a long night. I do a good drunk, though I say it. Better than yours, because I know when I'm doing it. The medals – they mean nothing. I bought them from a box from a one-legged peddler. If you look closely, you'll see they're French. They will be consigned to the river. You must crawl out from under your rock, track down that young lady and procure the other half of the cigarette from her, if she has it. That will help you, too."

"In what way, specifically?"

"Your haggard bird pushed between the two of you on that platform, correct?"

"Like someone had rocked on his tail."

"How were you standing?"

"Right beside the lady, with both my hands on my stick in front of me."

"She might have seen your hands. If so, she's the only person in the whole wide world who was in a position to see that you did not give the haggard bird a shove. Tell her you sought her out to persuade her to go to Chubb, to keep the police from breathing down the back of your neck."

"Why can't I go tell Chubb about her? That's simpler."

"Always looking for the simpler way. Tsk, tsk. Why not go to Chubb? Because he thinks you've done a flit. If he claps an eye on you, he's liable to slap you in a cell just for safe-keeping."

"And I'll be killed in my cell."

"I don't care if you are or not. How does that help me recover my message?"

"Who's thinking about himself now!"

"For the common welfare. You'll never persuade Chubb to search a young lady's person and effects for half-a-cigarette that may prevent a catastrophe the size of which he cannot imagine. Kill two birds with one stone. Find her. Persuade her to go to Chubb for the sake of your neck – and, while you're at it, if she has that cigarette, bring it to me."

"How do I find her? I don't even know her name."

"I do."

CHAPTER XVI

Herron had been slumping down in his chair. At this, he abruptly sat up, nearly tipping over the wine bottle. "Do you!"

"My contacts on the force discovered her name easily enough. She was the only person who gave a statement at the station who fits our description. Many pretty girls might have possessed the right age and coloring, but only one was traveling with a woman in a Bath chair and a Skye Terrier. No, don't summon the waiter to bring you a pencil. *Write nothing down*. Commit her name to memory."

"As if graven on the palms of my hands and as a frontlet between my eyes."

"She is one Miss Angelica Trickett. Currently residing with Lady Calthrop."

"Trickett, eh?" He set his wine glass down. The worries for his own safety melted away as his mind became occupied with the young lady from the Underground station. He thought he dimly perceived how to effect an entrée into her society, and for that he required a clear head.

The Major evinced surprise. "You know her?"

"No. I may know the family obliquely, if it's the same name. My father had an old crony named Lemuel Trickett."

The Major raised his whiskey glass. "*It is not for kings, O Lemuel, it is not for kings to drink wine, nor for princes strong drink: lest they drink, and forget the law, and pervert the judgment of any of the afflicted. Give strong drink unto him that is ready to perish.*" He rang his glass against Herron's. "Cheers."

Herron wondered if the man he was dining with was quite right in the head.

"Was this Lemuel Trickett a personal friend of your father's?" the Major asked, after a swallow or two.

Herron shook his head. "Hardly that. My father did not make personal friends. He kept everyone at arm's length. Even my mother."

"You must have been conceived in a very interesting fashion. Your father kept you at arm's length? Is that why you are driven to seek love everywhere?"

Herron thought this was getting a wee tad too personal. His personal life was his own. "Old Trickett was a friendly business rival. He was on his way out by the time I came along. I didn't think I'd ever met any of his family, but I must have at some point because that young lady looked confoundedly familiar."

"Don't forget the old lady, either. She's the one with the address."

"Lady Calthrop . . ." Herron dutifully repeated. "I've heard of her. Well, of her title. I've never heard the family name."

"Relict of the late Lord Calthrop. One daughter, died eighteen months ago in a riding accident. Horse stumbled or something. Threw her, anyway."

"So she's in double mourning. Husband and daughter."

"Miss Trickett came to work for her some time early last year."

"I think my aunt may be within the radius of Lady Calthrop's Society circle, but I'm probably an unknown quantity to her. Unless she buys her doggie biscuits at Strangways'. Where does she live?"

"Park Lane."

"What number?"

"Do I have to do everything for you? Use a directory. Now, be a good boy. Run along and make a duty call with that cigarette paper, and find its counterpart."

"How do I find it – assuming it's is there at all?"

"Oh, that's totally up to you. I give you a free hand."

"Thanks another bundle."

"I cannot impress upon you too strongly – it is imperative that you persuade them to let you in and to find the other half of that paper, if it is there. And look pretty sharpish about it. We meet again for the final time this evening. Oh, and once you have the other half of that paper, until I show up do try to work out what on earth *hip* and *gam* have to do with a lopsided square."

"Can't your people do that sort of thing?"

"My people can do all sorts of things. But they can't guess what might be on a paper no one has seen."

"They can't retrieve half-a-cigarette on their own?"

"If it's there it might be anywhere – in her clothes, her hat, her reticule . . . Have you ever tried to comb through the articles in a typical lady's reticule?"

"No. They've always been mysteries to me. They look small, but they're like one of those thingamajigs that you pull whatever you need out of. What's it called? You know, it's a musical thing."

"Cornucopia?"

"No." Herron snapped his fingers. "Horn of plenty! I knew it was musical. Reticules look small, but ladies do seem to pull whatever they need out of them."

"The other half of that cigarette paper may not exist at all. If it does exist, the chances are high it is *not* with Miss Trickett. That platform was full of warm bodies. They all wore clothes."

"I should hope so! There are very few people in the world, Major, who are properly equipped to strut around their birthday suits."

"They all have birthday suits."

Herron conceded that, "But they don't all fit just right."

"But back to the paper."

"Are you sure the paper you want there?"

"I'm sure I don't know. If the haggard bird had the other half of the cigarette in his hand when he fell, the other half of that message may be lying on the tracks and we're wasting our time. I'd rather waste your time than mine. There is one chance in dozens that we've back the right horse with this Miss Trickett. You have a way with women. If she doesn't have the other half of the cigarette paper, it's a pleasant way for you to spend what may be your final afternoon."

"Thank you!" Herron reached for his wine-glass again.

"By Jove, if my comrade knew what I saw, he'd never have given it to her."

Before he drank, Herron's eyes snapped up from his glass to the Major. "What do you mean? What do you know about her?"

"I don't want to prejudice you going in. I'd rather tell you what I did not see. I *did not* see the haggard bird slip anything into anyone else's pocket but yours. Therefore, I suspected you had it all. That was a serious blunder on my part. After seeing what you had, I'm more in the dark than ever."

"You're determined not to help me, aren't you?"

"Miss Trickett, *if* she saw your hands at the time of the incident, is the linchpin of your continued freedom and safety . . . from the police, at least. Get in that house. Find the cigarette, if it's there. And whatever else you do – *be careful.* This young lady may prove the most dangerous conquest of your career."

"And you can't tell me why?"

"Oh, no," the Major smiled, extending the "no" sound to about seven o's. "I hate to keep you in the dark. I like to work with informed people. If the haggard bird knew what I know, he'd be alive today."

"Oh, for God's sake," bawled Herron, his voice ringing out through the dining hall, "must you be so cryptic!"

"No, no, no, my dear boy!" smiled the Major, as eyes from all over the (by now) nearly-full dining hall turned to them. "The punch line goes, 'I wouldn't send a knight out on a dog like this.'"

Sitting back in his chair with smoldering eyes, Herron said, over his wine glass, "Before I die, my good man, just for the record, I just want you to know I thoroughly dislike you to the core of your being."

"The feeling is mutual, dear boy. But that's no reason not to work in tandem." For a moment, the Major tumbled out of character. He spoke in a lugubrious voice that must have been his own, since no one would adopt it.

"A catastrophe is coming. Mister Strangways. No, I don't mean a coming war, that's still up the road and we may yet dodge it. I mean an imminent catastrophe. I could decipher that much just from what you showed me last night." He clenched a fist. "It's so close!"

"The catastrophe?"

"And the means of preventing it. If we can only acquire *all* of that cigarette paper—God willing—maybe we can stick a spoke in their wheel. You must get it all to me by this evening at the latest, or hundreds of thousands may perish."

"And all those souls are just waiting on me to chat up Miss Trickett?"

"Oh, I sincerely hope not. Yet I fear you are their only hope. God save them."

"They can't kill hundreds of thousands in a single catastrophe."

"Yes, they can. So, you see, you are merely one of a hundred thousand. The only difference is, the other ninety-nine thousand, nine hundred and ninety-nine aren't aware of it. It's like the old poem by Thomas Gray, '*Alas! Regardless of their doom, the little victims play.*'"

"You find far too much time to read."

"If that paper exists, Strangways, you must pinpoint it and give it to me, and we will have done the greatest deed of salvic work since the Crucifixion."

"Of course it exists. I have half of it."

"One-half of a cigarette exists . . . or, existed. It's incomplete – singed along the edge. Our man sneaked half of it into your pocket. I saw him do that. I did not see how he disposed of the rest. Cross fingers, this Miss Trickett has it."

"I thought you said you didn't know the haggard bird."

"I didn't. I thought he was merely picking your pocket."

Herron lunged angrily forward. "And you didn't try to stop him!"

"I mind my own business. Only when he was shot did I realize what he must have done. When I saw him die, I knew he was my man, and that he had probably slipped something into your pocket. I tried to swim through the crowd to reach you, but Stoker got to you before I could engage you in conversation."

"What sort of conversation?" "Oh, ar! 'Jist arskin' for a shillin', mate!'" Returning to the Major's voice, he said, "Then, while you were counting out your change, I'd have snuggled up next to you and plucked out of your pocket whatever the haggard bird put in. If you had returned to the Underground station that night, I might still have picked your pocket and left you in ignorance."

"And saved me a lot of bother."

"No, you wouldn't be bothered at all, right now. You'd have no cares in the world. You'd be dead."

"Dead?" Herron squeaked.

"If I'd been able to take the cigarette. I'd never have visited you in your room last night. Stoker and his pal would have. They'd have gunned you down in cold blood in your own bed and you'd never have known the reason why. That decision you made to take a cab home from the Underground station Saturday night saved your miserable hide. We are held accountable for all our decisions by a Higher Power. God. Kismet. Lady Luck. Karma. Fortune. Destiny."

Herron was no mood to muse on the whimsies of Fate. "Let's get back the female in the sketch."

"It's difficult to pick two pockets simultaneously. Can we really believe the haggard bird slipped the half a cigarette in your pocket, and another pocket on the other side at the same time – and that on the run?"

"What was he running from?"

"He was running *to*, I think. He must have seen Stoker. In his shoes, I'd have tried to dart in front of the train, to put that steaming mass of metal between myself and my pursuers. He might have made it if he hadn't been shot."

"He wasn't shot! Unless Miss Trickett has perfected a soundless gun! Well, what happens if she doesn't have the other half of this paper?"

"You may not have had eyes for anyone else in that station, Mister Strangways, but you and she were not the only two people there, whatever you think."

"We're the only two people in the world right now, so far as I can see. I exist solely to find her, and she exists solely for me to rummage around her person for half-a-smoke. I don't know why you can't just break into her room like you did mine, chloroform her and take a look around."

"We must respect the sanctity of the British home. Our people cannot barge into a private citizen's house and root around for something that mayn't be there."

"What if you knew the paper was there for a certainty?"

"We'd be in like a shot."

"And what happens to me?"

"We're back to that."

"Well, I'll have to be beneath a stranger's roof under false pretenses? If I can find the dashed cigarette, I'm in clover. If it's not there, I'll look a frightful ass."

"We don't want to interfere with your methods. What you do at that point is totally up to you."

"You are such a very present help in trouble!"

"If all else fails, you have that gun you were bragging about. You are under the misapprehension that you are the only one who is working. My 'people' are desperately trying to locate every person who was on that platform. We have the list of everyone who was on the platform from our operative at the Yard. Names and addresses. But it takes time. Some of those persons did not have fixed abodes in London. They consist of every race and nationality, and they speak every language known to Babel. Since they come from various cultures, they must all be finessed differently. You don't approach an Indian maiden in a sari the same way you'd approach a hard-bitten cowpoke or a proper English gentleman. Get to that young lady as fast as you can *and recover that cigarette* – if she has it. Have that information to hand at our next meeting. And hurry. I don't know how much time we have on the clock to avoid a disaster."

"When shall we meet again, in the sweet by and by?" (Herron grimaced. He was beginning to talk like Merridew.)

"When you find out whether the lady had the cigarette or not, return to your bedroom. I'll be there."

"How will I know you?"

"How many men are you expecting in the arm chair in your bedroom?"

"And how will you while away the afternoon while I'm forcing my way into the stately homes of England at gunpoint?"

"I'll be looking for one final piece of evidence to clench my case."

"Which is?"

The ersatz Major calmly said over his cup, before taking a placid sip of coffee, "A marriage certificate."

CHAPTER XVII

Herron leaned far over the table; he wanted to grab the man by his bandolier and shake him until his brains rattled back into place. "Did this conversation just get switched on to another track? A marriage certificate is part of my problem?"

"We are many members, yet one body. Just you do your part, and I'll do mine. Repeat back to me what you must do today."

"One: Get out of here alive. Two: Pay a call on this Lady—" he did not to mention the title aloud "—at one of the swankiest addresses in the Empire. Three: Once I have infested her house, I'm to grope about the person of a young lady for half a cigarette that may not be there, if I have to threaten her with a gun to make her strip – and then kindly ask her to go to the police and tell them I'm innocent. Four: take my leave from the ladies and skulk furtively through the streets, taking pot-shots at anything that moves, until I can join you with the goods in the bedroom of my closely-watched house."

"It's that simple. Do it. And tell no one where you're going."

"Not even my man, Merridew?"

"No one! There may be men in this club, waiters and members alike, who would not hesitate to accept a little silver – or, indeed, a lot of silver – just for repeating your exact whereabouts."

"Merridew wouldn't sell me out."

"You'd trust him with your life?"

"I already have done."

"Well, don't. You tell him where you are bound. A waiter overhears a stray remark. Suppose one of 'them' is a member of this club in good standing? He's hired to watch you discreetly, but you manage to slip the lead. He might say—"

Here the Major, in a private performance, adopted a the accent of an old boy talking like he had a hot potato in his mouth.

"'—I say, where did that rascal Strangways go? Here's a fiver.'" He returned to the Major's clipped voice. "And the waiter will say, 'I 'eard 'im tell 'is man 'e went to blah-blah.' Money will change hands. Farewell, Strangways."

"Who is this Lady Calthrop, anyway?"

"I thought you knew her."

"My aunt knows her. I've only heard the name."

"She's of good birth and family, I believe. Married one Lord Calthrop, who died last year. Cousin of the Queen. In the military, retired as a Lieutenant Colonel. World traveler, big game hunter. Preservationist. You know those chappies. They like their game hot and on the hoof, so they put limits on hunting for others, to keep the animals all to themselves. He was also quite a collector. I've heard his collection is the finest in private hands."

"What collection?"

"You'll see, once you're in the house."

"She sounds tedious enough. It'll be a dreary tea, if she lets me past the door."

"Get through their door—yes, even if you must terrorize them with your pistol. By God, I'd tell you to shoot them both right off the bat, except that you wouldn't do it. That is why you are going to die, Herrie, me buck. The people you're up against will kill you without blinking an eye. If you try to kill them first, you'll blink; and in that split second you're dead."

"Tell me, how do I get out of here?"

"Do you want me to stage an elaborate *Les Miserables* flight through the sewers? I fear I don't know the layout of your club, or of its drains; and I haven't time to study them. Your escape must be after I am gone. I cannot be seen to have any connection with you."

"They'll know you asked for me."

"*Major Hobbes* asked for you. By that time, the distinguished military gentleman you are dining with will have ceased to exist."

"I know! You're not going to use it again – give me your uniform!"

"You really do want to de-bag me, don't you? And make me wander London in my underthings."

"You can have my clothes!"

"And beautifully tailored they are. I'm a trifle wider in the shoulders and chest than you are. No, I came in as Major Hobbes, that is how I will depart. One Major Hobbes enters, *one* Major Hobbes leaves. You must free yourself, even if you do crawl out through the drains. Then pay your respects on Miss Trickett."

"I doubt she would receive a caller who had been crawling through the drains. When I go to meet you, will I be safe at home?"

"Safe as houses."

Considering how safe his house had been the night before . . .

"The police left a guard at the door, Herrie, but no one inside."

"And the not-police?"

"Stoker's boys will assume you're too scared to put a foot through the door."

"Very perceptive of them. Will they have posted someone to watch for me?"

"Certainly."

"So how do you recommend I get in? Put a cabbage on my head and pretend to be a delivery from the greengrocer?"

Hobbes stroked his upper lip with a finger. "No. But it's a good idea. Impractical for you, but an enterprising burglar always finds an alternate way."

"Very few people burgle their own homes. And what about you?"

"Don't fret about me!" The Major winked. "I can walk through walls. Do hope Miss Trickett has the other half of the cigarette. The sooner our information is complete and we have baffled the opposition, the sooner we may send word through official channels that you are no longer to be molested by the police."

"How long will that be?"

"Who can say?"

"And you don't know *what* they're going to strike, nor *when*?"

"There are an infinite variety of targets. The naval review on the twenty-seventh is a prime possibility – remember the *ii*. If someone is planning to start a war in Europe, it will be well to commit a bit of sabotage to keep the British gunboats out of it, since those are presently the world's peacekeepers."

"Blow up the gunboats, and Britain is scratched from the running."

"And there's the Procession tomorrow, the twenty-second. *ii*."

"What can 'they' possibly do against a parade?"

"A good marksman may shoot the Queen and/or the Kaiser's mother. Protocol demands they both sit facing forward, so they can't be in same carriage – but from a reasonable distance I could shoot them both with a .303 Lee Enfield bolt action rifle in – ohhh – eight seconds. We live in an age of assassination. There was an attempt on the President of France just a week ago Sunday."

"Yes, I saw that in a paper. A bomb, wasn't it?"

"A bomb exploded as he approached some shrubbery on the *Avenue des Acacias*. The righteously indignant crowd beat, to insensibility, a detective they mistook for the assassin while the real criminal escaped. Bombs are growing in popularity as the means of assassination."

"Hardly worth being king these days, is it? So you don't even have a notion what day the catastrophe will fall, or against whom? Yet you want me to risk my neck to find the other half of what you have declared gibberish."

"What did Hamlet say?"

"God knows. It was Greek to me."

"That's *Julius Caesar*. Hamlet said, 'If it be now, 'tis not to come; if it be not to come, it will be now; if it be not now, yet it will come: the readiness is all.'"

"Oh, my God!" Herron reached for the wine bottle again. "How did that play ever run for three hundred years!"

CHAPTER XVIII

Luncheon was over. Major Hobbes departed, never to be seen again.

Herron had a final sip of wine.

A waiter bowed up to the table. "Anything else, Mister Strangways?"

"Yes. *Café noir*, please. And put this on my bill."

"Yes, sir."

That made him feel better. He put an excellent bottle of wine on a bill he'd almost certainly never live to pay.

When the waiter returned to pour the coffee, Herron asked,

"Is there a room free where I may meet privately with my man, my man?"

"We can find you some accommodation during the dining hours, sir."

"Good. Is Edgar on the premises?" He produced another sizeable gratuity. Even with the meal going on his credit a the club, Herron was nearing bedrock of his immediate funds.

"Edgar may be on duty by now, sir. I will check."

"I want to see him with Merridew, if he's available."

2

The private room arranged for Herron to meet with Merridew was the bath room, which had a row of tubs individually partitioned off. Since they had running hot water, the rooms could get very steamy.

It was the middle of the day, so Herron was sure to have the entire bath room to himself. Nearly everyone in the Club who bathed at all bathed in the morning, in the evening, or both. (It was after lunch time, and they stopped talking whenever anyone stepped in to wash his hands.)

Edgar found Herron in a steaming tub, sweating out the wine and being closely shaved by his valet. Merridew was not badly troubled by his flesh wound, though the soreness made him nick Herron with the straight razor. This gave him a wound on both cheeks.

Herron had all but forgotten Merridew's wound until he received the nick. Then he asked Merridew how his arm was and Merridew said it was fine.

"Was it a limb you hadn't been shot in already?"

"No, sir. It's a new one."

"Too bad. I'll slip some extra into your pay envelope next time."

"Very kind of you, sir."

The Major said a private room was a bad place for a clandestine meeting. As Herron's pretty, twentyish governess used to tell him when he was twelve or thirteen and taking his first, faltering steps toward seducing her, *Walls have ears.*

And the walls of the bath room seemed to echo more than most. But Herron, scrubbing himself down with Pears' Soap, had to be clean and pressed for his meeting with Lady Calthrop and Miss Trickett.

"Merridew," said Herron, putting an end to the shaving before Merridew nicked a vein and washing any remaining lather off his face, "I'm going to have to reach into your pocket. I must see a lady—"

The valet's eye, while not absolutely censorious, suggested in a slightly-raised eyebrow that his employer chose the oddest times . . .! Merridew gave further no indication of emotion. It was one of those occasions where the gentleman's gentleman was forced to play the gentleman.

"–and I left the house rather hurriedly, without grabbing a lot of loot. I doubt I have enough to cover cab fare. Do you have any of that ten-spot I gave you last night lingering in your pocket?"

"Yes, sir." Merridew produced the necessary cash.

"Edgar, when to the waiters perform their changing of the guard?"

"At half-three o'clock, sir."

"That late?"

"It's when the dining room closes for luncheon and the cooks prepare supper."

"How much would one of those red waiter's coats cost?" Edgar mentioned a sum, and Herron raised an eyebrow. He recounted his cash. "That's more than my present finances can stand. Perhaps I can borrow one?"

"Why?"

"To leave in one. Looking like a waiter."

"The waiters don't scram in their coats, Mister Strangways, sir. The waiters buy them out of their wages; but they leave 'em on the premises so none of 'em gets up to nothin' they shouldn't oughtn't of be doing' in the Club coat."

"Is that a rule of the Club? In the by-laws? And I was on the rules committee, confound it. I should have attended the meetings. Is there a waiter with my beautiful dimensions?"

"Which size is that?"

Herron had his clothes made to measure, but he never kept up with details. He glanced helplessly at Merridew.

"I'll go down, sir," Merridew assured him, "and check the sizes."

"Thank you, Merridew. Edgar, tell the waiters I will give them ten pounds each to leave the club in their waiters' kit, complete with wigs, at half-past three. I'll have to write out a cheque, but the Club will honor it."

Edgar did not possess the insouciance of a gentleman's gentleman. He betrayed agitation at the mention of this princely sum.

"They may be sacked, Mister Strangways, sir, for leaving in their clothes."

"In clothes they own?"

"But which stay put here."

"They're only going a few steps. Then they can all prance right back inside and have tea at my expense. The only uniform that's leaving the premises for more than five minutes will be riding on my back. If there's trouble, I'll try to slip it by the stewards. I'll tell them it was a wager, or a prank. If that doesn't work –

I'll make it right somehow. If they get sacked I'll try to get them unsacked, and if they remain sacked I'll hire them all for Strangways' in some capacity. So, take Merridew down to look at the uniforms and find one I'll look least abnormal in."

Herron was in his tailored silk undergarments when Merridew and Edgar returned to the bath room.

The satin knee-breeches had proved to be no problem, nor did the stockings, the waistcoat or the wig. The shirt didn't fit, but it would be covered by the coat.

The coat was small. It didn't look bad lengthwise; it was supposed to be cut short in the front and the tails in the back were long. The lace cuffs, however, shot far out of the coat-sleeves. So many inches of white shirt extended from the coat, Herron felt like an ape in fancy dress.

Nothing could be done about the shoes.

Herron had larger feet than any of the waiters. It was, in fact, a standing wager that Herron had the longest feet in the Club, and he tromped over all challengers. So Herron was wore his own shoes and spatterdashes.

He pocketed his pistol, the cartridge box and the cigarette paper in his pockets and crammed several of his calling-cards in with them. He left all his valuables behind, including his card- and cigarette-cases.

"Will you be requiring my services, sir?" wondered Merridew.

"No. You stand pat here as a hostage – collateral for my cheque."

"Is there anything else I can do?" "Sorry, Merridew. You are a wounded noncombatant. I'd be lost if anything happened to you." To Edgar. "I suppose waiters normally don't take cabs?"

"No, sir."

"We'll make an exception. I suppose the waiters leave by the side door?"

"That, they do."

"And that way leads round to the street in front of the Club?"

"Yes, sir."

"Have a cab waiting out in front—"

"Can't do that sir. This street is closed to traffic."

"Blast!" Having seen the parade route in the paper, Herron quickly worked out the nearest street not closed to traffic and told Edgar, "Have a cab there!"

"It'll mean leaving my post, sir."

This was getting unnecessarily complex.

"Edgar, If you get the sack, I'll hire you at Strangways', as well. I'll put you on the door and give you an even nattier uniform. All gold braid, from top to toe. Give the driver this." He dug into his ready cash for several impressive coins. "Be standing beside the cab with the door open. I will not speak to the driver. You will have told him to drive the moment I'm inside, and I don't care where to. Once I'm away I'll give him fresh instructions. See to it, if you please."

3

The street of the Hemlock Club was well done up for the Queen's Procession.

One entered the street between specially erected Corinthian columns. The street was lined for its entire length with tall Venetian-type masts topped with imperial crowns. Interlaced evergreen festoons stretched across the street from masthead to masthead. From these boughs hung baskets of flowers and globes of red, white and blue glass. During the day the colored glass globes reflected the sunlight in quivering, prismatic lights dancing all along the street.

Those lights might confuse anyone watching for him. If sunlight enough seeped through the clouds to affect the globes.

And, in fact, the sun shone bright at half-past three that afternoon, when every waiter in the Hemlock Club departed by the side door.

Dressed in a frilly shirt-front with lace cuffs sticking far out of his short, cherry-red coat – and topped by a pig-tailed wig – Herron shuffled himself into the center of the pack. He hadn't realized before just how much a fool a man felt in satin knee-breeches and white stockings and a wig. He wondered how people living a century and a half ago could bear the humiliation of it.

He supposed it was one that ever-changing kaleidoscope of society Jessop had rattled on about. The men in the white wigs and knee-breeches had their rules; so did the somberly-clad post-industrial Victorian; so, he assumed, they would have in that far-off year of 2001. The fads and fancies changed, but the rules of these societies had one thing in common: they were ephemeral.

All the eyes in London seemed to be weighing down on him. The desire to look around to see who might be watching for him was like an itch he could not scratch. Yet he knew he must not, by any means, make himself conspicuous.

He also didn't know what to watch for.

He fingered the pistol in his pocket. Whatever happened, he would sell his life dearly before dying in this get-up.

As the waiters strolled down the street in a pack, Herron kept expecting a bullet to come whistling to a stop in his brain. For the first time in his life he wished he wasn't so tall. The other waiters were shorter, so any armed enemy had a clear shot at removing the top of his skull.

The Club was not far from the end of the street, but the walk took forever!

As they rounded into Piccadilly, Herron began to believe the deception had not been discovered.

At the corner of the next street down Edgar was standing ostentatiously at the kerb in his doorman's uniform, next to a hansom cab. His gloved hand held open the door. Edgar's eyes were peering in the opposite direction, as if expecting the fare he was waiting on to come from that way.

Smart man, Herron thought. That was an angle he hadn't considered. Edgar might sound punch-drunk, but he had a good head on his shoulders – what remained of it.

Herron stepped up to Edgar like he wanted an innocent word with him—

—and he heard a voice from behind shouting, "That-un's wearin' spats!"

Herron dived into the cab. Edgar slammed the doors.

The cabbie, who had already been more than paid and tipped, and who had his orders, whipped up the horses. Just as they sped off, Herron heard the sound of flesh striking flesh.

No doubt seeing a hand making a grab for the cab, Edgar had applied his old pugilistic training. It soothed Herron to realize that many of life's problems could still be alleviated by a good right uppercut.

As the cab clattered away, Herron peered out the small rear window. Men were bursting through the crowd, chasing him. One of them aimed a pistol and fired a shot at a venture, and a hundred people around him scattered.

Herron cursed his luck that it was mid-summer. The days were long and warm and clear. The fog was long-gone, leaving behind it a beautiful summer day. Sunset wasn't until very late.

A man wandering the better streets of London in a red velvet tailcoat and white satin knee-breeches would stand out like a cherry on a white cake.

4

When the cab had jostled aimlessly for a few streets, Herron rapped on the trap door above his head with a white-gloved hand. Opening it, the cabbie peered in.

"Park Lane." Herron did not provide Her Ladyship's address, since he did not intend for the cab to halt there. If the people who had chased and shot at him had taken down the number of the cab, they could easily find the driver later and threaten (or bribe) him into telling where he let off a memorable fare.

Herron's one glimpse of Lady Calthrop, at the station Saturday night, had left an unpleasant taste in his mouth. But he wanted no harm to come to the innocent, even innocent harridans.

And if Miss Trickett *was* the woman standing beside him at the station – Herron adopted a wait-and-see approach to keep from building too many castles in the air – he certainly wanted no harm to come to the beautiful, either.

The Major had been leery of Miss Trickett. He said "they" used female assassins. Was Miss Trickett the one who had shot the haggard bird—?

Codswallop.

The haggard bird had not been shot, as the Major insisted he was. That made Herron think the Major had not seen anything at all. Perhaps the Major had been on his own private fishing expedition in Herron's brain.

Then again, if the haggard bird *had* been shot by some sort of silent gun, Miss Trickett was certainly close enough to do the job properly. Anyone further away would have had a poor view, through that crowd. And Herron had been looking down the tracks, away from her.

Herron doubted Miss Trickett's complicity. A woman so fair could not possibly be involved in so foul an affair.

No, he had no fear of Miss Trickett – but he was mightily perplexed at how to go about forcing his way into a Park Lane home to coerce an introduction to her.

Herron was not looking forward to his coming interview with Lady Calthrop.

To say nothing of the dog.

CHAPTER XIX

Lady Calthrop always took to her bed after her elevenses and did not descend again until tea at four-to-four-thirtyish.

Having slept the first part of this afternoon, she was awake when Herron Strangways left his Club shortly after half-three. While he was speeding to her address (well, so fast as the traffic and pedestrians allowed), Her Ladyship summoned Angelica Trickett to read to her.

The upstairs (and downstairs) maid, Doris, had pulled the curtains and draperies to block the sunlight when Her Ladyship turned in. A simple girl, Doris; pretty enough to be chatted up by all the tradesmen, but perhaps not overly bright. Or overly diligent.

Doris was the sort of maid who never actually shifted anything. She merely tickled *objects d'art* with a feather-duster, so that whenever a vase was lifted a ring of dust marked the spot.

Lady Calthrop professed to be afraid of electricity. And though she was known to be one of the richest women in London, she was too niggardly to pay for sufficient gas to brighten her own bedroom.

It was broad daylight outside; but when Angelica entered the *chambre*, with its murky illumination of a single paraffin oil lamp, and its dreary black velour curtains, it might have been the middle of the night. The cork-lined room was quiet and Lady Calthrop, nestled down in the coverlets with her terrier, looked like a corpse laid out in an undertaker's parlour.

Angelica sat close to the lamp-table, slanting the little book toward the flame and squinting into the small print.

The hardbound book was small enough to be carried in a lady's reticule. Its print was so minuscule, Angelica wondered if they used monkeys with small fingers to fit a printing-press with such tiny type.

Judging by the literature she typically read to Her Ladyship, Angelica would not have been surprised to learn the monkeys also wrote the stuff.

She wasn't dressed for company. Lady Calthrop did not mind Angelica dressing down at home – in fact, she encouraged it, since Angelica never had visitors and Lady Calthrop did not intend for her to go out that day.

Though her own dress never deviated from the prescriptions of society, and whenever they went out Angelica had to be dressed as Society demanded, Lady Calthrop had been an early member of the "rational dress movement." Angelica had the freedom to dress comfortably in their domestic arrangements.

Angelica was dressed casually in a light blue blouse that rode up high on her graceful neck. Its wrist-length sleeves that puffed out at the shoulders, and it was set off with a navy-blue, ribbon-sized string tie. A fawn waistcoat, buttoned tight up her narrow midriff, accentuating her bust. Most women wore corsets for narrow waists. Angelica did not need a corset, but she did need the waistcoat as extra support for her breasts, to keep them from being altogether too mobile. She did not want their butler to get an eyeful of jiggle.

His eyes showed too much interest in her physical configuration as it was.

From the waist down, she wore a light-brown cycling skirt. It looked like a skirt, but it was bifurcated and could be tightened at the ankles to provide Angelica the convenience of trousers for bicycling.

Just now, it was loose and looked like an ordinary ankle-length skirt. When Angelica crossed her legs with the book propped on her knee, she displayed a narrow triangle of fancy black stocking between the lower hem of her skirt and the top of her button shoe.

Angelica was disappointed that she had not gotten permission to venture out that afternoon. It was not her regular afternoon off, to be sure; but the Queen had arrived at Paddington from Windsor early that afternoon, and Her Majesty's path down the Edgeware Road toward Buckingham Palace passed practically by their door. Though Lady Calthrop visited Buckingham Palace from time to time, Angelica had never seen the Queen and she wanted take a peek at her.

Lady Calthrop had already claimed she could not spare Angelica on Tuesday morning during the Procession. Since Her Ladyship declined to let her out of the house this afternoon, Angelica was resigned to never seeing the Queen at all. Her Majesty, who rarely stayed in the nearby Buckingham Palace, was almost eighty, and unlikely to enjoy a seventieth-anniversary Jubilee in 1907.

Though chafing inwardly at being refused that simple request, which would not have been an inconvenience to Her Ladyship (who was asleep anyway) she maintained a placid demeanor. Angelica might not have had a care in the world.

Lady Calthrop asked, "Where had we got to, my dear?"

A trifle snippily, she responded, "Daisy Lill had just learned that the man who jilted her is planning to affiance himself to a woman with larger dowries."

"Oh, yes. Girls these days. They will attach themselves to the most disreputable persons. Arranged marriages are always best, my dear. They have all the unpleasantness of other marriages, without that shock that comes from a fading love when you realize what the wedding knot has tied you to."

Angelica had no sympathy to spare for Daisy Lill. *It's just a novel*, she thought. *And a not-very-interesting novel at that.*

Angelica liked books where things happened. She was devoted to those yellow-backed novels sold at train stations, where innocent bystanders were plunged from their complacent lives into one dire predicament after another.

Lady Calthrop liked novels whose events were improbably mundane.

Angelica thought a preference for books exhibiting 'a just picture of real life' showed a deficiency of imagination. *If you want real life*, she thought, *just go out of doors once in a while, and you'll quickly get a belly full of it.*

Angelica lived real life. She read for fun, and for experiences that never happened in reality. In short, she read books that were interesting.

And the only interesting thing that had ever happened in Daisy Lill's insipid little life was her being jilted. And that, as far as Angelica could judge, it was the irritating little simp's own fault.

I grew up in a secluded, simple way, and I could see a country mile off that this double-timing Lord Marmaduke was no good. Angelica shook her head. Daisy Lill, she believed, was getting no better than she deserves. She got far better than she deserved merely by having a novel written about her.

Daisy Lill did not have a brother. Angelica did. If some man had hoodwinked Angelica that way in real life, and she somehow managed not to murder him, she expected her brother would be man enough to horse-whip the blighter on the steps of his club. Or challenge him to a duel.

Dueling was illegal, but a challenge would show the right spirit.

Yet Angelica believed, with all her heart, if she ever were deceived, it would not be by a man named Marmaduke. That would be too unutterably goofy.

Sighing, she flipped to where she had left off, cleared her throat, and begin:

> *"And now, Lord Marmaduke, what have you to say to me?" asked Lady Rudbeckia, seeing full well the proposal quivering on his lips beneath his direful moustachios. "But, first–!" she asked, coyly, "when did you hear last from Miss Daisy Lill?"*
>
> *Lady Rudbeckia asked this last with a meaningful purr.*
>
> *"It is a streak of cruety in you to ask such a question. I have not seen Miss Daisy Lill since her promise of marriage."*
>
> *"No, you did not show up on your wedding day. I do not see why you should get me alone to tell me anything that is so publicly known."*
>
> *"Cruel Jade! Even when I told you of my engagement to Miss Daisy Lill, I told you that another woman possessed my heart. Do you not know to whom I alluded?"*
>
> *"Indeed, I did not, Lord Marmaduke. I am no sorceress, to read your little mind."*
>
> *"You are sorceress of my heart, Lady Rudbeckia–!"*

Angelica rolled her eyes. Her first rule was, any man who proposed to her must talk like a human being.

Not that any man was ever likely propose to her.

She attracted men of her own class the way the prettiest flowers attract bees. Unfortunately, men of her class were typically shorter than she; and Angelica firmly believed if she brought beauty, intelligence and a superb physique to the match, the man ought at least to bring height. She wanted to turn her face up to the man she kissed. She did not want to look down on him, or bend her knees to him, or prop him up on a stool.

And a man of her own class, whatever his dimensions, would not be rich. Angelica lacked a dowry. Though she liked to think of it as a sustaining force, sheer reason told her a couple could not live on love alone. A little bread and cheese was also necessary.

She knew the words of Kit Marlowe,

> *It lies not in our power to love or hate*
> *For will in us is overrul'd by fate.*

And she considered them bosh. God commanded her to love her neighbors and her enemies, so love was an act of the will, not a whim, or a sudden fever.

She had seen too many marriages of fatal love amongst her school-mates, some of whom had gotten hitched in a passion; and when the passion burnt out they didn't even like the man they had "loved." Her brother said it was the same with men, taking cold, objective looks at women they had married in a white-hot heat.

Love was a decision, then; and when Angelica made that decision, she determined it would be for life. She would not let passion overrule her reason. Love would be guided by reason, and so far, she had never met a man who rose to her reasonable specifications.

She gave her hypothetical lover plenty of elbow room in regard to actual physique. God would designed him, after all, not Angelica Trickett. But she would not fall for the first good-looking smooth-talker who happened up. She had a lot of offer and she wouldn't sell it cheap. And passion came cheap.

"Am I then, a witch?"

"Dare I say that you have bewitched me, and you it is whom I love and wish to marry!"

"It is strange indeed that you wish to marry me, considering that you are engaged to Miss Daisy Lill."

"I will not marry where I do not love. I cannot speak too highly of Miss Daisy Lill; and I confess, with all my heart, I would make her an excellent husband because of my sterling qualities. But I love her, I do not. Miss Daisy Lill is a timid fawn. My mate must be a woman."

"Why did you not think of that before you asked her to marry you?"

"In truth, I ought to have done so."

"And you ought also to marry her, since you are engaged to her."

"It is impossible that I should marry Miss Daily Lill. It would be wicked to do so, since my heart belongs altogether elsewhere. May I expect a positive answer from you, my own, dearest love?"

"An answer to what, pray, Lord Marmaduke?"

"You know what."

"I cannot answer until you have asked. What is your question?"

"Just this: Lady Rudbeckia, will you be my wife?"

Angelica was brought up short by a gloved rapping at the door.

"That's Dapifer's knock!" groused Lady Calthrop. "What a time to interrupt! See what he wants, my dear." Angelica laid the book aside. She was careful not to mark her place by laying the book face down on the bedside table, for Lady Calthrop had warned her that cracked the binding.

Lady Calthrop wanted the books in her library to look as if they were never touched. And they did. Angelica herself always donned gloves before picking them up, and marked her place with a velvet ribbon before laying them down.

Opening the door so as to block the butler's view of the invalid in bed, she found Dapifer extending a silver platter bearing a pasteboard card.

Angelica took the platter and closed the door. "It's a calling-card, Lady Calthrop. From a visitor."

"Whose?"

It was difficult to read with the lamplight so far away. Angelica had a smooth forehead, but it wrinkled easily. It wrinkled now as she read:

Herron Strangways

"Let me see, girl."

Angelica passed the platter to Her Ladyship.

"Herron *Strang*-ways?" She looked if the card emitted a bad aroma. "Who is Herron Strang-*ways*?" She reached for the bell-pull by the bed and began yanking it, yelling, "Dapifer! Dapifer!"

"You don't want him to see you in bed, do you, Lady Calthrop?"

"No, no. Help me up, my dear."

A soft, gloved rapping again sounded at the door. "I am here, m'lady."

Lady Calthrop had two wheeled chairs for use in the house, one upstairs and one downstairs. As she needed help on the stairs, she employed Dapifer, a husky, broad-shouldered butler, to carry her up and down from floor to floor (though Angelica sometimes mentally suggested stuffing her into the dumb-waiter).

Angelica Trickett was a valuable companion because she possessed a well-toned upper body that was nevertheless not lacking in femininity. She was able to assist Lady Calthrop out of bed and into the upstairs wheelchair.

Once Her Ladyship was in her chair, Angelica threw a rug over her legs and a shawl over her shoulders before admitting Dapifer.

Lady Calthrop waved the card at the butler like a challenge to a duel. "What sort of creature is this man?"

Dapifer winced. "Most unsuitable, madam. Dressed as a maccaroni."

Women of Lady Calthrop's class did not readily show emotion; but her voice jagged up an agitated register, playing every note on the scale. "A *maccaroni*?"

Angelica was perplexed. "He's dressed as a pasta?"

"No, Angelica," Her Ladyship wearily corrected. "A maccaroni is an eighteenth century fop."

"Oh, you mean like the song? 'Yankee Doodle went to town, riding on a pony, stuck a feather in his cap—"

Her Ladyship waved Angelica to silence.

She shrugged. "Does he have a feather in his cap, Dapifer?"

"No Miss."

Lady Calthrop asked, "How is he dressed?"

"In," the butler cleared his throat, "white satin knee-breeches. And a red, velvet cutaway coat with tails. And a white wig with . . ." Dapifer was barely able to bring himself to finish, " . . . a pig-tail."

"A white wig!" said Lady Calthrop and Angelica, in unison.

"With pig-tail. And," the butler added, perhaps as a palliative, "spats."

"Spats!" spat Lady Calthrop. "Should I admit such a complete stranger to my house in that outrageous garb because he happens to be wearing spaterdashes?"

Angelica feared spats would only render the sight more gruesome.

"He said to tell you he is the nephew of Lady Wilding, the wife of Sir Triant."

"That would make him the son of Eleazer Strangways," murmured Angelica, close to Her Ladyship's ear.

"Oh." Lady Calthrop was still unimpressed. "*Strangways*, of Emporia? Their tea is good. *Herron* Strangways is the boy, then? Yes, I do know Lady Wilding, and he is a prime topic of her conversation. She never mentions him by his name, only with a horror-struck 'my nephew. Do you know him, my child?"

Angelica firmly shook her head. "Our fathers were acquainted, but I never met any of the Strangways family. I hear he's one of the richest men in London."

"Well, what *can* he want here? Does he make his own deliveries like that?"

Dapifer had an answer for that. "He first asked for Miss Trickett. I answered that she was not receiving."

"For *me*? I can't think why."

"You were quite right, Dapifer. The nerve of the man. His aunt describes him as a *roué*. At best. You will have nothing to do with him, Angelica."

Dapifer kept up with the scandals of society. "I have heard, Your Ladyship, he is a sporting young man and much given to pranks. If he does not know Miss Trickett, his visit may well be the results of a wager, or a rag."

Lady Calthrop pursed her lips tight, making use of every little wrinkle around her mouth. "I've heard that, too, from his aunt. I'm surprised he had the temerity to use her name as a key to open our door. I do not appreciate my house being turned into either a wager or a rag. Do we, Angelica?"

"Indeed not, Lady Calthrop." She was not offended that he called on her, but she was more than a mite indignant that he should ask for her, as a total stranger, dressed as he apparently was.

"What shall I tell the . . ." Dapifer raised a soft glove to his mouth to cover a meaningful little cough, like a sheep about to offer an insult, "gentleman?"

Lady Calthrop sighed deeply, to let them all know what a bother this was. "Show him into the drawing room, Dapifer. You will not offer him refreshment."

"Very good, Your Ladyship. Tradesman's entrance?"

"No. Let him use the front door, if he's all that rich. Make him feel like he's welcome. It will bruise his pride all the more when we pitch him out."

Dapifer fought a sly smile. "Yes, Your Ladyship."

"Angelica, you will go to your room and stay there. I shan't be long. If he insists on seeing you, I will tell this Mister Strangways you are ill."

"That's not true. I am never ill. Please do not lie on my behalf."

"I would scarcely employ you if you were. Your room, Angelica. Stay there."

CHAPTER XX

Herron's journey had not been easy.

Park Lane was not far from the Hemlock as the crow flies – but he didn't go by crow. And the ever-present crowding problem was exacerbated by the Queen herself being out in the streets.

The Royal train, arriving from Windsor, had glided into Paddington Station at half-past twelve. Queen Victoria descended dressed in her customary black mourning for her long-dead husband (but with white egret plumes in her little bonnet). Her slow carriage-ride from Paddington Station south down the Edgeware Road was less crowded with spectators than the grand Procession planned for Tuesday morning – but not by much.

If Herron had left the Hemlock immediately after Major Hobbes, he might not have been able to squeeze into Park Lane at all.

Even with the Queen safely ensconced at Buckingham Palace by the time Herron left his Club, many of the spectators that had clumped together to view the queen's carriage ride still loitered underfoot along Edgeware Road and Park Lane. Park Lane being one of the most famous streets in London, many of the out-of-town visitors took this as an opportunity to saunter up and down the street, gawking at all the fancy houses.

Rather than hiding back in his cab when it turned into Park Lane, Herron leaned forward, over the apron. His face was clearly visible, but stealth was unnecessary. His pursuers had undoubtedly taken the number of the cab. They would go to the nearest telegraph office to inform their mates to keep their eyes peeled for it. Seeing Herron's face would be no worse than seeing the cab itself.

Park Lane was not one of his ordinary haunts, so Herron had to lean far out to acquaint himself with its layout. Adjacent to Hyde Park, Park Lane contained several of the stateliest residences in London. Herron had no notion which might belong to Lady Calthrop until he had taken his bearings.

After traveling slowly down Park Lane, Herron called for the cabbie circle the Park. At some distance from Park Lane, he shouted for the driver to slow down enough for him to hop out.

Advising the cabbie to whip up the horses once he had disembarked, Herron leapt out of the cab and bolted through Kensington Gardens and the Park – which he knew intimately, having finalized the terms of many assignations there. He trotted over the bridge at the Serpentine and across grass, leaping picnics to the shouts of angry picnickers.

Reaching Park Lane, he strolled briskly to Lady Calthrop's mansion.

He tried to behave casually. However, in an age where dark clothes were the fashion, a man wearing red-velvet cutaway coat whose tails flopped against the calves of his white satin knee-breeches could never truly be inconspicuous.

Fortunately, he believed, 'they' had no way to connect him to Lady Calthrop, unless they had seized the Major (or whoever Jessup might be just now) and tortured the information out of him. Once Herron was inside her house and off the street, he would be safe.

If they let him through the front door.

2

Herron approached the house with trepidation.

Her Ladyship's wealth did not intimidate him. Given the success of his Emporia he could have bought out almost any mansion in London, and its occupants, paying cash down.

Nor was he intimidated by Lady Calthrop's title. England, he believed, would, in coming years become more like America. The autocracy of privilege would yield. In a hundred years, Herron Strangways was certain, England would be a land where neither birth nor station would signify – only what a man or a woman, by dint of hard work (or even harder inheritance) could cram into his pocket-book.

To his mind, Lady Calthrop, reputedly one of the richest crumbs in the upper crust, was among the last of the dinosaurs.

Glaring distastefully at the Georgian monstrosities he passed, he was glad he didn't live in this neck of the woods. Every night (or early morning) when he mounted the front steps for bed, he'd feel like he was going to sleep in a museum.

The actual exterior of Lady Calthrop's house left Herron aghast. It was English Palladian architecture gone mad, with a great, extended front entranceway and two wings. Fortunately, squeezed between other mansions on either side, it was not able to extend its horrid wings too far.

Herron did not think he could sleep in such a place without nightmares that the house might fly away on those wings with him in its talons.

Though he had no fear of her money or title, and he still believed in his ability to talk around old ladies . . . Herron paced nervously back and forth before Lady Calthrop's front door several times before turning in at the gate.

The plain fact was, in the hours since the Major had left him, Herron had ironed out no plan of campaign for insinuating himself into the house. Lady Calthrop *might* honor his calling-card enough to let him within smelling distance; and since he was perspiring from running in a heavy coat and wig in sixty-three-degree heat, smelling distance didn't have to be all that close.

In his gut, he realized what an awful time a perfect stranger might have in a tea-time tete-a-tete with one of London's legendary beldams, especially when she discovered he had called solely to finagle a private conversation with a young lady in her employ during working hours.

Lady Calthrop might be a dinosaur, but he doubted the dinosaurs ever had any notion they were dying out. So far as they were concerned, their razor-sharp teeth and claws gleefully ripped flesh off bone right to the bitter end.

And even on the off chance he should succeed in getting past Her Ladyship's defenses – what should he say to Miss Trickett?

(*"You may have heard how I knocked the top hat off a Member of Parliament back in '93 from forty paces with an old aubergine just outside Saint Stephen's entrance - but I'm actually here on secret business for Her Majesty's Government. Hush-hush, don't y'know."* Said with a loathsome wink).

Herron wondered why the aubergine incident hadn't made Chubb's little book. Perhaps the Inspector, gauging the trend of Herron's character, had not bothered to read that far down. Herron had a good explanation for that one. The MP had been an old school chum – or so he thought, until he turned around.

Then, spotting a man eyeing him – a stranger with grey hair, wearing correct evening dress at three in the afternoon – Herron decided that whatever happened in the presence of Lady Calthrop (assuming he got even that far), he was safer off the street.

"They" no doubt knew the number of his cab; their associates might already have found and interrogated the cabbie. Inspired either threats or bribes, the cabbie might have told all about the slow troll down Park Lane. He'd identify where Herron had leapt from the cab and hared into the Park.

They might follow his trail from there. He tried to walk with the air of a refugee from a street fair, but he knew he stood out. His attire had undoubtedly been noticed. Especially since he was running, and leaping picnics. Herron had done everything within his power to ensure he was conspicuous. They were on his trail. He needed to find shelter.

Hopping up the front steps, he pulled the knob by the door to ring the bell.

A silver knocker hung on the front door; but it was unlikely anyone in this mausoleum would hear it, unless they were sitting in the vestibule with their ear against the panel.

The giant-sized door-knocker was surrounded by an oval, highly-polished and extremely reflective silver plate bearing the Latin legend: SPES TAMEN EST UNA. *There is only one hope* (or words to that effect – Herron had never been among the keenest scholars of dead languages).

He shivered inwardly, fearing the house might prove a nest of religious fanatics. He had not noticed a Bible along with the lady's parasol and terrier, but any amount of evil could be hidden in that pile of bombazine.

Might that beautiful young girl he had eyed at the station ask him if he was saved? Nothing chilled Herron Strangways to the marrow more than a beautiful young lady he had his eye on asking if he was saved.

He usually confessed he was High Anglican and let her make up her own mind.

3

Though he identified himself as High Anglican, Herron held no specific personal religious beliefs. He never attended any religious services – including marriages, funerals or (most of all) christenings – unless he was trying to impress someone (usually female) by his attendance.

Herron's religious principles resembled his patriotism. His country was, and he accepted it as such. God was – or wasn't. That was a matter for God to decide. A God existed, or not, whatever Herron Strangways believed in one.

And he believed most people sought God for the same reason he sought women: for what they could get out of Him.

Herron preferred religiosity to religion, since religiosity typically assisted (rather than inhibited) his conquests. Young ladies of a high moral tone were often less challenging than they appeared.

If the women were out-and-out hypocrites, and all their religion was so much show, Herron was half-way home. Such ladies did not really give a hoot what they did so long as no one found out about it.

Women who actually *believed* the tenants of their faith presented a firmer challenge – but Herron Strangways relished a challenge.

If his quarry was genuinely imbued with the notion she was a sinful being in need of Redemption, Herron employed that very fact as leverage against her scruples. As Herron once heard in a play he had been dragged to, *the devil can cite Scripture for his purpose* – and so could Herron Strangways. He hadn't attended the best schools for nothing (despite appearances).

I, too, have fallen from time to time, he assured them, with as pious a face as he could manage – though his features seemed to suffer not so much from piety as constipation. "All have sinned, and fallen short of the glory of God." Amen? *The perfect have nothing to repent of. That's why sin is so precious.* "There is joy in the presence of the angels of over one sinner that repenteth." *Have something to repent of – make the blessed angels happy.*

Whatever guilt those women wrestled with afterwards was, fortunately, not his problem. He journeyed on to plough fresh fields.

If a woman with a religious bent weren't as stupid as all that – well, it was simple for a tall, handsome young man brimming with *joie-de-vivre* (and money) to appear as the answer to a kneeling maiden's earnest prayer. A virgin saving herself for "the right man" more easily recognized a Divine Plan in Herron Strangways than stubby and/or impecunious and/or unattractive nonentities. Herron Strangways, on the other hand, looked like manna from Heaven.

He had no certain beliefs, but Herron did have a theology; it just wasn't Godcentric. Women were at the core of his theology, and it was flexible enough to accommodate the views of whatever young lady he was trying to impress.

When he could not awe a young lady with his cribbed theological notions, he was always a willing convert to hers, becoming a studious learner under her tutelage – until his conquest was achieved, or he until his prospects were doomed.

And no one doomed his prospects more quickly than a young lady who actually understood what she believed, and practiced her beliefs—not as ritual, or as forced obedience because an eye in the sky was peeping down on her, but from a genuine joy in her heart. That sort of joy was always Herron's Waterloo.

Herron had met the rare woman or two who would not even let him speak to them at all. They did not even tell him *Get thee behind me*, in case he misunderstood. They refused to fall for his favorite ploy, that he was a sinner in need of redemption and required her tender hand to lead him to the light. He found that was an invaluable first step to helping women blunder into darkness.

Is Miss Trickett inflicted with morals? Herron sighed. He sincerely hoped not. Or, if she had morals, he hoped they were only skin deep.

Sometimes he wished he'd lived in his grandfather's day. Herron believed he might have prospered cheerfully in those Regency years, when a wealthy man spoke frankly when he wanted to mount a filly (equine or human). The Regency bucks boasted about their huntin' and ridin' and drinkin' and wenchin' – and the women wore bodices revealing practically all their wares.

Instead, Herron's days were ruled by a prim, black-clad widow-lady who was rarely amused. Women wore blouses whose necklines barely plunged beneath their chins. Their upper slopes were so well-packaged no interesting formations ever poked visibly out in cold weather.

It had all started after the untimely death of Albert the Prince Consort, at the young age of forty-two, way back in '61. Moralizing youngsters rebelled at the ways of their blunt-speaking parents and brought revolution to the land.

They were they fresh young "bloods" of the '60s, fighting to bring new, "Victorian" values to a society that seemed to have lost its sense of social justice. In their new justice they covered the "limbs" of tables for propriety, and separated male and female authors in libraries, so they wouldn't rub together. They divided chickens into dark meat and light so they didn't have to say "breast" and "leg." They forbade words like "body" in polite conversation in mixed company.

The problem with young bloods, as Herron saw it, was that when they became old bloods their ideals never matured. The ideals suffered the same hardening of the arteries as their holders. Those selfsame '60s radicals who lorded their new ideals over their parents' "unjust" generation now oppressed their children.

In this year of our Lord 1897, the '60s radicals were grey-headed antiques who should have been put on display as an example to others, and dusted only occasionally. Yet these oldsters, still posturing themselves as rebels (though their views were predominant in society) clung tenaciously to their delusions.

They were still legislating their short-sighted morality and dictating how the world should be run – as if their exploded notions of human nature had any relevance to a powerful nation on the cusp of a new century.

They had made days difficult times for meetings between unintroduced men and women. Herron despised it—

—but, in his heart, he knew the societal taboos he despised were actually what made "the game" so much fun, requiring both skill and resource.

He predilections might never have thrived in the Regency, when a man's mistress was an open adjunct to his household (and he cheated on both).

Of course, Herron's grandfather had been no man of leisure. He had toiled his life away building up a small business, which Herron's father had bought and turned into a huge business.

Also, if Herron had lived in the days of his grandfather's youth . . . he'd be dead by now. That was the fate he had come here expressly to avoid.

Herron smiled. Here he was, at the very door of the most beautiful young female he had ever seen (recently) and survival, rather than conquest, was his foremost consideration.

Even catching a glimpse of Miss Trickett, though, might be impossible. Society ladies rarely condoned strange men barging into their homes and demanding presentation to young ladies under their protection.

Even he, the eternal optimist (and egotist) wondered if he possessed as much charm as he would need. This day had squeezed most of the juice out of him already, and lots of daylight remained.

4

For Herron, time dripped slowly by before the bell was answered, though it was really only about a minute and a half.

When the door opened, heh was confronted with a vast expanse of white shirt and waistcoat, barely enclosing the chest of the most formidable young butler he had ever seen. This chap was Edgar's match in sheer brawn – and a foot taller, ten years younger and much better looking. And no waist to speak of – just enough to put a belt around to hold up his beautifully-creased trousers.

He even had a few inches of height on Herron himself, and Herron rarely looked up to anyone.

Herron fumbled out a card. "Mister Herron Strangways to see Miss Trickett."

He cursed the Queen for not getting that minor knighthood to him when his father died. He wished he could say *Sir Herron*.

The butler looked dubiously at the card, as if suspecting its *bona fides*.

"Tell her I'm the nephew of Lady Wilding, wife of Sir Triant." This was a shot in the dark. Aristocratic Society was only so large, so Lady Calthrop must have stumbled over his aunt; but, for all he knew, they fought like cats every time they came in hissing distance.

"Miss Trickett is not receiving. I will present your card to Lady Calthrop and ask her if she is in."

The door closed in Herron's face.

Herron had hoped he would be allowed to wait out of sight in the foyer.

He didn't know why he should be looked on with suspicion by a mere butler. His demeanor, his speech, all declared he was a gentleman.

But, to be fair, his dress must have appeared peculiar.

Herron frowned at his own distorted reflection in the silver plate around the knocker – then, with horror, he reached up and tore the pig-tailed wig off his head.

He had only finished smoothing down his natural sandy hair with ginger highlights, and wishing he had a mirror to perfect the job rather than a plate around a door knocker that made his head look like a pinkish rugger ball, and upside-down to boot, when the butler returned.

"If you will follow me, sir?"

In the antechamber, Herron peeled off his white cotton gloves and handed them to the butler . . . and, in lieu of a hat, handed him the wig.

Pinching the wig distastefully between thumb and forefinger, the butler led Herron to Her Ladyship.

For such a large man, the fellow moved soundlessly as he led Herron through an antechamber that was wide enough to house an extended family in the poorer sections of London. Following him, Herron felt like an empty coal car bounding along behind a massive locomotive engine.

They passed into an enormous hall that could have doubled for a ballroom. A grand staircase scythed up the right-hand wall. At the top of the staircase stretched a gallery leading to what Herron took for the "bedroom floor" in either wing.

Because of the gallery, the ceiling – which seemed to be all sparkling gas chandeliers – was actually two stories high over the front hall.

It would never be an effective ballroom, however, since glass cases were scattered all over the intricate parquet floor. These cases, ranging along the walls and throughout the room in a waist-high maze, contained some interesting specimens of Lord Calthrop's collection.

Herron was, as the Major prophesied, properly impressed.

The front hall and the gallery were decorated with all shapes, sizes and varieties of weapons. The late Lord Calthrop seemed to have collected at least one example of every imaginable armament. His a-b-c of weaponry went from the assegai to the zweihänder sword of the German Renaissance.

Lord Calthrop had the entire evolution of the firearm under glass, from blunderbusses, arquebuses, and hand cannons to modern rifles. Pistols were lined up according to size, from an enormous four-barrel howdah pistol used in India on tiger-hunts, to an itty-bitty derringer like that employed by a Democrat actor to blast the brains out of Republican president Abraham Lincoln.

Knives and swords were splayed out on the walls in arcs and circles, and they wheeled up wall of the curving stairway.

Fine wall displays were also made out of maces.

Many of the weapons were primitive – the sort of things high-ranking soldiers picked up as souvenirs of far-flung campaigns in Afghanistan, India, and Natal (or on scientific junkets to Africa or South America). Therefore, wall displays were also made out of axes, clubs, jittes, knobkerries – even a *nunchaku*.

Herron wished he could borrow a few of these pretty things for the rest of the afternoon. He had a pistol in his pocket; but it was a tight pocket and he wondered if he would have time to extricate even a smallish pistol if his life was threatened. A solid, iron-headed mace, however, was ever-ready, and persuasive.

Herron saw no examples of cannon, but this was just the front room.

Dapifer wheeled left, then stood to one side at the doorway of a fancy front drawing-room, which was long enough to have a second door opening from the ballroom further along.

"Mister Strangways, Your Ladyship," the butler announced, as Herron squeezed by him.

This room, too, was decorated with weapons, though only on the walls.

Directly opposite the front window, on the wall above the settee, was a large portrait of a man in a beard like a fungus devouring the lower part of his face. The portrait, presumably of the late Lord Calthrop, was draped in black crepe.

On the sofa sat the aged *volaille en demi-deuil* from the station, in bombazine and her jewelry – and with that same, tacky parasol lying across her lap. She looked precisely the sort of '60s radical who overturned society thirty years earlier and more, and succeeded in cramming her narrow morality down everyone's throat. Herron had little sympathy for her and the society she built.

He heard the terrier barking somewhere in the distant offing, so it was no danger. He only had to worry about Her Ladyship.

Not only did it have two doors opening to the ballroom, the drawing room had an open door connecting it to the next room down. Herron had a partial view of a wheel chair just inside that door. Lady Calthrop might appear in Bath chairs at public, but in her own house she displayed no sign of her infirmity to visitors.

On the table beside the settee was a small, silver casket engraved *I.II.* Whatever that meant! He'd never seen Roman numerals with a decimal in them.

"Mister—" Lady Calthrop held his card up and glanced at it again through a lorgnette, though she knew the name perfectly well, "*–Strang*ways?"

He bowed. "Lady Calthrop."

"I will not ask you to sit. I believe we are not introduced?"

For a moment, Herron thought about his ruse of a garden-party . . . but with his life or his freedom at stake, he decided not to employ any imposture. If she caught him in one lie, nothing else he said would be believed.

"I have not had the pleasure, Lady Calthrop."

"Though we do have an acquaintance in common." She waved his calling-card before her, like a fan. "Your aunt. Thank you for bringing her to my attention. She has told me a great deal about you."

Herron's heart sank. End of interview.

"I trust you will excuse me, Mister Strangways, but this is Monday; Saturday evening I went through a very trying experience—"

"Yes, I was there. That's what I wanted to speak to you about."

Lady Calthrop lifted her lorgnette, which was secured around her neck with a fine gold chain. One glance through those spectacles had been known to turn strong men to stone. She glared this Strangways over, to see if he recalled anything to her mind.

"You mean, when that careless man blundered in front of the train?"

"Yes. I was right beside him."

"Oh." Interest sparkled in Lady Calthrop's eyes. "Nevertheless, the coincidence of being simultaneously in a railway station with one hardly entitles one to an introduction, or the run of one's household."

"No."

"*Before you go,*" a not-too-subtle hint, "I must ask . . . if you *are*, indeed, the son of Eleazar Strangways–?"

"He was my father."

A sharp intake of breath; then she muttered, "A tradesman."

She had known this, of course. She merely wanted him to hear the word, and her opinion of it.

"Mister Strangways, your father's sister had the sense to marry above her station. I am well acquainted with your aunt. We are members of the same circle. She is the *only* reason you were admitted through my door. You may take pride in being always in the forefront of your aunt's conversation."

Herron's spirits were down in his spats. His aunt was no hypocrite. She talked the same way to his face as she did behind his back. He knew exactly what Lady Calthrop must have had heard about him. Worst of all, it was nearly all accurate.

"You belong to a disgraceful club and are forever in trouble with the police."

Herron might have argued that he belonged to half-a-dozen clubs, the best his father could buy his son into. But, as he hardly ever darkened the door of any club but the Hemlock, he thought better of using that argument.

The words *Give a dog a bad name* trembled on his lips . . . but her summation was substantially correct. He might have quibbled that he was not always in trouble with the police – but he had never been more in trouble with the police than he was at present and he had come here in an effort to shake them off.

"I understand you came here asking for Miss Trickett. No doubt you saw her Saturday as well. I will not, Mister Strangways, allow you use your tenuous connections to me, or to a young lady under my protection, as an excuse for making my home a haven for your disgusting assignations."

"I say—!"

"Do not 'say,' if it interrupts. Miss Trickett went to school with my own, late daughter. When she and Lord Calthrop died I needed a companion, and I brought Miss Trickett into my household under my protection."

"Your ward?"

"No, but she is an innocent girl who takes people at their face value."

Herron almost smiled. He had a special interest in the education of young ladies who were still innocent enough to take people at face value.

"I stand *in loco parentis*. Do you know what that means?"

"I did study Latin at Cambridge." *Just not too assiduously.*

"Good. Mister Strangways, I resent your advances to a young lady in my household, whatever her status; I resent what you are trying to turn my house into; I resent your coming to call on me in that . . . that outlandish garb. And furthermore, Mister Strangways, your cards come from a cheap printer."

"Lady Calthrop, I need to speak to Miss Trickett to . . . to . . . I want need to speak to you both together."

"Dapifer?"

The huge butler appeared in the door behind Herron. "Your Ladyship called?"

"Mister Strangways is leaving."

"*Very good*, Your Ladyship."

Reeling a dainty watch, so small Herron wondered how it could possibly contain twelve numerals, from somewhere in the folds of her bombazine, she cracked open its tiny lid.

"It is Monday afternoon and it is nearly time for my tea, if you will excuse me. Angelica has had a very trying two days and is not well enough to see anyone."

"Oh, pish-posh!" came a voice from stage right.

Herron, who had been eyeing the carpet a good deal during the latter stages of the interview, looked up.

In the second doorway connecting the drawing room with the ballroom stood the young lady he'd sidled up to at the station.

CHAPTER XXI

Herron had only seen Miss Trickett in profile in poor lighting, and then with half her face veiled by the slope of a straw hat.

Viewing her full-on with daylight streaming through the front window-blinds, he was gratified to observe that both halves of her face were symmetrically lovely.

And, as memory tends to brighten faces with idealized haloes, he was happily surprised to observe she was lovelier than he remembered.

Face-to-face with Miss Trickett, Herron absorbed her like a sponge. Full lips, finely-etched cheekbones, divinely tall . . . her nose was perhaps too flattish and broadish, and her chin too dimpled, especially when she was serious, for perfect Gibson-Girl features. But Herron did not appreciate perfection.

From Herron's point of view, beautiful faces blurred indistinctly together. Women who were all perfectly beautiful were practically indistinguishable, as were all men who were uniformly handsome.

Herron liked the small imperfections that made beauty distinctive. Miss Trickett's nose and chin made her more beautiful because they made her unique.

Her mass of dark honey-blonde hair was still pinned up on her head, revealing small, well-shaped ears. Like Gibson girls, little wisps and locks of hair fell winsomely away from her pinned-up at the edges – one directly over one eye.

She stood casually in the doorway, but with her shoulders back in a way that thrust her breasts daringly forward. Her thumbs were tucked into the pockets of a curiously bifurcated skirt that reached to her high-topped button shoes.

Herron stood nailed to the spot, gaping at her, until Lady Calthrop hammered her parasol on the Persian carpet.

"Angelica, you have had a shock and I insist you remain in your room."

Angelica looked ready to fire another *pish-posh*, but good manners intervened.

"Lady Calthrop, I do so appreciate your bringing me into your home, and all you have done for me. Please, do not lie on my behalf. I am not unwell."

Herron opened his mouth to address her directly—

Lady Calthrop banged her parasol once more, authoritatively, interrupting him. "This is most improper. Angelica, you are not dressed for receiving – and you know my rules. Furthermore, you have not been introduced to this gentleman."

"Then, please introduce us," said Angelica, sounding not in the least rude.

Miss Trickett might be physically present in the room with him, but Herron had to speak to her through Lady Calthrop, like a man at a séance communicating to a spirit through a medium. "Lady Calthrop, I require only one minute of your time, and that of Miss Trickett's. I crave your indulgence that long."

Crave your indulgence? Even as he heard those words come out of his mouth, he wondered *What kind of talk is that?*

Lady Calthrop considered this request, then gave a single, sharp nod. She dangled her tiny watch in front of her. "You have precisely sixty seconds."

"Thank you, Lady Calthrop."

"So!" said Angelica, seating herself on the edge of a chair and looking expectantly at Herron under half-staff eyelids, "you were at the do on Saturday?"

"Angelica!" shot Lady Calthrop, with another parasolic *thump*. "I would not describe a death by mischance a 'do.'"

"It did for him."

"*Angelica.* Besides, we do not know whether this man is telling the truth about his being there."

"Oh, that's all right, Lady Calthrop. I noticed him."

"You did!" Herron's heart leapt. He remembered an exchange of glances, but he knew how a woman might look at someone but take no notice of him.

"I did. I even recognized you. We have friends in common, and I've seen you in passing."

"Have I seen you in passing?"

"I really can't say, Mister Strangways."

"I think I'd recall one so lovely."

"Thank you. I have heard you are frightfully wicked. Is that true?"

"Absolutely."

"Are you?" Her strong, white teeth broke out in a smile that nearly teetered him off topic.

Her teeth, too, were beautifully imperfect. While neither bucked nor chipmunky, her two front teeth were noticeably longer than the rest.

Her teeth gave Angelica a youthful appearance. For the first time, Herron began to fret about her age. She was tall and as fully grown as a woman could be without appearing top-heavy. But her teeth recalled a fast-developing girl he'd once met – who had *almost* taken him in. He never found out if that girl was thirteen or sixteen, but she was in that range and looked all of twenty-four. That had been a close shave. Just like his wines and his cheeses, his women had to be properly aged. Herron had a strict age limit for *the game.* Angelica Trickett's youthful-looking teeth made him wary of a mantrap.

"Thirty seconds, Mister—" as an affectation, Lady Calthrop gave his card a sidelong glance through the lorgnette; then her tried to burn a hole through the glass at him, "—Strangways. You are not making the most worthwhile use of your time. *What do you want?*"

Having been given a full minute before he crept out with his tail tucked between his legs, Herron wanted to ask Miss Trickett right away if she was a witness to the fact that he had not pushed the haggard bird in front of the train. And, if so, please relay that information as quickly as possible to Inspector Broughton Chubb of Scotland Yard.

Instead, he decided to be humorous. The fact that all his recent jokes had been dying on their feet should have caused a still, small voice in his ear merely to ask for Miss Trickett's help with the police – and then belt up. But he was Herron Strangways, with all the self-confidence that implied.

"As a matter of fact, I came to ask Miss Trickett for a cigarette."

Herron offered this lightly, to break the ice. n fact, he left both women frosted.

He realized immediately he'd taken a wrong turn in trying to engage their enthusiasm; but he couldn't suck the words back in from the air.

Lady Calthrop demonstrated her disapproval by saying, with a voice dripping like an icicle, that there was no smoking in her house.

Angelica's face and voice sank to a placid gravity. "I fear I do not fully appreciate the joke, Mister Strangways."

"No—but you will. You see, when I got home that night I found—"

Don't tell them about Jessup! He thought, desperately. *If I start babbling about secret agents in my bedroom they'll have me thrown right out on my— my—*

"—I . . . I . . . I found a half an unsmoked cigarette in my pocket."

This conversation was clearly *not* intriguing Angelica. She seemed disappointed, as if she had thrown back the lid of Pandora's box to expose the diabolical, and instead uncovered the fatuous. She might make allowances for wickedness, but not buffoonery. This man's polluted imagination had dreamt up some practical joke, and for whatever ungodly reason he made her the butt of it – and they weren't even introduced! The best she could hope for was that he was intoxicated. That would not be to his credit, but if he had come here dressed that like and talking like that stone cold sober—! That would be hateful.

Angelica had supposed a man with Herron Strangways' notoriety would, if nothing else, have a diverting story for practically forcing his way into the presence of two respectable ladies in such peculiar and ill-fitting clothes. She was wrong. That vexed her. She did not like being wrong.

Whatever this was about, it had ruined her day.

Herron divined the plummet in his market value. Her thoughts might not be quite on the level of, *"How art thou fallen from heaven, O Lucifer, son of the morning—!"* But his stock had clearly bottomed out.

He had entered the room a rich young man, made fascinating by good looks and a bad reputation. He was about to be thrown from it as a fool and a gadfly who intruded on the privacy of strange ladies to make insulting insinuations.

"Do you smoke, Mister Strangways?" she asked dully, automatically making perfunctory polite conversation to run out the clock until Herron was pitched bodily out the door by the mighty Dapifer.

"Like a bad flue. But this wasn't my brand, you see—"

"Yes, I can imagine the shock." Angelica rose from her chair. She had been standing casually before, but now she was as ramrod straight as a guard at Buckingham Palace. "I appreciate your coming by to share your experience with us, Mister Strangways. We have both had shocks. I saw a man die violently and you smoked a bad cigarette. You have my sincere condolences. I believe in talking these things out. I hope this visit has eased your mind. I am not unwell, as you may see, but I do have many duties to attend to. Thank you once more for dropping in. Good-bye. Please do not trouble yourself to ask after me again."

CHAPTER XXII

Herron felt like he had fallen in the river and was fighting desperately to keep his head above water.

"I . . . I'm trying to say . . . I didn't smoke it, don't you know. Not all of it. I—I can show you the paper—"

"You need not produce the evidence, Mister Strangways. Your word is quite satisfactory. I am *so* sorry I cannot linger, but I really am *very* busy. You see, I have a *job*."

"Miss Trickett, please hear me out."

"Oh!" Lady Calthrop was unable to totally suppress her glee, "is there more to this harrowing incident? I'm astounded your hair hasn't gone quite white overnight. Though, according to Dapifer, it was when you first arrived."

Herron did not blame her for her attitude. He'd started off on the wrong foot and every subsequent step had taken him deeper into the mire.

Lady Calthrop's eyes shone with a triumphant gleam. Miss Trickett was doubtlessly due for her share of *I tried to protect you*-s and *I told you so*-s as soon as their visitor was hustled out of doors.

Fortunately for Herron, Lady Calthrop bought him a little more time by climbing up on a ever-higher horse.

"Mister Strangways, do you know what King James said of smoking in his *A Counterblast Against Tobacco*?"

"Who, the Bible chap? Uh—no, I haven't perused his latest."

"King James called smoking, *a custome lothsome to the eye, hatefull to the Nose, harmefull to the braine, dangerous to the lungs, and in the blacke stinking fume thereof, neerest resembling the horrible Stygian smoke of the pit that is bottomlesse.*" A faux-Scottish accent emphasized the horror of her description.

"Oh. I see." "After talking to you, I think it must indeed be harmful to the brain."

Lady Calthrop snapped the lid of her watch shut. "Your time is well up. Good afternoon," she said, with the finality of a slammed coffin-lid.

Herron desperately produced the cigarette paper from his pocket. "Here is it! Please, Miss Trickett, do look at it!"

Angelica refused to touch it, but she lifted her eyes slightly, as if she could see it perfectly well from across the room. "How very interesting. Thank you again for sharing it, Mister Strangways." She started to withdraw.

Swinging the silver watch before herlike a hypnotist, Lady Calthrop said, with chilling politeness, "I am sorry you must leave us so soon, *Mister* Strangways. When I see her, I will inform your aunt you dropped by to pay your respects."

She tinkled a little crystal bell standing on a table beside the settee.

Dapifer had been lurking just out of sight. At the sound of the bell, he appeared in the doorway behind Herron, standing with his arms slightly away from his sides, with a clenched fist at the end of each.

Herron made one last, desperate effort.

"D-do you smoke, Miss Trickett?"

She turned to him, offended. "Certainly not!"

"Not a surreptitious puff or two in the bushes when you've slipped the collar?"

Lady Calthrop slid sly eyes toward Angelica, perhaps listening for information she could hold over her paid companion's head. "Mister Strangways," (Angelica's eyes fixed on the labyrinthine pattern in the Persian carpet) "I have tried to be kind. When that failed, I tried to be diplomatic. I find I must be blunt and ask you to leave. Please respect my wishes and *go*."

"So if—"

"Mister Strangways, please, before you become a nuisance—"

"Before!" Lady Calthrop echoed.

Herron struggled out, "So if—!"

"Dapifer," rapped Her Ladyship, "summon the police."

"—*so if*!" Herron repeated more loudly, "*If* there is half a cigarette in the clothes you wore Saturday night, or in your hat, or in your reticule, it would not be *yours*. And its paper might very well match this half?"

Angelica did not raise her head, but she cut her eyes up at him from beneath her dark-blonde eyebrows. She was trying to decide if he had a point, despite was madness in his method; or whether she was just being led further into his sick practical joke. She was tempted to turn on her heel and go in either case.

"Please, Miss Trickett, I beg you—look at the letters written out on this paper. My life hangs on the other half of this riddle being on your person. It might be in your clothes. Your hat. Your reticule— "

"Mister Strangways!" Angelica cried, "Please! The clothes I wore that night have been cleaned. If anything was in them, it is gone forever. There was nothing in my hat. If you will wait here, I—" she cut her eyes to the settee "—I will bring down my reticule." She dropped a curtsy. "Your Ladyship permitting?"

Lady Calthrop advised, "Ring for Doris to fetch it for you."

"If you will permit me, Lady Calthrop, I would rather go myself."

Herron had the impression that Angelica wanted to go herself so she would waste as little time as possible in the company of a loathsome man.

Lady Calthrop dismissed Angelica with a flick of her fingers.

Angelica curtsied again and glared squarely into Herron's eyes. "If there is not the smallest portion of a cigarette in my reticule, Mister Strangways, will you promise me you will go away and never have the temerity to call on me again?"

Herron traced an X over his chest with a finger. "Upon my honor." Lady Calthrop gave a horsey snort, to indicate what she thought of Herron Strangways' honor.

2

With Angelica's departure, a chill quiet settled over the drawing-room.

The only sound was the ticking of a clock in the next room. Herron had not heard the clock before. Its noise underscored, rather than broke, the stiff silence.

Herron could sense Dapifer's presence behind him. The butler was ready, on Her Ladyship's signal, to snag Herron by the collar and the seat of the trousers and propel him out the door at a brisk walk.

While Lady Calthrop, Herron and Dapifer remained rooted to their spots, the maid Doris appeared (on standing instructions) to set up tea in the drawing room.

Herron rarely took tea; but, feeling quite dried out, he thought he could drink the entire pot. He doubted, however, he would be asked to partake.

By force of habit, he noticed that Doris was a cute, petite blonde who struggled with the silver service. At any other time, he'd have leapt to help her, perhaps giving her a wink or a suggestive smile – or, depending on how she smiled back, even slipping her a note with his address written on it.

Doris shifted a low table before the sofa and laid it with teaware and an assortment of goodies on three-tiered serving trays: finger sandwiches (probably fish paste or cucumber or both), bread and butter, dainty cakes, pastries—

Herron heard his empty stomach grumbling. His breakfast was all used up. He wished he'd partaken of lunch; especially since he had been buying.

When the table was laid, the maid was dismissed with the slightest of nods.

The tea (and sugar, and cream) sat on the little table before the little wizened Lady. She poured none for herself. She deliberately offered nothing to Herron.

As they waited, the ticking of the clock grew louder, like a ceaseless drip heard on a sleepless night.

Lady Calthrop stared at him, unmoving, unblinking, unspeaking. It was almost like a show-down in a dime novel of the American west. Herron would draw half-a-cigarette at Lady Calthrop from Miss Trickett's reticule – or Her Ladyship would draw her lorgnette, and Dapifer would hurl his body out into the gutter.

At long last, Herron heard young feet pounding downstairs. Angelica, flushed, swept into the room dangling her silk, beaded reticule at the end of her fingers like she was holding a dead rat by the tail.

"I will examine this in your presence, Mister Strangways."

Her Ladyship thought it all sounded like so much nonsense and said Angelica should not waste her valuable time.

Setting the reticule on a side-table, beneath a framed painting of a country estate, Angelica proceeded to remove more items from her bag than Herron believed it could possibly accommodate. As she extracted one item after another, pyramiding them onto the table with precision, she called each by name.

"Handkerchief, cambric, initialed. Comb, one, tortoiseshell. Hair brush, one, ditto. Mirror. Small bottle of gardenia scented scent. Nail scissors, one pair. Thimble. Penknife. One button-hook. A box of Her Ladyship's visiting cards. Pencil. Small writing tablet. Pin cushion, one, with needles . . ."

Herron remembered a line from that play he'd seen once by accident, *Who steals my purse steals trash*—

". . . hair pins . . ."

A cold shiver tickled Herron's spine. They reminded him of female assassins.

When the side table was completely covered with what Angelica might have called "articles, various," she leaned forward with her hands flat on the tabletop, staring down at the varnish – and squaring her fine shoulders against him.

"That is all. No cigarette, Mister Strangways. Thank you again for coming."

Herron was unable to raise his eyes even to ogle her superb dorsal regions. He had lost her forever. Even his imminent death (and his odds of his living until nightfall were not worth quoting) no longer concerned him.

Still, he had to broach the matter of the police. "Before I go—?"

"No," replied Lady Calthrop. "We have been more than generous. Goodby, Mister Strangways. Perhaps you do not understand the meaning of the word?"

Herron heard the butler's cat-like steps from behind. His back tensed, anticipating Dapifer's enormous hand gripping his collar – probably twisting it, to half-throttle him before pitching him headlong to the pavement.

While her bag was empty, Angelica decided to clean the lint and detritus that had collected in its corners. She wiped around the inside of her bag with her handkerchief. Drawing it out, she was puzzled at a dark, flaky matter dotting the cambric. There did seem to be an awful lot of it. She sniffed it.

She didn't like the smell. Turning the reticule upside-down, she shook it once.

And, for good measure, once more.

Half a cigarette, twisted at one ends and leaking horribly, dropped silently to the Persian carpet. It bounced once, then landed on the bias between them.

Angelica gaped at it.

Dapifer, who had just gripped Herron's collar, paused and turned questioning eyes up to his employer.

Her Ladyship produced her lorgnette and scrutinized the cigarette. Then, in her most casual tone, she asked, "How do you take your tea, Mister Strangways?"

CHAPTER XXIII

Angelica's enormous mound of effects had been swept back into her reticule, which hung by its drawstrings over the back of her straight chair. She kept her pencil and her small writing tablet out, to making notes. The two halves of the cigarette paper (the right-hand half belonging to Herron) lay in the center of the glass-topped tea table, surrounded by a clutter of cups and plates – all empty, for Herron had recovered his appetite with a vengeance.

Lady Calthrop remained cool, making stray comments throughout the meal that Herron had probably sneaked the cigarette into Angelica's reticule himself to contrive an introduction to a naïve young lady; but, despite her censure, her manner displayed a piqued curiosity.

And, once Herron had a firm tea invitation, Lady Calthrop proved a perfect hostess – apart from one peccadillo.

Had the table been a clock face with Lady Calthrop twelve o'clock, Angelica would have been four and Herron, eight. But whenever Lady Calthrop passed anything to either Herron or Angelica, she passed it over their finger-bowls.

And once she said, as if raising a toast, "To the wee gentleman in velveteen."

Herron knew she wasn't referring him. His coat was red velvet, but a gentleman nosing over the two-yard mark in his stocking feet was hardly "wee."

Her peculiarities did not perturb Herron unduly. He had attended enough teas to know elderly ladies had their fancies, but they rarely became violent.

They made innocuous small talk during tea. Mostly, this was a running dialogue between Her Ladyship and Angelica. Herron didn't know what they were talking about or whom, and felt one had to be there to get the gags.

Angelica poured and the cut the cakes. Occasionally, she scurried to the kitchen to fetch something Doris had forgotten.

Whenever Angelica left the room, a stark silence fell between Herron and Her Ladyship, as if they were separated by a thick sheet of glass.

After tea, Lady Calthrop sat quietly on the settee while the two young persons, leaning forward with their foreheads close, pored over the cigarette paper.

The two halves did not fit perfectly, since the paper was singed at the join. Knowing just how long a cigarette should be, Herron spaced them properly apart.

Angelica gnawed her malleable lower lip. "It's not jolly much to go on."

"Angelica!" The chatelaine rang her teaspoon against a china cup. "Slang."

Angelica's assessment, however, seemed accurate. Herron's half read:

hip
chine
GAM
rt yjr esyrt
ii

and a square dancing on one angle.

Angelica's half contained the words (roughly on line with Herron's):

Ai
Inferna
RE
lomh p

The most troubling line to Herron was the second.

inferna chine

Lady Calthrop suggested 'chine' might be Oriental.

Herron and Angelica both recognized the words as English.

She had grown up as an avid readers of sensational fiction (along with the Bible and classics). Herron barely read anything beyond his newspapers; but newspapers often used terminology similar to "shilling shocker" novels.

Between them, they reckoned these words meant "infernal machine."

"And what, Angelica," wondered Lady Calthrop, "is an *infernal machine?*"

"A bomb," Herron answered.

"Rather," Angelica clarified, with greater precision, "an explosive device."

"A bomb is an explosive device," countered Herron.

"All bombs are explosive devices, but not all explosive devices are bombs."

"Never mind the syllogisms. Let's just say we've cracked that nut."

Angelica conceded the point and they travelled on. The third line read,

RE GAM

Angelica ran a hand through her hair. "What can that mean, do you suppose?"

"*Re gam?*" Herron smiled. "Oh, they want us to *gam* again."

Angelica suggested that if this message was in earnest, they ought not make jokes. "It must be important. It's in all capitals."

"Unless it's one of those things, you know, that use initial letters."

"Acronym?"

"If you say so."

Angelica noted this possibility on her tablet "Are *re* and *gam* one word?"

"Not an English word." Herron spoke as if he'd memorized the dictionary.

"Three letters and a space are missing between *inferna* and *chine*. Is there such a word in any language you know spelt *Re*-three letters-*gam?*"

"Could one letter be a blank between two words?"

"Neither *re* nor *gam* stand alone very well." Angelica started through the alphabet, trying possible letters. "Rea. Reb. Rec. Red. Red? Red's a word."

Herron was dubious. "*Red*-blankety-blank-*gam?*"

"No, that's not helpful. There must be a vowel before gam, surely?"

"Keep going on 're.'"

"Ref? Reg?" She rattled on to "r" and found nothing. When she tried "s" she started to move on; but Herron shouted,

"*Res!*"

"What's that?"

"Latin. A thing, don't you know."

Angelica cocked a wry half-smile. "'Thing' is not particularly helpful, either. Just now, London is full of things."

"All wearing hats. It's also used to strengthen a what-is-it. A—a superlative."

"You don't strengthen superlatives. A thing is, unique, say, or empty – which I thought your head was when you first burst in here – or it's not."

"I mean, you might say, 'the most beautiful *thing*...'" Herron stared at the top of her head while she bent over the papers.

When he was silent for more than five seconds together, she glanced up – and smiled as she caught his meaning. "Get back to business."

"There are all sorts of common terms using *res. Res gestae*... uh, 'things done'... oh, ah... *res non verba*, 'things, not words'... *res ipsa loquitur*, 'a thing speaks for itself'—which I wish this paper was doing!"

Herron's fount of Latin, derived more from his court cases than his expensive classical education, was quickly evaporating.

Angelica was unconsciously running her hand through her coiffure, incrementally unpinning her long hair. Wobbling stray locks were curling down her forehead and cheeks. "Maybe we should focus on words ending in *gam*."

But words were harder to conceive in regard to their wagging tails; and 'gam' did not strike either of them, right off the bat, as a popular word ending.

After running through the vowels (*agam, egam, igam, ogam, ugam*) Angelica took Herron's half of the paper to the window and held it against one of the panes.

"I wish I had a magnifying glass in my reticule."

"That's about all you didn't have... What do you see?"

"A little dot here, on this space you burned."

Herron, who had risen with her, joined her by the window. "A full stop?"

She jabbed a fingernail beneath the dot. It was on line with the top of the *g* in *gam*. Only Angelica's keen young eyes could have spotted it.

"By George, you have good eyesight." He gazed down at her. "And dashed lovely eyes, don't you know."

"Thank you."

They stared into each other's eyes silently for a few moments; then Angelica dragged them back to the matter at hand as they returned to their seats. "It must be all that remains of a letter before *gam*. What sort of letters (presumably lowercase) might leave a hanging hook? The only vowel might be 'u.'"

"A '*k*' might."

"A '*k*' might also have a mark below it for the down-stroke. A '*c*' would have a dot right beneath this one." She put her eyes practically on the paper.

"The crossbar of a *t*?"

"Maybe a lowercase '*r*.'"

"*rgam*?" Herron was dubious. "I think *erga* is a Latin word. And *ergo*. Given the size of the burn (if that is an '*r*') *Res* and *rgam* must be one word with a vowel in between. *Res-argam? -ergam? Res-orgum?*"

178

She giggled. "That sounds like what Americans pour over wheatcakes."

"My Latin vocabulary is not what is used to be—never was, really. Lady Calthrop, do you have a Latin dictionary?"

Her Ladyship rang her crystal bell and Dapifer entered – too quickly for Herron's liking. He was waiting just out of sight – a lurking, unseen threat.

She asked him to fetch a Latin dictionary from the library.

Returning with a fat book called *A New Latin Dictionary* published in 1884 by Harper Brothers, the butler plopped it on the table (rattling the china and blowing the cigarette papers off so Herron and Angelica bumped their heads retrieving them from the floor).

Rubbing his noggin, Herron flipped to *Res* – and found four densely-written columns of fine print. He skimmed down, reading, " . . . thing, object, being; a matter, affair, event, fact . . . Heavens! Too much information."

"That's better than when we had too little."

Before venturing into that wilderness of words, Herron thumbed through the huge tome for a –gam word that stood alone, without needing a *Res*.

No *argam, ergam, irgam* or *orgam*.

His eye flickered down at *orgam* and he idly read aloud, "*organum* . . . *orgessum* . . . *Orgetorix* . . . *orgia*—" Grinning, he looked dangerously close to reading "nocturnal festival in honor of bacchus—"

Angelica cut him short with reprimanding eyes.

Clearing his throat, Herron passed swiftly on.

This was manifestly getting them nowhere. He skimmed to "u" to to look up "*Urgam*" while muttering, "*Res—urgam—*"

And he stopped as if thunderstruck.

Angelica glanced up again to ask why Mister Blabbermouth was suddenly quiet – and was distressed by his eyes. He was staring straight at her, but through her, as if trying to focus on an object on the wall behind her head.

"What's wrong?"

"I'm thinking."

"That must take a lot out of you," purred Lady Calthrop.

"Let me check . . ." he flipped to *R* and, after fumbling through the columns, shouted "*Resurgo!*" like a cry of jubilation.

He extended the book to Angelica, marking the place with a perfectly-manicured fingernail.

"Look here – '*re-surgo, -surrexi, -surrectum* . . . to rise or raise one's self again . . .'" His hands trembled. "Jove! '. . . of convalescent persons: resurgam . . . to rise again, to rise from the grave . . .'"

He slammed the huge book triumphantly shut.

Her cool eyes glowered over crossed arms. "Where does that leave us?"

Herron's smile faded. Frankly, he didn't know.

CHAPTER XXIV

"*Res(ur)gam*," Angelica repeated, imitating his pronunciation as she dutifully copied the word down in her tablet in all capitals. "That is, at least, a word in a dictionary. But whatever can it mean?"

Herron shrugged. "Rising again from the grave? Vampires?"

"Perhaps it's some sort of religious tract about the Ressurection."

"Really, Angelica," smirked Lady Calthrop. "In a cigarette?"

"It makes me think of *Destroy this Temple and I will rebuild it in three days*." Herron stroked his chin. The words had a familiar ring. "What's that from?"

"A little thing called the Bible. You may have heard of it. And we haven't touched the top line. Yours reads *hip* and mine says *Ai*."

Angelica pointed out the top line:

Ai hip

"Ai is a Biblical town," she informed him.

"I fear you are altogether on the wrong track, Miss Trickett."

Surprisingly, Lady Calthrop said, "If this is as serious as this young man pretends, any avenue is worth investigating. What happened at Ai, Angelica?"

"It was a town where the Canaanites were licked by the children of Israel, after their initial success at Jericho. In their first attack, the Israelites were forced back from Ai – a scholar in these matters once told me *Ha-Ai* means *the ruin.*"

"That is a peculiar name for a city, Angelica."

"The site may have been a ruinous outpost manned by a garrison that was defending that approach to the all-important Amorite city of Gibeon. Perhaps that's why Joshua was overconfident going in, because it was a ruin, and he expected little more than token resistance, if any. The men at Ai, under a leader who might have been a warrior sub-king from the city of Gibeon, ambushed the Israelites and beat them back. After the defeat, Joshua despaired."

She closed her eyes, reciting,

"And Joshua rent his clothes, and fell to the earth upon his face before the ark of the Lord until the eventide, he and the elders of Israel, and put dust upon their heads. And Joshua said, Alas, O Lord God, wherefore hast thou at all brought this people over Jordan, to deliver us into the hand of the Amorites, to destroy us? would to God we had been content, and dwelt on the other side Jordan! O Lord, what shall I say, when Israel turneth their backs before their enemies! . . . And the Lord said, Fear not, neither be thou dismayed: take all the people of war with thee, and arise, go up to Ai: see, I have given into thy hand the king of Ai."

She blinked her eyes open and finished the story in her own words.

"Joshua struck Ai again, but this time he ambushed them. He attacked with a small force, then made a tactical retreat. The defenders at Ai overconfidently chased the Israelites. The 'fleeing' Israelites doubled back on them so the men from Ai were caught between an Israeli force in front and behind. After that, Joshua may have razed the rest of the ruin of Ai, laying Gibeon open to attack. The king of Gibeon tricked Joshua and the Israelites into a wary peace treaty—"

"Thank you, my dear," said Lady Calthrop, with a faint hand-clap. "I think you have it. Two of your words are traceable to your Bible. *Ai*, the ruin, and that word meaning rising again."

"Or destroying a Temple," said Herron, forgetting that had been Angelica's addition and not actually part of the message. "Whatever Temple it means." "I have no reason to doubt Angelica's knowledge on such matters – but we have no way to verify it either, since I am not religious and do not keep a Bible in the house. I do not hold with religions. They cause trouble. They throw monarchs off their rightful thrones, just like Joshua did. If I were a monarch I would end all religious strife by abolishing all religions. Rousseau wrote *'jamais Etat ne fut fonde que la religion ne lui servit de base.'* I would prove him wrong."

Angelica translated aloud to herself in imprecise French. "'A state was never melted—' sorry, melt is *fondre*, isn't it? '—founded that does not use religion as his basis.' My brother Schuyler might know if that is true or not."

"I'd like to prove it wrong," Her Ladyship dryly repeated.

"What about the French Revolution?" asked Herron, who had once read a sensational novel set during that period. "Weren't they a bunch of atheists?"

Lady Calthrop narrowed her eyes and looked like a snake about to strike. "Even they were forced to contrive a so-called 'Republic of Virtue' in an effort to replace the insidious influence of Christianity to earn the hearts of the populace."

Angelica fought a smile trying to break out in the corners of her mouth. "Didn't the 'Republic of Virtue' lop off all those heads at the drop of a hat? A-theism may not be a religion—"

"As you say, it is not a religion. It has no dogma, no doctrine—"

"Except the one absolutist doctrine that there is no god."

"If there *is* a conspiracy behind this secret message," Lady Calthrop hissed, "and I am not persuaded there is, a religion lies behind it, mark my words, like a serpent behind a rock. They're all alike—ordering their initiates to kill.""Christianity doesn't," Angelica said gently. "The Christian Scriptures, from Matthew to Revelation, teach altogether the opposite."

"Nonetheless," said Lady Calthrop, with a voice as cold and sharp as an icicle, "they have done. What could you know about it, anyway?"

If Lady Calthrop's voice was cold, Angelica's, which until now had been indulgently jocular, stiffened like a good meringue.

"Please, don't confuse 'Christianity' and 'the Church.' *Christianity* is the belief that the Jewish Messiah came as in an Incarnation as one of the Persons of the Trinity, and that He died as atonement for our sins and rose from the dead. *The Church* is a way gentile worship of the Jewish Messiah may be adjusted according to personal preference. The Church cannot save us or improve us, only the One the Church worships. Gentiles had to develop an alternative form of worship; we were brought into the faith under a new Covenant—"

"I do not want to listen to a lot of nonsense. Is the Church innocent or guilty?"

"Yes, in part or in whole, the 'Church' can plead 'guilty' – whenever it followed, or was closely allied to, the secular culture of the time. Every time the Church mirrors the surrounding culture it becomes despotic. When it stands aloof, seemingly alone in the world in the pursuit of otherworldly ideals, it doesn't."

"That is also when it ceases to be relevant, child."

"And I *do* know. My brother Schuyler read history at Oxford. I've done scads of reading on my own, and we discuss history at length on our picnics. He explained how murderous lapses in the Church, like the Spanish Inquisition, were always political, rather than religious, decisions. He says it's invariably politics that kills. Politics is all about control, and anyone who goes into politics, whether they are cloaked in ancient religious robes or in modern dress or scientific smocks, just want to control other people. I tend to agree with him."

"Do . . . you . . . child?"

"On a purely intellectual level."

"Oh. An *intellectual* level?'" Her tone carried no offense, except the all-but-imperceptible implication that the 'intellectual' was not a level to which Angelica should aspire.

"People with similar natures do tend to enter the same sorts of businesses. In this case, it wasn't the beauty of orthodoxy or the mystery of the Incarnation that attracted those sorts people to the Church, but the power. Now they get themselves elected to secular public office, because that's where the power lies."

"But religions are all so exploitative."

"Let's play 'pretend,' Lady Calthrop. Remember when Krakatoa belched all that detritis into the air back in '83 and the weather got colder? We know, therefore, that contaminating the air causes worldwide cooling – and far more vivid and beautiful sunsets, so it has a lovely side, too. Let's pretend a charlatan, with the heart of a medicine show snake-oil salesman, seized upon a cooling trend and went around the country in his wagon taking up collections to halt a 'new Ice Age' which would kill us all like it did the wooly Mammoths."

"I would say," said Herron, "that's between him and the gullible sapheads who try to buy improved weather. A fool and his money, don't you know."

"That should be your area of expertise," agreed Lady Calthrop.

Angelica said, "That's a good word, 'saphead.'"

"I picked it up on a recent tour of New England. Go on, do, Miss Trickett."

"Then, let's pretend the charlatan builds on a scientific hypothesis that the cooling will continue – and he uses that hypothesis to *politicize* the weather. He manages to get himself elected to office on a platform of halting a new Ice Age. He actually tries to pass laws on the pretense that *mankind can can control the weather by an act of Parliament*."

"My God!" said Herron, shocked. "He's struck the mother lode!"

"Yes, but he got his money before he went into office. What this charlatan wants is control over humanity, cramming the new morality of his new, scientific, Revelation down everyone else's throats. He has done exactly what churchmen are criticized for; only, instead of exploiting faith, he's flim-flamming the people by exploiting science. Let me give you another example."

"Oh. Must you?"

"After Christ finished a forty-day fast in the desert, Satan came to Him with a very simple and sensible suggestion. The fast was over, so Satan said, 'Change these stones into bread.' But Satan wasn't worried about Christ's physical welfare. He wanted *control*. He wanted Christ to perform tricks – and even do something so simple as eat – on his say-so. That's politics. Satan is a politician, and control over others is always Satanic. The British Association and the C of E need never fear each other, as they promote separate but equal disciplines. They *should* both fear unscrupulous people in governments who try to arrogate, exploit, politicize or suppress them – for control over science or religion."

"That hypothetical case," said Her Ladyship, frigidly, "was a silly one. No one would be so foolish to think the weather can be controlled by force of law."

"Never underestimate the length to which people will allow the wool to be pulled over their eyes," Herron advised. "We're selling junk from my stores we couldn't give away before just by hand-painting 'Jubilee' on it."

"As Mister Strangways says," Angelica said, "so long as this weather quack is padding his pockets with gullible money, it's his business. When he starts making laws affecting all our lives, he's—to my eyes, there is no difference between a medieval Inquisitor, and a charlatan who claims to stands between us and death by Ice Age. It's the same sort of people wanting control over his fellow men. Unfortunately, telegraphs or railroads have made the modern state far more dangerous than the 'Church' ever was – if there ever was an 'a Church.'"

"But doesn't it say in your Scripture," asked Lady Calthrop, with a sweetness in her voice that grated on Angelica – because she knew the vindiciveness that lay beneath it, "the world will be destroyed by heating, rather than ice ages?"

"*The heavens shall pass away with a great noise, and the elements shall melt with fervent heat, the earth also and the works that are therein shall be burned.*"

"Nonsense. Turn to science. Science is progress. Religion is an obstruction to progress. Religion cause strife. The only way of solving that strife is to found a new kind of state where religious worshippers are forbidden."

Herron didn't have a dog in this fight, but he had to throw in a little devilment. "If the winter wind blows too icily under the door, rip it off its hinges altogether."

"And there are so many religions," Lady Calthrop went on, ignoring him, "and gradations of religions in your own faith. Why can't they simply coexist?"

Angelica almost pointed out that Lady Calthrop's first complaint was that all religions were alike. Now she was saying they were all different.

Her Ladyship usually encouraged Angelica to speak her mind, though this was the first time she was so outspoken. Angelica had been given a fair length of latitude already today, and she did not know how much latitude remained before she sailed off the map – and into unemployment.

While Angelica vacillated over highlighting Her Ladyship's inconsistencies, Herron, noticing her struggling silence, chimed in with another point.

"It's because," answered Herron, whose knowledge of historical geopolitics was virtually nil, "they all think they're right. When different factions, all of whom think they are right, rub shoulders against each other, there's bound to be friction. Sparks fly. Human nature. Happens all the time at the Club. Not over religion. Don't think one of 'em's stepped over the threshold of a place of worship since they were in knee pants." (Lady Calthrop noted Herron still was in knee pants, and Angelica disguised a smile with a cough.) "I mean, it's that way with everyone who thinks they're right, in any sphere. Particularly politics. If dueling were legal these days, half the members of my Club would be shot dead one misty morning, over trifles."

Angelica was quick to follow Herron's lead. "Strife is not limited to religions. Different political parties squabble all the time because they all think they're right. And economists. Capitalists and the communists don't try to coexist. They go after each other tooth and claw. A-theism is an absolutism that thinks it is right. Should it be abolished? Is every sort of free thinking that leads to disagreement to be wiped off the slate for a cookie-cutter society? What are we all to think, if we cause strife by thinking anything that conflicts with another?"

She wished she had the temerity to itemize cases she had witnessed where Lady Calthrop herself had severed diplomatic relations with acquaintances and neighbors over trifles, where they both thought they were right and neither would concede. Angelica hesitated to rip the veil away from Her Ladyship's hypocrisy, condemning others for doing what she did to her kin and kith on a daily basis.

Sensing Angelica's turmoil, Herron stuck up for her again.

"Show me a 'Reformer' and I'll show you a chap who likes to smash things up just because he won't understand 'em. They think they're doing *the right thing, ergo* the other side must want to do 'the wrong thing.' They line all the angels up on one side and all the devils on the other, whether they believe in angels or not, and they never compromise. Whenever I hear a chap say he's doing *the right thing* (by whatever private yardstick), shivers tingle up my spine. Incalculable evil had been done in the world by people doing what they called *the right thing*."

This bemused Angelica. Herron had proved a helpful ally, but she couldn't listen to him talk utter rubbish. "What should people do, if not the right thing?"

"Everyone has a different notion of *the right thing*. People should do whatever makes them happy. But the people I've known who do *the right thing* aren't happy. Yes, they're grumpy sulks trying to make a world they can be happy in. What they want for their personal happiness is for everyone else to conform to the shape of their bottles. And they hate worse than H—er, they really hate anyone who disagrees with their own private brand of *the right thing*." He turned to Her Ladyship. "I mean, don't you think you're right?"

Her Ladyship had spoken to Herron – and acknowledged him – as little as possible. In this instance, answering him directly was unavoidable.

"No."

Herron raised intrigued eyebrows.

"I am right. But you have described exactly what religious people do, Mister Strangways. The religious fools who are antagonistic to medical advancements like vivisection, and who are trying to pass laws forbidding it, are an example."

"I'm against vivisection," murmured Angelica. "I hope their laws pass."

"I, also," Herron quickly added, though he hadn't an inkling of what the word meant. He'd seen it in the newspapers; but, as was too often the case, the press took informed readers for granted, rather than bothering to inform them.

"My dear," said Lady Calthrop, "without research on living animals, medical science would be a blind and groping guesswork. Vivisectionism has done so much to expand the fight against infectious diseases! Opposition to vivisection is a sort of disease itself – a disease of the brain, since its opponents are immune to facts or arguments. Enacting their narrow morality into law, they shut down science to the detriment of public health. That is what happens when religious people make laws based on belief rather than science. People suffer."

"Like the abolitionists?" Angelica challenged.

"An excellent example, my dear: the American abolitionists. The religious Crusade of the abolitionists forced their nation into a horrible war. And their Crusade against vivisectionism proves they are simply opposed to science."

"You might as well say," said Herron, who didn't know much about history but who retained a schoolboy relish for particularly bloodthirsty historical anecdotes, "Burke and Hare died as the atonement for the sins of science."

Angelica, momentarily dazed at finding opposition to fighting a war to end slavery, spoke up quickly to keep from associating herself with Herron's assistance. "I see no opposition between religion and science, Lady Calthrop, because they study different things. Science is in constant flux. Building a completely coherent picture of reality in science is like building on shifting sands. I prefer to build on a something eternal. I may be wrong—"

"If you are, join the club," said Herron. "We're all a little wrong."

"Religion, if you must use the word – I don't like it myself – seeks to understand unchanging truths about human nature in the universe and beyond—"

"What is beyond the universe?" Her Ladyship demanded.

"God knows. Science seeks observable facts to build a coherent knowledge of—well, not so much of Man as—as—as—"

Angelica was sinking. Not because she didn't know her arguments, but because she lacked acceptable terminology to adequately express them. As she struggled to find a suitable alternative for the politically inappropriate word "body" Lady Calthrop leaned in like a cobra about to claim its victim.

Herron tossed Angelica a word like a life-line. "*Corpus?*"

She nodded. She had read enough thrillers to know *corpus*. That helped her bob back up into the conversation.

"Thank you, Mister Strangways. Science studies the human *corpus* and its place within the limitations of the knowable cosmos."

"At best," countered Lady Calthrop, with finality, "religion is a kind of opiate. Life is bitter and unhappy for most people, so they hope there there is a god – out there someplace – to whom their dirty, cringing, unhappy suffering lives matter. If men need solace, let them have free access to genuine opium, to dream their lives away, rather than dreaming their lives away waiting for an afterlife that will never come, and paying priests for the privilege."

Still sticking up for Angelica, Herron played dumb – a role he limned remarkably well. "I read a lot in the papers about all these scientific inventor jonnies. Lady Calthrop, you don't like religions because they are all so different and don't get along – or because they're all alike, I can't remember which. But isn't it true all scientists don't agree on every single theory, either?"

"They agree," Lady Calthrop said, moving her lips but keeping her teeth clenched, "on fundamental facts."

Angelica began pushing her luck. "But facts are not truth."

Firing a salvo at Angelica through her lorgnette, Her Ladyship requested that she elucidate upon that remark.

"'Truth' is unchanging. If a thing is true, it's true for every time, every where. 'Facts' change. What's believed as a 'fact' today may not be considered 'fact' tomorrow. Science must be based on currently existing data, which may change as new 'facts' are discovered. After all, it was scientific not so jolly long ago to believe Troy was a myth, but that German fellow with the unpronounceable name dug it out. Every new generation of scientists discovers new facts that alter the way previously-known 'facts' are interpreted."

"One does not interpret fact. Facts are."

"I respectfully submit, Lady Calthrop, that 'facts' of any kind must always be interpreted *within their context*. And they must all be studied in their a wider historical context. Look at the earth-centered model of the universe—"

"Must we!" sighed Herron, thinking the conversation was drifting too far afield from the cryptic cigarette. Why, they might have been playing a leisurely backgammon match, rather than trying to unravel a message from a secret agent who had been murdered for the papers lying between them.

"My brother Schuyler," said Angelica, after flashing a patronizing smile on Herron to shut him up, "says we can't discern the Earth is moving, from the Earth. We must gauge the earth's movement relative to the stars. That's what they were unable to do in Greek times or the Middle Ages. Before Copernicus' time, scientists lacked the necessary optical equipment to observe the sky. They had no telescopes or microscopes or barometers. Their scientific knowledge came from 'facts' at hand, based upon empirical observation and reason. One of those scientific facts declared that the earth does not move."

Her Ladyship upped her ante. "In case you have not heard, my child, it never was a fact that the earth doesn't move. The earth does move."

"The world's greatest thinkers at the time thought it a fact, that it did not."

"They also thought the earth was flat."

"No, they didn't. They couldn't have. These days, one joins the scientific fraternity by acquiring mystical parchments declaring their higher degrees; back then, in precisely the same way, scientists joined the Church. So they must have known Scripture. Doesn't the prophet Isaiah say, *To whom, then will ye liken God? . . . It is he that sitteth upon the circle of the earth . . .?*"

"I do not know, child," Lady Calthrop replied, dryly. "I don't read fairy tales."

Herron demanded, "Do you have that whole blasted book memorized?"

"Not all of it, Mister Strangways, though I'm trying. That last bit comes in the same chapter where the nataions are called *a drop of a bucket*, so it's easy to keep in mind. But please, allow me answer Lady Calthrop." Angelica turned to her employer. "No one ever seriously thought the earth was flat."

"Then why," wondered Herron, "did seamen in the old days hug the shore?"

"They didn't. 'Hugging the shore' would be a good way to hit a reef or run aground. They had no means of measuring longitude. You can't derive longitude from the stars. Navigating without longitude is jolly dangerous. You can go half-way round the world on a given latitude before you bash into the place you're looking for. And you're more likely to bash into someplace else; or all starve, if your food runs out while you're going back and forth on the right latitude trying to find where you're looking for. And the old ships were dodgy. But that didn't worry the Vikings. They settled as far as Greenland, until the climate changed and the weather changed so cold they had to abandon their settlement."

"They should have had a word with your chap who can stop global cooling."

"Yes. The climate changes throughout history, usually for the cooler, but you'd have to be a silly to think a man can cause it or stop it. Anyway, the Vikings might even have got to America. So, there. They didn't believe the earth was flat. Medievals did, however, believe it was the center of the universe."

"Another 'fact,' I suppose," Her Ladyship drawled. "When all respectable, modern intellectuals know the *sun* is the center of the universe."

"The earth-centered universe was a scientific fact back then. My brother Schuyler explained it to me. The medieval scientists inherited from the Greeks a cosmos consisting of concentric spheres. The infinite outside was the abode of God. Counting down from God, the spheres grew smaller and smaller. The smallest sphere, in the center, was the earth. It was considered the *least* important place in the cosmos because it was the *farthest place from God*. Copernicus was appointed *by the church* to examine the stars methodically and report on why church astronomers noted anomalies in the sky that did not fit scientific fact. The only way Copernicus could account for those anomalies was to hypothesize a sun- rather than an earth-centered universe. The Earth was *elevated* by Copernicus to being as important as any other place in the universe. That's how science works: new facts alter the interpretation of old facts."

"It never was a *fact* that the earth was the center of the universe. It's untrue."

"The fact that it's untrue is important, isn't it? I would think what goes wrong in any experiment is as important as what goes right. The Earth probably is not the center of the universe (I've never seen an complete map of the universe, so I won't hazard a guess either way in ignorance). Some 'facts' we believe today will be deemed untrue in a hundred years. It happens all the time in science."

"It happens all the time in *life*," murmured Herron. "I remember once—"

Lady Calthrop was firm. "Facts are facts. Truth is subjective."

"*Quid est veritas?*" Herron drawled.

"What's that mean?" asked Angelica, who didn't want anything said in the conversation she didn't comprehend.

"Latin." Herron obligingly translated. "'What is truth?'"

Angelica made a sour-milk face. "That's the question of Pilate."

Lady Calthrop did not recognize the name. "Who?"

"The Roman governor of the province of Judea. He said that just before sending Christ to crucifixion. *Jesus answered, My kingdom is not of this world: if my kingdom were of this world, then would my servants fight . . . Pilate therefore said unto him, Art thou a king, then? Jesus answered, Thou sayest that I am a king. To this end was I born, and for this cause came I into the world, that I should bear witness unto the truth. Every one that is of the truth hereth my voice. Pilate saith unto him, What is truth?* He was a Roman so he'd have used Latin."

"You do have the whole book memorized," Herron muttered.

"Pilate is correct," said Her Ladyship. "Truth varies from person to person."

"I hesitate to disagree with you, Lady Calthrop, but—if you will permit me?"

"Please do."

"Liberty Hall," chimed in Herron, forgetting this wasn't his house.

"Remember the story of the blind men and the elephant?"

Herron and Lady Calthrop both shook their heads.

"Five wise men who had the misfortune to be blind were trying to gain a comprehensive picture of an elephant by groping its various parts—"

Herron clucked his tongue. "Sounds most unlikely. Were they all blinded in one accident, or were sightless wise-men rounded up specially? They can't have put an ad in the paper because none of them would have seen it—"

"Valuable though they are, Mister Strangways," said Angelica, in a voice she might have used in talking to a child or a puppy, "please reserve your comments until I finish the story, or I might lose my thread."

"Silent as a tomb!" he promised, ostentatiously crossing his heart.

"Each men groped only one part of the elephant. One grabbed the tail and said it was like a rope. Another felt the trunk and said it was like a snake. Another fingered the ear and said it was like a fan. Another wrapped his arms around the elephant's leg and said it was like a tree trunk. One, rubbing his palms over the body, said it was like a wall. *Facts* garnered from empirical observation led them to erroneous conclusions. Yet, however much they disagreed on the facts they gathered, the elephant itself was ultimately undeniable."

"Do you have a point, my dear?"

"The elephant is a metaphor for *Truth*. We may argue about our composite picture of Truth based on the facts as we observe or understand them. To deny that there is a Truth, even if we don't like it when we finally perceive it in whole or in part, is denying the elephant."

CHAPTER XXV

Her Ladyship's wattle vibrated furiously beneath her chin. "That's absurd."

"Let me try to explain it in a more personal way, if I may?"

Lady Calthrop's eyes were slits as she suggested Angelica had been quite personal enough. But she allowed her to continue.

"At school, I had a friend who was trying atheism on for size. We had many arguments. And we had actual arguments, rather than muck-raking shouting-matches. A few were heated, but it was mostly a fair give-and-take. We never pulled hair or had duels with scissors. Neither of us persuaded the other."

"Then you wasted your breath arguing with her, and she with you."

"*All things work together for good to them that love God, to them who are the called according to his purpose.* Our arguments helped me hone exactly what I do understand as Truth. She believed in an eternal, empty blackness governed by implacable physical laws. I believe in a beneficent Creator who passed and codified those laws in an ongoing Creation."

"On-going?" This bewildered Her Ladyship. "Didn't it take six days to make everything in the cosmos according to your Bible?"

"My King James Version – for, under the Stuart kings, even the Bible needed a governmental imprimatur for publication – says no such thing."

"What does it say, then?" wondered Herron.

"*In the beginning God created the heaven and the earth.* Very straightforward. There is no indication of how long it took. It doesn't even say 'the beginning' of what – though my Hebraic scholar friend said this verse might better be translated, '*When God began creating the earth . . .*' I like that. The King James version sounds like God started Creation in a rush, like a man running to catch a 'bus.

"The King James Verson encapsulates the Creation of all the Cosmos in ten words. It gives no sense of how the cosmos came into being, nor what it was made from, nor how long it took. Nor could it! Our sense of 'time' derives its year by the period it takes a rock to whirl around a great ball of fire; and we count our days from the speed that rock takes to spin. A Deity outside the cosmos can't be forced to adhere to such an arbitrary calculation. God does things properly. In a literal reading, the 'six days' come *only* when God focuses on the earth."

"The Earth is at the center," Herron teased. "God worked from the outside, in."

"You may be more correct than you realize, Mister Strangways. On the first day, there was *darkness upon the face of the deep. And the spirit of God moved upon the face of the waters.* What a beautiful image! Then God divided the Light from the darkness. All the Earth was water; then dry land appeared in one place, and it began moving out into continents. On the fourth day – and here is where you may be right, Mister Strangways – the light from stars began to appear. How fast does light travel? It was on the fourth 'day' of the Earth – not the fourth day of the cosmos – that the light from the nearest stars reached us. God took *light years* of time, working from those stars down to the Earth."

Her Ladyship looked confused. "Why did you say creation is on-going?"

"Scripture says God rested from all his work on the seventh day. The context, as I understand it, refers only to work done up to then."

"God just downed tools for a day, and upped Feet?" asked Herron.

"That's right: it's a living metaphor. Scripture does not mention the eighth day, but there was one. There would be no new stars, no new anything, if Creation stopped on day seven. An eighth day is as undeniable as an elephant. If the Divine Feet are still up, God wouldn't be much use these days."

Lady Calthrop couldn't resist a dig. "And so your god isn't. But speaking of putting his feet up, doesn't it say the earth is your god's footstool?"

Angelica closed her eyes for several long moments. Then she recited, *Thus saith the Lord, The heaven is my throne, and the earth is my footstool: where is the house that ye build unto me?*"

"Absurd. No explorer has discovered gigantic feet anywhere on the Earth."

"What about that book I'm reading to you, Your Ladyship? Lord Marmaduke says 'Daisy Lill is a timid fawn.' She isn't a fawn. She's (for the purposes of the book) a human being, if paper-thin. It's metaphoric imagery. That means is—"

Her Ladyship's icicle voice dripped, "I know what it means."Angelica could not suppress a laugh. "You just thought I was too dumb to." Trying to be courteous, she choked her laughter back down. "It's as if God is forbidden, by some unwritten law, to make a metaphor."

"God *is* a metaphor," answered Her Ladyship. "If you take your Scripture as literal truth, you can't suddenly claim metaphors."

"Oh, sorry. I didn't know the rules of the game. God is omnipotent, but he can't be allowed to make a metaphor. But . . . mayn't a metaphor be true?"

Herron, who had never met a metaphor, was strategically silent.

"I believe Scripture is the word of God," said Angelica. "Therefore, I take it seriously. Well, it says, *Let thy garments always be white*."

Giggling, Angelica leapt to her feet, reached her arms straight out, then slapped her hands flat on her hips; demonstrating, to extremely good effect, her blue blouse, fawn waistcoat, and brownish skirt.

2

When she stood, Herron leapt to his feet like he'd sat on a wasp, his chair clattering back behind him. He dashed around the table to hold her chair for her and, when she was safely ensconced in her place, he picked up his own chair and plumped down, shaken.

Receiving a double-barreled blast of Angelica full in the face at close quarters had boggled what he had always lazily referred to as his mind.

Jessup had been right. Herron realized, until the day before, he had always existed in a state of boredom. Angelica Trickett was (physically) everything Herron always desired to assuage his *ennui*. More than than, she was witty and intelligent, to boot. And bold as brass. She was a treasure.

Herron had only known her an hour, but he could not imagine ever being bored in her presence. He could spend the rest of his life plumbing her depths. He wondered why he had to meet her so late in his life – perhaps on his very last day?

He barely heard Angelica continuing, "If we all must be clad in white by Divine fiat, why do most preachers dress in black? It's metaphoric imagery. And then, there is the most profound metaphor in history, *"This is my body."*

It certainly was, thought Herron, running a hand over his fevered brow.

"How do you know what is metaphoric and what is not, Angelica, dear?"

"I use my reason. God gave it to me . . . for a reason." So that wouldn't sound too smug, she said, "Scripture, too, must be evaluated within its context."

"I thought," said Her Ladyship, with hauteur, "the important thing about religion was fervency—earnestness. A lack of hypocrisy."

"Oh, goodness, no. Sincerity is meaningless. Napoleon was sincere; he sincerely wanted to control the world. Every lunatic who believes he's Napoleon is sincere. You can sincerely believe any unreasonable folderol. Back before James II was run off the throne, Protestants preferred to believe his newborn son was a changeling smuggled to his wife's bed in a warming-pan rather than accept the truth. The *truth* shall make you free. *Sincerity to an untruth locks you in a cage.* I would rather face up to an ugly truth than sincerely serve a beautiful lie."

"So . . . how do you use your reason, my child?"

"In the middle ages, according to my brother Schuyler, every city wanted a bigger cathedral than the last. Cathedrals reached higher and higher to Heaven. And they were constructed with stone, roof and all. When they got too high, higher than any building ever went, the builders found the walls were prey to the stresses of weight and atmosphere.

"Those gorgeous Gothic flying buttresses shooting from cathedrals," Angelica arced her hands out to demonstrate their shape, "are not frills or frippery. They fortify the walls so they won't fall down. The gothic builders found a way to give the buttresses beauty as well as utility.

"Cathedral walls, with their high, stained-glass windows letting in a spectrum of multi-colored light, are my metaphor for faith, which is defined as '*the evidence of things not seen.*' The visible flying buttresses represent reason. We can't always be certain of unseen things, so stresses rise in faith – as in the Parable of the Sower. It's like the pressure on cathedral walls. When the stresses of wind and weight assail my walls and I begin to doubt, I use my reason."

"So faith . . . is not sufficient."

"As one man said in Scripture, *I believe; help thou mine unbelief.*"

"You dismiss sincerity very lightly. I suppose dismissing sincerity is necessary in a faith full of hypocrites."

"The world is full of hypocrites," said Herron, finally coming up for air. Though he yet unable to face Angelica again without risking a relapse.

Angelica shrugged. "That is not for me to judge. From my experience, '*Hypocrite*' is just a nasty word nasty people sling around – until they take a hard look in the mirror. It's a way one man has of controlling another, by forcing him meet a standard he won't live up to himself. From what I've seen, most people who use that word probably should apply it to themselves first."

"So you don't reject the word 'hypocrite,' my dear?"

"Fictional characters like Daisy Lill must be either fish or fowl. In real life, people are more multi-faced than diamonds."

Diamonds again! Thought Herron.

"We like to stuff people in jars with labels on, but no one can avoid little inconsistencies in character. Nasty-minded people trumpet these inconsistencies as 'hypocrisy.' Oh, very real hypocrites do exist, play-acting that they're one thing when they're really another. But a real person living with absolute fidelity to a single fixed idea is probably a dangerous monomaniac who should be locked in a cell in a straight waist-coat, with keepers sitting on his head."

"Do you mind being called a hypocrite?" Her Ladyship asked in her most feline manner.

"I don't like it, but inconsistencies in my character will be with me the rest of my days. They only show how much room I have to grow as a person. And as a Christian. No human being is perfect, and therefore all are hypocrites to a degree."

"Everyone?" demanded Lady Calthrop. "Am I a hypocrite?"

Angelica answered carefully. She wanted to be honest, but, given the circumstances, she needed to be as diplomatic. "I fear so, Your Ladyship."

"In what way?"

Instead of highlighting examples of Her Ladyship's hypocrisy, Angelica said, "Only you can answer that question, since only you can see into your heart."

"Am I a hypocrite?" asked Herron.

"What is this, the Last Supper, and everyone asking, '*Is it I?*'" She looked so squarely into Herron's brown eyes his whole body tingled. "Yes, Mister Strangways, I believe you are an out-and-out thoroughgoing hypocrite."

"In what way?"

"You try to maintain a front of wickedness which I do not believe is in you. Pretending to be wicked and not living down to it is the same as adopting an air of righteous you don't live up to."

"I think that's your point, Miss Trickett," Herron conceded; though, still stunned by the full-frontal view he'd had of her, he probably would have conceded the point to Angelica whatever she said. "Though I am really wicked, you know. Cross my heart."

3

"My atheist friend and I," Angelica said, looking peeved by Herron's admission, "both believed Truth was real, whether or not we could adequately comprehend it. Truth didn't have to be what I believed, or what she believed. *Belief does not make Truth,* any more than advertising. Or sincerity.

"We were trying to comprehend the one genuine Truth from different angles, through a glass darkly. Since Truth exists apart from belief, it might not correspond absolutely with any of our preconceptions. However, we both agreed that, as reasonable creatures, we would be fools if we closed our eyes to Truth if we caught a glimmer of it through that dark glass."

"Sort of like height!" Herron put in, trying desperately to redeem himself.

"I beg your pardon?" Angelica looked totally lost at sea at his remark.

"One is tall or short. Oh, one may wear thick soles, or stand on encyclopaedias, but when we're all in a line in our stocking feet we just have to accept our personal elevation. There are no 'height exercises.' Once we reach twenty-five or thirty we simply have to accept that we're never growing taller."

"Yes, Mister Strangways, thank you for that observation." Angelica's tone sounded like a mother congratulating a child for falling face-flat into a profundity. "Unfortunately, too many people try to twist the Truth to conform to the shape of their preconceptions – like Mister Strangways' horrible people who do the dreaded *right thing*. They will never accept that their 'right thing' is wrong unless they accept Truth, and are honest enough to look at their *right thing* objectively."

"Is anything objective in life, my child? Even Truth, if it exists?"

"Lady Calthrop, if there is no objective Truth separate from, and higher than, you, or me, or Mister Strangways here, Truth has no more substance than the imaginary playmates we had as children." Herron looked at her strangely. He never had imaginary playmates. His father could afford to 'bus in the real thing.

Lady Calthrop smiled pleasantly. "You still have imaginary playmates, my dear, only now they are in the Father, Son, and whatever the other one is."

"Your Ladyship, if you will please forgive my being so fulsome—"

That's surely God's fault, thought Herron, misunderstanding the word.

"You ask for forgiveness a lot," crackled Lady Calthrop. "It's so easy to be forgiven, isn't it?"

Laying the bread-and-butter knife at right angles atop the knife she'd used to cut the cake, Angelica said, very quietly, "No, it isn't."

"What were you saying, Miss Trickett?" wondered Herron, irked at Lady Calthrop for interrupting. Secret message or no, after his eyeful of her he now hung on every word spilling from her sweet lips.

"What *was* I saying? Oh . . . Only that for one to declare there is no ultimate Truth strikes me as an attempt to cram one's own ideas down another's throat in such a way as to choke off further discussion. Let's say

Mister Strangways here declares Truth is subjective – his Truth is his, my Truth is mine. Then when I try to make a declaration of my beliefs, he shuts his ears to it, or throttles the talk off.

"If we were playing field hockey, that would be like – right after the starting whistle – one team flicking the ball into its goal and immediately declaring the game over. 'We got our point,' they say. 'That's all that matters.' If I try to score a point by stating an alternative viewpoint to his, he might call a foul, standing me in the penalty corner and barring me from play, as if I've stolen something from him by trying to refute him."

"And so you have, my dear. His declaration that Truth is subjective broad-mindedly allows you to keep your little beliefs. It's unkind to challenge his."

"In doing that, he's stolen one of my basic rights as a human being."

"What right?"

"The right to defend my beliefs. He's given me his viewpoint: truth is subjective and plastic. That is an unproveable statement of faith. Then he thinks it's mean of me to counter that with my unprovable statement of faith. He's had his say, but he's censored mine. That's the height of – to use your word – hypocrisy. There is no other word for it."

"I never—!" Herron started to protest his innocence.

"We may never agree on Truth. We may debate it until we're both blue in the face and keel over; but it's wicked to deny anyone the right to that debate."

"You hold your beliefs very dear, my dear." "Yes, Your Ladyship. I do."

"Don't you ever entertain doubts?"

"Yes. That's why, for me, faith and reason must go hand-in-glove. From time to time I wonder if there is only one Way, or if there is really a beneficent god. I will have doubts until I no longer see Truth through a glass darkly, but face-to-face. Don't you ever doubt there is no god? Not even of any kind?"

"Never."

Angelica breathed in a whisper, too softly for Lady Calthrop to hear, "Which of us is the more doctrinaire, then?"

A little smile kinked up one side of Herron's face. He earnestly hoped that was the end of the digression.

4

Her Ladyship refused to let the matter rest. "Is anything wrong with a belief in no one, eternal Truth, my child?"

"Oh, Lady Calthrop—yes! If no Objective Truth exists outside ourselves, 'right' and ''wrong' are matters of personal aesthetics. I refuse to accept that."

"Does your refusal to accept it make it false?"

"No, Your Ladyship. But if Truth is subjective . . . anything is permissible. If, aesthetically, one does not like people who have a certain race or religion or hair color or politics, one may with impunity murder them all. Moral impunity, I mean. When there is no objective, beneficent Deity outside ourselves and the cosmos who says '*Thou shalt not kill*' – meaning murder – you may kill anyone without guilt or responsibility. That's the first step to becoming Jack the Ripper."

"Guilt is important to your religion, is it not?"

"It is not. My faith teaches me the acceptance of personal responsibility – but *freedom from guilt by forgiveness*. I know people who feel a terrible guilt over – oh, the Saint Bartholomew's Day Massacre, or something which happened centuries ago and which they had nothing at all to do with – but who feel absolutely no personal responsibility for anything they actually do. That's hypocrisy of a most repellant species. A 'preacher' who uses a phony air of righteousness to take advantage of an innocent is not a whit more hypocritical than a man who feels guilt over the treatment of the Saxons, say, but never feels personal responsibility over anything he's done to offend God or man, or—"

Angelica began pressing her luck by mentioning Her Ladyship's own foibles,

"—who never takes action to make up with offended relatives and neighbors."

"That's a long sentence," said Herron. "I must diagram it later. What if this ultimate, objective Truth is a negative, as your atheist friend believed?"

"My reason cries out against it. If I were an atheist, I would be must troubled by the problem of 'good' in the world. Where can it come from? Not from mankind, from what I've seen of them. There *must* be a positive Truth – that is, a beneficent Creator. Without that, Society itself would be impossible. We would all be driven into barbarity by hedonistic impulses. We three disagree on many things. Yet here we are, having a pleasant afternoon tea and a diverting discussion. We're not chasing each other around the table waving hatchets."

"Diverting," Herron said, deciding they had wasted enough time, "is just the word. What we should be doing—"

5

Angelica had not finished her thought, and Herron politely backed down.

He wished he had brought his watch along. He had to get this message to Jessup that evening – and as early in the evening as possible.

"Human nature being what it is, that we are able to form societies where we respect each other's God-given rights proclaims the existence of a Supreme *and* beneficent Creative Deity. That's a statement of reason. Where Christianity takes its unique step of faith beyond that, is identifying that Deity as Personal."

"Well, child, I thought you believed in free will?"

"Yes, Your Ladyship."

"Is the ability to *not* respect others, that is, to hate – and kill – free will?"

"Yes, Your Ladyship. As much as I dislike saying it, to deny anyone the right to hate is infringing upon his freedom. A man abuses his natural freedom by hating, but that freedom is nevertheless a blessing, by God, to *individuals*."

"Individuals only?"

"Yes, Your Ladyship. Neither by God nor by that eminently sensible document, the United States Constitution. Scripture says, *proclaim liberty throughout all the land unto all the inhabitants thereof*. There is no free will in herds. A herd mindlessly follows leaders in stampedes, or into the abattoir—but never out. All freedom must have the individual as its foundation."

"What about governments?" asked Herron, harking back to his talks with Jessup and the Major. "May freedom rise from groups banding together for mutual security into societies, and agreeing to governments?"

"Governments do not grant freedoms. The best are only there to guarantee and protect natural freedoms. Of course, if we all lived according to the Golden Rule, *Do unto others as you would have them do unto you*, there would be no need for government! What a jolly happy world we'd all have, then. As the Apostle Paul wrote, *For, brethren, ye have been called unto liberty; only use not liberty for an occasion to the flesh, but by love serve one another*. If we all used our free will to love and serve one another, we could put up a sign, 'No Governments Required.' We'd have no wars, since governments make wars; no laws limiting personal freedom, since only governments pass such laws. We'd need no police or hangmen. We would have no politics. Why, we'd need no taxation!"

"Good God!" Herron ejaculated. "Paradise!"

"My dear child, doesn't your Scripture say to pay your taxes?"

"It says *Render to Caesar the things that are Caesar's*. It doesn't say Caesar is right in demanding an ever larger slice the pie. The modern Caesar, government, is a vampire leeching off the blood of the working wage-earner. I want to see social justice, and taxation is hardly ever just."

"Amen," said Herron. "My gov'ner taught me all about it."

"Yes," Her Ladyship purred, "let us drink from the fount of your knowledge."

"Well, taxation, don't y'know, takes money out of the private sector for the government. When money in the private sector is lessened or depleted, the private sector – that's people who own shops and businesses, like me, don't y'know – don't employ so many people. Result: fewer jobs, more unemployment. Unemployment means people have less money to spend. That means less spending, especially in shops like mine, blast it. When that happens, I have less profit. Since my profit is used to pay my employees, my employees lose jobs when people don't buy from me. When more workers are out of work, it means less tax revenue. So, for the government to cover its expenses, which are legion, they raise taxes *again*, God blast them, taking more money from private pockets, costing more jobs – it's a vicious cycle, both to my employees and to me."

Angelica had another slant. "I employ no one. I simply see taxation as economic feudalism. In feudalism, the overlord owes obligations to the peasants, and in return the peasants owe their overlords a obligation, which keeps them in their place. In lieu of physical obligations, vassals made a monetary payment, or *scutage*. Like scutage, taxation is a monetary obligation paid to government overlords, who keep the peasants in their place. That's why folk heroes are almost always warriors against taxation: Lady Godiva and Robin Hood and George Washington. Every revolt I can think of was against taxation. Wat Tyler, Jack Cade, the American and French Revolutions. The rebellion of 1715—"

Lady Calthrop shot her eyes to Angelica. "What's that?"

"Oh, James Stuart was trying to take the throne from under the Georges. The father of Bonnie Prince Charlie, I think he was. I believe he said he'd do away with the tax on malt. Then there's the Boston Tea Party, when over-taxed tea was flung into the harbor by rebellious Americans. Tyrannical governments always institute higher taxation, and revolts for freedom and the individual nearly always have a fight against taxation at their base."

"Hear, hear," rumbled Herron.

"Unfortunately, we hardly ever follow the Golden Rule in our free will. It's not easy. This goes back to your people who do 'the right thing.' Portia in *The Merchant of Venice* says '*If to do were as easy as to know what were good to do, chapels had been churches and poor men's cottages prince's palaces.*'"

"Ah," said Herron, subdued. "I fear you lost me on that turn."

"Most people do not use their God-blessed liberty to love or serve. They hate and hurt, because they think of themselves first. Governments are instituted among men to restrain our freedom, since all human life is precious."

"Is it?" asked Lady Calthrop.

"No. I am wrong. All human life is not precious. It is sacred."

"You are young. When you're my age, child, you'll understand that some lives are not worth living."

Given her invalid status and her mourning, Herron understood her to be talking about herself; and, for the first time, he felt a pang of pity for the elder lady as well as the younger. Unlike Herron, the wheelchair-bound Lady Calthrop, too old for amours or prospects, might not care if intruders riddled her with bullets.

"Freedom is absolute to individuals – but," Angelica added with staccato firmness, "*not choice*. One does not always choose what one does in life to make a living. Yet we do have the freedom to *try* whatever we want. What does the American Declaration of Independence say?"

"I'm sure I don't know, child."

With a quiver of his head, Herron indicated that he'd never read it.

Angelica recited again, "'*We hold these truths to be self-evident, that all men are created equal, that they are endowed by their Creator with certain unalienable Rights, that among these are Life, Liberty and the pursuit of happiness.*' It's not Scripture, but it's like my faith: God gives us the freedom to try anything. We *do not*, however, have the right to succeed. In fact, many of our desires should not be achieved, especially when it involves dominance over others. Humans, I very much fear, lack the character to exercise personal responsibility. So, we have laws – and policemen and hangmen – limiting the full exercise of God-granted liberty. That's why all governments are necessarily evil."

"*All?*" asked Lady Calthrop and Herron, in unison. Both were shocked.

"Each to its own degree. They are evil because all governments are instituted among men *specifically to inhibit the Divine blessing of individual freedom.*"

Herron shifted uneasily in his chair. "Doesn't that imply a sort of moral equivalency between governments, however rancid they are?"

"Not at all. The better governments forbid *negative* freedoms, like stealing and rapine and killing, while guarantee *positive* freedoms. The freedom of speech is positive, and of thought. The freedom to write and publish whatever you jolly well like (especially, in the scurrilous press). And so on."

Herron smiled and subtly patted the pocket where his "bulldog" revolver lay.

"Even the best government," Angelica continued, "must pass laws limiting freedom, to provide a basic protection to its citizens. To enforce those laws they must establish military forces and police, so if you violate another individual's freedom they can take your liberty altogether by decanting you in the jug."

Lady Calthrop again upbraided Angelica for using slang.

Angelica grinned at the criticism. "All governments have those things in common. But you can easily dispense any with moral equivalency. Look at which governments build walls to keep their own citizens in, and compare them to the governments who build walls to keep an eager queue of immigrants out. That's one way to sort the good apples from the bad."

"What kind of walls?" wondered Herron, trying to think of any country that had surrounded itself with bastions like a fortress.

"Ellis Island in America is a sort of wall. America fosters freedom around the globe. It's a haven for those seeking a new life in freedom. But if a midwife takes home all the babies she delivers, she can't afford to feed herself."

Lady Calthrop sniffed. "The Americans are worried about immigrants – after they were all immigrants who dispossessed the native population."

"Just goes to show how important it is," said Herron. "That would never have happened if the Indians had instituted tighter immigration controls."

Trying valiantly to finish her point amid all the pointlessness, Angelica asked, "Which is preferable: a country that must turn away hordes trying to get in, or a country that jails or even shoots at citizens tying to get out?"

"So," said Her Ladyship, "you blithely determine which country is good and which is bad. What about people? Do you believe in that old tale about Original Sin? Are all people evil? Or are they either good or bad?"

6

Angelica answered slowly. "I believe the natural impulse of all human nature inclines toward evil. I cannot divide humans into 'good' and 'bad.' It's written out unmistakably in Scripture that we all will be judged by the same standards we mete out to others."

"We build the gallows," joked Herron, "on which God hangs us?"

Briefly, so Her Ladyship could not see, Angelica stuck her tongue out at him. But her eyes showed that he had guessed right.

"And what about people like me," said Lady Calthrop. "I never accept arguments from one holy writ or another. But I can clearly see that some people in the world are good and some are bad."

"By whose standard? Mister Strangways' busybody who does *the right thing* always thinks anyone who disagrees with him is a bad person. And no matter what one is guilty of, one never places one's self in the 'bad' column."

"I do," said Herron, hopefully. "I'm very bad indeed."

Angelica made a face at him. "I fear when a man isolates certain individuals as 'bad' he runs the risk of concluding that he'll make the world a better place by eliminating them. Most of the evil in the world is done by people trying, in the worst possible way, to make the world a better place – for themselves – by removing from the world whatever people they have defined as 'bad.'"

"I made that point about an hour ago," Herron groused.

"As I see it, no human being is wholly 'good' – or 'bad.'"

"Every heel," said Herron, with the self-importance of one stating an eternal maxim, "must have a sole." He glanced back and forth between the women. "Sole? Soul? It's a play on—"

"Even Adam and Eve," Angelica cut in, "fell into evil by trying to do *the right thing*. They wanted to be like God. In their eyes, that was the ultimate good. And they went about *the right thing* in the wrongest possible way. People nearly always choose the worst way, especially in forming governments."

"And especially," said Her Ladyship, with a note of triumph in her tone, "if they set their governments up on religious principles."

Herron thought Angelica might respond to that. She didn't. Angelica let Her Ladyship have the last word.

And it was almost the last word Herron ever heard from Lady Calthrop before he was taken out in the country that evening to be shot in the back of the head.

CHAPTER XXVI

Herron exerted his utmost charm to shepherd the ladies back to the papers.

"Yes," said Lady Calthrop. "Let us return to that, so Mister Strangways may be on his way. From your guesses, one of those words means an attack from a ruin, and the other that they will destroy a Temple. The connection is clear."

"Is it?" Angelica bore a puzzled expression at those conclusions.

"*Ai*. These people are plotting to attack from a ruin, as at *Ai* in your Bible. Perhaps it's a coup against the government by a cult meeting clandestinely at an ancient pagan shrine site. There's a ruined pagan temple somewhere, from which these people mean to attack. *Resurgam* means they intend to rebuild the pagan shrine and dedicate a new society based on their cult."

Herron was dissatisfied. He thought they had strayed from the actual message.

"Miss Trickett," he pointed out, "your *Ai* is on my *hip*."

"I beg your pardon?"

"On line with. On the paper. I think *Ai* and *hip* may be part of the same word, and I smoked the letters in between."

Lady Calthrop clucked her tongue at *Ai-hip*. "What sort of word can that be?"

"Really, Mister Strangways," chided Angelica, "I wish you hadn't burned your half. It smells perfectly foul."

"It was poor quality tobacco."

"You should not be smoking at all."

"A man must have an occupation. Now, let's think. Ai? Aib? Aic? Aid—"

"'Aid' *is* a word." Angelica doubtfully screwed up her elastic mouth. "Aim?"

"Let's do what we did before, and look at it from the other end."

"That was with '*gam*.' '*Hip*' is a complete word in itself."

"I'm not happy with it. Let's try, anyway."

"Wasting time," said Her Ladyship, "when you have a reasonable hypothesis. I warn you, Mister Strangways, I will countenance no advances to Miss Trickett."

Herron shouldered on, regardless. "What letters may go in front of *hip*?"

Angelica shook her head, waggling her stray locks. "None that make sense. But what does, with bombs and rising from graves? 'Chip.'"

"Ai_chip? Aim chip?"

"The only other single letter I can think of is 's' for 'ship.'"

"Ai _ ship . . ." Suddenly, in a pitch of excitement, Herron uttered a word not condoned in mixed company. He apologized profusely, then shouted, "Airship!"

Angelica wrinkled her brow at him. "What's that?" Lady Calthrop clapped her hands, then gleefully stretched her arms into the air with her fingers outspread. "It's a balloon." Her tone and body-language seemed to suggest who altogether ridiculous it all was.

"It's not a balloon, precisely," Herron corrected, though this was no time to go into rigid internal structures he barely comprehended himself.

He cursed himself for not spotting *airship* sooner, but it was only obvious in retrospect. The two sides of the tear did not fit perfectly together, and they curled up toward the middle. It was not obviously one word.

"Americans have been seeing airships over their middle western states and in Canada for months. Vaguely cigar-shaped vehicles, moving against the wind, which therefore much be guided by some powerful engine. Steam, electricity—"

"Such vehicles do not exist, Mister Strangways," said Lady Calthrop, coldly, decisively. "Now *you* are becoming unscientific."

"*Resurgam*," murmured Angelica, mussing her coiffure so more wisps of hair dangled down. "'Rising again' suits an airship." One lock of hair obscured an eye; Angelica brushed it up, and it fell right back down. "Granting that—what?"

She glanced at the notes of what they had worked out:

Ai(rs)hip
Infern(al ma)chine
RE(sur)GAM [?]

"It's merely a lot of stray words, if words, with tenuous associations. Yet this part may truly be code." She pointed with her pencil to:

lomh p rt yjr esyrt

"I thought it might be Welsh," Herron offered, flaccidly. "Not many vowels."

"There was a Welsh girl at my boarding school. Welsh is the most lyrical of languages. This is hidden for a reason. You know, Mister Strangways, I think if we crack it, everything else may fall right together."

Lady Calthrop, looking bored by these proceedings, tinkled her crystal bell. "If you two will excuse me." When Dapifer appeared, she said, "I hate leaving you two attractive young animals alone. Don't get up to mischief."

Angelica hurried to fetch the wheeled chair from the next room. When she sprang from her chair, Herron rose with her, watching her bustle about.

Dapifer lifted Lady Calthrop from the couch to the wheelchair. Pushing her from the drawing room, he wound her through the glass cases toward the stairs. There, he would carry her upstairs and transfer her to the upper-story wheelchair. Returning to the table, Angelica offered Herron a reassuring smile.

He dodged round the table to hold her chair, then he reclaimed his own seat.

As they faced each other over the table, Herron asked,

"What, exactly, do you do here, Miss Trickett?"

"I read to Her Ladyship. Brush the dog and take it for airings. Some shopping, though Cook goes to market. I accompany her on visits, push her wheelchairs indoors and her bath chairs out." She glanced around to make sure no extra ears had slipped in. "When I was hired, I was led to believe I would have charge over the staff. That never materialized. Dapifer is the power in the servants' quarters."

"You're a general dogsbody." (Angelica shot him a stern glance.) "Er, sorry, poor but you know what I . . . (ahem) Lots of staff needed to run a joint this size?"

"It's a small staff, actually. And – I hate to speak behind their backs – they seem intellectually below average, apart from Dapifer. Dapifer even acts as groom! Her Ladyship been divesting herself of staff ever since her husband died. She gave the downstairs maid her notice long ago. I never knew why – nor why she kept poor Doris on."

Herron thought he wouldn't let Doris go, either.

"I was informed flower-arranging would be in my duties. That sounded jolly. I'm a good flower arranger. Well, it turned out she wanted me to catalog samples of flowers and skeletal leaves her husband had collected in his travels; and to arrange and catalogue floral slides she uses for her microscope."

Herron was astonished. "She has a microscope?"

"In the library. It's really more a laboratory than a library. It's a good job you asked for a Latin dictionary rather than a great work of fiction. Her few books that aren't scientific treatises are soupily romantic novels."

"She's a far cry most Society ladies. So, no flowers in the house?"

"A few potted ferns. Sadly, no living flowers. I do think a house without flowers looks so bare. She never notices flowers have beauty as well as utility."

"Nor people, I imagine."

Herron was looking squarely at her when he said this, and his implication was unmistakable. Angelica's color rose and her eyes dropped.

"Do you really need to work for her?"

"Yes. Your firm is prosperous. My father's company died with him." She puffed up at the hair dangling in front of her eye. It fell right back. "Frankly, it was dying long before that. He imported from the southern United States. Their war ruined him. He never turned the firm around. He had hopes – then he died." While she was talking, Herron had been gaping. "By Harry! I have it!"

"Well, keep it to yourself."

"Where I've seen you before, I mean. My gov'ner hauled me kicking and squirming to your old ma—er, your father's funeral. He told me it 'showed the right spirit.' Crikey! You were a just little girl!" He had seen Angelica at the funeral, but he hadn't *noticed* her, even at the raw age of seventeen. Girls lacked all the wonderful attributes he enjoyed most in women.

Recalling where he had first laid eyes on her, he was impressed at how the little girl had grown up.

"Thank you for coming," she said. "Even kicking and screaming. I was so distraught I don't know who was there. I think it was not well-attended—"

"Yes, that was hard cheese."

"—but it was a long time ago."

"Can't be more than ten years."

"Ten years feels longer when you're twelve."

"Yes, too bad. I'm sorry. Still," he said, remembering what Major Hobbes said, "*All flesh is as grass* and all that, don't you know."

"*The grass withereth, and the flower thereof falleth away.* Or, as it says in that Shakespeare play, '*women are as roses, whose fair flower being once display'd doth fall that very hour.*'"

"Exactly. Get 'em while they're young."

Dwelling on the past, she missed that remark. "Pardon?"

"I mean . . . uh . . . do you actually like Shakespeare?"

"It's one of the great pleasures of my life."

"Never could make heads or tails of it myself. Too much like Scripture. All that 'theeing' and 'thouing.' Well, it does appear you've fallen on your feet."

"Or on my head."

"Are you happy in this bally museum?" He dropped his voice. Walls, he recalled, have ears. "Lady Calthrop strikes me as a bit of a tartar."

Angelica nodded regretfully. "It's her sarcasm that's hardest. She can be very cruel that way. You never notice the edge in her voice unless you hear it every day. It's like the woman in Shakespeare, '*How fine this tyrant can tickle where she wounds.*' We're fortunate Lady Calthrop is in a good mood today, or I wouldn't be wasting the afternoon over puzzles."

"Say," said Herron, thinking of places where they might meet her again – if he lived – "will you be stepping out watch the Procession tomorrow?"

"Lady Calthrop refuses to let me leave the house. She can't abide crowds."

"She doesn't like crowds, so you can't join them. You're like Cinderella."

"No, I am not. I'm here of my own volition. I can quit, you know. Though it won't be easy to find other work."

"I'm sure you can. You're smart as a whip. Can you be a governess?"

"*Jane Eyre*? Caring for a child with a darkly handsome and mysterious guardian whom I marry in the end – with a mad wife in the attic? No, thank you."

Herron had no idea what she was talking about, and he was afraid to ask.

"I don't deal with other people's children. They have same the faults as their parents – but writ in a large typeface, since they haven't learned the art of subtlety. Children are too close to the original sin they were born with for my comfort."

"Well, do you have any private yearnings or ambitions?"

"Yes."

"And they are?"

"Private."

Herron waited for her to elaborate. She didn't. "Have any good skills?"

"I know typewriting, Pittman shorthand . . . even Morse."

A broad grin split Herron's face. "How wonderful. That's just so much tippy-tapping to me. And none of those appeal to you for earning a living?"

"There is no appeal to the idea of working for a typewriting agency in a room with fifty other girls endlessly banging away at it all day. I enjoy quiet here, and I get out with the dog a few times each day. Except for tomorrow."

"Why not work as a telegrapher? You can be privy to everyone's secrets."

"This is a good position—"

"Is that what the Gorgon keeps telling you? Can't be much fun here."

"I am not an independently wealthy woman. I don't work for fun."

"I trust you are well-paid?"

"I am not paid at all."

Herron cocked an eyebrow up at her. "No?"

"But all my needs are met. She gives me a clothing allowance to buy anything I want. I wear clothes I could never afford as a typist. I have more than enough to eat. In fact, Lady Calthrop lets me have whatever I need."

"Except company."

"Mister Strangways, I cannot afford idle away summer days. And I can't just up and leave working for one London's richest invalids on the off-chance of finding an equal or better job right away – if ever."

"Call me Herron. Better yet, Herrie."

"We should keep our relations strictly formal until we know each other better."

"Would you like to know me better?"

"I can only know you better, since I know nothing about you now – except that you display an extremely poor sartorial sense."

Herron glanced down at his cherry-red tailcoat and white satin knee-breeches. "At least I didn't wear the buckle shoes."

"Yes. That was a mercy."

"I told you during tea why I'm in this fancy-dress."

"You were holed up in your Club by someone you didn't want to meet and had to play like a waiter to escape."

"You sound disapproving."

"I try never to give credence to gossip . . . but I have heard that you are a man much given to practical jokes. This does seem to confirm it. I will not ask what you did to this man you don't want to meet—"

"How do you know the fault is on my side? I may have a reputation—"

"We agree on that! He can't be a creditor. Strangways' Emporia won't be in the hands of the bailiffs. I remember seeing men cart away my father's property. Not just the tables and the chairs and the beds, but little things he and my mother had bought when times were better, and which were special to them. All to be sold on the block to pay his creditors. My father never raised his eyes again and never smiled again until the day he died. You're not in that situation."

"Oh, I have creditors. I can easily pay my bills, I just don't, always. One must show them who's boss. Also, I may play a prank or two, but—"

"I have also heard that you drink too much."

"From whom?"

"I do not repeat gossip – and betraying gossipers is just another form of gossip, is it not? Since our fathers knew each other well, and were in similar businesses, naturally we have friends in common. Some of them know you pretty well."

"It's nice to know you have friends who know you pretty well who are quick to tell nice young ladies behind your back that you drink too much or that you once put soap in the Trafalgar Square fountain."

Her eyes brightened. "Was that you! My brother covered that for his paper. He thought it was funny."

"He's about the only one who did. Say, maybe I'll hunt up one of our common friends have him introduce us. That way we needn't be so formal."

She gave a wry-half smile with her expressive mouth. "I don't know that I want to be introduced to someone who smokes too much and drinks too much and plays nasty pranks and pays calls at tea-time on strangers, dressed like that."

"You don't drink?"

"I do not."

"T for Totaller?" he gently chided. "Church of England Temperance Society? Will you honor me a tambourine solo?"

"I'll play it off your head. I drink wine, but I do not take it to excess."

"Ever been tiddly?"

"That is none of your business."

"If an answer isn't 'no' – it's *yes*. You must tell me about it some time."

"I doubt Lady Calthrop will ever admit you again. You have what you came after; and she suspects you slipped that little bit of paper it my reticule yourself."

"Do you suspect that?"

After a ruminative pause, she drawled, "No." "Why not?"

She did not meet his eyes. "Because I don't want it to be true."

"I thought you said we should not close our eyes to the truth."

"Is it true?" she asked, very softly.

"No." Seeing Angelica's eyes fixed on her crossed arms, Herron leapt back into a jocular vein. "Ever tried whisky? Just a sip? For medicinal purposes?"

She shot a disgusted glance up at him through the stray lock of hair on her forehead. "Mister Strangways, you cannot induce me to—"

"'*Do you realize? That clothing insures your comfort by affording protection from the heat or cold? . . .*'"

Her eyes grew wide. In an appalled whisper, she said, "I *beg* your pardon?"

2

"Quoting. Shh, don't interrupt, I'll lose the flow. ' . . .*That books and newspapers insure you against ignorance? That a pure malt stimulant taken regularly, will insure your health, and keep you toned up? That to insure getting the purest and best of malt preparations, you should obtain–*"

He cupped his hand over his mouth and blew what he meant to be a trumpet-call (though it was closer to what rhyming slang referred to as a raspberry tart).

"'—*Duffy's Pure Malt Whisky. Which never fails to give strength and vigor to those who are weak or run down. Nothing so quickly overcomes exhaustion and debility. Nothing compares with it for stirring up the sluggish blood and building up health. For curing and preventing coughs, colds, the grip and pneumonia it is absolutely unequaled. All grocers and druggists keep it*!'"

Angela giggled, "What on earth are you running at the mouth about?"

"An advertisement I saw in an American newspaper. They say 'druggist' or there, not 'chemist.' I thought it was better poetry than 'Casabianca.' '*Stirring up the sluggish blood*'— the poet laureate could not have written that line in a million years. Who is the poet laureate, by the way?"

"Alfred Austin."

"Never heard of him."

"He's probably never heard of you."

"Bet he buys all his nibs from Strangways'. What did he write?"

"No idea. Sorry. Did you try 'Duffy's Pure Malt Whisky' while in America, Mister Strangways?"

"How could one resist?"

"And?"

"Couldn't stomach the muck. But I never had a cough."

"Do you often get coughs?"

He nodded. "Can't imagine why. I stay out of drafts." He licked his lips. He could use a cigarette just then. "One must preserve the only health one's got."

"And you believe the best way to do that is by drinking whisky?"

"It must be true. It was in the newspapers."

"My brother Schuyler writes for the newspapers. Ask him some time about their reliability. But getting back to *these* papers—?" she said, firmly.

Rising, Herron paced the length of the room. He had been trying to wheedle Angelica back to this subject for an hour; now that he had her alone, he didn't want to waste life on side issues. Half London might be gunning for him, but if he could arrange a tryst with Miss Trickett he'd die happy.

"How can one think of papers in such charming company?"

"Thank you." She thanked him guardedly. She'd heard *a lot* about him.

"I believe your family is from Bristol?"

"Yes."

"I'd never have known it."

"Because I don't talk like Long John Silver in a cheap theatrical production of *Treasure Island*? 'Ar, Jim, m'lad!' My father was Bristol born and bred and never talked like that. He did have a *slight* accent—"

Herron could just imagine.

"—but my mother's accent was quite different and she balanced me out. And, of course, I had Finishing School."

"While I just got finished at school."

"School was all my parents could afford to do for me. I must make my own way in the world. So, I work, and live, here."

"A bird in a gilded cage, as the song says."

His allusion put the starch into her manner. "That song is about a woman who marries for money. I *earn* my living, thank you."

"Yes, I bet you earn every blessed farthing. *You* wouldn't marry for money."

"If ever I do marry, it will not be for money."

"What will it be for?"

She glued her eyes to the table. "*Not* for money. And I will never, I trust, be a mere flower in a rich man's buttonhole. I will earn my own way in the world."

"Is earning your living really so important?"

"It is, when you've nothing else to rely on. Beyond boarding school and finishing school, my poor father left me nothing but a memory of love. I will stand on my own two feet in this world partly because I want to – but mostly because I must. I will earn my own keep and pay my own way."

"But you'd take a door out of here if one opened up at your feet?"

"I won't take a way out that cheapens me."

"Are you so high-minded you'd refuse a caller who has a pot-full?"

She glared up at him. "Mister Strangways, do you *want* me to like you for your money?"

"If that's what it takes."

"And maybe one day you'll sweep me away into a mercenary marriage? I'd rather be poor and happy than rich and miserable."

"And are you happy?"

"Happiness does not depend on outward circumstances."

"Again – that wasn't a 'yes.' Are you happy?"

"Happiness . . . doesn't enter into making a living." She looked down again.

"I shouldn't think so, here. *This* is what you meant when you said we don't always have the choice to decide what we want to do in the world for a living."

She stared at him, amazed. "I owe you an apology, Mister Strangways."

"For what?"

"I didn't give you the credit for being as half so perceptive."

"I fool everybody that way."

"I didn't think you were listening."

"I tried not to; but I drink in every word that drips like honey from your lips."

"Then drink this honey: *if any would not work, neither should he eat.* In my case, it's imperative. I can't choose to eat if I don't work. My father made poor business decisions, and he was also affected by circumstances beyond his control. He died owning nothing but shattered dreams. It was all he left behind and he tried to make sure his children did not receive them as an inheritance."

"I'm sorry–"

"Please don't feel sorry for that – or for the Saint Bartholomew Day's Massacre. Or the Saxons. My father's firm failed, and his heart failed with it. Even if your father had profited off my father's failure, no one could blame him."

"No. Survival of the fittest and all that. That's life, don't y'know."

"And no one would blame you, anyway, since you had no hand in it. I am not poor because you are rich; you are not rich because I am poor. But you are rich and I am poor. I can't even afford to shop at your Emporia—"

"Emporium," he muttered, unnecessarily. He'd habitually corrected people so much, he confused himself. "The prices are what the market will bear, plus a little extra for profit. You can't sell things for less than they cost to make or import, don't you know. And you close your doors if you don't make that little extra bit on top. Profit pays your employees, and your employees work better if you pay 'em. Even the employees who do nothing but procrastinate tend to take that procrastination elsewhere. Profit is also what you use to pay for overhead and expand your business to hire new people, to keep the ol' economy humming."

"I do understand economics. I wasn't complaining, I was simply stating fact. Your wares are probably priced reasonably for their value, but they are too high to fit into my purse. Oh – Lady Calthrop has mentioned that you sell good tea."

"We do."

"Is this it?" She nodded at the pot.

Herron didn't really drink enough tea to know his brand from another – or if there really was any difference between teas other than the label. "I'll send you some, so you may taste it for yourself."

"I'm no beggar, Mister Strangways. I want no hand-outs. Our circumstances may be drastically different, but I do not envy yours. Envy is not an attractive emotion, and covetousness is against the Law of God. I do not covet your money or your place. Please do not pity mine. You earn all the money you can, however you can, so long as it's honest. Let me earn my living in my own way."

She dropped her eyes again.

"In fact," she said, in a lower tone, "if I did find you attractive . . . and charming . . . and funny . . . and even nice, in spite of yourself . . . I'd wish you weren't awash in such a sea of money. I would not want it to appear that I liked you for your money. Because I don't."

"Don't like me? Or don't like my money?"

Angelica adamantly refused to answer.

"Money's not a bad thing."

"It's a wonderful thing. I wish I had—" She made stern eye contact with him. "But whatever I have, I will earn it and it will be mine. I reject your pity."

"I don't pity you, Miss Trickett. I pity anyone who crosses you. But, cooped up in this museum as you are, has anyone told you lately – how lovely you are?"

Her eyes dropped again. "Not for a long time."

"Incredibly lovely green eyes."

She smiled them up at him. "They do say green is God's favorite color."

"But He uses it sparingly in eyes, I think. And that dark tint must be very rare indeed. They makes you very special. They must mirror a beautiful soul. Pardon my asking, Miss Trickett, but do you have any regular gentlemen callers?"

"Lady Calthrop does not allow me to receive callers. That was stipulated when she first employed me."

"How does she expect you to meet people?"

"I think she expects me not to meet people."

"So you just hunker down in the house and never get any exercise?"

"Lady Calthrop encourages exercise. My brother and I are both avid cyclists. She lets me have a day out with him once a week – but only in his company."

"Cycling with Mister Medieval Architecture can't be much fun."

"He's my brother and I love him and he's very interesting."

"*Chacun a son gout.* So long as I'm not exposed to it. Where do you go?"

"We take a train out to the country. We cycle out and have a picnic."

"It sounds like a lonely life."

"I don't find Her Ladyship's 'no callers' rule unreasonable. This is her house. She doesn't have to employ me. She told me the rules. I accepted them."

"Apart from cycling junckets, do you get the odd afternoon off?"

"Of course."

He stared squarely into her eyes. "I have every afternoon off. If you went for a saunter in the Park, and – quite by coincidence, of course – I happened to be sauntering there, too, would you object if we took our saunter in proximity to one another? Or must you run to Lady Calthrop and ask permission?"

She stared long into his eyes without betraying any emotion. "No, Mister Strangways. I would not object." Then, firmly, "Furthermore, I am twenty-two and capable of looking after myself. I do not require permission. Nor protection."

3

She allowed a moment of silence for that to sink in, then added,

"You do look better without the monocle. It makes you squint your features so. In one of those interminable novels Lady Calthrop adores, where nothing ever happens and women seem to get married for no deeper reason than sheer spite, one woman considers marrying a man with an eyeglass, though she said *I shall dream at night that I am looking at the extraordinary face of a magnified insect.*"

"A magnified insect? Is that how you think the monocle makes me look?"

"Just quoting. Like you, with your horrid malt whisky advertisement."

"You quote extraordinarily well," he said, stuffily.

"One remembers better when one read aloud. Like they used to in the middle ages. According to—"

"—your brother Schuyler. Yes, yes. I've never met the chap but I seem to know him better than I know you. I was wearing my eyeglass at the Underground station. You were staring at me. Don't pretend you weren't. You smiled at me!"

"I was trying to keep from laughing out loud at you."

"Oh." Herron's face fell.

"You have beautiful eyes. So softly brown. Don't cover them up."

Her compliment restored his jocular mood. "I'm surprised a woman with Lady Calthrop's deep pockets was using the Underground at all Saturday night, don't y'know. Doesn't she have a carriage and four? Or five, even?"

Angelica giggled. "She hates the Underground. She's totally irreligious but she said if there was a Hell it would be just like the Underground – full of noise and fumes and soot and thick with aimless people lost and groping in smoke."

"Yes the 'Stygian smoke.'"

"What is 'Stygian,' anyhow?"

"It comes from the River Styx, separating Hades from the land of the living."

"If you call it living, in this city. The streets are always congested. These days a carriage can hardly move through town, even without a Diamond Jubilee."

"I visualize Her Ladyship standing up in her carriage like Moses, raising her chintzy little parasol and commanding the traffic to part."Angelica pursed her lips tight. One did not joke about wheelchair bound invalids. "Lady Calthrop has been uncharacteristically charitable in allowing you remain. And in allowing me to remain unoccupied for so long."

Herron reached to his waistcoat pocket for his watch – and remembered he left it in Merridew's care, along with the rest of his personal effects. "Has this been a long time to remain unoccupied?"

She shook her head. "You really can't comprehend what a job is, can you?"

"A job of work, you mean?"

"Her Ladyship has been uncharacteristically indulgent. And you have broken bread with her. I do not think you should use this precious time as an opportunity to abuse her. If this cigarette paper really means anything, we should try to finish our work with it before her mood changes and she commands you to shog off."

"'Our work' has a lovely ring—"

"If it is 'our work' *we* ought to get on with it."

"It's odd, isn't it? Our being drawn together by a dead man."

"Please don't express it in quite those words, Mister Strangways."

"Does it give you the creeps?"

"The dead man, you mean, or our being drawn together?"

"On second thought, don't answer that. But a man died trying to deliver this message. I don't understand it. I can't think of anything worth dying for."

"Can you think of anything worth living for?"

"You bet! But I've only got one life. What is worth giving it up for?"

"Surely, one's country—?"

It was against Herron's policy to respond to a pretty woman with *balderdash*. "Didn't someone once say that patriotism was the last refuge of scoundrels?"

4

"Samuel Johnson. His context was clear. It was a critique of scoundrels, not patriots. A scoundrel plays on the patriotism of others to work his evil ways, like a trickster playing on another's religion or cupidity. Like the hypothetical scoundrel I mentioned who used science as a refuge to play on fear, by saying he can pass laws to control the weather. He did not mean to imply patriots were scoundrels. He meant scoundrels who, when all else fails, cry, 'Don't question my patriotism!' when no one ever did. A true patriot will die for his country."

"Pardon me, Miss Trickett, but do people really die for a spot of dirt?"

"I should have said countrymen. *Greater love hath no man than this, that a man lay down his life for his friends.* That's the patriot. And the country – the country is not the dirt, Mister Strangways. Oh, it is in some places, I suppose. Lady Calthrop is much taken with a modern scientific theory that soil has influence on the national characteristics. And there was the French Revolution, which denounced God and called for *'la religion de la patrie.'* And the Germans are always thundering about their precious 'Fatherland.' Most nations are held together by a glue of ethnicity. When they say, *'We're special,'* they refer to what they describe as their national character. Those sorts of people only need a Napoleonic scoundrel to lead them. And they will follow him – straight to Hell."

"But every country thinks its special. That's why none of them are."

"You're almost right. As I understand it, citizens of the Athenian democracy thought they were exceptional because of a special blessing *to them specifically* from the goddess their city was named after. Christendom believed all humans were sacred and inviolable – not so much for themselves but because they were stamped with the likeness of God. But then – there are the Americans."

"Them again!"

"They truly are an exceptional nation. Not, I hasten to add, because they have exceptional 'national' characteristics – they don't. It's because they were the first people to say, '*We share our certain rights with all persons in every place.*'"

"Didn't other people say that?"

"Individuals. Lady Calthrop quoted Rousseau—"

"Whoever he was."

"—that no country was ever founded without religion as its base."

"Or, melted, as you pointed out."

"Oh, be quiet. She wanted to prove that statement untrue. Well, it already has been proven untrue. The United States of America was the first country founded on the principle that *all* human beings, from the highest to the humblest, possess identical, and unalienable, human rights. True, there is an unmistakable Christian influence in the idea that all men are special just because they are."

"In the image of God, as you said. And a grubby image it is, sometimes."

"Yes. But the United States rose from the yoke of oppressive colonization to become a great nation because of the ideal that *all persons, whatever soil they were born on, whatever their outward circumstances, have identical – and intrinsic – rights*. They have these rights regardless of their nationality or race or gender or salvic condition. They have those rights whether they are rich or poor. *They have those rights for no other reason than because they were conceived and born and live and are who they are.* That was the new idea that a new nation was founded upon. In Mister Lincoln's words '*a new nation, conceived in liberty and dedicated to the proposition that all men are created equal.*' That is why America is exceptional. And sometimes I think the exceptional ideas America was based on are all that keeps the entire world from being one, big, hierarchical class system, like a beehive, with workers on the bottom and warrior or guardian bees above – and a queen bee perched on top."

"You seem to know a lot about our cousins over the pond."

"I'm half-American. Oh, close your jaws. I thought you mightn't guess that. My mother was born and bred in the state of Georgia, within 'a whoop and a holler' from a city called Savanna. Being American, goodness knows what sort of blood she had pumping in her veins. America is a mongrel country held together by the glue of Constitutionally guaranteed individual freedoms. When Americans say they are patriots, they certainly aren't referring to their dirt; they mean they love their individual freedoms, and the right of others to exercise their freedoms, to the extent that they would die for them. As they proved in their recent war."

"I wondered why you were always prattling on about them."

"My mother taught me well. That's why we have them. To teach us right."

"And while some Americans repeated the jargon of Liberty, they kept slaves."

"Nothing turns on a sixpence. That sort of liberty was – and remains – a novel idea. But they got around to rectifying the situation."

"And it doesn't bother you that they took so long to address the situation?"

"My mother was a southerner, so maybe some of my ancestors dealt in slaves. I neither know, nor care. It was all over and done with fully ten years before I was born. Anyone who feels guilt for something they were not responsible for needs to visit his friendly, neighborhood alienist. Slavery existed everywhere through history – but Americans actually died to abolish it. The United States was formed in 1789. Therefore, under their flag as a nation, they endured slavery—"

Closing her eyes to think better, she did a quick count off her fingers.

"—seventy-six years. Already, there has been no slavery in the United States for thirty-two years. In the year – oh! – 1941, the United States, under their Constitution, will have existed as long without slavery as they did with it. In another hundred years, when everyone who ever owned or sold or bought a slave is dead – and their children, and their grandchildren – this new 'original sin' of slavery will cease to be relevant. Why, America may one day have a president of African descent. He'll be a Republican, of course, as they were the party of abolition, and I'm sure only the most despicable among them will even note anything so superficial as his – or her – pigmentation."

"Miss Trickett, you rely too much on reason. You don't understand how precious a man's grudge is to him. Especially in America, where a feud can break out because of what one's great-grandfather did. Lots of Scots in America."

"What's that got to do with it?"

"You know what the Scots are like. The MacCambells and the Glencoes can start killing each other because someone stole a pig in the time of MacBeth."

"Mister Strangways, I will not sit here and listen to foolishness. If you are just going to run people down, you may leave and I'll go back to work."

"No, please! I was just saying – America isn't perfect."

"Perfection is an attribute of God. The American Revolution is *still* the only Revolution that has not simply exchanged one form of tyranny for another. Charles I for Cromwell; Louis XVI for Napoleon. Americans threw off a tyranny, and colonization, and established rule by consent of the governed."

"What is a tyranny, anyway?"

"It's where the people fear the government, because it is greater. In America, the people are greater than the government. They are still struggling to implement the grand design, but they've always espoused equality – not equality of outward circumstances, which is impossible and impractical and desirable only to lunatics. When they say 'equality' they mean the equal intrinsic worth of each individual. Their Constitution guarantees each individual identical freedoms. To say what they jolly want. To worship when and where and what they choose, and if. To peacefully assemble. To publish what they want even if it's against a current administration. To protect themselves – by force of arms, if necessary. And to exercise that liberty which allows every individual to strive to improve their own lot by work of their own two hands – even if that struggle seems doomed."

Herron didn't think he would strive to work at anything that seemed doomed.

"It's not quite the same with us British," she grinned. "We've died to stop slavery in various parts of the world, but at home we're too caste-conscious, thinking various ranks in society are different in their intrinsic worth. For instance, Lady Calthrop thinks you're a glorified shopkeeper and Dapifer wanted to make you the tradesmans entrance."

Herron fumed. "I'll take that from a Lady, but I'll be dashed if a butler—"

"In America, anyone can come in through the front door – if they wipe their feet and don't spit on the floor. Still, we British, at least, are not affected by 'soil.' We are spread over the globe in all colors and nationalities. And 'English' blood is really the blood of Vikings and Normans; Britons, Romans and Celts."

Herron had never thought of his blood with that perspective.

"I may be only half-English, and I may have a soft spot for America, but I was born and reared *here*. I am a British citizen. I'm a patriot for Britain – not just for dirt colored on a map, but, for the rights inherent in my British heritage. Though, ironically, I only know my rights by learning them from my American heritage."

"Sort of the way I only got the hang of English grammar by taking Latin. You talk a good fight, Miss Trickett. But you can't even vote for your rights."

"Mister Strangways, one doesn't vote for rights, since rights do not derive from any government. They are inherent in our nature as human beings."

"Only if you believe in God."

"Don't tell me – you don't believe in a God? Not even of any kind?"

"I'm not qualified to have an opinion. But I believe in governments, and they can always strip rights away from their citizens."

"The best governments exist by the consent of the governed."

"Which implies voting. Would you like the vote?"

"Certainly! But . . . tell me the distinction between liberty and democracy?" Herron shook his head. "Is there one?"

"A big one. Freedom is God-given. Humankind is free – because it is. *Ipso facto*, to use some of the little Latin I have. God provides every man the liberty to go to Hell his own way, if you'll pardon my phrasing it quite in those terms. God tells us in Scripture what He prefers we do, but we're not forced to do it, like automata. God lets us built our own roads to utter damnation."

"Surely," said Herron, getting back at her when he brought up superlatives, "'damnation' needn't be modified?"

"True. Sorry. God gives us liberty. Liberty is the ability *of the individual* to do and say and think. This Liberty can thrive without democracy – in fact, through most of history it's had to, where it's existed at all."

"And Democracy?"

"As I understand it, true 'democracy' is fifty-one percent of the voting public dictating to the other forty-nine percent how to live."

"Only where one hundred percent of the people vote. Otherwise, I suppose it's a very small group that lords it over the bulk of the population."

"Yes. And in countries when there is no freedom, 'democracy' is altogether a meaningless pantomime. *Voting, in a free country, is speech.* In an unfree country – well, a vote cast under intimidation is worthless. What use is the vote, if their government denies them their God-given freedom to dissent? It's the government sucking the meat out of the egg and leaving the shell for us. I don't want to earn the vote only in an outward show of 'democracy' – and then being denied my God-given right to speak my God-given mind."

"I don't even know why women want the vote. It only changes one group of crooks and charlatans for another. I can vote, but I never do."

Angelica was aghast. "You don't!" "No. It's a lot of trumpery."

"Mister Strangways, people have died to secure you the ability to vote."

"I didn't ask 'em to. Besides, as you keep saying – I'm rich. If I want laws that better my life or my business—well, I have plenty of friends in Parliament. Both houses. All parties. Politicians *are* all the same, Miss Trickett. Whether Tory or Liberal or whatever, they will give me a hearing because of my money."

"And you *buy* laws favorable to yourself? That's reprehensible."

"Isn't it, though? All politicians want is to reach into my pockets and make free with the contents of my trousers."

"Mister Strangways!" Angelica looked demurely away.

"My money, I mean. Believe me, if I didn't push sacks full over the transom, they would take it in other ways. They'd raise my taxes – targeting me, perhaps. They'd pass any laws they could to keep *me* from enjoying my money if they can't. In America, they'd pass a law calling me a monopoly and break me up."

"Strangways' isn't monopolistic. There's Harrods', and the Fontaines—"

"Old Harrod is a greengrocer. Strangways' is a real store. But Parliament can pass a law saying you're anything, and that's legally what you are. From my heart, Miss Trickett—as far as politics go, I want no part of 'em. Businesses should stay out of politics – *and vice versa*! Yet I assure you, there's not one chap in Parliament who cares for anything in life higher or nobler than my wallet. They force me to play their game, and I'd rather play it when the rules are in my favor. If I don't slip them money on the sly, they'll swoop down on me and seize my money in a way less happy for both of us."

"How sad. For all of you. And the rest of us. But we live in a free country, Mister Strangways, whether we all vote or not. I can go to Procession tomorrow and rail against the Queen. So long as I don't physically damage her, I can shake my fist and call her an old ratbag all day long. I have the right to do so."

"You don't even have the right to step outside."

"That is not a fair distinction. This is my job."

"Tomorrow is a national holiday."

"This is a private residence. I accepted the house rules and am bound to live by them. I still have freedoms here . . . such as, to speak, so long as I don't hurt her with words. In my personal life I have freedom so long as I respect the rights of others. What did Shakespeare write?"

"God knows!"

"Henry V. *'Every subject's duty is the king's, but every subject's soul is his own.'* One day, God willing, I'll be able to cast a ballot—in the same way you don't. And I won't appreciate your going behind my back to pay politicians to do one thing, after I and my fellow citizens have told them to do another by vote."

"I'll give it up, then. *When* you get the vote. Will you vote for women?"

"Maybe. It's not a fetish. You see, I believe do in the equality of the sexes."

"Good! So do I! Absolutely!"

"Paul wrote, *there is neither male nor female: for ye are all one in Christ*."

"Er . . . if you say so."

"By 'the equality of the sexes' I mean women are just as vain and mean and stupid and rapacious as men. And politics will only make it worse. When women are elected, they will prove the theory that all persons who go into the business of making laws that control people's lives are the same. When I have the vote, I won't pay attention to a candidate's superficial attributes, gender or hair color or what. My vote will be based on whichever candidate talks the least nonsense."

"There's not usually much to choose between them. Must freedom come first? Can't you have the democracy first and then vote for freedom?"

"I thought we had clarified that. One final time—one does not vote for freedom. *My liberties do not derive from government.* But they may be taken away by votes, if a country votes in a scoundrel."

"Your mind is so refreshing, I wish you could vote."

"And I wish you would! I do not play games; and a show of democracy without freedom is just a game. It will come, though it may not come easily. Some may yet die for the privilege." "Which brings us full circle. Why should anybody die for a thing they can't enjoy when they're dead?"

"Some *must* make sacrifices for liberty so others may enjoy it."

"Did Brother Schuyler tell you all that?"

"No one *tells* me things, if by that you mean I blindly accept what anyone says, even a person so dear to me as my brother. I can reason for myself that if no one is willing to die for a thing, that thing will be lost for everyone."

"Why?"

"If a thing is not worth a sacrifice, it's not worth keeping. That should be clear to anyone with a modicum of intelligence."

"The notion is totally foreign to me."

Rather than reply with the obvious riposte, Angelica said, "You'd rather see everyone lose their liberty, rather than one person dying to preserve it?"

"If I'm the one – yes! Why should someone willingly sacrifice their life, and their rights, so someone who might not be so worthy . . . someone like me, say . . . can enjoy them?" A frisson shimmered through his frame. "I-I-I just don't like the notion of people dying for me. It makes me uncomfortable."

"Because you'd then have to feel gratitude? Or . . . responsibility?"

Herron thought she had summed that up just about right.

"Come back to the table, Mister Strangways. Let's finish cracking the code."

"Why? I don't how we can get any further forrader. Those words at the bottom make no sense. And I'm utterly flummoxed by the rebus!"

"What 'rebus'? Where?"

"That square or rhombus or whatever it is standing on tip-toe."

Angelica gave a golden, dulcet laugh. "Don't you know what that is?"

"No."

"That's the difference between men and women. It's why they need each other. Why they ma—" She caught herself before saying *marry*. "Mister Strangways, *airship* would never have occurred to me. Even if you physically wrote the '*rs*' down between *Ai* and *hip*, I'd have dismissed 'air-ship' as a meaningless portmanteau word. But I recognized this symbol at once."

"That square dancing a jig? What is it?"

"A diamond."

CHAPTER XXVII

Diamonds again!

Herron bent over the papers. He saw the diamond shape, once it was pointed out to him. "Aye-aye!"

"Pardon?" she smiled up at him.

He tapped the *ii* on the paper. "A friend of mine wondered if this message might refer to a terrorist action taken against the Queen's parade – which is tomorrow, the twenty-second; or the naval review on Sunday, which is the twenty-seventh. Do you see?"

"No."

"May I use your pencil and writing tablet? Thank you. You see, twelve is written this way in Roman numerals." Herron scribbled out:

xii

"Like on a clock," said Angelica. "I know that."

"Yes. This is twenty-two." He wrote an *x* before the *xii*.

xxii

"And twenty-seven is this." Below xxii, he wrote

xxvii

"The double-i on my half of the paper may stand for tomorrow, the twenty-second – the Procession. Or for the naval review at Spithead on the twenty-seventh. Dammit!—We still can't narrow down which date they mean to strike!"

"Really, Mister Strangways, if you only hadn't smoked it! She stooped over the table. "There's something else here. On your side. Like that dot we found near *gam*." She tapped it with a fingernail. "The remains of a letter, you think?"

"Is it an x or a v?"

She strained her eyes at it. "I can't tell."

Not only was that area singed, the mark was tucked in a wrinkle where the cigarette had been crushed out. Herron wondered if it was only a speck of tobacco ground into the paper. "Why don't you use Her Ladyship's microscope?"

"She keeps it under lock and key. She doesn't want anyone 'playing with it.'" Her eyes brightened and she snapped her fingers. "But, if you recall, I am cataloging her flowers and skeletal leaves! I have access to the slides!"

"A lot of good they'll do—"

But Angelica had already bounded from the room.

She returned about a minute later, gripping a few slides like a squirrel holds a nut. "Mister Strangways, help me move this table over by the window."

They shifted the table to the window. Angelica opened the blinds.

She laid a slide over the burned area and, dipping her finger in her finger-bowl, dribbled a few drops of water on the glass over the double-*i*.

"The water all forms one big drop, see? And that magnifies."

"Good Lord!"

She knelt beside the table with her fingers on the glass top, and lowered her eyes right over the drop of water. "I can see the tips of both the upper and the lower cross-bars. A *v* would not have such a mark at its base. It's an *x*." She looked up earnestly. "It must be *xxii*. The twenty-second."

"They're striking tomorrow! They're going to drop an explosive device on London from an airship *tomorrow morning*! In just a handful of hours."

CHAPTER XXVIII

Rising from her knees, Angelica whispered, "Oh, dear God."

Herron, on the other hand, shouted a gleeful, "Hoo-ray! We've cracked it!" With the table moved from the middle of the room, he curveted around the carpet. "By Jove! Something that explodes will be dropped from an airship over the city tomorrow, possibly on the Queen's Diamond Jubilee Procession!" The appalling significance of that statement finally jarred on him. He stared hopelessly at Angelica.

In a hollow voice, she said, "London is full of military detachments."

"Armed with rifles and bayonets. They won't be much use against an object floating in the clouds."

"They have artillery! They can shoot an airship down with big guns."

"Miss Trickett, artillery shells must find their range. There will be misses. Are they likely to lob up shells that are bound to come down with a *boom* in the heart of an over-crowded London? They'll kill hundreds, maybe thousands, of innocent people – and dignitaries from nations the world over!"

"They can evacuate – or hit the airship before it reaches town."

"And from which direction is the airship coming? We can't ring London with artillery in that time. And where is the airship going *to*? Until we know where 'they' will strike, evacuation is impossible."

"The papers said the Procession will only be six miles long—"

"—that message doesn't say they're going to strike the Procession. It only says it will strike *the day* of the Procession – if we're reading even that much aright. I saw the map of the route. The parade passes some notable landmarks. We won't need terrorists dropping sticks of dynamite on the Royal Gallery or Buckingham Palace if the military blows 'em up first."

Angelica leaned forward on the table, desperately scanning the paper. "So where will they drop the explosive device?"

"I think it's *Resurgam*."

"Well—what is that?"

"I don't know. At a place nicknamed *Resurgam* an infernal machine will be dropped from the air."

"But is *Resurgam* a nickname the terrorists used, or that man who wrote this?"

"We don't know. One place hardly matters. If the airship is fully stocked with dynamite, terrorists can sit in the sky all day, lazily smoking cheroots and lighting dynamite fuses from them. And no one can do a thing to stop them."

Angelica was silent for a long time. When she spoke, her voice was deceptively calm. "Lady Calthrop said there's no such thing as an airship." "And medieval scientists said the Earth revolved around the sun."

"The Earth does revolve around the sun."

"Not now. Sure, so far as anyone knows, outside of American papers there is no such thing as an airship. That inventor over there, the electricity man—?"

"Franklin?"

"Edison. *He* said, barely two months ago, there was no such thing as an airship. I saw it in a newspaper. He said it would only be a toy, anyway."

"Then this must all be a joke."

"A joke," he hastened to point out, so she would not think he was pulling a fast one on her, "that the haggard bird was murdered for."

"What haggard bird?" She wondering if the conversation had gone off the rails.

"That's what I call that chap who had the bad manners to die at our feet Saturday night. He's the one who slipped us each half of his smoke."

"That man who jumped out in front of the train? Suicide, or an accident."

"Murdered. By one of several parties interested in our mutual cigarette. So, at least one man has died delivering this message."

"*To us.*"

"Well, not specifically *to us*, but that is how it turned out in the end."

"Murdered—how?"

Herron stared silently at the door, listening acutely, as he whispered, "A pal of mine said the haggard bird was shot."

"Shot!" She violently shook her head, brushing her shoulders with her loose hair. "Nonsense. Those Underground stations are little tin boxes. Even a small pistol would have sounded like a boiler explosion."

"I know. I don't understand it, either—"

He turned back to her – and saw her clenching her fists firmly on her hips and burning her narrowed dark green eyes into him. "Mister Strangways, if this is one of your pranks, I promise you I will hate you forever."

He stepped briskly over to her, extending his hands. She automatically reached out one of hers, and he clasped it firmly but gently between both of his.

"Miss Trickett, a few minutes ago you were talking about people risking their lives for stuff. A man died for this paper. He lived just long enough to give each of us half of it. For all I know, a long queue of people may have died ahead of him. I don't want to be next in line."

She responded quietly and sensibly. "There remain the words you mistook for Welsh. Let's crack that. When we have that information, we'll go to the police."

"The hell with that – oh, *pardon moi*. I'm going now! We've gone as far as we can go. We're amateurs – let the experts take over. What are they paid for, if we do all their work for them. Miss—oh, hang it! Angelica!" He swept up the cigarette papers in one hand and closed her fist on them. "Please keep these. They must not be found on me, or my-my person." (He didn't want to say *body* – not because the word was unbecoming in mixed company, but because he didn't want to think about his own *corpus* cold and lifeless as a beached cod).

"You can't leave them here. You'll need to know what they say."

"I have a good memory. I'm only just beginning to understand that it's useful for more than memorizing trifles from the newspaper. I wish I'd known how good it could be when I was swotting for exams. They really ought to let kids have fun and make them go to school when they're old and know more about life. Uh—I'm sorry to run, but I have to hurry to meet a man in my bedroom."

"What?"

"That is, I have to see a man about a blessed marriage certificate."

"*What*?"

"I—I'll explain next time we meet."

"But shouldn't we inform someone?" "I'll pass the information along. I'll let you know what happens tomorrow. Her Ladyship's tame gorilla may not let me over the threshold, but whether I show up merely to be turned away, or whether I send my man Merridew, or whether I telegraph, I'll contact you first light tomorrow. *If you do not hear from me again by morning* – or if anything untoward happens to you or to Lady Calthrop because of my presence here – please contact Inspector Broughton Chubb of Scotland Yard. He's a funny little bloke, but I think he knows what he's about."

"Could you write the name down down?"

"I don't want to leave any evidence I was ever here." Dropping her hand, he retrieved his calling-card, which Lady Calthrop had tossed carelessly on the side table beside her crystal bell. "Please remember the name: Broughton Chubb."

She repeated it.

"Oh, also – your staggering loveliness knocked it right out of my mind – the police are sizing me up as the haggard bird's murderer."

"Preposterous. You couldn't harm a flea, unless you were pulling its legs."

"They think I was playing a prank and gave the haggard bird a shove."

"Fiddlesticks. You were standing right by me and that man shot right between us like he had come out of a cannon. You had both your hands on your stick."

"You noticed my hands!" he said, holding them up with a rising heart.

"I noticed your stick," she corrected, folding the cigarette papers together and tucking them into a pocket. "It was gorgeous."

"A mark of esteem from my Club. Do go tell Chubb about my hands. That will stop the police from throwing a net over me. Chubb will have your statement. He'll believe you. I say, *can* you get out of this mausoleum in the morning to see the police? Or will Lady Calthrop give you the sack?"

"Mister Strangways, if this rigmarole of yours is even partially true—terrorists attacking from the air! Well, if I would sacrifice my life for my country, I ought to be willing to risk my position. It amounts to the same thing. If I'm sacked, I'll probably starve. But before I risk anything—!"

She stared hard into his naked eyes.

"I've heard too much about your shenanigans. Look me straight in the eyes and tell me that this business is really—real."

He extended his hands to her at arm's length, and she took them. Staring hard into her eyes was difficult for him. They were so beautiful they kept melting his firmness. He finally breathed, "It's a damned deadly business clear through. If 'they' followed me, I've brought danger to your doorstep."

"What danger?"

"I don't know. The more I know . . . the less I know. If you can sneak out in the morning, you may need someone tagging along who can handle himself."

"Dapifer?"

"I don't like the smell of him. Dapifer's more Lady Calthrop's dog than that flea-bitten terrier. Go to the Hemlock Club. Ask for Edgar the doorman. Tell him I sent you. He can punch his way through anything."

She wavered. It was one thing to read a suspenseful story for amusement on a tedious train trip. It was quite another thing to be thrust into such a story *in media res*. It sounded so outrageous—

—and Herron Strangways had such a shoddy reputation.

"Promise me, Miss Trickett, I beg you."

She studied his eyes for almost a minute before warily saying, "I promise."

"Promise what?" a gleeful voice cackled from the upper doorway.

Dapifer was wheeling in Lady Calthrop, who seemed delighted to catch these young people holding hands.

They started out at arm's length, but as they spoke they had crept incrementally closer until they were clasping all four hands practically beneath their chins.

Angelica ripped her hands out of Herron's clasp like she had picked up a hot poker; but she was clearly peeved at her employer and not at Herron.

"I knew you two would be up to mischief the moment my back was turned. What did you promise him, Angelica? What did I warn you, Mister Strangways? *No* assignations. You two must have sorted out the scribblings on that paper, if you're making love. But whatever your promises, there will be no covert amours in my house." She emphasized this point by hammering her bamboo parasol on the floor with each word. "Are you finished playing your game?"

"We are, Your Ladyship," Herron answered. "It's time for me to pop off. I only hope I haven't placed you and your household in jeopardy."

Lady Calthrop snorted. "You're dramatizing to impress an impressionable young lady. I believe you scribbled that nonsense on that paper yourself and slipped it into her reticule while she was standing beside you Saturday night, since you had no way to speak to her otherwise."

Angelica's eyes shot him a worried, sidelong glance. The suggestion was not impossible. And this story sounded so absurd! *A bomb from an airship–!*

Herron had a respectfully suave tone. It was often useful. He utilized when (for instance) he was caught holding hands in conservatories by aunts and guardians who materialized through the shrubbery like ectoplasm.

"I apologize if I led any danger here, Your Ladyship."

"The sooner you go, the sooner it will dog off after you. I think your visit has indeed lasted long enough, Mister Strangways. If you have sorted out your little word puzzle, Miss Trickett has other business to attend to. And you must have many more calls of a similar nature to make in the neighborhood, I am sure."

"Thank you, Your Ladyship." Turning his back on the ladies, he fetched Angelica's reticule and handed it to her by its drawstrings. Extended it the length of his arm, he offered her a comic bow, doffing an imaginary hat.

"Your bag, Miss Trickett. With my compliments. Use it in good health."

Angelica could not refrain from smiling at his sudden reversion to silliness. She thanked him gracefully – and wished she drop a cutesy curtsy in reply. But she could not act up beneath Her Ladyship's gimlet eye.

Lady Calthrop dismissed Angelica, who disappeared upstairs with her bag.

Herron inclined his head. "Lady Calthrop, I thank you for your hospitality. I-I enjoyed seeing your collection. I have heard so much about it."

"It was my husband's. I do not believe arms belong in private hands and I keep it only as a memento. On my death it reverts to his family."

In lackluster politeness, he asked, "If I may make so bold, what is your personal interest, Lady Calthrop?"

"The reconstruction of humanity."

"Oh." Herron wished he had his stick. When people said that sort of thing to him he liked to put the ivory knob in his mouth. "In what way?"

"Mister Strangways, do you know the length of the average man's intestines?"

"Uh, no haven't taken a tally lately."

"Twenty-five feet! Therefore, it's mostly full of food that is never quite fresh. Human beings are decanters of putrefied food."

"Oh, I say!" Herron was shocked by this sort of language.

"And there is so much ugliness in the world."

Herron agreed with that, though he did not comprehend her next comment.

"Twin babies born with their heads fused."

Yes, definitely, he required his stick to deal with stray remarks like that.

"So many ugly, squalid and unfit people in the world. And they believe in a Creator! Why would a beneficent Creator make something ugly?"

At that moment, Herron would have given unto the half his kingdom to tell her to take a wee keek into a mirror once in a while—

"This should be a world a beauty, Mister Strangways. And since it is not, it must be made so. The only real sin is ugliness. It must be eradicated for the purification of the Earth. A world where twins will not be born with their heads fused, where children with backward minds must not be possible. While lesser men call upon a Creator, the intelligent man knows there must never have been a Designer or there would not have been so much intestine. Therefore, man must be redesigned. A better society must be created where ugliness is not conceivable."

"Oh. Well . . . good luck on that."

Actually, Herron thought that was the most gimcrack idea he had ever heard. Since he was rich, prospective inventors were always pestering Herron with gimcrack ideas, so he knew one when he heard it. Lady Calthrop's idea should have won a prize. It reared up on its hind legs above all other gimcrack ideas like an angel topping a Christmas tree brightly lit with Edison lights. If anyone else had said it, Herron would have accused him of being brightly lit, himself.

But Herron meant to get on Her Ladyship's good side, insofar as she had one; so he nodded sheepishly and tried not to let a dumbstruck look creep into his eyes.

Lady Calthrop continued, "Health, you see, is a public duty."

"Oh. Quite."

"Good health is an obligation one owes society. When one can no longer give society good health, one has an obligation to leave it."

"And go . . . where?"

She gave a disparaging flicker of fingers. "Health *is* beauty. It is our duty to be healthy and to enforce health in others. To weed out ugliness, humanity, like musical instruments, must undergo a fine tuning. It is quite the *haute science*, the newest and most sensible scientific thing. Are you familiar eugenics?"

Herron shuddered, recalling a French *fille* named Eugenie from the Folies Bergere with whom he was very familiar . . . But Lady Calthrop couldn't know about her. If word of that ever got back to Angelica—! Or the photographs!

"*Homo sapiens*," Her Ladyship went on, "will never truly be perfect so long as men are made out of meat. However, that is no excuse to stop trying. You are smitten with her, aren't you, Mister Strangways?"

Herron felt a momentary panic – until he realized she was talking about Miss Trickett and not Eugenie. He tried to throttle off that direction of the conversation. Whatever Herron's other failings, he never discussed ladies openly. For all he told anyone, he might have been as celibate as the Pope.

Her Ladyship broke in again:

"You are smitten with Angelica because she is a robustly healthy animal. If she had exactly the same features, but lacked her obvious good heath, you would not look at her twice. She's intrigued by your shady reputation, but that alone is not enough for a woman. She sees your healthy, tall, upright body."

"I say!" he said, not liking to be spoken of so intimately by elderly ladies. "In any case, I intend to better my reputation."

"People cannot change, young man. People are who they are, in their race and class and physique. The late Lord Calthrop—" her eyes strayed to the crepe-draped portrait over the couch, "—spent many years studying the class distinctions among the lower races, and he drew many interesting conclusions. One of them is that we are all prisoners of our biology. Angelica might have proved a suitable *parti* for you. She is on your level. But I am *in loco parentis* where she is concerned, and I deem you a most unsuitable companion."

"But you agree we would have been a corking match?" She waved a dismissive hand. "Your father was a short man, I believe?"

"No. He was tall, but he had a counting-house stoop. I am taller than he was."

"Then, that is an advancement in the species. Angelica's father was nearly as tall as you. Angelica's brother is exactly her height. That is regression. He would not be allowed to continue at that height in a sensible, scientific society."

Herron smiled. It would serve Angelica's medieval-minded brother right if they sent him to the rack for stretching in a torch-lit dungeon. The way he must bore people with medieval history and architecture, Schuyler Trickett deserved every twist of the winch.

"Angelica is tall for a woman. Therefore, she is advancing the species." Her eyes became sly. "You may have heard of my own father? Count Roehenstart?"

Herron shook his head. He wasn't up on Debrett's.

"He was the son of the Duchess of Albany." She slanted her head to one side as if that angle helped her perceive him better. "You may have heard of her? Robbie Burns wrote a poem about her." She recited,

> *"Alas the day, and woe the day,*
> *A false Usurper wan the gree,*
> *Who now commands the towers and lands -*
> *The royal right of ALBANIE.*

> *"We'll daily pray, we'll nightly pray,*
> *On bended knees most fervently,*
> *That the time may come, with pipe a' drum,*
> *We'll welcome hame fair ALBANIE."*

Poetry was not Herron's *forte*, and he was unfamiliar with this egregious slab of it. He knew Burns wrote a poem about the plans of a mouse that ganged agley, and he wasn't too sure he understood even that.

"You may know of my great-grandmother, Clementina Walkinshaw?"

"I'm sorry, we were never introduced."

"Then, farewell, Mister Strangways" she extended a cold hand.

He took her hand and bent over it. "Not *au revoir?*"

"No. We shall never meet again."

"On the bonnie, bonnie banks of Loch Lomond. Very well, I'll take the high road. Thank you for a pleasant and instructive afternoon, Lady Calthrop."

Dapifer showed him out. Though he didn't grip Herron by the collar and the seat of the trousers, he looked like a butler whose fingers itched to do so.

In the antechamber, Dapifer said, "Sir's gloves."

Taking the white gloves that came with the uniform, Herron wiggled his hands into them.

"And sir's . . . periwig."

Herron clapped the wig on his head with one hand while reaching into his pocket with the other—

—and remembered he had no cash or coins on his person. When Merridew cashed his cheque at the Club, Herron distributed all his funds among the waiters, and the cabbie who had been paid in advance. He couldn't tip the butler.

And he couldn't take a cab home. He would have to walk through some of the better streets of London in his waiter's garb.

With an embarrassed bow he slunk away from Dapifer and out the door.

2

When Dapifer returned, Lady Calthrop asked him to carry her up the stairs.

He carried her up, set her up in the first story wheelchair, then wheeled her across the gallery overlooking the ballroom, to the door of her bedchamber at the end of the corridor. On her orders, he went to Miss Trickett's room, in the opposite wing on that floor, where he knocked with a softly-gloved hand.

"Come in."

Dapifer opened the door only slightly. "Lady Calthrop has had a most trying day, Miss Trickett. She wishes you to read her to sleep."

"Yes, I'll be right with her."

Angelica breathed a sigh of relief when he closed the door and left her.

When she first took the reticule from Herron, she was puzzled that felt much heavier than when she had brought it down. When she swept all her paraphernalia carelessly back into it, she might accidentally have shoved in some bric-a-brac from the table . . . but the extra weight felt like a brick from the side of the house.

On reaching her room and closing the door, she dumped the contents of her reticule out over the bed. It needed rearranging anyway.

She had been examining the clutter with dread when Dapifer knocked, and she toseed her pillow over the debris before inviting him in. When he closed the door, Angelica grimly lifted one corner of the pillow.

A revolver of the "bulldog" breed, and a box of ammunition to suit, it lay nestled in amongst her effects.

For the first time, she harbored no doubt in her heart that Herron Strangways was fully in earnest.

CHAPTER XXIX

Herron, meanwhile, was immensely pleased with himself.

His prestidigitation proved that if he could transfer a revolver and a box of cartridges from his waiter's tight pocket to a woman's bag without detection, a trained "dip" might easily slip half a cigarette into a man's coat and a woman's reticule simultaneously in a dark and crowded Underground train station.

Herron did not regret giving away his gun, even with what seemed like half London fee-fi-fo-fumming for his blood. He wanted Angelica to be safe, whatever happened to him.

Perhaps that's what it's like, he mused, scenting, for the first time, the fragrance of having something to risk his life for. *England, home and beauty . . .*

He revised the sentiment. *Well, perhaps not England and home.*

He had an inkling of why one man might go to a Cross so others might find eternal forgiveness – a thing that had never made any sense to him, either.

He certainly was not ready to endure *crucifixion* for Angelica; but if making a present of his pistol kept her flashing that devastating smile and laughing that golden, dulcet laugh – then he was willing to risk walking a few streets to his house without any more protection than his own two sprinting feet.

He tried to focus Jessup. He had so much to tell! So he wouldn't forget, he muttered the information he and Angelica garnered from the cigarette paper over and over. An airship dropping an explosive the twenty-second – tomorrow!

They did not know where nor more precisely when; but one can't have everything. They'd know where when they spied the airship coming.

He tried to keep his mind on Jessup—but on this street where she lived, he was unable to tear his thoughts totally away from *Cinderella*.

It was, perhaps, a regrettable fact that, in reality, all Cinderellas did not have a Ball roll into their lives. But if he survived this imbroglio, Herron was determined to see Angelica Trickett had one.

Or, if not a ball precisely, a new position. He had any number of Club and business acquaintances who needed paid companions for elderly relatives, or personal secretaries who could type.

Finding Angelica a new position was not altruism on his part. Nor did he see it as meddling in her affairs. Lady Calthrop made it plain Herron was no longer welcome in her house. He had to find Angelica a decent position in a home where he could arrange his rendezvous.

*Yes—dash it—*he admitted to himself, Lady Calthrop was right. He was smitten with her.

In all his previous experience with the female of the species he had maintained a steady equilibrium. Other men might fall into love like they had tripped on a top step they didn't see. Not Herron Strangways. He appreciated all the women he had known, especially in a Biblical sense, in a love-your-fellow-man-dy kind of way. Even the one he ducked behind dustbins to avoid.

What surprised him most was that he *didn't* want to seduce Angelica. That would be like holding a barn dance in a church. He didn't want to touch her, or kiss her, or hold her. He merely wanted to bask in her radiance.

Though she rejected any association with the song, Herron began to sing:

> *"She's only a bird in a gilded cage,*
> *A beautiful sight to see.*
> *You may think she's happy and free from care,*
> *She's not, though she seems to be—"*

He desperately wanted to see her again! But, given her *loco parentis—*
> *"—'Tis sad when you think of her wasted life*
> *For youth cannot mate with age;*
> *Her beauty was sold*
> *For an old (wo)man's gold—"*

A closed carriage rattled down Park Lane. When it was rolled even with Herron, it was pulled so violently to stop it nearly strangled the horses.

Two men rushed out from the long evening shadows of the Park, threw a rug over Herron's head, and bundled him inside.

The driver flicked his whip. The carriage rolled on.

In broad daylight, it took fewer than ten seconds for a red-coated and bewigged Herron Strangways to disappear completely off the face of the earth.

CHAPTER XXX

Angelica hated stuffing Herron's cigarette slips in her pocket, for they stank of low quality tobacco, slightly singed. But she had promised to keep up with them, and she was a woman of her word.

She had a few precious moments of freedom, before attending to Lady Calthrop, to make clean copies of those faintly penciled words.

After restoring everything to her reticule except the revolver and cartridges, she laid the torn pieces of cigarette paper carefully side-by-side on her bed – after spreading brown paper beneath them so their burnt margin and tobaccoy stench would not ruin her counterpane.

Crawling onto her hands and knees by the bedside, she reached under the bed. Her well-turn hips arched up and waggled lower the farther she eased her long body beneath the fringed bedspread. Her skirt hiked up, revealing a black expanse of stocking between the hem of her skirt and the tops of her button-shoes.

Soon, she was so far beneath the enormous four-poster bed that only her two shapely calves were visible, kicking the air and pumping her further out of sight.

Then her legs went rigid. Slowly, she wiggled out backward. Her clothes were wrinkled and disarrayed and her hair was dotted with fluff when she sat upright against the bed with her knees drawn up.

Angelica sneezed once from the dust (Doris never cleaned under beds).

Though she was alone, she yanked down her skirt. Even in the privacy of her room she tried to preserve her modesty.

Reaching her well-toned arms under the bed once more, she gave a final tug, yanking out a Remington Stardard no. 2 typewriter, with a shift key and a standard "qwerty" keyboard.

It was Angelica's own typewriter. She had picked it up second-hand and it was all the property she owned. On accepting this position, she was told all her needs would be provided for; but when she first cycled up Park Lane, the typewriter was slanted up in the wire basket on her handlebars.

Her job with Lady Calthrop did not require typewriting. She occasionally acted as Her Ladyship's amanuensis, answering letter and invitations; but Lady Calthrop believed in hand-written correspondence, and she appreciated the legible swirl of Angelica's cursive hand-writing.

The typewriter was her constant companion because Angelica wanted to write stories. That was the private aspiration she declined to share with Herron Strangways. She dreamed of supporting herself one day by fiction, and kept the typewriter close to hand in case the muse should strike.

It hadn't struck yet; but one never knew, with muses.

Quickly, before Lady Calthrop dispatched a second summons, Angelica heaved the typewriter onto the bed, where it sank lopsidedly in a depression in the feather-soft mattress. She sat with a poor typing posture, hunching over the machine with one leg on the floor and the other tucked beneath her. Rolling a piece of stationery into the carriage, she typed out the secret message.

She planned to duplicate the message exactly as it appeared on the cigarette paper, leaving gaps between the halves and bracketing the letters she and Mister Strangways had assumed. *Ai* [rs] *hip*; *Inferna* [l Ma] *chine*; *RE* [sur] *GAM*.

She was a fast typist. She would never be among the fastest of typists because fast typing required seeing words as nothing more than strings of letters, while Angelica wanted to comprehend what she read even when she was typing it. But the typing took her no more than a few seconds.

In her hurry, Angelica forgot that haste makes waste.

Her haste certainly wasted her stationery. She typed without looking at the keys; but it had been so long since she had typed anything at all, she positioned her fingers one letter-key to the left of where she wanted them.

Therefore, when she proofed what she had typed, "*chine*," became "*xgubw*."

She sighed. It was all nonsense. No – not quite *all*.

The genuinely inscrutable words of the message, *lomh p rt yjr esyrt* now read:

king o er the water.

Angelica thought "*o-er*" must be one word, but Herron—
—she caught herself. That was too familiar.
—*Mister Strangways* had inhaled the rest in a stream of smoke.
What might the word be? The burned space was narrow there. One letter? Ober . . . ocer . . . oder . . . She reached "v" before she found a word that made sense: *over. King over the water.*
Airships . . . rising again . . . kings over water!
Angelica buried her face in her hands. Her honey-blonde hair, now thoroughly unpinned, flopped forward over her knuckles.
She had thought, once they cracked that line, everything else would fall into place. Instead, the message was even more cryptic!
Angelica peeked at the message through a lattice-work of fingers.
What on earth could it mean?
Oh, a tenuous connection might be linked together between "airship" and "rising again" and "king over the water."
In her writer's imagination she fancied a monarch in full regalia, replete with crown and scepter and a red cloak trimmed with white ermine, rising again in an airship and floating like a cloud over water to bomb London from the air.
But what king? Over what water?
Well, she reasoned, *England is an island. Wales and Scotland had kings once, but no more.* An invading king – the Kaiser, for instance – must come over water.
In an airship?
Should she alert the Police? The Military? The Coast Guard? All of them?
How? Lady Calthrop did not have a telephone, and Angelica wondered if she could afford a telegraphic message long enough to explain it. And she wondered how she'd ever explain it if she didn't understand it herself.
She had come to London with some money. She'd spent little of it, since Her Ladyship met all her needs and her wants were few. Therefore, a telegram looked most likely. She would be more lucid in writing than in shouting over the bad connection one usually experienced with telephones – with an operator between her and the disembodied voice on the other end, like a medium at a seance.

No, she decided. She would make no move—yet. She would not panic anyone. Or make herself look foolish by issuing warning about the Kaiser possibly attacking in an airship and dropping a bomb on his own grandmother! For the Kaiser's mother was Queen Victoria's eldest daughter.

Besides, Mister Strangways was going at that very moment to deliver the import of this message to someone. Wasn't he? *Isn't that what he said?*

No, he said he was going to meet a man in his bedroom about a blessed marriage certificate.

Angelica's curiosity on that point was less than satisfied, but that made about as much sense as everything else that had happened on this most peculiar of days.

She determined that when Lady Calthrop dismissed her that evening, she would lock herself in her room and attempt to make sense of this message if it took her all night.

Even if she did not hear from Herron Strangways in the morning, and had to deliver those foul-smelling papers to Scotland Yard herself, she would act *only* when she had massaged some meaning out of the message – if one existed.

Glancing at the squat blue Royal Bond porcelain clock by her bed, she realized she had delayed Her Ladyship too long already.

Angelica left everything where it was – except the pistol. She couldn't leave that lying around! It looked like a toy, but even small guns had loud bangs. Angelica meant to hurt no one before she had to.

Angelica knew a little about firearms. She broke the revolver open to see if it was loaded. Yes, it was. Seeing no reason it should be loaded until she had a target to shoot at, she extracted the cartridges for safety.

Snapping it shut, she slipped it into one of her deep skirt pockets.

She slipped the cartridge box into the other pocket. In Lady Calthrop's dark room, she would never see the lumps in Angelica's pockets. Leaving the typewriter and the papers *in situ*, she threw her pillow over them as a cover.

She didn't want the aroma of those tobacco-scented papers transferred to her pillow . . . But if they were important enough for haggard birds to die for, they ought to remain hidden. She'd send her pillow cases to be laundered tomorrow. She wasn't expecting to sleep tonight, anyway.

She doubted anything would happen to the papers . . . but she had once read a novel to Lady Calthrop about a miserly weaver who had his gold stolen the one night he did not lock his door; and she had taken that lesson to heart.

Locking her bedroom door with her key, she dropped the key into the pocket with the cartridges. She was in such a hurry, she neglected her hair.

It swung free down her shoulders and back, though she swept away the stray locks dangling in her face and tucked them precariously behind her ears.

Angelica's bedchamber was near the top of the stairs, on the stage-right wing of the gallery. Lady Calthrop's room was at the far end of the left-hand corridor. To reach Her Ladyship's *chambre*, Angelica had to cross the gallery overlooking the main entrance hall.

The gallery was decorated with a few, small potted ferns, occasional tables of bric-a-brac, and a small display or two of weapons, including two long, crossed daggers from the Italian Renaissance. Inexplicably, it also had a French painting of vague water-lilies that Angelica rather liked, but which looked incongruously pretty in a house where all else was coldly intellectual.

Pausing on the gallery and leaning over the balustrade, Angelica could not suppress a winsome grin as her eyes flicked over the ballroom. With all the weapons in the house, she wondered why Mister Strangways considered it necessary to slip her an extra sidearm?

Well, she was grateful for it. Most women who had male callers were laden with emerald rings or ruby bracelets or diamond necklaces. Angelica had never heard of a woman whose first gift from an attractive male caller was a gun. That certainly left an indelible impression.

It also left her normally placid nature a trifle disquieted.

She did not put it past Herron Strangways to wangle an introduction by waving a gibberish message before a gullible female, saying they two must decipher it together in the interest of national security. And once he had persuaded her that she had saved England—

She could think of only one reason a man would give the gift of loaded revolvers – which she might well use on him if he was lying to her. Some earnest danger loomed in the offing. If Mister Strangways thought the trouble was so dire and immediate that she needed a firearm that night—

She glanced down into the grand entrance hall again, as if expecting to see masked enemy agents, in cloaks and wide-brimmed hats, concealing themselves under the display cases or secreted in the darkened chandeliers.

A slight frisson of excitement shimmered through her. Continuing on to Lady Calthrop's room, Angelica feared the saga of Daisy Lill was not going to hold its reader spellbound tonight.

CHAPTER XXXI

It was just as well Herron had left the pistol with Angelica; the way the men in the closed carriage patted him over for weapons, they'd have confiscated it.

Once they were sure he wasn't armed, the men blindfolded Herron, tied his hands in front of him, threw him to the floor between the seats, and used him as a footrest. He bounded along in that undignified position until they left the city.

This time, Herron was utterly lost.

In London, one could count turns. Some streets were cobbled, some had been macadamized. A church with distinctive bells stood on nearly every corner.

Beyond the city, if they avoided towns, he might never hear a recognizable bell. And Herron did not know one bumpy, unpaved country road from another.

It was also impossible to tell if they went straight on any fork, or slanted off.

Since the men turned Herron over repeatedly while searching him for weapons, and he didn't know which way they'd originally flung him down in the floor of the carriage, Herron did not even know which direction they were heading.

They changed horses twice on the road, but that was all he learned. And that meant nothing. They might have gone a roundabout route no more than a few miles from London, rumbling through a bewildering maze of unpaved roads; or they might have gone fifty, sixty, or even seventy miles as the crow flies.

Eventually, after what seemed an interminable journey, Herron heard gravel crunching under the wheels, like the drive of a country estate.

When the closed carriage finally ground to a halt, he recognized the familiar footfalls of men walking with large dogs.

The men who had taken him prisoner yanked Herron out of the carriage by his ankles, so that he bounded down into the gravel on his posterior.

Herron had no chance to observe the house. His captors did not remove the blindfold until he was well inside the front door. His hands were not untied and he was hauled forward by his bonds to a room in the back of the ground floor.

The blindfold was ripped off so he wouldn't stumble; but Herron's visibility remained limited. If the house had gas laid on, none of the jets were burning. Nor was there a fire in the house.

One of his guides knocked at a door and called, "Strangways, sir."

"Come!"

The door was opened and Herron was shoved unceremoniously through. The door slammed behind him.

At first, all Herron saw was a paraffin oil lamp on a beautifully-lacquered walnut Refectory table covered with stacks of papers. Everything else was dark. Herron didn't know what time it was. This might be an internal chamber with no windows. It might be night outside any windows that existed. Or the windows might be heavily draped. It was just dark, except around the lamp.

Behind the table, an ostentatiously well-dressed and -groomed man in a tail-coat and a red tie leaned forward into the light. He neither rose nor greeted Herron in anyway. He did not even lower the pen Herron heard scratching behind the stacks of papers.

"Herr," he glanced at a few papers lying to his left side, "Strangways."

Herron gave a bow. "May I sit?"

The man smiled up genially. "No. You will not be here long."

He spoke with an unidentifiable accent. It wasn't strong, but its traces were unmistakable. His 'w' sounds were slightly sharpened to 'v.' And, to Herron's annoyance, his accent made the man pronounce "Strangways" as "Strankface."

"You have a thing we want, Herr Strangways."

"Do I?"

The man rose from his seat. He was tall (though slightly shorter than Herron) with thin, almost feminine wrists. A winning smile beamed out from under a thin, two-part moustache flanking his philtrum. The nostril-warmer, which probably needed a can of wax a day, did not stretch straight out, like Napoleon III's; nor did it curl up like the Kaiser's. Rather, the moustache sagged down but its ends boxed up sharply in an L.

Herron could not look the man in the eye. He was fascinated by the movement of the stiff moustaches when the man spoke.

"Two halves of a cigarette paper. You will commit them, please."

"Do what?"

"Commit them. To my keeping."

Herron's first plan was to play the nincompoop, a part he performed with considerable dexterity whenever relatives or officials wanted anything from him. "What sort of papers?"

"Cigarette papers."

"Turkish or Virginian? I prefer Old Dominion myself." Herron snapped his fingers. "Oh, sorry. Forgot my cigarette case. I was invited here in such a rush."

The man playfully wagged a finger at Herron. "Ah-ah-ah! You are in no bargaining position, Herr Strangways. You will hand them over or we will search your dead body. Inside and out." "What if I don't have them?" Herron cheeped, worried about the word *dead*.

"There are only three other places they are. In your home, in your club, or in the house you visited this afternoon." He gave Herron a reassuring wink. "All will be combed like fine teeth."

"Gone over with a fine-toothed comb?"

"That is what I said."

It may be what you meant, thought Herron. *God only knows what you said.* Clearly Herron had to watch his own words words with this one.

So, he was in the den of "they." And "they" knew about the Park Lane house.

Herron was doubly gratified he had given Miss Trickett the pistol. If any of "they" ransacked her house, Angelica had the chance to take a potshot at "they."

Nevertheless, by leaving the papers with her he had landed her in the soup. He had stood on the rim of the bowl and splashed her right in.

The man referred to one of the papers he plucked from one stack on his table. "You were also in a cab this afternoon, but you are unlikely to have secreted private papers in a public conveyance." Almost like he was finishing a joke, he added, "You're not clever enough to locate them again."

"I promise you, I do not have them." Herron scratched an X over the left side of his chest, where he assumed his heart to be – though he felt it moving up into his throat. "Nor," he added, truthfully but misleadingly, fighting to maintain his insouciant exterior demeanor, "do I have any notion where they are right now. I'm not even sure you have the right man. Whom did you want, again?"

The man produced a photograph of Herron. A good likeness.

"This is you."

With a huge sigh, as if he was tired of wasting his life in meaningless talk, the man took up another sheet of paper and wearily began reading,

"Strangway, Herron. Born, 1 January, 1870. Died, Monday, 21 June, 1897."

"Oh, I say—"

"Father, Eleazer Strangways, born, 1830, died 1889. Shipping merchant, dealer in tea and Indian and Oriental goods, including opium—"

"I don't think that's germane—"

"Mother—"

"Leave her out of—"

"—Millicent Strangways, nee Herron, born, 1837, died, January 1870, probably from complications in childbirth. You always were a troublemaker. Your father bought you the best. Charterhouse—Cambridge—no degree taken. Sent down—"

"Okay, you win. I was sent down."

"Member of many clubs. Here is a list." He flashed it at Herron, just long enough for him to gauge its accuracy.

"You've left off the Beefsteak."

"I did not like the name. You have done nothing since Cambridge except spend your father's hard-earned money. At least he worked – exploiter of the workers though he became."

Herron was about to correct the man's English by saying *employer* of the workers, when the man ripped up the picture and threw the pieces away.

"You used to be Herron Strangways."

"I confess. That's my name. So?"

"I do not know if your shiftlessness is clever camouflage, or if you are the useless eater you look, but we have no more time to discover which. Goodbye."

Herron's insouciant front began dissipating like bubbles popping in bathwater. "Where am I going this time?"

In a tone he might have used to describe an upcoming picnic, the man replied, "You will be taken away by persons who will shoot you in the back of the head."

His voice sank to an amiable confidentially.

"It is an advantage of a large country estate. Bodies are not so difficult to dispose of. In the country, one goes out shooting, so gunfire is not out of place if trespassers overhear. And there is plenty of good, rich dirt to bury you in."

"Before I d-die, will you at least tell me what this is about?"

"No."

"You're no gentleman."

"No."

"How 'bout a bite to eat? Every condemned man is entitled to a last meal!"

The man flashed his broadest smile yet. "Think, do, Herr Strangways. Is it not a waste of necessary resources to feed you when you are immediately after going to be shot?" He clucked his tongue a few times at Herron's selfishness.

Herron nodded. "I can see how that might affect one's appetite."

"Besides, I doubt you would enjoy anything I give you. I am a strict vegetarian. Nothing is served or eaten in this house, and nothing is this house is made or used from the exploitation of our cousins the animals. It is my deeply-held belief that no animal must ever be harmed to benefit a human."

Herron's jaw dropped. "How's that, again?"

The man turned away and pulled a bell cord by a rear door. "The callousness of your British women! They do not think of the pain inflicted on birds when their feathers are plucked out of their living flesh – for the adornment of hats! The American Indian hunted bison almost to extinction, driving them over cliffs in their hundreds. I have heard, Herr Strangways, from Mister Hawkins, that you had a genuine ivory knob in your stick?"

"Yes. Presentation from my Club, don't y'know."

"Do you not know an elephant had to have its tusks removed for the ivory?"

"Sorry. I don't know much about dentistry. Still, it's just the waste of a perfectly good pachyderm not to use his tooth, once I have it. You don't want the poor chap to have endured all that extraction in vain. But that's fascinating. I'd like to hear more about your ideals about helping our furry, little cousins. Except the elephants. They're not furry. Do tell me more. I am a keen learner. Oh, I should report that your people whipped up the horses to get me here faster."

Though he was regaining his outward nonchalance, Herron was frantically bargaining for time.

And The man behind the Refectory table knew it. He waggled his finger again. "You are trying to buy time and I have none to retail. This is no

American wild west show. No Buffalo Bill is riding to rescue you in a 'nick of time.' Why should we put anything into a brain that soon will be spread all over—"

Herron perked up his ears to hear a the name of a county or an estate.

"—the ground." The man consulted a large watch he reeled from a waistcoat pocket. "It is late. And so must you be."

"Be—?"

"The late Herron Strangways." He twisted his head to one side and peered Herron over with a sidelong glance. "I will tell you this much while we wait, I suppose because men will speak of their pass-times. We are architects, as much as was your Christopher Wren. Wren designed churches. We design societies."

"How interesting!"

"Please, no flattery. There will be a revolution in this country, Herr Strangways. It is one hundred and fifty years overdue."

"That long? How time flies. But the people don't seem to want a revolution just now. Look at how happily they're reacting to the Queen's Diamond Jubilee."

"The people," the man replied jauntily, "are like children. They lack the nuance to understand what they need. They will take what they are given."

"Don't 'the people' make revolutions? Pitchforks to the Bastille and so on?"

The moustache laughed indulgently. "Do not derive your history from novels, Herr Strangways. The French Revolution was made by the middle class. Robespierre, Desmoulins, Barere, Danton, Couthon – all lawyers from respectable families. Robespierre wore knee-breeches and wigs – just, ha-ha, as you do!"Herron's wig had gone lopsided in the carriage, and he hadn't had a chance to straighten it. Lifting both bound hands, he peeled it off his head and laid it on the Refectory table with so much care, it might have been Exhibit A.

"The educated, Mister Strangways, must lead the ignorant. The ignorant merely want vengeance. They have been poor, maltreated, hungry, oppressed. In the beastial way of such people, so long as they make their old masters poor, maltreated, hungry and oppressed under their new whips, they are happy. It is the intelligentsia who raises new governments from the ruins of revolution. The ignorant masses require meaningless 'magic words' – *liberte, egalite et fraternite*, for an instance. New governments need order. That means new laws."

"Oh, are you a lawyer?"

"I do not answer personal questions. The personal life is dead."

"What do you do if 'the people' don't like what you're doing?"

"In France, more than forty thousand Frenchmen died in what narrow-minded historians call a 'Reign of Terror.' Most were peasants. And a good thing. Poor people have more babies."

"So, bottom line, you want fewer poorer people, is that it?"

"The masses have their uses – all tools do. Our Revolution will begin with a demonstration of our power tomorrow. Long after, we shall tell the masses that *your* like saw them only as living fuel to burn for the engines of exploitation."

"Oh, I have a like? Which like?"

"You are a greedy employer making a fortune off exploitation of the masses. You see them only as replaceable cogs in the machine that makes money for you."

"And what do you see your useful 'tools' as?"

"Bees."

"Bees." Herron echoed, in a flat tone. The conversation seemed to have switched lines on him unexpectedly and he missed his stop.

CHAPTER XXXII

"Human culture, especially the masses, should resemble that of bees."

Herron, keeping a weather eye out for holes to insert his charm into the conversation, was disconcerted. "We are talking about *human* masses?"

"Just human, yes."

"All bees look alike. Don't 'the masses' have faces?"

"No more than bees."

"Oh." Herron rememberd that he himself had seen no faces in the crowd for the past fortnight, until Angelica happened.

"Take a hard look at revolutionaries, Herr Strangways. You do not see the dingy countenances of the poor or down-trodden. You see the educated faces of lawyers and gentlemen."

"Two distinct groups."

"They cannot be part of the Lords Temporal, so they overthrow the old lords and establish themselves as the new lords. As we will."

"Who are *we* when we're at home?"

Ignoring him, the Moustache pulled the bell-rope again, a trifle impatiently.

Grasping wildly for any wedge to jam into the machinery of his predicament, Herron said, "I always thought architects *built*."

"Architects destroy to build. Old buildings are demolished so new buildings may be erected. Or, like old Saint Paul's, burned down. That is the way great minds have always operated."

This sort of talk apparently sparked the Moustache; while they were waiting for an answer to his bell, he fell into the cadence of a public speaker.

"Nero wanted no more shabby wooden Rome. There was a fire. Perhaps an accident, perhaps not. Nero said, 'This is our moment' and he seized upon it. From the smoldering remains of a squalid wooden town rose the marble metropolis we recall as Rome.

"Christopher Wren submitted his proposals for rebuilding old Saint Paul's Cathedral on May Day, 1666. On 27 August, after a close and argumentative vote, the committee assented to Wren's plans to tear down – I repeat, *tear down* – the central tower of the old Church of Saint Paul, and replace it with a dome. Less than a week later, on 2 September, the Great Fire of London started – so they say – in a baker's house. London burned for days. And old Saint Paul's—"

He lifted up his hands and flowered out his fingers.

"Poof. Gone. Burnt, so there would be no dissent. Reactionary fools might have objected to tearing down part of their Cathedral. No one would object to Wren's carting off blackened rubble of the entire Cathedral and replacing it with a structure he had on the drawing-board. The Great Fire was most convenient."

"The Great Fire wasn't convenient for those who were charred in their beds."

"They matter not. The new London was Wren's as surely as the new Rome was Nero's. Did Nero and Wren spark the fires to destroy the old, so the new might rise from the cinders, like the Phoenix? Or did these great men not want to waste a good crisis? There are stories of incendiaries spreading more fires *during* Great Fire of London. Such stories were also current in Rome. Were they Wren's minions, and Nero's? Were they ensuring complete destruction, ignoring the death toll for the betterment of the community as a whole?"

Herron assumed these were rhetorical questions. They were.

"The building you were taken to by my associates, the night of the 'accident' at the Underground station, was meant to be demolished, no? So a clean new building might be erected that was of better use to the community. To build, Herr Strangways, one *must* destroy. True?"

In his role as convert, Herron nodded rapidly. "Righty-o. Sounds reasonable."

"That rule also serves for human beings. For some to live, others must die."

CHAPTER XXXIII

Herron didn't want to make a madman madder by correcting him, but a slender hope existed that the Moustache might listen to a tremulous voice of Reason.

Like a man sticking a toe in water to test its temperature, Herron said, "Does that invariably follow? Please enlighten me where I'm wrong. It sounds like you're saying when you earn a pound on the exchange, someone must have lost it. Economies don't work like that. Properly nurtured economies grow. *Everyone* may earn pounds as businesses expand. Or lose them, worse luck, since there's invariably a bally 'correction' in the market sooner or later. Now, with people—"

"The planet is overcrowded, Herr Strangways. For the majority to live better and healthier lives, the minority must yield."

Herron supposed *yield* was Moustache's friendly euphemism for *die*.

The whole of the previous fortnight, Herron had been thinking there were too many people underfoot. The difference was, Herron hadn't wished them all dead. He just wished they were elsewhere, and having a good enough time to stay there.

"Overcrowding is insanitary. It unnecessarily stretches limited resources. Even when the government seizes all the wealth of your like, there will not be enough. *There will be no sea of humanity swamping our boats.* For the hygiene and health of the many, the few must die. In our new society, the population will be strictly controlled, so that we have only those people who are necessary."

"Who decides which human life is necessary?"

"The Guardians of the new republic."

"The . . . what, now?"

"The new republic. So the government will not be spread beyond its resources, the new republic must strictly control the population."

"Oh, yes, limit the people rather than the government, by all means. Do we have enough bullets for the backs of inconvenient heads?"

"Political power may be acquired by the barrel of a gun, but other ways exist to ease out of society the elderly, the infirm, the crippled physically and mentally. We euthanize old horses and sick dogs, do we not? And the young—well, a sapling growing awry it is easier to uproot than a grown tree, is it not?"

This had a superficial resemblance to Angelica's statement that *some must make sacrifices* . . . but she meant self-sacrifice. The Moustache wanted the new republic to choose sacrificial victims, probably against their wills.

And Herron had an unsettling feeling he was the first sacrificial victim earmarked for chunking into the volcano.

"I don't know horticulture," Herron said, "but I see your demolish-old-for-new philosophy. So, the old folks at home will be first on your list to pack their grips and shuffle off?"

"Old growth must be timbered so it does not choke out new, or there will be no forests in the future. It is time for the elderly to look to the end of life, and yield if they are no longer productive members of society."

"Only productive members need apply?"

"*Ja.*"

"What sort of government is it?" Herron forced an excitedly expectant look into his eyes, as if he was thinking it was about time something new toddled up.

"You probably consider governments primarily as protectors, with their police and military keeping order against enemies, foreign and domestic."

"I did suppose," Herron answered, almost apologetically, "that if a government ever rolled up its sleeves and got down to work, its first priority might be to fend off enemies. For a little thing called 'existence', don't y'know."

"Our true enemies are hunger and cold and nakedness and poverty and want."

"Extremely laudable. I approve. Here's what I want—"

"Those are the enemies we will fight with our *kulturkampf*."

"I can't see eye to eye with that, I'm afraid."

"You are a traditionalist?" "No. I'm just not much for German. What was that word again?"

"The culture's history and tradition must be changed."

"How do you change a history?"

"That is simple enough. No one knows much history."

"True. I only picked up on the salacious bits, myself."

"We revise history to suit our requirements. Traditions are more difficult. People follow their shibboleths long after forgetting how they began. They do not like to change traditions even when they no longer know what they mean."

"Well, shouldn't they be looked at case-by-case? You don't want to throw the baby out with the bath water."

The man pounded the table. "In our war for pitiless benevolence, babies must be tossed out if they are in the luke-warm bath water of tradition."

Herron did not care much for babies, so on a literal level he wasn't distressed overmuch by that image. "Which way will your – what was it? – yes, thank you, your *kulturkampf* aim your guns? At foreign enemies, or domestic?"

"At property."

"Of course."

"*La propriete, c'est le vol!*"

"I think I missed that serve. 'The property, she is the thief?'"

"No, no. owning property is theft."

"I think it's closer to the mark, old man, to say *stealing* property is theft. Well, it's a free country and we may agree to disagree on small points, and still, I hope, remain friends. But doesn't property represent freedom? To my way of thinking, 'freedom' is a man going out and doing whatever he wants – and making as much as he can cram in his pockets for doing it."

"Rubbish."

"Yes, if one wants to cram rubbish in his pockets, that's freedom. However, I am flexible enough to be persuaded to your point of view."

2

Herron preferred being figuratively open-minded to having a bullet blast a yawning hole in his skull. He'd be Mr. Moustache's right-hand man if he could talk his way into it – until he saw an opportunity to leg it out of there.

Nevertheless, this was a sore point with him. Herron had met many men of this kidney. They wanted a revolution where no one would be rich – except, of course, themselves.

Oh, they talked a good game. They preached that everyone should have a level amount of water in their buckets – but only so long as they controlled the spigots. Herron was rich, but he didn't want to keep other people from being rich. So far as he was concerned, the more, the merrier. The wealthier society was, the more people would buy from Strangways'.

Herron wanted to control no one else's life or wealth. All he asked in life was that no one try to manipulate him or his.

Because he was wealthy, he had been on the receiving end of this sort of cant often – and some of it had been deucedly personal. *Why,* he wondered, *do some folks need to make politics so vitriolic?*

Herron was not from a propertied class. The only land he possessed lay beneath his stores. But his stores were his babies. Unlike most babies, Herron's babies made money for *him*. He didn't want them tossed out with any bathwater. Sure, he spent his money freely. But, on the advice of his Scottish manager, Grouse, he sowed a sackful of his profit back into his business. When his profits allowed him expand, he expanded, opening more stores – and creating genuine jobs, so more people could pay for the upkeep of their more fleshly babies.

And no one ever showed Herron the least appreciation for it.

Once, when he was an adolescent, his aunt had dragged Herron to a play about a merchant in Venice, where Herron feared he might be forced to gnaw his own leg off to survive. He tried to put this traumatic episode behind him, but a few of the play's pithier sentiments stuck in his head. Just now, he recalled the lines,

> *You call me misbeliever, cut-throat dog,*
> *And spit upon my Jewish gaberdine,*
> *And all for use of that which is mine own.*

The character who said that (his aunt explained afterward, in the debriefing) was of Hebrew persuasion, against which there was prejudice in Elizabethan days.

As an adult, Herron had many friends business associates who were Jewish and he knew for a fact that anti-Jewish feeling was not limited to the Elizabethan theater. As the world prepared to whip round the corner into the twentieth century, Herron sensed a rising tide of anti-Semitism among left-leaning anti-establishment types. They pointed to high-profile cases, like the Rothschild banking family or Tory Prime Minister Disraeli. They alleged a lot of unhinged "Jewish conspiracies" consisting of banking, financial and even military cabals.

No personal Devil existed in Herron's paper-thin theology; but if anything in the world was satanic to him, it was this anti-Jewish prattle.

While acknowledging the anti-Jewishness aura of the play he had witnessed, it nevertheless seemed him that these days it was the *Merchants* who were increasingly spat upon and kicked as curs – or robber barons.

Herron himself was a target of personal hate from many sides.

In England, with a landed class who disdained business, and who devoutly believed money should be married for, the Strangways family might purchase their way into good Society. But the aristocracy who invited Herron to tea still looked down on him as a glorified storekeeper who should know his "place."

The poor, on the other hand, perceived the Strangwayses as robbers. Because they had money, it was assumed they got it in the same manner as highwaymen. The Strangways earnings came by hard work and thrift – at least, the hard work and thrift of Herron's forebears. But a general impression lingered that the Strangwayses and their ilk were Robin Hood in reverse – robbing from the poor and giving to the rich. This was hogwash, of course, and thin hogwash served up cold; but it was an *idée fixe* impossible to rectify.

Herron was therefore the scorn in both the upper and lower classes in England – and the envy of both, since both classes wanted his money.

Herron had spent many recent months in America, meeting with American businessmen and observing their practices (both at business and in the saloons). There, he had witnessed the attitudes Americans exhibited to those who owned steel mills, who extended railroads, who produced oil.

With freedoms in America they lacked in England, and no layer-cake class structure, businesses were the merrily-running engines of robust economic times – and employment. Without employment, hunger and poverty held sway.

And in America, men and women were ostensibly free to achieve their best without a landed upper class keeping them in their "place."

Yet even in America, a rising aristocratic class, the politicians (who adopted an English-aristocrat scorn for tradesmen) erected barriers in the path of mercantile achievement, and stoked the fires of hatred in their citizens for employers.

Everyone wanted more jobs in this increasingly technological world; but everyone hated, and tried to do down, the very tycoons who opened and maintained the companies and factories which made more and more jobs possible. *Fine*, Herron always thought. *That was only fair play. In a free country, despising the boss is a perquisite of earning a pay packet.*

But hate was hate, and Herron believed it all bubbled out from the same spring. He did not necessarily believe, as Angelica Trickett did, that the Bible was a gateway to Truth. But he had heard it said, *Whosoever hateth his brother is a murderer.* If the Bible was right in supposing all men were brothers, in the terms of that play Herron strongly suspected just as many people murdered Merchants by hate in their hearts, as murdered Jews.

3

Herron assumed that play he had seen about the Merchant in Venice was by Shakespeare (everything seemed to be, though he wasn't prepared to lay a wager on it). Recalling another good line, and he started to say,

"*Hath not merchants eyes, hath not they hands, elbows,* er—"

"Herr Strangways, we are architects building the *Wolfahrtsstaat*."

"Anything sounds invested with importance if you phrase it in German. What does that magic word mean?"

"It is a method of social justice by government intervention."

"'Justice' is a tidy word. Doesn't it look different, depending on the angle at which you peek at it through the bars?"

The man smiled. "Justice, in any society, is the advantage of the strongest."

"In France, it was justice to run a string of inconvenient peasants through the chopper. Who'll decide what constitutes justice this time around?"

"Justice will be determined by the intelligentsia."

"Oh, yes, you've mentioned them. And they are—?"

"Those with heightened intellectual superiority."

"Such as yourself."

"*Ja*. And by 'social justice' we mean that instead of a few owning a concentration of property and businesses while others have a pittance, the government will assume responsibility for workers' physical and mental needs—"

"So everyone will have a pittance."

"—and directing his industry. The public must be led, or driven, like any other form of cattle."

"Directing his industry? What the deuce does that mean?"

"Let us envision a carpenter. It is the socially just thing for a carpenter to ply his trade. There is no justice in a carpenter who does not carp. The government will take no interest in persons who refuse to work. Everyone fit to work, will."

"Where will the jobs come from if no one has a business?"

"There will be a fit worker for every job and a job for every fit worker."

"Oh, employment by slogan. How do you intend to arrange the employment?"

"By making work available to the masses."

The circular reasoning made Herron dizzy. "What about the unfit, then?"

"There will be no unfit."

"Oh? How will you manage that?"

"They will cease to burden society."

"Where will they go?"

The man did not answer that question directly. "In the crisis after the Queen's death, we will mobilize the youth with the cry, 'Ask what you can do for your new republic' – and when they ask, the new republic will send them."

"Wherever it can keep its closest eye on them."

"Ushering in an era of united service to the government, by the government, and for the government. And in return the republic will meet their needs."

"I'm no historian, but didn't 'bread and circuses' bankrupt Rome? I think I heard something about that in a class, though I tried very hard not to listen."

"We will give the masses more than mere bread. We will give them *hope*."

"Cunning. It's cheaper to feed people on hope than bread."

"The government will nationalize the bread industry to keep the masses fed."

Herron was amazed. "*Is there a bread industry?*"

"All the bakeries will receive their consignments from the government."

"That is true equality for you. *No one* has bread that's altogether fresh."

"No one will be making obscene profits at it, either."

Herron was aghast. "*Do* bakers make obscene profits?" He had never thought of money as an *obscenity*. In this culture, obscenity meant nudity or something fun. He supposed everyone had their own ideas of prurience. But money?

"There will be caps on all salaries, whatever the field."

"Got to keep those greedy hounds of bakers in their place. Will there be any cap on what the government garnishs from wages through taxation?"

"No. Persons die. Governments live on."

"And on and on. What if the rank and file don't rubber-stamp all this change?"

"The new republic values consensus over conflict. Therefore, dissenters will not be allowed to remain."

Herron wanted to ask *remain . . . .what?* Instead, he took another tack. "What about someone who doesn't want to work? I've employed a few of them. They seem to like payday well enough—"

"One who is unwilling to work as the state directs is a parasite. Parasites must be deloused, so they are not a drain on society's life's blood."

"What about a person's personal decisions? His private callings? His self-interest? Your carpenter, for instance, might just delight hammering wood. And, come to that, who doesn't? He might not find much carpentry where the new republic sends him. He might have to do other work for his stale-y bread."

"There will be no room for the *laissez-faire*, either in economic or personal relationships. Also there will be no *laissez-faire* individualism. The mystique of the individual will cease to exist. There will be no private callings or decisions, no locks on doors. Think of the new republic as a single factory, even as a single office – the state – with every worker working for a single goal. Not for his own selfish wants, but for the good of the organic whole of the communal health. There will be only the community, and in it workers will work as directed."

"Singing their work songs as they go traipsing merrily out in the state-run plantation. The Americans fought a war to end that. What if the happy workers decide to follow your example, and make a little revolution of their own?"

"Naturally, for the safety of the organic body as a whole, individual constituents in the society will be disarmed – for their own protection."

Even with his faint grasp of historical geopolitics, Herron knew every tyranny seized all weapons, so their oppressed citizens would not rebel against *them*. Totalitarian troglodytes probably forbade the personal ownership of rocks.

The man continued, "So there will be no impulse to rebuild a concentration of capital, workers will not be paid."

"Ah-ha! I can advise you there, from my knowledge of workers."

"What can you possibly know about workers?"

"I know they don't like not being paid. Where is their incentive to work if they can't curse their pay for being too small? Even professional procrastinators will shuffle off to procrastinate elsewhere, when they're not paid to shrug work off."

"Government will provide all their needs. This will end greed."

"Except in the government."

In unison, Herron and the man repeated, "Persons die. Governments live on."

"Yes, yes." Herron shook his head thoughtfully. "People like hard cash they can jingle in their pockets. You're not going to have many takers."

"A man who is unwilling to work must be willing to yield."

Work or die! Herron conceded, *Effective slogan. Extortion is always a powerful stimulus. Too bad I can't put signs like that up in the Emporia.*

"The masses will be given tickets for everything – for food, clothing, health services. This will help us fight dissent. If any person disagrees with our programme, he will get no ticket and he will be unable to buy anything. No one can buy or sell without our permission, from a loaf of bread to a cricket team."

"What if folks have a little gold hoarded away?"

"It will be of no use. No monies of any kind will be used in the new republic."

"You can't do away with money! You need it for international trade, if for nothing else. Y'know, I think you people will require my expertise—"

"There will be international currency, but no internal currency. Workers will be given tickets redeemable for their earnings. Eventually."

"With exactly the same amounts, I suppose? Since all men are equal, as the Americans say (and brothers, as Scripture will have it). Though, if I recall correctly, the first murder was an affair between brothers—"

"No, no! *Equality* is a myth. We say, 'From each according to his ability, to each according to his needs.'"

"Wait," said Herron, frantically. "That's from the Bible, too, right?"

"How can government take from each according to his abilities, if all persons are equal? How can we provide according to their particular needs, if all persons are equal? That dictum makes no sense if there is equality in the human species. Our dicta must be right. Ergo, men are not equal."

"'Provide according to their particular needs?' There go the self-sufficient, down the drain. If anyone doesn't need you, you don't need them."

"In the *Wolfahrtsstaat* workers will be paid according to their place—"

"I thought it was according to their needs."

"That would not be beneficial for the genetic hygiene of the nation."

"What would be beneficial for the genetic hygiene of the nation?"

"To eliminate poverty."

"Good. I'm all for that. I wish I had the shekels to make everyone a millionaire just by handing them bags of swag. Unfortunately, you can't just shovel money at people. You know how some folks are. They can't husband their resources. They make small fortunes out of large ones. They'd go straight out to watch the doggies run, and blow it all in a wad on a pooch with panosteitis. There, again, a few will parlay their piles into larger piles. Instead of all being millionaires, they would be billionaires and trillionaires. And the billionaires would start saying the poor millionaires are poverty-stricken and the trillionaires ought to give them some of what they have to balance it out."

The man laughed. "You have grasped that 'poverty' is a word of convenience."

"Not to those living in it."

"All words vary by definition from one mind to another. That is fundamental to the new republic. We will write laws as the people vote. But if we do not like the way people vote and do not want those laws, rather than change the law we will change the meanings of words in the laws. However, there is genuine poverty in society, and we wish to combat and eliminate it. *Ja können wir.*"

"Didn't some chap say, *the poor you have with you always?*"

"Let us leave religion out of it."

"Religious folks have done a lot for alleviating poverty through charity. The Salvation Army, the Red Cross, Forence Nightingale, er—"

"Charity does not eliminate poverty." "No, but I admire those who give to charity. Let them do it 'til their ears pop. Just so long as it's voluntary."

"Charities will be unnecessary. The government will take from one person's bounty, and will give it to another in need."

Treading carefully, Herron said, "I see two problems with that. First, if earners think their earnings will be taken by the government swooping in like a big bird, they have no incentive to make earnings. Second, if you nationalize all businesses and do away with people's earning capacity, how will anyone have any bounty?"

"It will be a gradual process. Until we can eliminate money in society and nationalize all industry, this taking and giving must be done through taxation."

"It would be, yes." *The government will play its thieving game of Robin Hood.*

For the governments to decide who got whose money struck Herron as similar to the government deciding which human lives were "necessary."

"I despise charity," declared Mister Moustache, with a wave of his fist. "It is worse than futile. It is *counterproductive*. It helps people survive who ought not. These religions and philanthropists are damaging the fabric of society with it."

"Then, what is your program to eliminate poverty?"

"The only viable method to eliminate poverty . . . is to eliminate population."

CHAPTER XXXIV

All that evening, Lady Calthrop was more than usually wrought up. She was so distracted, Angelica doubted Her Ladyship heard a single word of the Daisy Lill saga, even though she kept Angelica by her bed until nightfall.

Angelica supposed Her Ladyship's agitation was attributable to their caller.

Lady Calthrop often took immediate dislikes to persons, but never one so marked. Her umbrage almost made Angelica giggle, and she had to take especial care not to laugh while reading the dreary tragedy of Daily Lill.

About nightfall, Lady Calthrop dozed off. Angelica marked her place with a ribbon, laid the book aside, scrolled out the paraffin lamp, tiptoed from her employer's *chambre*, and scurried to her own bedroom.

Unlocking the door with her key, she opened it just wide enough to slip inside. Pausing only to lock the door and turn up the gas, she made a beeline for the bed and tossed her pillow aside.

Her typewriter was still where she left it . . . but the cigarette paper was gone.

It had been a lovely summer's day and Angelica left her window open to air her room. A breeze rippling in might have carried the lightweight cigarette paper off her bed, even from beneath a pillow—

Then she noticed that the stationery she left in the roller of the typewriter, containing a copy of the message, had also vanished.

That had not floated away on a summer zephyr.

In her haste, Angelica *might* have taken the paper out of the roller and put it absent-mindedly in "a safe place" which she didn't recall. She had done that sort of thing before. Her foremost concern, after all, had been for the disposition of the pistol. That might have distracted her.

But performing an unusual action – in this case, laying a pillow over a typewriter – had fixed the scene in her mind's eye.

Several times during her reading, Lady Calthrop had interrupted to inform Angelica that their "gentleman" caller (whom she never referred to by name) had seen her at the station, followed her to find out where she lived, and over Sunday concocted a cock-and-bull tale to gain admittance to the house. It would be like him, by all accounts she had heard from the young man's aunt.

He's ruined so many young women, Lady Calthrop confided.

And, Angelica silently tacked on, *so many young women are quick to let themselves get "ruined" by smooth, handsome and rich young men.*

Confidence tricksters, she believed, preyed more on the greed of their victims than their gullibility. In the same way, Angelica believed men like Herron Strangways preyed on the concupiscence of the women they seduced. Angelica had a strong will. She would not be humbugged by a pretty face and a lot of sweet talk. *Or by a moneybag, Mister Strangways.*

Even after discovering a gun in her reticule, Angelica found Lady Calthrop's argument persuasive. A rich idler pressuring his way into a respectable home at tea time, spinning an implausible yarn about an airship and national security?

Really, Angelica, said Her Ladyship. *You cannot believe such talk. An intelligent woman like you?* Despite its weight tugging on her skirt, she patted her pocket to reassure herself that she still carried the pistol. Without its reassurance, Angelica might have believed her employer – and she'd have hated Herron Strangways forever for lying to her. If that young man showed the cheek to speak to her in the Park on her afternoons off, she'd have cut him directly, looking him straight in the eye and walking by him without acknowledging his presence.

On the other hand, while hating him for deceiving her . . . she would have admitted that his falsehood had breathed excitement into a life which, she grudgingly conceded, had become almost as dreary as Daisy Lill's – lacking even the color of Daisy Lill's thwarted romantic escapade.

2

Angelica had entered Lady Calthrop's household with high expectations that her work experience might, apart from providing sustenance, give her fodder for the stories she hoped one day to write.

Yet this afternoon was the first incident that had ever happened on Lady Calthrop's premises worth remembering.

Angelica read, and wanted to write, stories with twists of mystery and adventure. Yet everything in this house was so regimented, the only mystery she ever noted was one Tuesday when cook sent the wrong sandwiches for tea.

Now Angelica had a genuine mystery: where were those papers?

Had she had not been convinced of Mister Strangways' truthfulness by the weight of a gun resting against her thigh, the disappearance of the papers would have tipped the scales in his favor. They had not blown away, and she had not misplaced them. Person or persons unknown had stolen them from her room.

She wondered why they had swiped the stationery with the gobbledegook she had typed with her fingers in the wrong place? The only sensible line was "king o er the water" – and that didn't even make sense. *None of it makes any sense.*

3

How had the intruder gotten into her bedroom?

The door was locked. She unlocked it when she came in.

No outsider could have scaled the side of the house to her window. Her bedroom window opened onto a sheer drop to the rear garden.

They might have gotten in by a rope tied to a chimney pot, but that was unlikely. *And*, she thought, *there is quite enough hullabaloo in this joint tonight without adding marauders swinging down from the eaves!*

Just in case an ape-man *had* scaled the outside wall, she stuck her head out the window. A glance was sufficient to prove no one had gained entry that way. Dust was thick on the sill.

That Doris—!

Anyone going in or out the window, whether climbing up on a ladder or swinging down on a rope, would certainly have smudged the dust.

She slammed the window shut against the night air and pulled the curtains. Turning and leaning back against the sill, her eyes slowly swept her bedchamber.

Angelica was not absolutely certain no secret passages opened into her room; but that was altogether too romantic for this prosaic house. The chimney over the coal grate might admit an organ-grinder's monkey, but that was all.

A narrow transom window stretched over the door, but it didn't open and its stained glass was intact.

Once more, she felt out the key in her pocket. She knew she couldn't have gotten in herself if she'd lost the key, but she had to make sure it was still there.

With the windows, the chimney and sliding doors in the wainscoting eliminated, the only access to her room was through the door. Angelica hardly ever locked her door, but she had tonight. Whoever had stolen the papers had come in through the door. Dapifer had spare keys in his pantry.

Angelica yanked the bell-pull. She hated waking the staff, but she decided to question Doris before charging the formidable butler.

In a few minutes, Doris clumped down the two flights from her attic room. She jiggled the door handle, then rapped on the upper panel.

Angelica forgot she had locked it behind her. She opened the door, and the gas-light in he room fell on Doris, wrapped in a red-plaid dressing gown. Her hair was braided down for the night. Still half-asleep, she wavered on her feet.

"Yes, Miss?" she asked, with a shallow curtsy. She was afraid if she went too low, she'd topple over. Her tone carried more than a touch of asperity.

"Doris, did you clean this room today?"

"No, Miss Angelica."

(Angelica had been certain of that, but she had to ask.)

"Have you been in here at all?"

This question caught Doris yawning and wiping an eye. Unable to answer promptly in words, she shook her head – and nearly gouged the eye out.

"You didn't clear any papers out of here? By accident, perhaps?"

"No, Miss. Lady Calthrop gave me strict orders never to touch no papers."

Angelica ruminatively gnawed her nether lip. Then,

"If you do ever do come to clean this room," (she said, rather pointedly), "and the door's closed, what do you do?"

"I knock. If there's no answer, I jiggle the latch."

"And if it's locked?"

"I knock louder on the door and say 'Miss?' and if there's still no answer I go to Mister Dapifer. He has spare keys in his pantry."

Angelica pursed her lips. Had Dapifer's carelessness allowed the spare key to her room to be stolen or duplicated by a house-breaker? Or had the butler himself been in here – rummaging around, since the papers were not in plain sight?

If Dapifer's been in my bedroom, Lady Calthrop will hear about it – if not the police. Invading my privacy, taking papers entrusted into my care—!

She started for the butler's bell-pull. "I'll ring for Dapifer, then. You will wait here, Doris, until he comes—"

"He ain't here, Miss."

"He ain't? I mean . . . ohhh!" She cut her eyes to the clock. It was half past eleven. "Where has he gone at this hour?"

"Said he was sent out on some errand by the old — by Lady Calthrop, Miss. He told me he might be some time and if I hear someone coming in late it'll be him, so it wouldn't scare me. He was still out when I went to bed."

Angelica was quiet so long Doris was afraid she'd been forgotten.

"Is that all, Miss?"

"What? Oh, yes. Thank you, Doris. You may go."

Another quick curtsy and Doris fled, hoping to get back to that same dream.

She'd been dreaming that her vocal talents had been noticed by a passing impresario who had grabbed her by the wrist, yanked her into the Savoy Theater, and shoved her right out on stage to star in a revival of *The Mikado*.

Unfortunately, Doris *did* return to that dream. When she started singing "The Sun whose rays" to a packed house, she realized she didn't know the words.

And then she perceived she was naked, to boot.

She stood onstage stumbling over the words – and fumbling to cover three intimate areas of anatomy with only two hands – until she was wakened by the gunfire erupting downstairs.

CHAPTER XXXV

"Eliminate . . . population?" Herron cautiously parroted, trying not to sound as distressed as he was by those ominous words.

"We will tell every citizen he has a right to a job, a right to a house, a right to medical care and food. Any man with a brain knows we cannot keep that promise to all, with the population in its current trajectory."

"So to meet your promise to everyone, 'everyone' must be fewer."

"It will not be easy. We cannot simply eliminate population by lottery."

"Oh, can't we?"

"No. As a first step, undesirables must be scientifically identified, isolated, and gradually eliminated by making no work available for them."

"Undesirables?" Herron tried not to say the word distastefully, but it was a word that lent itself to distastefulness.

"Ones the state deems ugly or fat or skinny or short. The crippled, physically and mentally. Anyone atavistic who might corrupt proper human breeding."

"Fine. First, we identify our undesirables. What's our second step?"

"Wages will be rigidly set, at a deceptively high *minimal* level for all jobs."

"A government-enforced minimum wage?"

"Yes."

"At a set rate everywhere, across the board?"

"It will vary. Comparable work will receive comparable pay."

"And when these minimum wages rise – and they will –what happens?"

"Workers will receive more money."

"Some of them will."

"All. It will be the law."

For the first time, Herron began to be combative. "It may be your law, mate, but it isn't the law of economics! Some will be making more money, and others will be making double their salary – *times zero*."

"Explain, please."

"Listen, I run a fairly large concern. Well, I don't, but I can. I can absorb a certain amount of your thieving taxation and regulation. But small businesses employ most of your precious workers. Not the huge cotton mills or gigantic ironworks, but just shops. All businesses, large and small, have rigid budgets. When the government forces a business to arbitrarily raise an expenditure in one area – in this case, employees – businesses can't just pull money like a rabbit from a hat, *abracadabra*. Or print worthless scrip like the government. They'll be forced, by law, to hand some workers the sack. Unemployment will skyrocket."

"Businesses may increase their prices to compensate."

"We can't arbitrarily raise our prices up a peg. We've got to peddle our wares at prices the market can bear. If prices shoot too high, folks won't buy the merchandise. They'll go where it's cheaper, or they'll do without. And it's easy to do without the exquisite, luxury imports sold at Strangways'."

"And a good thing. You lure buyers in and make them think they need these 'luxury imports.' It will serve you to lose business."

"It won't serve my employees. I can't keep them all on when the old firm is hemorrhaging money. When you run up with a hatchet and start hacking up my tree, you think you're hurting me – but it's employees who are shaken loose by the vibrations. You're putting more people out into the streets with no livelihoods. Added to your high minimum wages, you're forcing more destitution."

"Did you not start the destitution with low wages?"

"I'm all for every worker receiving a livable wage. I've given orders to that effect to Grouse, my manager. But everyone will lose, all the way round the mulberry bush, whenever arbitrary expenditures for employees (or anything else) are enforced by a crack-brained government fiat."

"You misunderstand the purpose of our minimum wage. We will pass laws ensuring all workers in the *necessary* population retain their positions."

"Oh? Oh! This 'minimum wage' will prove handy at further excluding your carefully selected undesirables from eking out a living."

"Correct."

"Even though undesirables have to eat, too."

"Why? You say you 'starve a fever,' do you not?"

"Y'know, I never really knew which way that ran. It could be 'Feed a—'"

"It is also important for the genetic health of the species to starve bacterial infections from the body politic. Either the infection dies, or the body. I suppose you are not picky about whom your company hires, Herr Strangways?"

"Not so long as they do their jobs effectively."

"Situated as it is in the beating heart of an empire spread over the globe, it would be fair to say that you hire those of various races and cultures?"

"We're branching out, but primarily we're a monger of imports. We need buyers on the other end who can purchase quality at suitably low prices, which we can sell them here for suitable profits. Our buyers must know their cultures. If they're part of those cultures, so much the better. And over here, I have a Scotch manager and an Indian head book-keeper—whiz at numbers, that chap. Don't know how he does it. Never so much as looks at his fingers or toes."

"And you pay employees higher and higher wages for better work? Bonuses? Extras? You are liberal with workers you deem worthy?"

"We want to keep good people on. The way to do that is to pay them better than the stinkers. It's my money; I can do as I like with it, and I like rewarding good people for good work."

"Even if it means paying undesirable genetic types more money than better genetic types, just because they happen to do their jobs efficiently?"

"If an employee does a day's work for a day's pay, he's an acceptable genetic type so far as I'm concerned. And a rare type, too."

"In the new republic, employers will not be tempted to hire undesirables to fill vacancies if they have to pay them at ever higher rates. That way, the problem of undesirables, and the poverty they cause, will be well on its way to alleviation."

"Through starvation."

CHAPTER XXXVI

"Starvation is – *was ist?* – yes, a *loaded* word."

"Did you want to eliminate the starvation, or the word?"

"Words have no meaning other than that which someone ascribes to them.""Good Lord!"

Herron was astounded. He'd never thought of that before. If he had only realized it earlier, he might have been saved a lot of bother with words like *love* and *marriage*. He'd used them sparingly and only as a last resort. He'd never been so free with them as to be charged with breech of promise; but a time or two he'd put his head in a noose that might've been drawn tight.

He suddenly realized how he might freely use the word *marriage*. All he had to do was believe the word had no ultimate, intrinsic meaning. If no Platonic ideal of 'marriage' was tucked away in another dispensation, Herron could keep his own, private definition of *marriage* in his head, and think only of that when he slung the word around. What *she* took the word to mean was *her* lookout. He felt like Copernicus. This opened a new cosmos to him. He *had* to live!

"Of course," the Moustache continued, "we may much more easily avoid ever again having a famine, such as the famines presently plaguing India."

"Uh? Oh, yes. That'll be a neat trick. How will you do it?"

"By redefining what constitutes famine conditions. And redefining how we collect our data. We may happily say, one hundred years from now, there has never been a famine in the new republic. And there is no starvation."

"Whatever their definition, it still means the people don't eat."

"True, but it will look better in our books for statistical purposes. We do not want to alleviate the reality 'starvation' for undesirables in the overpopulation."

"So they get no work or food?"

"We must – what was your word? *Ja*. 'Husband' our resources. It was generally thought before, where everyone works there will be enough for all, if only just enough. As your Saint Paul said, 'If you do not work you do not eat.'"

"Not particularly my Saint—"

"But our best estimates prove that is untrue. Fools like you still cling to the idiocy that all we need is for industries and shops like yours to expand, to provide more jobs for everyone. You invoke employment as the panacea for every social ill. Our studies demonstrate that even when everyone in a society works, it does not necessarily follow there will be sufficient for all to eat."

"What if your studies are wrong?"

"Our studies will not be wrong."

"I'm glad you have such confidence in them. We wouldn't want your studies taken out and shot. Did you do much field work?"

"Field work is unnecessary. Statistics do not lie."

"I think Disraeli said there are 'lies, damned lies, and statistics.'"

"He was a Jew."

Herron fumed, "What does religion have to do with it?"

"The *geldjuden*, the rich Jews who control everything that goes on in the government, must be forcibly dealt with. Otherwise, I do not care about religion, since it does not matter in the least. My reference was to his biological type."

"So far as I know, his biological type was 'human.' That's the sort of person I employ. I may be a bit of a bigot, but I've never yet hired a non-human."

"But there are human types and . . . sub-human types. The more advanced species of human, naturally, would show diversity – say, in hair color. Species without that diversity are not so advanced. But those types are necessary, as well, in a certain quantity. What we are most interested in are those humans who consume more than they produce. Do you read Malthus?"

"I admit, Malthus has never been my first choice of reading matter to curl up with on a wet Sunday afternoon. What did he write?"

"He wrote 'the power of population is indefinitely greater than the power in the earth to produce subsistence for man.'"

"Oh. Does that mean anything? In particular?"

"Population must be kept low or people will always outgrow agricultural production. Malthus noted, even in his day, that more people are born than die, even with pestilence and the scythe of war to keep the population in check."

"I thought the ratio of births do deaths was always one-to-one?"

"Overpopulation will be dire in the new republic, with no more war—"

"Oh, that's wonderful. 'No war' is always good for merchants. We're the first casualty of any war. Wars interrupt our trade routes."

"So you only oppose the shedding of blood in war only on a monetary basis?"

"It's good enough. Make money, not war. Why is the new republic anti-war?"

"We violently oppose war because we cannot control it. Also, we believe war is murder. All warmongers will be declared undesirable."

"And shot?"

"When we bring peace to the land, and our scientific policies end disease—"

"End disease? That'll be jolly. What's the plan for that?"

"We have docketed all diseases. Since there is no god and no creation, there can be no more diseases than we have listed. Everything that exists, exists, and no god can make more of it."

"No brand-new plagues popping up, you mean? That's comforting. There are quite enough as it is."

"The government *will* fund experiments to find the cause of each disease. When that cause is isolated we *will* find a cure." He made it sound like a threat. "Undesirables will assist us, proving that even they have limited uses."

"That's fine. Will they be nurses, or—?"

"They will be injected with diseases and we will experiment potential cures on them. By their deaths, they will save the lives of those persons of the species who will make a better breed. This will end the torture of animals in vivisectionism."

"I see you've given this plenty of thought."

"Unfortunately, the end of war means the population will grow exponentially. And when we end disease, people will live too long."

"And how will you address the crisis of citizens outstaying their welcome?"

"There is no god; but if there were, god would not run the government. We must. So the Guardians must be collaborators with the deity in matters of life and death. Undesirables in the state must be scientifically identified, isolated—"

"And starved."

"You keep injecting that word. There are many more expedient methods of paring off a bulge in the population statistics. We call it 'negative selection.'" The man gave a rather sad toss of his shoulder. "Is it not better that the people who die be chosen scientifically, rather than seeing the haphazard process of overpopulation destroy humans who may have more of a right to live?"

"Do some people have more right to live?"

"If they are beneficial for breeding purposes."

"Ah, yes, you've got to preserve the thoroughbreds."

"Undesirable breeds will be eliminated, but we will otherwise fight hunger. The new republic's strict governmental policies will ensure that the necessary population never quite starves."

At this point they heard footsteps shuffling behind the rear door. The door was flung open, revealing Stoker. Hawkins, his face browned from the elements and prematurely lined like a walnut, peered over his companion's shoulder with a flabby cloth cap drawn low over his eyes.

CHAPTER XXXVII

After dismissing Doris, Angelica gave her bedroom a 360-degree once-over from where she was standing.

She gnawed her malleable lower lip, thinking. She *might* have misplaced the papers herself. She was *almost* certain the papers were no longer in her room, but a *soupcon* of doubt nagged in the back of her mind.

Since she couldn't tackle Dapifer right away, she commenced a methodical search of her room. Even if the papers didn't show up, it would kill time until the butler returned. And she might find a clue as to who had been in her room.

Angelica rifled all her drawers, turned out her reticule thrice, and finally crawled around the carpet on her hands and knees, examining even impossibly small flecks of paper that Doris had missed in what she hyperbolically termed "her cleaning."

Angelica found neither the cigarette papers nor the stationery sheet from her typewriter with her spoiled copy of the message. Nor did she see any indication that another living soul had violated her privacy (especially not Doris).

Magazine detectives distinguished foot marks on carpets; but Angelica, whose eyes were keen, could discern only slight indentations. Upon comparison, she discovered those were made by the heels of her own high-topped button-shoes.

After rearing up from peeking under her bed for the third time, she sat with crossed arms on the floor, her spine resting against the bed rail and her elastic lips twisted in a grimace.

Rising to her knees, she stared out over the bed and examined the room from that vantage-point, looking for anything she had missed.

Angelica was a tidy person, though not meticulously so. Everything was more or less in its place (even after several searches).

Rising, she yanked the butler's bell-pull. Dapifer did not answer.

Despite the hour, Angelica was far too wakeful for bed. She knew she'd never sleep with the unsolved "Mystery of the Papers" rankling her. This needed deeper thought; and for Angelica, deep thought invariably required tea.

Angelica's mind was a bit fuzzy. It was long past her bed time. She rose at half-four every morning, and that was only five hours away. It had been an unusually trying day, since she'd had to entertain company. Herron Strangways had taken a lot out of her. She hoped tea would help her sort things out. Forget fish – tea was her brain food.

She had little compunction about waking Doris or Dapifer; but she would not venture into cook's lair and rouse that dragon from her slumberland. She would go down and make her own tea.

That way, she would be downstairs when Dapifer returned! Then she would have a word with him . . . !

CHAPTER XXXVIII

"What detained you!" demanded the Moustache, turning on them.

"Eatin'," said Hawkins, in his laconic American accent. As if to emphasize the point he picked green matter from between his teeth with a fingernail. "You feed us like gol-darn rabbits, but we gotta have sumpin' to keep our strength up."

The Moustache said, "Are you ready, Mister Strangways?"

"In a moment. Let me see if I have this straight." Though more than a little distressed, Herron fought not to show it. He had this man talking, and he meant to keep it up. "The government, advised by its Guardians, provides all jobs?"

"*Ja*. Eventually. There will be an unavoidable period of transition, but hopefully in fifteen years it will be an accomplished fact."

"Look here, as I understand it – and please, correct me if I'm wrong – cute little government make-work jobs sound to me like just another name for the workhouses. Fine. If changing the definitions of words haphazardly doesn't bother you, it doesn't bother me. Still, the government needs money for all these wonderful programs. The government, though – and I'm trying to phrase this as delicately as possible – does not, itself, have a job. Its only money comes from confiscatory taxes and rates."

"Money can be printed."

"And putting more money into the system causes inflation. In the Emporia, when we foolishly stock too much of an item no one wants, we price it down, lowering its value to move it off the shelves. When we have high-quality items that are hard to get in this hemisphere, we stick a high prices on them. The latter have move value because there are fewer of them walking the streets. It's the same with money. When there's more of it about, its value decreases – and, since merchants have to eat, too (at least until you guys take over) prices will rise. When pounds are plentiful, anything priced in pounds goes up accordingly, to compensate. You can't devalue your money and expect prices to remain constant. Printing more money causes inflation."

"That is not correct."

"It is."

"Is not."

"Is."

"You are no thinker."

"Agreed. I was just pointing out from practical experience—"

Mister Moustache waved his hand in Herron's face, like he was brushing away a fly about to land on his nose. "We cannot have objections to the ideas of our finest minds on the basis of something so insubstantial as experience."

"I'm only repeating what I've seen. Think of King Midas. Everything he touched turned to gold – fine. What does that do to the gold market? Right down the w.c., if you pardon my German. And if he sat in the w.c., that would be gold, too. A gold w.c. must be darn cold in the wintertime. You can't use gold for exchange when everyone's cellar is bursting at the seams with it and everyone's sick to death of it. When everything you touch turns to gold, gold has the value of dirt. I suppose you might say all the dirt where he walked had the value of gold, so to speak. Unless he wore golden slippers. What I'm getting at is, you can't just print money to solve problems. The more you print, as my old gov'nor taught me, the more you have inflation out the . . . well, we'd have plenty of inflation."

"Won't."

Herron was tired of running around that particular Maypole, so he didn't argue that point any farther. "I suppose, for governments, the word 'revenue' is invariably synonymous with 'taxation' because so few people in a government seem to have any experience actually running anything *except* government. If the politicians all had to go out and work for a living rather than sitting around on their Committees thinking up ways to spend other people's money—"

His sentence was too long and convoluted. Herron got lost, and started over.

"Anyway – let me give you a word of advice, because I dearly want to see you rise in the world. It sounds, until you can eliminate money altogether and have your institutionally mandated jobs, this new republic will simply demand ever higher taxes and tax rates."

"Well?"Herron had been administering what he thought tantamount to a symbolic kick in the slats. He thought everyone despised taxes and rates as much as he did. Instead, the man was unphased by the accusation.

"I-I know, this is only on the basis of experience again, but higher tax rates thwart the growth of businesses that create more real and lasting jobs."

"No, government spending will create more jobs than reducing taxation."

"I hate to take issue with you," said Herron, "because I've really come to like and respect you . . . but you're talking through your hat."

"I am not wearing a hat."

"Oh, my hat . . .! Listen, please! You need to keep money in the private sector. Taxation confiscates money from the private sector. With less money being sucked out of my pockets, I can truly help economic growth by creating jobs through expansion. If I found more money in my till because the government took less, I would open an Emporium in, oh, Whitby, say. If I don't' have one there already. I lose track. Well, wherever I set it up, it would employ people there. The more workers I employed, the more revenue the government could sneak from a tax base that would then swell like dough in an oven. It's infallible. If you jack taxes up too high, and especially if they target corporations, I may just tuck my stores under my arms and toddle off to America. It's quicker shipping there from the Orient, and America's brimming with *nouveau riche* eager to stock up on the sort of goods I peddle. If I removed my stores to escape a Frankenstein's monster of a tax code, you would cause even more unemployment."

"Mister Strangways—"

"No, please let me get to the punch line. What you need is *a larger tax base*. That means more people earning money. More jobs. More jobs come from more money in the private sector, rather than the government sector. Everyone knows the government's full of crooks anyway, and the expenses of everything they do is padded, while businessmen who have a bottom line to meet streamline their expenses, so everything done by the private sector costs less. When you lower tax rates on blokes like me who employ others who will make money and more money, the government end of the take grows. Easy as pie."

"That is nonsense."

"Perhaps you didn't give the proposition sufficient thought in half-a-second."

"It disagrees with me and therefore is incorrect."

"Oh, give it a chance. With a larger tax base there will always be more tax income, so long as the government doesn't go on a spree over the weekend and wake up Monday morning with empty pockets and one dickens of a hangover."

"Herr Strangways—!"

"I'm only trying to help. Since the government doesn't *earn* money, it *takes* its pelf from innocent bystanders. It's a mugger-economy. Where will the new republic get its money to support the workers when there are no earnings to tax? How will you ensure a vibrant, growing economy?"

"Your howling error is easily pinpointed, Mister Strangways."

"Well?" "Your error is thinking we want a vibrant, growing economy."

"Oh. Don't you?"

"Oh, no. We want *control*."

"Righty-o. That is where I made my bloomer. Thanks awfully."

"Seize him," said the Moustache.

Immediately, Stoker and Hawkins seized Herron by the arms.

"Our pleasant chat is over, Mister Strangways. Your time is over. The time of all your kind soon will be over. I would like to kill you at this moment, but that makes too much mess indoors. You must be taken out for shooting. Good-bye."

CHAPTER XXXIX

Normally when dismissed by Her Ladyship at bed-time, Angelica carefully brushed her long hair one hundred times. An ordinary, perfunctory duty like that might have soothed her present mood.

Instead, she had totally forgotten her hair, which was mostly unpinned, awry over her head and shoulders, and flecked with dust. She had no opportunity to muse on hair, since Herron Strangways had turned her world upside down and given it a good shake. He he dropped into her life like an explosive device from an airhip, and nothing made the slightest bit of sense.

Gentlemen paid calls in red velvet coats, knee breeches and white wigs.
Cigarettes bearing cryptograms were stashed in her reticule.
Papers typed with nonsense vanished from the tight typewriter rollers.
Butlers ventured out on nocturnal jaunts.

Stepping out into the corridor with a low-burning paraffin lamp, Angelica found the house all dark and shut up for the night. It was the first normal thing she had experienced since tea-time.

She descended the stairway scything down from the gallery. Near the semi-circular curtail step, an archway opened to her left, leading to the ground-floor right-hand wing of the house, with steps spiraling down to the kitchen.

Beyond the arch, only just glimpsed in the lamplight, was the green baize door leading to the butler's pantry and the bedrooms of Dapifer and cook.

Angelica decided tea could wait. Dapifer might have slept through her bell. If he had returned from his mysterious errand, she had to confront him there and then. She didn't care if she woke him up, even if she caught him in pyjamas!

CHAPTER XL

Stoker and Hawkins bustled Herron out the rear door of the dark room and down several flights of stairs. He hadn't come up any stairs to enter that room, so he rightly figured the land sloped dramatically away at the rear of the house.

They pushed him out a back door, down a creaky set of wooden steps, and out toward the stables.

The Moustache supervised the Strangways removal. He and the still wrist-bound Herron leaned against the wall by the stable door while Stoker and Hawkins disappeared inside.

Herron was impressed by the size of the stables. "How many horses?"

"None. We do not ride animals. That is cruel. This is a modern and technologically advanced society. We use clean and healthful motor-carriages. They weary less and control better."

"Control," Herron repeated. That was the word that best expressed the new republic. If you control the bread, you control the world; he recalled Angelica's example of Satan trying to control Christ's turning the stones to bread.

Clearly, this new republic had to own access to all the bread and all the work: to make the people dependent upon government. *Make them look to the government for what they can get out of it,* Herron thought.

Aloud, he murmured, "Like God and women."

The Moustache reeled a watch from his waistcoat pocket and flipped open the lid. "If we do not hurry, the date of your death must be changed. It is almost the twenty-second." He snapped the watch closed and shoved it back into his pocket.

"So, if the people do not do and say precisely as you order, they get no bread. Won't they be hungry?"

"Not for long. But it is necessary. If we do not control the people, they will do what they want. That will be chaos."

"No, we can't have people doing what they want."

"No."

"It might even be immoral." "I thought you were an educated man, Herr Strangways," the Moustache laughed. "Morality, Herr Strangways, is a matter of . . ."

He fought for an English word with a lot of, *was ist*-ing and *how you say*-ing. Herron helpfully suggested the word Angelica had used at tea.

"Aesthetics?"

"*Ja, ja*, 'aesthetics.' Mores sixty years ago were 'hunting, fishing and wenching,' is that not so?"

"Er – you don't pronounce the 'g' on the end. 'Huntin', fishin'—"

"Now, morality is calling meat 'light' and 'dark' so you do not say 'breast' and 'leg.' We will lay a new foundation for morality. To replace the obsolete morality of the Church and the Jews, even Robespierre and the French Revolution had to introduce what they called 'The Republic of Virtue.'"

"They're the bunch who made a virtue of lopping off all those heads?"

"Correct."

"Oh yes, they set a high standard for morality."

"What has gone on beneath this Queen must be called immoral and we must become the Guardians of the new morality."

"Oh, so the Guardians also enforce correctness. Make sure never is heard a discouraging word, or whatever the Guardians deem a 'bad' word from day to day. Since 'morality' is just a word."

"*Ja*. Even more than most."

"Like 'starvation.' And 'justice.'" *And love, and marriage.* "'Morality' will mean whatever the dickens your Guardians decide on any given day."

"*Ja*. The insidious dichotomy still exists between what the masses call *good* and *bad*. They do not realize these things are mere prejudices. All persons want to think they do things that are 'good' and they themselves are not 'bad.' So, we in the coming revolution call what we do 'moral' and make it a fight for right. The ignorant masses will follow. They are not equipped to question closely."

Herron Strangways was, to put it kindly, no major intellectual himself; but he had some intuitive comprehension that when one declared that words had no real meanings, one controlled their meanings. From controlling the meanings of words, it was a only a short hop to controlling what people thought.

The new Guardians wanted external control over the populace, by dictating their jobs and their pay and their bread. It appeared they meant to attain internal control of their citizens by dictating the way their brains digested communication. Herron understood that languages had to change or die, like Latin. Or French. But Herron did not approve of people tinkering around inside his private head.

"We will build a new morality, clothing our beliefs in the garments of truth."

"'Truth,'" Herron said, "being just a word." *Quid est veritas.*

"Less than most. However, we must possess that word to fight the enemy."

"What enemy?"

"The people."

Herron refrained from asking where the *republican* part came into their 'republic.' Their 'republic' talk, so far as he could gauge, was all flapdoodle.

"Say, what about the agitators who thunder against 'conventional morality'? What will they say when this neo-morality becomes conventional?"

"Nothing, for they will agree with us."

"And give birth to new agitators against 'conventional morality.'"

"No. The new republic will crack down on all forms of dissent – in the interest of order, which is conducive to the public health."

"Your enemy, the people, won't like being told 'shut up' by the government."

"The British," the Moustache explained, "are patriotic for their freedoms. The lowest and stupidest man in a public house proudly proclaims, 'This is a free country' before giving his worthless opinion on – whatever it is uneducated persons talk about. The new monarch, 'she who is to come,' must transcend Britishness. She must stand above country, or empire – or even the world. Like a divinity. And slowly we will make the people think that a 'free country' no longer means unmeasurable intangible trifles like thought and religion and speech."

"A friend once told me that freedom was inherent in nature."

The Moustache uttered a German word that didn't sound at all polite. "Freedom *does not* exist in nature. Nature is an implacable enemy, not a bestower of freedoms. A naked man facing down nature alone is a pitiful creature. Intangible freedoms exist no more than other intangibles – gods, or angels, or ghosts. As there is no intangible freedom, *we must change what people think of as free.* We must transform their idea of freedom to tangibles. Goods. Services."

"No personal freedom? Only free *stuff*? Your 'freedom' is very materialistic."

"Nothing exists that is immaterial. If freedom is to exist, it must refer to the material. That is what we will mean, when we say 'freedom.' Free . . . stuff."

"'Free' meaning 'paid for by someone else.'"

"*Ja.*"

"Like me."

"'Like you' is the proper term. Not you, for you will be dead."

Herron heard shouts from Stoker, inside the stables. Then he heard bizarre snorts and coughs as a motor carriage engine sputtered to life.

"Ah!" The Moustache clapped his hands and rubbed the palms briskly together. "Your transport to your grave awaits you."

CHAPTER XLI

The butler's pantry was unoccupied, as she expected. Itching for a confrontation, Angelica continued on to Dapifer's bedroom.

No light gleamed under Dapifer's door. She rapped on the door with gentle knuckles, hoping her knock was loud enough to wake him, but not loud enough to disturb the ill-natured cook three doors down.

"Dapifer?" she called, softly.

Receiving no answer, her temper flared momentarily and she slapped the flat of her hand against the door's upper panel.

"Dapifer!"

Imitating Doris, she jiggled the latch. The door was locked.

Her hair had been altogether shaken loose, but many of her hair-pins remained. She'd read stories where fictional detectives opened locks with them. Sliding a hair-pin from her coiffure, she set down her lamp and shoved the pin in the lock.

After maneuvering it carefully around for a few minutes, she realized that worked only in detective stories. All she got was a hopelessly bent hair-pin.

Squatting down by the door, she peered through the keyhole. It was too dark to make anything out.

Cupping her hands around the keyhole, she called, "Dapifer!"

Finally, she put her ear to the keyhole and listened for fully a minute. Nothing stirred. All indications suggested Dapifer was still out on his errand.

Rapt in thought, Angelica took up her lamp and wended her way to the kitchen.

CHAPTER XLII

Choosing his words carefully, Herron raised his voice over the echoing roar of the motor-carriage engine warming up inside the stables. "Let me see if this is the way the snow blows. 'Freedom' is intangible. Therefore, it does not exist."

"*Précisément.*"

"I guess that means 'yes.' Freedom therefore can exist only through things, rather than ideals like religion, thought, and the empty air of speech?"

"Ideals do not exist in nature. In the house are many books cataloging natural forms and species. I see 'freedom' nowhere categorized. I see no examples of it pinned to boards. I cannot dissect it. Nor 'ideals.'"

"Since nothing exists that is immaterial, intangible ideas do not exist."

"If you can grasp that, all the masses can. Speech is not real. Nor thought. But hunger is real. And nakedness. And homelessness. Therefore, freedoms must meet real and physical needs rather than emotional or metaphysical needs that cannot be weighed or measured. Animal needs like food, shelter, sex, medicine. These are what we will teach the people belong to them by 'right.'"

"Equally free access to ideals, to speech and thought, to personal choice and taste, to religion – dammit, to life – isn't that what makes all persons equal?" It was in the world according to Angelica Trickett, a world he wanted to live in.

"Only the natural world exists, *ergo* only tangible freedoms exist. As they give according to their ability and must be doled out to according to their needs, humans are *ipso facto* unequal. And since many lack tangible freedoms, since we need an enemy to get the masses on our side, we must say others, like you, are keeping them from enjoying those tangible freedoms. You have too many goods, Herr Strangways, therefore you have too much freedom and it must be taken from you. That is what it means to live free. To have the government take from people like you to meet the needs of others who are chosen by that government as more worthy to own them."

"To 'live free' equals 'living off others.' Well, you are original thinkers, I'll give you that. Just make sure you toe the government line. If it doesn't smile on you, you'll be pushing up the daisies. You said your 'Malthus' chap says population will always outstrip resources? Thus, as you said, for the government to foot everyone's bill, a statistical slice of the population pie must be deducted from the whole. Targeting the poor, of course, since, as you pointed out, they have more babies. And your pesky 'inconvenient' biological types."

"Let us refer to those biological types as 'scientifically selected persons' whose removal will be genetically beneficial to the health of the larger body."

"And for those who remain, while you're telling them 'freedom' means free loot, you'll be stripping away their abilities to speak, think and travel freely."

"We take nothing from them. These things have no weight or volume or mass and so they do not exist. Those ideals will be surrendered of their own free will."

The last time they'll ever use it, Herron thought. "You're sure they'll all give up their ideals of equal freedoms of their own volition?"

"*Ja*, if they want to eat. We will build a new ethics overcoming animal individualism, so our citizens may find fulfillment in an ego-less collective. It is only in the collective that the individual is truly able to express himself."

"Eh?"

"We must bring people together."

"By utter control, mind and body."

"Is there another way? People never come together in harmony, without dissent, without some level of oppression. Without that oppression they think what they like, do what they want. To have a country in unity is, ultimately, to control what everyone thinks and does. Thus, the new republic must control what its citizens read in books and the daily press. We must forbid people from hearing any matter speaking against the new republic – in the name of fairness. It is only fair to us that there be no dissenting voices, so the citizens will live in harmony."

"Your candor is refreshing. What if someone declines to be 'brought together' under your parasol?"

"Then we will call him a divisive troublemaker."

"Let me see if I have this cow by the right horn. When an establishment is in charge with whom you do not agree, such as currently exists, you and yours are divisive troublemakers. However, you'll show no tolerance for the young divisive troublemakers of tomorrow?"

This was a difficult sentence for the Moustache to follow. When he finally worked it out, he answered, "There is a difference, Herr Strangways."

"Oh?"

"Unless you come together in the new republic in peace and harmony you will be labeled as undesirable."

Herron knew what that meant. *Bang*. "Yes, that is a big difference. I'm so glad you pointed that out. It certainly encourages me to mind my p's and q's."

2

That expression soared right over the man's head. While he was bewildered by the pease and queues, the moustache paused long enough for Herron to say,

"All these new foundations will cost lots of money. Which equals taxation."

"Taxation will be painless." "That's a clever new twist! I've always found it sore as a bad tooth. How do you intend to alleviate the pain? Have the revenue people administer laughing gas to the patient before picking his pocket?"

"Taxes will be deducted from pay tickets before they are distributed. Workers will not even notice we are garnishing their wages."

"Their mandated wages. And mandated prices, I assume, too, rather than what the market will bear."

"There will be no market."

Herron was shaken. "A free market is the essence of freedom, surely!"

"Is that what your father told you?"

"I don't need the dear old guv'nor on that one. Anyone who has a problem with a free market has a problem with free*dom*, full stop."

"It is not fair. Some succeed and some do not."

"That's called 'Life,' old man. Experienced by those who live out in the real world. I don't know if you can glimpse the real world from your lofty ivory tower. Oh, sorry, you don't like ivory, do you? Elephants don't come in inconvenient biological types. You may not know this, old man, but you can't control natural economic forces any more than you can control the weather. Prices fluctuate. They go up; they go down, blast them. Controlled markets cause shortages. They create 'black markets' where people really are exploited. Placing arbitrary controls on markets that should be free is like slapping a lid on a boiling pot. If you leave too tight too long it'll blow its top."

"No one will use the excuse of a market to steal money by profit." If the Moustache was representative of the new republic, Herron had a queasy feeling the dodo birds were not extinct. They would be running the government.

The words *genetically beneficial* made it all sound rather worse. This chap seemed so pleasant, so gracious and good-humored . . . yet the things he was saying were all so perfectly monstrous.

And Herron wondered, *Who is 'she who is to come'?* The Moustache had mentioned her briefly, almost accidentally, as if he didn't want Herron to hear of her. Who was she! A new queen pulling the strings from behind the curtain?

This was the only daylight he saw. If only he could be let alone in a room with a woman, he believed he could work his magic on her and possibly stay alive.

And if he could stay alive, he could get the dickens out of England before all this arrant nonsense was rammed down its throat.

Is 'she who is to come in this house?' he wondered, eyeing the rear of the large country manse. If so, how might he meet her?

CHAPTER XLIII

Somehow, Herron had to meet this 'she who is to come.' Perhaps making the moustache angry would make him to haul Herron before his superior.

Herron fell back on his own personal philosophy, *If you have nothing to say, keep talking until something springs to mind*.

He started, "Let's get back to individual achievement—"

"Since you have no achievements of your own, Herr Strangways, it is not a good topic for you."

"*Touche*." Herron was a fair man who always gave credit where it was due. Trying to sound like he had his learning cap on, he said, "But what I mean, don't y'know, is, say some johnnie invents a thing. An airship, maybe—?"

The eyes above the moustache flickered.

"Or, rather," Herron altered, hastily, realizing the airship was a misstep, "a better mousetrap. He puts this better mousetrap on the market, the world beats a path to his door, and he makes a gazillion pounds. Or, dollars, since he'll probably be an American."

"That man's wealth must be spread to those who truly need it." "But, I say! You mean this hyper-what-ical mousetrap chap who thought it up and made it and marketed it will have his money taken away and awarded to some bloke who never gets out of bed 'til the crack of noon, and then only to fetch another bottle and take a loving whack at the wife?"

"I do not think 'a gazillion' exists. If this mousetrap is successful and the inventor makes a septendecillion pounds on it, why should he keep it?"

"Because he made the mousetrap."

"On the backs of others."

"No, I'm sure he'd use a workbench."

"He took his money from those who bought his overpriced mousetrap—"

"Of course he did. And they got fewer mouses in the bargain."

"—and from those who worked for him, who earned a fraction of what he gained. His money should be returned to its rightful owners."

Herron thought that met Angelica's description of sheer covetousness.

Some Commandment covered covetousness... He had heard it read out at school, between dozes in chapel. That Commandment stuck in Herron's mind because it included coveting one's neighbor's wife; and when he was a lad the man who lived across the street had a wife who was an absolute stunner.

Oh, it wasn't just about wives, but coveting anything that was thy neighbor's – presumably including thy neighbor's wallet.

Merridew would know... But an argument from Scripture wouldn't hold much water with a moustache like that. So Herron decided to continue talking the only thing he really understood beside the art of seduction, business.

"As far as the customers go," Herron tried to explain, "it's a fair exchange: his mousetrap for their money. I've been selling commemorative Jubilee rubbish like hotcakes, don't you know. I don't want the Jubilee rubbish. I want the money. Some other bloke wants the Jubilee rubbish and can part with enough ready cash to legally take the junk out of my stores. At the conclusion of our exchange, we're both as pleased as Mister Punch. If you take the mousetrap man's money and give it back to 'the people' who paid him for his invention, then the chap with the mousetrap is giving the sweat of his brow away for nothing."

"And?"

"Eh?"

"He will be paid the minimum wage at whatever job the government has given him. Any idea he has on that job will belong to the government."

"No matter how much money the government reels in off his better mousetrap, he'll be paid whatever the self-appointed Guardians choose to dole out to him?"

"He will receive tickets for his work, like all other government employees."

"Doesn't every moral law screech out that a man or woman should profit by his or her own... er... what they call 'intellectual property' – hm, sounds like the property is smarter than they are – to sell for whatever the market will bear?"

"That is why we need to redefine morality for a new ethics. Your mousetrap man makes exorbitant profits, while the workers made the mousetraps."

"No, the *man* made the mousetraps. The mousetraps exist solely because of *him*. If his mousetraps were a bust, he'd lose all the time and capital he'd invested in 'em. And if they're a best seller, he's in a real pickle. When there is a demand, supply must meet it. When there is too little supply, the prices are high. When there is a glut on the market, the prices drop.

"With a high demand, he can't, with his own two, little mitts, hammer together all the mousetraps the eager public is clamoring for. If he has nothing to sell than the mousetraps he can make in one day all by his lonesome, he'd have to ask an impossibly high price for them. I haven't taken a survey, but I'm almost certain it's the poorest houses that have the most mice, and the inhabitants of the poorest houses would most need a mousetrap. For the mousetrap price to be affordable at every level of bank balance, our man must churn the things out by the barrel. The more you have, the cheaper things are – as I was saying with the money supply. That means he must hire workers to make the mousetraps for him, and he must hire them at previously agreed wages. After all, if the mousetrap bubble bursts, it's the mousetrap man who loses shirt. It's his mousetrap."

"And he fires his workers!"

"Certainly. The primary goal of a business, old chap, is to stay in business. It's not a sort of orphanage for the unemployed. When times are good, more employees are hired. When times are not good, employment is terminated. The man earned his money for what he did. The workers earned their money for what they did. Those workers spend their days constructing mousetraps they couldn't have thought up in a million years. If it hadn't been for *his* idea they wouldn't be working. They'd be on the pavements busking to Musical Hall ditties with their hats held out for coppers. At least, with their contracted wages, they're inside.

"Salaries, you see, are an *expenditure*. It's the mousetrap man's business. To keep it afloat when there is no longer a demand for the mousetraps, he must wave *adieu* to workers. Or, he hopes, *au revoir*. He wants his business to get back on its feet like Lazarus. But if he's kind-hearted and keeps all the redundant workers on—the business goes bust, and they're all busking on the street together."

"That does not excuse the inequity of this man making more money than his workers, or taking money from the poor to pad his pockets when he has enough."

"Who defines 'enough' – oh, yes . . . the Guardians. Think of it this way: maybe the mousetrap man isn't in it for the money. Maybe he just has a dread fear of mice and wants to see them exterminated for the hygienic benefit of humanity. He has to make millions of them to sell them cheaply enough to force the little vermin into extinction."

"He still makes a greedy profit."

"Merely for the health of the community, our hypothetical Mousetrapper wants to make and sell better mousetraps. But making 'em costs money. That's pure expenditure. If he went into hock for the capital to make first mousetraps, he may be in debt for ages. And we who run shops have so many other expenditures on top of mere material. I, for instance, don't make things, but I run a shop full of goods I have to buy. Other expenditures are worker's salaries. Shop space. Repairs. Taxation. More taxation. Implementing new regulations gouges the ol' pocketbook. The more he doles out, the less he has to expand and hire. Our mousetrap man will acquire lots and lots of overhead."

"To keep the rain out, *ja*."

"When he's finally out of the red ink and turning a profit, he'll expand his company and hire more workers to make more mousetraps, making them even more affordable! If the tide of profit keeps rising, he'll kick the salaries of his workers up a notch. Perhaps, after meeting the needs of his workers, his company, and himself, he gives the rest of his profits to the deserving poor—"

"And perhaps," the Moustache countered, "he builds himself a big house he fills with useless bric-a-brac and has rich foods and expensive wines."

"Did you say 'expensive wines' or 'wives' . . . never mind, same difference. Well, why not? Whether he gives it to the poor or keeps it to satisfy his own lusts – *it's his money to do with as he jolly well likes*."

"That is where we disagree, Herr Strangways."

"I was afraid it might be."

"He could put any price on his mousetraps – a hundred pounds apiece."

"I doubt it. Try selling mousetraps for a hundred pounds apiece. You won't be in business long. Cats come cheaper. The market sets prices."

Herron was increasingly perturbed by the this fellow's arrogant obtuseness.

"The workers," said the Moustache, "should collectivize. Demand more."

"You don't know what they're making."

"It's still not enough."

"Greedy little swine, aren't they? Just like bakers. Fine. Change the laws. Let the workers collectivize and I hope they have a sunny day for it. And if the workers demand more and more money all the time, they'll eventually reach a tipping point: tipping the business into bankruptcy and tipping themselves into unemployment. All the new republic's policies seemed designed to foster unemployment. You may think the net is spread only for your undesirables—"

"Do not change the subject, please. A man cannot be allowed to retain so many dollars, or pounds, when others are starving!"

"Why not? You just said men were unequal. And you didn't seem to give a hang about seeing people starve five minutes ago."

"But the inequality must come from the government. An entrepreneur who makes so much money should have his aluminium taken from him by right!"

That left Herron totally fogged. "I think you've strayed from the point."

"No, you are not addressing the real point, which is that you and your kind are ticks bloated from sucking blood from the veins of the worker!"

"Oh, I say, steady on."

Herron certainly had gotten the man's dander up. His dander was so far up he looked ready to pull a gun and shoot him down in the stable yard.

"Profits," he went on, "are evil and must be seized by the government and spread for the benefit of the collective."

"You're willing to ensure everyone will be equally poor and miserable, just to destroy the wealth and livelihoods of a few successful entrepreneurs?"

"But, of course. Crooks often pose as entrepreneurs."

"And because a few people who call themselves something might be crooks, you have to forbid it for everyone? You might as well say everyone in the populace is guilty before being proven innocent."

"Oh, we will," said the Moustache, off-handedly. "Everyone is guilt of some minor infraction of the law that can be made larger for our purposes."

"And set up accounts so everyone will receive a pittance from the government – rather than allowing anyone to break out of their straightjacket and succeed at what they're good at?"

"Ja. Because that is a definition of individualism, Herr Strangways, and that must not be allowed. The age of individualism—"

"—has gone the way of all flesh. So I've been told. Say, what about creativity? We've flushed entrepreneurs down the drain. What about those who make money from the arts? Aren't artists individualistic? Will you put caps on what artists can demand for a picture, or for book royalties?"

"Please use your brain, Herr Strangways. Shakespeare was hailed as 'the Starre of Poets' after his death, was he not?"

"Was he?"

"He was. That was three hundred years ago. Now it is nearly 1900 and his writing is barely comprehensible. It *will* be incomprehensible in another two or three hundred years. Like Chaucer. Men die, Herr Strangways, from generation to generation; stars and planets, from eon to eon. Perhaps universes, after longer periods, go dark. What use will your Shakespeare be then?"

"Not really my—"

"When neo-dinosaurs replace man as the dominant species on the planet, what use will they have for Shakespeare? Or for Bach's 'Mass in B Minor' – or 'Daddy Would Not Buy me a Bow-Wow.'"

"Say, that's a good one," said Herron. Not knowing how else to handle this lunatic, he thought he might interest him in a sing-a-long. "'Daddy wouldn't buy me a bow-wow—' here, you echo, *bow-wow*, 'Daddy would't buy me a—'"

"What use," said Mister Moustache, showing no inclination to sing, "will be the daubings of an artist on canvas? Or the jottings of a novelist whose book no one can read in ten thousand years? Given that – what is the point of art and music and culture? *Eitelkeit der Eitelkeiten! Alles ist Eitelkeit.*"

2

Herron brooded over that. Oh, it was definitely, hard cheese for Bach, he thought – and presumably for Mozart and Beethoven, too.

To tell the truth, he didn't feel too badly for them. They were dead; and, so far as Herron cared, so was their music. He didn't go to concerts and the only songs he knew were the latest offerings from the music-halls (the risquer, the better).

His favorite song had been sung in the halls by Lottie Collins a few years earlier. It had the edifying chorus,

> *Ta-ra-ra-boom-de-ay!*
> *Ta-ra-ra-boom-de-ay!*
> *Ta-ra-ra-boom-de-ay!*
> *Ta-ra-ra-boom-de-ay!*

Then continued, after a modulation,

> *Ta-ra-ra-boom-de-ay!*
> *Ta-ra-ra-boom-de-ay!*
> *Ta-ra-ra-boom-de-ay!*
> *Ta-ra-ra-boom-de-ay!*

He was certain Ludwig Sebastian Mozart could never have penned anything like that, even on their brighter mornings!

But the idea of huge reptiles mangling his beloved things underfoot (underclaw?) in ten thousand years made Herron melancholy. The Moustache had a point there. Everything faded and died. What was the point of doing anything?

"What about beauty?" Herron wondered, grasping at straws by this time. "Artists add beauty to the world."

"Utility *is* beauty. Look at bees."

"You've got bees in your bonnet, old man."

"Do you realize the human species has not changed since the Pleistocene?"

"I didn't even realize there was a Pleistocene. Sorry I missed it."

"Humans modify slowly. They produce as few as three generations to a century. That gives no time to modify. They require another solution."

"I don't see what you can do about it."

"For perfection of the species, humans must be selected for breeding."

"That is rather faster than natural selection, I suppose." "Herr Strangways, natural selection is a selection by death, and humans are manifestly not dying in sufficient numbers to make change possible."

You'll probably take care of that first thing you gain power, Herron thought.

CHAPTER XLIV

While her kettle boiled, Angelica ransacked the kitchen pantry for tea.

Rather than steeping the generic blend Lady Calthrop bought for the servants to use, she decided to find Lady Calthrop's cache of tea from Strangways'. She wanted to know if it was really as good as advertised.

In the light of her lamp, she laid out a small China teapot, one cup and saucer, and a tin of Strangways' Darjeeling (she found other varieties, and regretted she could try only one at a time.)

Knowing kettles never boiled until one left the room, she stepped briskly to the cellar door, where tradesmen made deliveries.

Angelica's Monarch bicycle leaned against the wall just inside the entranceway, since Lady Calthrop occasionally sent her on errands requiring speed. She rolled the bike outside, into the area, to be ready in case Herron Strangways did not get back in touch with her and she had to find that Inspector.

Isn't that what he said? 'If you do not hear from me—'?

So many people as would be in the streets that morning! When she was in the area she heard them out there now, before midnight, going to find places to stand for the Procession. She doubted even a bicycle could squeeze through.

I'll require an airship, I think. And before going to the police, I need to find those papers, or they'll think I'm a lunatic. They probably will in any case. Airships! Kings over water!

Passing through the kitchen again, she gave the kettle a suspicious glance. It was just sitting there. She didn't want to turn the gas higher. Instead, she went abovestairs again with her lamp, to take one more forlorn turn around her room. She was certain the kettle would be whistling merrily by the time she returned.

Ascending the grand staircase, she noticed one of Lord Calthrop's trophies had gone missing from a wall-display.

She couldn't remember what filled that the blank space; she was so used all the displays she never noticed anything until it wasn't there.

The object was missing from an exhibit of long, primitive weapons. In the halo of light from her lamp, the gap made the display look like a wheel with a spoke missing all the way across.

Idly, Angelica wondered if Dapifer had taken it with him. Depending on the neighborhood he was venturing into, he might have needed it for self-defense.

No, your mind's still fuzzy, Angelica! she scolded herself. If he needed protection, why not one of the pistols from the cases in the front hall? Firearms would be preferable to – well, an Esquimau harpoon; or a *dung* (which she had learned as a rather unfortunate name for a double-edged Tibetan spear).

But Angelica had too much on her mind to mull over the eccentricities of peregrinating butlers. Her business lay upstairs.

As her head came level with the gallery, she noticed a soft glow off the wall of the left-hand corridor. She wondered what might cast such a light.

Stretching herself flat on the stairs, she reached up and slipped the lamp onto the top step. Then she ascended on her hands and knees, keeping her head low until it was even with the floor of the gallery.

Laying her cheek flat on the carpet, she saw a pinpoint of light shining from beneath Lady Calthrop's bedroom door at the far end of the corridor.

Her Ladyship had tried to plug the slit with a pillow or blanket, but she had missed a spot and the light shot up onto the wall.

Stretched face-down on the stairs, Angelica rested her head on her fists and squiggled up her face.

Why was Her Ladyship up at this hour? *I thought I left her asleep!*

And with so much light in her bedroom! Lady Calthrop made Angelica read to her in the dim light of a small paraffin lamp, rather than letting her use the gaseliers. She forbade burning the gas too high in any room, even in the "museum." *It's like burning money*, she whined, though she was extremely rich.

That's how one becomes rich, Angelica always thought. *By denying one's self small comforts.*

Angelica had grown without many comforts by necessity rather than choice. At twenty-two, she had already decided would rather live with small comforts and remain relatively poor, than to become a rich and uncomfortable miser. And she vowed that if she ever became rich – hopefully by her writing – she would deny herself nothing. She was sick and tired of thrift!

She almost laughed: that would make her a perfect female counterpart to Herron Strangways. He was rich and profligate. *I wish I were!*

Oh, well, Angelica thought – a bright light under Her Ladyship's door in the middle of the night was just one more enigma added on to the rest.

But it piqued her curiosity.

Her calf-high button shoes, black on the bottom with fawn suede uppers, were not easy to remove. As she didn't carry a button-hook in her pocket, she could not slide her feet out of her shoes and slip to the door in her black-stockinged feet.

Leaving her lamp on the top step, she tip-toed fully shod across the gallery and down the corridor to the door of Lady Calthrop's *chambre*.

CHAPTER XLV

"I reject survival of the fittest," Mister Moustache continued. "It is enough, for me, that robber baron industrialists cling to the notion of survival of the fittest by natural selection to rationalize the evil they perpetrate on the worker. Even if you proved natural selection is true I would reject it on the basis of who accepts it."

"Listen, if it's human stud you want, I will be more than delighted to help you breed away. I've been told that I'm an advancement on the species—"

"You!"

Herron had no answer for that. "Just repeating gossip. Say, don't physical barriers keep humans from producing new generations as fast as bunny-rabbits?"

"Indeed. Thus, for the health of the world, change for the betterment of the human species *must* be forced through engineering. In a modern, technological society, everything changes for the better by engineering. So will humans."

"I see," Herron lied.

"Humans must change, and quickly. Therefore they must be changed scientifically. They must learn to grow more like bees within a few generations."

"Oh . . . ah . . .? You mean, striped, with stingers in their—?"

"Until we guide the development of *homo sapiens* by science untrammeled, changes must come *via* the culture. Social changes first, then physical."

"You're trying to force *Utopia* down people's throats?"

Moustache wagged a finger in Herron's face, just an inch from his nose. "*Utopia* is a novel. Creating worlds that do not exist, whether one is a priest or a storyteller, will be forbidden. Ours will be a rational world. We have no room or tolerance for make-believe."

"Down go the arts, then. Right down the pipes after the entrepreneurs."

"Some artists will be useful at promoting societal change. For instance, we cannot simply strip away wealth. The masses are so conditioned, it will at first like theft. Therefore, there must be a long-term propaganda campaign designed to let people know that they are entitled to the wealth of others."

"A propaganda campaign to persuade people wrong is right?"

"Right and wrong, Herr Strangways, are—"

"Words?"

"—prejudices. At first, we will simply spend all the money we have in the Exchequer and then some, building up exorbitant debts."

"Bankrupting the country in a deliberate fiscal crisis. Good."

"*Ja, gut.* Then we will use the occasion of the crisis as an initial step to seize private property and put its revenues in government hands, to make it appear we are helping the poor man who is hurt by economic collapse. Then we will commence our reeducation programme, teaching it is immoral to deprive the poor from the freedom to take another's property if he requires it."

"That doesn't really sound like a recipe for universal harmony. What's to keep the whole country from wholesale looting and vandalism?"

"That is why the government must be the intermediary and take property for distribution through taxation. High taxation will not only strip useless eaters like you of your wealth, they will discourage others from becoming rich lest they, too, be punished for it. When enough of a voting bloc exists of persons convinced that they are entitled to live off the fruits of another's labor, we will have another campaign to persuade them that there should be no private property at all. *La propriete, c'est le vol.*"

"That's right, the property, she is the thief."

"But all our concurrent propaganda campaigns will employ only so many hands. Therefore, artists must be put at work – not at their alleged callings but where the state requires them. They will be paid as the Guardians decide. Like all others, their pay will be deposited directly into carefully numbered accounts in nationalized, government controlled banks, This number will be used by all citizens as identification; when they acquire a home, or get employment, or—"

"Oh! I see! People used to be able to disappear. They could sell out all they had and use the proceeds to move to another vicinity and start a new life under a new name, without the baggage of the old. When your citizens are given special numbers they must use as identification wherever they go and whatever they do, the new republic can always find them! Because they are always 'guilty' until proven innocent of some minor infraction. They can't run. They can't hide."

"The insidious yoke of individualism is broken. Our culture must be more like bee culture. Like bees, everyone will work for the greater good of the collective in a strictly enforced distribution of labor."

"Aren't there solitary bees, too?"

"There will be no solitary bees in the new republic."

Finally grasping the connection between the new republic and bee culture, Herron understood why Mister Moustache always referred to "the worker."

CHAPTER XLVI

Two doors away from Lady Calthrop's bedroom, Angelica eased onto her hands and knees and crawled the rest of the way, listening acutely. She heard a sound that was familiar – and, at the same time, strange.

She recognized it at once, of course. Morse code.

Someone inside was sending and receiving telegraphic messages.

But no telegraph wires were attached to the house!

CHAPTER XLVII

"You said 'voting bloc.' You'll have elections?"

"Oh, we will grant universal suffrage."

"A lady of my acquaintence will be gratified to hear it."

"The broader the electorate, Herr Strangways, the fewer persons who will take advantage of it. Which is good, since a larger electorate means a lower average mentality of voter. I was in America not long ago, and I saw voters swayed neither by the best argument, nor the most logical, but the most *recent*. America is a revolution we must use as a model not to follow."

"It looked awfully successful to me when I was over there."

"But you do not see the seductive, the pernicious evil intrinsic in their founding documents, like their *Declaration of Independence*."

"I haven't read it."

"'*We hold these Truths to be self-evident, that all Men are created equal, that they are endowed by their Creator with certain unalienable Rights, that among these are Life, Liberty and the pursuit of Happiness.*' Ignominious!"

"Yeah. Shame on 'em. Who do these Americans think they are?"

"There is no Creator, so we were not *created* equal. And we proved, when we said, 'From each according to his ability, to each according to his needs' there is no equality. Rights are 'endowed' by creator? Since there is no creator, *ergo*, there are no rights. When we eliminate men clinging to their gods we will change the abominable notion that 'Rights' are found in nature. When does one animal respect another's rights? When does the fox respect the rights of the hen in its mouth? Or the dog, of the fox it is chasing? *Homo Sapiens* is an animal, though one with a slightly higher thinking capacity. We delude ourselves we have special 'rights,' but in fact we are all prisoners of biological impulses. We hunger, we thirst, we crave shelter and sex."

"Now you're talking."

"The myth of intrinsic rights is perpetuated by governments who think being protectors of intangibles is easier than doling out food and services."

"And what the government giveth," Herron added, badly mangling the book of Job, "the government may taketh away."

"As necessary."

"So, no life, liberty or pursuit of happiness."

"Life? The despicable notion that life is a right for the human species has led to our surplus population."

"And the pursuit of happiness?"

"The pursuit of happiness is a vicious anarchy of persons running in different directions for *individual* achievements, wasting wealth in *personal* pleasures. We should all run together for the genetic hygiene of the collective."

The disgust he used to accent words like *individual* and *personal* was worse than Herron had ever heard from any pulpit-jockey railing against *sin*.

"The myths of rights to life, and pursuits of happinesses," the Moustache concluded, "have brought the world untold misery."

"But 'the pursuit of happiness' is so vague you won't even need to redefine it."

"Everyone cannot achieve their happiness, so many are disappointed."

"It only says we have the right to pursue it, not to catch it."

"Others are disappointed when they receive what they thought will make them happy, and it does not. The best solution is to eliminate from people's thinking they have a right to anything more than they are given."

"Misery loves company."

"*It is only when all organs function together for the greater health of the whole that happiness is possible.* When a tooth aches, the entire body is affected, is it not? You are merely one organ in the body politic – and, I think, a vestigial one."

"If you say so. Oh, you forgot to mention 'Liberty.'"

"No," Moustache laughed, his good humor apparently returning. "It simply is not worth the mentioning. Liberty is a myth. Men are prisoners who have constructed their own cells by their pursuit of their individual lusts."

"I was never a prisoner until today. I'm a free agent. I like being me."

"All 'Individualism' is a prison, Herr Strangways. Americans cherish their so-called 'rugged individualism' – and look at whom they elect."

"Ah." Herron beat his brains to recall the name of the chap who had been sworn in as the new American president.

"Lincoln!" the Moustache spat.

That's going back thirty years and more. "What's wrong with Lincoln?"

"Lincoln was not erudite, not in the intelligentsia. He was a backwoodsman. Herr Hawkins called him 'a dum-dum.'"

"Hawkins has a great way with words. I thought the only requirement for presidency was to get elected by any means short of shooting your opponent."

"Did he get elected? Did he?" The man's moustache quivered excitedly.

"There is a popular rumour to that effect."

"He *lost* the popular vote in 1960 by more than *nine hundred and fifty thousand* votes! Nearly a million more voters cast ballots for other candidates! He received less than forty percent of the vote! But because of American's silly Constitution he was able to finesse what they call their 'Electoral College.'"

"Lincoln was popular, by all the accounts I heard when I was over there."

"The most unpopular president! Divisive and uncompromising. In 1860, when Lincoln was selected, the American flag had thirty-three stars. He was so divisive, in seven months a full one-third of those stars in the American flag seceded, refusing to be in a union that had such a fool as president. Among them was that state that gave birth to many heroes of their so-called 'liberty' like Washington and Jefferson. Lincoln is the divisive sort of fool we do not require in our new republic. We want to bring together citizens in cooperation and unity."

If they agree with you, thought Herron. *Otherwise, you're Atilla with telegraphs and a railroads.* "Lincoln's first act as president was to maneuver southern confederacy into a war, ostensibly to preserve the union but—! as the war advanced he changed his goal from 'unity' to 'freedom.' It was no longer a war for its stated cause, but for his insidious hidden agenda."

Herron had never thought of freedom as insidious, but Mister Moustache was on a roll and Herron did not dare interrupt.

"Even Lincoln's 'freedom' was a sham perpetuated by *dis*honest Abe! His so-called 'Emancipation Proclamation' freed no one, since it affected only states where it had no force of law. Those slave-owners within his so-called Union who did not secede were exempt – including the state where he was born! Where, no doubt, he was appeasing his slave-owning friends. So his war to massacre young American males was for no good purpose. Lincoln – Faugh!"

Herron was quite taken aback. He never knew anyone said 'faugh' in real life. He thought it was a term relegated to second-rate novels.

"The war was good for his friends – financiers like Morgan and Cooke, who made fortunes from Union bonds; and the railroaders and the industrialists whose steel replaced agriculture America's big business. He probably invaded the south merely to seize their cotton to make it cheaper! A war for cotton!"

"He was elected again, though?"

"Lincoln *nearly* lost his second election to a Democrat candidate who – unlike Lincoln – was a war hero with genuine military credentials; and who, though he might have led the Union to victory, instead vowed to stop that stupid, wasteful war for cotton Lincoln had blundered stupidly into. McClellan merely meant to bring healing to the open, bleeding, festering sore that Lincoln had made America. Lincoln himself waved some phony credentials he had fighting some thing called the 'Black Hawk War' but it is certain he never showed up for any fighting."

"Is that so?" Herron asked, distantly. He was no longer listening to Mister Moustache, who – like Stoker and Hawkins seemed to have done in the stables after cranking their motor-carriage – had gone away and left his engine running."Lincoln was a fool. He said, at a turning point in the war, he went to his room and locked the door and knelt before his Almighty God and prayed for victory. What sort of fool is it who, at the helm of a nation, goes whinging and begging before an invisible divinity! Lincoln—again–faugh. They lionized Lincoln when he was dead – because then they had no more fear of him. America impeached its next president, who had been Lincoln's hated vice-president; but if Lincoln had lived, it would have been he who was impeached, and rightfully so – look at the death he caused by his unnecessary war, started and maintained by lies, deceptions and hidden agendas of freedom and enriching his friends!"

"And rumor had it in my old school that the south started the war."

"Lincoln used the paltry firing on Fort Sumter as a *raison d'etre* for his evil war, even though no blue coat died there! After that, Lincoln bled two nations of its youth, murdering those young men as surely as he had done it with his own hands. They should have tried him for murder, and hanged him by the neck until he was dead! And longer! Why, Fort Sumter probably was not even shelled by the Confederacy! The evil Lincoln no doubt faked it, bombing it with his own warships, with the complicity of the Jews! And Lincoln was ugly, too."

2

"That sort of ugliness," Mister Moustache prattled on, "must be eradicated from society by scientific breeding. In America, they have a government ostensibly – as that fool Lincoln said – of the people and by the people. And look what a mess the people have made. The masses are not mentally equipped to understand political theory. They have no comprehension of economics. The new republic will have its origins with the intelligentsia, and we will be the Guardians. Whatever the rabble says or votes for, we will do as we want."

"Another victory for Democracy," said Herron. "I can't wait to be controlled body and mind by a lot of self-righteous egg-heads who think they're smarter than everyone else in any given room. Get the old 'Varsity dons up there running things. 'Those who can, do; those who can't do, teach; and those who can't teach run the government.' Say, I was at Cambridge, and even attended a lecture once in a while, for a lark. Can I be one of your guardians, deciding who will live and who will die? Because there are a few chaps I know—"

"That will not be necessary for more than one generation. The population must be controlled by more than the mere ability to delouse parasites like you. Until now, marriages have been slap-dash affairs, with mates pairing off with no consideration for the genetic health of the state."

"I've never taken the plunge myself, but if I ever do, I confess that consideration will probably rank on low on my list of priorities."

"All marriages must be approved by the government, and will be approved only to those we think who will have children who are fit by heredity."

"Oh, yes. Can't have children without marriages," Herron winked.

"Having children will be what it should be: a privilege allowed by the government. Only so many children will be allowed per household and this number will be strictly enforced – by abortion or sterilization, since we have not yet found a way to control keeping husbands and wives from coition."

"You could pass a law forcing couples to keep log-books of mileage."

"If undesirable and inferior persons should procreate, and especially if they breed, they must be considered enemies of the state."

"The parents, or the children?"

"We will decide that when the time comes."

"I hope this doesn't indicate a prudishness in our new republic?"

"No. Coitus will be promoted for health and mental hygiene. If a marriage is of superlative heredity, couples may be allowed to have many children."

"I thought you were losing sleep over the surplus population."

"Of undesirables. Fewer *and better* children is what birth control means."

"And the state decides which couples marry? And which may have issue?"

"The average person cannot be trusted to make such decisions. Look whom they do marry, in most cases."

Herron winced. The man had him there. He almost said, *touche* again. He was well aware of why so many couples closed their eyes when they kissed.

"In the New Republic, marriage will be civil—"

"That's a change for the better! I've known few that were."

"Marriage, Herr Strangways, must have centuries of religious mysticism scoured away from it. This is the nineteenth century, not the dark ages of superstition. If we remake and redefine marriage enough, the very word will be meaningless, and we may remove both the word and its meaning from our lexicon. This will help in decoupling procreation and marriage."

"Decoupling procreation?" Herron echoed, intrigued.

"It will aid in our desire to decompose the family, so that children are raised by the larger village or community, at public expense. So the original breeder couple we refer to as 'parents' will not teach children anything harmful."

Herron thought of Angelica. *My mother taught me well,* she had said. *That's why we have them. To teach us right.* "What do parents teach that's harmful?"

"Anything about religion . . . or against the new republic or its economics. When we have eliminated the need for marriage and the family, citizens may pursue as much coitus as they desire, without the ramifications of disease and unwanted children. The tyranny of the individual is over, Herr Strangways. We are breaking the shackles of the individual, reversing that dogma of the cult of the individual, to evolve toward the higher and more genetically beautiful collective."

CHAPTER XLVIII

Herron finally understood what had happened to him.

He was not in a privately-owned house at all.

He was in a home for the criminally insane.

Or, at any rate, the criminally gormless.

A few of the worst lunatics had mutinied and seized control. Then they had kidnapped him from some perceived grievance – perhaps the unforgivable evil act of employing and paying workers.

Here was a (presumably) sentient being claiming that words had no meaning.

He was actively defending the notion that an entrepreneur who risked his own capital and spent his own time and effort to nurture his brainchild to a market was not entitled to keep the profits he earned, or to do as he liked with his earnings.

To him, 'freedom' was insidious and 'individualism' a prison. He was a man wanted to breed humans to become more like bees so they would work cheerfully for the broader collective rather than in the pursuit of their own happiness.

Here was a man who wanted to 'decouple procreation' for the abolition of the family, to raise children like cabbages in taxpayer-subsidized farms.

In Herron's most charitable assessment, the man was off his trolley.

Yet, harebrained as it all sounded, he could see it making popular headway.

Miss Trickett, he recalled, did not approve of covetousness. Yet envy and covetousness were driving forces behind much human behavior.

The idea of stripping money helter-skelter from the rich would certainly appeal to certain intellects – those, for instance, who were fed up with the risks of robbing homes and banks and trains.

Freeing copulation from moral or familial restraints was certainly a winning hand to any man who saw women as objectives rather than individuals.

Herron might have joined them, had he not been first in the queue for euthanizing.

Yet, it seemed to Herron, even with his limited political vision, that what Lugner and his lads wanted was a new form of slavery – at least, a stripping away of true freedom. And the free stuff, including copulation, was simply keeping their slaves amused, and not letting their minds stray to the freedom they had lost.

And, if Lugner's sloganeering campaign of posters designed by conscripted artists wasn't uniformly successful in deluding the masses – why, lunatics with bombs and airships might prove exceptionally persuasive.

2

Actually, Herron was already doubting the airship.

A message scribbled inside a cigarette was just another nod to lunacy.

The pursuit of the haggard bird's cigarette might conceivably have been a cockamamie variation of "drop the handkerchief" played between the barmy factions of this booby-hatch.

"I appreciate," Herron smiled, ingratiatingly, humoring the lunatic, "you're altruistically trying to accelerate the advance of mankind."

"Don't be childish forever, Herr Strangways. There is no 'mankind.' It is a myth, like equality, invented and fostered by religion. The priests invented single primogenitors, therefore we must somehow all be in one 'brotherhood of man.'"

"Worried about leaving out woman-kind? As if that weren't an oxymoron—"

"You utterly misunderstand me!"

"Oh, I sincerely hope so."

"Tell me, where is mankind? A man is an Englishman or a Frenchman or another collective. He is a white man or a brown man or a yellow man or a red man. Or, worst of all, that blending of everything, an *American!* Pah. Americans gave the world the absurdity of all human species in all places possessing identical – and inalienable! – rights simply because they were conceived and born and live. Americans will be scorched to the earth."

"You'll retain their females, I trust?"

"Do you wish to breed with that mongrel race?"

"It had crossed my mind from time to time."

"'Mankind' is an illusion, like *religion* and *the individual* and *the personal life*. Illusions must be crushed. This is a world of reason."

"I suppose, then, that if all men are not, as the preachers tell us, brothers, but we're only groups of diverse collectives, some collectives must, *ipso facto*, be better than others?"

"That goes without saying."

"Not to me. I suppose the superior collectives know who they are?"

"We do."

"I had a premonition you were going to use exactly those words. And you're really going to have me taken out and shot in the head."

"*Ja.*"

"And I can't smoke?"

"If you light a cigarette I will shoot you through the lungs."

"Righty-o. That proves that smoking is deleterious to the health."

"People have their place, Herr Strangways. Only in games do pawns become queens. But pawns have their uses. A select few must be kept on the board."

"Amen. Where's the fun of being superior if you can't have a fawning claque of pawns ready to sacrifice themselves for you?"

The man's eyes shot to Herron. "*Il vaut mieux être marteau qu'enclume.* You are shrewder than you look, Herr Strangways."

"I fool everybody that way."

"To look at you, one would think you had not much more brains than a bird in a clock. It is too bad we cannot use your brain in our new republic."

"Why can't you?"

"Because your brain soon will be splattered out all over the ground." "Will society roll over and play dead for this fancy programme of yours because you say 'please' and 'thank you'? Or does firepower tip the scale?"

"Education will play a vital role."

"Oh, yes, the cabbage farms. Government ownership of schools. While one nationalized industry cranks out sausages, another cranks out the veggies, little wards of the state with carefully-selected indoctrination."

"You have a gentleman's education. You know what you know because you were taught it. All education is necessarily selective. We will change not the process but the selection. This will be inculcated into the youth: individuality and privacy are outmoded by-products of an obsolete religion;

and *untermenschen* who cling besottedly to them will have no berth in the modern state."

"What are you going to do, bomb the churches, synagogues and mosques?"

"Nothing so vulgar. Initially, of course, we must seize control of the empire by terror and fear." He said that in the same tone another man might have used to say which train he'd be boarding to start a journey.

"Then you'll say it is a crisis only your puppet-master, 'She who is to come,' can control? All bees must rally 'round their queen. Will your new republic will keep the Empire intact?"

"*Ja*. Rome rolled roads over three continents, and in the *Pax Romana* Christian missionaries exploited those roads to spread their little stories of their dead Jew carpenter. We will use the empire – and Britain's naval might – to spread our ideals over the globe. After all, Herr Strangways, when you start to build a new bridge over a river you cannot just blow up the old one."

Herron shook his head. "Lost me there."

"Traffic cannot be stop. Old bridges must be kept open until new bridges is complete. Then utterly destroy the old bridge. The same with your religion—"

"I'm not really much of a church-goer, though I claim to be High—"

"—will die a slow death. Religion had its place in the childhood of man, when everything could not be scientifically explained. This is the nineteenth century. We know everything. And we are going into a bright, sparkling new twentieth century that will see the perfection of the human species by engineering."

Dismissive as he was of the Jewish carpenter whose stories were spread by Christian missionaries, Herron desperately wanted to point out he was still clinging besottedly to a dating system based on that Jewish carpenter's birth.

"The priests," the man continued, "and rabbis and imams who live off society are parasites. Parasites are genetic dead ends. But those with childish minds will cling to their religion. Therefore, if they cannot be persuaded by a massive campaign of re-education, the parasites must be surgically extracted from the larger body. Your religion is noxious as it teaches that all men are equal in the eyes of your deity, and that all persons therefore have intrinsic worth. You are like men in a raft after the ship has gone down, who, seeing an importance in all human life, try to save every drowning soul – until the raft sinks beneath the weight of its overloaded, writhing mass of stinking human flesh."

"For a foreigner, I must commend your flair for solid English imagery."

"We must channel that 'will to believe' from a hope in Salvation to a new hope that we, their elected leaders, will achieve our stated goal of equality."

"I thought you didn't believe in equality."

"I said, 'our stated goal.' We must appear to be liberators. Only when we have established our liberation will there be reprisals."

"Ah!" Herron tapped the side of his nose. "Box clever there. You'll have the *volk* following you like a white rabbit through your private Wonderland."

Probably due to his detestation of fictional worlds, Mister Moustache was unfamiliar with the work Herron referenced. Thinking Herron had gotten the wrong end of the stick with his talk of rabbits, he tried to explain,

"For the betterment of society, the superstitious barrier between the organic and inorganic, between 'soul' and 'body,' must be dissolved. It will not be easy to dissolve at first, so there must be an initial misdirection."

"Like a conjuring trick."

"*Ja.*"

"In simple terms, you'll lie through your bloody teeth."

"The cosmos has no god, no invisible forces. Freed from the rules of conventional morality, we may – *must* – say whatever will help us succeed."

"'Lie' being only a word." Considering Merridew, Herron said, "They'll be hard nuts to crack, these religious folk. I know. I've tried."

"We shall 'crack' them. The French Revolution made the mistake of introducing the Cult of the Supreme Being – which was too much of a concession to their enemies. Slowly, but surely, we will replace the idea of an Objective Deity floating on a cloud with an earth-bound religion that prefers the salvation of the world's manifold ecologies to that of man."

"Yep. Got to look after the dirt first. Will you stop the coming Ice Age, too?"

"For recalcitrant believers, there are more expedient ways of cutting a cancer from the body politic. We *will* disintegrating the mysticism of man as a superior creature beloved by a creative deity. Gradually that myth will be replaced by the knowledge that we all are animals alike. From there it will be a short step for the masses to accept that unfit or unattractive bipedal animals should be euthanized."

"Yet you won't eat meat.""Nor cheese," he added, proudly, smiling as he said the word. Apparently, he did not perceive Herron's irony.

His "cheese" smile faded as Stoker and Hawkins, who had warmed up the motor-carriage engine to their satisfaction, drove to the open stable doors.

3

Since they could not shoot him twice – he hoped – Herron decided to give the moustache a poke in the eye before he was taken away.

His hands were still tied in front of him, but two fists were better than one. After all, the fellow had two eyes, and Herron thought he might as well bung them both while he was at it.

The front of the motor-carriage appeared in the stable door.

"Herr Strangways: Will you surrender those papers?"

"Will you let me live if I give them to you?"

"No."

"If I don't have a chance, I don't have the papers."

"We will search every place you have been. And every person in those places. You may save them a lot of unnecessary pain and suffering."

"I can tell you what the message says, so you won't have to look for it."

"We know that. It is about our plans. We want no one else to know. We have worked too hard too long to have tomorrow ruined by bumblers. Anyone who knows our plans, or whom we suspect of knowing, must die. You first. Now."

Mister Moustache turned his head, to snap a few orders to Stoker and Hawkins.

Making the most of this opportunity, Herron lunged and smacked the man in the eyes with both fists. The movement was so swift, neither Stoker nor Hawkins had time to react at first.

Hopping out of the auto, Hawkins grabbed Herron around the waist.

Herron clutched the front of the motor-carriage with his bound fists. Hawkins and Stoker each grabbed one of his legs, stretching his legs out – and apart – in a desperate attempt to tug him loose.

"I have friends in high places!" Herron fired this last salvo between grunts as his legs were yanked harder and harder, both out, and apart, like a wishbone. "They'll wonder—umph!—where I am!"

"In twelve hours, Herr Strangways," said Mister Moustache, massaging the tender spots under his eyes, "the disappearance of one man hardly will matter."

"Before I die—umph!—at least tell me—oh!—who killed the haggard bird! I can't die without knowing. I'll be curious for all eternity!—umph!"

"No one on this estate killed him."

Strangely enough, Herron believed him. The man might have the soul of a merry wholesale slaughterer; and his ability to change the meanings of words in an instant revealed the heart of a confirmed and chronic liar of truly titanic proportions. But on this one occasion, he was telling the truth.

Herron had no more opportunity to think. Stoker and Hawkins tugged him loose and he hit the rutted ground face-down with a *thump*.

"I am weary of you, Strangways. Tomorrow is a big day. I am sorry you will not live to see it. Good bye."

Stoker and Hawkins yanked Herron around the rear of the motor-carriage whiel the other man slowly trundled off with his moustache, back inside the big house.

CHAPTER XLIX

Hawkins handcuffed Herron to the rear of a Knight three-wheeler, which had two larger wheels behind and one (slightly) smaller front wheel steered by a tiller.

John Henry Knight designed this motor carriage for two persons. Stoker and his companion occupied the seats, while Herron bounced uncomfortably along with them, strapped across the back. The stench of petrol fumes was so strong Herron nearly suffocated on the way to his grave.

These newfangled vehicles were unquestionably superior to older modes of transportation. Horses, which pulled a vast variety of vehicles, deposited unhygienic traces throughout the cities. Trains were smoky and sooty.

Motor carriages used clean fuels that cost less than upkeep for horses. They looked shinier and smelled marginally better, and so were healthier and more efficient. They didn't get tired. They didn't require whipping. They were not, like trains, bound to tracks.

This motor-carriage made more than its fair share of noise, but Herron felt this problem would be reduced with refinements to the engines. That was a matter for the intractable laws of supply and demand.

But he had no time to mull over the pros and cons of nascent automobiles. He was gripping the sides of the vehicle with all his might to keep from tumbling off and being dragged to death by his wrists.

2

It was night. The faint white glow of the last-quarter moon shone valiantly through a rising fog.

Herron realized they were in the fen country, east of London toward the North Sea. It was a part of the world he'd never visited in any depth – although it was not very far from his nominal *alma mater*, Cambridge.

The fens consisted of wetlands made profitably arable by clever drainage. Farmland reclaimed from useless wetland had proven so fruitful for farming, food prices had dropped. Plentiful food at lower prices genuinely assuaged hunger – without the necessity of scientifically sloughing off swaths of population.

The huge estate was criss-crossed with narrow, paved roadways. Bridges, dykes and locks carried the roads over running water.

With a sinking heart, Herron realized he had little chance to escape. Even if he managed to hocus-pocus his way free from the manacles and make a break for it, he'd wind up crawling through ditches and over dykes, splashing through drains and meres, swimming streams. And all while dodging bullets.

Since Herron's own doom was sealed, his final thoughts were for Angelica Trickett. In the morning, she had to sneak out from under Lady Calthrop's basilisk eye and get word to Inspector Chubb.

But word of what? And would Chubb protect her on the basis of a cigarette paper of doubtful provenance? The story reeked of implausibility even to Herron, who was about to have his skull splintered by a bullet because of it.

He hoped she would leave that house. Since he had dropped the handkerchief on her, Angelica was second in line for the new republic's abattoir.

3

When the vehicle finally stopped, Herron was afraid they'd make him suffer the indignity of carrying the shovel.

Fortunately, Stoker and Hawkins trusted him with nothing he might use as a weapon. Hawkins carried the shovel across his shoulders with his wrists hooked over the handle.

When they decided on a suitably remote spot, Hawkins solemnly threw the shovel straight up in the soft ground, where it quivered in front of Herron.

"Dig," said Stoker, aiming a gun at Herron's brisket.

His companion laughed. "Makin' him dig his own grave. That's a good 'un. You allus was a card, Jake."

Herron could not imagine where Hawkins got the idea his associate was 'a card.' Stoker's beady eyes had an unwavering seriousness.

Wrenching the shovel from the earth, Herron applied himself to the hardest manual labor he'd ever done in his life.

The earth was soft. Digging wasn't difficult, but Stoker wanted Herron buried deep.

Soon, the white cotton gloves accessorizing the waiter's uniform were shredded. So were Herron's hands. He regretted he wouldn't be living long enough to raise blisters.

He had always kept up with games and exercises, including swimming; but digging gave him aches in muscles he never realized he had.

During the excavation Herron had, with the permission of his guards, stripped off his coat, waistcoat, stock and collar. He was clad only in his breeches and shirt sleeves when the hole was deep enough for Stoker to order a halt.

"Okay, Strangways. Toss out the shovel."

Herron hurled the shovel from the pit.

Stoker motioned with his pistol. "Out of the hole."

"Why git 'im out once he's in it?" demanded Hawkins.

"He might duck down when I shoot, dunce. Let's make it easy on us. Get up here, Strangways."

Herron hadn't thought to dig steps into a grave. Climbing from the hole, Herron trembled from an involuntary judder of muscles unaccustomed to manual labor. The digging had not done his manicure any good, either.

Squirming over the rim of the pit, Herron briefly toyed with the idea of diving for the shovel, knocking Stoker's pistol away with it, and braining Hawkins.

Unfortunately, the men were standing too far apart. Only one of them actually had a gun trained on him, but both of them were armed. Herron might take *one* of them with him, but the other would kill him just as dead.

"Kneel on the ground with your head over the hole. It'll be cleaner."

Reaching into his inner coat pocket, Hawkins begged, "Let me do 'im Jake."

"You had the first shot yesterday – and, obviously, your performance was less than adequate. It's my turn to shoot him first."

"That wasn't fair. I didn't get a clear shot at 'im."

"You get the first shot next time. We agreed to the rotation."

Hawkins drew a greasy deck of pasteboard playing cards. "Cut you for him."

Stoker sadly shook his head. "Why don't we just do eeny-meeny-miney-moe, catch a tiger by the toe?"

"Okay."

Rolling his eyes, Stoker said, "Just go stand behind him and apply the *coup de grace*. I doubt we'll need it. I've potted smaller birds with one bullet."

"Hey!" said Herron, "Don't I get a blindfold and a cigarette?"

"This is not a firing squad, Strangways; it's an execution."

"Yeah," echoed Hawkins, snorting a chuckle through his nose, "where do you think you are, a firing squad or sumpin'?"

"You've wasted enough of our time as it is. Besides, I do not smoke, so I have no cigarettes on me. And my friend here has none ready-made. Just try to relax. Stare into the pit and it'll all be over before you can say Jack Robinson."

"And I'll do the cootie-grah," said the other.

"Now," said Stoker, "throw all those clothes you cast off into the pit. We don't want them found by trespassing busybodies, do we? Right."

Herron kicked the clothes into the hole. As he knelt and extended his head over the digs that would be his home for the rest of eternity, he realized the man with the twisted moustache had been right about one thing – if only one. No one was riding to rescue him at the last moment.

After all that digging, Herron was too weary to fight. He hadn't the energy to run, even if he wasn't gunned down before he found his feet.

He felt he deserved a good, long rest. And he was just about to get one.

His only hope was that Angelica would get through with the key to the whole mess. *Not that it'll do me a hell of a lot of good,* he thought.

And the key hadn't made sense, even when they cracked it. Herron was literally and figuratively going to his grave in the dark.

As he heard the large pistol being cocked, Herron said, "Won't they find me?"

"Naw," answered Hawkins. "We'll set a bush out over yer. The way this-yere country stinks, they'll never get a whiff of a stiff bein' under 'aire."

Looking up at his executioners, Herron saw by their expressions that pleading would have no effect. He did his best to keep his old-school upper lip stiff.

Never give the other fellow the gratification of seeing your fear.

His aunt always predicted he would come to a bad end. Herron was unable to imagine a worse end than being shot in ignominiously in the back of the head and buried in a frilly white shirt-front and satin knee-breeches. Fortunately, Herron was almost too weary to feel the horror of it – even of the lace cuffs he'd wear until the Judgment Day.

He had not read many novels in his life, but when he was a boy he read a lurid piece of fiction with the lines,

The worms, they crept in, and the worms, they crept out,
And sported his eyes and his temples about.

What an ignominious thought to die on! He was glad he'd been forced to dig the hole. That final exertion of his life left him barely sufficient strength to realize that this was the end of twenty-seven useless years. And all that time spent relentlessly pursuing women . . .

. . . well, he grudgingly admitted, one corner of his mouth jabbing up in a smile, his twenty-seven years had not been a *total* loss.

He was unable to peer down into the hole. He did not feel compelled to see it right away – he'd be in it long enough. Instead, he kept his eyes trained on the barrel of the gun Stoker aimed at him.

Stoker inclined his head to his companion, who stepped forward with a grin, ready to finish Herron off if they didn't do the job in one.

He recalled what Jessup had said: *their sort have no scruple about shooting a sitting bird.* Or, indeed, a kneeling one.

He expected Stoker to step up and fire point-blank into his head. Instead, Stoker took aim and fired from where he stood.

Stoker's single shot rang out and reverberated over the fens. No *coup de grace* was necessary. Death was instantaneous and irrevocable.

Two dim figures, one with a smoking pistol, remained silhouetted in the moonlit swirls of fog on the fens, staring at the headless body in the grave.

Tuesday, June 22, 1897

CHAPTER L

When Angelica crawled across the carpeted corridor to Lady Calthrop's door and put her ear to the keyhole, what she heard was not the metallic tapping of telegraph keys. It was more like – like a buzzing. Morse code delivered by bees.

And it was extremely faint. If she hadn't had twenty-two-year young ears, she'd never have heard it through that heavy door.

The large pendulum clock downstairs began to ring the hour. It chimed first, then clanged out midnight. That kept Angelica from being able to hear a thing.

Only when the twelfth ring died away could Angelica piece together the message:

-A-Y-S-D-E-A-D-C-O-N-F-I-R-M-E-D-R-E-P-E-A-T-S-T-R-A-N-G-W-A-Y-S-D-E-A-D-

Biting the knuckle of her right index finger to keep from crying out, Angelica rushed to her room and flung herself face-down on the bed. Feeding a corner of the counterpane into her mouth, she stifled her moans until she nearly choked.

What in God's Holy Name is going on? She wondered. Herron Strangways – dead? He *couldn't* be! He was having tea here just a few hours ago.

He was a silly young ass . . . but dead? How?

After a few minutes, Angelica composed herself. She could almost hear Herron's voice,

"If you do not hear from me again . . . or if anything untoward happens to you or to Lady Calthrop because of my presence here . . . please contact Inspector (something) *. . . of Scotland Yard."*

Herron had not wanted to write anything down – and a good thing, considering what happened to things in this house that got written down! But her mind was a bit fuzzy after the shock of hearing about his death – no, his *confirmed* death. The Inspector's name did not spring readily to mind. Well, she had heard from Herron, in a way. She had to sneak out.

CHAPTER LI

Long before her usual time to rise, Angelica lay wide awake and fully dressed atop of the covers on her bed. She'd even kept her shoes on.

Normally, she was quite a good sleeper. This night, she had lain on her back staring into the blackness, unable to keep herself from reliving the last few hours of Monday over and over and over in her mind.

She occasionally misplaced things, when she was flustered or in a hurry; but she had not lost the cigarette paper, and certainly not the paper she left in the typewriter roller. They had been stolen and she knew by whom.

Dapifer is more Lady Calthrop's dog than that flea-bitten terrier, Herron had said. Angelica had not returned to that inscrutable butler's room for a show-down. She no longer cared even to bid him fare-well. He had been in her room – in her space! Without permission. *How dare he!* And Monday ended with that buzzing telegraph message. That message kept pulsing through her brain from the time she laid down until now – a telegraph message sent to a house *connected by no telegraph wires.*

Was that why Angelica had to read to Her Ladyship in the dark, with the shades drawn? So that her young and inquisitive eyes would not notice a telegraphic machine hidden in Lady Calthrop's bedroom?

Was that why Doris was kept on as upstairs (and, these days, downstairs) maid when nearly all the other servants were given their notice? Lady Calthrop might cover a telegraphic machine with nothing more than a bushel basket and rest assured that Doris would never find it!

And the message was so horrible! *Strangways dead*. Confirmed.

Trying to convince herself she was out of practice and had misunderstood the Morse, Angelica's fingers spent more than an hour tapping out the letters on the counterpane, trying to rearrange them so they spelled – *anything* else.

She could find only one possible construction for that cold message.

Strangways dead. Confirmed.

Why – confirmed?

Not that it mattered. Hearing it hurt just as badly whether his death was confirmed or not. Having seen them at close range, she could not contemplate a world where Herron Strangways' brown eyes were forever closed.

Even less could she imagine them being blasted out from the front of his face by .45 caliber slug from a Smith and Wesson model 3 Schofield revolver.

And why should Lady Calthrop be told about it . . . at midnight! . . . by a private telegraph? And why hadn't it sounded like a telegraph?

Her decision to sneak out to that Inspector with her story had hardened over the hours into a determination to leave Lady Calthrop's service without notice.

I'll be shut of this house come dawn, she swore silently, vowing she would take nothing with her but her typewriter and the clothes she came in.

And the pistol, her sole gift from Herron Strangways.

Everything else in her possession had been provided by Lady Calthrop.

That embarrassed Angelica, in retrospect. She called herself "earning a living" but her duties were light. Oh, she had to be on call twenty-four hours a day, and she had to perform some unusual tasks.

When Lady Calthrop held dinner parties, she dressed Angelica in gowns with balloon sleeves and pleated skirts – cut low to display her exquisite back to good effect, as well as more than a hint Angelica's well-sculpted decolletage.

Angelica was a modest young lady. Proud as she was of the way her *poitrine* had developed, she preferred gowns and dresses that were conducive to gentlemen looking into her eyes rather than down her front.

Her chest was not for the delectation of the general public. She attended these functions equipped with a fan, which she used as a screen for anything below her neckline. She barely touched her food on these occasions, since it was hard to eat and hold a fan simultaneously.

She felt like an exhibit rather than a guest, like a shop window display in a red light district. She was always thankful when each dinner party ground to a close.

In return for her duties, all Angelica's physical needs were provided for.

In the sleepless night she realized, to her chagrin, it was making her an addict.

A chronic opium-smoker listlessly dreaming his life away curled up in a pipe would be unable to function in real life if the pipe was removed. Angelica had struck the same sort of Mephistophelean bargain with Lady Calthrop.

By having all her needs provided for, under the pretense of earning her own way, she would eventually be debilitated by mollycoddling disguised as liberality.

She recalled the song Herron had quoted at her. In her present position, she actually was no better than a woman who married for money. She was Lady Calthrop's "bird in a gilded cage."

I'd be a jolly sight happier as Herron Strangways' kept woman, than Lady Calthrop'! At least he is a lively young man.

She corrected herself. *Was.* Dead. Confirmed.

Whatever happened to her, Angelica decided she would no longer be a woman kept by anyone. She'd break free.

Come dawn, she would leave the house of secrets. She would go straight across the river to her brother, knock him up, and inform him she had left—

—the service of one of the empire's richest women. A cousin and intimate of the Queen. A grandame who provided a better home – in exchange for few actual duties – than any other employer could, or would.

After boasting about standing on her own two feet, what would he think?

Well, he'd love to see more of her. He'd offer to put her up. But she couldn't sponge off him. She would have to find work.

She adamantly refused to return to the drudgery of a typewriting position.

Was work as a paid companion for another invalid lady impossible?

When she applied for another situation, they'd ask for references.

If she mentioned she had worked for Lady Calthrop, they would be impressed.

Why did you leave her employment?

What could she say? *I felt too cosseted?*

Then they would contact Her Ladyship, who would tersely reply that Miss Trickett had vanished into the night without giving notice.

No one would ever hire such a person.

She could be a telegrapher! That wouldn't require references, only skill. The idea of finding employment (and, maybe, advancement) by skill rather than by looks or connections appealed to her.

She had been a rapid telegrapher at one time. And like Herron Strangways said, she'd know everyone's secrets.

That brought her full-circle. *Strangways dead.*

She wondered what that secret could mean.

No matter which way she shifted it, the only meaning she could squeeze from it was that Herron Strangways was dead. And that news was so important to Lady Calthrop she had to receive it at midnight. And with a confirmation!

She desperately wanted some tea—

—and for the first time remembered leaving the kettle on the gas stove. The water would have boiled away and the kettle would be burnt to a crisp. The kitchen was probably thick with smoke and the stench of roasted copper.

In an hour or so Cook would rise to start breakfast and find an unholy mess!

No more waiting. Angelica could not face the wrath of Cook. She rose gradually, so the bed would not squeak.

Then she recalled: the clothes she first came in were in the laundry!

Even if they had been in her wardrobe, Angelica might take an hour to dress and do her hair decently. By that time, the house would be stirring and escape might prove impossible.

She decided to leave in what she wore: her bifurcated cycling skirt, blue blouse, fawn waistcoat, black stockings and button-shoes.

Angelica felt that walking out in them was stealing from her employer.

But I'm not Lady Godiva, she told herself.

She couldn't swallow her modesty and leave all her clothes behind. Wending nude across London, darting from doorway to doorway, lamp post to lamp post, bush to bush, was impractical.

It was the day of the Diamond Jubilee Procession, which would begin in a matter of hours. The streets would be filled with people who had already staked out places to stand. She'd give them more of an eyeful than they bargained for!

And her prim and proper brother, a good fifteen years older than she, might have a word or two about her showing up on his doorstep *au naturel*.

She could probably keep all the clothes in her wardrobe, so far as the household was concerned. They had been bought to measure for her. They were far too big and young-looking for Lady Calthrop. Doris was too dainty for them, particularly in the bust. They were of no use to Dapifer even if he could pour his enormous frame into them. It was inconceivable Lady Calthrop would find another companion of exactly Angelica's dimensions, especially in the waist.

It was the principle of the thing. Angelica considered them stolen clothes if she left in them. She would mail them back here when she had bought replacements from her own savings.

The straw hat she'd come in was damaged long ago and discarded, so she would leave without a hat – or a coat or cape, since every one in her armoire had been given to her by Lady Calthrop.

She hated to leave with neither a hat nor a cape, but it had to be done.

Money. She double-checked the remains of what cash she had brought with her. All present and accounted for. Dapifer, or whoever had been in her bedroom (that still sent chills shivering through her frame) had not come for cash.

Property. She owned a bicycle and a typewriter. She had arrived on her bicycle with her typewriter in the basket. That was how she would leave.

Gazing around her room again, she saw that everything there – down to the squat, blue-tinted porcelain Royal Bond clock by her bed (which she had never liked, and which showed almost a quarter of three) – had come with the job. Lady Calthrop had not expressly forbidden it, but Angelica had never brightened the austere décor by any personalizing touch. She wondered why.

She looked to the bedside table at her right. The pistol lay pointing away from her and the cartridge box stood sentry beside it. Those were hers, too, gifts from Herron Strangways. She thought she had unloaded it, but one couldn't be too careful with firearms. Angelica had taken the pistol out of her pocket so, if she managed to catch any shut-eye, she wouldn't shoot herself squirming in her sleep.

Sitting on the bedside, she broke the revolver open. All the chambers were empty. She filled them with cartridges. Snapping the pistol back together, she slipped it into her right-hand skirt pocket. The ammunition box, she squeezed into the left pocket.

She had a little money, the clothes she stood up in, a bicycle, a typewriter and a loaded revolver. What more did an aspiring author require to begin a new life?

Typewriter in hand, she crept to the door. Easing the door open, Angelica leaned out and peered both ways along the darkened corridor.

The corridor was clear all the way to the gallery overlooking the entrance-hall.

The wings were separated from the gallery by faux-Tudor archways. Sidling along the wall, Angelica tucked herself into the corner of the arch.

The ginger-breaded archway was merely a fanciful architectural detail. Since it was not load-bearing, its legs were too slender to conceal a healthy young woman. The tips of her long shoes and her well-supported breasts jutted visibly out in the halo of light from the lamp she'd left burning at the head of the stairs.

So did the heavy typewriter.

She peeked around the arch, then tip-toed to the curving grand stairway.

Just as she reached the stairs, the door at the far end of the corridor opened. The seated form of Lady Calthrop was silhouetted in the doorway of her brightly-lit *chambre* with her parasol across her knees.

Foiled in making a surreptitious, nocturnal flit, out of courtesy to Her Ladyship Angelica stood her ground for a conversation she feared might turn unpleasant.

2

As the wheelchair creaked closer and Her Ladyship rolled into the light of the lamp, Angelica's jaw dropped.

Lady Calthrop had cast off her widow's weeds. She was clad in a thin, *white* gown. Her hair was done up in Regency Grecian style, with a diamond tiara sparkling in her coiffure. Around her neck she wore a rope of beads capable of anchoring a small watercraft. In her lap was the silver casket reading *I.II.*

The parasol beneath the casket was the same tatty bamboo affair she had carried to the train Saturday night; but though Angelica registered that fact, she did not grasp its importance.

"My dear, why aren't you in bed? You're fully dressed."

"I'm sorry, Lady Calthrop. I . . . I couldn't sleep—"

"Thinking about your man, I'm sure. Don't you worry about him. His aunt has told me many stories about the way he treats females. He won't be back for you. Don't give him another thought."

Angelica winced. That was like the stories she had heard of him, too. Her doubts about Herron began to resurface.

Then she remembered Her Ladyship had been the recipient of that horrible telegraphic message. Lady Calthrop knew for a fact Herron Strangways would not be returning, because she knew Herron Strangways was dead. *Confirmed.*

She cocked her head. "You look flustered, child. What is the matter?"

"I . . . I just thought I'd saunter out for a breath of air."

"In the middle of the night? With your typewriter?"

Lady Calthrop wheeled slowly along the banister in the gallery until she sat sideways between Angelica and the stairs.

"I'm afraid I cannot let you go out. Unless you are giving notice."

Angelica started to offer an explanation—

Lady Calthrop cut her short.

"And then it must be a fortnight in advance. You must still live under my roof and obey my rules for two weeks, my dear."

Lady Calthrop's voice changed subtly. Only someone who heard her every day would pick up on the slight variation in tone. It had that honed edge she always used when putting Angelica in her place while still sounding pleasant to company.

Angelica wished she had run downstairs before letting herself be confronted. She couldn't get out of it, now. Lady Calthrop's sidelong chair blocked the stairway. A narrow space opened on either side of the chair, but Her Ladyship handled her chair expertly; she could roll back and forth, as necessary, to clog the passage. To reach the stairs, Angelica would have to leap over her.

Her Ladyship's reptilian neck craned up to the side, toward Angelica.

"If you leave without notice, I must let you go without a reference. If anyone called on me about you, I'd say you were a flighty girl. You'll never find another job, I'll see to that. I'll say you received gentlemen in the house behind my back."

"That's a lie!"

"That's not a nice thing to say."

"You disapprove of the way it sounds? It's not the truth."

"*Quid . . . est . . . veritas.*" Lady Calthrop cackled. "So far as I know, you have had men up here behind my back."

Angelica's face flushed angrily, but she retained her temper. "You know very well I have not, Your Ladyship. Since I've been in your house, except on days off I've never been so far away you couldn't whistle me up whenever you liked."

"What about that young man you go cycling with? You call him your brother, but he doesn't much look like you. How do I know what you two get up to in the country? Even if he is your brother – such things have happened. I might just be forced to say, all around London, that I had inadvertently employed a Sieglinde."

Though she had not seen Richard Wagner's *Die Walkure*, Angelica recognized the name. She had learned from sniggling girls in her boarding school about the sister in the sibling incest presented in that opera.

Angelica was so upset by this allegation, she was about to say something even more uncivil to Lady Calthrop. Then she remembered she wasn't here to bandy words but to leave. The implication that she and her brother were lovers was the last straw. As soon as she saw a break in the conversation she would give notice and depart with dignity, without another word.

"For all I know," Lady Calthrop shrugged, "you do sneak men in. If I were young and beautiful like you – I would. 'Gather ye rosebuds while ye may, Old time is still a-flying . . . !' So, unless you intend to marry for money – and I've no doubt a woman with your attributes can sell herself high – you'll be bereft if you leave and I spread that word about you. And do not pursue that Don Jeu-an who was here yesterday, thinking marry his money. You'll never see him again."

Angelica's mouth was dry as she rasped out, "Why not?"

She knew why not. She wanted Lady Calthrop to explain.

Her Ladyship merely gave a slight toss of one shoulder. "Men are all alike."

They are when they're dead! Angelica silently seethed.

"They only want one thing," Her Ladyship rattled on. "They have contempt for you if you're weak enough to give it to them; and if you're adamant that you won't give it to them until your wedding night they have contempt for you then, too. And this Strangways," (the way she snarled his name, it appeared to give her mouth a bad taste) "was a most unsuitable young man, with a foul reputation. He reminds me of the line in the poem by Burns, *'there's a youth, a witless youth.'* No, he won't be back for the likes of you, child."

Angelica wondered what to do. More than ever, she was certain she was right in leaving, even without notice, though her departure could not be covert.

Unfortunately, she could not just slip past. Lady Calthrop might just be cruel enough to catch her and squeeze her legs between the chair and the banister.

She might have trotted down the back stairs – but Her Ladyship was talking to her, so Angelica waited until she could sneak a word of farewell in edgewise.

And then . . . what?

She would be out of a job and unemployable. If Lady Calthrop carried through with her threat to sully her reputation, she would have to leave London.

Why, if a woman with Her Ladyship's power in Society intimated that Herron Strangways had been known to visit Miss Trickett on the sly—

—Angelica might have to change her name.

Deciding to bait Lady Calthrop into revealing what she knew about Herron Strangways' death, she grimly interrupted,

"Lady Calthrop, I know typing, shorthand – and Morse."

Lady Calthrop might have been on a pivot, she wheeled around so quickly to face Angelica. Her eyes were those of a cobra about to strike.

"Then you probably realize, my dear, I only admitted that Strangways to this house because I had already received a message about him."

That was a bolt from the blue. So far as Angelica knew, the first either of them had heard from him was when Dapifer presented his card.

"*Herron Strangways*! Since you were present when I received his card I pretended not to recognize the name. Yet, I had already sent men out looking for him. And then the fool marched straight up to my door. I let him in to find out what he knew. Nothing much, as I expected. The man was every inch the fool he looked, even without the eyeglass. Nevertheless, even fools are dangerous when they play with dynamite. So I had planned to dispose of him here."

The full import of these words wasn't registering on Angelica's still shocked mind. "You were about to have him thrown out."

"I was going to kill him if he knew anything. And if he didn't, I would have Dapifer throw him face-down in the street. He might be alive now if you had not rushed down and interfered. And when you found the other half of that cigarette paper, and I watched you two piece together the whole story, I knew he would have do die, as little as he knew. And so must you."

Angelica kept her perfect posture, but mind was reeling. "What?"

"Your message must never leave this house. The cigarette paper and your copy of their message have both been destroyed. Only two minds knew what that message was. One of those minds, if you care to dignify it with that name, is spread out in a bloody mess over the fens. The other mind is yours."

Lady Calthrop's clinging white gown revealed no weapons. *Is she going to try to club me to death with a bamboo parasol?*

It was time to go. Whatever Lady Calthrop meant to do, Angelica was unafraid that a wheelchair-bound invalid might pursue her down flights of stairs. The pistols were on the ground floor, and the boomerangs were on the walls out of Lady Calthrop's reach. Therefore, Her Ladyship could not shoot Angelica, or stun her from behind. If Angelica could not sidle past her and escape down the front stairs, she would run down the back stairs.

Nevertheless, she felt obliged to utter a polite word or two before taking to her heels. "Lady Calthrop," (because of her emotions, Angelica heard her voice rising a jagged octave) "you've been very kind to me–"

"Yes. My daughter told me you were a perfect specimen."

Angelica was so profoundly repulsed by the word, she staggered back a few steps. Lady Calthrop might have slapped her face.

"*Specimen?*"

"Tall. Fine posture and shoulders. Good dorsal region. A strong upper torso with well-toned shoulders and arms and gently sloping but rounded, pertly tip-tilted breasts."

"Lady Calthrop—!" cried Angelica, indignantly.

"Perfect pelvis, buttocks, legs. That hair! – those emerald eyes! Ah! You were so much the opposite of that discharge from my womb, which I should have drowned in a bucket. How ugly she was! I want to spare future mothers from such a sight. We must selectively breed for beauty."

Angelica remembered Lady Calthrop's daughter: short with stubby, fat legs; pudgy; dark; freckled; short-sighted. With a slight overbite.

"When my daughter went to school, I told her to keep her tiny, piggy eyes out for someone perfect and to make friends with her. When she told me about you, at my request she spied on you everywhere. In the bath—"

Angelica dropped her typewriter. Her hand shot to her mouth as if to keep her from throwing up. "Oh, dear God."

"—in the changing room. She crept to your bedside at night and stared down at you while you slept. Occasionally she gave you a sleeping draught I sent her, and examined your body more fully—"

"Oh, no! Oh, God, no!" An image flashed through Angelica's mind of herself drugged in bed with Lady Calthrop's daughter undressing her and groping her over. She recalled some mornings at school when she woke up listless and sore—

And headachy from being knocked out by drugs . . . !

Why, she might have died if that girl had slipped her too much of the drug!

And Angelica was afraid to think who else might have taken advantage of her while she was unconscious. *Even Herron Strangways wouldn't stoop to that!*

"When she first told me about you, her voice was worshipful. She adored you. I knew then I had to have you."

"H-have me?"

"Your repellent notion of perfection of the soul through the Cross is *passe*. Science has eliminated the need for any creator. The industrial society has eliminated the need for a soul. Man is a machine, and like all machinery must be perfected through science. Adaptation is far too slow and chancy. Mankind requires perfection by technological engineering directed through eugenics."

Even if Angelica had been familiar with these concepts, she would not have pieced together the fragments of what Lady Calthrop was talking about. Her mind, working under much pressure and no sleep, was utterly revolted by those revelations she could understand. Angelica heard these final words indistinctly, muffled by a mist settling over her brain.

Yet even in her adled mental state, she grasped why she was brought into the house. And why she went to dinner parties in gowns cut low front and back, with "Doctor This" and "Professor That" from the "Univeristy of Somewhere." They were a creepy eugenics circle dominated by Her Ladyship. Angelica *had* been on display, like so much prime meat. Or a beast in a zoo.

"That, my dear, is the future. The future is where we must all live. Tradition is the past. History must be swept away and forgotten."

She wheeled incrementally closer. Hemmed in at the wall, Angelica could no more run than a rodent fixed in the hypnotic stare of a snake.

"I hated you when I first saw you. I made it look like grief over that person I suffered to birth . . . but I loathed *you*. You were everything I never was, and everything I could never produce. Yet I loved you, too, more with more motherly affection than I ever felt for that spawn of mine. Lovely. Tall. Strong. Intelligent. You are the woman of the future!

"Strangways asked me what my interest is. I hinted, but he obviously didn't know what I was talking about. I'll tell you straight. Just as my husband collected these awful weapons, I, too, am a collector – of perfection. We have a new society rising, Angelica. A technological society, full of electric lights and typewriters . . . and airships. But it is *so* disunified. Everyone does as they please without regard to the genetic hygiene of humanity. We must cease to think in categories. We must no longer perceive the political, the economic, the social, the scientific – or the 'personal' – as separate. In a truly modern state there will be no such distinction. All will be part of the organic whole of the village – and it all must be *controlled*. With technology we have nearly perfected the world around us. Now we must perfect the human race that runs roughshod over it."

As she spoke, Lady Calthrop was slowly raising her parasol.

Angelica fought the mists gathering around her brain. However rude it seemed, whatever the ramifications of her actions, she must break off the conversation and leave this madhouse. She no longer cared if Lady Calthrop spread the word that Angelica Trickett had turned her house into a brothel. She refused to remain another minute in the company of this horrid person.

She wished she could write the woman off as a lunatic. Her Ladyship's eyes, however, told Angelica she was sober and coldly rational.

"Lady Calthrop, I am leaving. Please get out of my way."

"You know, Angelica, I would like to have seen you two healthy specimens copulating. It would have been a beautiful sight."

Angelica, reaching for her typewriter, froze in mid-stoop.

Her Ladyship smirked at the look on Angelica's face. "Our absurd society believes it has overcome our animalistic impulses, so it teaches young animals like you to be shocked at such sentiments. 'You are better than the animals,' they tell you, 'therefore when you mate, it must be concealed from sight, in a locked or lightless room, or even under covers.' It is treated like a shame, than a matter for rejoicing – even between persons like you two, who were so beautiful together. That is how far our society has lost its moral bearing. We must eliminate that morality build a new morality, clothing our beliefs in the white garments of truth."

"Truth!" spat Angelica. "Which you don't believe in!"

"Most people do believe there is a truth of some sort. We must fight the enemy where he is."

Angelica's head was spinning. "What . . . *enemy*?"

"The people. High-minded people who think they are they are God's 'special creation.' In the new morality we must and will make citizens aware that they are animals who should, like other animals, give in to and delight in all their natural impulses. I've never seen dogs blushing with shame when a male dog pushes the female like a wheelbarrow! Why should men and women not be the same? And, along with the release of our natural impulses, we must carefully teach that some human animals are vermin who need to be isolated and destroyed for the betterment of society. The two ideals are inseparable. If we have a society that breeds freely, we must purge those types whose breeding would prove harmful to the species. That would solve the problem of the surplus population as well.

"All through tea, while you two were wasting your lives over that doomed bit of scribbling, I was fancying what you would look like in various poses, with him pressing you down on the carpet – or you, him."

She laughed at Angelica's scandalized stare.

"Hypocrite. I know you were thinking the same thing. I wanted so much to tell you both to rejoice and revel in your animalistic youth. How I wished circumstances were different, so I could encourage you to cast aside the tea things and your clothes and release your pent-up impulses. He did have a fine exterior – but he had to die because of what he knew, so it's just as well he was a nitwit. Strangways' mental equipment was light, and I did not want so perfect a specimen as yourself to produce issue that might have your looks but inherit his idiocy.

"I know, we should breed males like him especially, so the male of the species will eventually have even less brain than they have now, so they no longer even fancy of themselves as dominant. Ah, but you, my dear, are everything humanity should be. You deserve something special!"

From somewhere deep in her throat Angelica coughed out, "Lady Calthrop—!"

"I've been saving you for Dapifer."

This time, Angelica staggered and fell back against the wall with her hands over her face. "No . . . !" "Look at the fool blush!" snarled Lady Calthrop "Your modesty is nothing more than prejudice. You have so fully embraced the conventions of Society. *'Which of us is the most doctrinaire, then?'*"

"Lady Calthrop, you are insane! My God, you must be!"

"You will enjoy the process. I know for a fact Dapifer's a perfect specimen. He proved it to me – even before my husband died. And he has a brain. It's irked him to be servile to congenital idiots like that Strangways. I told him it was only a matter of time. I've been eager to see what sort of offspring you and he might breed. Oh, don't worry about any children. You won't have to raise them. I know what a pesky bother children are to a woman who wants to live free. Humans should raise their young in a collective, without the outmoded tradition of love of parents for individual children! Why, in bee culture the queen bee gives birth to the whole hive – but she doesn't have to sully her hands in rearing them! All children will be reared together – and those who do not advance the species will be weeded out, just like pruning the bad limbs off a tree. I am old, my child. I cannot be a queen forever. But you – you might be the queen bee of a new master race. In terms of the old superstition, you might be a new Eve, who may mate freely with no fear of consequences—"

Angelica had heard all she could stomach. "Shut up!"

This made Lady Calthrop angry. "That was uncivil, child. *Never* be rude to me." She raised the parasol to her mouth.

"Lady Calthrop, Get out of my way. I don't want to hurt you."

Over the handle of the parasol, she answered, "You haven't the guts to hurt me." A triumphant gleam lit Lady Calthrop's face. "In any case, you may as well concede. Everything is set in motion. Soon, no one will have anyplace to run to."

Placing an end of her parasol between her lips, she aimed the other at Angelica.

Angelica backed away. She meant to reach the back stairs, though she'd have to abandon her typewriter. With her mind on how to wiggle back around the Tudor arch, she forgot to feel her way – and she toppled over an occasional table.

She and the table crashed down in a mess of broken bric-a-brac, porcelain and the remains of an ugly fern. When she hit the floor, the base of her skull thumped upright against the wainscoting.

Something struck the wall far over her head. Angelica rolled her eyes up and saw a feathered dart sticking out of the wall where she had been standing immediately before the accident.

Herron Strangways had said, *"A pal of mine said the haggard bird was shot."*

By a blow-gun!

CHAPTER LII

Angelica yanked at the pistol in her pocket. Its hammer caught on the fabric of her skirt, and she gave it three increasingly desperate tugs before it emerged with a ripping sound.

Lady Calthrop was reloading. Seeing the pistol, she lowered her parasol slightly and extended her wrinkled hand, palm up. As if talking to a recalcitrant child, she said, "Hand over the gun, Angelica."

"NO!" Angelica extended the revolver at the length of slightly trembling arms. Both her hands were wrapped around the grip and both index fingers were on the trigger. Clenching her left eye, she sighted her right up the barrel at Her Ladyship.

Lady Calthrop purred, "If you would prefer to saw me right in half, there's a loaded howdah pistol in the case downstairs, for tiger hunts. Four barrels. *Boom-boom-boom-boom.* As if you could shoot anyone!"

While she glared at Lady Calthrop with one eye – to Angelica's amazement, Her Ladyship set the silver casket on the floor and pushed herself upright from the wheelchair until she was standing on her own two feet.

"Lady Calthrop," Angelica said, feeling foolish while stating the obvious half-way between laughing and crying, "You can walk."

"*Resurgam.* Of convalescent persons – I shall rise again. Give me the gun."

"No!" Angelica's face was beading with sweat, and she felt moisture forming on her torso. Her hands were damp. Though Her Ladyship had attempted to shoot her once already, Angelica held her fire.

Lady Calthrop calmly reloaded her parasol with another dart. "I hate to lose you, child. I don't know when I'll ever find a specimen quite so marvelous. It is such a waste. Especially as not one life will be spared by your death."

Angelica's mind was still hazy so she didn't catch all that, but she clung to a realization of her danger. "Lady Calthrop," she fought to keep her voice level, but she heard a quaver in it, "if you raise that parasol again, I will shoot you."

"Shooting me accomplishes nothing. In fact, it will only go worse for you."

Angelica's voice sounded huskily unfamiliar to her own ears as she said, pronouncing the words very slowly, "Put the parasol down. Now."

"If only you'd listened to me! If only you had learned. You're not stupid, but you never would learn. Good-bye, Angelica."

"I swear by God, Lady Calthrop, I will shoot you."

"A stand-off? You aim at me and I aim at you and neither of us can kill? Brinksmanship will achieve nothing, my dear. You cannot leave here alive."

Lady Calthrop believed Angelica lacked the backbone to shoot her.

Even so, Angelica had to be euthanized quickly. The girl was obviously frantic. A sweating bint with jangled nerves might spasmodically yank the trigger accidentally. Even if Angelica missed with a frenzied shot, gunfire in Park Lane at three in the morning might attract the wrong sort of attention.

She thought Angelica was likely to shoot only while she was agitated. Hoping to mollify her into a false sense of security, Her Ladyship lowered the end of the parasol to the floor.

"If you shoot me, child, you *will* hang for it. Have no doubts about that."

"Why should they hang *me*?" Angelica growled between clenched teeth. She had to keep her vision clear, but forehead flop-sweat was drizzling around her eyebrows and running into her eyes. She tried to blink the moisture away."They will hang you for my murder, child. Dapifer will swear you shot me down in cold blood – an old lady bound to a wheelchair."

"You're the murderer!"

"I?"

"You killed that man at the Underground station."

"I swatted a fly. The world is better off without him. *And* without Strangways." She observed Angelica narrowly. "The demonstration I have put in train for today *cannot* be stopped. It is too late. You and your recent caller are the only persons alive who had an inkling of things to come. He is dead already."

"That's not true!" she spat, not knowing quite why.

Instead of blinking, she was winking to keep one eye trained on Lady Calthrop at all times. But her eyes were stinging so from perspiration, she risked wiping them with the heel of a hand, which went immediately back up to the pistol.

"It's another of your lies."

"He *is* dead. On my orders. While you two beautiful young animals romped together yesterday, I came upstairs with Dapifer and contacted certain persons with my wireless telegraphic set. I kept Strangways here long enough for them to arrive, and they took him away and shot him in the back of the head. I received confirmation of that at midnight. I heard the clock strike downstairs."

Angelica had heard the telegraphic message. She knew Herron was dead. The story of how it happened was new, and Angelica felt like Lady Calthrop had stabbed her in the heart with words.

The moisture in her eyes may not all have been due to hidrosis.

"And you are dead, too, Angelica. Even if you volunteer to join us, it is too late. I can't trust you. I must be absolutely secure in the loyalty of my people." "I will never join you!"

Lady Calthrop's eyes brightened with a sudden happy thought.

"Listen, my sweet, you will not leave this house alive. So! How will I kill thee? Let me count the ways:

"*One*: you can shoot your way out through me – but if you kill me, Dapifer will tell the authorities you murdered me and he'll see you swing for it.

"*Two*: if Dapifer arrives downstairs during our *impasse*, I will order *him* to shoot *you*. And he will. We will tell the authorities you went hysterical and started shooting at us, and we had to kill you in self-defense.

"Thanks to *you*, circumstances have progressed too far for an amicable solution. Because of this situation *you* caused, *one of us must be shot*. If it's you, you're dead. If it's me, you're hanged. You will die, regardless."

Angelica said nothing . . . but she had the sick feeling of being trapped. She could no longer even spring up and make a dash for the back stairs; Lady Calthrop would fire one of those hellish, no doubt poisoned, darts into her back.

"But we may count a third way, child. The most convenient way for everyone! It will spare your family the shame of seeing you dying on the gibbet.

"Think of your brother. Would it not be better for him, and for your own posthumous reputation, if we reported that you killed yourself, rather than forcing your loved ones to watch you die ignominiously at the end of a hangman's rope?

"Just turn the gun around and ease the barrel in your mouth. Then pull the trigger. You'll never feel it. That will be so much better for you. It will be *your* choice, *your* decision. Please, my dear, go out with *dignity*. Take charge of your own life! Let no man master you! Become the master of your own destiny!" Angelica dared not remove either of her fingers from the trigger, but her eyes were burning fiercely from salinity. She drew in her elbows, bringing the pistol closer to her face, thinking she could give them a quick wipe.

Lady Calthrop, watching with gleaming eyes, apparently mistook this move for Angelica's relenting. Thinking the young lady was persuaded that her only alternative was to blow her own brains out, her voice became mesmeric.

"That's right. Just turn the gun around. Slide the barrel in your mouth and pull the trigger with your thumbs, my dear. I promise, you will never even hear the shot. It is the best for everyone. We'll pay for a quiet funeral. You're a good, religious young girl, aren't you? You believe in an afterlife. Your young man is there, waiting for you. He needs you. He's waiting for you with open arms. Now, sweetie, turn the gun around, place your lips around the barrel—"

"No."

"—and pull the trigger."

"No!"

"I'm doing you a kindness." Lady Calthrop's almost hand imperceptibly inched up her parasol—

"Put that down!"

"Foolish bitch, now you're being foolish!"

The front door opened and closed.

"Dapifer!"

"My lady?" Angelica had never known the butler to use the front door before. His long legs would quickly bring him to the curtail steps of the stairway.

"Come here, Dapifer."

"Yes, m'lady."

"With a pistol."

"Which, my lady?"

"The Howdah. If I ask you, will you please blow Miss Trickett's pretty head clean off her shoulders?"

"Yes, my lady."

Angelica heard the sound of shattering glass as Dapifer chose his weapon. He had not wasted time fetching a key to the case.

"Don't come up here!" Angelica's voice came out harsh and throaty, but she calmed it enough to say, with only a slight tremor, "*Please*, don't you come any closer, either, Lady Calthrop. Tell him to go away! If he starts upstairs, I swear I will shoot you! God as my witness." She sat up away from the wall, her arms stretched to their full length. She ignored the stinging sweat in her eyes.

Lady Calthrop finally realized Angelica was not going to kill herself. She was on the brink of hysteria with a loaded firearm and she was very likely to carry through with her threats. "Fool—you'll have to shoot us both, now!"

She wanted to point out that this was why private citizens had to be forbidden dangerous weapons, but it was no time for a lecture.

Then she saw Angelica's open right eye was no longer trained on her. She was anticipating Dapifer's approach up the stairs.

Since Angelica was on the floor, Her Ladyship would have to bring the blow-gun up at only a shallow angle. Knowing it would be safer to announce Angelica's death from an inexplicable cause, rather than going through the bother and messiness of gunshots, Lady Calthrop yanked up her parasol in both hands—

Angelica caught the movement in her peripheral vision.

As Her Ladyship put the parasol to her mouth, Angelica pulled the trigger with both index fingers.

She flinched at the unexpectedly loud blast from the gun, and as the recoil pounded her hard back against the wall lower than before.

CHAPTER LIII

While the roar of the gun still reverberated in her ears, Angelica heard the *thunk* of Lady Calthrop's dart in the wall immediately above her head. The recoil had driven her painfully but into the wall, but it saved her life.

Meanwhile, Angelica's bullet had found its mark. It knocked Lady Calthrop down into her wheelchair, which rolled back a foot closer to the stairs.

Lady Calthrop's right hand clutched at her left shoulder. Blood flowed freely through her fingers. Her face was a twisted mask of rage.

Angelica's spirits sank. She had missed any vital spot by as good as a mile.

The butler was her primary concern, now, and she could not divide her attention between him and Lady Calthrop. She had to shoot Her Ladyship a second time. And since the parasol had fallen out of reach, the second shot would not be in self-defense.

Tensing for the recoil, Angelica pulled the trigger again.

With the second explosion, a scarlet blossom flashed out on the white dress at Lady Calthrop's abdomen.

"At least," grunted Lady Calthrop, still alive but slumped down in her chair with blood spurting from her intestines, "you cannot stop . . .

what is in motion." Straining for every breath, she said, "My end . . . is my beginning."

After the second shot, Dapifer's footsteps ceased. Angelica heard nothing, but she suspected the butler was creeping silently up the stairway.

As if to confirm her suspicions, she heard the cocking of pistol hammers from just below her line of vision.

Lady Calthrop's clinging, satiny dress had hiked up her shins. Slipping as low as she could against the wainscoting, Angelica aimed the revolver between Her Ladyship's ankles, where blood was dripping.

Spreading her own legs so she wouldn't shoot herself in the foot, Angelica watched for the top of Dapifer's head. In an unconscious habit of intense concentration, she extended her tongue to her upper lip.

Slowly, Dapifer's dark, slicked-back hair eased into view. Angelica sighted the pistol and waited until she caught a flash of his forehead.

A splash of noggin appeared . . . then his eyes! Angelica fired between them.

When the pistol boomed again, Dapifer ducked. At that range he should have not heard the explosion before the bullet smashed into his skull. She had missed.

Angelica had braced for the recoil, but she badly bit into her tongue. She barely felt the pain and was unaware of the trickle of blood threading down from the right-hand corner of her mouth.

Footsteps were pounding down the stairs.

The butler was no longer on the attack. He was going to fetch the police!

He'd tell them a young lady in his house had gone berserk, that she had already murdered Lady Calthrop and she was firing indiscriminately at everyone.

If Angelica didn't stop him, she would hang for sure.

She was by now nearly flat on her back. Bucking up on her shoulders, she flicked her long legs out like whips and kicked the wheelchair with both feet.

As the chair tumbled backward down the grand stairway Lady Calthrop, still alive, cast terrified eyes down at Angelica. She fell from view and the chair bounced down the stairs, *thunk! thunk! thunk!*. At the curve of the stairs it struck the wall and tumbled in a savage free-fall.

Lunging forward, Angelica peered down through the rounds of the banister.

Dapifer was nearly at the foot of the stairs when the loaded wheelchair caught him in small of his back. The chair twisted sideways against the curved wall and carried the butler limply along as it spun the rest of the way down.

When they all pounded down together onto the parquet floor, Dapifer lay covered with blood – but alive. He had dropped his enormous pistol, but it landed *almost* within the reach of his fingertips.

Lady Calthrop's chair had him pinned; but he was a strong man. If his back hadn't snapped, he would have no difficulty extricating himself.

By the look on his face, he was determined reach the gun even if both his legs had been chopped off at the hips.

Angelica broke her bulldog revolver open and refilled the three empty chambers with trembling hands (fortunately, the cartridges were self-extracting, or she might never have worried them out of the chambers in her present state).

She had to get outside the fastest way. That meant going past the butler.

As she snapped the gun together, her eyes narrowed down on Dapifer. He was already writhing out from under the twisted remains of the wheelchair and its lifeless occupant.

Mounting the banister and balancing herself with the highly-polished wood between her breasts, Angelica slid face-forward, aiming at Dapifer all the way. It wasn't easy. Sliding down, she had to extend the gun forward in one hand, compensating for the curve in the stairs, while stretching the other arm out to maintain her equilibrium.

Holding his side like he had broken ribs, Dapifer clutching the howdah and slammed his body back so he was sitting upright against the wall at the curtail step, while steadying his weapon at Angelica.

But he had to take aim, while she already had him in her sights. She fired.

The recoil flung her off the banister. She thumped to the floor and rolled against one of the display cases. Rolling over, Angelica lay face-down, aiming the revolver across the floor at him.

The moment Angelica's shot struck him, Dapifer fired off all four barrels of his own pistol. He had been aiming up; the bullet's impact forced his arm even higher, so he merely peppered the chandeliers.

Anglica observed him for a few moments, over the barrel of her gun. He was breathing, though with difficulty. As the butler's chest heaved for breath, a splash of red widened on his white waistcoat.

Angelica didn't waste time feeling gratified that her aim was improving. Seeing the fight was shot out of Dapifer, she sprang to her feet, dashing out the door, down the walk and into Park Lane.

Heedless of her direction, she ran for all she was worth.

Angelica was hatless and her long hair flowed wildly behind her. Her casual attire was dirty and unkempt where she had been climbing under beds, rolling around on the floor and sliding down banisters. Her hair was full of dust and soil and bits of fern, and one side of her skirt was torn. Her blouse had ripped open down to the third button when she was hurled from the banister, and she was bleeding at the mouth. And she carried a naked gun with a freshly-fired aroma.

None of this occurred to her; and her first impulse was to find a policeman.

The parade route, as she understood it, was to be lined with the military and the police. Had she run south, she'd have stumbled onto the route of the Procession – and into the arms of more policemen than she could count, who would take her where she would field some uncomfortable questions.

But she ran toward the Edgeware Road. She did not pause in her stride until she reached Marble Arch at Oxford Street.

Even at three in morning, the atmosphere was noticeably light on longest days of summer. Slinking into the shadows of the arch, Angelica caught her breath, peering out into the damp morning twilight like a hunted animal.

What would she say if she found a policeman? Or if one found her?

I just shot Lady Calthrop. And her butler, for good measure.

What if Lady Calthrop and Dapifer weren't dead? If either of them could speak, they'd have a noose around her neck.

And if they were dead, Angelica's position was equivocal at best.

Why did you shoot Lady Calthrop?

Why not?

Was Lady Calthrop armed when you fired two bullets into her at close range?

She was threatening me with her parasol . . .

It was just as well Angelica was not a native Londoner, or at Marble Arch she might have realized how eerily close she was to old Tyburn tree, where gallows had broken the necks of London murderers for six hundred years – including the fine necks of a few notoriously beautiful women.

She was fortunate that she ran north instead of south. She might be sheltering at the Wellington Arch at Piccadilly – which was on the Queen's route. In just a few hours the Queen would be rattling up Constitution Hill to turn at the Wellington Arch only Piccadilly. There, a disheveled woman carrying a freshly-fired pistol might have attracted unwanted attention.

She was a fugitive and every man's hand was against her. Yet, dire as it was, Angelica was not primarily concerned about her own predicament.

Something unspeakable was going to happen in a matter of hours, and she was the only living soul in all the world who knew it was coming.

Even she saw it only in a vague outline. Terrorists financed by Lady Calthrop were going to drop an explosive from an airship. Fine. She did not know where. Nor when, within a range of hours. Nor on whom or what.

But she, Angelica Trickett, had to stop it!—if she had to threaten the Queen herself at the gates of Buckingham Palace with her little revolver.

But . . . could Angelica prevent anything? Even if she managed to save the life of Her Majesty (assuming she was the target), the terrorists might drop their bomb on any of the hundreds of thousands of souls clumped together in London. Should she save one old lady and risk the lives of countless innocents.

She could just imagine the attitude of most policemen.

A bomb from an airship, *Miss? What airship is that, then?*

Even if she found someone to believe her . . . how did one stop an airship?

Having passed through the front stretch of hysteria, Angelica realized Lady Calthrop was right: what she had put in train probably could not be stopped.

But Angelica was determined to give it a try, whatever the consequences.

Herron. She had to find Herron. He'd help her.

No, Herron's dead . . . dead. Lady Calthrop ordered him shot in the back of the head. Because he came to see me! Oh, God! Oh God! Oh God!

Despite the pre-dawn chill, she was still sweating profusely. Perspiration drizzled over her eyebrows. When she wiped it away, she didn't realize she was dragging a loaded pistol across her forehead.

Herron's dead. Dead.

She grit her teeth. She had to do whatever she had to so alone. *No, not alone!* She had to find—*What was his name?*

It was fishy, but she could not angle it from the depths of her memory.

Pike? Carp? Hake? Bass? Kelp? . . . Gudgeon?

Then a name floated up in her memory like a corpse in the muddy Thames.

SPES TAMEN EST UNA: There is only one hope. For Angelica, that hope was Edgar, the Hemlock Club's doorman.

Edgar! *Edgar!* She kept whispering the name, forgetting everything else except that. If anyone had asked her own she'd have replied "Edgar."

Repeating the name automatically, she fought through her misty consciousness to take her bearings.

The Hemlock Club was in Saint James, Herron said . . . *Saint James–what! Street? Square? District?* She was so addled, she even considered Saint James Park, as if the Hemlock Club were a tree-house.

Her brother belonged to a Club, and he was hard pressed to keep up the dues. She had often lingered outside her brother's Club, hanging onto the iron palings out front while waiting to spend her free afternoons with him.

Schuyler's Club was on Pall Mall. Was the Hemlock Club nearby?

She fancied it was. Normally, she and her brother took their afternoon strolls in Green Park, along Piccadilly. To reach Picadilly they rounded a corner and passed it many times. Once – only once – Schuyler raised his stick and pointed the Hemlock out to her with horror.

To locate the Hemlock Club, she first had to reach Pall Mall. And she was on Oxford Street!

Think, Angelica! She only knew major thoroughfares in this part of London.

She nearly backtracked down Park Lane. Shuddering at venturing past Lady Calthrop's house again, she mapped a path in her head.

South at Oxford Circus onto Regent Street. Good. Piccadillly Circus. Lower Regent Street south. Right. Go.

Darting east on Oxford Street, she kept to the shadows of the shops and away from the gas lamps – still unmindful of the naked gun in her right hand.

CHAPTER LIV

On this morning of mornings, London's streets were filling, even at half-past three. Men, women and children of all classes and nationalities had lingered outside all night. Many had slept, for the first time in their lives, in public places (like Trafalgar Square) so they would be on the parade-route when they woke.

Thousands more were stalking to the parade route to stake out good spots to view the once-in-a-lifetime Procession, even at this time of the morning. Oxford and Regent Streets were filling with a flowing tide of humanity.

At first, Angelica hid in the shadows of shops and crouched in doorways whenever anyone passed. The furtive senses of a hunted animal kept her mind alert and focused so she had no time to panic. She might have gone the wrong way at Piccadilly Circus, except that her brother had taught her: until she learned all the streets, to follow the bow of Anteros. Her eyes flashed by habit up at the statue of Anteros, who more or less pointed out her way. Anteros felt more than usually important to her today.

The lower end of Regent Street cross Pall Mall, which was on the Procession route. As she continued south and more people flocked out into the clammy morning twilight, doorways no longer provided concealment. Angelica walked openly down the sidewalks, increasingly wedging and shouldering her way through the tide of humanity in a most unladylike manner.

When she reached Pall Mall she would be on the Procession route – meaning police and military street-lining parties, and more *people*. The parade did not start for more than nine hours, but she feared there might be a strong police presence and she was in constant danger of being detained on circumstantial evidence alone. It was not actually a smoking gun, but it retained the odor of recent firing.

No doubt many people wondered at this rude ragamuffin who, ebowing brusquely by, muttered "Edgar" rather than "Excuse me." No one wanted to upbraid a woman perfumed with the scent of gunsmoke.

2

The morning twightlight atmosphere was noticeably brighter beyond the thin sheet of fog when Angelica found the Hemlock Club. She might not have recognized it, but she remembered the legend carved over the door (beneath the bow window of the library): *Do as thou pleasest*.

That street was particularly well-lighted, so Angelica did not mistake the building her brother had pointed out to her.

As she mounted the front steps beneath a bow-window, a broad-shouldered man with a twisted nose blocked her way. "Sorry, Miss, you can't go in there."

"Edgar." She repeated the only word she had said for three quarters of an hour.

"Yuh? Does I know yous, lady?" He hoped she wasn't a disreputable slice of his past come to do him dirty on the Queen's big day.

All she could answer at first was a repetition of the doorman's name. Then she remembered she had shot and probably killed two people, and she hadn't even had her morning tea. "Herron Strangways—!" She gasped. "Please God, help me!"

Edgar looked her over. A wild-eyed woman – totin', as they said in the western stories, a sidearm.

Many times wrathful brothers or fathers arrived on the steps of the Hemlock Club with horse-whips, bull-whips, and pistols (usually in boxed sets of two).

For a young lady to appear personally – disheveled, bleeding at the mouth, fern leaves in her hair, gripping a reeking gun in her fist—!

Young Mister Strangways must have forgotten himself, indeed.

Edgar's sympathies lay with the young lady; but he had his job to do. He was not paid to take sides in quarrels, but to bar admittance to non-members and troublemakers. However disgraceful young Mister Strangways' conduct had been, however much he deserved to be gunned down in the street—that was a matter for the police and/or the Membership Committee. It was not Edgar's place to judge one of the Club's most admirable tippers.

It was easier on his own conscience to keep her out, knowing Herron Strangways had left in a cab more than twelve hours ago and had never returned (to the chagrin of a young waiter whose uniform Strangways was wearing).

Since he knew Herron Strangways was not on the premises, Edgar would not have to tell falsehoods to protect him from this female's just retribution.

"He ain't here, lady."

Angelica's mouth drew down at the corners. She had gamely outdistanced her hysteria all the way by channeling it through the physical exertion. Having arrived at the Club, the hysteria gained on her. She began to tremble.

"Oh, God! He must be killed!"

Edgar mistook her words for threats. "I don't know where he's holed up."

His heart did go out to her. If he had a daughter like this, Edgar would have hoped she might administer a flesh wound, at least. But he would not be guilty of aiding and abetting a *crime passionnel* (even if he had known the term).She felt her voice rising a register, but she was unable to lower it. Hysteria had her in its grip. Barely cognizant that she still clutched a firearm in it, she shook her fist at him. "There'll be a bloody sight more killing if you don't help me!"

Edgar took a backward pace or two toward the doors, to fetch reinforcements.

Angelica's agile young body dodged around his bulk. Stabbing her pistol into his back, her writer's imagination came up with a suitably tough-sounding line. "Move without my say-so and I'll by God blast your spine out your fat gut!"

Edgar feared no man's dukes, but he could not fight against the velocity of a bullet. "Mister Strangways' man Merridew is inside. Maybe he can help you."

"Take me to him!"

"You can't go in, Miss! Them's the rules! I didn't make 'em!"

"I've killed two people already." She screwed the pistol harder into the small of his back. "They can't hang me thrice! You don't make a move without me!"

"Can I go to the door?"

"I stick on you like a tick. And I'm getting better every time I kill."

Edgar went to the door with Angelica directly behind him, their legs stepping together. He called for one of his co-workers, just inside the door, to summon Mister Strangways' man.

"What if he's asleep?"

"Wake him up!"

"Chop-chop!" shrieked Angelica, as the door closed.

Soon, Merridew came bounding out of the club, pulling on his coat. He blinked a bit when confronted with a strange young lady who did not appear altogether safe; but he had been under fire before, so he showed no outward indications of perturbation. He gave her a bow. "You wished to see me, Miss?"

Pressing her pistol firmly against Edgar's backbone, Angelica spoke over the doorman's shoulder, "Mister Merridew?"

"Just Merridew, Miss."

"I trust I didn't get you out of bed?"

"I usually rise about this time to start the day. How may I be of service?"

"Herron Strangways—" She didn't know how to tell him he was dead.

"I'm sorry, Miss, but I haven't seen him since he left the Club yesterday afternoon, to pay a call."

"On Miss Trickett?"

"He did not confide his destination."

"On . . . ah . . . Oh! On Lady Calthrop?"

Merridew did not know that name, either. But he did, from his years in military service, recognize shock when he saw it.

Under Merridew's phlegmatic influence, Angelica's hysteria was subsiding; but her eyes were growing even wilder as she was beginning, in the clammy light of burgeoning reason, to realize the hopelessness of her situation.

She had shot two people. If they were dead, she might be tried for murder. And hanged for it.

On the other hand, if either or both of her victims were alive, they'd say Angelica had shot them in a rampage. She'd hang for that, too.

Even with the mitigating circumstances of the darts, shooting a wheelchair-bound Lady – twice – and then booting her down a staircase was unlikely to move a British jury in Angelica's favor.

"Merridew, I was Herron's friend. Whatever I've done, you must believe that!" Merridew studied her. The young woman's clothes were a disgrace and she needed a good wash and brush-up. Her manner left much to be desired. But her dulcet voice, agitated as it was, carried the refined intonations of a lady.

Having been chivvied and shot at and wounded, Merridew did not, like Edgar, assume the young lady had gotten into her present state through any malicious actions of his employer. Somehow, she had become mixed up in the excitement he and his young master had endured in the past thirty-six hours.

But on which side? Was her pistol for shooting – or for shooting back?

He wanted to trust her, but his arm still ached as a reminder of their danger. And for all her politeness, she *was* holding an innocent doorman hostage.

"I am sorry, Miss . . . can you prove you are a friend of Mister Strangways?"

She flushed angrily, wondering what sort of proof might verify her acquaintance with Herron Strangways—?

With an acuteness he had never displayed in the ring, Edgar noted her momentary inattention. Throwing himself back, he pressed her hard between his bulk and the iron railing.

It was a risk on his part, but it paid off. She dropped the pistol on impact. It clattered down the steps to the pavement.

Edgar and Angelica both leapt after it. Edgar was closer, and heavier, so he had gravity on his side as he shouldered her aside and scooped up the revolver.

"Let me see that, please, Edgar," said Merridew, stepping calmly down.

Edgar did not hand the gun over, but he gave Merridew a good gander at it.

Merridew's stint in the service left him with an astute eye for firearms. "How did you come by this weapon, Miss?"

Edgar had barreled Angelica into the sodden gutter. Sitting up and peeling her hair out of her eyes, she answered,

"Herron Strangways gave it to me. And these." She wriggled the cartridge box from her pocket. Her head sagged forward and she raised her grimy hands to her face. "He wanted me to call him Herrie."

The pistol might not have been absolutely distinctive; but Merridew knew a box of cartridges he himself had purchased.

He handed the box back to her. After all, he had the gun. What could she do – shove the bullets in manually?

"She says she done in two people." Edgar tried to speak confidentially, but his voice was not conducive to whispering. "Came within a cat's whisker of three."

The valet opened a palm at Edgar. "Allow me?"

Edgar handed him the pistol. Merridew broke it open.

"Only one empty chamber, Miss."

Angelica dropped her hands. "I reloaded."

Merridew nodded.

"I didn't know how many times I would have to shoot them, you see?"

"Ah." Merridew extended a hand to her.

Catching a glimpse of his proffered hand through a veil of hair, she reached up to it and allowed him to help her to her feet. "And," she said, delicately wiping her stern conscious all the while of being under the observation of two men. "I would have shot them again and again until I could get away."

"What has happened to Mister Strangways, Miss?"

"They said he was dead."

"Who said, Miss?"

Merridew was only an inch or two on her, and she reclined her forehead against his shoulder. "Oh, God! Oh, my God, I've killed Lady Calthrop! She said he was dead! But he can't be! Dear God, he just can't be!"

Merridew did not like hearing the Deity addressed by title in that casual tone, but he had become inured to worse in the army. This young lady was clearly distraught, and he only wanted to help her.

"There, there, Miss—"

She backed three paces from him, her red-rimmed eyes glaring furiously through her stringy hair. "Don't dare patronize me! We've got to stop it!"

Edgar and Merridew exchanged wary, sidelong glances.

"Stop . . . what, Miss?"

"*I don't know!*" Throwing herself across the club steps, she grabbed the iron railings and peered through them like bars of a prison. "But whatever it is . . . I'm the only one who can stop it! And I've got to stop it before they get me, too!"

Edgar winked at Merridew and tapped his temple with an incredulous knuckle. His professional opinion, in technical terms, was that the lady was unhinged.

Offended by this pantomime, Merridew drew himself up and gave Edgar the withering stare only well-trained valets can manage. Approaching Angelica (cautiously) he suggested, "Perhaps Mister Strangways has gone home."

He didn't sound altogether sanguine about the possibility. Unlike Edgar, Merridew knew from the pain he felt in his arm pulling on his coat, there was a *they*. *They* might well have gotten Mister Strangways already. For now, he needed to calm this young lady down and maybe get a rational story from her."Edgar, I'll take the young lady to Mister Strangways' home. Please send for Inspector Broughton Chubb to join us there."

"Chubb!" Angelica echoed, perking up. "Yes! Find Inspector Chubb, Edgar, for the love of God! Please! Find him!"

"Yes, do find him, my good man," said Merridew, properly.

"Where's he at?" Edgar's body language showed he didn't appreciate a valet, with no gold buttons or epaulets on his coat, referring to him a "good man."

"Scotland Yard," Merridew wearily replied. "Does the Club have telephones?"

"No. Lots of young gentlemen have asked to get 'em installed – I think, to get in faster touch with their bookies. But I know where there's a call-room nearby."

"Call, then. I believe they have telephones at the Yard. If not – shame on them. If Inspector Chubb is not there, they will know where to find him."

"Tell him to hurry!" called Angelica, shrilly. "For God's sake, hurry! Please!"

The three of them walked to the end of the street, with Angelica squeezed between the two men. There they split up, Edgar to find a telephone, Merridew (with Angelica on his arm) to find a hansom cab another street down.

Once ensconced in a cab, Merridew sat facing placidly forward, his arms down between his knees, swinging the pistol in both hands. He had no intention of shooting the young lady. Nevertheless, with one wound in his arm from Sunday evening, he was unwilling to tuck the weapon altogether out of sight.

Still slightly befuddled by shock, Angelica drooped back against her side of the cab. Her head was down, but her eyes stared frantically up from beneath her dark-honey eyebrows and spidering hair. Transferring all her distress to her teeth, she clamped down on the first joint of her left index finger until it bled.

The din of the city was never still, day or night – especially on such a day as this. On top of that, the rattling of the wheels and the clip-clop of the horse filled Angelica's ears with discordant noise.

Yet somewhere, in the midst of the clatter—

She cut her eyes to Merridew. "Is that *you*?"

"No, Miss. It was probably the horse."

"I mean, humming."

"Oh, ah, I suppose so."

"'Onward, Christian Soldiers'?"

"Oh, yes. Do you know it?" He began singing the verse he'd hummed up to:

> *Crowns and thrones may perish, kingdoms rise and wane,*
> *But the church of Jesus constant will remain.*
> *Gates of hell can never 'gainst that church prevail;*
> *We have Christ's own promise, and that cannot fail.*

For the first time in hours, Angelica smiled. Daubing her eyes with the heel of her hand, and with a rising inflection (probably due to the residue of hysteria) she joined Merridew on the chorus,

> *"Onward Christian soldiers, marching as to war*
> *With the Cross of Jesus going on before!"*

CHAPTER LV

When the cab slowed before Herron's terrace, Merridew pointed at their broken-in front door. "That's it, Miss."

Wrenching the gun from his hands, Angelica leapt from the hansom before it stopped completely and rushed inside. Merridew went yipping at her heels.

"Here, you!" shouted the cabbie, raising his whip.

Remembering the gunfire that had broken out the last time he was there, Merridew, pausing to pay for the cab, shouted for her to remain with him on the steps, waiting for the police.

Not hearing Merridew or deliberately ignoring him, Angelica darted inside. In the foyer, she gripped the pistol tight in both hands, at arm's length, aiming it on the floor at a forty-five degree angle. She was ready if she had to shoot fast.

Against all hope, she shouted, "Mister Strangways?"

Her voice fell, uncertainly.

"Herron?"

She bolted upstairs.

"Herrie?"

On the first floor, she threw all the doors open, one at a time, calling his name. Finally, she burst into his bedroom – and staggered back with a startled gasp.

A gentleman in evening dress (including a shiny silk top hat and a white blossom in his buttonhole) sat upright in an armchair facing the door. His head sagged forward like he'd nodded off.

For one moment, in the extremely dim light, she felt a rush of optimism that it might be Herron. Then, as she slowly neared him, she saw the hair beneath his topper was grey.

She didn't like the way he was sitting. His posture, with his shoulders back, was too correct for a sleeping body.

Stepping up to him, she kept him covered with the pistol – until she saw a spear-point sticking out between the second and third studs of his shirt-front.

A Zulu *iklwa* had been plunged through the back of the chair and the man's body. His shirt was red below the point, but most of his blood had already dribbled down his dark tailed coat and had pooled on the carpet.

In that instant, Angelica realized what had been missing from the weapons display on Lady Calthrop's stairway. She recognized it as the *iklwa* because Dapifer had once explained to her that the Zulus named it for the sound it made when they yanked it from the wound. That left an impression on her.

She realized what Dapifer's nocturnal errand must have been.

He had been waiting in this room. But not for Herron Strangways.

Her spirit all but broke. *He wasn't waiting for Herron Strangways – because he knew Herron Strangways was dead. He came to wait for this man.*

Clutching a tall post at the foot of Herron's bed, she laid her cheek against it.

She didn't know how long she leaned against the bed-post. She may even have dozed on her feet for a few minutes, until she heard the clang of the front door-bell. It was operated by a bell-pull and sounded not unlike a set of cowbells.

Leaving the bedroom, Angelica slipped along the banister in a crouch until she saw the front door through the arch separating the front room from the foyer.

In the foyer, Merridew was admitting a tubby, less-than-dapper little man in a brown bowler hat. The man's small eyes rolled around as he passed through the archway. Spotting a female on the ill-lighted gallery, he ripped off his hat and held it over his chest with both hands.

"Is Mister Strangways t'home, Miss?"

"Are . . . are you Broughton Chubb?"

He twisted his head curiously. "That's what my mother told me."

She descended the stairs half-way. "I'm Angelica Trickett."

"*Who?*"

She drew her eyebrows close together, wrinkling her otherwise unblemished forehead. "Herron—Mister Strangways—didn't tell you about me?"

Chubb shook his head. "Why don't you tell me about yourself. After you've said where we can locate the said Mister Herron Strangways. There are a few points we at the Yard would like that young man to clear up for us."

"You don't know where he is?"

"No. Is-is something the matter, Miss?"

"No—no."

"Why are you holding that pistol?"

She stared at it stupidly. She was still staring at it when Chubb padded upstairs and quietly disarmed her. Her hand was limp so he didn't have to wrench the revolver from her fingers.

Examining her in the dim light, he held a handkerchief out to her. "Spit."

She spat on it, and he wiped away the dried blood from her dimpled chin.

"Say 'Ah.'"

"Ahhh!" Like she was with a physician, she stuck out her tongue.

Chubb saw where she'd bitten her tongue. That accounted for the blood.

"Don't shoot the police, Miss," he winked, wadding the handkerchief away into his pocket. Chubb sniffed her pistol. "I'll go on up, have a little look-see."

Angelica threw her arms across the stairs from the wall to the banister. "No—"

"I'm sorry, Miss, but pursuant to my dooties I must ask you to step aside."

She wavered – and stepped back against the wall with her hands tucked into the small of her back.

Sidling in front of her, he mounted the steps. She followed him resignedly.

She'd only murdered two people and would soon be discovered alone in the house with the corpse of an elderly gentleman who had been stabbed clear through with a weapon taken from her place of employment.

God only knew what she would say if they found Herron's body stuffed away in a wardrobe!

Angelica had no doubt the Inspector was going to slap the . . . *What*, she tried to recall, *did they call handcuffs in the magazine stories?* "Darbies." Inspector Broughton Chubb was going to slap the darbies on her and haul her off to prison. Still not thinking quite clearly, she had the odd impression they were going to hang her as soon as they had her in the hoosegow, without the bother of a trial.

As if by instinct, Chubb was drawn directly to the bedroom. His eyes were not so keen, so he spotted the body in the armchair only when he turned up the gas.

He was well-enough acquainted with dead bodies to recognize one when he saw it, though the *iklwa* raised even his jaded eyebrows.

Chubb approached stealthily, stepping over the pooled blood and keeping a weather eye out for any clues, while Angelica stood just outside the door, leaning with one shoulder against the jamb.

"Who is he, Miss?"

"I don't know."

Chubb entertained little doubt about the stranger's condition; but, just to be on the safe side, his fingertips found the man's wrist.

"Yep. He's been dead a nice little while. Nasty wound, that. I seen men stabbed just like that in the Natal wars – only, not in armchairs. Never thought I'd see it in London. Just proves folk are the same, world over."

"I didn't do it. I—I arrived with Merridew. He can vouch for me."

"Merri-who? Oh, the man out front. Yes, he showed me in yesterday – no, I'm a liar, it's the day before, Sunday. Don't let's bother him. And don't you worry, neither – I don't suppose you stabbed this gentleman, Miss. If I may say so, you have very nice shoulders—"

"Thank you."

"—what I can see of 'em. Good poise. But it would take more than you've got to ram this pig-sticker through the chair and the body. No, I don't think for a moment you did it. Nor do I think it was a sudden invasion of Zulus."

"No." Her tone was accusing. "You think it was Herron Strangways."

Bent in a squat, studying the wound carefully without touching the body or the blood, he asked, distractedly, "Now, why would I think that?" "He said you've had your eye on him all along."

"Who said?"

"Mister Strangways."

"Are you an angler, Miss?"

"Fishing, you mean? No."

Chubb stood. He'd been careful not to touch anything bloody, but he wiped his hands on his handkerchief anyway.

He glanced at the handkerchief curiously; then, suddenly remembering why it felt damp, he tossed it aside and wiped his fingers on the dead man's coat before continuing with his thought.

"I've been playing with that young gentleman for two days. I baited him. I've been giving him line, you might say. Because even if he ain't guilty of what happened Saturday night at an Underground station, he knows more than what he says. There were many times in the past two days I was ready to reel him in, if I found one shred of hard evidence."

"This is pretty hard," she whispered.

"Yes, Miss. You can't argue with a corpse. It's definite proof."

Her heart sank. She squashed her nose into the door frame.

"Of his innocence."

She blinked at him. "P—pardon?"

"He's always up to monkeyshines, that lad, but he could no more calmly skewer a man in cold blood in his bedroom with that thing than I could. Probably less, the way I feel some mornings. Try to get to work in this traffic! Did you ever hear of psyche-ology?"

"Uh . . . something to do with the mind." "Yeah. Phrenology was guessin' a bloke's character by feeling the bumps on the outside of his head. Psyche-ology is guessin' a bloke's character by feeling the bumps on the inside." He gave his own large, not quite round head a tap. "The psyche-ology of this ain't right for that scamp. He might get a good laugh seein' this ol' bloke break his bloomin' neck slippin' down a flight of buttered stairs, but he ain't up to this." He examined the man some more. "And this ol' bloke ain't so old, neither. He's painted up, like an actor."

"Oh!" said Angelica, as if remembering an appointment, "I-I must confess, Inspector—" She jammed herself in the door frame with both arms, standing like Samson between the pillars just to remain upright, "—I've shot Lady Calthrop."

"Very probably, Miss. By the smell of that gun somebody's been shot and it might as well be her. Dead?"

"I wasn't certain. I kicked her downstairs onto her butler—"

"To make certain?"

The question confused Angelica. While she was gaping at him, Chubb bent his head under one of her arms, shouting,

"POTTLE!"

The Inspector's tall assistant appeared on Angelica's other side like a genie popping from a lamp. He was tall, and peered over her shoulder.

"Run 'round Lady Calthrop's—?" Chubb, still twisting his neck down and around to talk beneath her arm, looked quizzically up into Angelica's eyes.

"Park Lane," she replied. She feared the absurdity of this conversation might make her laugh. It raised her spirits, but the way she felt, once she started laughing, she might not stop until the men came to throw a butterfly net over her.

"Get that, Pottle? No! Where are your ears, man. Park—Lane! No, you won't need a warrant! There's been a shootin'. It's a suspicious circumstance.

Police are probably there already. Find out what you can and report back here!"

As Pottle saluted and dashed off, Chubb returned his attention to Angelica.

"Let's see if we can learn just who this feller was."

Taking one of her hands, he led Angelica to the bed and sat her on the edge. Only when she sitting on it did she realize the bed was at a peculiarly catty-cornered angle, like someone had pushed it up against the door.

While she watched, Chubb made a methodical search through the dead man's pockets. He found only one crumpled sheet of paper. Giving it no more than a glance, Chubb wadded it away into his own breast coat pocket.

Whistling a merry tune, Chubb said, "What have we here?"

Angelica leaned far over, gripping the bed-post, to see what he had discovered.

He pulled a corner of a paper from behind the man's shoulder.

"Stuck. Could you lend a hand, Miss? A foot, rather?"

"What do you want me to do?"

"Put your left plate up against this fellow's chest, just beneath the point."

"Why?"

"So maybe I can wrench Exhibit A out of our victim."

"Shouldn't we leave everything—?"

"For the authorities, Miss?" he winked. "I'm the authorities. I doubt the police surgeon will have much difficulty pin-pointing a cause of death. I *think* he'll rule out suicide. But knowing him—!"

Angelica screwed up her expressive lips. "Must I?"

"I would very much appreciate your cooperation, Miss."

"Very well." Bracing herself against the bed, Angelica shoved one of her button shoes into the dead man's chest while Chubb tugged the *iklwa*.

"There she comes!" he said, waggling the weapon loose from the chair.

When Angelica lowered her foot, the body rolled forward – at her. She leapt up onto the bed in a bound while the corpse sprawled forward onto the floor.

Chubb peeled a paper away from the dead man's back. He had been sitting against it as if hiding it. The *iklwa* had pinned it to his back, and the blood from the wound made it stick.

"What is it, Inspector?"

"Hm. A marriage certificate."

"Oh, no! Not a blessed marriage certificate!"

Chubb cut his eyes up at her. "What do you know about this?"

"Herron Strangways told me he had to meet a man in his bedroom with a marriage certificate."

"If you will pardon my saying so, Miss, I think you know a dam-sight more than I do. Now, why don't we go downstairs and have Mister Stangways' Merri-man make a pot of coffee, and we can talk it out."

Angelica nodded weakly. Now that she had found someone to listen to her, all the remaining energy fizzed out of her body. When, over coffee, she could tell the Inspector all about the bombing, she believed she could throw her body across that bed and sleep for a week.

She didn't think it would be unseemly. After all, Herron Strangways wouldn't be using it again. Herron Strangways was dead. *Confirmed.*

Unfortunately, it would be a long time before Angelica Trickett found any rest.

CHAPTER LVI

Merridew first considered cooking a full breakfast for his guests. Correctly gauging their mood, however, he instead provided a lighter repast of toasted muffins with fresh butter and honey. He also opened a tin of biscuits.

While Merridew prepared and served tea and coffee, the Inspector interrogated Angelica with as much delicacy as he had at his disposal.

Taking her time, and savoring her coffee while she spoke, she filled him in on everything that had happened from the moment Herron Strangways appeared at Lady Calthrop's doorstep until she found the body in his bedroom. Holding nothing back, she even revealed that Lady Calthrop had chosen her as a paid companion primarily for breeding purposes.

Chubb did not care about the progressive new science of perfecting humanity through eugenics. The moment Angelica related their interpretation of the secret message written on the cigarette paper, he became preoccupied with the bomb.

Inspector Chubb was not a man who knew, or cared, a curse about politics or science. He was a simple man, who did not like seeing things blown up.

The route of the Queen's Procession was no secret. A detailed itinerary had been published on page 8 of the *Times* on June 11.

Herron had not retained that paper; but a sketch-map of the Queen's route through London had appeared on page seventeen of the *Times* on

Monday, June 21. Merridew located the paper and Chubb fanned it out over the kitchen table.

Though he knew the itinerary by heart, Chubb paced the kitchen while Angelica, whose eyes were keener, sat at the table and read the Queen's route aloud, her fingernail digging a groove in the map.

Chubb exhibited a particular fondness for Herron's stockpile of biscuits, and he seemed to have a voracious appetite this morning. While listening to Angelica, he constantly munched biscuits he dipped in his tea.

For her part, Angelica ate nothing.

Merridew thought she might be nervous. Really, she was too intent on the map to bother with eating. She actually felt more relaxed than she had all morning.

Merridew believed, to the core of his being, that the best way to cope with any emotion was with an application of food. To encourage Angelica to partake, he kept quietly producing provender, humming,

> *"Guide me, O Thou great Redeemer*
> *Pilgrim through this barren land.*
> *I am weak, but Thou art mighty;*
> *Hold me with Thy powerful hand.*
> *Bread of Heaven, Bread of Heaven,*
> *Feed me till I want no more,*
> *Feed me till I want no more"*

He unconsciously hummed "Feed me till I want no more" whenever he delivered some new comestible to the table.

Angelica was familiar with the song and found herself humming along with him, and occasionally warbling a few words in her mezzo-soprano . . . but she wasn't encouraged to eat. Her mind was fixated on the Queen's six-mile route, which she read, and read again, and again . . .

At a quarter to nine, troops collected on the Embankment along the north side of the Thames would begin their move toward Buckingham Palace. The Procession itself would consist of two major sections: a Colonial Procession, consisting of the premiers of various territories (such as the Prime Minister of Canada) and detachments of as many regiments as possible from all over the Empire (with samples of artillery); and a Royal Procession – sixteen carriages stuffed full of royalty, by rank, with other princes riding as escort. The Prince of Wales, for instance, would ride along with the Queen's carriage.

The Queen's carriage (followed only by Her Majesty's Horse Guards) would leave Buckingham Palace at 11:15 and travel up Constitution Hill to Piccadilly. From Piccadilly, she would move south onto Saint James Street until making a sharp left-hand turn into Pall Mall. Her Majesty would pass along the north side of Trafalgar Square, in front of the National Gallery. Rolling east along the Strand and Fleet Street to Ludgate Circus, she would ascend Ludgate Hill Street to Saint Paul's Cathedral for the Thanksgiving ceremony at twelve o'clock precisely.

As the forty-six thousand, nine hundred and forty-three troopers of all ranks, gathered from the eleven million square miles of the empire, arrived at the Cathedral, they would array themselves around the western churchyard. Calvary, gun-carriages and escorts would halt on the north side of the Cathedral. Infantry would rank, in close order, along Ludgate Hill on either side of the street.

For the high noon Thanksgiving ceremony, the Queen's carriage would pull directly alongside the steps of the Cathedral's west front, facing south. The upper set of Cathedral steps were blocked off except for a narrow path leading up to the great west doors. This blocked off areas would be bulging with clergymen. The bishops and archbishops officiating in the ceremony would stand in the center.

After the ceremony, the Queen's carriage would skirt around the southern periphery of Saint Paul's. The Royal Procession would lead the parade along Cheapside, turning south down King William Street to cross the Thames on London Bridge.

Angelica recalled the song, *"London Bridge is falling down, falling down, falling down—"* Addled from lack of sleep (and everything else that had happened since Monday afternoon) she had an impression disaster might strike there.

Noting Angelica's distraction, Chubb said, "London south of the river is delighted to welcome the Queen. She'll go south on London Bridge and north by Westminster Bridge. They'll be closed to traffice. But to keep hoards of spectators from stampedin' south, to tell their grandchildren they saw the Procession on both sides of the river, all the bridges in between are closed, too."

"Oh?"

"Yep. Westminster, Waterloo, Blackfriars and Southwark and London."

"That must cause an inconvenience."

"They tell me upwards of one hundred thousand pedestrians cross London Bridge alone every working day. And about twenty thousand vehicles. Today is a holiday. Even so, an awful lot of traffic is gonna be bottled up on one side of the Thames or the other." He smiled at Angelica. "Feel better, now?"

"Yes, Inspector." Shaking off the effects of the nursery rhyme, Angelica dully, dutifully repeated the route south of the river for the umpteenth time in a voice growing hoarse. "Borough High Street. Borough Road. Saint

George's Circus. Blackman Street. Westminster Bridge Road. Westminster Bridge. North of the river again. Bridge Street. Parliament Street. Whitehall. Through Horseguard's Arch. The Mall. Back to Buckingham Palace. The end."

She glanced hopefully up at Chubb.

"Once more," said the Inspector, dipping a biscuit in his now ice-cold tea.

Angelica had come to believe Chubb never actually drank tea, but only used it to dampen biscuits.

Taking a deep breath, Angelica started again. "The Queen will be leaving Buckingham Palace at eleven-fifteen. Up Constitution Hill. Piccadilly. Saint James Street. Pall Mall. Trafalgar Square, in front of the Gallery. The Strand—"

Chubb watched her narrowly. Though not, perhaps, the most sensitive of souls, Chubb had a vast experience of dealing with persons in tense situations. He understood that this simple, ordinary task of reading the paper might be all that was keeping Miss Trickett from becoming unglued.

Just then, she perked up. A fresh connection struck her. "The Courts of Justice! They might make a good target to a man who thinks he got cheated of justice at one time or another."

"As I said, it's a holiday."

"There will be grandstands there. They'll kill people."

"There are grandstands all along the route, Miss. Nearly every building on the way has been turned into furniture. All packed full. What we need to figger out is, do our mad bombers have a method to their madness, as the fellow said. Do they want to bomb par-tick-lar places, or par-tick-lar persons? Or do they just want to blow up a building or a few hundred people for the lousy, stinkin' hell of it? That cigarette message you recited for me – you're sure you got it all right?"

"I hope I remembered it correctly." She closed her eyes. *"Airship. Infernal machine. Resurgam. King o'er the water.* At the bottom, a diamond, and *xxii* (we think)." She opened her eyes. "I don't remember the original of the *King* line, but I can reconstruct it if necessary."

"It don't make sense when it's English. It'll make even worse sense when it's gobbledegook. If that bomb ain't dropped today, but on Saturday's regatta of gunboats, what would the Roman numbers be for that?"

"Sunday?" Angelica had forgotten the date. She tapped her fingers on the table as she counted the days off. "The twenty-seventh, x-x-v-i-i, Herron Strangways told me. You don't read Roman numerals?"

Chubb had his mouth full of soggy biscuit, so he shook his head.

She wrote the two numbers out in the top margin of the newspaper: *xxii, xxvii.*

"But there was a burnt space that kept you from tellin' exactly which it were."

"I feel in my bones it's today, Inspector."

"Your bones ain't exactly admissible in court. Still, you and Mister Strangways did a good job on breakin' that secret cigarette message."

"Thank you, Inspector."

"Only, it don't help us an awful lot."

"Don't it? I mean . . . oh!"

"The thing is, Miss," Chubb said, dunking another biscuit, "for that message to help us thwart a bombing, it had to contain everything we need to know. To wit, how, what, when, where and who."

"And why."

"In my experience, you don't often know 'why' 'til you got your man in bracelets. And he might never give any better reason for killin' a whole family than saying, 'They were home.' Let's review what we know. *What?*"

"An infernal machine."

"*How?*"

"Delivered by airship."

"*When?*"

"Today, the twenty-second."

"According to your bones. Presumably the bomb will be dropped on the Diamond Jubilee Procession that's going to start—"

He reeled a huge watch from a waistcoat pocket.

"Hm. Forgot to wind it. Never mind." He tucked the watch back into his waistcoat and it a pat. "Let's just say, 'too soon.'"

"Don't you think we ought to notify the authorities?"

"I am the authorities. Can you see why your message don't help us much? It don't tell us the most important things. *Where* will that there bomb be dropped? And for 'when,' I'd like a more exact time than 'Toosday.' Then, there's 'who.'"

"We know *who*. Lady Calthrop was behind it."

"Yes, Miss. So you told me."

"You sound like you don't believe me."

"I ain't paid to believe things, but to sneak as close as I can to the truth. Even if I can't get provable truth, I got to get enough facts to make a case. If what you say is true, this Lady Calthrop was perched at the top of the flagpole. Fine. You may have put her up in the clouds this mornin' – we'll know her condition when Pottle gets back – but alive or dead, she ain't steerin' no airship. It ain't a solitary assassin we're lookin' for, but a gang. What sort of gang? Where? Where are they now – and *where* and *when* are they gonna strike? Every gang has a bee in their bonnet about this or that. If we only knew who, we might guess where. If, that is, they're gonna blow up a place or a person with a reason."

Angelica looked glumly down into her coffee cup.

"And there are two things in that cigarette paper I don't quite understand. That word you said was Latin—"

"Meaning 'I shall rise again,' Mister Strangways said."

"I wouldn't trust to that young feller's education. He didn't strike me as bein' par-tick-lar-ly studious. So we got that Latin word, and we got the phrase 'king o'er the water.' That last bit sounds more like the '*who*' to me, if we can figger out what king it's talking about. One thing Lady Calthrop can't be is a king."

"I wondered about that all night, Inspector."

"If 'king o'er the water' means *who*, that Latin word is all we have left to tell us *where*. The problem is, we just don't know which is *where* and what is *who*."

That last sentence was a bit much for an Angelica without sleep.

"Inspector, with all my heart, I believe the Latin word referred to Lady Calthrop. 'Of convalescent persons: *resurgam* . . . to rise again.' She rose again, both from her chair and from her mourning. That's our *who*. In my heart I believe the 'king o'er the water' must be a code for *where*."

Chubb observed that her heart wasn't what he would call solid evidence.

"Don't let's fret much about *who* right now. What we got to figger out is which of them clues tells us *where*. Right about now, I'd rather stop a disaster than make an arrest. We can't move 'til we get the 'where' nailed down."

"Why?"

"They may mean to chuck out bombs on all and sundry, but to do any good we got to assume they mean to bomb someplace in par-tick-lar, and then evacuate that place. And since neither of us knows that place, we're stuck."

Angelica looked hopelessly at the map. *Six miles* of territory to cover. Nearly fifty thousand armed troops – and all powerless against an air assault.

Angelica wearily rested her forehead on the heels of her hands.

Chubb pitied her fatigue; but she was the only link he had with this imminent disaster, and he had to keep her from conking out on him.

"Miss, we go to keep in mind, people that blows things up in peacetimes ain't right in the head. I've known dynamiters to bomb just about anywhere. They've even set their bombs off in the Tower, of all useless places – all that'll be killed there is blackbirds and American tourists. Some chump tried blowin' up Greenwich observatory in February of '94 – but fortunately, he blowed himself up instead. Now what good was that – was he angry at Time itself, 'cause he didn't never have enough of it? We'll never know. Well, we can't bank on these people bein' so dumb they'll blow themselves up. Our only hope of saving anybody and stopping a disaster is to say they're going to bomb something or someone specific. And we can't sit around here playin' guessin' games. 'If I was a mad terrorist, what would I bomb?' You got a message. We got to figger out if there's a connection between any of that message and any place on this route. And we're marchin' up and down that Procession route until we find it."

"It doesn't mention many sites on this little map."

"That's okey-doke, Miss. I'm a Londoner born and bred and when you're in the Force you know where everything's at. You just keep readin' off the streets. I know what's on 'em better than a cabbie."

"What if our mad bombers are . . . mad? If they just mean bloody murder?"

"In that case . . . it don't matter a cuss what we do. What if we knew for a fact they mean to strew hundreds of bombs from one end of town to the other? We can't evacuate all London. Miss, we've dropped a coin at night, and our only hope of finding it is looking under the lamp-post."

"It's not very satisfactory."

"Think this over. One bomb will kill – what? A dozen tight-packed folks?"

"Assuming they have only one bomb."

"What happens if we run out into the street shouting 'The sky is falling'? Half the folks will think you're barmy, and the rest will start runnin' – tramplin' over each other and maybe runnin' right into the place bein' bombed. Jack the Ripper killed fewer women than I got fingers and in one part of town and he got all London in an uproar. If we found a way to announce there was just one bomb bein' hurled out from the clouds, we'd get all the millions of souls in town in a panic. That would get ugly fast. We'd be better off sittin' here, enjoying our tea and biscuits while a dozen or two people got blown to smithereens."

Angelica doubted she could enjoy a meal in those circumstances.

"But *if*," Chubb continued, "our mad bombers do have a par-tick-lar target in mind, whether it's Her Majesty or someone – or some thing – else, we might figger it out, and evacuate that one spot."

"They might still drop their bomb elsewhere, out of spite."

"We can only do what we can do and leave the rest to God."

"I try to be a Christian, Inspector, but—where is God while this is happening?"

"Where He always was, Miss. Shakin' His head at what folks can get up to, to hurt each other."

"Why doesn't God send someone to stop it!"

"He sent you."

She raised her head from her hands. That was a dreadful thought.

But it was true. Angelica alone of all the people in London – alone of all the people in the world! – had seen that secret message that no longer existed. Whoever was targeted today, Angelica's memory was the only slender strand those lives had to cling to for safety.

With the weight of those living souls resting on her shoulders, she did not want to be the handmaiden of the Lord.

But she had to acknowledge that Chubb was right. The haggard bird would have slipped half a cigarette into her reticule even if Herron Strangways had not sidled up to her. He had expedited her discovery of the cigarette, but if Herron had not been drawn to her, he would never have gotten within the haggard bird's reach. Whether she liked it or not, she was the chosen one.

Angelica believed in free will. She had a clear choice: accept the cup given her, whatever the cost, or deny that those lives were her responsibility (and hide out until the tragedy was over).

In a still, small voice, she asked, "What do you need from me, Inspector?"

He gave her shoulder a kindly pat as he paced around the table. "Just stick by me. As for what we need—Gawd! I wish I knew! You may see a connection we're missing. I think it's in them two lines we don't understand, either that Latin bit or the mumbo-jumbo that was worse mumbo-jumbo once you found out what it said. For the foreseeable future, we ain't shiftin' from this spot."

"Inspector, I would be convinced our *where* clue lay in the Latin word, if I hadn't seen Lady Calthrop rise up from her wheelchair. And in that white gown! She's been in black since she hired me nearly eighteen months ago."

"Did the man who passed you the cigarette know Lady Calthrop?"

"I don't know."

"She was right there at the Underground station when he died. That's proved. We got her statement."

"And mine."

"Did the man recognize her? *Was he running from her – and her darts?*"

"I don't know."

"Did he suspect she was rising of her chair, and her mourning, in three days?"

"I don't know."

"That's our problem, Miss. So long as we keep saying 'I don't know' we can't rule nothin' out. We can't jump on just any train and hope it goes by our stop."

Angelica pushed her chair away from the table. She'd been staring at the map until her aching eyes were blurry. She rubbed them, wondering if they were permanently crossed.

So far as she was concerned, they only needed one more clue. They knew who, what, when and how:

inferna_____chine. The what. A bomb. Forget hair-splitting distinctions between bombs and explosive devices. It was a bomb and designed to kill.

ai__hip. The how. The method of delivery.

The when required a little imagination, but the diamond helped. June *xxii*, 1897. Today! That it would happen during the Procession was a safe assumption.

RESURGAM. Angelica was convinced RESURGAM had nothing to do with the Procession. *RESURGAM* was their *who*. Lady Calthrop.

It made no sense that she could see in any other context.

The only part of the message that still made no sense was *king o'er the water*. Those words had to contain them the all-important clue to *where!*

Despite Angelica's restlessness to be up and doing . . . *something* . . . unless they discovered that *where*, they were doomed to fail.

They were probably doomed anyway. An airship coming from – well, any direction – was going to drop a bomb on London. Who could stop it?

London was stuffed full of souls, and they couldn't halt an airship if they all banded together and formed a human pyramid with Angelica climbing on top to shoot the at airship with her little revolver.

She lifted the back of her left hand to her mouth to cover a yawn. "Maybe we should think of the other end. Where are they starting *from*? Lady Calthrop never talked about owning any country estates where she might hide an airship."

"She might not have owned it in her own name. Even if she did own it outright, it'll take hours for us to track it down and get to it. The airship would be *here* before we could get *there*. It'll come on a beeline, while we got to depend on roads and trust in horses."

"It might at least tell us what direction it's coming from."

"So we could all run out and wave at it as it passed overhead. Very friendly."

"Inspector, what do you suppose is the importance of the marriage certificate?"

"We won't know 'til word gets back from the Court of the Lord Lyon."

Her eyes opened wide. "The *what*?"

"It's sort of the Scottish College of Arms."

Angelica shook her head. She wondered if Broughton Chubb had gone as mad as the bombers – or if, while she'd been tucked away in Lady Calthrop's house, the whole world had gone askew and she hadn't noticed.

What could airships blowing up queens have to do with marriage certificates going to the Court of the Lord Lyon – whatever that was!

"Did that poor man upstairs have anything else?"

"This was clutched in his hand." Chubb laid a monocle on the table.

Angelica frowned at it. It reminded her of Herron. "I meant a paper you picked from his pocket."

Like a cheap conjurer, Chubb produced a folded sheet of paper from his breast pocket and handed it to her.

Angelica looked it over. It was difficult to read where it had been crumpled He found another paper in the man's hand. It was just a doodle. It said, *Even Thrasymachus blushed*. Chubb knit his brow over it and handed it to Angelica.

"You know what that means?"

She shook her head. "Please, God, not another code!"

Chubb tossed the paper side.

Still thinking of the *who*, she said, "The Kaiser is a 'king over the water.'"

"Miss, there must be at least twenty, twenty-five claimants in succession between the Queen and the Kaiser. It would take a plague—Or a big bomb, since most of the Queen's surviving children and grandchildren will be in the parade. I could find that out in a jiffy. All they'd have to do is blow up all the Queen's male children and their issue and they start ticking down the women. The Kaiser's mother is the Queen's eldest daughter. She'll be in the Procession."

"Protocol will have her in a completely different carriage than the Queen. They can't have a bomb big enough to blow them all."

"Can't they? Science is always up to doin' things I thought impossible. If they can make an airship, they can make a big bomb to throw from it."

"There was nothing I saw or heard from Lady Calthrop in all the time I worked for her that predisposed me to think she wanted the Kaiser to be king in England."

"You didn't see nothin' that presupposed you to think she could walk, neither."

Angelica glumly admitted that was true. "Even if they have a bomb that a can blow everyone in the Procession to hash, so long as one child survives descended from the Queen's sons, the Kaiser can't be king."

"Oh, no?"

"In any case, that would be too terrible. The man's a fool."

"And he ain't in London, neither. Maybe he's behind it – or maybe these people with the bomb want to leave nothing but a choice so horrible that a compromise candidate would be preferable to either a child or the Kaiser."

"You know, Inspector, my brother Schuyler told me that when the last of the Stuarts died – Queen Anne – Parliament passed some sort of law that jumped over as many as fifty claimants to put the German Georges on the throne."

Inspector Chubb responded that nothing Parliament got up to would surprise him. "If all that's left of the royal family are a few tots, Parliament might just jump over half again as many claimants to keep Germans *off* the throne."

"Anything would be preferable to the Kaiser."

"Maybe that's what Lady Calthrop's brood was bankin' on. Or maybe they'll keep on bombin' cities until we agreed to their terms."

"I know I brought it up . . . but it sounds ridiculous."

"Flyin' machines sound ridic'lous to me. We live in an time of political murder, Miss. There was an attempt on the President of France a week ago. It's becomin' a more popular way of changing the government than elections."

Angelica's shook her head. "The more we learn, the less we seem to know."

Chubb heaved a sigh of agreement.

"Lady Calthrop must have been mad. She talked like it in her last minutes."

"I don't hold with the idea, Miss, of calling people 'mad' just 'cause we don't like what they say. I think a lot of times we do that because, if we admit other people done terrible things while they was sane, we're afraid to look in the mirror at ourselves. I seen a lot of murderers in my business, Miss. And it's taught me one thing: anyone can kill. It's just a matter of provocation and opportunity."

"If I accept Original Sin, Inspector, I'm forced to agree with you."

"I don't know much about theo-lol-logy, but if that Original Sin means anyone can do just about anything awful, it's true enough, judgin' by what I've seen. Even if she was mad, mad people can inflict terrible damage."

"Maybe the whole thing is mad. Maybe the airship isn't coming, and all those people won't die."

"If it don't come, the only person that'll die may be you. By hanging."

CHAPTER LVII

Herron had shifted his eyes from Stoker, who was actually aiming the gun at him, to the approaching Hawkins. So, as the staccato shot barked crisply from Stoker's firearm, even before it reverberated away over the fens Herron saw the American's face explode out toward him.

Blood, brains and skull fragments spattered all over Herron even before the body flopped forward, revealing Stoker standing directly behind him with a smoking pistol.

Before Herron could registered surprise, Stoker kicked the body into the grave. "Roll down in the hole and take off your clothes."

"I beg your—?"

"Quick, you blithering idiot, or I'll do you, too." He cocked his gun a second time and aimed it down. His eyes were scanning the flat, wet countryside, but he could easily shoot the kneeling Herron using just peripheral vision.

Herron rolled into the pit beside the headless corpse. He was not overly squeamish in the normal way, but he tried not to look at the place where the head had been as his trembling hands began undressing the deceased.

"Why can't *you* undress him? I wager you've done this sort of work before."

"We need a look out."

"I wager I have better eyesight than you." "Do you know what to look out for?"

Not much, Herron thought, since the low fog on the fens had risen.

"Faster!" snapped Stoker. "Put on his clothes and dress him in yours. Then throw the dirt back in the hole."

"His clothes are sodden with blood."

"We'll tell the boss it was an unexpectedly messy execution. It happens. Underclothes, too."

Herron was appalled at the condition of Hawkins's flannel union suit. "Why?"

"What are you wearing? Take your trousers off."

Herron stripped off his by-now shabby and torn waiters' satin breeches. Stoker sneered at Herron's knee-length underwear, "Silk? Tailored?"

"Liberty's, actually."

"Hawkins' sort don't wear that. If anybody comes to check whether you're really in that hole, we want them to find him in *all* your clothing."

"They are pretty thorough, if they'll check his – you-know."

"They are thorough. I know."

"Who are *they*?"

"Shut up and finish."

Herron had difficulty dressing the late Hawkins. A lifeless human body is an unwieldy thing, and Herron was used to having someone helping him dress himself of a morning. The undergarments alone were nearly impossible. Herron thought he'd have more luck putting his clothes on a bag of turnips.

Finishing at last, he donned Hawkins's shoddy clothes. Naked, he'd felt like a fool. Dressed, he felt like a clown. The shirt was too large for Herron's frame. The dungarees were more *dung* than *rees*, and when Hawkins's suspenders were adjusted, the dungarees rose over his ankles – and up into his crotch.

When Herron scrambled out of the pit, Stoker put him to work refilling the hole. It was warm work; but, judging by the whiff of Hawkins's togs, a little more perspiration would hardly matter.

He was tamping the earth over the grave before he dared speak again.

"What's going on here, anyway? Why didn't you shoot me?"

"Second question first. God knows. Totally unprofessional. Endangering the whole operation rather than swatting a gadfly."

"First question?"

"I don't know, altogether."

"Third question: whose side are you on?"

"I told you the truth when we met. I work for Her Majesty's government."

That hardly eased Herron's mind. Her Majesty's enemies wanted him shot, and so far as he knew Her Majesty's government wanted him hanged.

"For years, I've been worming my way into *their* good graces, earning their trust. I'm all ready to make my arrest while they're in the commission of their crime. All I needed, after all my years of hard work, was some nincompoop like you blundering in. I came out here with half a mind to shoot you just on general principles. Blowing you into that hole would get you out from underfoot."

"Funny way of keeping me out from underfoot, putting me in the ground."

"You've been a deal of trouble, young man, prying where you have no business. I tried to warn you off Saturday night."

"And Sunday evening you tried to shoot me."

"I don't *try*. You've just seen, I hit what I shoot at. When you were on your ledge, I had a clear shot from the window of your end room."

"You didn't shoot me, even though you had orders to?"

"I sent Hawkins to the room where I thought you were cowering. Hawkins would shoot you and you would be off my conscience. Cap, too." Seeing Herron's blank stare, he added, "Hawkins's cap. Put it on."

Fortunately, the cap had been blown up and away by the explosion of Hawkins's head, so it had only a sprinkling of blood on it. When Herron slapped it onto his own head, it slid low on his eyebrows. It was stopped from swallowing his head whole by his slightly protuberant ears.

Herron trusted that Hawkins' bigger head was not indicative of brains. At least, it wouldn't fly off if a sharp wind blew up. Whatever disgusting pomade Hawkins used on his hair, it adhered the cloth to Herron's forehead.

"Shoes and socks and let's clear out. You've been nothing but a thorn in my side for three days. Just like that fool at the station."

"Oh, yes, the haggard bird. Was that fellow with the moustachios telling the truth when he said no one here killed him?"

"*I was sent to kill him*. I wish I had, before he got to you. He defected from here knowing too much. This close to zero hour there was an intensive lockdown. When he made his break Saturday, he was careless. His trail was so easy to follow, he might as well have dropped breadcrumbs behind him."

Herron admired Hawkins' socks, which were quite colorful – or had been. Like everything else he wore, they were dingy and were not altogether clean. Wiggling his feet in them, he said, in a strained voice, "The haggard bird missed his train, but it didn't miss him. Why did you nab me?"

"You might have been his contact. I also wondered if *you* killed him."

"Me? I've never killed anybody. That I know of."

"I've seen good assassins disguised as persons even more vapid than you. When you wear that eyeglass you look like you have just sense enough to put on your hat without assistance – but not your tie. I had to know if you were his contact, his murderer, or if you were only the loitering numbskull you look."

"And what did you decide, after grilling me?"

"I couldn't make up my mind. So I thought, if these people want to control every aspect of our lives I'll let them see what that means. I sent as much as you told me up through channels. Sunday night, word came down to kill you."

"They really thought I was a threat?"

"They're mobilized for action. They haven't time to assess every threat, so they'll kill anyone on the off-chance."

Fortunately, Hawkins had big feet. Herron knew he couldn't wear own shoes and spats to accessorize his present get-up. He was afraid, if Hawkins's low-top boots proved too small, Stoker's solution would be to shoot off Herron's toes.

In fact, Hawkins's shoes were roomy. Herron was glad Hawkins had never sauntered into the Hemlock to accept the standing challenge against Herron's tootsies. Hawkins's boots were good for length, but far too wide. Herron might have walked on water in them if their flat soles hadn't been spotted with holes.

Herron, with the shovel, and Stoker strolled casually back to the motor carriage, each in a snappish mood toward the other.

"So, you're sort of the bloody-minded thug to whom I am supposed to owe the freedom I was always taught was the right of every Englishman." "And you're the lazy sort of layabout I risk life and limb for every day to insure the freedom of."

"I do not lay about."

Stoker gave a mawkish bow. "Pardon *me*, m'lord. Get a move on. The earth's soft yet over the grave, and it's big enough to accommodate two."

"And what'll you tell home office when you return alone?"

"I'll tell them you fought back and killed Hawkins, but I got you. On second thought, I'm not sure that keeping you alive is in Her Majesty's best interest."

"Oh, she'll take a shine to me once we're introduced."

"I haven't taken a shine to you."

"Nor have I to you, friend . . . what is your name? Hawkins called you 'Jake.' I assumed your name was Jacob."

"The fool misunderstood something he heard. 'Stoker' will do."

Herron sat in the motor carriage passenger seat with the shovel upright between his knees.

Taking the tiller to steer them back to the compound, Stoker sat as far away as he could from Herron, to keep fresh blood from smearing his suit.

The fog was too thick on the fens by now for them to see if any listening ears were posted nearby. The Knight three-wheeler was advertised as "silent," but it certainly made enough noise to drown their words.

Herron raised his strong voice to ask, "Why did you change your mind about – as the western novels say – pluggin' me back there?"

"I did not change my mind. You deserve pluggin'. I simply considered the ramifications. As with everything else you own, you owe your life to your father."

"Did you know him?"

"I hardly move in the august circles of the rich and famous."

"No," said Herron, sarcastically, in his best public school accent, "I don't remember ever seeing you at Ascot."

"Stow the blarney. Your father made, or bought, friends in high places. And you're the sort of young whippersnapper who went to school with the high and mighty, who appears in the newspapers too often, and whose disappearance would cause questions to be asked in Parliament. Your rich and your political friends, desperate to find you or your body, would mobilize Scotland Yard overnight."

"Yes, they do think a lot of me."

"Of your money. Lots of lolly to be divvied up from a man who has no children, no siblings, no close cousins and probably no last will."

"Even if I had drawn up a will, you wouldn't be in it. So what's in it for you?"

"Having your friends and relations sic detectives and reporters sniffing down your trail might force these people here to change their plans. I've been through too much to have them up and change plans on me. If they change plans or decamp, I may know less than I know now!"

"I was told the haggard bird was also working to get to the bottom of whatever's going on around here."

"Told? By who?"

"Whom, I think." Herron related his various meetings with Jessup. "I had a date with him tonight. With the haggard bird and you both working here for the same ends, I'm surprised you two didn't know each other."

"We knew *of* each other, but we'd no clue we were working on the same side. More than one organization works in the shadows on behalf of Her Majesty. We often arrive at the same place by different paths. Like two people eating from different ends of the same sausage."

Herron wouldn't have minded the vision of Angelica's sweet lips chomping toward him on a succulent sausage, with a kiss in the middle; but he was appalled at the mental image of chunky, balding, toothbrush-moustached Stoker and the dreary, hag-ridden haggard bird doing the same.

"Strangways, we didn't set down our grips and say, 'Pardon me, I'm new here. Where do all the spies mingle who are trying to undermine your operations?'"

Herron had been brought up to understand how to run a business – he had simply never lifted a hand to do it. He was appalled at the lack of organization in Her Majesty's secret services.

"You people ought to get together. You're unnecessarily duplicating work."

"What do you know about work?"

"I know I don't want it duplicated. I don't want to do the same job once, much less twice. Wouldn't it be simpler to have the information from these various organizations funneling through one office?"

"It's also simple to talk after the fact. If he'd gotten clean away, he might have jeopardized their plans. He fled from here *to expose and undermine the plot*."

"Isn't that what you want?"

"No! I want them show their hand, here and now, so we can arrest them in the act. Do think, once in a while! If they're thwarted, they'll merely reform and strike again, and I may not be able to get myself so intimately involved next time."

"So you'd have shot the haggard bird even though he's your side?"

"I have a job to do."

Herron shrugged. That was no longer his business. He was alive, and he just wanted to get into his own bed. "Well, I've enjoyed my trip to the zoo. How do I get home through the heightened security?"

"You don't."

"If you want to avoid questions being asked about the disappearance of dashing young Strangways of Emporia fame, I must reappear. And soon!"

"Therefore, you will make yourself known. You're going to write letters to friends saying London's too crowded and you've zipped over to Paris."

"Inspector Chubb asked me politely to stop in London. The police won't like my sudden flit to the continent."

"Nor will they like scouring Paris to locate you when you're not there."

"So I'm *not* going to Paris?"

"If you try to leave the compound before I say, I will shoot you in the leg."

"Just as well. Paris won't be worth visiting again until they've dismantled that skeletal eyesore, Eiffel's tower. They've destroyed their tourist trade."

"I haven't seen it."

"Don't bother. It's rubbish. Must I not go to Paris?"

"Don't go to anyplace you like! You're a man who does things on whims. Tell your friends you've—" Stoker struggled to think like a bored, rich traveler, "—you've suddenly gone off yachting with a friend to fish off Norway."

"Fishing?" Herron grimaced.

"Then—you're taking a cruise down to Monte Carlo, then. Incognito."

"That sounds jolly. I'd be much happier not going there."

"I couldn't care less where you don't go."

"When don't I leave?"

"As soon as possible. Write your notes the moment we return. I'll see they are delivered. Then you stay in our cantonments where I can keep my eyes on you."

"Won't your boss recognize me?"

"He probably didn't even look at you. People don't matter to him. You were an annoyance, like a flea. Once you are exhumed, so they are certain I killed you, he'll believe your particular itch has been scratched."

"After all that effort I put in burying myself, they're going to dig me up?"

"They'll find a headless man about your size in your clothes. Pull the cap low, slouch, scratch yourself in public, and he'll never notice you're a changeling."

"Is the Moustache the big panjandrum around these parts?"

"I don't know who is running the show. They refer 'she who is to come.'" He leaned in confidentially. "I think it the person at the top of the tree is a woman."

"Do tell. Whoever 'she' is, she must be wealthy."

"They see her as some sort of cock-eyed goddess of beauty, peace and plenty."

"She better have plenty if she's doling out jobs – and salaries – at her discretion. And Mister Moustache is her lap dog? How do you put up with him? He's the most arrogant young ass I've ever met, and I went to public school and university, and I am pals with several members of Parliament."

"He may not be the big boss, but he is in command of operations here. Don't cross him. In shop-keepers' terms, he puts a low price-tag on human life." "He seemed pleasant enough. German?"

"Swiss."

"Swiss! How can he come over all high and mighty? They don't even have their own language!"

"He was in the Prussian army. He keeps holding his service experience over our heads. I know for a fact he went through something called the Bavarian Airship Flying School set up by that mad King Ludwig."

"That reminds me: what time does the balloon go up tomorrow?"

Stoker braked so abruptly he stalled the engine. "What's that?"

"Tomorrow – when the airship bombs the Diamond Jubilee parade."

Stoker was quiet until the "silent" engine again drowned their words. "You've pieced a lot together in less than sixty hours."

"I'm a pretty clever chap under pressure."

"You had the message in the cigarette after all?"

"Yes. How did your Swiss know that, by the way? So far as I know, only four people knew about that cigarette: Jessup, me, and the two people I went to visit this afternoon. I didn't even tell my man Merridew about it."

"The Swiss got a telegraph message Monday afternoon that told him the whole story. So it *was* a cigarette we were looking for. Where was it?"

"Half of it was nestling in my pocket all along. I didn't find it until the next day when I tried to smoke it." "Hawkins said we should have searched you over. We'd have found it."

"Too bad you didn't."

"If we had, we'd have assumed you were the contact of our late friend at the station and we'd have disposed of you at once in that abandoned building."

"Shot me?"

"Probably not. Reach into the left-hand breast pocket of Hawkins's coat."

Herron did – and found Hawkins's Bowie knife. Herron felt ill. That knife was what Hawkins meant to use on Herron if they needed a *coup de grace*.

"Hawkins knew his ropes. He was a rigger. We equip our riggers with Bowie knives to cut themselves loose if they get tangled up in the ropes. A gunshot might have attracted unwanted attention Saturday night, in London. Hawkins would have dispatched you with that very silent weapon you have in your hands."

Herron slipped the knife back into his pocket. "And you'd have watched him."

Stoker gave a careless shrug.

"I know. You have a job. And you'd have toted me down to the river?"

"We might have let the rats dispose of you. What did the cigarette say?"

"Huh? Oh . . . ah . . . Just scattered nonsense. I only had half of it. With Jessup's help I met up with the party who had the other half and we worked out 'Airship' and 'Infernal Machine.' There was a Latin *non sequitur* and a Roman numeral that we decided was 'xxii.' A symbol that looked like a diamond. And a line of utter rubbish we never made heads nor tails of."

"Well, the Diamond Jubilee has come and gone. All that remains is the Procession this morning and the regatta on the 27th. Frankly, I thought they were going to bomb the ships. England is a powerful country, but its navy – and even its army – can't even leave this island without boats. But then, I suppose the gunboats will be able to shoot the airship down, once they find their range. They can't do that in London. They'd kill too many innocent people. That's why the good guys usually lose – they don't want to kill too many innocent people. The people here don't care who they have to kill to get power and keep it."

"The queen – and millions of others – will be in the streets today."

"Until Saturday, I hadn't been to London since we arrived back on this side. One good bomb will kill a couple of hundred people, they way they are packed."

"That many? In one blast?"

"They have truly infernal machines here. And many more will be trampled in the stampede. That's what happens with crowds, when there's a panic. Since you know so much, there are a couple of things you might tell me."

"And they are?"

"Where the bomb will be dropped, and precisely when."

Herron gurgled a strangled cry of indignation. "After all I've been through, Her Majesty's agents know exactly what I found out! And not one blasted thing more! How I *hate* duplicating work!"

CHAPTER LVIII

Stoker, too, was indignant. "You mean – you had this mysterious secret cigarette paper with the details of the bombing, and you haven't a clue about where they're dropping the bomb? Or when?"

"You live in the heart of the organization! Don't you know where and when?"

"We are rigidly compartmentalized, Strangways. I'm really attached to the aerial department, but since I'm handy with a gun and have no compunction about killing whenever necessary, they use me on outside jobs."

"Bloody-minded assassin!"

"Let's call me an *agent provocateur*."

"Let's not pull any of Mister Moustache's cute little word-games and say you're the same sort of murdering swine they are."

"If that's true, just remember that it's never good policy to insult murdering swine. What you blithely dismissed as 'a line of utter rubbish' is probably the crux of the message. Can you recall it?"

"Not as words." Herron rattling off a stream of letters.

"Woah! I can't put it together in my head! Write it out when we get back."

"I didn't think you blokes wrote things out."

"If it'll make you happier, I'll eat the paper when I've committed it to memory. What was the Latin word?"

"*Resurgam*. It means 'I shall rise again.'"

"Probably a code word chosen at random – code words usually are – by an operative who wanted to show off a fancy public-school education."

"And dictated by space. There's dashed little room to scribble on a cigarette paper, and *Resurgam* is only eight letters long. All capitals, by the way. That reminds me of a joke. What's the capital of Ceylon? Capital 'C' of course."

He gurgled a laugh.

Stoker must have been too preoccupied on his driving to grasp the point of the joke, as he didn't so much as crack a smile.

"*Resurgam* is a code word," Stoker said, "But is it a code they use here on the compound, or was it a invented by the haggard bird and *his* people?"

Herron was reminded that Angelica Trickett has posed the same question. "I believe the haggard bird thought it would ring a bell with the old folks at home."

"The haggard bird probably didn't know *where*. Only the man who drops the bomb may know where it will fall, the way they compartmentalize here."

"You *did* know about the airship?"

"I said – I'm in the aerial division! You can't compartmentalize an airship."

"So there is a real airship? I've doubted its existence."

"It exists. Dreamt up by a Californian inventor. He thought it would make war impossible. Well, a nice, devastating weapon would make war impossible – if one honest broker nation had it and no one else did. But once other nations get their hands on 'em, we're all back to scratch."

"Always Americans! I think they're really God's chosen people."

"This American's work took a lot of tinkering, all across America and the Atlantic. We never thought we'd make it viable in time."

"And you flew it jall over America for months. It was in the papers."

"We couldn't have test-flights in Britain. We have too many quaint, bloody little villages. In those American and Canadian plains you can fly – and crash – dozens of prototypes where they'll never be found."

"Isolated farms, though, sprinkled across the plains?"

"Populated by isolated farmers, whom no one will ever believe."

"How did you get the airship over here?"

"We flew," was Stoker's matter-of-fact answer.

"Over the Atlantic?" Herron whistled. "You are advanced."

"Twenty man crew. Pilot and back-up pilot; two glider pilots, including me; a few riggers, including Hawkins; and mechanics and repairmen."

"And the American inventor? Where is he?"

"From what I've been able to learn, he's currently reposing – and decomposing – at the bottom of San Francisco bay."

"Which is why he's not claiming his rights. Where does the Swiss come in?"

"He is our main Pilot."

"Him? They trust that dolt to pilot an airship? A man who seems to judge a thing by its usefulness to his doctrinaire political agenda? He'll be gauging height and direction by political efficacy. I wouldn't go up in the air with that lunatic."

"That 'lunatic' just had you kneeling at your grave, Strangways. You were a squeeze of my forefinger away from eternity."

"What's his name, anyway? Even a man who believes in dehumanizing humans must have some moniker."

"Barak Lugner."

"What the hell sort of name is that?"

"A man named 'Herron' asks me that! I looked it up. It's in Scripture."

"They have a Bible here?"

"I went to a library on one of my ventures out. Listen. *Deborah, a prophetess . . . judged Israel at that time . . . And she . . . called Barak the son of Abinoam out of Kedeshnaphtali, and said unto him, Hath not the LORD God of Israel commanded, saying, Go . . . And Barak said unto her, If thou wilt go with me, then I will go: but if thou wilt not go with me, then I will not go. And she said, I will surely go with thee . . . for the Lord shall sell Sisera into the hand of a woman.*"

"Kedeshnaphthali?" Herron shook his head. "That can't be right. Don't tell me Lugner reads the Good Book?"

"His parents obviously did. And once, I did find a slip in the house that reads: *Sie sprach: Ich will freilich mit dir gehen; aber der Ruhm des Weges, den du gehst, wird nicht dir zufallen; denn der Herr wird Sisera in die Hand eines Weibes ubergeben.* That's, *The Lord will sell Sisera into the hands of a woman.*"

"He's barking, you know that? He clings besottedly to his political ideals with an earnest and fundamental faith. What was that expression he gave me? 'The will to believe.' That's what he has. In spades. And he believes such horrendous things. Is all that hooey he spouted really on the agenda of the conspiracy?"

"Strangways, ours is the *only* working airship right now, so airship pilots are scarce. 'She who is to come' – whoever she is – must take what she can get where pilots were concerned. Lugner has been piloting all our prototypes."

"So Lugner may be a stooge for larger interests. He hates money, but he'll work for 'she.' And if she can build airships and own an estate large enough to hide it on, she're pressed down and overflowing with shekels."

"Money is power."

"All mine has only gotten me is a nasty set of second-hand clothes."

"I'll tell you what his blether reminds me of. 'There shall be in England seven halfpenny loaves sold for a penny . . . all the realm shall be in common . . . there shall be no money; all shall eat and drink on my score, and I will apparel them all in one livery, that they may agree like brothers and worship me.'"

"That's Lugner's entire party platform. Right down to the greedy bakers."

"It's from Shakespeare's *Henry VI*."

"Shakespeare again! I've been bumping into him everywhere."

"In the play, a Duke was actually funding Jack Cade's rebellion and if it succeeded it would have put all the rich folks in the tumbrel – except him."

"I suppose that's the way it is with these revolutionists. They claim to hate money, but social engineering costs a wad. 'She' must be sitting on a pile of money. You haven't an inkling who this 'she' may be?"

"No. I care about only two things: these people have an airship and a bomb; and they intend to use them. Today. If he chooses me as the glider pilot on this mission, I will try to apprehend him in the act. If he chooses another glider pilot—" Stoker stopped. The ramifications were too horrendous to speak.

Herron muttered. "And what happens to me?"

"We'll play it by ear. Sit tight. *Talk to no one* – Hawkins's speech was very distinctive. If you utter one word in your plummy, public-school accent—"

"I know." He extended his index finger. "*Bang*. Who was Hawkins, anyway? If I'm to play him I ought to know my life story."

"We picked him up in their 'wild west.' He was in what they call a 'ro-day-oh.' It's sort of a circus on horseback."

"I saw Buffalo Bill's Wild West show when he was over here."

"Hawkins's outfit wasn't nearly so impressive. Spavined broncos and the like. He roped calves. Lugner hired him as a rigger. He was also what they call a 'crack shot' – and he was totally unscrupulous. He doubled as a trouble shooter."

"Literally."

"He knew nothing about the conspiracy and cared less. I'm sure he was unimpressed by Lugner's folderol. Hawkins has no politics beyond his pockets. So long as they paid him, he didn't care what else they did."

"It's bad enough he doesn't seem to own a collar, but did I really have to wear his foul underclothing?"

"Yes."

"They'll double-check your handiwork? And they'll take him for me?"

"You and he were similar in height. You're slimmer, but that won't matter. His face had to be totally removed. Your face looks nothing like his."

"That's the kindest thing you've ever said to me. Now that I'm settling in here, probably under the bed, my principle worry is for—" He baulked at mentioning a woman's name.

Stoker finished the sentence. "—the little filly you had tea with?"

"How do you know about her?"

"If you don't wish to be seen in a house, Strangways, draw the shades. Does she have those papers?"

Herron shot him a glance. He didn't want to trust Stoker that far, just yet. He could imagine Stoker murdering one of his own associates in cold blood just to persuade Herron of his *bona fides*.

For a lark, Herron almost told him Lady Calthrop had the papers. But even if they went for the old lady, Angelica might be injured as a bystander.

Stoker understood his silence. "Good lad. Don't trust anyone, even me."

"May I see it?"

"What?"

"The airship?"

"We're not on a sightseeing holiday! We've no business there, and it'll get reported back. We return straight back to our eugenicist friend Lugner and tell him you are dead and buried. Then we go to find you a cot in a bunkhouse, where I will spread the word you had a sudden attack of laryngitis out in the damp."

"Look, Stoker, old chap, if you want to stop whatever is going on, why not just nobble the airship while you're here?"

"This is an armed camp, Strangways. The screws on our already tight security have been twisted even more after Saturday night's fiasco. It's unlikely anyone can get in or out without the proper authority. If the airship is damaged, they'll look for a saboteur in their midst. And they will find him. I will die for queen and country, but not while alternatives remain.

"Too, they're building another airship. It's up on a scaffolding, but the internal structure is complete. All it needs is the skin. They can't possibly prepare it for today but—if I damage the airship they have ready for today, what happens?"

"Lives are saved."

"Today. That's the short-term. They will strike again. When? Where? If they isolate me as the saboteur and I'm killed, the government can't depend on getting another agent as intimately involved in it as I am. Saturday night alerted these people to very real spies in their midst. They were paranoid to begin with, and Saturday's fiasco has made them trigger-happy. *I must stop them today.* To do that, Lugner must leave the compound *in* the airship *with* the bomb, and in my company so I can catch him red-handed."

Stoker's eyes became almost wistful.

"And then . . . I hate to destroy the world's first functioning airship! It's so majestic. I couldn't damage it. It's like a living being – something with a soul."

"I assume even Hawkins had a soul of sorts? You destroyed him easily enough. 'She' may be Miss Moneybags, but there must be an organization behind this who wants to seize control of the government by this act of terror. Who is it? The Fabians? The Anarchists? The Communists? The Capitalists?"

"The Jacobites."

CHAPTER LIX

Herron was shocked. "What—the French?"

"No! The French Revolutionaries were Jacob*ins*, deriving their name from a Parisian Club they had in a defunct Jacobin monastery. These are Jacob*ites*. It comes from the Latin version of James, 'Jacob.' Or Iacobus, to be precise."

"Thanks. I'd never have recognized what the devil you were talking about without that extra layer of precision. What the devil are you talking about?"

"Iacobus. Jacob. James. They didn't have 'J' in Latin, I'm told."

Herron became testy. "No, they didn't have 'J' in Latin. Or 'U.' Or lowercase letters, for that matter. They also didn't have airships. Why do you?"

"Have you never heard of the '45?"

"The forty-five what?"

"*1*745. It was called 'Charlie's Year.'"

"Lately, every explanation I've received has only served to make everything more cryptic. Start at the beginning. And skip 'In the beginning—'"

"This will be a bit of a history lesson—"

"Back in ruddy grammar school. Please – take me back and shoot me!"

"You may not think this history is relevant, Strangways, but an hour ago it had you kneeling by the maw of a gaping pit, with a cocked pistol aimed at your head! And it may yet! Shut up and listen, or forever hold your peace."

"Mum's the word, old man."

"After Queen Elizabeth died in 1603, the Stuarts got sucked into the power vacuum. Four Stuart kings followed her, James, Charles, Charles and James."

"Sounds easy enough to remember. I wonder why I didn't."

"James I was the son of Mary Queen of Scots, Elizabeth's cousin and next in line for the throne. Elizabeth had Mary beheaded, so James bobbed up to the throne. He was King James VI in Scotland, but he was the first king named James in England, so he took the name James I."

"Was he the Bible chap?"

"Yes. His son, Charles I, was overthrown and beheaded by the rebellion led by Oliver Cromwell. It was eleven years before Charles II regained his father's throne. When Charles II died without legitimate issue so his brother, James II, at that time Duke of York, became king. James II was remembered in a song.

> *'The grand old Duke of York, with forty thousand men*
> *Marched up the hill—and then marched down again.'*

He marched into battle – and then funked it and wouldn't fight."

"With forty thousand men? What were the odds against?"

"The number is probably hyperbole. Just remember that James II was the last king from the House of Stuart, and he was deposed in 1688."

"And that's why everyone I've met for three days has taken potshots at me? He was deposed more than two hundred years ago? I had nothing to do with it!"

"If you don't want to listen—!"

"Okay, I'll bite," Herron sighed. "Why was he deposed?"

"Because he was a Catholic."

"Oh, I say, hard cheese?"

"Not *altogether* for that reason, but like most people, you want this short and sweet, for the simplest, and probably most inaccurate, understanding of history."

"That was all donkey's years ago! Wo cares?"

"His descendants, some of whom think they are more entitled to the throne than the German family currently occupying it."

"German family?" That meant nothing to Herron.

"The Queen's family came from Hanover. The first Hanoverian king, George I, could not even speak English while ruling Great Britain."

"Which is mostly English-speaking. Except for Scotland."

"It galls these descendants of the Stuarts that old Victoria's been sixty years on a throne they consider rightfully theirs by strict primogeniture."

"Say 'strict primogeniture' three times fast. Do they have a good claim? Did James II have children? In a marriage?"

"James II had several daughters—"

"Who don't count."

"—and one infant son who accompanied him into exile. James II's eldest daughter, Mary, was married to William of Orange."

"I could do with an orange myself." Herron was so hungry he could almost smell the fresh aroma of an orange even over and above the stench of the fens.

"'Orange' was a Dutch principality. They were Protestant, Prince William and his wife, Mary. When James II was deposed, Parliament sent representatives of both parties to ask Mary to be their queen. So much for your '*they don't count.*'"

"My apologies to Queen Mary."

"She brought her husband along to reigned jointly as—"

"William and Mary! Yes, I've heard of them."

"Wonders *will* never cease. Mary died and William ruled alone until he was killed from injuries he received during a ride. His horse tripped on a gopher hole and he died. Eventually. Ever after, supporters of the Stuarts would drink secret toasts to 'the wee gentleman in velveteen' – meaning the gopher."

"'Wee gentleman in velveteen,'" mused Herron. That phrase rang a bell. "Please, go on. You are interesting me strangely."

"William and Mary's throne passed to Queen Anne—""I saw her statue outside Saint Paul's Cathedral. Where does she fit in?"

"Anne was Mary's sister. Another daughter of James II. So much for your—"

"—saying daughters don't count. I apologize to Queen Anne from the depths of my black heart! So, Queen Mary and Queen Anne were sisters of this infant male heir to the throne James II smuggled into exile when he was deposed?"

"Half-sisters. Yes."

"All in the family so far."

"So far. Then Queen Anne died without heirs."

"Judging by her statue, it's no wonder. Was King James II out of daughters?"

"Yes. That was in 1714. James II had died in 1701. He had made a stab or two at retaking his throne, but – he was the 'grand old duke of York' who marched to the top of the hill and then marched down again."

"After all his sisters died out, the tyke who was exiled with the old king Jimmie the Two was presumably an adult who wanted his throne back."

"Unfortunately, like his father, James II, young James was Catholic."

"Oh, yes. I was talking to a lady just yesterday about how much stink you can stir up in these parts with religion."

"Try becoming an Ottoman Sultan when you're C. of E."

"Things are tough all over. What was the boy's name?"

"James."

"Not much imagination in the family nomenclature. James the first, James the second, and James the nothing. So James II's son James has grown up watching his sisters—"

"—*half*-sisters."

"Two half sisters make a whole sister. And he's been watching them reign on a throne he thinks has his name carved on the seat. Why didn't he just come home to England and say he '*Voila*, I am a Protestant?'"

"Strangways, some people actually believe what they profess to believe and don't change it for political expediency, whatever the personal cost to them."

"More fools they. No wonder he didn't make it in politics. Politicians all shed their principles faster than a snake casts off its outer epidermis."

"This James, who you call James the Nothing, was smuggled out of England when his father was deposed. They called him the Old Pretender."

"This is getting awfully complex. He was old?"

"He was in his late twenties when he first tried to regain his throne."

"So he was pretending to be old."

"'Pretender' comes from some Frog word meaning 'claimant.' He was very mixed up with the Frogs."

"Must have been covered in warts. What happened after Queen Anne?"

"When it was clear Queen Anne was going to die without an heir, Parliament passed 'An Act for the Further Limitation of the Crown and Better Securing the Rights and Liberties of the Subject.'"

"Is that all one bill?"

"That was in 1701—"

"Dates, too!"

"Forget the date, who cares!"

"If they're trying to shoot me for it—I do."

"The Act said '*That whosoever shall hereafter come to the possession of this crown shall join in communion with the Church of England as by law established.*' It only goes to prove that anything called 'a bill to secure rights' will pass, even if it strips rights away. That Act named Electress Sophie of Hanover and her heirs as the rightful inheritors of the throne after Queen Anne." He added, "Sophie was a granddaughter of James I."

"The Bible chap. Got him, this time. The first Stuart king and the father of the king they ran out of town because of his loyalty to the Pope."

"Good shot. James I had had a daughter named Elizabeth—"

"And Lizzie is the sister to James II and therefore *aunt* to Jimmy the Nothing, the Old Pretender."

"Right on the button."

"Really? You understood that I said? I'm not even sure I did, and I said it."

"James I's daughter was Elizabeth, and Elizabeth's daughter was Sophie. Sophie married the Elector of Hanover—"

"What did he elect?"

"Don't you know anything?"

"I used to think so. Please continue. You are no longer interesting me strangely, but we must pass these long summer evenings."

"An 'Elector' was a member of the Holy Roman Emperor's so-called 'Electoral College' – that's a group of bigwigs (literally, at that time) who Elected Holy Roman Emperors. Parliament's Act in 1701 overturned the laws of succession so this Sophie could follow Anne as Queen."

"Parliament established their own queue for the throne? Can they do that?"

"They did that."

"That doesn't sound like cricket."

"It was worse than that. Parliament's Act passed over *fifty closer claimants* to the throne to get to this Sophie – and some of them were Protestant."

Herron's eyes widened. "That must have trodden on some toes. Ten toes each – that's more than 500 toes altogether. Think of the corns. Ouch."

"Sophie was eighty-three when she died. She collapsed after running indoors from a rainshower. She predeceased Queen Anne by only a few weeks."

"Hard cheese, again! Knowing you're going to be a queen if you keep breathing longer than the incumbent, then turning up your toes a tad early because you're afraid you'll melt in a dab of rain. A lesson to us all. When in doubt, take an umbrella. So what happened?"

"Do you really care?"

"On the edge of my seat! Actually, if I sit on the edge of my seat, this rattletrap motor-carriage will probably fling me overboard. But if this has anything to do with why folks want my brains blasted to powder, I need to know it. Curse it."

"Sophie predeceased Anne, but the Act naming her as successor had a clause that included Sophie's children. Sophie's eldest son therefore became the new king of England. His name was Georg Ludwig. He chose to be called George I."

"Thank God he picked right! To think Britain came within a gnat's eyelash of having a King Ludwig!" A shiver of horror shook him.

"George I's son was George II. George II's grandson was George III—"

"George III was the chap that lost us America and talked to the trees!"

"Yes. He was also the first Hanoverian King whose first language was English – after nearly fifty years of Hanoverian rule."

"And these are the folks you called 'the Germans.'"

"Didn't you learn *anything* in school?"

"Mostly on the playing fields. Isn't that where they stopped the Armada?"

"No. The Duke of Wellington is supposed to have said the battle of Waterloo was won on the playing fields of Eton."

"Really? I had the impression that happened off in Belgium someplace."

"They should have used your head for a football. That's all it's good for."

"It also supports a wide collection of hats."

"George III was followed by two sons in turn: George IV and William IV—"

"Ye cats! His name wasn't George? How did they expect to tell him apart?"

"King William's next youngest brother married one Victoria of Saxe-Coburg."

"Just one?"

"Will you listen? Their daughter was named Victoria, after her mother. Upon the death of her uncle, King William IV, son of the chap who, as you put it, lost us America, the young Victoria was raised to the throne in 1837."

"Queen Victoria!" Herron whistled. "I get the drift. Toting up children, grandchildren, and the sisters and their cousins and their aunts for two centuries—why, there must be hundreds of people who feel they're closer to the throne than Queen Victoria. But what can they do about it?"

"One of them thought she could build an airship and blow the Queen up. Or at least hold the country hostage by air until the Stuarts are returned to the throne."

"And that person is trying to kill *me* because almost two hundred years ago Parliament wanted to ensure a Protestant succession? That's insane. Religion!"

Herron hated to think it, but Angelica had been wrong and Lady Calthrop had been right – religion only causes trouble.

"It's too bad they're not like the modern, up-to-date, scientific nineteenth century. From our perspective, religions all look alike."

"Do they?"

"They all offer pie-in-the-sky solutions. I want to slice my pie here and now.""And all political systems, Strangways? The Tories and the Liberals and the Unionists all think if their ways are followed we'll all be happier – are they all alike? Are all economic systems alike? The dogmatic followers of capitalism and communism both think they will usher in an economic Utopia if only they are followed dogmatically. Are they the same?"

"Uh, I suppose not."

"Neither are all religions alike, fool."

"Are you a Bible-thumper, friend Stoker?"

"Not me. I don't believe in anything I can't shoot."

CHAPTER LX

"You've provided a lot of less-than-exciting historical information, Stoker, but you haven't explained why I was invited here. Who, really, is holding me?"

"I have an inkling. I told you to remember King James II being deposed."

"Did you?"

"I did. Did you?"

"No. Refresh me. When was that again?"

"1688. He was the Catholic king forced off the throne, whose daughters reigned after him. Then the Germans, from George I to Queen Victoria."

"Oh. Yes. What happened to James II, deposed king and Catholic?"

"I told you that. He died in 1701. "

"All flesh is grass."

"His heart and brain were removed. His brain went to the Scot's college in Paris. His heart was sent to a nunnery in Chaillot. Both disappeared in the French Revolution. Well, I happen to know Lugner has the brain of James II in a silver casket at the estate. It's marked *I.II* – I. for Iacobus, II for the second."

Herron gasped. He suddenly had a good idea where James II's heart lay. He had seen a silver casket marked *I.II* in Lady Calthrop's house.

"James II had a son, you may recall," Stoker put in. "Oh, right, James the lesser. The young Old Pretender. Last heard from itching to sntach his father's throne out from under those rotten Germans."

"When Prince James grew up, he styled himself 'James III.' He tried to regain the throne from George I in 1715. He failed. James married a Polish princess and they had a son, Charles. Charles was the rightful heir to the throne of Great Britain by strict primogeniture, and he made an attempt to overthrow the Hanoverians in 1745. Remember 'the '45'? That's where I started. In 1745 Charles Stuart tried to recover his grandfather's throne. 'Bonnie Prince Charlie.'"

"'Bonnie Prince Charlie!' Even I have heard of him. Why was he bonnie?"

"I don't know! Since Charlie grew up in exile on the continent, his Jacobite supporters referred Bonnie Prince Charlie *'The king over the water.'* Some of the more obsessive Jacobites still pass plates over finger bowls to show their support for this King Over the Water."

"Don't tell me he's still alive!"

"Bonnie Prince Charlie died in 1788."

"Well, one hundred and ten years back is getting warmer, but it strikes me as a long time to give a good blankety-blank. I recall telling a young lady not to underestimate how long folks could carry a grudge. So they want Charlie to be king even though he's dead? King over the water? 'King under the dirt' is more apropos. That Bonnie Prince Charlie chap came jolly close, didn't he?"

"Not close enough. Liket the grand old duke of York, he funked it and headed for the hills. 1745 was the last serious effort Jacobites made to seize the throne."

"*Seventeen* forty-five. And this is *eighteen* ninety-seven. A century and a half plus two. I'd think death would have come to call on anyone who cares."

"The struggle for power never ends."

"You should meet a pal of mine named Jessup. You two run on parallel lines. I suppose that's why you never meet. You're not really trying to sell me the notion that Scottish nationalists are responsible for building this airship to scatter bombs over London to kill the Queen?" "I'm absolutely certain the Scots themselves have *nothing* to do with this affair. Only individuals who used the Jacobites as an excuse for a power play."

"End the suspense, if any, Stoker, old man. Did some cockeyed descendent of Bonnie Prince Charlie acquire this airship to blow up the queen today in hopes of restoring the Stuarts to the throne of Great Britain?"

"That depends on whether Bonnie Prince Charlie had descendents."

"Holy Moses! Well? You're the eighteenth-century expert. Did he?"

"There are many schools of thought on that."

"A man has descendants or he hasn't."

"Charles railed against his own father, the Old Pretender, for bringing children into the world when they could not have the throne . . . but, yes, 'Bonnie Prince Charlie' in his turn had one child. A daughter."

"And we've proven daughters can have the throne. If nothing else, there's a Procession in London today to honor someone's daughter who's been on the throne sixty years, and who looks likely to keep ticking out the century."

"The problem with Bonnie Prince Charlie's daughter was legitimacy. Bonnie Prince Charlie's marriage is common-law at best."

"Common-law children have been legitimized."

"Charlie thought she was legitimate enough. He got up an Act to legitimize her. It was signed in 1784 by King Louis XVI of France and his foreign minister, Vergennes. I think the Pope also wormed in on the Act and okayed it."

"We know what happened to Louis XVI. Off with his head."

"Bonnie Prince Charlie said of his daughter, *There is one hope*. One hope remaining, that is, of regaining the throne of Great Britain, which he believed lawfully belonging the Stuarts. He moved to Florence. There, he styled himself 'Count of Albany' and he called his daughter the 'Duchess of Albany.'"

"A Count called his daughter Duchess? Did she have any claim to the title?"

"Charles insisted she had the best possible claim – that he was a *de jure* king and could grant whatever he bloody well pleased."

"'Duchess of Albany' sounds deucedly familiar."

Herron had read 'there is one hope' just the day before – on the silver plated door-knocker on Lady Calthrop's house. "*Spes Tamen Est Una!*" he cried.

"What's that?"

"Latin for 'Watch Out for Falling Rocks.' What about the daughter? Would be about two hundred and particularly decrepit for her age? Being pushed around London in a Bath chair and looking like the devil's grandmother?"

"She died in 1789."

"Did they take her pulse?"

"She's dead, Strangways."

"Again . . . any children?"

"Charlotte the pseudo-Duchess of Albany had three children by the Archbishop of Bordeaux, Ferdinand Maximilien Mériadec de Rohan."

"How do you remember this stuff? By mnemonic devices? 'Ferdinand de Rohan was never Samoan—'"

"There *may* have been a secret marriage. Married or not, they had two daughters and one son, who styled himself—"

"Count Roehenstart!"

Stoker glared at Herron curiously. "Now, how did you know that?"

"Just a lucky guess. Where did the title come from?"

"He made it up. It's part 'Rohan' and part 'Stuart.'"

"Did this so-called Count Roehenstart have any children?"

"Not by any of his legitimate marriages."

"He was married more than once?"

"Yep. And he also did lots of work out of the home. His own legitimacy was questionable at best, so none of them are in line for the throne, anyway."

"If Count Roehenstart had a daughter, what must she do to prove her right to the throne?"

"She has no right to the throne."

"Let's pretend. Humor me. I might want to write a novel about it."

"Who would believe it? Okay. Here goes. If Count Roehenstart had a daughter who wanted to be queen, she must: first prove that Count Roehenstart's mother *was* secretly married to Archbishop Ferdinand Maximilien Mériadec de Rohan. That would legitimize the Count. Then Parliament must, by law, recognize the Act Bonnie Prince Charlie signed to legitimize his daughter, who was Count Roehenstart's mother."

"The second part is easy enough. Parliament can do anything by law, even passing a law leap-froging over fifty claimants to the throne to find the chap they liked best, and tag him as 'it' even if he can't speak English." Herron's mind felt heavy with all this new information, but it was grinding away. "If Count Roehenstart's mother and the bishop had a secret marriage, they would require—Great Scott! *A secret marriage certificate.* Is that possible?"

"Such things have been known to happen, Strangways. I don't see how that is relevant in this case."

Herron mentally corrected him. *It's relevant as all hell.*

He had been going to meet a man looking for a blessed marriage certificate when these nutters nabbed him. And, just as he left for home, a woman told him frankly that one Count Roehenstart was her father. *Lady Calthrop.*

Married to Lord Calthrop, one of the richest men in the kingdom, who had the scientific interests (and the ready cash) to bankroll an airship or two.

And Lady Calthrop was inexplicably in that Underground station when that haggard bird was killed. *No, not killed! Shot.*

Herron still wondered about that. He had heard no shots. But Lady Calthrop was close enough for a clear shot at the haggard bird.

And so . . . dammit! . . . was Angelica.

Angelica! Beautiful, intelligent, witty, spirited. What a woman!

No – zounds, what a *person*.

He suddenly realized Angelica Trickett was exactly what he had sought so earnestly all these years: a female counterpart to himself!

Yes, but could he trust Angelica? She seemed genuine. Yet, was it likely she could work in a house where such a plot was hatched and not know? She was more like Her Ladyship's protege than her servant. No mere employee would be so outspoken as Angelica had been over tea. If Lady Calthrop turned out to be the ringleader of this affair, where did that place Angelica, her right-hand woman?

Had Angelica been *too* outspoken? Had all her bickering with Her Ladyship been a show, played out for Herron's benefit? In the end, Herron did surrender those all-important papers to her. Had it all been a sham to trick them out of him?

In the dining hall of the Hemlock Club, Major Hobbes had said, *Some of the best assassins I've ever known are women*. Herron would certainly be prey to any intriguing spies and assassins fitting Angelica Trickett's description, and filling out her dimensions.

Herron hoped he wasn't indicting her on flimsy evidence . . .

. . . Angelica . . . *Damn her, she did keep me lingering around the house long enough for Lady Calthrop to summon those apes to bundle me up in a rug the moment I setpped out into the street.*

As hard as it was for Herron to credit . . .

. . . *Angelica might be in this conspiracy up to her pretty, little—*

Herron interrupted himself. "So all this," he said, waving an arm around the fog like he could see the entire compound, "is a plot to restore angry Stuart descendents of Bonnie Prince Charlie to the throne? Poppycock!" "Stranger things have happened."

"Name three. In descending order by height."

Instead, Stoker said, "I only wish I knew the identity of 'she who is to come.' I haven't shinnied to the top of that tree."

Herron started to say he had; but first, he needed a smoke to settle his jangled nerves. He was more distressed by this information than he had been when he was about to stop a speeding bullet.

2

Fumbling for a cigarette, he found a tobacco pouch in one pocket and cigarette papers in the other. Hawkins was a man who rolled his own.

With the bouncing of the motor carriage over roads laid quickly and roughly over the fens, Herron proved less than adept at rolling his own.

He poured half the tobacco in the pouch over Hawkins's faded dungarees before he collected enough in the paper for even one cigarette.

Smoking didn't help. It jangling his nerves worse than ever.

Though Herron possessed had haggard bird's cigarette paper only slightly more than thirty hours, he felt like he had done little else all his life but handle it.

It was the darkest part of the short, summer night, and foggy on the fens . . . but Herron had a good tactile sense.

And he did not like what he felt.

Hawkins's cigarette papers were identical to the haggard bird's.

Herron had his own cigarettes specially prepared, so he didn't know the varieties of cigarette papers available. Maybe in this vicinity of the back side of nowhere, only one brand of papers was stocked by the local boutique.

And his first puff gave him a decided sense of *Déjà vu*. It was the same tobacco he had tasted in his bed Sunday evening. Jessup's tobacco!

Suppose . . . just suppose *Hawkins* had been an agent in cahoots with the haggard bird. Furthermore, suppose a Stoker loyal to Lugner knew it.

By killing Hawkins, he eliminated a danger to himself and earned Herron's trust at the same time. Killing two birds with one bullet.

Stoker said he had Herron in his sights Sunday night when he and Hawkins had broken into his home . . .

But it was actually *Hawkins* who had repeatedly "missed" Herron, first firing through the bedroom door, then out the bedroom window. A 'crack shot.'

And, on the face of it, Stoker's elaborate story sounded thin.

Jacobites? Supporters of the late (more than a century late!) Bonnie Prince Charlie, trying to hijack London by terror with an airship?

Herron mentally repeated, *Poppycock*! He didn't believe that angle one bit.

His world was twisted off its axis by his smoke. In this new world, the late Mister Hawkins, with his repellent pomade and manners, might have been his friend. In this new world, he had solid grounds to *distrust* Angelica Trickett.

Herron had been guided through the last three days by a simple faith: that the more he learned about this whole affair, the more he would know.

Instead, he was more confused than ever.

And in more danger.

Even if he could trust Stoker, Herron was in an enemy camp of terrorists, pretending to be someone whose voice he couldn't imitate to save his soul.

And Angelica? *Lord! If Angelica is* not *a part of the plot—*

These people showed a mania for silencing anyone who knew about the upcoming bombings. Even if they only suspected it. And if Lady Calthrop was 'she' – she had watched them piece the story together by cigarette.

Angelica might be dead already!

Herron could imagine Lady Calthrop wheeling down to Angelica's bedroom and slipping a venomous serpent into her bed.

Yet if. . . if Hawkins, was the one I should have trusted – I'm a sheep in cheap clothing. And I'm dead. I simply haven't stopped writhing yet.

CHAPTER LXI

"I really didn't want you involved in this, Strangways," said Stoker, as the main house of the compound came into sight.

"Not, I trust, from a deep-seated concern for my personal welfare?" "Because amateurs always muck things up."

"Tell me . . . a lot of people had little pieces of this puzzle. You were here, the haggard bird was here. Why couldn't your lot and his lot and the police ever talk to each other and share information?"

"Demarcation, mate."

Another question gnawed at Herron's mind. "You and Hawkins worked together a long time. Was it difficult, shooting him?"

"Hawkins and I were shoulder to shoulder on our long flight across America. We shared everything. I associated intimately with him for years. So, naturally, I loathed him with a hatred you can only feel for those you know well. If you want to love your neighbor, Strangways, the best thing you can do is raise as many barriers to understanding as possible. Once you really know your neighbor you'll be unable to love him. Hawkins would do anything for money and never ask questions about where it came from. He deserved to be shot down like a dog."

"Spoken like a true assassin. Why don't you throw in with the eugenicists?"

"If I killed for pleasure, Hawkins would have died a long time ago. If I'd given in to emotion when the airship passed over the ocean, he'd still be swimming."

"How about the haggard bird?"

"I didn't know him well at all. Nor did I kill him. Nor Hawkins. He wasn't even there. You show a ticket to get on that platform, and we decided I should buy the ticket while Hawkins remained in the Brougham, guarding the door."

"How did you decide?"

"Coin flip."

"You decided a man's life on the flip of a coin."

"Two lives were decided by that coin-flip – the haggard bird's, and yours. If Hawkins seen the haggard bird brush by you in his final moments, he might have knifed you in the crowd and searched your body in the confusion."

"Great. The very fact that I'm alive is all due to someone calling 'heads.'"

"'Tails.' I'd have shot that fellow you call 'the haggard bird' without a qualm to keep him from delivering any information that might have stopped the bombing. *I want Lugner's nefarious air-bombing plans carried through.*"

"All but the bombing part, I hope."

"If possible. Where there's no action, there's no crime. Whether I arrest Lugner and his cohorts in the commission of the crime or shortly after, it's all the same to me."

"Don't you care who dies?"

"Do you?"

Herron never had before. He'd been too concerned about himself. But Stoker's weird notion of calmly letting a terror crime happen before making an arrest made him queasy. Did both sides require the blood of innocents?

"Lugner wanted the haggard bird back alive, if possible, to force him, under torture if necessary, to tell where he was taking the information . . . and to find out if he knew any other 'collectors of information' on the premises."

"What if the haggard bird wouldn't talk?"

"A man always talks, Strangways. It's a matter of finding the right points and finding the appropriate (ahem) incentive."

"That doesn't sound like playing the game."

"This is no game, Strangways. Stop thinking like a schoolboy. Lugner and his lot laid down the rules: no rules. Fine with me. It's a no-gloves match between us, and I'm weighing the life of society against one man's discomfort."

"Sounds like you've gone over to Lugner already."

"You fight fire with fire."

"And aphorism with aphorism. 'For every aphorism, there is an equal and opposite aphorism.' And what if the haggard bird had talked under torture, ratting out other government agents undermining the Jacobite conspiracy?"

"No fear. If I won the coin toss, I meant to shoot him and say he almost got away and I only meant to wing him. If Hawkins had won the coin toss and we had captured the haggard bird most alive, I'd have made sure he died 'trying to escape.' I didn't want the haggard bird spilling any beans to Lugner. Too many good people have died already trying to find out what was going on with these terrorists. Why should good people on the right side always be the one to die? It's time a few people on the other side died. Lugner and his brood think humans are animals – then I'll treat them like the animals they are."

"The R.S.P.C.A. might not approve of your damaging even such a creature as Lugner. And if you can capture Lugner—what? Would you actually countenance torturing a man to make him talk?"

"If comes down between that man and a bomb that's about to be dropped on a crowded city and killing innocent women and children – one of those potential victims being the Queen? I would not turn a hair torturing him. Or you."

2

"Why do they need *you* for the airship? Is it some sort of safety code to equip every airship with a hired gun?"

"I told you – I'm a glider pilot."

"Oh, yes, I recall. Bit chunky for that, I'd have thought."

"Been gliding for decades."

"You should have stayed off the starchy foods."

Stiffly, Stoker continued, "That's how I wangled myself into their company from the first. I've had to do other things to stay in their good graces."

"No wonder you called yourself Colonel Philgrave."

"Every new recruit here has to kill someone. Lugner gives you a name and you go out and kill him. If you come back with a job well done, he trusts you."

"And . . . giving him a crime to hold over your head."

"Yes. And you must talk the talk. 'She who is to come' needed an airship pilot and found Lugner. Lugner needed a glider pilot and I let him find me. But if I marched out of step with his hare-brained agenda, he'd have 'fired' me—"

"As you dismissed Hawkins from his employment, no doubt."

"—and he'd have hired another gun who might not be such a good glider pilot, but who was more politically efficacious. Politics and loyalty matter more to him than skill. Therein lies our hope."

"I don't believe in hope. In three days it's become a four-letter word to me."

As they drove up the two miles of gravel walk to the manse, Herron took it in the enormity of the estate. "This compound seems isolated from the rest of the world. How do they contact this 'she who is to come.'"

"Wireless telegraphy."

"Oh? And how does that work?"

"As an undercover agent, I know all methods of sending messages, including telegraphy. But I haven't a clue how the wireless set works. It won't quite reach from here to London, so there's a relay station about half-way. And a few more scattered over the compound, for quick communication. That's all I know."

"More demarcation."

"Yeah."

"Well?" said Herron. "We're almost home."

"Well – what?"

"Time for you to preach to me about freedom."

"How's that?"

"Every person I've run into lately has given me a new view of freedom. Three different views, one each.

"The first fellow said 'freedom' comes through humans banding together to find security in Society, against anarchy.

"The next person said freedom is a natural state given by God via nature. The anarchy is included in freedom. Without freedom, we can't even form societies.

"The third person said people are prisoners of their biology. There is no real freedom in nature, since it can't be booked and cataloged. Man – and woman – is just another animal who should be carefully controlled – preferably by government zookeepers – and euthanized when inconvenient. Control means teaching that genuine 'freedom' assuages biological instincts like hunger and shelter and sex, the way the devil tried to control Christ by telling him to turn stones into bread to assuage his hunger after one hell of a fast. Unquantifiable intangibles like speech, thought, personal choice, religion and individualism need not apply, but must be quashed for the safety of the collective.

"It's your turn. What's your view of freedom?"

"I'm no political philosopher, Strangways," growled Stoker. "I'm a simple common-or-garden glider-pilot-cum-*agent provocateur* with an expertise in eighteenth century history doing undercover work for Her Majesty. I have a job to do and I'm doing it. And if you don't shut up I'll change my mind about shooting you through the middle of your forehead and give you a third eye."

They did not exchange another word until Stoker halted the Knight three-wheeler before the front steps of the mansion.

As Stoker killed the engine, a voice with a foreign accent called out, "Herr Stoker!"

The gas had been turned up in the front room. Lugner was silhouetted in the doorway. He skipped down the steps and over the gravel.

Herron slumped down, pulling Hawkins's hat low over his eyes, like a weary assassin, after a hard day's murder, dozing in the satisfaction of a job well done.

Peeking out from a corner of his cap, Herron was gratified to see the Lugner's eyes were darkening and swelling. He was pleased by the symmetry.

Lugner rubbed his palms together. "We have had a message from above."

Herron glanced up, half-expecting to see an airship dropping notes in bottles. Then, remembering the need to hide his face, he looked down at his scuffed boots.

"What message?" wondered Stoker.

"'She who is to come' wanted us to know they have the papers, so there is no more need to worry about them. The young woman will be dealt with quickly in her sleep in a way that is silent and undetectable."

Herron seethed. His Cinderella might be seventy-five miles away, sleeping the night peacefully away while a snake was gliding through her linen. How he envied the snake. And he could never reach London to help her, even by airship!

He was no religious man, but he trusted God would answer an intercessory prayer even for the likes of him.

God, if you will hear me, help Angelica get out of that hell-house with her life!

"'She' asked about Strangways. I have sent a return message by wireless transmitter that Strangways is dead and we have confirmed it. You have served us well, Herr Stoker. We sent men after you to observe. They could not see the execution for the fog but they exhumed and examined the body and they telegraphed back how efficiently carried out your orders."

"You never doubted my loyalty, sir?"

"Frankly, Herr Stoker, we must be wary of everyone, even our friends, since the incident two nights ago." He reeled out his watch. "I am sorry. Three nights ago. It is well after *mitternacht*. That spy you chased three nights ago had been with us for the better part of the decade."

(He pronounced the word *decayed* and it sent chills up Herron's spine).

"Therefore, we trust no one. I was very pleased to receive the news about you. One shot was heard, one shot euthanized Strangways, cleanly removing his cranium. You did very well. You will accompany us today on our great venture."

Stoker saluted. "Thank you, sir."

"We must be over London at the very prick of noon."

"And what of my assistant, Mister Hawkins?" He nodded to Herron.

"He will remain here. We do not require his hands on the ropes on the way to London, though he must be at take-off. You will excuse me, I have many things I must make ready. Go now to the shed and see your glider is in good repair."

Lugner skipped back up the steps into the house, humming "Die Rote Fahne."

When Lugner was out of earshot, Herron whispered, "You can't leave me here alone. If anyone who knows Hawkins speaks to me, I'm dead."

"No! I forgot you'll be necessary at the launch. Blast it, those ropes will shred your feather-soft hands."

"They're already in a bad way from digging."

"Hawkins's palms were like leather. Do you have a fear of heights?"

"Only falling from them."

"I can't leave you here on your tod – for *my* own protection. If Lugner finds out you're here and Hawkins is in that hole you dug, I'm dead as mutton. This is your lucky day. You're going to get a dekko at the airship after all."

CHAPTER LXII

"Airships!" said Herron, as they bumped along another road through the vast country estate. "Wireless telegraphic transmitters! With all the new inventions, these people must make a fortune off their patents."

"These people have bigger fish to fry."

"Don't mention food. I haven't sunk a fang into a bite since tea. You know how old ladies are with their tea – toy sandwiches that look like they were made for small dogs rather than grown men. And the girl! When you're with a truly lovely young lady, friend Stoker, you feel you don't need food. You feast off her beauty. It's the best cure for any man on a diet." That made him glum. He hated to think of five feet seven of wonderful body rotting away in the ground. "It's too bad you can't work that wireless transmitter."

"I didn't say I couldn't work it. If it transmits like a telegraph, I'm sure any telegrapher can send and receive messages. I just said I don't know how it works. I'm told it sends messages by radio-pulses."

"Thank you for clarifying! What the deuce are radio-pulses?"

"I'm no an electrical engineer. Two scientists – Tesla in America and Marconi over here – have been working on wireless telegraphy; but so far as I know, these people have the only few working sets in existence. Since only another wireless set can receive those radio-pulses, the message Lugner sent to 'She' about your death probably wasn't even encrypted."

Just then, Herron saw an enormous shed rising on the horizon. It was still vague in the fog, but Herron thought the shed didn't go *up* so much as *out*. It looked like a covered cricket field, including seats and pavilion.

"What on earth is that?"

"That's the shed where we store the dirigible."

"The what again?"

"Airship. The word comes from the major problem with airships, which has always been dirigibility—"

"The what again?"

"Directional control. Based on a French word."

"Oh . . . ah . . . yes, I know it . . . *diriger*! To direct, or steer, or something like that, right? Shove an *–ible* on the end and you have 'steerable.' As opposed to balloons." Herron had tried to explain that problem to Merridew Sunday morning, and here it was just an hour or two after midnight on Tuesday – good God, had there only been one full night between then and now?

"Balloons do not have dirigibility – or directional control, if you prefer. Oh, they have no trouble finding the direction of *up*. Nor the direction of down – especially fast downs."

"Crashes, I think they're called."

"So balloons do have up-and-down directional control. But once they go up, they really are at the mercy of the winds, and they have to keep climbing and descending to find winds going their way. A true air-ship travels in any direction, with or *against* the wind. This is the first airship with an engine strong enough to allow dirigibility in all directions – even in the teeth of the wind. Jump out of the motor-carriage now. Sneak around to the side of the building. The noise of our 'silent' engine will cover your thrashing about. Once I'm inside, I'll loosen a board in the shed wall for you to squeeze through on this side."

Though the Knight motor carriage was speeding at 7.5 miles per hour, Herron risked a jump. He hit the ground hard and rolled to a painful stop.

Pushing himself up on his arms, he saw Stoker braking the motor-carriage before the huge shed, then idling the "silent" engine long enough to cover Herron's footfalls.

Herron scurried to the side of the shed in a crouch. Seeing a few dangerous-looking toughs converged on the motor carriage, Herron crawled the final few yards to the shed on his belly.

The toughs knew Stoker on sight and even greeted him by name; but that was not sufficient for security. Herron heard them exchanging sign and countersign.

"'*There is only one hope*,'" said a guard.

"'*She who is to come*,'" Stoker answered.

"We wasn't expecting you."

Stoker shrugged. What they expected was no concern of his. "This is the day. We need to make sure everything is in order. I am going up in *Darnley*." "We heard a shot in the distance."

"We were disposing of a problem."

"With only one shot?"

"One shot is all I need to dispose of most problems. Lugner will be here shortly. Open the door."

Enormous locks on enormous chains across the door were unclasped. Working together, the guards pushed one of the great shed doors. The doors were layered on tracks. The guards telescoped the doors just wide enough to admit Stoker. When he was inside, the toughs slammed the doors tight and relocked the chains.

Herron crept on around the shed on hands and knees.

Guards pacing all the way around the shed, in both directions, passed him regularly, but the light was poor and the fog was thick, so Herron had plenty of shadows to crouch in. In these parts they must have had plenty of hares to distract them; if they heard Herron's movements, they took him for a hare and didn't so much as shine their dark lanterns in his direction.

Stoker must have known the guards' rounds. When they were both out of sight, Herron heard a scratching. Though there were no lights outside, a glow appeared in the side of the shed when a board was wiggled out loose from the bottom. It was immediately pulled up again, to douse the light.

Herron marked the place and slithered to the board. He lay quietly until the guards passed again and were both out of sight; then he pulled the board up and wormed through the hole – snagging Hawkins's faded yellow shirt on a nail.

"Hurry!" whispered Stoker.

Herron worried with the nail, but couldn't extract his shirt.

Stoker grabbed him under his arms and yanked him in, ripping the shirt down one side. "Worry about your life, not your apparel."

As Stoker replaced the board, Herron stood, and froze, gasping, "The airship!"

"Yes, *the* airship."

CHAPTER LXIII

The gigantic shed had no external lights, but its interior was brilliantly illuminated by generator-run electric lights lining the tops of the walls.

Having been freshly inflated for use that very day, the airship was moored in place and floated off the floor of the shed. The lower edge of the car hovered just at the top of Herron's head.

The airship was more vast than Herron imagined. It looked fully as long and nearly as high as Saint Paul's Cathedral, without the dome and lantern. In fact, at six hundred feet, the airship was longer than Saint Paul's. Its inflated diameter, only seventy-nine feet its broadest, meant the Cathedral was 286 feet higher.

The airship's skin was a membrane coated with a shiny gold varnish.

"The envelope consists of two layers of fabric with India rubber in between."

"Sort of like a mackintosh?" asked Herron.

"Sort of. It's stretched taut to eliminate drag."

As they neared the front of the great ship from the side of the shed, Herron read the word *DARNLEY* in black capital letters on its beak-like nose.

The ship's name rang a bell with him. Herron couldn't dredge it out of the dark well of his historical memory, but he knew it had some Scots connection. That gave some validity to all this restoration of the Stuarts nonsense.

If he had been able to place the name immediately – he might have scooted right back out of the shed and tried to make a break for it on foot, whatever dykes and bogs he had to battle through, whatever bullets he had to dodge.

Along the underside of the bulging airship, about six feet down from the envelope, ran a metal keel just wide enough for a man to walk on if he held on to the struts and steel cables all along its length.

Slung beneath the keel was a metal cockpit Stoker referred to as the "car."

Stoker pointed along the keel. "That's for increased lateral stability."

"Okey-doke." Herron didn't know the meaning of "lateral stability," but it was his policy not to argue with an armed man.

"Our next airship will have an even sturdier keel, built right at the bottom of the envelope. As you can see, on the new model, over there, they are building two cars, one on either end. Though *Darnley* is a fully-functional prototype, it's all still experimental. There's a lot we don't yet know. But even with what we do know – we can sit in the skies and bomb a city all day without fear of retribution."

Stoker looked admiringly at the vessel as they strolled the airship's length.

"When the sun strikes that gold skin, it's like a star descending from the heavens. When it flies low, it's an awesome thing to see hanging over you, when you've never seen anything fly but birds."

"And bats."

"Yes, and bats! Its bulk is so enormous, but it looks weightless in the air."

"It looks weightless in the shed. I don't suppose it is?"

"The empty weight of the airship is nearly eighty-one thousand pounds."

Herron could easily see why.

They were actually strolling slowly between the two airships. The second ship, resting on a plywood scaffolding that made it level with *Darnley*, was merely a mass of metal girders, a skeleton without skin. It was just far enough away so *Darnley* could be maneuvered out the front doors without pounding into it.

Nineteen twelve-sided rings, spaced about thirty-three feet apart, comprised the airship's "ribs." (Comparatively) smaller rings were on the nose and the tail. This frame gave the airship its long cigar shape, tapering symmetrically to a point on either end. The rings were attached by metal girders.

Thirteen main girders and twelve intermediary, smaller girders stretched lengthways down the ship from ring to ring, all around the frame. They were reinforced by metal x's between the girders. Steel cables kept the frame taut.

Herron was amazed that *Darnley*'s light and fluffy exterior was supported by a clunky, rigid internal skeleton. He waved an arm at the unfinished ship. "It's hard to believe all that weight flies through the air with the greatest of ease."

"What was the *Great Eastern*?"

"Er . . . oh, I know. It was a huge ship. Water-bound ship, that is."

"Six times larger than any ship afloat, in its day. Capable of carrying 4000 passengers around the world without refueling. And it was *iron*. One hundred years ago, it was hard to believe iron would float. Now, you find it hard to believe metal can fly. Never underestimate technology. Anything you can imagine is already on someone's drawing-board. Or in novels."

Girders that had not yet been fitted into the new airship's skeleton slanted up against the scaffolding. Herron tapped a fingernail on one. "What is this stuff?"

"Aluminium."

"Not steel?"

"Steel is too heavy."

"If you want lightness, why not use wood?"

"Wood warps. Aluiminium is light weight – compared to steel. But it's tough. When we made low altitude turns in the American west, we learned that girders of a lighter material would buckle. Aluminium is just right. Lightweight and strong. If your girders aren't strong enough, your ship might snap right in two in a turn. Best of all, unlike steel, aluminium resists corruption."

"We should make politicians out of it."

"Don't you ever stop being flippant?" demanded Stoker.

"I try not to. But all the while I'm joking, the little mind is clicking away. Just like this: how can your people have purchased such a quantity of aluminium without it being noticed? You can't just waltz out of a store unnoticed with an aluminium girder tucked under your waistcoat."

"We 'borrowed' most of it from Hiram Maxim."

"The gun johnnie?"

"That's right. Maxim bought up large amounts of aluminium for an airship company he's started for a Klondike expedition. Wherever there are airship experiments, Lugner's organization has wormed 'inside men.' They find out secrets, pilfer materials. Our plant in Maxim's Atlantic Pacific Arial Navigation Company kept two sets of books about aluminium coming in – and going out."

"And you brought it over by airship?"

"No, it was too heavy. We shipped it from San Francisco to King's Lynn."

"And no one ever noticed such a quantity of aluminium missing?"

"Maxim wouldn't report it – it would be too much of an embarrassment."

"He must have made a lot of money off guns to write off all this aluminium."

"Oh, he didn't just make guns. He also invented a newfangled mousetrap that earned him a mint."

Herron stopped, stunned. He recalled Lugner's words, *A man cannot be allowed to retain so many dollars, or pounds, when others are starving! His aluminium should be taken from him by right!*

Herron's hypothetical example of a mousetrap maker hadn't been so hypothetical. Luger and his crew had used that defense to justify stealing aluminium from Maxim on such a vast scale, they were able to construct two airships – plus whatever ships they had crashed in America.

Stoker stopped and turned. Snapping out of his reverie, Herron caught him up.

2

"It's a huge monster," Herron said, breathlessly.

"The larger the airship is, the better its effectiveness. And there's no practical limit to their size – at least on paper. *Darnley* is just over 600 feet long. Imagine an airship of 700 feet – 800! A thousand!"

"It would mean so much more metal!"

"Maybe. But the gas area becomes *cubed* with size. So much more lifing power. No larger than *Darnley* is, she floats like a cloud – yet lifts sixty-six tons."

"And the ship is – oh – about thirty-six tons? It lifts more than it weighs?"

"The *ship* is merely a glorified storage container. It's the gas that lifts."

"What sort of gas?"

"Hydrogen. Fifty-two thousand cubic feet of hydrogen will lift one ton, and we have one million and a half cubic feet. If we filled it to capacity, which we never do, we'd be able to lift much more."

Herron cast his mind to what little chemistry he ever knew. "Don't they also call hydrogen *inflammable air*? Isn't that stuff awfully dangerous?"

"Can be."

"Do you just puff it up like a balloon?"

"The earliest airship inventors aped balloons. A hydrogen balloon is so light, just the sun shining directly on the envelope expands the gas and makes it shoot up. Every time the sun goes behind a cloud, the balloon falls down. Peeking in and out of clouds, the sun would jerked a hydrogen balloon up or down like a bandelore. Pockets of hot and cold air around the balloon have the same effect. And, being spherical, a very light hydrogen ballon will tend to rotate."

"Nasty."

"The cigar shape is more aerodynamic."

"And it requires all this heavy, bloody network of metal?"

"A non-rigid airship, that is, an airship without all this bloody network of metal, has to have the same long aerodynamic shape – but its shape must depend upon *internal* gas pressure. When the shape depends on the gas alone—what?"

"Oh, are you teacher, now? Okay, I'll play. Sir, I don't know, sir."

"When gas is lost, non-rigid airships sag in the middle. Others get humped in the middle. That's what we call 'hog-backing.'"

"Sounds fun. But not, I assume, aesthetically pleasing to the eye."

"And damned dangerous. This is the best shape for an airship, and it must be *rigidly* maintained by that heavy network of metal. Even non-rigid airships aren't just open bags. They maintain their shape by adding ever more ballonets."

"What are ballonets?"

"You'll see. Right now, think of them as little bags of gas."

"I know a few of them from the Club."

"Stow it!"

"That's what I keep telling them."

"Listen! Everything I tell you will be important to your life. Do you care about your life, Strangways?"

"You betcher. I've been clinging to it by my fingernails for three days."

"Then listen. Our ballonets are distributed throughout the ship for trim."

"Where's your hydrogen kept?"

"We store it in pressure tanks—"

"If it lifts so well, why don't I see the tanks floating around?"

"*Heavy* pressure tanks, compared to the hydrogen inside. Screwed down."

"Where does aluminium come from?" Herron wondered. "I don't think I've ever heard of it before, except a mention or two in the papers."

"Actually, there's quite a bit of aluminium in the world; but as I understand it – I'm a glider pilot, not a metallurgist – you don't simply have aluminium mines where you can excavate the stuff in a pure form. It has to be extracted from other ores. Someone called it 'silver made from clay.' Common as it is, aluminium was more valuable than gold only a few years ago because it was so difficult and expensive to get at. Napoleon III had a feast where most of the guests ate off gold dinner sets while he dined on aluminium plates."

"They must have given him indigestion. Oh, sorry – humor is verboten."

"Now, they're beginning to making aluminium cheap as dirt by a process involving . . . I think the word is 'electrolysis.'"

"Are they really? Electrolysis, eh? What's that when it's at home?"

"I'm not altogether certain. I've been meaning to look it up."

"When you find out, send me a wire. What makes this thing all dirigible?"

"You mean, what gives it forward propulsion? Why, an engine, of course."

3

"Is that all?" Herron was disappointed. He was hoping for terminology that made *Darnley*'s propulsion sound magical.

Stoker became huffy. "You can't just slap an engine on a balloon, can you?"

"Can't you?"

"No. Balloons are the wrong shape to go forward with an engine."

"And this ship is the right shape to take off with an engine?"

"No! Airships use gas for lift and require propulsion only once they are in the air. That causes problems on the ground. The airship needs a lot of power to make any way in the sky—"

"Any what?"

"Way. An airship without powerful engines will lose its way—"

"Like Hansel and Gretel?"

"'Way' in the sense of forward momentum."

"You mean like a rowboat making way on a river?"

"Not a very exact comparison; but, for your uninformed mind, we'll compare it to a rowing-boat. If you're rowing a boat against the current and then you stop rowing, the current carries the boat in whatever direction *it* chooses. Like a rowboat battling the current, an airship's progress must remain constant."

"So no sitting by the roadside on a summer's day."

"Just try to comprehend that airships must maintain their forward momentum. *Darnley* can't move *slowly* on its engines. It's too light."

"Its lightness is what lifts it into the air."

"It's so light, it cannot make any forward momentum against the gentlest ground-winds at low speeds. *So when the airship is taken out from the shed the engines are worse than useless.* The ground-handlers must do everything."

"Yet the engines, which are worthless at moving slowly, are powerful enough to combat atmospheric winds?"

"Barely. The new ship there will have higher horsepower. You'd be astonished how stiff the winds get 'way up there. If the engines fail altogether once we're in the sky, we're worse than a balloon."

About half-way along the underside of the keel a roughly cylindrical, metal container was soldered. It extended down several feet, though it was still over Herron's head. It had netted vents like air holes all around it. "What's that?"

"I don't know. I asked Lugner about it the last time we went up and he told me it had to do with increasing the lateral stability. Considering how detailed his other descriptions were – all the information I'm telling you, I got from him – the way he described what was in there has been remarkably terse."

"It's not the bomb, is it?"

"Probably not. The way it's soldered on, no one can remove it to drop it. Whatever it is, it's a permanent fixture."

4

"What makes the thing go up, anyway? You just fill these bags with lighter-than-air air, and—*pfft*?" Herron fluttered a hand up over his head.

"It goes back to Archimedes."

"The chap who said *Eureka*?"

"That's right. He sat in his bath and said, *Eureka* – 'I have found it!'"

"The soap?"

Stoker shot a warning glance. "He saw the water rise when he sat in his bath."

"I noticed that when I was three."

"And then what did you do?"

"Probably played with boats. Not much else you can do in a bath. At three."

Stoker possibly had second thoughts about letting Herron live. "A king showed Archimedes a new crown. He wondered if it was pure gold."

"The goldsmith might have had his thumb on the scales, you mean?"

"Yes. Archimedes realized that a gold crown and a chunk of gold with the same volume as the crown would have the same weight."

"Archimedes had a flair for the obvious."

"Then tell me this, Strangways: how do you measure the volume of a crown, whose shape is extremely irregular?"

"I don't even know what 'the volume of a crown' refers to."

"When Archimedes saw how his body displaced the water in his bath, which rose and spilled over the sides of his tub, he realized that a gold crown submerged in water would displace an amount of water equivalent to its volume. He leapt up shouting, *Eureka* and ran through the streets without even dressing."

"Probably didn't matter too much in Greece back then."

"Sicily."

"Either way. If they all dressed like their statues, 'scantily' barely covers it. What does this have to do with airships?"

"Air is like a fluid. Airships swim *in* the air, rather than float *on* it. For too long no one understood that. That's why dirigibility – directional control – was never achieved by oars or screws attached to balloons. Airships, surrounded by the atmosphere, are more like fish than ships. An airship is immersed in, and totally surrounded by, air . . . and air pressure."

"Does air have pressure?"

"Of course it does."

"I don't feel it." Herron glanced up dubiously, as if some visible weight of the aether was about to squash his skull. He wondered if a squeezing pressure of the air was what gave him his morning heads.

"You really didn't learn anything in school, did you, Strangways?"

"It was my policy not to. It was my little method of rebelling against the system. They could make me sit in classes, but they couldn't make me learn."

"And you're proud of that, are you?"

"We must all make our little stands in life."

"Custer certainly did. Do listen, your life may depend on this. *And mine.* A body submersed in a fluid displaces that fluid, right?"

"If you say so, old man."

"Don't call me 'old man.' A body rising into the fluid of the air must have a lifting force equal to the mass of the air it displaces."

Herron responded, with a rising inflection, "Hmmm?"

"Air in the atmosphere has a greater specific weight than the hydrogen."

"The hydrogen . . . is *lighter*, you mean?"

"Precisely."

"Why didn't you just say that in the first place?"

Stoker shoved his hands deep into his coat pockets, probably to keep from socking Herron in the jaw. "Balloons," he continued, "are fine for fun, but they are rotten as transportation and impossible for load-bearing. They're lifted by hot air, which is *twelve times* heavier than hydrogen. That's not much lifting-power. A hot-air balloon can never lift or carry loads effectively. And you can't steer them. And this time of year is not the most conducive for weight-lift of any kind. It's better in the winter."

"Why? Isn't the air cold in the winter?"

"Cold air is denser."

"I'd think that would make it worse, to take off in snow."

"Don't be stupid. Ice and snow add to the weight of the ship! I mean, clear, cold days. For upward buoyancy, the airship must be significantly lighter than the ordinary atmosphere. Normal air, that you might breathe in the Park, weighs around seventy-five pounds per one thousand cubic feet."

"Who on earth spends their lives measuring these things?"

"Pepys wrote that when King Charles II established the Royal Society he laughed at them 'for spending time only in weighing of ayre, and doing nothing else since they sat.' Unlike King Charles, I'm delighted they weighed the air. It helps make an airship possible. So, normal air weighs about seventy-five pounds for one thousand cubic feet. One thousand cubic feet of hydrogen is only about *five pounds*. Do you see the difference between five and seventy-five?"

"It's a difference of seventy, I think, though I'm counting with my shoes on."

Stoker merely shook his head and went on. "My point is, *the lighter the gas relative to the air, the greater its lift*. In the winter, the air molecules contract, and in the summer they expand, because heat causes expansion."

"Oh, yes. That's why days are longer in the summer—"

"Did you ever think of taking your line of repartee into the Music Halls? It would keep you in fruit. Stop babbling."

"I always babble when I've nearly had my head shot off."

"Next time it won't be 'nearly.' As I was saying, the heavier the surrounding air, the better the gas will lift. Cold air is roughly *fifteen times* as heavy as hydrogen, while hot air is only about one-twelfth as heavy. Whatever the mission is today, since it is the start of summer and the air is about as warm as it gets in these parts, our airship is stripped down to its very basics for optimum lift."

Herron decided to end to this sort of talk. Hearing words like "optimum" made him nervous. "How many airships did you construct to learn all this?"

"We didn't just hammer together a lot of prototypes and smash them all across America. We used wind tunnels. We dragged models through tanks of water."

"The science lesson takes the fun out of the whole experience, doesn't it?"

5

As they came to the rear of the massive ship, Stoker pointed to engines slung under the major body of the airship, all of which were connected to enormous propellers – five in all.

"What sort of engines do you use?"

"Internal combustion. They are an absolute boon to mankind."

"What make?"

"Our own. We looked at Daimler, but they were still using combustion engines at the time. Combustion engines are not a good mix for airships."

"Why not?"

"The combustion engine has a platinum tube fed with petrol – and an *open* flame. Exposed burner . . . inflammable air . . . "

Engines typically sputtered and banged. That was bad enough. Herron realized that an open flame in close proximity to hydrogen was liable to spark a louder bang than was strictly necessary.

Stoker continued, "Combustion engine technology was a dead end for airships using hydrogen gas. We power our airship by water-cooled *internal* combustion engines. We had to develop that technology on our own, parallel to companies like Daimler. Since airship engines, unlike motor-carriage engines, must run constantly to maintain their forward momentum, we had to come up with engines that wouldn't shake themselves to sawdust when they ran for long periods; water-cooled so they wouldn't get too hot; and all the while increasing the horsepower to fight those so-and-so atmospheric winds."

"'Horsepower' is a curious term for something speeding through the air. Unless you mean Pegasus. Oh, I forgot, you only have Greek science, not lore."

"We have five four-cylinder engines capable of eighty horsepower."

He went on to describe how the cylinders were chambers, and that the fuel was fired inside those closed chambers to move the pistons, which made the difference between combustion and *internal* combustion . . .

In all this scientific and technical description, Herron felt like a man who accidentally walked ankle-deep straight into a boggy tract of land; and every step he tried to take *out* instead found him sloshing deeper into the mire. Herron felt the clammy scientific muck closing in around his thighs.

Stoker realized he was losing the sympathy of his audience and decided to give Herron an example of how a piston was fired by the fuel. "Did you ever set a fuse to petrol in a small pot to blow a potato through the air?"

"No. Not a potato."

Herron was not more forthcoming until the statute of limitations expired.

"We considered using the hydrogen itself to fire the pistons, but determined that was too dangerous—"

"Look, this is all very nice, but what makes it *go*?"

"Each of the five engines is attached to a propeller. And above the propellers, near the rear of the dirigible, are the gun turrets."

"Gun—!"

"For mounting Maxim machine guns. We acquired a few of those, too, while swiping the aluminium. They meant to do more than merely drop bombs, but they haven't worked out how to fight the slipstream to keep gunners at their posts."

Herron did not want to dwell on the gun turrets. "How fast can this monster go – compared to the motor carriage?"

"I believe the Boliee motor carriages can make up to twenty-five miles per hour with an engine of much less horsepower than we have. With all our engines firing, our airship is capable of cruising at more than . . . oh . . . thirty knots – say thirty-three or more with the wind; thirty against, tops."

Herron whistled—then became angry when he did a little arithmetic in his head. "Malarky! Nothing goes that fast! The liner I went to America in only made fifteen knots!" When Herron shouted, his words echoed through the shed.

Stoker slapped a hand over Herron's mouth, pushing him back against the solidly-built scaffolding of the second airship.

"Shh! I'm supposed to be alone in here! Listen – I just said modern motor-carriages don't go much slower, and on less powerful engines." He lowered his hand. "Though, to be honest, I'd never have believed it myself if I hadn't experienced it first-hand. Plenty of money and effort has been poured into improving our engines. Even so, powerful though these engines are, the fact that they have to whirl those huge propellers – and make and maintain way against the wind – makes our speeds sound less impressive than land-based motor carriages. The Boilee engine has nothing like our horsepower, yet our top speed isn't that much faster than their motor carriage. But we're improving all the time. And we don't have to stick to roads. We literally travel 'as the crow flies.'"

"So you people had to develop the motor as well as the airship?"

"Oh, we had the airship in no time. A huge rubberized envelope with a rigid skeleton that rises when it's filled with hydrogen can be made by any fool."

"Yes, that adequately matches Lugner's description."

"Making the airship go any direction we wanted was well-nigh impossible with the engine technology we had when we started! We'd have had our ships up and running *years* sooner but for the engine. We started with even less than nothing. Our first internal combustion engines looked – and felt – ready to quiver apart if they ran for extended periods. Yet, airship engines must run *constantly*."

"So must the engines on motor-carriages."

"No, you're dead wrong. You can stop a hot motor-carriage under a tree by the side of the road and let it rest. If you stop an airship in mid-air, it's nothing more than a funny-shaped balloon."

6

At the stern of the airship, the electric lights lining the top of the shed cast an eerie, gauzy glow where they filtered through the great, three-bladed propellers.

The propellers were so large they might have come off a steam-ship.

"Hmm. Petrol combustion engine? Not coal or steam?"

"Coal engines require coal."

"Do tell."

"Add a hundredweight of coal to an airship's lift; then imagine trying to make forward momentum, dragging all that weight against the wind."

"Steam's not heavy."

"Steam engines are. And though our scientists pored over their drawing boards for years, they were unable adequately to reduce steam engines to a practicable size. And where does steam come from? Fire. Fires come from wood or coal, which must be taken aloft. And with it, the additional weight of men to stoke fires, like they have on trains. And fires do not play well with hydrogen."

"*Ka-boom.*"

"Precisely."

"I can see where your internal combustion engine was, as you said, a boon."

"A Frog named Henri Giffard used a steam engine to propel an airship filled with hydrogen at the speed of six miles an hour – carrying a heavy weight of coal with him! He somehow lived to tell about it. But steam airships were a dead end. Literally. Our spies tell us a German chap named Diesel has a promising new engine type; but in its present state, it's far too heavy to suit our purposes."

"But . . . like hydrogen, isn't petrol highly flammable?"

"Can be. But it's so manifestly useful! Petrol generates a lot of power for its weight, and you may keep quite a lot of petrol in a comparatively light tank. Too, the petrol will be used up as we go, which will have the same effect as casting off ballast. It won't explode so long as it's kept enclosed in the internal combustion engine, or in its tank. It's cleaner than coal or wood."

"Sounds ideal. Maybe I ought to buy shares in the stuff."

"Unfortunately, we cannot restock petrol in flight. We can drop down to chop down trees for more wood to power a steam engine, but we can't set down a massive airship in someone's yard and ask if we can borrow five hundred gallons of petrol. Before starting out we must always work out how far we can go on the petrol we have, and then turn around before we reach 'the point of no return.'"

Herron thought the words *point of no return* had an incredibly ominous ring.

And Stoker meant it quite literally. When they ran out of petrol the engines would stop and they would be at the mercy of the winds.

"Are these internal combustion engine things new?"

"They've been around. In the early days inventors actually tried gunpowder – and hydrogen – in the cylinders to fire internal combustion pistons. It was only when they began using petrol that they became viable. We got a few de Dion Bouton motor-carriage engines – they're sold separately, you know—"

"Oh, yes?" Herron had lost interest. This reply was cold politeness.

"—yes. And we took them apart, saw how they were made, and set to work improving them. And they needed so much improvement! Two point two-five horse-power engines are useless against atmospheric winds."

"What did you do, make them bigger?"

"Fool. The airship can't be weighted down by ever bigger engines. If you try to increasing the horsepower by enlarging the engine, the weight of the engine will nullify any advantage you gain in higher horsepower. We had to study to improve the engine to get *higher* horsepower from a *lighter* weight of engine. The problem our inventors had to focus on was not the physical size of the engine, but the *ratio of the weight of the engine to its horsepower.*"

Herron's interest returned. He recalled mentioning *the power-weight ratio of the engine* to Merridew not two days earlier. At the time, he didn't know what the words could possibly mean. He was beginning to get an inkling.

Most of Stoker's scientific description whizzed over Herron's head like so many airships. All that piccalilli about Archimedes and displacing fluids meant less than nothing to his mind.

But Herron was beginning to glimpse through a glass darkly that an airship engine had to achieve ever higher horsepower to make progress against the winds – while staying compact enough to keep from weighing down the payload.

The power-weight ratio!

That's why viable airships were impossible for so long! The technology had not been available, or men might have been flying around in dirigibles for ages!

Astronomers before Copernicus, who lacked the instruments necessary to properly examine the stars, were unable to guess that the earth revolved around the sun. Now a new technological revolution was in the making, driven by petrol-burning internal combustion engines. No wonder even deranged people like Lugner were high on progress! They were all whipping around a corner into a bright and shining twentieth century, full of progressive technology like motor carriages, telephones, typewriters, Kodaks and phonographs – and now air travel!

And the Lugners of the world wanted to control that progress and technology –and mankind, through eugenics – the way Satan tried to control Christ by sensibly suggest He satisfy His hunger cravings by turning stones into bread.

But first, Herron meant to tell Merridew he understood the power-weight thingie – assuming he ever saw Merridew again.

"All this took years of intensive work – and a pile of money," said Stoker.

"Good thing it was from the private sector. If the government footed the bill, it would have cost more and had layers of bureaucracy lining their pockets from it—all picked from my purse! A pal of mine once called a pickpocket a 'dip.' The government is full of dips. You had wealthy patron, then?"

"Either a rich patron, or a conglomerate."

"But you don't know who?"

"I never was able to climb that tree, either."

Herron knew who was on the uppermost limb of that tree. *Lady Calthrop.*

But he decided not to share this information with Stoker, for two reasons.

First, his suspicions might be totally wrong and he'd look an awful ass.

Second, he still didn't know how far to trust Stoker.

Stoker might have been boring Herron into complaisance all this time, spinning idiotic stories about Bonnie Prince Charlie and Archimedes, to make it easier to pick Herron's brain. To finally learn how much of the operation was known, abroad before finally blasting that brain altogether out of Herron's skull.

Herron wondered why had Stoker brought him here at all? Lots of equipment lay around, but he saw no real hiding-place inside the shed.

He thought he'd be safer back at the barracks, cowering under a bed.

CHAPTER LXIV

At the airship's stern, four . . . *things* stuck out from the airship. If *Darnely* were a fish, Herron would have thought of them as fins. One was on top, another on the bottom. Two jutted out from the sides.

"What are those?"

"The flippers on the top and bottom are for horizontal stability. We call this shape of the airship 'aerodynamic,' but left to itself it will tend to slue around broadside in the direction of motion. In the worst case, with its engines running, it might end up wheeling around in circles. So we need those tail flippers as stabilizers for horizontal control. And the flippers on the sides are elevators."

"What do they do?"

"When the elevators are slanted one way, the airship noses up; when they're slanted another way, the airship noses down. Nosing the airship up just slightly actually gives it more dynamic lift. Nosing down presses the airship downwards."

"Which way is which?"

"God and Lugner only know. And Lugner probably would be distressed to learn I put God in his august company."

"How long does it take this ship to turn?"

"The diameter of its turning circle is four thousand feet."

"Good heavens. You had better not forget anything and have to go back home to fetch it. What's that insignia painted in red on the top fin?"

"It's an ancient hindu symbol. Right-facing, it's the symbol for eternity, and the evolution of the universe."

"It looks like a bloody swastika."

"It is, you fool. It's supposed to be a good-luck charm. Lugner wanted it."

"I thought he hated religion. Isn't superstition a kind of religion?"

"'She Who is to Come' must have requested it. In any case, I suppose a symbol for eternity can stand for their 'bringing people together.'"

"And 'strengthening cooperation between peoples without dissent.' By euthanizing unnecessary human animals. I don't like the red against the gold."

Stoker shrugged. He had nothing to say about color-coordination.

Where the airship tapered toward its tail-fins, a glider was attached to the underside of the keel by a hook over an aluminium bar that looked like a trapeze. It was on a universal joint keeping it in trim whatever the disposition of the airship. It was, Herron perceived, easily released by a lever.

The glider was a flimsy-looking contraption of spruce and fabric. Herron thought it resembled an eight-foot-high dragonfly.

This was Stoker's baby, and he proudly explained that its insect-like segments pivoted independently on ball-bearings. It had a cruciform tail segment hinged on a universal joint, which was designed to maintain the glider's equilibrium whatever the angle of the wind.

To Herron, that was just so many words uttered by the yard.

The glider's long, twin wings (each one fifteen feet long and five feet from their leading to their trailing edges) were shelved above each other, making its dragonfly wings look like two long boxes with no sides.

It was all tied together with piano wire.

"Stoker, my lad, I've never seen anything that more adequately fit the description '*death-trap.*' Dashed thing looks like it's made of paper."

"Weighs twenty-three pounds."

Herron cast disparaging eyes on the glider. He wished he had his monocle so he could glare critically through it. "It'll drop like a rock, with a man on it."

"It's a two-seater, one behind the other. It carries two men."

"Two rocks."

"You're forgetting the weight of the air."

"Silly me. What's the glider for?"

"Escape. If you can get to it in time."

"Wh-what do you mean by that, exactly?"

"I mean no more or less than what I said. About a fortnight ago, there was an accident at Tempelhof Field in Berlin. That's the Prussian Army Airship Battalion where we got 'Boss' Lugner."

"The Airship Battalion with no airship."

"Oh, they had one ten days ago. An inventor named Karl Woelfert was trying out his specially-designed airship. Two-man crew, himself and one other fellow – a mechanic called Knabe. When Woelfert cast off he proved his airships's up-down dirigibility immediately, by shooting three thousand feet into the air."

"That's good." Seeing Stoker's sneer, he meekly added, "Isn't it?"

"An airship should float gracefully up into the clouds. It shouldn't pop up like a rubber toy held at the bottom of the bath. Woefert was actually using a Daimler hot tube ignition engine. Naked flame—petrol—hydrogen . . . not a good mix."

"Not a successful trip?"

"Two vibrant streaks of flame bursting out to either side was the first indication that all was not well. Ground observers heard a distant *thump* when the petrol tank exploded. They reported hearing one single, piercing scream from the midst of the conflagration. Fire shot through the ship like a bullet. The blazing car dropped off the envelope and slammed down into a nearby timber yard."

"Sweet Genevieve! What happened?"

"Who knows? The flame in the combustion engine may have ignited benzine used in the steering motor. When he shot up so fast, Woelfert may have vented hydrogen, and it caught fire from the burner. There was not really enough evidence to make a proper evaluation."

"Oh, well, 'what goes up—' Oops, sorry. Anyone hurt?"

Stoker turned cool eyes on Strangways. It wasn't worth the time to explain that an explosive fireball plummeting three thousand feet to an utter smash was not conducive to survivors.

Herron craned his neck, peering all around the glider. "Are you sure that doodad is safe? Not the glider, that is, but the passengers."

"Perfectly. You can glide on that for a thousand feet."

"Then what?"

"To finish your quote—you 'must come down.'"

"That's what I'm afraid of."

"Don't be."

"And you'd actually let yourself down from an airship in that thing?"

"I'd rather be in the glider than the airship. Lugner's the airship pilot, and when I'm up in the sky in the car of the airship, I am at his mercy."

Little though Herron would trust Lugner's tender mercies, he said, "You won't catch me going up in that thing."

"You don't go up. Gliders must always take off from a height, and descend on the air like a feather."

"And its passengers *thump* to the ground like overripe cantaloupes."

"Well, there's only room for two on the glider: me and Lugner."

"Why did he choose you to go with him?"

"I'm the best glider pilot on the compound."

"And you didn't know you were going up until just now?"

"Nope. They keep an eye out for treachery in the ranks. 'Treachery' meaning political dissent. And security is tight since that incident Saturday night."

"Do you mean to tell me that if Lugner and his thugs doubted the *political* loyalty of their best pilot, they'd trust their second-best pilot to operate this gruesome flying coffin?"

"These people are idealists. They put loyalty to their political cause over proficiency any day."

"That's not idealism – that's lunacy. Look here, all I do is run is a store. I put a man named Grouse in charge of it. Grouse and I heartily dislike each other. We disagree on all political and social issues. He despises my lifestyle and he has a fund of robust Presbyterian language to inveigh against my lifestyle. But I gave him his position because I want the thing done right. *And my stores never leave the ground*! Trusting any job to someone based on political expediency rather than competence is dumb on the ground. In the air so blue, it's suicide."

"That's the way Lugner operates. He prefers loyalty to competency."

"And that's the way the fool will run a country. If he takes over I'd almost rather you'd shot me and got my suffering over quick. But, look here, I can't see that my position in this shed is lot better than it was before. In fact, it seems a lot worse. If they find me here, won't they shoot me and ask questions later?"

"Maybe not."

"No?"

"They may ask questions first – with torture. To find out who you're working for. And the torture will probably be prolonged, since they'll think you're lying when you tell them you don't know anything. That excuse might have bought your life from me Saturday night, but you didn't leave well enough alone. You know too much, whether you know it or not."

"Is being tortured for info I don't have any worse than riding in your glider?"

"Oh, gliders are perfectly safe, if you know what you're doing. And they are mostly quiet, except for the wind whistling around you. Have you ever swung a sword and heard it *whish* through the air?"

"I was best at athletics in school. My father bought me a well-rounded education, and I'm pretty fair at fencing, both *epee* and saber, though I do say it."

"That *whish* you hear when you sling your sword is the air it's slicing through. The weight of the air is quite strong enough to support that glider with two men on it. You know, when we were in America testing our airship prototypes, I heard about an American named Herring doing work with a *powered* glider."

"Powered flight?"

"It's a dead-end. It takes the *glider* as far as it will go. It's as impractical as heavier-than-air flight. Even though the ground-handlers must do everything for an airship until it rises into the atmosphere, I believe lighter-than-air flight will be the wave of the future. Heavier-than-air flight is for the birds."

CHAPTER LXV

They circled the airship, and were just coming even with the car slung on undercarriage in the forward part of the keel. "The first design for the car was boat-shaped," said Stoker. But Luger thought that was too 'sentimental.'"

"This is the most amazing thing I've ever seen. And I've seen . . . well, quite a lot. It's too bad these people have learned the wrong lesson. They want a nation where 'the state' pays for everything, but this hulking ship, and all their little claim-jumping inventions, were constructed by private enterprise."

Herron firmly believed Lady Calthrop was wrong. Religion was not the biggest obstruction to progress and science – government was.

Stoker shrugged. He didn't care who made it, only what it was made for. "I've given you the grand tour outside; now – up in the car. After you, m'lord."

With a mawkish bow, Stoker indicated a net made of thick, very strong, but extremely coarse black ropes hanging down from the open doorway of the car.

Herron's eyes followed the netting up. "You're sure nobody is in there?"

"The airship is typically unmanned until it's pulled from the shed."

Feeling he had no choice, Herron clambered warily up the net, into the car.

The car consisted of one room, about twelve-by-twelve square. It might have been *slightly* longer from back to front, but it looked square enough to Herron.

From waist-high, to the roof, the car had windows on all sides except the rear, near the open door. The walls flanking the door were bare, save for a set of crossed swords, draped with a Jolly Roger. It was the only personal touch there.

A rope coiled by the door was attached to a grapnel at one end and a winch on the other. Herron supposed the grapnel was used for an anchor.

Just under the front windows were a few levers, though Herron couldn't guess what they controlled, and he wasn't about to ask Stoker, who had come up behind.

Ask him what time it is and he'll tell you how to build Big Ben.

Counters, presumably for charts – and coffee mugs, though he didn't see a pot anywhere, nor any way to heat one – took up space at the side-windows.

The counters contained a few odd devices. Stoker pointed out an aneroid barometer (like a huge pocket watch); an inclinometer (like a upside-down protractor with a plumb bob attached, with the string of the bob showing the angle of inclination); a thermometer; and a compass in a brass binnacle.

Since balloons were the only method of extended air travel anyone knew about, Herron first supposed the charts rolled on the counters were little better than ancient parchments used by mariners that read, "HERE BE YE DRAGONS."

Unrolling the charts, he recognized them as complete diagrams of the railways into London from all directions. "Why do you have railway maps?"

"Think, Strangways. So far as anyone knows, only balloons fly, and they're at the mercy of the winds. Since no one is navigating in the air, there are few maps for air travel. Airships may navigate by the stars at night, but during the daylight hours we follow the tracks. We practiced that all across America. We flew from Oakland to Sacramento on the Central Pacific lines to Ogden, Utah, then Union Pacific lines to Omaha. Most of the crew wanted to go from Omaha to Chicago, but Lugner wanted the practice. Omaha to Kansas City to St. Louis, then north again to the Great Lakes, where we exploded one prototype. From there we followed a wiggly route to New York state and Maine. Then up into New Brunswick and across the Atlantic."

"Must have been a very cold journey that far north over the ocean."

"Airships like the cold. The crew was nasty, but we reminded ourselves we were better dressed and protected than the Vikings who went the other way to Greenland in open ships."

"The world was warmer then. We all cooled off with the Krakatoa explosion in '83, when it polluted the air worldwide. I learned all about that, yesterday. The papers reported your airship being in Idaho and Texas and lots of other places."

"Everyone wants to get their name in the papers, so once they started reporting on us, every light in the sky became 'the airship.' Unfortunately, there's more fog in England than on the American plains. It often blankets railroad lines."

"That sounds jolly dangerous, flying through the fog."

"Cruising from the fens to London at three thousand feet, few, if any, natural features pose any danger. And since we're the only flying vehicle in the skies, other than the odd balloon, the possibility of an accident is remote."

A funnel-like device hung down from the ceiling by a hose. "What's that?"

"Speaking tube. So someone here can talk to a party in the envelope."

The actual steering mechanism was operated by a wooden ship's wheel. Another wheel was set in a slot in the deck at right angles to the ship's wheel.

"What's that second wheel for?" wondered Herron.

"The elevators. Here, see this regular ship's wheel? It turns the rudders – those are the fins at the top and the bottom of the airship's stern."

"Just like a real ship."

"Just like. By flipping these switches here, the rudders may be maneuvered together or independently. The fins on the sides are the *elevators*. They are worked by this wheel in the floor. The angle of the elevators is of the utmost importance, because the pressure of the air rushing over the elevators raises or lowers the nose. If you do the wrong thing, your airship is a smear across a field. If the rudders and the elevators aren't worked in perfect synchronization—"

"Down will come baby, cradle and all!"

"The pilot must also be a good judge of the weather. Hmm. The barometer calls for a smattering of light rain today, but otherwise ideal flying conditions when the fog clears. To be honest, Strangways, I don't like Lugner, but I do admire his skill at working these two wheels. It's like it says in Scripture, not letting your left hand know what your right is doing. Then there's the wind."

"Eh? I thought the engines nullified the wind."

"You thought wrong. The higher you get, the more treacherous the winds are – and the more uncertain. Winds are stronger at any altitude. At the top of Eiffels' tower in Paris, they say the winds blow as much as four times as high as winds at the base. It's worse on an airship cruising at three thousand feet. So we fly low. Though, as a rule of thumb, we rarely fly lower than half again the airship's length – and, that's dangerous, too!"

"You might barge into something. Why not fly higher?"

"Height affects the hydrogen. The gas expands at heights and must be valved off. And since we need as small a payload as possible in the hot time of year, we do not carry spare pressure tanks of hydrogen. Therefore, the gas we valve off cannot be replaced mid-flight."

"That fellow in Berlin ten days ago didn't have much luck valving off gas at three thousand feet! Say – what's this?" Herron reached for a cord with a handle dangling just over the wheel, slightly larboard of the pilot.

Stoker grabbed Herron's arm before he could touch it and wrenched it painfully down. "Don't pull that, y'fool! That's the whistle!"

"Like a steam whistle on a train?"

"Only louder. It doesn't work by steam, but by a jet of compressed hydrogen. If you pull that, you'll have every guard on the compound in here. Shooting you."

Herron looked around. The weight of every single item in the airship had to be considered for lift – including himself. An eleven-stone disparity in weight would alert them to a stowaway. "Where will you hide me?"

"Not in here, obviously. Climb up. We'll tuck you away in the envelope."

In the dead center of the car, a ladder stretched up into the superstructure.

Herron studied the ladder censoriously. Its rungs were extremely thin rounds, attached to a central metal pole rather than side-rails. "Will it hold my weight?"

"Climb up and find out."

Herron gingerly crawled up a rung or two, then waggled his weight up and down on his toes to see if the metal bent.

Stoker came close to smiling. "They risked using steel for the ladder. To keep the weight down, they tried to make it as thin as possible."

"They succeeded in making it as thin as possible. Good job the rungs are round – if they were flat, they'd have only one side to 'em."

When his head raised up out of the hatch, Herron saw the top of the car was even with the keel, leaving a gap between the car and the envelope. Going into the envelope while flying, they would have to climb through six feet of open space. With all that heavy air blowing around them.

"If there's trouble," said Stoker, "Lugner and I will escape up to the top of the car and, holding on to the struts, move along the keel to the glider. If there's a hydrogen explosion, we won't even have time to yell 'Fire!'"

At the top of the ladder, in the dark superstructure, he paused. "Will they search this thing over before they take off?"

"They unearthed Hawkins's body to have a peek at his underwear. Yes, they'll serach. If we hide you well enough, they won't find you – 'til we're aloft."

"Then what?"

"They'll probably pitch you overboard like so much ballast."

"Not the death I'd prefer."

"You'd better pray it kills you. We lost a man overboard in America. He wasn't killed, but the impact crushed almost every bone in his body. He didn't have enough rigid skeleton left for us to lift him onto a stretcher. It was like trying to shift a beached jellyfish."

"What did you do?"

Stoker patted his coat where his pistol nestled in the inside breast pocket. "One shot. Left him for the wolves. Pray you land near someone who is armed, or you will lie there, slowly dying, in inconceivable pain."

"You won't try to stop them from throwing me overboard?"

"And blow my cover?"

"So . . . what chance have I got?"

"Only one: Don't get caught! That entails keeping your trap shut."

It was dark until Boothby flashed a dark lantern around. Herron knew of such things, but he had never seen one up close. It was a paraffin oil lantern with a handle like a pewter stein. The lantern part was enclosed in metal, except for a hole where the light shone out like a bulls-eye. This hole could be shuttered with a shield. Virtually undetectable when the shield was closed, the dark lantern shot out a comparatively dazzling shaft of light when the shield was opened.

Herron hadn't known what to expect, but he fancied the inside of the envelope would be a vast, open area like a cathedral.

Instead, despite an external size of six hundred feet long and seventy-nine feet high, the interior of the envelope was cramped. It was filled with girders, supplies, and about twenty inflated bags, like balloons. Herron saw little of the bags in the narrow beam of light shooting from the lantern, but he supposed the bags were all about twenty-five feet long and twice as high.

As Stoker darted his light around the envelope, Herron perceived wooden catwalks here and there, between girders and beams, for the storage of supplies and ballast. They were carefully designed to balance the weight, and keep the airship in trim. The floor space sturdy, but limited.

The catwalks were all dangerously open at the sides.

As they walked along a narrow catwalk from the wide piece of flooring around the hatch to a wider area of flooring near the stern, Stoker said,

"It looks like we're taking a full complement of fuel. We can carry thirty-five thousand pounds. I wonder why Lugner needs so much fuel for a jaunt to London and back? That should use little more than about five hundred pounds."

"What are these balloon things?" Herron wondered.

"They're the ballonets I mentioned. You don't want to just fill the envelope of the airship, like you're puffing up one big bag."

"Don't I?"

"No. ballonets are safer. And when you valve off gas, it's better to release it a little at a time from each of the ballonets."

Herron ran his fingertips along one of the ballonets. "They aren't full."

"They're full enough. As we go higher, the air pressure outside the envelope will decrease. The hydrogen must have room to expand. If you don't give the hydrogen elbow-room, it won't take you up very far. And when the gas expands too much, we valved it off."

"You mean, these ruddy things might blow up, and up and . . . explode – *bang*! And let out all that poisonous hydrogen? And when those balloons all explode and the hydrogen seeps out, we'll fall to earth we know not where?"

"No, no. The ship will rise no farther than the gas ceiling. In any case, we're flying to London, not over the Alps."

Herron was not soothed by the answer. "What are the ballonets made of?"

"Goldbeater's skin." Seeing Herron's blank look, Stoker explained, "When they were pounding their gold into thin sheets, for gilding parchments, gold beaters put gold between two layers of the stuff."

Herron stroked a ballonet. "It feels funny. What's it made of?"

"The intestinal lining of an ox, treated with India-rubber."

Herron yanked back his hand. "We'll be held up in the air by *tripe*?"

"Tripe comes from stomachs. These are more, properly, chitterlings. Think of us as being in the 'bowels' of the ship."

"Doesn't Mister 'I'm-Superior-To-You-Because-I-Don't-Eat-Cheese' object to cutting cattle open and stealing their guts? Oh, that's why he said, in specific language, 'Nothing in this house' was made from animals. I suppose he never lets the airship in the house and especially not up on the furniture."

"And he's just pragmatic enough to know gold-beaters skin is gas-tight. We made a deal with the stockyards to buy the stuff in bulk."

"It's appalling!"

"It's sturdy. When we used fabric, the maintenance men occasionally tripped and fell right through it – into the poisonous hydrogen. That's another reason Bowie knifes were handed out. So fallen men could cut out of the bags. Or, if they were succumbing to the gas, they could make a faster end of themselves. And this might interest you, as a passenger. When an airship is in motion, ballonets rub together. When fabric rubs fabric, *they might produce a spark from static electricity*. And, since we're totally surrounded by hydrogen gas—"

"All right, you win. Are all airships designed this way?"

"There is no officially functioning airship, so there is no 'right' or 'wrong' way to do things. We've sent observers to every launch of promising young airships. Some inventors use envelopes like balloons, open from one end to the other without the ballonets. A few have even used aluminium covering for the airships rather than fabric, so the airships will keep their shapes from the *outside* rather than from an internal skeleton."

"Which way is preferable?"

"As I understand it – and around here you have to learn to ask questions without seeming inquisitive – pumping hydrogen into one large bag will mix it with other air and degrade its purity."

"'His strength was as the strength of ten, because his gas was pure.'"

"And degraded purity makes the hydrogen more volatile."

"Again—*ka-boom*."

"Yes. It won't take much to send hydrogen up in flames. We exploded an airship in America a few months ago – a prototype we didn't need anymore. I think they were testing to see just what an explosion would do."

"After keeping your airship so secret even Mister Edison was sure it didn't exist, weren't you afraid of being found out by exploding one?"

"I think a few pieces were found, but most of it is resting comfortably at the bottom of Lake Huron."

"Was it a big explosion?"

"There's never been such a destructive man-made fireball in human history."

"Was it unmanned?—or was it an experiment with Lugner's undesirables?"

"Unmanned. We had observers in boats near the site of the explosion. I watched from several miles away. I pity anyone in the vicinity of that holocaust."

Herron swallowed hard. One little mistake, and he might be in it.

One good thing: the lesson in aerodynamics was manifestly over.

When they reached the stern of the airship's innards, Stoker led Herron to a large bladder-like container near the tail. It was constructed of canvas sailcloth and stank of tar. When he threw back the lid and shined his lantern into it, Herron saw it was three-quarters full of murky water, bulging like wine in a goatskin.

"I can see where it may be a thirsty journey, but . . . ick."

"It's not drinking water, Strangways. It's ballast. We keep a thousand pounds of water ballast in several containers. It helps keep us maintain trim."

Herron patted his flat belly. "I keep trim without ever touching water, unless it's mixed with a dab of whisky – to keep it sterilized and kill harmful bacteria."

"Did you ever think the whisky might eventually do to you what it does to bacteria? One day it'll sterilize you. By *trim*, I mean we try to keep the ship level. Some early airship inventors had their crews move weights back and forth to maintain trim. Crossing the ocean with as many crewmembers as we had, we found we could adjust the trim by moving men's bodies forward or aft, as necessary. Losing trim causes drag. Drag means less speed and less control."

"Where did twenty-three of you sleep in this hole?"

"We took shifts in hammocks slung across the girders. On that trip we realized, for the first time, how cramped we were in here. Moving across the American plains we landed often. You can't land in the ocean. Their next ship will be larger. Larger is better, with airships. The larger the ship, the more cubic feet of hydrogen."

"That's the rumour."

"And more powerful, and capable of carrying a larger payload – of bombs. And maybe have the gun turrets working. That's why we must stop them today, or die in the attempt. Here. We'll smuggle you aloft in the water ballast."

"*In* this muck? I say, doesn't 'ballast' get dumped over the side!"

"Yes. Unfortunately, the sluice vents are far too small to suck you out."

"Can't you drain that dismal liquid before I dive into it!"

"And flood the shed? They'd assume one of the bladders had sprung a leak and they'd check each of them. They'd find you, and—"

"*Bang.*"

"*Bang* for me, too. By protecting you, I protect myself."

"And that's the only reason you're doing this, friend Stoker?"

"Pretty much."

"What happens when we get back? How do you smuggle me out again?"

"I'm playing this totally by ear, lad. I made a snap decision back there not to shoot you, and things moved so fast, now I'm stuck with you. I couldn't leave you in Hawkins' place in the ground crew, obviously. I'll hide you. Maybe I can thwart the mission and we'll be safe. Maybe not. But you'll be safe enough once we're aloft. The only problems we've ever had with the water ballast is when we flew too high and it froze."

"Setting me into a block of ice like a flower in a crystal paperweight!"

"We won't go that high."

"I might freeze anyway!"

"Maybe not."

"Is 'maybe not' good enough?"

"It is for me. Remember, if you're found dead in here, it'll look bad for me."

"Oh, I'm *so sorry* for you. Couldn't I hide in one of those ballonets?"

"Sure. We might be able to squeeze nearly all the hydrogen out of one, except for trace elements. Go ahead, cut one open with Hawkins's handy Bowie knife. Let the hydrogen out. Wave your hands in front of it to scatter the gas. Have you ever seen a man die of hydrogen asphyxiation, Mister Strangways?"

"Not that I'm aware of."

"It's not pretty. Do you want to know how it feels when it happens to you?"

"Not particularly."

"If you can't hold your breath for eight hours – get in the water."

"If the airship is scaled down because the gas doesn't lift so well in the summer, won't they notice my extra weight?"

"Just in case, I'll take out another bit of disposable ballast."

"Disposable ballast! That's what I am."

"You will be if they find you."

"What good will my being here do? Presumably this airship will go on its merry mission to blow up the Queen or whoever and start a major panic in London, and then toddle back home to put its feet up. I've made a circle and I'm back where I started. I don't see that I'm much safer flying the round trip."

"Actually, you're a lot safer *flying* than *landing* – if 'landing' is the right word, since airships ideally remain afloat even when they dock in port."

"Why is flying safer than landing?"

"In landing, we must valve off hydrogen. When we get close to earth, one of the mooring ropes might touch the ground, giving off static electricity. If a single spark of that hits the hydrogen we're valving—"

Herron started for the hatch. "Let me know when you get back—!"

Stoker grabbed the tail of Hawkins's yellowed shirt and slung Herron around. "I'm thwarting this mission in mid-air if possible. You may have to help me."

"Will it be possible?"

"I don't know. We want to catch them in the act – and also, if practicable, we want to save the life of the Queen. Don't we, Strangways?"

"Do *we*?"

"You saw the size of the car. They won't require a large crew. And since we won't be landing in London, just dropping bombs and turning around, we won't need to bring riggers."

"Can we cut the car loose?"

Stoker shook his head. "Soldered on. But, maybe two of us can handle a small crew. I'll try to wrest control of the bomb if nothing else. In the best case, I will seize the bomb and dispose of it by flinging it out into an open field, or a lake."

"In the worst case?"

"I'll be forced to detonate the bomb in mid-air. At that moment I will be dissipated into a rubberized whiff of gas in a massive hydrogen explosion. You, too. It'll at least be a pretty way to die."

"Will it?"

Stoker waved his arms around the ship. "All these ballonets are filled with hydrogen. If they blow up together, this airship will be the greatest firework ever seen. Then two hundred yards of blazing rubber will crash on London and cause the biggest conflagration since the Great Fire of 1666. Now, get in the water."

After that description, Herron thought *in the water* was precisely where he wanted to be. "Can't I take off these clothes? They're loathsome enough dry."

"And let one of Lugner's thugs find them in here before takeoff?"

Fully clothed, Herron stepped into the bladder and slowly lowered himself into the clammy water.

Stoker was impatient. "Come on! Come on!"

A man does not settle quickly into a cold bath, and Herron let the weight of his body displace the slick and oily fluid by slow increments. He sat with his knees drawn up, for the bladder was only about half the length of a bathtub.

Stoker used a scoop to ladle water from that container into others, so the water level would feel about even in all the bladders from the outside.

"Look," said Herron, "do I have to stay in here all the time?"

"We don't want them finding wet footprints."

"What if I have to go—you know."

"It won't hurt the water to add a little to it." He slapped down the flap used for a lid. It wasn't air-tight, but once it was buckled down on all sides, Herron found little breathing-room. The oily aroma nauseated him.

"Also," Stoker called through the flap, "whatever you do – *don't smoke!*"

Herron gave a sardonic laugh har-de-har-har. The tobacco and matches he'd found in Hawkins's pocket were hopelessly soaked, and the cigarette papers had practically melted.

2

Late Saturday afternoon, Herron had entered an Underground station to catch a train home because his steps were wobbly. He had stealthily sidled alongside the loveliest woman he had ever seen recently.

Now, in the wee hours of Tuesday morning, with dawn just rising somewhere beyond the shrouded fens, he was in a dead man's clothes, half-submerged in murky liquid, in a gold-varnished airship bound for London to blow up the Queen.

As he had to remain in this container at least until take-off, he was a virtual prisoner in the airship.

This is a switch, Herron thought, wetly. *It's a cage in a gilded bird.*

CHAPTER LXVI

Merridew had refilled Angelica's cup. She sat up so abruptly she nearly spilled hot coffee all over herself. "Hang *me*?"

Chubb nodded. "You'd better pray it ain't a mad woman's ravin's."

"Why? I don't want anyone blown up with a bomb if I can stop it. If it is coming, I can't stop it; so the next best thing is to hope I'm wrong and no one will die. *Including me.*"

"Well, if it is a wild-goose chase . . . you tell me Herron Strangways is dead. The man Strangways meant to meet about his blessed marriage certificate is dead. Lady Calthrop may be dead. The cigarette paper you said had a hidden message is gone and no living soul on the face of the planet has seen it but you."

"I see."

"See this, too: Lady Calthrop had some powerful friends. They won't be well-disposed to anyone who shot her. Live or dead, if you try to blacken her name in court with a yarn about conspiracies, and airships that never materialized, they'll only get furiouser. You won't be the first pretty young lady to take the drop, and her friends in high places will see you take it."

"So," she said slowly, to make sure she had it straight in her sleep-deprived mind, "I'll be tried, whatever happens. If she's alive, I go to prison. If she's dead, I go to the rope. Unless an airship bombs innocent people all over London."

"Yep. Can't get by that. You shot her. If she dies, I'd plead self-defense; but a jury might think you used excessive force, a revolver against a parasol."

"My only hope of *not* being hanged for murder is for this airship to scatter its explosives over London? Over the Queen and dignitaries and children watching the Procession on their father's shoulders and God only knows who else? They've got to die so I can live?"

Chubb nodded gravely. "If that airship appears and drops its bombs, you're safe. And like you said, if it really is comin' there ain't no way to stop it."

"No."

"So we might as well resign ourselves to the notion that dozens, maybe hundreds, will die before this day's over – in the bombing and then in the ensooin' panic. If that happens, you'll probably not be hanged."

"Is that supposed to be a comfort?"

"Anyway, in that case Lady Calthrop's will be one death in a passel. You'll be arrested for shootin' her, but you can claim Lady Calthrop was at the bottom of it and all and she was trying to kill you, personally. Maybe that butler will back you up, if he's alive; maybe not. If there ain't no airship, your fate depends on how much your daft little tale persuades a British jury."

"Then, the only chance I have for freedom is for the airship to appear."

"No. Not 'appear.' You claim you shot your way out of Lady Calthrop's house in a desperate effort to warn the world of bombs being strewn from on high. If an airship does appear, and all it does is fly over London and go merrily on its way, it won't help your case one wee bit. It must drop bombs and kill people."

"And there's no evidence that'll keep me from being hanged if it doesn't?"

"We might convince a jury you wasn't actin' in your right mind."

"And spend the rest of my natural life locked away in Bedlam. I think I'd prefer the short, sharp drop."

"Not so short. We want to break your neck, not strangle you like a chicken. And not too long neither, or the snap at the end might yank off your head."

A shudder shimmied through Angelica's frame.

"Don't worry. If there's no airship bombing, the drop will be carefully measured. It'll be just right for you."

2

Pottle returned eventually, shouting his way through Herron's house before finding everyone collected in the kitchen.

His first announcement was that it was broad daylight outside, though lightly overcast. After being snippily informed by Chubb they did not require a weather forecast, Pottle outlined his journey to Park Lane.

Lady Calthrop was dead. The cause was for the coroner's jury to decide. A few bullet holes dotted her, but also every bone in her body looked broken.

Angelica, who had seen Her Ladyship's sad eyes as she started backward down the stairs, knew she was guilty of killing her whichever way the verdict went.

"Well, that's that," Chubb confirmed. "You're innocent 'til proved guilty, but them wounds he described are consistent with your story. Go on, Pottle."

Pottle continued. The butler was alive and talking. Frightened of the authorities in his weakened condition, Dapifer made a clean breast of his doings.

His confession had not been altogether helpful, or even lucid. He admitted his strong-arm work for Lady Calthrop, including murdering the man in Strangways' bedroom. He wished he could have done the same to Herron Strangways for not tipping him. In a gasping wheeze, the butler confessed he would have murdered Miss Trickett or mated with her, whichever Lady Calthrop commanded—

(Angelica shivered again, more from the latter than the former.)

When Pottle questioned him, Dapifer maintained his ignorance about conspiracies, or airships, or bombs. He did say that when he first brought Strangways into Her Ladyship's presence, Angelica was not meant to descend—

"That's true," Angelica broke in. "Dapifer carried her downstairs and I was given strict orders to keep to my room."

"Which you did not see fit to obey," Chubb pointed out.

"She was going to tell a lie about me and I refused to countenance it." She giggled from sheer weariness. She started out trying to keep from spreading lies and ended up gunning down two persons, one in a wheelchair.

Eyeing the giggling Angelica guarded, Pottle went on with Dapifer's evidence. The butler explained that Her Ladyship's intention was to kill Strangways with her blowgun. Dapifer would hide the body and dispose of it later. Angelica's arrival saved Herron's life (temporarily) and gave Lady Calthrop the much safer idea of summoning agents via her wireless telegraph to seize Herron the moment he set foot out over her threshold. That way there would be zero chance of witnesses seeing a dead body toted from her house.

"Clever!" said Chubb. "If the bomb plot fell through and questions were asked about his disappearance, you and she and the butler would all agree about the last time he was seen alive, walkin' out the front door on his own power. It would have been one of them great mysteries, like the Iron Man in the Mask."

Angelica shook her head, whipping her loose mane of hair from side to side. "And I kept Herron occupied until Lady Calthrop's thugs arrived!"

"But you saved his life – then – because you are a headstrong woman."

"She encouraged me." *Because she wanted me to be perfect.* She added in bitter silence, *And sheepish women are not perfect . . . ugh . . . specimens.*

The butler, Pottle said, thought Her Ladyship had it in for Strangways. She hated the *nouveau riche* as a threat to her class, and she complained that the government should lay a heavy punative taxation on the Strangwayses of the world to keep mere shopkeepers from buying their way above their station.

Chubb had no time for social engineering and told Pottle to stick to the crimes. "Was anyone else in the house, Pottle?"

In the kitchen (Pottle read from his note-book) he found a wild-eyed old lady screaming blue murder over a burnt-out tea-kettle. Upstairs, a terrified young maid, hearing shots, had barricaded herself in her attic room and refused to open her door even when Pottle identified himself as the police. And, finally, between the upstairs and the downstairs, Pottle found a hairy, dog-like creature who tried to taste his shinbone.

"What 'authorities' was this butler-fellow scared of?"

Pottle read his note that police officers had been alerted by gunfire, and had approached the house from the south.

(Angelica silently thanked God she'd been guided to run away to the north.)

The police on the scene had already developed a working hypothesis of a botched burglary, Pottle concluded. He had not mentioned Miss Trickett.

"Good work, Pottle," said Chubb. "We don't need them fishing in this pond."

Pottle then produced three needle-like darts, which he had stuck in the lapel of his coat. He had wiggled them out of the wall of the gallery overlooking the entry hall, where Miss Trickett had her shoot-out with Lady Calthrop.

Angelica, who had seen the darts only in her peripheral vision, found they were long and thorny, and would have stung like the dickens in her face and throat. And then they would undoubtedly have paralyzed and killed her with poison.

The poisoned darts hardened any residual guilt Angelica might have felt about shooting Lady Calthrop. She'd claim self-defense even on the gallows.

From a spacious inside pocket, Pottle extracted a silver casket engraved *I.II.*

"What now, Pottle? You didn't steal the silver?" Opening the casket, Chubb took a bewildered look at its contents. He tipped it up to give Angelica a view.

She peeked inside – and cringed away.

"Well," said the Inspector, snapping the lid shut, "it's a part off somebody. But who and what, it's hard to tell at this remove."

Pottle had returned laden with a wireless telegraph in a wicker box.

He had ridden back on a bicycle he found near the cellar door. He brought the wireless telegraph machine in the bike's basket. The wire basket on the bicycle was large enough to hold the picnic hamper she used when she and her brother went on cycling day-trips in the country, and the wicker box with the wireless telegraph fit in it at an angle.

Pottle hadn't known what to make of the machine. Poking about upstairs, he had heard it buzzing what he took for Morse.

Opening the box, Angelica couldn't make much of it. It was full of tubes and internal wires. She did recognize was a rubber listening tube, like those sold with gramophones she had seen in store windows. The tube was bifurcated near the end, and the separate tubes ended in metal balls that fit in the ears.

She slipped into this head-set, with the tubes hanging down beneath her chin. A moment later, she located what *seemed* to be a transmitting key. Pressing it—

She yanked her hand back. It shot sparks! Seeing the sparks wouldn't hurt her and the thing hadn't blown up in her hand, she pressed the key again.

The sparking key emitted the buzzing her keen ears had heard through Lady Calthrop's door. The pulses were much clearer through the listening tube.

Pottle didn't know Morse, but he recognized it when he heard it. He had diligently transcribed the strange pulses as he fancied he heard them, and he offered to go out and find a telegrapher.

"I know Morse," Angelica offered, removing the tubes from her ears.

Pottle handed her his note-book and she puzzled over it with a wrinkled brow. He had chucked the message down so fast, many of his dots looked like dashes, and many of his dashes looked like nothing on earth.

Painstakingly, Angelica spelled out:
-H-I-P-A-L-O-F-T-R-E-P-E-A-T-P-L-E-A-S-E-A-N-S-W-E-R-A-I-R-S-

Calmly, Angelica said, "Our airship, Inspector, is flying this way." Tossing her pencil aside, she slumped down in her chair with her head back. Crossing her arms beneath her breast, she breathed out a long, slow sigh of air. She showed no emotion. She had no emotion left. "And nothing on earth can stop it."

The airship was gliding toward them with its infernal machine. Even if it saved Angelica's neck, people were going to die *somewhere*.

Chubb had been right from the start. Until they cracked the code in the cigarette completely and learned the *place* 'they' meant to bomb, she might as well camp out cozily in this kitchen, with its soothing aroma of percolating coffee.

She might as well enjoy it. It might be her final taste of freedom.

Angelica felt like crawling upstairs and flinging herself over Herron's bed – she didn't think it was unseemly since he was dead – to make up her missed sleep.

Then she remembered Chubb had moved a lot of clothes, then laid out a corpse in evening dress on Herron's bed. She decided not to flop down there, after all.

Sleep or not, she'd read about the blood, devastation and horror of the terror attacks in tomorrow's newspaper. From that moment on, she would cope with the guilt of her failure every day for the rest of her life.

For she felt responsible. Angelica sojourned in the house where the plot was hatched. She had undoubtedly hob-nobbed, in gowns displaying too much décolletage, with men and women wading up past their Wellies in the conspiracy.

And she had guessed nothing. *Perhaps*, she admitted, *I didn't want to see it*. Noticing nothing, doing nothing, she had been a tacit part of the conspiracy.

I should have shot down her a year ago, if I had to swing for it.

Yet, Angelica had seen no reason to rifle through her employer's effects on the off-chance she was conspiring to bomb London from the air. Her Ladyship had been nasty, but not murderous. Nevertheless, much had obviously happened right under Angelica's nose; she should have gotten a whiff of it.

Sensing her attitude, Merridew refreshed her cup with piping hot coffee and offered her a muffin.

Ignoring the muffin, without sitting up she uncrossed one languid arm and drew the cup to her lips. "Is this coffee from Strangways' Emporium, Merridew?"

"That's right, Miss."

She sniffed it, then took a sip – and nodded approvingly.

"On his way out, Mister Strangways often shoves a canister into his pocket." He spoke with a tinge of revulsion. He didn't think anyone should take anything out of a store without paying, even if that person forked over for the entire stock.

Chubb cleared his throat in a contrite manner. "My turn to confess, Miss Trickett. I never quite believed your story. Not—!" he added quickly, seeing she was about to lodge a protest, "—that you was deliberately misleading the police. Just that you got the wrong end of the stick. But Pottle scribbled down this Morris Code. Even his lousy hen-scratchin's make him a reliable witness."

"If you still harbor doubts, you may easily confirm my interpretation."

"Oh, we will."

"By that time, you may even see the airship floating overhead."

"May be. But you got to admit, young Strangways' story sounded mighty peculiar. What's next, that's what I ask meself."

Her voice barely audible, Angelica answered, "Nothing next, pray God."

"The butler claimed to know nothing about the conspiracy or the airship. *If* he survives he *might* find religion and tell a jury you shot Lady Calthrop in self-defense. If there ain't no airship, and the butler dies – there ain't one shred of evidence that you didn't just go berserk and shoot willy-nilly at anyone who breathed in your vicinity. You'd better pray that airship blows up somebody."

CHAPTER LXVII

Daylight on the fens. A gentle breeze had dissipated the fog to a light gauze by the time the airship *Darnley* was guided out from its shed. Lugner could not have ordered better weather than shone on him this morning.

The ground handlers and riggers (who would have included Hawkins, had he not been stuffed down a hole a few miles away) were dressed in striped shirts and dungarees and topped by the black caps of seamen. Since the airship floated above the ground, as the ground-handlers stepped out with precision they looked like they were carrying its its vast, fat bulk smoothly along on their shoulders.

Dozens of ground handlers were necessary. *Darnley*'s high horsepower engines and five propellers were useless at low speeds.

When the ship was eased out of its shed, the handlers and riggers moored it to metal staves, then stood at rigid attention at every rope.

Stoker strolled admiringly to the car with one hand in the small of his back and his body cocked slightly forward. He was still amazed at this floating behemoth.

From the far side of the car, Lugner called, "I can not find Herr Hawkins."

"I'm not his keeper!" Stoker shouted back.

Lugner marched briskly around the car, buttoning on a bluish-grey, double-breasted greatcoat that reached to his calves. Tying a long, silk scarf around his throat, he said, "Herr Hawkins was with you when I saw him last."

"I dropped him at the barracks and drove on to the shed alone. You can ask the guards who were on duty here last night. They'll tell you I arrived without him, and here I've been here ever since. It was his own look-out to get here on time."

"I will deal with him on our return. The glider is in excellent working order?"

"Tip-top."

Lugner wore a pistol in a holster beneath the greatcoat, on his left side. Stoker had earlier noticed that the pistol's grip faced forward, so Lugner would have to reach across his body and thrust his right hand into the coat to extract it.

He filed that bit of information away in his mind for future reference.

Lugner reached his arms out and an assistant strapped a Prussian saber around his waist. As the baldrick was secured over his shoulder, Lugner gave the saber a loving pat. That done, he thrust his hands into heavy, leather gauntlets. Finally, he waggled his head into a pickelhaube another assistant had been holding ready.

He lowered a pair of goggles that were strapped around his helmet with an elastic band, wincing as they chafed against the black eyes Herron had given him. Then he clapped his gloved palms and rubbed them together.

Lugner had already double-checked the weather, the temperature, the humility and the barometric pressure. He raised his nose, as if enjoying a sniff of the miry stench of the surrounding fens on this perfect flying day.

"It is a glorious day for a demonstration, Herr Stoker."

"A trifle cloudy."

"High. Cloud cover will protect the skin of the airship from direct sunlight, so the gas will not overheat. Come, we must reach London by noon."

"How many in our crew?"

"Two. I pilot the airship; you, the glider."

"If we need it."

A peculiar look gleamed in Lugner's eyes, but they were difficult to read through the goggles. "Yes. *If* we need it."

"Can you handle the airship alone?"

"I will not be alone. You will do whatever menial tasks I demand."

"But—?"

"Do not be inquisitive. In our new republic everyone must learn to do as they are bid. Let us hurry. We cannot let a good crisis go to waste. *Albion wird abgebrannt!*" he shouted, raising his gauntleted fist. Lowering his hand, he said,

"May I see your watch, Herr Stoker?"

Lugner's own watch was in waistcoat pocket, buttoned beneath his greatcoat. Stoker had on his stiff, cloth cap with its goggles, but he was only just sliding his arms into his own long, tan greatcoat; his watch-pocket was still convenient.

Stoker held his watch up by the chain and dangled it dryly before Lugner, like a cynical hypnotist.

"We must give ourselve three hours flying time to reach London by noon. Traveling thirty-three knots."

"Will the engines withstand that speed all the way?"

"Are you the pilot of the dirigible now, Herr Stoker, as well as of the glider?"

"No. Sir."

"No sir! You must trust your leaders. They are better than you. You know we destroy each obsolete prototype utterly so no one else can use it. Our new machine will be better. It will surpass forty knots. This prototype is good enough for a demonstration on a fine day, but this is its last, glorious flight."

"So when we return to base we'll be destroying it and reusing the parts?"

Lugner had already warned Stoker about questions, and he did not issue warnings twice. He detailed his flight plan as if Stoker had not spoken.

"For most of the journey we will remain at three ship's length above the ground. We will fly higher closer to London, to make our descent all the more effective. It will also make us certain to be out of gunshot range. It would be most ignominious to be shot down."

Stoker absorbed this expressionlessly, though he was faintly amused. This would certainly alert the world to their presence. One noticed six-hundred foot, gold flying machines sailing at less than twelve thousand feet on a sunny morning. Lugner sent a few burly men inside the airship to poke around. Not from precaution, *per se*. It was a final check, to ensure all was airworthy. They had plenty of time before starting, so this final scrutiny did not need to be cursory.

As Stoker reckoned, the men did not peek inside the containers of water-ballast, though they felt them over from the outside to make sure they were full.

While this was going on, Lugner stowed away a silver casket reading *I.II* – which contained the brain of James II, the last Stuart king of Great Britain.

When the ship was declared airworthy, Lugner asked Stoker to hand up a wicker box carried by an aide.

Stoker handed the box up. Lugner laid it gently in one corner of the cabin.

"Picnic basket?" Stoker wondered, laconically, joining the pilot in the car.

"It is a vital thing we need for our mission."

Stoker had given the airship his own once-over that morning. Since the airship was stripped down of all non-essentials due to the warmer weather, his search had not taken long. He was acquainted with every possible variety of bomb. He had located none of them on board. He guessed what lay inside the wicker box.

Smiling faintly, he wondered if Lugner had bought the box at Strangways'.

Lugner signed to the master of ground-handlers. The master shouted orders, and the ground-handlers eased the silent airship up by its ropes to two hundred feet. At that height, they moored it again.

Secure at two hundred feet, Lugner started the five engines, one at a time. He listened acutely to each for a few minutes, to ensure they were all running well.

Only when he was satisfied with the performance of every engine did he start them all, to warm them up.

When he deemed the engines were sufficiently warm to achieve and maintain their necessary rate of knots to London, Lugner signed again to the master of ground-handlers, who fired one barrel of a shot-gun.

Since voice commands might not be head over the engines, Lugner used a gunshot to alert the handlers to release their ropes simultaneously.

At the sound of the shot, the ground-handlers unknotted the mooring ropes. They held the ropes while the master signed back to Lugner. The pilot signed for the master of ground-handlers to fire the second barrel.

At the second shot, the ground-handlers released their ropes simultaneously.

Pulling a lever in the car, Lugner emptied some of the water ballast. Lugner laughed at the men scurrying away from pouring water. "Look at them run!"

Snapped his own goggles over his eyes, Stoker breathed a sigh of relief at being airborne, alone with Lugner. Cracking the pilot's scrawny neck, disposing of the bomb and thwarting the mission looked too easy to be true!

And he was so right.

CHAPTER LXVIII

Herron, who had no sleep Monday night, had dozed off in the water.

As the engines coughed to life, he was shocked fully awake. Never having heard such a din, he tried to fight his way out of the bladder, thinking the bomb was exploding around him.

Concluding, at length, that he hadn't been blown to smithereens, Herron stopped trying to scrample out of the tightly-buckled bladder and sat tight.

Until Lugner released the water-ballast.

The water in Herron's vat flowed out through vent-holes whose slots were operated from the cabin. The holes were not large enough for Herron to be swept out with the water, but he clung sputtering to the oily canvas bladder.

Coughing out murky water, Herron felt waterlogged and wrinkled all over. Desperate to see what was going on, he sliced his way out with Hawkins's knife.

Darnley's envelope had no windows. Guided by the shaft of light rising from the hatch, Herron sloshed along the catwalk and the swaying bridge. The engines smothered the slopping of Hawkins's wet boots.

Then Herron heard a gunshot from the outside. Not knowing it was a signal to the ground handlers, he threw himself flat on the swaying catwalk. Hearing the second shot, he again recognized he was still in one, soppy piece.

Lying on his belly, he eased forward until he could peek through the hatch.

Resting his chin on the backs of his hands, he peered out through the six-foot area between the top of the car and the bottom of the envelope, just as *Darnley* nosed up into its ascent. His ears popped – a new, and unpleasant, experience.

When the ship leveled off, it only gradually dawned on Herron that everything on the ground had suddenly become very small.

Lugner circled the airbase several times, to make certain all the controls were operating to his satisfaction.

Even when they were in trim, Herron didn't fully understand how high he was – until he noticed that his own hands were larger than the shed, whose roof was just visible through the final, curling wisps of morning fog.

Darnley was lighter than air, but its eighty-one thousand pounds of rigid internal structure kept it stable. If it didn't move quite like silk, it was certainly the smoothest ride Herron had ever experienced. Horses and carriges jolted. Railroads bumped over crossings and points; they swayed around bends. Herron felt less rocking than he endured on a ship at sea. Only a tingling in the pit of his stomach informed him they were moving at all.

It didn't dawn on him for a minute or two. Then the thought jabbed home like a hatpin through his brain: he was up in the sky with nothing between himself and the ground but air!

The thought made him uneasy at first. Nothing to catch him if he fell.

Then, in his small window of sight, he saw the reclaimed arable land of the fens, with its low walls of local stone and its fields of varying summer colors. It made all the world look like it was covered with a cozy quilt.

And he realized he was having the most marvelous experience of his life.

He was *flying*. No – floating!

In a train or a carriage, trees and telegraph poles whizzed by. At this altitude, fields, hedgerows and isolated farmhouses crawled slowly below them.

He had the proud sensation that they must be the highest men in the world. Forget saints stuck up on pillars in Asia Minor, or Sherpas hopping over the Himalayas, or Andean goat-herds. Whatever their altitudes, those folk were still *in contact with the ground*. Herron was drifting leisurely above it.

Apart from the incessant drone and vibration from the engines, the ride was so smooth Herron could almost believe the airship was hovering in place like a (a noisy, vibrating) cloud while the earth spun beneath them.

He wanted to climb right down into the cabin and gaze through the windows on three sides. Had he known Lugner and Stoker were alone in the cabin, he might have risked it. But he could see little of the cabin, and he didn't know who else might be down there or how they were armed.

Satisfying himself with peering from on high at an angle through the hatch, Herron nearly cried out in surprise when he heard Stoker demand,

"Aren't we flying too low? You said three lengths."

"The wind is not so much turbulent near the ground. This conserves petrol."

"We're bulging with fuel. We've more than enough get to London and back."

" . . . back . . . *ja* . . . " said Lugner, distractedly.

Herron decided it was time for him to get back – into the bladder. In his wet clothes he thought, *It isn't half cold up here*.

And he had no way to get warm, or dry. If he found two sticks, he couldn't rub them together and stoke a fire, surrounded by one million and a half cubic feet of hydrogen gas.

Still, the thrill of flying to some extent offset the discomfort of the cold.

If only, he thought, all the people of earth could see the world from this perspective! How small the earth looked! The lines on maps were invisible from a height! When men saw the earth like that, then, as the Bible said, *They shall beat their swords into plowshares, and their spears into pruning hooks; nation shall not lift up sword against nation, neither shall they learn war anymore.*

Then, Herron reminded himself that the only people who had ever seen the earth from this perspective had fixed machine gun turrets on their airship.

Crawling back into his bladder, at least Herron didn't return to submersion. Nearly all of the water in his vat had drained out when Lugner released the water ballast. But the container was damp and Herron's seat and boots were in puddles.

And however badly the oily container stank when full of water, its empty stench was even more miserable.

2

He had been *in situ* about ten minutes when the lid of the water-container was flung back and a dark lantern bulls-eyed down into Herron's blinking face.

"Who's that?"

Stoker turned the bulls-eye of the lantern up under his chin for one second before winking it out again. Leaning into the bladder he said, just loudly enough to be heard over the roar of the engines,

"I'm making a casual round of the airship. Come out and take a look around."

"I'm sure the view must be beautiful."

"Not the view, idiot. *Take a look for the bomb.* I thought Lugner brought it aboard in a wicker basket, but that was his wireless telegraph. He's already used it. And the blasted thing sends out sparks with its radio pulses! He telegraphed – oh, probably 'She Who Is To Come' – to say we're aloft. He got no response and that put him in a foul temper. Thankfully, he doesn't realize I know Morse. I can understand whatever he sends. Or receives."

"So – where is the bomb?"

"It must have been aboard all the time."

"We might have defused it last night!"

"Certainly not! I'd have left it just where was until we were airborne. I wanted nothing to give us away, and any tinkering with the bomb might have been noticed. If we find it bomb now, that's enough evidence for me to arrest Lugner. We can either defuse it or pitch it out into a stream or an unoccupied field."

"Do I get a vote on whether we tinker with it or toss it out?"

"No. Here's what you can do: appear as a witness to attest to the a bomb, and that he meant to use it. Your name will carry weight with a jury. You know, Strangways, from the first time I met you Saturday night, I've heartily disliked you. And my distaste for your company has grown over time. But you're the perfect witness: the abducted head of Strangways' Emporium."

"Emporia. Will you charge him with kidnapping? Attempted murder?"

"Since I'm the one who dragged you out to murder you, I'll overlook that."

"Thanks a bundle. You don't want to wait until he's about to pitch it out?"

"No! For all I know, the bomb might have a trigger device he can set off while he's holding it, and we'll all go up together. And that isn't the worst of it."

"It gets worse?"

"Yes. In that case, the hydrogen will blow up over London, the airship will descend in one, big, burning mass—"

"I remember. The biggest conflagration since 1666."

"I can't arrest a man until he's broken a law. But if we find the bomb we'll have more than enough reason to arrest him, and charges enough to hold him, while we wear him down with (ahem) interrogations about his organization. And 'She.' Well, I can't stop here chatting. Lugner and I are alone. He'll miss me."

"We have him outnumbered! Overpower him now! Take control of the ship!"

"Not yet. There's no law against a man taking a cruise in his private airship. *I need the bomb.* So long as the bomb remains hidden, where we can neither defuse nor jettison it, Lugner is inviolable."

He opened the vents on his lantern again, making Herron blink again.

"When you find the bomb, Strangways, come to the ladder and get my attention. *Then* we'll overpower the ruffian and seize the ship."

"Leave me the lantern, at least!"

"And let Lugner see a light darting around up here? Besides, there's a flame in it. I'm not going to let you have any fire near all this hydrogen."

With that, Stoker slouched off to the cabin, taking his light with him.

Herron had never felt colder in his life than when he stepped out of the bladder a second time. The airship had gone higher than its initial altitude, and he felt he was about to get hypothermia in his damp clothes.

Slipping off Hawkins's filthy cap, he shoved the cleanest part of it in his mouth to keep his teeth from chattering. That was unnecessary. His teeth would never have been heard over the roar of those engines.

He gazed around the dark. *If I were a bomb, where would I hide?*

And how would he find it? Even if he possessed usable matches, Herron would not have dared igniting one – given the nature of the inflammable air filling the twenty or more ballonets. His search was confined to the merest groping.

It wasn't pleasant. The girders all felt a little clammy from dripping moisture; and he didn't want to touch the goldbeaters' skin any more than he had to.

He walked the length of the superstructure many times, his squishy footsteps drowned by the engines. He climbed up, down and through the network of girders. He reached around the ballonets, feeling for anything bomb-like. Naturally, Herron didn't know a bomb from Adam. Magazine illustrations depicted them as round, black balls. Like Christmas puddings, only with burning fuses shoved in their tops rather than sprigs of holly. Beyond that, he was stumped.

Herron found nothing in the least bit bomb-like. But he'd continue searching, even if it blew up if he touched it wrong.

Herron wasn't much at self-sacrifice. However, his hours alone in the dark water-bladder had given him time to consider all he had heard of what Lady Calthrop, Lugner, and their acolytes had planned. The cold horror was finally sinking in on him. *Or maybe it's these clammy clothes.*

Either way, he was determined to find that bomb and thwart the mission, if it killed him. He'd already died once. After his experience at the pit, he had no more fear of death. He had looked death in the eye, and death had blinked.

He only hoped Angelica had already fled Lady Calthrop's house and had found sanctuary with Inspector Chubb. That way, she was safely out of this mess.

Herron was determined to find and dispose of the bomb, overpower Lugner with Stoker, and turn the airship about so no one in London could get hurt.

He was the first to admit he was no hero, and he was still acting primarily on an impulse for self-protection.

Yet, he did want Angelica Trickett safe. And for her sake, he was determined to thwart this mission and keep London from being bombed.

CHAPTER LXIX

Angelica gloomily shook her head. "Is mine the sort of life that hundreds of men, women and children should die to preserve? I'm only twenty-two. I don't want to die. I've never even known love."

"Neither have I. Just marriage."

"If their lives actually *depended* on my dying – oh, my God, I'd go to the gallows. I won't say I'd die happy at the hands of a hangman. But I'd die if it meant no one else had to. At least, I-I hope my nerve wouldn't fail. But for—Lord! how many people to die! To save me? I couldn't live with that."

"You don't have a choice, Miss. Nor me. It's all up to the airship."

"Then . . . Inspector?"

"Yes, Miss?"

"If it does come to it . . . will you arrest me?"

Chubb was silent for several long moments. Then, "Yes."

"Thank you. I'd rather it was a friend. On my first arrest."

"Even if the airship does appear and we have a bombing outrage, you may have to answer a few touchy questions."

"I'm beyond humiliation. But it is so horrible. How will I live with myself?"

"The same way most everybody else does, Miss: one day at a time. As it stands, our blessed Lady Calthrop will receive a glowing obituary in the

Times, and anyone who reads it will be touched, I'm sure, by the violence of her passing. But if we can't stop this airship her obituary will hardly be noticed."

Angelica stared hard into her coffee cup, like she was trying to see the future in it. Merridew refreshed the coffee and she gave him a thank-you smile, but she didn't touch it right away. This was the worst she'd felt since her father died.

Chubb watched her for about a minute – then slapped a fist into the palm of his hand. "If that airship doesn't come—well, the police got a theory, don't they?"

"I beg your pardon, Inspector?"

"They believe it was burglars, right? Well, let 'em. Oh, if they do tumble onto any hard evidence against you, I can't shield you. I won't obstruct 'em. But I won't volunteer any information, and neither will Pottle. Right, Pottle?"

Pottle raised his face from the biscuits long enough to second that statement. Then he dived back in.

"That's very kind," said Angelica. "But—?"

"—but if this butler fellow lives, he may do you down just for vengeance.

Tell me, Miss, did you know Lady Calthrop well?"

"Not at all, apparently! When she looked at me . . . Oh, God! I've never seen hate – genuine hate – actually distorting a person's features until this morning."

"That sort o' hate ain't pretty, Miss. And it makes my job a lot worse."

"I hope I never see that much hate again. And I pray earnestly to my Savior I never feel that level of hate, ever, in all my life. What a horrible way to live. It makes you pity someone who can hate that way."

Chubb was noncommittal on that. "How long did you know Lady Calthrop?"

Angelica had just shoved her hand over her mouth, pushing yet another yawn back down, so she had to pause before replying.

"We met for the first time at her daughter's funeral."

"You read about her death in the papers?"

"No, I never read the papers. My brother's a journalist – a job rather than a vocation – and he advised me that there's never anything in the papers I need to know for a happy life. Lady Calthrop sent me a card, informing me that I was her daughter's only friend I might want to know she had passed away."

"What was she like? The daughter?"

"Oh, a pitiable, mousy creature – as you can well imagine, with such a mother! Shy and dark and with freckles like a sprinkling of pepper. She looked up to me. The other girls laughed at both of us. I was poor, and I shot up to be the tallest girl in the school, and gawky with it. But the other girls were all a little in awe of me, so they didn't actually bully me or laugh in my face. She was rich, but her hair and posture and figure were hopeless and she didn't know how to fight. They bullied her and I stuck up for her. Young people who feel like they're the left-over odds-and-ends fall together into their own cliques. Yet—though I'm ashamed to admit it—I looked on her like a mascot I let tag along with me."

"It didn't hurt for an attractive young lady who felt awkward with herself for being tall, to have a sidekick others could compare her favorably to in looks."

"Maybe. I feel so sorry for her now."

"Because she's dead?"

"That's part of it. After learning what her mother was, I wonder if I was the only person who ever showed her *any* sort of affection. Maybe I was given a chance to help someone—and I failed. She needed a better friend than I. But I knew her parents were big pots, so I didn't feel too much sympathy for her.

"We can be terribly unfair to the rich, can't we, Inspector? They say there's one justice for the poor and another for the rich. But there's also a prejudice against the rich we tend to overlook. There's a tendency to think whatever their struggles and heartbreak, the rich can always find solace in cold sacks of gold."

"I wish I had a cold sack-full, to ease mine."

"My parents struggled in their last years. My Oxford-educated brother makes ends meet in a job he despises. After school, I was looking forward to a life of scrimping by on a pittance from a rotten typing job, unless I had success in my writing or I married out of my class. So I didn't feel much sympathy for the sole heir of wealthy parents. Yes, she was ugly, but she would never have to do a stroke of work in her life. I don't suppose this is making a lot of sense to you?"

Chubb stolidly declined to answer. He was long accustomed to letting people run off at the mouth, while patiently listening for anything incriminating.

"Inspector, did you ever have a close friend you never particularly liked?"

"All of 'em, I think."

"She was probably crying out for love, but I was bigger and prettier and could write better than any girl in the school, so I was high-handed and patronizing to a rich girl. Then, after my school-days, when I went home to Bristol and worked for a typewriting agency in an airless room with fifty other sweating girls, I never gave her another thought until I got her mother's card. Her mother said she worshipped me. Maybe she did. Because I was . . . kind to her."

Yet, Angelica shivered, thinking of that girl spying on her in intimate moments. Drugging her, stripping her, and reporting Angelica's most personal details home to interest her mother – and (Angelica realized with revulsion) her father. Had Lord Calthrop listened to his daughter's description of Angelica's smoothly contoured naked body with a less than scientific detachment?

"Why did you work for the mother?"

"A few weeks after the funeral, Lady Calthrop invited me into her home as a paid companion. I saw an opportunity plumped down in my lap."

"To take her daughter's place?"

"Dear God, I hope not. It's sickening enough, as it turns out. I thought she was just a well-meaning if cranky lady whose family had all died and who needed someone in her home who wasn't quite a servant. And, she decided to reward me for befriending her daughter. It was like a story. Too much like, in retrospect."

"How were you treated? Like part of the staff, or one of the family?"

"In-between."

"Did you eat with the staff?"

"I usually dined with Lady Calthrop. She liked to have someone to talk at. And she showed me off at dinner parties. On the few occasions she went out without me, or had visitors she didn't want me to meet for whatever reason, I dined alone in my room. Or, rather, with a good book. One is never absolutely alone or lonely with a good book."

"But you've got to close the book some time. Ever get lonely?"

"My brother is years older than I and we were only siblings. My father died when I was twelve and my mother when I was at school. I had few friends at school. Most of the girls went around in twos. I went around in ones. Then I met Lady Calthrop's daughter. I'm told she worshipped me. I don't care for being worshipped. It was just another way of setting me apart, so I was lonely even when I did have a friend. My first job was in a room full of typewriter noise, and a supervisor who made sure we girls didn't waste time talking. Now I'm living in a strange town where I know no one and no one knows me – except my brother. I aspire to being a writer, which means I aspire to spending long days in an airless room with only a typewriter for company. Loneliness is my lifestyle."

"Were you ever curious about why you were sent to your room?"

Angelica managed a winsome smile. "I was always curious."

"But you was too well-bred to listen at doors and rifle through drawers."

"Until this morning. I had no reason to. If you can tell me, Inspector, do you have anything on your charge sheets about Her Ladyship? Or Dapifer?"

"Not . . . as such. No actual charges against them."

"You have looked them up, then? Why?"

"M'lord and lady were a rum couple. Lord Calthrop offered to endow a zoo in New Orleans, U.S.A. They turned him down because he insisted on putting an Esquimau human being in a cage as one of the exhibits, as well as a pygmie."

"How horrible! He sounds beastly. I'm glad I never met him."

"Did you like Lady Calthrop?"

"Not particularly."

"Why did you stay on?"

Angelica peered up at him with one eye hidden by her tangled coiffure. "I was well-compensated for light duties. I never new want, or cold, or uncleanness."

Except from Doris, she silently added.

"What about errands? Didn't she send you to stores to buy stuff?"

"Always on credit. When she sent me on errands requiring money, she rigorously counted the change, down to the last ha'penny."

"Didn't she trust you?"

"I don't know. I think she was an old skinflint."

"But you was took care of."

"I had a full wardrobe. I had as many meals as I wanted, with excellent cuisine. Cook was ornery, but she knew her job. I had hot running water and I never again had to use a tin bath half-filled with pump-water heated lukewarm on a wood stove. I had a sound – if limited – library. I was pampered. Within margins, she let me speak my mind. Yet, she always meant to keep me afraid of her. We're all naturally afraid of invalids, anyway, handling them like they were made of glass. She scolded me, often unfairly, and upbraided me with cutting sarcasm. I kept telling myself it was making me stronger to stomach her hot air and turns of ill-temper. Otherwise, the job was not too arduous. So I stayed."

"Would it surprise you to learn that there has been, all along, some suspicion that Lady Calthrop was concerned in her daughter's death?"

"Nothing would surprise me today. I thought it was a riding accident."

"A poisoned dart from a blow-gun can cause a riding accident, either on the horse's part or the rider's. If we had noticed them darts earlier—!"

Angelica could see where Lady Calthrop might have considered her own daughter an unfit "specimen" and eliminated for the hygiene of the species.

"So," Chubb continued, "she probably – though it can't be proved at this remove – killed her own daughter. And, knowing all about you—"

Too much about me, thought Angelica,

"—invited you to the funeral."

"It wasn't really an invitation, just a notice of death thanking me for the 'kindness' I had shown her daughter. And I was vain enough to believe it."

"But she knowed you'd go to pay your respects because you're the sort of person that would. So, she met you and lured you into her home – a widow lady, just lost a daughter—and so bloomin' rich. You was unattached and might want a job with lots of benefits and nominal work."

"Just, no money. One of the richest women in London never gave me a—"

"No, she wasn't."

"Wasn't what?"

"Wasn't rich. I looked into her affairs at the time of her daughter's death."

"Why?"

"I was suspicious. Once a person gets away with doing a thing, they think they've out-clevered everyone. Having done it successfully once, they'll do it again the same way, thinking they'll have the same result. They always go back to the well once too often. Her Ladyship was nearly skint, even then."

"Skint? You mean . . . bankrupt?"

"Friends ponied up for her daughter's funeral. No wonder she counted the change when she ever gave you any. Every penny counted."

"She was rich as Croesus! Where did it all go?"

"Airships cost money, I suppose. I'm surprised she wasn't in the poorhouse."

"She might have liquidated her house."

"She only has a life interest in it. It reverts to her husband's family after her death. She lived on tick. But she had just enough credit in her reputation to keep you so pampered you wouldn't be tempted to look for other work. And she kept you on a short lead so you wouldn't roam off and get married. If it ain't too personal, Miss, why ain't a good-looking lady like you married?"

Angelica had just taken a sip of coffee – which she spewed it back over the rim. *"If it's not too personal?"* she smiled. "Is this a proposal, Inspector?"

"Oh, no. Missus Chubb would have a word to say about that! It's the job. Asking in-time-ite questions out loud has got to be a habit."

"Frankly – I suppose there are many reasons. One, I'm tall. Women like taller men, and I'm no different! That lets out quite a percentage of the population as potential husbands."

"You and me, for instance, would look funny amblin' down the aisle."

"I'm too well-educated and refined to marry lower than my station . . . and I *won't* marry anyone in my 'station' –he'd be as bereft as I am. We'd have to live on something! I've no dowry, and no rich uncle in Madiera who'll leave it all to me if he breaks his neck in a steeplechase. I've only a few pounds to my name."

"That leaves your marrying someone rich."

"And I won't be called a fortune-hunter! So even if a Herron Strangways swanked in here we fell in love and he proposed, I'd refuse him!"

"Even if you loved him?"

Raising her cup to her lips, Angelica nodded.

"You *can't* marry someone poor and *won't* marry someone rich."

"That's not all. I . . . I don't know if you understand this, but want to stand on my own two feet. I want to write, Inspector. I want to chip out a niche in the world and be able to point to it and say, *this is mine*, even if it's not overly lucrative. I thought I was working toward that. I wasn't. I was hardly working at all. I fell prey to luxury, and became just another animal in Her Ladyship's menagerie – like Lord Calthrop's poor Esquimau. I might have ended up like the flowers Lady Calthrop has on coldly scientific slides."

And here, she thought to herself, *we see Angelica Trickett with her gently sloping, but rounded and pertly tip-tilted breasts.*

"And, of course," she continued aloud, "while I was in her house, I could not receive callers; so I never encouraged any. In fact, I never met anyone the whole time I've been in London, outside of my brother's small circle."

"And you didn't like none o' them?"

"Not much to choose from."

She knit her brow, thinking. Her face, with its elastic lips and unmarked brow that could produce many come-and-go wrinkles, was beautifully expressive.

"And then . . . this might sound jolly strange to you, Inspector—"

"After what I've heard these last three days? I doubt it."

"—but my parents were happily married."

"Mine were happily separated. So?"

"They had an ideal relationship. Not overly passionate, but loving on both sides. They actually *liked* each other, to begin with. Then they respected each other. Finally, they loved each other enough to marry. And they were both bound and determined they were *going* to love each other and *make* their marriage work *whatever* happened. Every married couple takes vows, my folks meant to keep them. For love really is a decision, isn't it, rather than an emotion? Or we wouldn't be told to love our neighbors – and our enemies."

"Who are generally the same folks."

"I suppose I've always been afraid I'd never find such an ideal – not with the insipid variety of men in my generation. Overall, I suppose you could say I was particular. Though I was in no position to be so, socially or financially."

Only physically, she thought. *And how long does that last? There's only one way to make a living off that, and I'll die before I resort to it.*

"Sorry if I've offended you with my questions. That's what the police is for."

"I just don't know whether to pray the airship materializes or not. If only we knew where it's heading!" She raised her cup again, hoping another shot of coffee was just what she needed for her mind to get into full steam.

"And then – what?"

After her sip, she said over the rim, "Send a message to evacuate."

He nodded. "But where? That's what's eatin' at me. We can evacuate one spot, but what's too keep them from pitching out their bomb elsewhere? Like I said before, we can't evacuate all London. All the Queen's hosses and all the Queen's men – and all the queen's field artillery – can't stop an airship that's already aloft. They want to kill people. If there ain't no people where they want to kill 'em, they'll kill 'em somewheres else. And we've no time left to find out!"

"The Procession doesn't start until nine."

"It's goin' on nine now."

"Is it?" She yawned, then said "The Queen won't leave the palace until eleven fifteen, according to the paper. We've time to go to Buckingham Palace—"

"If she's their target, we might be able to push our way through the crowds around Buckingham Palace in two hours to deliver a warning. But you won't stop the Queen coming out. What if we did get an audience with her – and she believed every blinkin' word we say? Which ain't likely. She'd want to show the world the Crown won't be intimidated. She'll never give in to blackmail. And quite right, too. Do you know, that Gracious Lady has been shot at seven times when she was out in open carriages? She's been shot at more than any sovereign in history, including Lincoln – and he had a war on. These days the favorite weapon of assassins is dynamite, but even if we told her they meant to blow her up, she still wouldn't stop the parade. Anyhow, no one's probably going to believe it until they see this airship – and maybe not even then."

"So . . . what can we do?"

"Well . . . maybe we can evacuate a spot. But to do that we got to know where that spot is. And I don't see how any place you mentioned has any bearin' on that message Mister Strangways brought you. Not as you stated it to me."

"Maybe it's not there."

"That man died gettin' that paper to you."

She frowned. That's what Herron Strangways had told her, too.

"If a feller's going to risk his life trying to deliver a clan-des-tine message givin' all the facts, I don't see how he can leave off the most vital fact of the lot."

"What about *King o'er the Water*?"

"Until it don't materialize, I'll accept your *airship* and your *infernal machine*. All the rest is supposition. A Latin word? A line of gobbledegook you can't understand unless you type it wrong? And I have to take you at your word for every inch of it, since I never saw the message."

"Did Lady Calthrop really have a hope of being Queen?"

"With an airship, these folks can hold the entire country for ransom while they threatened more outrages. 'You saw what we did on the twenty-second of June and we'll do worse if you don't give up the throne.' If they have more than one airship, and powerful bombs, they'll be able dictate whatever terms they want."

"I wonder what makes people want to blow other people up in peacetime?"

"Everyone wants to blow up somebody, Miss. Why are you smiling?"

"My brother once took me to a play by Gilbert and Sullivan – Schuyler is a Gilbert and Sullivan addict. It was this thing about an island kingdom governed by a monarchy tempered by dynamite. The monarchy was absolute – but it was written in their Constitution that if the monarch ever grew too imperious it was the duty of the 'Public Exploder' to blow him up."

Chubb didn't crack a smile. "And you find that amusing, Miss?"

Very quietly, "Within its context."

Chubb was in no mental condition see the humor in exploding a monarch. "Say – what was that Latin word again?"

By this time, all Angelica's hysteria was fully replaced by lassitude. She spoke lethargically. "*Resurgam*," she repeated.

"You're sure that's Latin?"

"It was in a Latin dictionary. I have to rely on Mister Strangways' pronunciation. My French isn't bad and I might manage a snootful of German under torture, but I don't know dead languages."

"So I'm gettin' it third-hand. Maybe there's a clue in the letters, like – what's them words made up of letters?"

His description was vague. Angelica guessed at his meaning. "An acronym?"

"Yeah. Write it down for me."

"I'll write it in the top margin of the newspaper. That way I won't have to say it again. And I'll do the last bit, too."

"I thought you couldn't remember them nonsense words?"

"I know typing well enough to reproduce it. Give me a moment to brood."

More than ever, Angela regretted losing the typescript of the message. In her exhausted state, she felt barely capable of holding a pencil. She told Merridew the coffee smelled welcoming, and he refreshed her cup again. She was going to need it if she meant to reproduce a typewriter keyboard.

She was sitting back in her chair, so she wrote the Latin word on the newspaper's top margin at arm's length. Just in case in might be an acronymn, she wrote it in all capital letters.

Chubb, meanwhile, was scrutinizing the map over her shoulder.

"Just now," the Inspector said, half-consciously, "with the Jubilee on, London's full of folks from all over the empire. And foreigners. Americans!" He said this last word as if he'd just bitten into a bitter nut.

Angelica smiled wryly. "You don't like Americans, Inspector?"

"Lets just say I ain't forgiven 'em. And a bombing where foreigners are killed might be what they call an 'international in-side-ent—'"

Chubb's vituperative rage at Americans choked to a halt. His eye had lit, for the first time, on the word Angelica had only said before.

RESURGAM

He snapped his fingers. "Sweet Mother of Pearl!"

"Inspector?" Angelica sat up quickly from her slouch. "What's wrong."

"I wish I'd made you write it out first thing, Miss, and we wouldn't've wasted so much mornin'! We might've been on the road hours ago. I don't know all them old languages to hear 'em, but I know a writ word when I see it."

"Do you recognize this, then?"

"Yep! And I know where they're going to drop the bomb, too – and when! If you'd got around town more, you'd know. Hurry, we got to get there—fast!"

CHAPTER LXX

As a last resort, Herron fished about in all the bladders of water ballast, wetting himself down again. The bomb just might be in a watertight container.

He splashed about in the water bladders (with the sound covered by the constant drone of engines) and each time he came up empty.

Not knowing what else to do, he squished to the hatch and squatted on the edge, his shiveringly trying to attract Stoker's attention by waving.

"I have been unable to contact 'She.'" Lugner was saying, closing the wicker box containing the wireless telegraph. "I have telegraphed repeatedly that we are aloft, and have received no reply. I will try again later. I do not want to overuse the transmitter and waste the battery."

Taking the lantern, Lugner marched over to the ladder and laid a hand on a rung, singing an old Jacobite song that really required a Scottish accent:

"I may sit in my wee croo hoose,
Wi' my rick and my reel tae toil, fu' dreary,
And I may think on the day that's gane,
And I will sigh and sab till I am weary,
I ne'er could brook, I ne'er could brook,
A foreign look tae own or flatter,

> *But I will sing a ranting' sang*
> *That day oor King comes o'er the water . . ."*

Herron remained motionless. The inside of the envelope might be dark, but with Lugner directly beneath him Herron's slightest movement might betray him.

He was trapped. The constant noise of the engines would cover his footfalls, but Herron doubted he could run effectively in Hawkins's shoes. They were too wide for his feet, and protracted submersion in water had not served them well.

And . . . where was there to run to? Since the ship had been stripped down to essentials, hiding places were scarce. And he had no chance to get away if Lugner flashing a lantern all over the place!

Knowing there was a stowaway loose frantically searching for the bomb, Stoker tried to keep Lugner from climbing the ladder. "Where are you going?"

"Just to take a last look round the ship that served us so well."

"Don't be sentimental. You can't leave the wheel!"

"Do not worry about it, from now on. It—what's that!"

Lugner's head twisted abruptly to the ladder. He had removed his gauntlets to operate the wireless transmitter, and a drop of water had plashed onto the back of his naked hand. He looked up.

With no time to spring away, and nowhere to go if he did, Herron merely waggled his fingers at Lugner with a sickly genial smile.

"Hawkins! Why are you here! No—not Hawkins! *Mein Nieren!* Strankface!"

Lugner fumbled at the buttons on his greatcoat and plunged a hand inside. Unbuckling the flap on his holster, he drew his gun. It wasn't fancy. Dark metal with a metal loop on the end, dark wood grips, and a barrel of about seven inches. But however ugly it was, it shot real bullets.

While Lugner was engaged in extracting his weapon, Stoker merely reached into his inside coat pocket and produced his own revolver, which was slightly longer than Lugner's in the barrel and had ivory grips on a wooden handle.

Catching this movement in the corner of his eye, Lugner spun his body half-around and aimed at Stoker rather than Herron.

In response, Stoker aimed his pistol *straight up*, toward the envelope – and the hydrogen ballonets directly overhead.

"Drop the gun," Stoker bellowed, "or I'll fire a hot bullet through your gas!"

Lugner smiled, as he might have at a child who had made a foolish remark.

"Herr Stoker, shooting hole in the bag will merely release the gas. Hydrogen is most volatile when mixed with oxygen. That is why we never valve it off in a thunderstorm. Even with a leak, you must have a direct source of inflamation. A bullet will not ignite it, whatever its temperature. You need a fire."

"Strangways! Do you still have your matches?"

Herron was about to say they were damp and flaccid; then he realized Stoker was bluffing. "Oh yes. Right here. Oodles of them."

"One's all you need to blow us all to hell. Have it ready. One of the ballonets is about to be have a hole in it."

"Right. I've drawn a match, Lugner. One false move and I swear I'll strike it!" It didn't sound like much of a threat, but it was the best he could offer. "Y-you're certain, *mein herr*—" Herron started, with a slight, nervous cough, "—that a bullet alone won't blow us all sky-higher?"

Keeping his pistol aimed at Stoker's face, Lugner slowly shook his head. To Stoker, "I am prepared to die for my cause! Are you?"

"Yes," rapped Stoker. "If I'm sure we'll take you with us."

"Wait!" Herron called through the trap. "Don't I get a say?"

Stoker and Lugner snapped their heads up at him, shouting "NO!" in unison.

"Then at least give me time to dream up something to die for! I came out a little short of causes this morning."

"Think of that girl of yours," said Stoker. "If we explode before we reach London, we'll have thwarted Lugner, and she'll live happily ever after."

Herron immediately spotted a flaw. "It won't do me a lot of good."

"Strangways, I'm going to fire! Stand back!"

"L-let's not be rash—"

The blast from Stoker's gun in the small, metal cabin was so loud Herron thought the whole airship had exploded despite Lugner's promise to the contrary. He threw himself back and clung to the catwalk, as if it would keep him from being blown to atoms.

The bullet smashed through the ceiling of the cabin, pierced the envelope, and punctured one of the ballonets.

Nothing happened. The only damage Stoker's bullet had done was to the ceiling of the car, and to their eardrums.

Deafened by the roar even at his perch above the car, Herron slowly peeked over the edge of the hatch.

Lowering his arm, Stoker aimed his pistol at Lugner. Their gun barrels, held at arm's length, were mere inches apart.

Herron wondered why Lugner hadn't fired. It had been a perfect opportunity to blow off Stoker's repellent toothbrush moustache, leaving him alone with an unarmed Strangways. And why hadn't Stoker shot Lugner in the first place?

Then he understood! Stoker didn't want to kill the airship pilot unless he had to, since he couldn't steer the airship.

By the same token, Lugner needed Stoker – to operate the glider.

Though they were threatening each other, and making professions of sacrifice, neither man was so reckless of his own safety as he pretended.

He could barely see Stoker, but Lugner was still almost directly below him. Taking out three days' worth of aggravation, he leapt down onto Lugner's back and wrested him to the floor (meticulously avoiding the point on the pickelhaube).

Lugner's fingers clenched when Herron struck him. His gun went off, missing Stoker's head by inches and shattering a pane of glass in the front window.

Lugner's elbow hit the floor, jarring his hand open. His gun squiggled away.

With Herron, Stoker and Lugner grabbing it, the pistol caromed off the ship's wheel, made a bank shot in the corner and, slithering between three pairs of hands, slipped out the open doorway of the car.

"That was a stupid thing to do!" Stoker shouted, as he and Herron shook the airship pilot to his feet between them. "I might have been killed."

Herron shrugged. "That was a chance I was willing to take."

While they were holding him, Stoker shoved his pistol up beneath Lugner's jaw. "Check, I think?"

"But," answered Lugner, "not 'mate.'"

Stoker pushed Lugner brusquely to the wheel "Take us down. Slow."

"No."

Herron had a sense he's seen this before. Stoker had his pistol aimed between the pilot's shoulder blades. But if Lugner adamantly refused to take the wheel, Herron didn't see how shooting him improved their circumstances.

Stoker clarified the situation. "I don't care if you do or not. All we need is the bomb. If you don't tell me where it is, I'll shoot you and Strangways and I will find it, or we'll get this craft down somehow. Once we dispose of the bomb, whether you are dead or alive, your mission is over. If we can't get the airship safely on the ground, Strangways and I will take the glider down leave you in a flying mausoleum. But if you tell us where the bomb is and turn Queen's evidence, it'll go easier for you. It's up to you. Where's the bomb?"

Lugner turned, his smile becoming supercilious. "You do not yet know?"

"Uh-oh." Herron frowned. "Er . . . just a thought . . . Who was Darnley?"

Stoker snarled, "Who?"

"Darnley! Chap whose name is on the nose of this behemoth. You knew all that history and don't know the Darnley? Lived in the time of Elizabeth."

Stoker shook his head. "I told you, the eighteenth century is my speciality. Mostly after the Commonwealth."

Herron rolled his eyes. "Demarcation in history, now. That's the way to insure everyone knows just enough to remain ignorant. I recognized the name the moment I saw it, but its importance escaped me. It's all coming back to me."

"Well? What about him?"

"Let me double-check. Just answer yes or no, *Mein herr*. Who was Darnley?"

Lugner smile was almost unbearable. "Henry Stuart, whose English title was Lord Darnley. He was the husband of Mary, Queen of Scots, titled Duke of Albany upon their marriage. He was progenitor of the Stuart kings."

"Oh. Right. That's what I was afraid of. Thanks awfully, don't y'know."

"So what?" demanded Stoker.

"Here's what," Herron answered. "The story of Darnley is one of those few historical tidbits that really delight a schoolboy who hates history. Mary Queen of Scots, you see, married this Henry Stuart chap after a whirlwind courtship. Well, you know, 'Marry in haste, repent in leisure.' She soon found him a vapid, boring chap. And since they were Catholics, divorce was *verboten*. That only left murder. So, probably on her instructions, some of her people *tried to blow him up by filling the cellar of his house with gunpowder.*"

Stoker's mood became somber. "Is that so?"

"I have this unhappy feeling, friend Stoker . . . that we *are* the bomb."

CHAPTER LXXI

Stoker nodded, slowly comprehending. "That's why we didn't find a bomb. No doubt explosives are hidden in one of the ballonets. If it's timed to released oxygen as it detonates—"

"*Ka-boom.*"

"That hardly expresses the explosive power of one million and a half cubic feet of hydrogen held in twenty ballonets."

One reason Herron had lingered in London, rather than taking an extended tour of the continent to escape the Jubilee, was because he looked forward to the fireworks displays.

He loved fireworks. Now he looked likely to be a big one.

"Not just exploding hydrogen," Stoker continued. "Aluminium shrapnel. And what's left of the metal be thirty to forty burning tons crashing down on the city. And the fuel! Of course! No wonder we're stocked with a full complement of petrol! If we explode over any part of London, it will be the worst man-made disaster in history. We need only fly low over some great building or over a crowd! Even if they shoot bullets at us at a low altitude, we've proven that won't harm us. We've been thinking too small, Strangways. That must be what your 'haggard bird' discovered Saturday! That's why he was in such a hurry to reach his people, even at the risk of his life. This will be the worst man-made disaster in history. Ghenghis Khan and Atilla together never imagined the like."

Lugner never heard of Wonderland, but he was smiling like the Cheshire Cat. Stoker's guesses were all too obviously correct.

"Crowded as London is," Stoker concluded, "we may be talking about hundreds of thousands dead, not just from explosions and panic, but petrol spreading an unquenchable fire."

"And we're in the bally beating heart of it!" Herron pointed out.

"Forget that!"

"You forget it! You worry about hundreds of thousands. I'm only concerned about one! Me!"

"Why don't you join Lugner's folk, then? You'd fit right in with their *Wolfahrtsstaat*. 'Everything's fine, 'cause I've got mine!'"

Herron started to argue, but Stoker shushed him.

"We're safe, now, Strangways. We control the ship! We're thwarting them in the act. We've caught them red-handed! Ha! It's better than I ever hoped. All we have to do is make sure this airship doesn't go anywhere near London!"

Grabbing the shoulder epaulet of Lugner's greatcoat, Stoker forced him to the wheel again. "Steer us away from London or die!"

"No."

Throwing Lugner back against the wall again, Stoker thrust his pistol into Herron's hands. "You know how to use this?"

"I'm told I'm not Wyatt Earp, but I can 'plug the varmint' at this distance."

Lugner sneered, "I think you have not the *darmen* to shoot an unarmed man."

"I never have done, but there's a first time for everything. In any case – if you cherish your kneecaps, you just keep still. I've had a hard three days— *Ahhh-choo*! And on top all that, I think I'm getting a cold. So I'm not in the merriest of moods."

"I'll take the wheel," Stoker said. "If he blinks, put a bullet in him."

"I thought you couldn't drive this thing."

"It should be simple enough to turn it around and find a farm or a lake to blow up in." Stoker tried turn the ship's wheel. After several tugs, even pushing down on it with all his strength, he found it wouldn't budge.

"What did you do with it?" he demanded, shaking the wheel. "It's locked!"

"Yes. It is locked," Lugner agreed.

"Unlock it!"

"It has nothing to do with me. It was programmed to lock."

"What do you mean? How were you going steer it down over the Queen or whatever you meant to blow up?"

"This point was where I meant to disembark with you in the glider."

"Don't lie to me! This ship can't steer itself!" He shot a quizzical glance at Herron, who shrugged. "Can it?"

Lugner's smile became so unbearably smug, Herron was tempted to shoot it off on general principles.

"I was to fly it so far – then it was to fly itself. There is no way to halt the ship, or turn it about. It is on a preset course."

"That's impossible!" But Stoker's *possible* trickled weakly to inaudibility.

Herron muttered, "I doubt I'll ever say that again. Tell us all about it, Lugner. But remember, I still have this thing pointed at you. I may not be the world's best shot, but at this range I'll hit something. And believe me, pal, it'll smart."

Lugner asked, "Did you ever hear of a man named Tesla?"

Stoker and Herron both shook their heads.

"He was a Serb – but clever, of his type. Tesla invented the Tesla coil—"

"Sounds like an exotic dance," Herron broke in.

"Shut up and let the man talk, Strangways," demanded Stoker, "if you want to know why you are about to die! Go on, Lugner."

"The 'Tesla Coil' is the basis of what they are calling 'radio control.'"

"Ah." Herron brightened up.

Lugner shot him a glance. "You have heard of it?"

"Certainly not."

For his part, Stoker saw what Lugner was hinting at. "It must be like the pulses in the generator that operates the wireless telegraph."

Lugner gave a single nod in Stoker's direction. "Five years ago, this man Tesla operated a toy boat at a distance, by radio waves. He claimed that it had a range of up to 25 miles. We thought, if a mere Serb can operate a small boat, we may operate a big airship. We could. We are being guided from London. And we are within twenty-five miles of our target. At this point, the ship's wheel was programmed to lock. We can not deviate from our present course."

Herron scratched his head. "Doesn't this Tesla chap have a patent?"

"Strangways," Stoker, broke in, exasperated, "these people are trying to kill and maim thousands of innocent people and terrorize millions more and burn down a city in order to usurp a throne by bloody terrorist blackmail. They're not much concerned about jumping a patent claim or two. Well, if we can't stop the ship, it's imperative we get to the bomb, which must be on a timer"

"Can't we go up and cut through the ballonets and find it?" asked Herron.

"Be my guests! Cut all the ballonets open. Fill the envelope with hydrogen. Try holding your breath long enough to find the bomb before it explodes. You'll be just as dead, but your death will be more protracted and painful than if it went off in your hands. There's only one way to handle this."

Taking the pistol from Herron, Stoker ostentatiously cocked it and aimed it between Lugner's eyes. "This relieves us of one worry. If you can no longer fly the airship, your life is expendable. Good-bye, Lugner. I hated knowing you."

"What's this?" asked Herron, excitedly. "What's this?"

"I can kill him, now. You and I can take the glider and warn London by telegraph to evacuate the target. There must be a post office in a village with a telegraph nearby wherever we land, this close to London!"

Herron perked up when Stoker mentioned taking off in the glider. Sticking his fingers in his ears, he leaned away from Lugner, waiting for the shot.

Addressing Lugner, Stoker said, "You know I have the *darmen* to shoot you in cold blood. Tell me right now—what's the target!"

A tense pause ensued, while Stoker waited for an answer.

Without lowering his smile even to half-staff, the pilot shook his head.

Stoker lowered his revolver. "You're right . . .You won't tell us any better with a bullet in your brain." He pocketed the pistol. "We'll try another method of getting the information out of you. And you'll wish I had blown your head off."

Rising nervously from his crouch, Herron removed his fingers from his ears and wondered, "W-what are you going to do?"

"You and I are going to make 'friend Lugner' tell us where we're heading. We know whatever is guiding us must be in a specific place. It's like the wireless telegraph – for it to function, it requires two sets, one to *send* and the other to *receive*. We must learn where that place is we are being drawn. Then we descend in the glider and find a telegraph office or a telephone. Lugner won't tell us the place of his own volition, so we will *coax* the information out of him."

Lugner maintained a superior smile. "Why not throw out a note in a bottle? A farm hand may find it, snap his fingers and say, 'I must stop the Queen's Diamond Jubilee Parade.' He can ride his plough-mule to Buckingham Palace, no?"

"I can telegraph to certain friends in Whitehall who will listen to me. The people I work for in London can find and destroy the device." He took a glance at the watch he reeled from his pocket. "Parade's already in full swing. And no one ever needs to know any of this happened."

"Except," Lugner answered, "my associates have already cut lines, or otherwise interfered with, all the telegraph offices in London."

"I don't believe you!" said Stoker – but his voice wasn't confident and the sentence drizzled to an ignominious mumble.

"And the National Telephone Company and other exchanges. Do you think we built one small airship to kill a few undesirables? This is a revolution. We own all lines of communication."

CHAPTER LXXII

The full panoply of the Procession was more colorful than anything London had ever seen – even in the middle ages, when colorful spectacles were closer to the hearts of men than in these drab, post-industrial days.

By the technologically advanced year of 1897, men and women had forgotten how to live spectacularly. Their lives were full of newspapers, printed books, Music Halls, barrel organs, bicycles and typewriters. Upright pianos stood in nearly every middle class home. Prices for Edison's phonographs and Bell's gramophones were high, for they did not yet have many uses other than dictation; but their prices were dropping as they became more popular.

With all this, ordinary people were losing the sense of self-made entertainment. They were becoming passive and drab even in the pursuit of their leisure.

The Medieval Londoner – whose nights, before gas lighting, were full of abject terror from man and beast and ghoul and whose only sewers were the streets – understood how to create spectacular pomp. Grandeur and beauty were becoming inconceivable to the modern, dark-suited, bowler-hatted bureaucratic mind.

The Queen's Diamond Jubilee Procession on Tuesday, June 22, 1897 changed all that. It was as colorful as a sunlit river of red and gold, mixed with a twinking of blues, greens, browns, tans and white.

Diamond Jubilee this might be, but gold shone everywhere. Uniforms were white-and-gold; red-and-gold; violet-and-gold, blue-and-gold. Gold buttons, gold braid, gold epaulettes, gold piping – gold badges, medals, stars and stripes.

Forty six thousand, nine hundred and forty three military men had bivouacked in and around London, to appear in the Procession or in the street-lining parties.

More soldiers, sailors and marines were in London than had ever collected there at one time in human history. The Romans had seen nothing like it, nor had the iron-plated warriors of the middle ages.

Every detachment in the parade had a distinctly colorful uniform. Scarlet was the conventional color for many British army uniforms; but some, like the Malay States Guides, a regiment raised only the year before, were set off by pagris colored emerald and yellow, and had green collars on their blood-red tunics. Khaki was also a popular color for uniforms, but the North Borneo Police set their khaki uniforms off with red pillbox caps.

Had their intention been mutiny, the multi-racial force would have numbered enough to seize and hold the capital of the Empire indefinitely.

2

Despite its extravagance, the Diamond Jubilee was not officially a state occasion. Ten years earlier, the festivities of the Golden Jubilee had set back the royal family alone fifty-thousand pounds; and the queen wasn't about to be stuck with the bill this time. If she had to celebrated her sexagenarian year on the throne, she wanted as much of it as possible to be voluntarily donated.

The garlands, signs, festoons and flags decorating every street were not erected by state fiat, but by individuals, alone or in groups, in the spirit of celebration.

It wasn't just the price-tag that discouraged Her Majesty. A full-steam-ahead State occasion meant the Queen would have to issue invitations to every smarmy head of state in the world to swarm unctuously around her. This way, the Queen didn't have to invite anyone who raised her hackles.

For instance, she stiffed Kaiser Wilhelm of Germany – her eldest grandson.

The first of Queen Victoria's nine children, also named Victoria (called Vickie by the family), had married the Crown Prince of Germany, who became Emperor Friedrich III. On that his death in '88, their son Willy became Kaiser Wilhelm II.

The Kaiser was a big bug in Europe. Grandson or no, Willy had a way of setting the Her Majesty's teeth on edge.

Part of this was his sheer flamboyance. A decade earlier, when Willy was still merely a Prince, he had attended the Queen's Golden Jubilee – and made an attempt to upstage *Großmutter* by wearing a stark white military uniform and a gold helmet topped by a gold eagle. As Kaiser, there was no guessing what shenanigans Willy might pull to try to steal the limelight.

Chafing on the continent this Tuesday morning, the Kaiser was soon to learn he was one of the few members of the Queen's close family who not in danger of being blown up in a massive hydrogen explosion.

Despite snubbing the Kaiser, Queen Victoria believed in bringing people together – and, as much as possible, bringing them together as family. From Britain in the Atlantic to the Pacific coast of Russia, nearly every crowned head in Europe was, by blood or by marriage, woven into an intricate web of kinship, with Queen Victoria sitting in the middle like a pudgy spider.

This was her way of trying to make war in Europe impossible: Peace through families. After all, families never fought, did they?

Actually, Her Majesty feared that if the ties of blood she had bound around Europe could not, ultimately, stave off a catastrophic European War, it would probably be Willy who started the snowball rolling.

3

If actual heads of state were few, lesser royalty from around the world took part in the Procession in large numbers – at Her Majesty's gracious invitation.

The Procession was chock-a-block with princes (including the heir to the Austrian Empire, Crown Prince Franz Ferdinand).

Especially important to the Queen were the princes from India. Victoria had invited all the Indian princes, though some were unable to attend due to local difficulties. Her Majesty was always gleeful at being Empress of India. She took her position so seriously, she even made a stab, late in life, at learning Hindustani.

Although few actual heads of state were in attendance, with so many Crown Princes in the Procession – and with the skins of rulers being notoriously thin – a single unpleasant incident, such as an off-hand princely homicide or two, could spark a series of pleasant, little wars. Or one big one.

4

The parade came in two parts.

First was the Colonial Procession, comprised of detachments from troops spread over an eleven-million square mile Empire the sun never set on. Some marched, others rode beautifully caparisoned horses – especially the princes. Mixed in were premiers, like the Prime Minister of Canada.

This part of the Procession was headed by an advance party of four Royal Horse Guards and the Band of the Royal Horse Guards. Behind them came mounted troops, then foot soldiers. The Colonial Procession included troops from possessions ranging, alphabetically, from Aden to Zanzibar.

Chinese from Hong Kong in sun helmets. Dayaks from Borneo in red, pillbox caps. Africans from the Gold Coast and Nigeria. Men from Singapore and Jamaica, Ceylon, Sierra Leone and Australia, India and British Guiana. Almost every shade of mankind, answering to almost every language, worshiping almost every extant god, serving in harmony under the flag of a dainty island kingdom ruled by a dainty woman in black. This was truly people coming together.

However much they might love their Queen – or say they did – every contingent in the Colonial part of the grand Procession represented peoples subjected to British law by the threat of force.

In that way, Queen Victoria might have agreed with the man flying a bomb to London to assassinate her: bringing people together, even when the ultimate intention is universal harmony, invariably entails some level of oppression.

Amidst the cavalry riders and infantry marchers were batteries with horses hauling caissons of artillery show-pieces from the world's finest armory.

But they had nothing suitable for shooting down airships over London.

Millions of persons were packed in the streets to be near the lovely Procession.

The crowd itself was orderly and good-natured, despite its cramped conditions. Since the military detachments rode or marched only a short distance apart, the crowd barely had time to cheer one group before another rode or marched by. They cheered everything that passed.

But they were all waiting most intensely for the Queen. It was her day, after all, even if she had no intention of paying for it.

CHAPTER LXXIII

After leaving Herron's house with Chubb, Angelica glanced repeatedly into the partly cloudy skies. She had no definite notion of what an airship was, but she expected to see it any moment.

The streets of the parade route had been closed to traffic for two days. The adjacent streets were jammed with people, and the surrounding streets were jammed with vehicles of every description.

The transportation problems had rippled out as far as Herron's street, which was so clogged with traffic it had become impossible in the five hours since Angelica and Merridew arrived there.

Even the police coach Chubb had used could no longer get through.

Forced to travel on foot, Chubb weaved through snarled traffic and pedestrians toward the parade-route with Angelica in tow.

Along the actual Procession route, the spectators were packed solid in a six-mile slab of unbroken humanity. Many had camped out in their spots all night (in some cases, they had been there since Sunday).

The thoroughfares crossing the parade route were blocked-off, and these streets were crammed with warm, human bodies a full street back. Some "spectators" were so far away, they had no hope of seeing so much as the plumes on the hats of the highest riders. But they cheered whenever the ones in front cheered.

As the echoing drums, the martial music, and the cheers of the crowd grew ever louder the closer they inched to the Procession.

As Chubb led her through the spectators packed thick in the block-off crossing street, Angelica thought it might be easier to push their way through a cheese.

Chubb had his stubby fingers clamped around her wrist; but several times their hands separated, and she and Chubb had to grope for each other between the bodies. Fortunately, Angelica was so tall she almost never lost sight of the Inspector's brown bowler hat.

The Inspector kept repeating, "Police . . . comin' through . . . Police . . ." It was questionable whether anyone actually heard him. Those who did probably believed Angelica was a law-breaker he was arresting in a powerful hurry.

Finally reaching the front row of spectators, Chubb and Angelica were confronted with an more formidable obstacle.

The entire parade route was lined by parties from the military or the Guards (or both). A strong police presence also lined the route. In some places, the military and the police were lined in double rows. One needed a police pass to pierce the intractable cordon of street-lining parties.

Fortunately, Chubb possessed just such a pass. Identifying himself, he produced the pass, saying he was on vital business from Scotland Yard. The street-lining parties opened for him – then shut on Angelica.

She was still dressed in torn and dirty clothes, and her hair was disgraceful. Having spent a morning in a home with all affordable modern conveniences, she had forgotten to wash her face or run a brush through her honey-blonde mane.

Angelica doubted they'd ever let her through. She couldn't hear anything he said, over the din of the parade and the crowds screaming in her ears, but Chubb somehow talked, cajoled or threatened them enough to let her pass. The street-lining parties grudgingly let her ooze through their ranks.

Once past the street-lining parties, Chubb took Angelica by the wrist again and they darted *into the parade itself.*

Angelica didn't know one military uniform from another, so she couldn't identify which group they were infiltrating. In fact, they were dodging between mounted detachments of the Trinidad Yeomanry light horse (in khaki uniforms and bush hats whose left brims were turned up) and the Cyprus Military Police, (wearing fez caps with black tassels, blue zouave coats edged with red braid, and red cummerbunds).

The horses were so extremely well-trained they had displayed no agitation at the screaming millions waving hats or white handkerchiefs (or commemorative Union Jack Jubliee hankies, as sold at Strangways'). The sudden appearance of Chubb and Angelica underhoof, however, made them rear. Despite the bucking hooves kicking around her head, Angelica kept her eyes not on the horses but the armed riders, all of whom were observing her and Chubb narrowly.

Oblivious to the horses rearing around him, Chubb spiraled through the street like a drunken man, his eyes darting around for a telegraph office he knew was lurking around there somewhere. Forgetting he was clutching Angelica's wrist, Chubb swirled her around behind him, nearly flinging her flat.

Spying a sign painted in a window, he shouted, "Telegraph office!" and made a beeline for it on his stubby legs. Angelica, bent at a low angle as he hauled her behind him, could only see the tops of the letters over the heads of the crowd.

Across the street, he showed his pass again, and they were – again, grudgingly – admitted through another solid line of burly policemen.

They didn't have to push so hard through the crowd this time. The people were far fewer on the southern side of the parade route. Angelica wondered why.

Releasing Angelica, Chubb burst through the doors of the Telegraph Office with her on his heels.

The telegraphers, in blue coats and caps, were in the front window, trying to view the Procession over the heads of the crowd by standing on their stools.

As Chubb and Angelica turned to them, the two men were already shaking their heads. They looked disinclined to elaborate until Chubb identified himself.

"I have to send an urgent telegraph. Police business."

"Commandeer a pigeon," answered the younger of the two telegraphers, who wore a fluffy growth under his nose that he optimistically referred to as his moustache. "Unless you can repair telegraph lines, you're out of luck, mate."

The other telegrapher, an older man more respectful of the constabulary, hushed his companion.

"What about wireless telegraphs?" Angelica enquired, politely.

The clerks exchanged bemused looks. "Ain't no such thing, miss," said the younger man, "'less you mean banging drums like they has in the bush."

Chubb thanked them and hurried out, again hauling Angelica behind him. He shoved her into an alleyway to one side of the Telegraph Office, standing on his toes and yelling into her ear over the cheering and the noise of the parade.

"Miss, what's the first thing you would do if you was running a revolution?"

Angelica had never plotted revolution, and at present she was in no mental state to give the matter her keenest consideration.

"You'd seize the means of communication. You wouldn't cut all them telegraph lines 'cause you'd be needin' some of 'em, so the revolutionaries can communicate with each other. Even revolutionaries got to talk to one another. Before they start killin' each other off, like they always do."

Toddling further down the alley, Chubb turned a dustbin over beneath a high back window on that side of the telegraph office.

Mounted the dustbin, he eased up on tip-toe and peered inside. "You stay here," he said, drawing the pistol he'd taken from Angelica. "Gimme a boost."

Angelica helped the squat Chubb squirm through the window into the darkened back room. After a few minutes his face popped up over the sill and he crawled out with the pistol tucked in his belt.

"It's what I feared. I found a couple of bodies tied up inside, in their shirt-sleeves. They must be the real tele-graphers. Easy enough on a day like this when all the authorities in town are makin' sure the Procession goes whiz-bang."

"I don't know about whiz, but we got to keep it from going *bang*. How do we get word there to evacuate!"

"Nobody can get there no faster than we can. See them policemen and military men, Miss? Police, military, marines, sailors, Guards – that line of 'em stretches unbroken right the way along. I can whisper in the ear of the closest man there that there's an airship going to bomb the Queen at noon and would he please pass it down. And they would, whispering it all the way, from ear to ear. But you know how that turns out. We'll say, 'You got to evacuate 'cause an airship's gonna bomb you to bits' and at the end of the line it comes out, 'My uncle thinks he's a pickled gherkin' or some other load of old codswallop."

"We must stop the parade, then!"

"How do you reckon on that doin' that, Miss?"

"We have a gun."

"Yes, Miss. Very pretty, too. Do you know who is in that there Procession?" He clenched his eyes to think better. "Royal Horse Guards. Canadian Dragoons. Canadian cavalry. Royal Canadian Mounted Police." He opened his eyes. "They always get their man, conceited snots – one of 'em smugly asked me the other day how the Ripper case is going." He closed his eyes again. "New South Wales Lancers. Victoria Mounted Police. New Zealand Mounted Rifles. Queensland Mounted Rifles. Cape Mounted Rifles. Natal Carbineers. Umvoti Mounted Rifles. Border Mounted Rifles. Ceylon Mounted Rifles—"

Angelica laid her hand on his shoulder. "I take your point."

"If you aimed your dainty pistol at 'em and yelled 'Stop,' they'd blast you full of holes like a colander."

Angelica had reached the same conclusion.

"It shows how powerful this airship idea is, blackmail-wise, Miss. Fifty thousand armed soldiers in town. Artillery. God only knows how many police. And the airship can't be touched. This was a good day chosen to demonstrate their power. They can keep blowing up folks and buildings and not bein' touched until we gives them just what they want: the throne."

"Lady Calthrop can't have it now."

"There's a lot of organization behind this. You cut the head off the snake, but its coils are still floppin' about.

Angelica glanced up. Most of the lines feeding into this telegraph office appeared intact, though they might have been cut inside. "Inspector, those two men might have been lying. They won't suspect we know they're fakes. We can use our pistol to overpower them and use the telegraph ourselves."

"I'm no tele-grapher."

"I am – remember?"

"You sure you want to try? It may be dangerous. They're killers."

"It's worth a try, if we can save lives. If we fail, and if the airship bombs London anyway, we're just two more dead."

"That's just what I'm afraid of. Did you notice the telegraph machines?"

"To our left as we go in, near the wall."

"You walk casually to the machines. If they try to stop you, I'll hold the gun on 'em. I won't shoot 'til I have to. To tell the truth, I ain't a crack shot. Ready?"

Angelica swallowed hard and answered with a grim nod.

Gun in hand, Chubb sidled to the Telegraph Office door with her behind him.

Peering obliquely through the window, they saw the two faux-telegraphers still perched on their stools.

"You go in first. Catch their eyes."

After what she'd been through already that morning, Angelica thought she would never be nervous again. Nevertheless, entering the den of two revolutionaries who had already tasted blood that morning, she felt butterflies tickling her innards in the vicinity of her belt-buckle.

The men turned to her as she entered. She smiled and sauntered past them.

Hopping off their stools, they converged on her, drawing pistols.

"Hold!" bellowed Chubb, leaping into the doorway. On bent knees, he leveled the revolver in both hands. "Scotland Yard! You're under arrest for murder!"

The two men spun around. When they turned away from her, Angelica threw herself down on the floor and squirmed behind one of the two telegraph counters as the gunfire erupted.

Chubb, with an advantage, fired off two shots – and missed. Belly-flopping to the floor, he rolled behind the other counter.

Chubb spun his bowler in the air as a distraction. Two well-aimed shots, striking the hat simultaneously, catapulted it to the wall, about four feet away.

While they were plugging his hat, Chubb fired a round over the counter, winging one man in the arm with a shot that was probably more luck than skill.

At the sight of first blood, the men burrowed to earth around a standing cupboard full of paper and supplies, about four feet from the rear wall. From hiding, both had clear shots at the front and rear doors, cutting off all escape. The wood floor creaked mightily. Even with all the noise outside, neither she nor Chubb could creep or dash for the door without being heard or seen, even with all the noise just outside.

Angelica sat upright with her back against one counter, her knees drawn up.

Crouching behind his counter on all fours, Chubb shook his head at her. "I don't think we shoulda come back!"

CHAPTER LXXIV

Displaying contempt for Stoker's pistol, Lugner sauntered to the corner of the car and patted the wicker basket in the rear corner.

"This is a wireless telegraph set. With the telegraph offices seized or decommissioned all over London, this is the only way to speak to anyone there. It can only contact another wireless telegraph capable of receiving its impulses. Only three such set exist within a twenty-mile radius of the capital. This, the relay set that transmitted messages from our compound to London, and another in the hands of 'She.' And," (he flashed a smirky smile from beneath his offensively waxed moustache) "since there now is a slow hydrogen leak directly above our heads, it may be dangerous to use a transmitter that sparks."

"Don't try to hoodwink me!" Stoker answered. "Hydrogen is lighter than air! It won't leak down from that hole and settle in the car."

"Perhaps not. But you cannot stop us. You must agree with that."

"Don't tell me what to agree with. You're not running your new republic yet."

"Stoker, you *will* suffocate if you cut the ballonets open looking for bombs."

"Then we'll crash-land somewhere."

"I say!" spouted Herron. "Steady on. Don't let's lose our heads."

"We'll override the lock on the wheel. Or find and damage the device that is drawing us to London. Failing everything else, we'll vent all the hydrogen."

"You know you cannot vent hydrogen enough to land before we reach our target. The ship will descend too slowly."

"One thing we can do is to *learn* your target. Once you've told us where you plan to blow up the ship, then we'll worry about how to get the information to the authorities." To Herron, "It's either Lugner, or hundreds of innocent lives."

"You intend to . . ." Herron swallowed hard " . . . torture him?"

"Yeah. You got a problem with that?"

"Not . . ." Herron cleared his throat, ". . . theoretically."

"I do!" said Lugner. "Torture is uncivilized. I am against it."

"But then," said Stoker, with a twinkle in his eye, "'torture' is just a word."

"Quite," agreed Herron, perking up. "I'm sure I've seen it in the dictionary. And according to Lugner's own rules, it can't be 'torture' if we don't define it as such. He was just telling me a few hours ago, we'll never have a famine again when he's in charge, because he'll redefine how 'famine' statistics are gathered. We'll simply redefine 'torture' to exclude whatever it is you intend to do to him."

"In your little mind, Lugner, words don't really mean *real* things—"

"In the Platonic sense," Herron amended.

"—in the, as you say, Strangways, 'Platonic' sense, all definitions are as arbitrary. Well, you're about to learn how arbitrary 'torture' is. You still look a trifle reluctant, Strangways, though we're not going to 'torture' him, *per se*."

"I confess, I am reluctant."

"He's going to murder God knows how many innocent women and children."

Herron shrugged. "I don't know 'em."

"They probably didn't lose a wink of sleep when I was about to splinter your skull with a bullet. It didn't keep you from going a tad white around the gills."

"I am a freedom fighter," snapped Lugner. "I will endure torture for, and become the first glorious martyr to, the progressive science of eugenics."

"Tie him up!" sneered Stoker.

Herron nodded. "Righty-o. I felt some rope in the envelope when I was groping for the bomb." He reached for the ladder.

"Don't leave me alone with this slippery customer. We don't want him jumping overboard before we can interrogate him. Use the grapnel rope."

Herron went to the the rear of the car, where the grapnel rope was still coiled near the open door.

As he leaned over for the coil – suddenly, he shot forward. Lugner had administered a swift kick to Herron's hinder regions, and he flew out the door.

CHAPTER LXXV

"Psst—Miss!" Chubb stood on three points – both knees and his left hand. His right hand held the pistol aloft. "You got more cartridges for this thing?"

Wiggling the box of ammunition from her pocket, she slid it across the open space between their counters.

Two shots echoed through the telegraph office. The first one struck the floor and ricocheted up. Angelica tucked her head in her arms, but the bullet thumped into the far wall and stayed there. The second bullet clipped one corner of the box, bounding it it to the wall in Chubb's direction, but leaving it exposed.

Peeking over her shoulder and around the corner of the counter, Angelica saw a bit of one of the men behind the cupboard. Probably – correctly – assuming she wasn't armed, the man was eyeing Chubb's counter.

With two guns, she and Chubb might try blasting their way out. But she wasn't armed and she saw nothing she could use as a weapon. If only she could find some way to distract those men without exposing herself!

The wall she was facing was blank. It had a few framed pictures high up, but she'd get at least two bullets in the back if she made a grab for them.

There were the telegraph machines on the counter, but Angelica doubted she could hurl one far. Besides, they had risked their lives in returning expressly to use those machines. Angelica didn't want to bust up any equipment they needed.

She rolled her head far back.

Just above the edge of the counter, she saw the chimney of a paraffin lamp.

Her mother, being American, called paraffin oil as *kerosene*.

Moving slowly from her hips to her knees, she inched her eyes high enough over the counter to confirm that the lamp was full of fuel. But it *wasn't lit*.

Ducking quickly down, she mimed striking a match to Chubb.

From his coat pocket, Chubb extracted the box of matches he'd shown Herron on Sunday. Holding it up, he raised questioning eyebrows. *This what you want?*

She nodded vigorously, and he tossed the box over to her.

They heard no shot. The match box passed unnoticed.

Catching the box and setting it on the floor beside her, Angelica proceeded to make a series of signs, asking Chubb to draw their fire by reaching for the cartridge box while she grabbed the lamp and lit it.

This was a complex thought to mime. Utterly bewildered by her signals, Chubb raised high eyebrows up another notch.

Screwing up her lips and crossing her arms, Angelica pondered how to get her plan across to the Inspector without shouting it at him.

Suddenly, he snapped his fingers. With another questioning look, he pointed to the box of cartridges, then at the lamp, and raised his eyebrows higher.

She nodded.

Raising his eyebrows to their utmost extent, the Inspector gave her a hand-signal that clearly suggested she was out of her mind.

She nodded again.

Easing his head around his corner to spy out the cupboard, Chubb gave Angelica a resigned nod.

Mouthing *Ready on three* he held up two fingers and a thumb to count down.

The thumb went down, and one finger. Shouting, "THREE!" Chubb threw himself backward against the wall, simultaneously firing at the cupboard and scrabbling for the cartridge box.

Angelica reached up and grasped the base of the lamp.

The Inspector did not appear especially mobile; but when he hit the wainscotting on his shoulders and grabbed the cartridge box, he rolled out of range and sat back against his counter very quickly indeed.

A few shots pounded into the wall near where he had been. The way he wiped his brow suggested he did not want to attempt that experiment a second time.

Quickly, Chubb reloaded while Angelica struck a match and lit the lamp. She gave it plenty of wick, so the flame would be high.

Their next move was extremely dangerous for Angelica, who had to make the first move. She tensed herself for it while replacing the lamp's chimney.

The cupboard hiding the men stood near the rear wall. Her intention was to smash the burning lamp low on the wall, with such force flaming paraffin, or kerosene, would spew out at (with luck, behind) them, forcing them from cover.

She had one chance, and had never tried the lamp-toss before. Since she couldn't throw a lamp effectively on target over her shoulder from a sitting position, to accomplish this feat she had to stand up and expose herself.

Facing her counter in a squat, she looked at the Inspector, to make sure he knew what he had to do.

Chubb raised a hand, showing crossed fingers.

She rolled her eyes. Her life was on the line and he crossed his fingers. But then, it had been her idea in the first place.

She just hoped he would uncross his fingers when he started to pull the trigger.

Extending a hand around his counter, Chubb fired a shot to ward the men back.

The instant Chubb fired, Angelica sprang up and flung the lamp overhand.

She never saw it land. A hard object thumped against her, smashing her back against the wall. As she collapsed to the floor, a stabbing pain struck her side.

Oh God! she thought, rather obviously, as darkness engulfed her, *I'm shot.*

CHAPTER LXXVI

Herron didn't know what happened. He only knew that, all of a sudden, nothing separated him from the ground except twelve hundred feet of air. He felt his stomach rising as he accelerated at the earth at 32 feet per second, per second.

As Herron sailed down through space holding the rope, he yanked the grapnel out after him. It opened like a giant flower as it soared out.

The rope ripped the skin off his palms, but Herron, out of sheer terror, clung to it until he jolted against the massive grapnel.

Designed to anchor an airship of eighty-one thousand pounds plumped out with hydrogen, the grapnel was necessarily huge. Had it not been so large, Herron might have been impaled on its sharp points.

The impact with metal nearly made him black out. He was certainly winded, and extremely sore in the thigh that had, by a fluke, hooked over a fluke. One leg and one arm were crooked over flukes, while his other hand clasped the rope.

At take-off, Herron had wished for a better view. Now he had view enough to last a lifetime.

The winds *were* powerful at altitude. The grapnel swung wildly beneath the airhip in the wind. Every time he spun around, Herron perceived, through the patchy clouds, London approaching from the west. It was only just a blur on the horizon, and it grew blurrier every time he swirled around.

He mananged to retain just enough consciousness to realize he would be smashed to a jelly if he fell. That was all the impetus he needed cling to the rope.

Clenching his eyes, he cried, "*Stoke-er*!" His voice trickled out like a shout in a dream – a cross between a whine and a dry whisper.

From up on high, Herron heard an explosion; then another. He wondered, vaguely, if it might be the bomb going off prematurely. He almost hoped so. He didn't want to fall, but, dizzy as he was getting, he was ready to die.

He was certainly glad he'd had nothing to eat since Monday tea with Angelica. He hoped Angelica wasn't feeling as bad as he was.

CHAPTER LXXVII

Angelica's plan went perfectly, apart from the fact that she was shot.

The paraffin lamp crashed behind the cupboard, against the wall just where it joined the floor. When the fuel burst out in flame toward the men, they rushed out from behind the cupboard with their clothes on fire.

Leaping up, Chubb emptied the pistol into them.

After they hit the floor, the Inspector ran to them and stamped out their clothes, possibly with more force than the small flames required.

Yanking a spare blue jacket off a hook on the wall, he smothered the fire the paraffin was spreading over the floor. Laying the jacket flat, he did a sort of flamenco jig on top of it. Only when the fire was thoroughly doused did he return his attention to the phony telegraphers.

One of them lay ominously still. The other writhed. Picking up one of their fallen stools by the legs, Chubb administered a dull *thunk* to the man's skull. He'd have a headache when he woke, and Chubb hoped it would be a doozy. He slapped irons on him, handcuffing him to the iron stove they used for heating.

Setting the stool down behind the telegraph counter – he at last saw Angelica lying with her head propped up against the wall, her arms out. Blood stained her blouse, her waistcoat, the floor and her open palms.

Falling beside her on one knee, Chubb took her pulse with his fingers. Then he lifted one of her hands and began rubbing it vigorously.

Her eyelids flickered, but didn't open. "I'm shot?" she moaned.

"A bit." He put his hand to her side, where the blood was still flowing. "Does it burn like all Hell?"

Gritting her teeth, she nodded.

Begging her pardon, he examined the gash caused by the bullet. Her clothes had been slit all the way to her skin like she'd been struck with a machete.

"It's only a flesh wound."

"Only!" she repeated bitterly, without opening her eyes or her teeth.

"Leastways, there's no lead in it. You musta got knocked out a few ticks when your head slammed back against the wall. Lordy, seein' you lyin' there, I feared the worst had happened. I hope all them revolutionists shoot that poorly."

After another minute, Angelica felt ready to move. He helped her to her feet, and she leaned forward on the counter.

Seeing the men on the floor she asked, solemnly, "Are they dead?"

"I did my best, but I think the score's tied one-an'-one."

"Good God, Inspector, how many people are going to die today!" Snaking a hand under her waistcoat and beneath her breast, Angelica felt the burning crease in her left side. It throbbed, just as the Inspector described, but her head throbbed worse. On the crown of her head, her fingers discovered a rising knot.

"You able to work them machines?" Chubb asked.

She nodded – and wished she hadn't.

While the Inspector reloaded his pistol – and emptied the cartridge box into his coat pocket – Angelica tried to send their message.

A few taps on each machine was all she needed. "Dead, Inspector."

"Blast. Now what!"

"Maybe the airship may be equipped with a wireless telegraph machine."

"So?"

"Let's go back to Mister Strangways' house. If we contact them and tell them their plot is discovered, maybe they'll listen to reason and turn around!"

Chubb was desperate enough to try any crazy scheme – even diplomacy.

"But we can't sit at Strangways' house dotty-dashing. Lots of good it does to talk to 'em if they don't turn around. We got to get to there first and try to make 'em evacuate before we contact any airships."

"How do we get there? It's miles. No vehicle can move within streets of the Procession route, and I'm not up running."

"You up to pumping your bike?"

"I don't know. I'll try. Once I've caught my breath."

"No time for breath. Pottle's at Strangways' house. I'll tell him to round up police and military enough to arrest telegraphers in their offices before stroke of noon. It'll have to be simultan-ous or they'll contact each other and scarper."

"What do we do?"

"No livin' soul can get there any faster than we can. We got to be what's-the-fellow's-name. You know, 'one if by land, two if by sea.'"

"Paul Revere."

"Yeah. I wonder what he'd have done 'if by air.' Never mind, let's go."

Dashing from the telegraph office, they pushed their way back through the crowd and the street-lining parties of police and military. Once more, they scooted through the parade, disconcerting a detachment from the Royal Malta Regiment of Militia, in white, spiked helmets and red coats, who hurled epithets after them that Angelica hadn't heard since finishing school.

CHAPTER LXXVIII

Herron felt the rope being winched up in a series of uncomfortable jerks.

When he finally reached the door and pulled himself inside the car, Herron saw Stoker, with blood streaming down his face, lying on the floor near the winch.

Lugner was gone.

Stoker wasn't dead, but he had a crushed and bloody nose.

His head spinning, Herron crumpled against the bulkhead. The insides of the car wheeled lopsidedly in his brain so quickly, he clenched his eyes – and then he felt like he was being slung around in the dark. He had all the rotten side-effects of drunkenness with none of the pleasant side-effects.

Stoker sat up beside Herron, his eyes trained up on the hatch. Herron didn't ask what had happened, but Stoker told him anyway.

"When Lugner kicked you, I winged him in the thigh; but he had enough strength left to dive head-first into me and bowl me off my feet, then stamped at me like he meant to kick off my moustache. Probably would have crushed my skull under his boot if he had been able to stand solidly on the leg I shot. He wrested my gun from me and ran to the ladder."

"You're a good shot. Why didn't you kill him with your first bang?"

"I want him alive! We must know where we're heading! Or, if we manage to override the locks on the wheel, *he must be kept alive to work these controls*! I can turn the wheel, but I'm not qualified to operate the elevators. I'm willing to try, but I'm more likely to steer us straight into the ground. I'd do it if I had to—"

"Never say it!"

"You have to catch him, Strangways."

"Let him go—good riddance!"

"You'll think 'good riddance' if he goes out the keel and takes the glider."

Herron didn't feel like standing upright, much less chasing an armed man along a narrow keel. "Why me? I'm the amateur. I muck things up, remember?"

"You do, yes. But I have to keep monkeying with these controls! If we don't override this mechanism that's drawing us, we'll fail." Dripping blood, crawled to the ship's wheels and began fiddling with them, running his hands over them to feel out any possible external controls. "Do you see him anywhere?"

Careful not to expose himself to gunfire, Herron craned his neck up the ladder.

"Don't worry about the gun."

"Why not?" It seemed a perfectly legitimate concern.

"It's a six-shooter. I put one bullet into Hawkins and one through the roof. A third is lodged in Lugner's thigh. I tried to shoot him again, and missed, when he barreled into me. I attempted to empty the chambers while we were struggling, but only fired off one more before he wrested the gun from me. That's five."

"One through the windscreen!"

"That was from his gun. When you fatheadedly jumped on top of him."

"Oh, right. Won't he have cartridges?"

"He didn't come anticipating a shoot-out in the sky. Besides, his pistol was a Sauer Reichsrevolver and mine was a Schofield, and different calibers. His ammunition won't match my gun. He has only one bullet left."

"That's all he needs."

"He can only shoot one of us."

Since, if he was the one who had to pursue Lugner, Herron had a better than fifty-fifty chance of being that one, his mind was not soothed on that particular point. "He has that saber, too."

"That can't hurt you from a distance."

"No, but if he's waiting up there, the first one of us who pokes his head up over the hatch gets a foot shorter and no place to wear his hat."

"Keep a weather eye out for him, Strangways. I'll try to find some way to override the lock on the controls!" Stoker continued nosing around the wheels. "If only we knew the target! You got every useless bit of trivia from that cigarette paper, but you don't know the one thing that really matters right now!"

"Don't you know *anything* about it?"

"Lugner said we must be there 'at the prick of noon.' That's probably when the bomb's set to explode and ignite the hydrogen."

"Why noon? Does the airship change into a pumpkin at the stroke of twelve?"

"No. We're going to turn into the biggest *bang* since Krakatoa."

"But . . . why noon, particularly?"

"Why not? Noon's an easy time to remember."

"Don't you know what happens at noon during the Procession? The Queen arrives at Saint Paul's Cathedral for a Thanksgiving ceremony."

While he was talking, Stoker had been slithering around behind the steering mechanism, searching for any possible way to override the lock. Now, his head rose slowly over the top of the wheel. "At noon precisely?"

"It was in the papers. The Archbishops of Canterbury and York will be there, the Prime Minister, the Cabinet, members of Parliament from all sides – Heaven knows who else. Probably every major figure in government, and most of the minor officials who do the real work. The Procession will speed up or slow down in order for the Queen to arrive on the dot."

"We'll blow the dome off! Kill anyone underneath. Start a major fire."

"And with the telegraph offices and telephone exchanges in the hands of the enemy, no one on the ground can do a damn thing to stop it."

Standing, Stoker gave the wheel a kick. "Or in the air."

CHAPTER LXXIX

"Whee!" squealed Chubb, waving his bullet-perforated bowler over his head.

"Please sit still, Inspector!" begged Angelica, who had never balanced her bicycle with a policeman perched on the handlebars.

Angelica's graceful figure was athletic, but she was no Amazon. Her strength was ebbing from stressful activities that including shooting people and being shot.

The bicycle wobbled precariously under Chubb's weight. Every ounce of strength in Angelica's arms and shoulders was required to maintain their equilibrium. She was already pumping her bike for all she was worth. And she had to contend not only with a lumpy Scotland Yard inspector perched on her handlebars, but also the wireless telegraph in the basket.

Fortunately, no crowds or traffic impeded the route Chubb had selected.

Angelica had wondered why so (comparatively) fewer people lined the parade's route on the south sides of the streets. Chubb instinctively understood it.

Crossings over the Thames had been closed, to keep multitudes from stampeding over the bridges to see the Queen's Procession on both sides of the river. No traffic was allowed to cross the parade route, including pedestrians.

Inspector Chubb realized this created a "charmed circle" along the north bank of the Thames.

This "charmed circle" was hardly circular. It extended from Westminster Bridge in the west to London Bridge in the east. It was bordered to the south by the river, and to the north by the Procession route.

No one could enter this "charmed circle" from across the river (unless they owned a canoe). None of the multitudes north of the parade could venture over into that territory without one of those scarce passes.

Most of the people already isolated within this "circle" were lining the parade route. This left the Embankment, along the river, virtually deserted.

They entered this "charmed circle" near Westminster Bridge. They thought that would be easiest point of entry, since it was at the tail-end of the Procession route. Too, it was extremely handy to Herron's house.

Since nearly everyone was at the Procession, Angelica rode her bicycle on the smooth walkway rather than the road. Whenever he saw pedestrians, Chubb waved his bowler and shouted, "Out of the way! Police business!"

After what seemed, to Angelica, an interminable wobbling, their bicycle passed Waterloo Bridge, and spun around the bend in the river.

Rounding the curve of the Thames, Angelica's trajectory allowed her to see the dome of Saint Paul's Cathedral humping up straight in front of them.

"Saint Paul's, Inspector!" she panted. "Dead ahead."

"Not dead . . ." Chubb gasped. "Not yet."

Angelica was having a hard time of it but Chubb's ride, while exciting, was not easy. He had never been on a bicycle at all, much less balancing on the handlebars with his knees tight on a heavy wicker box.

"We can't go through them buildings to reach the Cathedral, and so we got lots of ground to cover before we get anywhere near it. When we do get there, I'll show what that last bit of your cigarette message means."

"What," Angelica puffed, "are our chances of success once we're there?"

"On the up side, maybe they'll hear me out and evacuate the area."

"On the down side?"

"We'll never squiggle through the crowds. Even in the south, folks'll be thick at the Cathedral. If we do shove through, the military and the police may not hear us out. At the very least, we'll have ringside seats for the disaster."

"You're an Inspector. Won't they listen to reason?"

"To *reason*, yes. And they'll think I lost mine if I tell 'em a person or persons unknown is going to bomb the Queen from an airship. It's me they'll lock away."

This was a new twist for Angelica. It never occurred to her that no one would believe their tale with a man of Chubb's position lending it veracity.

"It wouldn't be the first time a hoax has caused a lot of to-do at a queen's visit to the Cathedral, Miss," Chubb called over his shoulder. "I don't have much in the way of schoolin', but I know a bit about crime. Way back in the early 1700s, good Queen Anne attended a Thanksgiving ceremony at Saint Paul's Cathedral, which had only just opened for business. There was a rumor rife that Jacobites had snuck into the Cathedral and loosened all the screws holding up the dome; and at a certain point in the ceremony the screws would pop out and the dome would crash down and kill everyone, Queen and all."

"The dome isn't held up by screws? Piers and buttresses, surely?"

"I don't know what holds it up, but it ain't screws, no. Them rumors in Queen Anne's day scared a lot of folks, even though there's no possible way it could have happened. Unfounded rumors do make the rounds. Bombing the Cathedral from an airship sounds as silly as unscrewing the dome!"

"Did you know the dome we see is only a shell?"

"Get away!"

"Really. There's a brick inner dome that does all the load bearing. The outer dome is connected to it by a lot of scaffolding, it's wood covered with metal. The brick inner dome supports the lantern and the ball and cross at the very top."

Almost immediately, Angelica regretted having spoken. The Inspector looked like a boy learning there were no fairies, not any more.

"I could be wrong," she offered, apologetically. "And I heard it was held together with great chains."

"Of being?"

"No, real chains. Huge chains. They girdle the dome to keep it from exploding out from the weight." She was in no condition to lecture, so she changed the subject.

"Couldn't we have sent one of those nice mounted soldiers ahead of us?"

"Flag down one of the Royal Scots Greys and ask 'em to ride on ahead and say mad bombers will swoop down from the sky? You and I know all the information. No sense in tellin' it to him here and him repeatin' it there, even if we could detach him from the parade. No, we can't stop an airship with a cavalry charge. Besides, I ain't altogether straight in my mind that there is a airship."

"But those men in the telegraph office—"

"Weren't in no airship! I won't believe it 'til I see it."

Boom!

Angelica leapt in her seat. Glancing at the Cathedral, she saw no smoke rising around the dome. "My *God*, what was that!"

"'leven-fifteen!" Chubb answered. "Firin' cannon in Hyde Park to announce that the Queen is leaving Buckingham Palace!"

Eleven-fifteen! Angelica moaned inwardly. Hearing cannon fire in Hyde Park, however distantly it sounded, indicated they still had far to go to the Cathedral, even though it was in sight.

She didn't know why the Inspector decided upon the Cathedral was the target, but if he guessed right, they had to beat the Queen there.

The sun, as if on cue, burst through the clouds at eleven-fifteen exactly.

She was approaching Saint Paul's from the south-west. When the clouds parted, Angelica saw an infinitesimal gold speck in the sky to the northeast. She wondered what it might be. She didn't recognize the airship when she saw it.

CHAPTER LXXX

Unlike Angelica Trickett, the Queen was no telegrapher.

At 79, the five-foot Victoria, her grey hair in a bun on her head beneath a white veil, had nurtured her growing empire until it included eleven million square miles of territory and a quarter of the inhabitants of the globe.

She could speak several languages, but she did not know Morse code.

Immediately before leaving Buckingham Palace, the Queen delivered a telegraphic message for all the empire: "From my heart I thank my beloved people stop God bless them stop V R and I."

She did not tap the message out herself. She only pressed one button – which alerted her telegraphic minions to proclaim her good news unto all the world.

At that moment, the Queen's message should have started speeding east from possession to possession across India and Hong Kong to hop the Pacific Islands. It should have skimmed west across the British West Indies to Canada. It should have met itself coming the other way on or about the 180th Meridian.

Unfortunately, by the time the Queen sent her message, all the telegraph lines in London had been seized or severed. Among the lines cut, thanks to Lady Calthrop's influence, were those leading from Buckingham Palace.

Pottle had already rounded up policemen enough to storm all the telegraph offices and post offices and telephone exchanges in London (with the able assistance of the military). They were to strike simultaneously at eleven-thirty.

So, when the Queen was joggled out from Buckingham Palace in her carriage, she went farther than her world-wide message. Three and three-quarter million souls dwelling in the Empire were deprived of Her Majesty's kind words of appreciation for their being subject to her.

2

Ten minutes behind the Colonial contingent came the Royal Procession, led by the captain of the Regiment of 2nd Life Guards, Oswald Ames – named for the great King of Northumbria who beat back a Welsh invasion in the A. D. 630s. He was riding in company with four troopers of the 2nd Life Guards.

Running mostly to leg and moustache, the 6' 8" Ames was probably the tallest man in the British Army. If stood back-to-back with Herron Strangways, Ames would have towered over him by more than half a foot.

The Royal Procession was escorted by Life Guards, hussars, dragoons, lancers – and it contained no fewer than seventeen fancy royal carriages, replete with drivers and footmen in cocked hats. Five carriages were laden with foreign envoys. The remaining carriages carried members of the Royal Family (in ascending order of rank according to protocol up Her Majesty). Princes and Royal Highnesses from around the globe rode as escorts to all the carriages.

The parade had been full swing on this sweltering day of seventy-five degrees for fully two hours before the Queen's open carriage rolled from Buckingham Palace at eleven-fifteen precisely.

At the gates of Buckingham Palace, blue-jacketed royal marines stood at attention to her right hand. To her left, the red-clad Queen's West Surrey Regiment presented arms. The military street-lining parties continued presenting arms as her carriage passed all along the route.

This was the moment all those millions of "trespassers" in London, who had harried and harassed Herron Strangways for weeks, were waiting for. They made their pilgrimage to London expressly to take a gander at the little woman being wheeled out for an airing in her sixtieth year on the throne. The Queen intended to give them an eyeful.

The Queen's carriage was pulled by eight cream-colored Hanoverian horses in four ranks of two abreast. They were equipped with golden harnesses, and they had purple ribbons braided in their manes.

Her Majesty's traditional black silk dress and mantle was embroidered with silver. Diamonds and white acacia sparkled in her black bonnet.

The Queen sat beneath a pearl-grey parasol. Prince Albert, her (thirty-five years) late consort, once bought a metal-lined parasol for Victoria's protection against bullets. No parasol, however well-lined, was protection against bombs.

The Prince of Wales escorted the Queen's carriage on horseback. So did her third boy, His Royal Highness Arthur, Duke of Connaught and Strathearn. The Queen's second daughter, Her Royal Highness Princess Helena of Schleswig-Holstein, rode in the carriage with Her Majesty.

From Buckingham Palace, the Queen rolled slowly up the barely discernable slope of Constitution Hill, where three attempts had been made against her life.

Judging by the raucous music of cheers the Queen heard all along her way, she expected no trouble today. No dynamite, no bombs like that hurled at the president of France a little more than a week earlier. She expected none of those gunshots that had irked her on seven previous excursions.

Everyone seemed so happy to see her!

At the Wellington Arch, near Hyde Park Corner, the Queen's carriage followed the Procession onto Piccadilly. The echo of the cannon fired in Hyde Park had only just died away in the ears of the spectators there.

Had her carriage gone north, she would have been on Park Lane, where a shooting incident had taken place in the pre-dawn hours. Information was scanty, but the police surmised a botched burglary, in which one resident was killed. The butler of the house was struggling for life in the hands of the surgeons.

From Picadilly, the Procession turned south on St. James Street. There it passed, amongst other sites of interest, the Hemlock Club.

All the charter members of the Hemlock (except one) stood in the bow window of the library, directly over the front steps (where, they understood, during the pre-dawn hours there had been some affair of an armed woman of degenerate appearance; but the details were vague).

The whereabouts of that scamp Herron Strangways had been questioned. It was assumed he'd found a female younger than Victoria to engage his affections.

Hoisting their glasses, the charter members of the Hemlock toasted "The Queen, God bless her!"

Herron was forgotten in the excitement of toasting the Queen. They weren't worried about him. After all, he was a man of irregular habits and he would turn up, as usual. No one expected he would be so irregular as to be outfitted in the clammy, second-hand clothes; or that he would "turn up" in an explosive airship currently sailing lower than one thousand feet, and descending.

From St. James Street, the Queen turned east on Pall Mall to Trafalgar Square.

As Her Majesty's carriage edged along the north side of the Square, men and women waved and cheered from stands erected in front of the National Gallery, as well as from its roof.

She only had the Strand and Fleet Street to go before her carriage made its approach up Ludgate Hill to Saint Paul's Cathedral.

3

All along the route, the crowd, which had been shouting itself hoarse for two hours at everything that moved (and singing the national anthem whenever there was any break in the action), cheered most wildly when they saw the Guards and others in the street-lining parties presenting arms, indicating the Queen's immenent arrival.

The spectators had been standing for hours along six miles of streets. They were crammed into the grandstands stands erected in front of, and atop, every major building along the route. They peered out of every window along the way, many of which had been rented weeks in advance.

As the Queen's carriage rolled elegantly beneath them, spectators in high windows leaned so far out they looked liable to fall headlong to the pavement.

On the pavements, little children sat on the shoulders of their parents. Shorter persons jumped excitedly up and down to peek over shoulders. A few of the more athletic young men shinnied up lamp-posts, where they perched like Zacchaeus in his sycamore tree.

Here and there, spectators swooned at the sight of the Queen; even so, the crowd so tight swooners remained upright.

From time to time in the past, the majority of Britishers could not have cared less for their monarch. Victoria had triumphantly outlived her critics.

4

Bundled down in the ceremonial robes and chains of his office at the west end of Fleet Street, the Lord Mayor of the City of London, Sir George Faudel-Phillips, was sheltering from the heat at the Child & Company Bank until he was alerted to the Queen's approach.

Mounting up, he waited on horseback until the Queen came in view. As the carriage slowed to a halt where the Strand flowed into Fleet Street, the Lord Mayor and his deputation dismounted and bared their heads.

Her Majesty's carriage halted beside a high monument topped by the statue of a rearing, winged griffin.

This monument, erected in the middle of street as a danger to traffic, marked the former site of the Temple Bar, a gate to the ancient City of London.

The Lord Mayor's sword-bearer bowed to the Lord Mayor and handed him a ceremonial sword with a pearl-studded scabbard. The Lord Mayor, in turn, extended this sword to Her Majesty – hilt foremost, of course.

This very sword had been used in this ceremony since the days of Queen Bess, whenever the Monarch passed through the City on state occasions. It acknowledged the Sovereign's overriding authority while she (or he) was in the (roughly) one-square-mile City of London.

Custom cannot cage a monarch. In reality, Lord Mayor of the City was in no position to decline the Queen entry. Nevertheless, it was a polite – and politic – custom for the Queen to ask the Lord Mayor's permission to enter the City. Especially when she was marching tens of thousand of troops through it.

And, of course, on fancy occasions like this, the ceremony made a great show.

The perfunctory presentation of the sword amounted to little more than the Queen laying a hand on the hilt. The ceremony took about a minute. The applause lasted much longer.

As it was the Lord Mayor's place to lead the Queen through the city, Faudel-Phillips scrambled back onto horseback.

Remaining bareheaded, but hatless and with his white hair shining, he led the queen's carriage into the City of London, holding the ceremonial sword aloft.

Fleet Street, that lair of ravening journalists, would carry the Queen to Ludgate Hill. From there, she would ride up to Saint Paul's Cathedral – where she intended to be at the very stroke of noon.

Yet, nothing done by government ever runs like clockwork. Not even clocks. True, this was no state occasion; but the Queen was government personified.

Even with no gaffes along the route so far, the Queen's carriage was going too slowly. She might be as much as a quarter of an hour late getting to the Cathedral.

5

During the ceremony at Temple Bar, word had not yet reached the Royal Procession of any disturbance ahead. Nevertheless, by the time the ceremonial sword was extended to the Queen, everyone east of Saint Paul's Cathedral was already looking up at the approaching airship, whose shape was, by now, quite discernable to those with keen vision.

The airship, run by private enterprise, was dead on time.

CHAPTER LXXXI

"I see him!" Herron, squatting against the bulkhead, pointed out through the rear door. "On the keel!"

"Go after him! Before he gets away!"

"A lot of people have been ordering me about in the last few days, don't y'know. And I'm getting bally tired of it. Let him go. Maybe he'll fall."

"Or maybe he'll take the glider."

"C-can he pilot the glider?"

"If he tries – may he break his ruddy neck! But even if he plunges to his death, he's left us stranded hundreds of feet in the air in a six-hundred-and-forty foot hydrogen bomb. Go get him."

"He's armed!"

Rising from where he had been slithering around the ship's wheel, Stoker wrenched one of the swords from the display near the door and handed it down to Herron with mock ceremony, much as the Lord Mayor of the City of London was just then offering a ceremonial sword to the Queen.

The look in Stoker's eyes suggested he was liable treat Herron like disposable ballast if he didn't confront Lugner posthaste.

Herron gave the saber, then Stoker, a disparaging look. In lieu of any other weapon, however, he accepted it.

Still dizzy from swinging wildly through the air on the grapnel, Herron could find his feet only by pulling himself upright by the ladder.

Clinging to the rungs, he leaned his cheek against the cool, metal pole in the center of the ladder as he rose. He wondered how he was going to maintain his balance on the keel.

Not that it mattered. If Lugner took the glider, they were dead anyway. To Herron, it was just a matter of whether he would wait to be blown to particles, or whether he'd leap to a smash.

On the whole, Herron preferred the former. Falling from a great height would afford too much time for reflection. Besides, he'd already met his recommended daily allowance for plummeting and he didn't want to try any more.

Gripping the saber in his teeth, Herron climbed the ladder to the roof of the car.

Squatting on the car, Herron eased woozily around the ladder and inched out onto the keel, falling, more than stepping, from one strut or steel cable to the next.

The aluminium keel was a narrow, but thick and solid, surface. Its network of struts and steel cables made excellent hand-holds for one who could barely stand.

And, Herron noted, if Lugner turned around, he would have a perfectly clear shot straight up the keel at his pursuer.

Fortunately, the wind faffling Herron's cheap, baggy suit around his legs also drowned any noise he made maneuvering through the struts after Lugner.

Then *Darnley* sailed through an unexpected crosswind hat that blew Hawkins's cap right off Herron's head. In the water-bladder, the cap had gotten wet, making Hawkins' disgusting pomade less adhesive.

Sailing off Herron's head, the cap spun away to one side and spiraled over the eastern outskirts of greater London. The airship, going more than thirty knots with the tailwind, quickly passed it.

Lugner stopped, staring at the cap. At this altitude, the cap could only have come off the head of a man behind him. He turned, pistol ready.

With no place to run, Herron braced himself on the struts and closed his eyes while Lugner, at the far end of the keel, aimed and fired.

He heard the bullet whiz by. He'd always been told if you hear the bullet, it can't have hit you. He hoped that was true.

Lugner's shot had not strayed far off the mark; but he ventured into these elevations to pilot airships, not to take target practice. He had not compensated sufficiently for the crosswind.

When the exultation he felt at not being hit was past, Herron had a second jolt of euphoria as he realized the revolver was now empty.

Lugner had not counted Stoker's bullets. He kept squeezing the trigger until it slowly occurred to him the gun was going to emit nothing but clicks.

Holding the pistol by the barrel, he flung it at Herron with an animal snarl. Again, his aim was off. The pistol arced down before it reached Herron, bounded with a *clank* off the keel, and twirled down into the fringes of London's east end, where someone might find it useful.

Slowly, Lugner drew his saber.

Herron's first impulse was to turn around and step gingerly back along the keel as quickly as he could.

No—he could not allow Lugner to reach the glider. As Stoker said, Luger might kill himself in it; and if he took it, Herron earnestly hoped he would.

But I won't laugh long.

Herron entered the sword-battle with trepidation. He had often dueled with sabers for exercise – and in even minor competition. But never while queasy.

Lugner's entire manner showed contempt for Herron. Though Swiss, Lugner had served in the Prussian military (so he claimed), while Herron was merely the idle scion of the rich loafing about town.

He offered not so much as a perfunctory salute, but lunged at Herron.

When he was firing his pistol, Lugner had not taken the wind into account. As he attacked Herron, what he failed to take into account was the active education of a British gentleman whose *nouveau-riche*, social-climbing father wanted him to better the scion of the aristocrats in everything, especially in sports like fencing.

Lugner also didn't consider that he himself was unused to dueling on a narrow metal bar whose struts limited the window of his attack.

Lugner's blade had thrust out like a snake; Herron parried with a twist of his strong wrist. The edges of their swords crossed with a crisp clank of steel.

Herron had barely parried the blow. For him, fencing was an art practice with Gallic science. Lugner was no artist. He came from the school where a man won however he must.

This was no "first-blood" game played for points, but a fight *a outrance* – literally, 'to excess'; but, in dueling parlance, to the bitter end.

Lugner knew that from the first; only in the first attack did Herron cotton on to the fact that he had to kill or be killed.

Good fencers sometimes boasted they could fight with foils through a wedding-ring. Unfortunately, Herron and Lugner were using sabers, which required more elbow room than a wedding ring usually permitted. The steel cables and struts allowed no opportunity for them to swing their weapons.

And the keel provided no space for fancy foot-work. Herron did not have the luxury of dancing with Lugner around an area the size of a ballroom. Even in competition, the fencing field might be six feet wide. In these cramped conditions a *coup passé* was impossible A "flying lunge" would keep the fencer flying all the way to the earth, and probably a foot or two further down. They battled toe to toe on a narrow keel, with weapons designed for use on horseback.

When Herron parried Lugner's first attack, he had no time to group. Since the struts closed his window of attack, Lugner kept it thrusting forward, attacking again and again and driving Herron back without even giving him even the breathing-space to turn and see where he was stepping.

Sword clashed on sword – but not with a loud, resounding rattle of steel, for they barely had room to separate their weapons.

Lugner thrust with an economy of movement . . . but he was a hothead. Prepared as he was to cooly condemn "scientifically selected" citizens for elimination by his eugenics, he got carried away by excitement of a duel.

Then Herron parried a blow that knocked Lugner's sword up. The saber dug into envelope, piercing one of the ballonets. Though the hydrogen was lighter than the surrounding air, they both leapt back, as if a trace amount might leak downwards and asphyxiate them both on the spot.

Herron recovered first. He stood with sword ready for another go.

For his part, Lugner kept backing – toward the glider.

Herron rushed him. Lugner thrust, to ward him back. Herron parried with the flat of his sword.

Catching Lugner's saber near the hilt, Herron used his forward momentum to force Luger's weapon over his head far enough to slip beneath it and land his shoulder in Lugner's chest. It wasn't by the book, but Herron had to win, and that meant forgetting fair play. He shouldered Lugner *hard*.

The pilot toppled back, hooking his elbows and knees over the struts. His wrist struck one of the metal struts jarring his fingers open. His saber dropped straight down and stuck quivering upright in a roof on the city's outskirts.

Herron stepped back a pace – and collided with Stoker, who carried the netting over one shoulder.

"About time you showed up! Why aren't you in the car trying to fix things?"

Stoker shrugged, "There's nothing more I can do and we're out of time."

"So the Cathedral is gone and so are all the people around it."

"Yeah."

"And the Queen and her family and the Prime Minister and the Archbishop of Canterbury and women and children and—everyone else in the vicinity."

"Yeah."

"And it'll cause a fire like none the city has seen since 1666."

"Yeah. So move it, Strangways, if we want to save our own miserable lives."

"Suits me."

Herron continued along the narrow rod of the keel, stepping over Lugner.

Stoker wrapped Lugner in the netting; he and Herron jerked the pilot to his feet between them.

"Right!" said Stoker, once they had Lugner between them. "Toss him over."

CHAPTER LXXXII

Perspiring freely from pumping her bicycle with all he strength on this warm day, Angelica came even with Blackfriar's Bridge and veered north. She continued as far as she could, until they were utterly blocked by the crowd around the southern periphery of Saint Paul's Cathedral.

At that point, they abandoned the bicycle and shoved through the pack on foot.

The crowd as thick here. Everyone, it seemed, wanted to be near the Cathedral for the Thanksgiving service for the Queen, even if they saw nothing.

Angelica was still dressed in the "cycling skirt" she'd been wearing when Herron Strangways barged in on her the day before. This was a bifurcated affair that could be transformed, for cycling, into something superficially resembling trousers. When Chubb asked her to cycle to the Cathedral, Angelica had made the alteration in private, at Herron's house. This facilitated her ability to poke, prod and knee her way through the crowd.

Chubb, to her right, was identifying himself as Scotland Yard and administering a vicious kick to the shin of anyone slow to get out of his way.

While they had hacked through a forest of people when they squeezed through the north end of the Procession to the telegraph office, Angelica and

Chubb battled no more than a few hundred souls in the "charmed circle" to the south.

"We come the right way," panted Chubb, when they reached the front of the line. "I doubt we'd ever have got through at all if we'd swung round from the north, unless we crawled over their heads and shoulders."

Angelica peered around the western churchyard.

The grandstands Herron had noted on his Sunday stroll, flanking either side of the Cathedral steps, were brimming to capacity. Bureaucratic English officialdom was fearful of accidents during times of pageantry. To be on the safe side, male and female dignitaries holding blue tickets for the Cathedral grandstands were mustered and seated as early as nine o'clock that morning.

Except for the Procession, all creatures great and small had been barred from the Cathedral yard by ten o'clock, even if they *were* privileged blue-ticket holders.

The grandstand flanking the right-hand side of the the Cathedral's west façade of was teeming with ambassadors, ministers, ladies and gentlemen of the court, and members of the diplomatic corps. Also cabinet minsters, MPs, Aldermen – anyone who could swap a seat in the Cathedral grandstands as a consolation prize for not being able to shoe-horn themselves into the Procession itself.

The left-hand side of the Cathedral, where official Colonial representatives were seated, was by far the more sumptuous. Richly-clad rajahs, resplendent in their turbaned finery, rubbed shoulders with Oriental ambassadors in silks.

Men and women were also stuffed into stands on the upper portico of the Cathedral's west facade. These fortunate few had found shade from the noon heat – but that also meant they could not *be seen*, which was half the joy of being present on this magnificent occasion.

The broad steps leading into the Cathedral from the west were blocked off on both sides. Only a narrow walkway remained for the officiating clergy.

The Anglican churchmen were all in their various copes. The Archbishops of Canterbury and York wore royal purple. The bishop of London had a cope of yellow. The bishop of Worcester, a member of the Order of the Garter, was clad in a cope of that Order's hue of blue. Other Anglican prelates wore copes of green, white, or gold.

The blocked-off areas were stuffed with representatives from non-conformist churches (including the Archbishop of Finland, representing Orthodox churches.

Behind the clergymen, on the second tier of steps leading into the Cathedral, was a cloud of white-clad choristers, boys and men.

Two military bands had also been squeezed onto the crowded steps.

The Queen would not be entering the Cathedral. Following a tumble she'd taken a few years earlier, Victoria had difficulty mounting steps without assistance. She refused to allow this immense crowd see her carried inside.

The planners toyed briefly with the notion of building a ramp for the Queen's carriage to roll bodily into Saint Paul's; but this was rejected in favor of an out-doors ceremony with the Queen's carriage parallel to the first step. That would allow the largest possible number of spectators to view the ceremony.

Though most of the clerical representatives were in their places, the clergy actually officiating on this occasion were not yet clogging the narrow walkway into the Cathedral. They awaited the Queen's approach in the shade.

Rubbing elbows with the Lords Spiritual were the Lords Temporal. Prime Minister Robert Cecil, 3rd Marquis of Salisbury, stood at rigid attention in front of the Cathedral steps, proudly wearing his blue ribbon as a Knight Companion of the Garter. Being overweight, Salisbury probably had wished for a cooler day.

The Warders of the Guard in the Tower ("Beefeaters"), in their peculiar (and peculiarly uncomfortable) finery of red and gold, were leaning on their halberds, to the southern edge of the Cathedral steps.

North of the Beefeaters, and spaced farther apart, were the Honourable Corps of Gentlemen at Arms, wearing black trousers, gold-braided coatees of vibrant red, and bright helmets topped with white swan feathers. Their captain, fifty-seven-year-old Henry Strutt, 2nd Baron Belper, watched on horseback while the infantry details deployed themselves on either side of the street as they arrived.

"Well," said Chubb, "we're here."

"But . . . now what?" Angelica pointed out the thin red line of Her Majesty's crack regiment of Coldstream Regiment of Foot Guards, topped by their fuzzy busbies. How would they chip their way through that line?

2

And the Guards were only part of the problem. Even as they watched, the entire western churchyard was filling with troops from the Procession.

The Procession was drawing in around the Cathedral for the Thanksgiving ceremony. The cavalry formed up to the north of the Cathedral. The infantry ranked in extremely close order on both sides of Ludgate Street.

Orders had come through that head-dresses were not to be removed during the services at the Cathedral; so kepis, pith helmets, busbies, wedge-shaped garrison caps and feathered bush hats rubbed shoulders with fezzes, pillbox hats, tarbooshes and a rainbow of colorful puggarees and turbans.

The Chinese contingent of the Hong Kong police wore conical sun-helmets. Submarine miners from Malta wore dark naval caps.

Forty six thousand, nine hundred and forty three military men, infantry and cavalry. The Coldstream Guards. Beefeaters. Honourable Corps of Gentlemen.

Spectators on the street. Spectators wherever they could be fit on the west front of the Cathedral. Spectators filling the enormous, multi-tiered grandstand across the street to the north. Spectators peering out from the windows and roofs of nearby buildings and grim warehouses. The people were like the camels of Midian, *without number, as the sand by the sea side for multitude.*

And Angelica and Chubb had to face them all down, to halt the Procession and evacuate them. Angelica prayed, silently and extremely fervently.

Chubb nudged her and rolled his eyes skyward.

She followed his gaze. "Oh, dear God, it's here. It really is here!"

It wasn't actually at the Cathedral. It was miles away, yet. But its shape was distinct and undeniable. It was a great, plump, golden airship.

"Never mind the bombs," said Chubb. "I think you're in the clear."

3

As word crept around the churchyard of a flying machine visible to the north-east, several of the prelates on the Cathedral steps milled down into the churchyard to take a peek – here the Right Rev. Frederick Temple, Archbishop of Canterbury, there the Right Rev. Dr. Mandell Creighton, bishop of London, who had been elevated to the chair of Saint Paul's Cathedral in January.

The Cathedral itself blocked the view to the east of many of the dignitaries and rajahs in the grandstands; but those who could see were craning their necks and pointing to a golden spot of light growing closer by the second.

Many of them thought it was a balloon – an unbilled addition to the festivities.

Those with the keenest eyes had already picked out the airship's distinctive shape. They might have read of the many futile attempts to construct a successful airship, but none of them had ever actually seen a machine flying. They might have been thinking, *What was a beautiful way to honor the Queen, keeping such a wonderful invention under wraps and producing on her day, in her honor.*

Unlike the clergy and the spectators, the military had to remain at attention, and they strained to keep their eyes straight. Yet it was difficult, for those whose view was not blocked by the Cathedral, to keep their eyes from straying to the golden oblong shape drifting easily toward the dome of Saint Paul's.

The airship was still far off, but it was descending upon the Cathedral.

Angelica and Chubb fought through the barriers to the Coldstream Guards. The airship might be unstoppable, but they were not going give up.

Once Chubb got word to the Prime Minister, he hoped to wash his hands of the affair and run. He really didn't have any authority here. He was Scotland Yard and Saint Paul's Cathedral was in the City of London.

If Chubb hoped his identity as a Scotland Yard inspector would be sufficient to worm through to the cordon of Guards at the Cathedral so he could have a quiet word with the Prime Minister, he was sadly mistaken. The Coldstream Guards proved far more obdurate than the street-lining parties had been.

"I can't let you through, sir. Them's the orders."

"I'm from Scotland Yard!" he reiterated.

"You can't get a seat without a blue ticket."

"I don't want a seat! I am Inspector Broughton Chubb of Scotland Yard, and I need to talk to the Prime Minister—that gentleman in the beard over there!"

"Still can't get in without a ticket, sir."

Chubb turned to Angelica. "We need a ticket to see the assassination."

CHAPTER LXXXIII

"'Toss him over!'" Herron echoed, appalled. "Kill him in cold blood?"

"We're over London! There's nothing more we can do! We'll take to the glider—and there are only two seats."

Stoker examined the outskirts of the city less than five hundred feet below.

"We'll be lucky to find a place to set her safely down, as it is."

Lugner protested. "You wanted me alive!" His eagerness for martyrdom melted when he saw the likelihood of being hurled ignominiously down to die in the streets with common riff-raff.

Stoker gave a casual toss of a shoulder. "We don't need you anymore. You can't override the device? No. So, you've outlived your usefulness, Lugner."

"You're going to kill me – just like that!"

"Oh, you might not *absolutely* die at this height—"

"I surrender. Unconditionally."

"Not unconditionally. These are my conditions, if you don't want to keep flying – straight down, very fast. Tell us what controls this machine!"

"It's a Tesla coil, as I said. It's there!"

He pointed at a device soldered on the lower edge of the keel, about halfway along, not far from where they stood. It had holes for the radio-waves to pass through. It had been painted grey to blend with the aluminium.

Moving over it in a precarious squat, Stoker tried to wrench it off. It didn't budge. Taking Herron's saber, he attempted to prise it loose, or work the point of the saber into one of the holes far enough to damage the device. All he achieved was to break off the saber's tip.

"I wish I had my gun! I'd shoot it off, even if I got killed in the ricochet!" Stoker poked his way back through the struts to Lugner. "And there is a device sending pulses from the Cathedral, to draw the airship, through that thing?"

"Yes. There is a device hidden the Cathedral! I do not know where! 'She who is to come' had access to private parts unseen by the public."

Herron winced. "More compartmentalizing!"

"I think it is hidden somewhere inside the outer dome."

"What if the airship gets there early?"

"It will remain in place until the explosion."

"Liar!" Stoker declared "A lighter-than-air airship can't hover in place."

"I would have thrown down the grapnel before we departed the airship in the glider. It would catch on the lantern on top of the Cathedral dome."

Herron shook his head dubiously. "Chancy, that."

"The device would settle immediately above the lantern. It would be a mere matter of hooking the grapnel to it. Once the airship was secured, it would not then matter if it was blown about by the wind. The explosion would be the same."

Stoker gave a nod. "I've heard enough. Strangways, give me his watch."

Herron didn't know what this petty theft portended, but he rummaged around in Lugner's blue-grey greatcoat until he located the timepiece.

He handed it to Stoker. "What did you want that for?"

"It's a nice Swiss watch. Don't want it to smash when Lugner smacks down on the pavement. He won't be able to use it when he's reduced to the consistency of cat's meat. Now – toss him over!"

"I won't be party to killing him that way."

"I've already let you live, Strangways. *Not* murdering two worthless slugs in less than twelve hours might set a nasty precedent."

"I've heard enough of this slug's schemes to make me reconsider the notion of wholesale murder as the answer to life's everyday little problems."

"Let me remind you, Strangways, that glider is a two-seater. I am the pilot."

"Ergo . . . you go."

"Correct. The passenger seat is the only one up for grabs. If I still had my gun I'd blast his brains out, if I can hit a target that small. Now, either we throw the slug over, or let him go up with the ship. Unless you two want to flip a coin?"

"I have an idea. If it doesn't work, we're not out anything."

2

Herron quickly outlined his idea.

London was a city of churches.

Saint Paul's Cathedral dominated London's skyline; but there were many high steeples, like so many congregations with their hands raised competing for who would be chosen to play on God's team.

The cross atop Saint Paul's Cathedral reached up to three hundred and sixty-five feet off the ground. London's other steeples and spires were lower, but *Darnley* was under five hundred feet by this time, and attracting much attention.

It was only a matter of time until they passed directly over a church.

Stoker, who had heard too much of Lugner's prattle about using "undesirables" for experimentation, savored the delectable irony of "experimenting" on Lugner.

For his part, Herron meant to bag the glider's passenger seat, but he wanted Lugner to have a sporting chance. If they left Lugner alive on the airship, he'd die by his own explosives. This way, he *might* survive.

First, Stoker relieved Lugner of his pickelhaube and goggles. These, he handed to Herron. "You'll need the goggles on the glider to keep the wind out of your eyes. The helmet won't save your life if the glider fails and you hit the ground head-first, but take it, anyway."

Herron also took the scarf.

Herron and Stoker both had fairly strong arms. Straddling the keel and lowering Lugner at arm's length, they waited.

Cocooned in his net, Lugner showed too much sense to squirm.

As Herron suspected, it was not long before another high steeple jabbed up directly beneath them. This one had a cross on top, which was even better.

Stoker knew more physics, so Herron left the call to him.

"NOW!" shouted Stoker, and they released Luger simultaneously.

With a high-pitched scream, Lugner fell away from them with all the grace of a bag of turnips. A length of the netting flutterered up in his wake.

Herron watched Lugner shrink smaller . . . smaller . . .

The net flapping up behind Lugner was very long, since it had to reach the ground when the airship at least sixty feet high.

"I think we missed," said Stoker, without a tinge of regret.

Indeed, Lugner soared down past the steeple. But the Cross on the top snagged a square of the net, snapping Lugner back before he struck the lead-lined roof.

Herron breathed a sigh of relief.

Then the wooden cross-bars on the Cross, which had been out in all weathers for years, snapped from the unaccustomed weight.

Lugner yowled in terror as the netting slid down the length of the spire.

He struck the spine of the church roof with a *thump*. Then the netting rolled in a semi-circle down the side of the roof and pitched out in front.

Lugner's fall was finally arrested by another good yank that left him dangling in front of the church like cargo being loaded into a ship.

"We'll tell Scotland Yard where to find him when we land," chuckled Stoker.

"Let's go tell 'em now!" said Herron, making for the glider.

Stoker caught Herron's shirt-tail. "Do you see anywhere to set a glider down?"

Herron didn't know precisely how much room a glider needed to land – but, over the eastern edge of the city with its dark canyons of streets between tenement houses, nowhere beneath them looked particularly promising.

"We go when I say we go! Get back in the car. Now that we don't have Lugner to worry about, I'm determined to do everything I can to keep this thing from blowing up before we abandon ship! And you're sticking with me!"

"Can't I just go sit in the glider and wait for you? I can't fly the blasted thing!"

"You might have a go."

In fact, Herron had intended to have a 'go' the moment Stoker's back was turned, if he insisted on waiting until the last possible moment before leaving. For all he knew, the clock attached to the infernal machine might be fast.

"Buck up, Strangways. You've got to be brave."

"I've been told that a lot in my life and every single time it preceded something nasty."

"Oh, shut up and come on!"

Sighing, he trailed Stoker back along the keel to the car.

The dome of Saint Paul's Cathedral lay dead ahead.

CHAPTER LXXXIV

Over the steadily increasing noise of the crowd at the Cathedral, no one heard a single horse galloping into the churchyard on his coal-black charger. The 6'8" Captain of the 2nd Life Guard, Oswald Ames, formerly leading the Royal Procession, arrived to see what was happening.

Word of the approaching airship had trickled down to the the carriage procession, still in Fleet Street. As no airship was listed in the programme, Captain Ames felt obliged to ride ahead to find out what it was all about.

A man in his position, bound to protect his sovereign's life whatever the risk to his own, did not like surprises.

Ames wore his full regalia, including the nickel-plated helmet with a long, white plume fluttering behind him. His scarlet tunic had a dark blue collar and cuffs with gold insignia, and was covered in front with a cuirass – at, least, a shining, nickel breastplate. Gold, braided shoulder-cords were slung from his epaulettes to the front of his breastplate. White, buckskin breeches were tucked far into his thigh-length boots. He also wore the gold star of the Garter.

In Fleet Street, his view had been blocked by the ugly railroad bridge and intervening buildings – including the dome of the Cathedral itself, since he was riding uphill from the west and the airship was descending from the east.

When he arrived in the churchyard, his attention zeroed not on the skies, but the commotion at the southern edge of the crowd.

Ames rode toward Chubb and Angelica. They were trying to effect an entry through the line of Coldstream Guards, but he knew the dumpy little man in the brown suit and bowler hat, and the tall and frowzy-looking female perspiring beside him, were not the well-heeled holders of blue tickets.

"What's going on here?" Ames bellowed, reining in.

Identifying himself for the umpteenth time that morning, Chubb did not bother relating his story. Rather than proceeding with a witness-box recital of events, he aimed a stubby finger at the flying machine. "There!"

Ames had anticipated the airship, but he was startled when he actually saw so large a thing floating like a cloud hundreds of feet high. "What on earth is it!"

"It's not on earth," answered Chubb. "There's a bomb in that thingumajig, and whoever's in it means to drop it on Her Majesty."

Chubb didn't know really know this beyond a doubt, but he thought that accusation would engage the full attention of a Captain of the Life Guard.

"How do you know?" Ames demanded, without lowering his eyes.

"I'm Scotland Yard. We know everything." He sincerely hoped Ames wasn't going to be like those snotty Mounties and ask the identity of Jack the Ripper.

"I'll send someone back to slow the queen's carriage. And we'll watch for objects thrown out of airships."

"Uh-huh. That's fine. And what if that feller up there realizes he's stymied, and decides to heave his explosives into that grandstand over yonder – four stories high and chock full of blistering humanity? If he throws out a bunch of dynamite, he'll kill a dozen, maybe a couple-dozen. Maybe a few hundred, if the grandstand collapses. And then we've got the panic. Look 'round – pavement, windows, grandstands. Thousands of people, maybe charging down Fleet Street in terror!"

Ames waved his gauntleted hand to show he understood. The potential death toll did not bother him. His primary duty was Her Majesty's safety. Even if she wasn't killed by a bomb, she might be irreparably damaged in a panic. He could see the stampeding thousands tipping her right out of her landau.

Ames shaded his eye with his hands, to study what he was up against.

Gleaming like an elongated second sun, the airship was approaching fast.

The Captain squinted an eye down at Chubb. "Are you quite certain they mean to bomb Her Majesty, Inspector?"

Flashing on the Captain an expression that might have curdled milk, Chubb slowly crossed his heart.

"And what do you recommend we do?" Ames realized at once that they were at a disadvantage. His being the tallest man in the British army was no use in this situation. If he climbed to the Cross atop the Cathedral and balanced the heels of his boots on the crossbars, he couldn't wave an airship away with his sword. Bullets and bayonets were equally useless. So was artillery, when shells that missed might rain down on millions of innocent bystanders.

"Well," Chubb countered, sardonically, "I can't wave my credentials and arrest 'em. This is out of my jurisdiction, and so is that. I'm just—" He turned to Angelica. "What's that bloke's name, again?"

"Paul Revere."

Warning Chubb and Angelica not to move, Ames dismounted (leaving Angelica the reins of his horse) and ran to consult with the Prime Minister, the Marquis of Salisbury. When he bowed to the Prime Minister and received permission to speak, Salisbury motioned for Baron Belper to join them.

Angelica stroked the nose of Ames' horse while she watched the Captain explain the situation to them. Salisbury and Belper both turned their eyes impotently up to the airship – then stared helplessly out over the crowd.

Tickling ears overheard their frantic discussion. Whispers passed from man to man, from warrior to warrior, that the airship meant damage to Her Majesty.

All the Queen's men were ready to fight for Her Majesty's defense. But, turning their eyes to the sky, they wondered what anyone could actually do.

2

Neither Ames, Prime Minister Salisbury, nor Baron Belper had an inkling of what they were up against. Even if they had known this was no a simple dynamite attack, they could not imagine the explosive power of bombs mixed with more than a million cubic feet of hydrogen gas and thirty-five thousand pounds of fuel.

Neither they, nor the other dignitaries and ministers who elbowed their way into their conversation, wanted start the panic they feared would ensue if they issued orders for an immediate evacuation of the Churchyard. Nor did they think it prudent. The airship would be directly above them soon, and if it didn't find targets at the Cathedral, it would drop its bombs elsewhere. (Unable to envision flying men, they spoke as if the airship had hatched the bomb plot on its own).

A full evacuation seemed impossible, but the Prime Minister hoped – somehow – to quietly clear the grandstands immediately around the Cathedral itself. Those grandstands were filled with dignitaries, than which there is nothing more intractable..

To Angelica's chagrin, the conversation roiled on. Two horseman cantered off in different directions. One of them was Baron Belper himself.

Captain Ames returned to Chubb in the company of Lord Salisbury, the Prime Minister. His Lordship's bushy beard bristled at the Inspector, and his bald head shined in the sun when he gave Angelica the lowest bow his girth allowed.

"Baron Belper," the Prime Minister informed them, "went to fetch the Metropolitan Fire Brigade, in case these terrorists have incendiary bombs. A member of the Guards was dispatched down Ludgate hill to stop the carriage Procession and bustle her Majesty to earth in Saint Martin's church. Before *we* move further—are you certain of your facts, Inspector?"

Chubb tossed a thumb toward Angelica. "This young lady has all the details."

"Is this true?" Lord Salisbury asked, kindly.

Angelica nodded.

"Please give us a précis of the situation."

All eyes turned on Angelica.

She had often wished to meet the Prime Minister; but not like this. For the first time that morning, she was conscious of her appearance. She hadn't even noticed that her blue blouse had become torn down the throat when she fell of the banister shooting at Dapifer. She didn't pull it together now, fearing to draw even more attention to her gleaming flesh with all these soldiers at hand.

Blushing, she curtsied and related all the vital information she knew. During her recital she ran a hand through her hair and found bits of fern and loam.

"How did you discover the Cathedral was their target, young lady?"

In fact, Angelica didn't know. That had been Chubb's doing. He told her it was Saint Paul's, and here they were. The airship proved his surmise correct.

"It's so," said Chubb. "I'll stake my pension on it."

"You certainly will," said one of the back-bench politicians who had dogged the Prime Minister's steps across the churchyard.

The Prime Minister thanked Angelica, then turned to Captain Ames. "May the Queen be brought to this Cathedral quickly, Captain? She might be safer inside here than where she is."

Ames, who knew how slowly the carriage procession had been moving, gave his opinion that it was impossible. "My Lord, I believe we would be exposing her unnecessarily. It's safer for her to shelter where she is."

"Very well. It will cause a peck of trouble; nevertheless, we must evacuate the Cathedral, including the churchyard and all the grandstands."

"What about the warehouse to the south, sir? And the buildings to the north?"

The Prime Minister shook his head. "I'm afraid there's enough work as it is. Do send someone through the buildings telling them to back away from the windows. And clear the roofs. That's the best we can do."

Angelica wondered what evacuating the Cathedral would accomplish.

These terrorists had come to kill, for reasons of their own. If they couldn't kill here, they'd simply fly elsewhere. The entire sky over London was their domain.

"We have artillery," said one politician who had followed the Prime Minister. "Shoot it down!"

The Prime Minister was adamant on this point. "If the airship truly means harm, there is no safe way for artillery to shoot it down without accomplishing just what those villains want: destruction, death and terror."

Some of the MPs and dignitaries who had tagged along with the Prime Minister argued that Saint Paul's should not be evacuated. The crowd, they insisted, should be led *into* the Cathedral, not away from it.

"The people are sitting ducks on the streets," insisted the politician. "Whoever is up there cannot pitch down enough dynamite to blow up an entire Cathedral."

The Prime Minister glanced up. "They may have a powerful bomb, indeed."

Many were disinclined to believe in the existence of a bomb that could damage anything beneath the Saint Paul's enormous, lead-coated dome.

"With all due respects," answered Lord Salisbury, in his famous words, "a half-hour ago I was prepared to disbelieve in the existence of an airship."

Unfortunately, by this time the argument had become general. Everyone – General officers, foreign potentates, clerics and idlers, had an opinion and attempted to weigh in with it.

Politicians who had never heard of airships before, and had no notion what kept them aloft, suddenly became experts on dealing with them.

Leaders of the opposition to the Prime Minister, who would naysay anything he suggested on general principles, began pointing fingers at his administration for causing the situation. They raised serious questions about the bona fides of the young woman who was the source of this clandestine information.

Some went so far as to hypothesize that the airship posed no serious danger; they demanded, in the interest of safety, Chubb and Angelica be arrested as troublemakers who were disrupting the public order. They would not believe in a genuine threat until they were blown up themselves.

Obstreperous "Little Englanders" thundered, with smug gratification, that the very multi-colored Procession proved that the Empire's chickens were coming home to roost. A few of them even voiced compassion for the terrorists, rather than for the men, women and children they had come to massacre.

They believed the terrorists must be striking from genuine grievances, rather than to seize the throne in the name of a descendant of Bonny Prince Charlie, who wanted to erect a governmental Leviathan that included a eugenics programme that would decrease the surplus population by any persons the government deemed poor breeding stock. Though they didn't know it (because they neither had, nor wanted, the facts), they were colluding with terrorists and eugenicists.

Angelica did not know Lugner's plans, but she considered that last group, otherwise good Englishmen, complicit in mass homicide.

Whichever side they took, Angelica soon had all the arguing she could stomach. "Oh, *Hell!*" she growled.

Wresting her gun back from Chubb, she darted for the Cathedral.

Coldstream Guards, Beefeaters, and Honourable Corps of Gentlemen at Arms all tried to grab her; but she had been a proficient field-hockey player at school, and she dodged adroitly around them all.

With nearly all the front steps of Saint Paul's blocked off, Angelica saw that her only access to the Cathedral lay straight through the officiating clergy. Diving into them for sanctuary, she was quickly swallowed by prelates and choristers.

Since she was taller than some of them, she charged up the steps in a stoop.

Chubb lost sight of her at first. Then he was able to follow her progress by the path she made burrowing through the white cloud of choristers, elbowing and head-butting them out of her way.

He glimpsed her once, when her head and shoulders popped abruptly above the white-clad choirboys with the indignant yip of a stung Pekinese. Presumably, one of them sneaked a pinch or pat on a place Angelica considered private property.

Then her head went down again. Chubb could clearly observe the her snaky progress, he didn't see her again until she sprang upright the top of the steps.

Tall though she was, Angelica was dwarfed by the enormous columns on the lower porch.

Clasping one hand on the top of her head, as if she'd banged it against a particularly unyielding choirboy, she raised her pistol in an outstretched arm and fired at a slant into the air until all the chambers were empty.

This started the evacuation off nicely.

Dignitaries in tail-coats or maguas, prelates in copes of many colors, white-clad choristers and dark ministers of state, all took to their heels as if Angelica had fired the starting pistol for a cross-country sprint with hundreds of contestants.

Some of it was more like a steeplechase, since the people were leaping and knocking over barriers – and each other – in their haste to get away.

The Coldstream Guards and the military began shepherding the stream of people as far as Ludgate Circus, where they flooded every street.

The Honorable Corps of Gentlemen at Arms, the Yeomen of the Guard, the Coldstream Guards and the military, all of whom by this time knew the airship's nefarious purpose, threw themselves eagerly into assisting the evacuation of the roofs of surrounding buildings and grandstands, while miniminzing the alarm.

The important thing was to keep London, whose normal population of four million was this day almost doubled, from wholesale panic.

3

Chubb, scuttling at a list with the heavy wicker box of the wireless telegraph gripped in one hand, fought his way up the Cathedral steps against the torrent.

At the top of the steps, he found Angelica struggling with several minor clergymen. They had applied for, and received, special permission to attend by the Dean of the Saint Paul's, the Very Reverend Robert Gregory, and had been standing in the rear of the lower portico, uncertain of what was going on below, until a desperate-looking woman began firing shots into the air.

While, unlike the choirboys, being scrupulously careful of her femininity, the clergymen had disarmed Angelica and were holding her arms behind her back until help arrived.

She squirmed and kicked her feet back at them, but they held her tight.

"Inspector Chubb!" he announced as he topped the steps. "Scotland Yard. I'll take custody of the lady. You get the hell out of this House of God."

Everyone was quick to take his advice. The clergymen who had wrested the pistol from Angelica handed the gun over to Chubb.

Pocketing the bulldog revolver, Chubb latched a hand onto Angelica's wrist. Together, they shouldered their way through the doors of the Cathedral against the evacuees pouring out all around them.

"Now," said Chubb, "if those airshippers have a bomb, I reckon the safest place to be under all that brick in the dome. Terrorists don't have much imagination, you see. Or, as we used to say in the services, they make good artillery but poor cavalry. Once they got an idea in their heads, they'll carry it through if it kills 'em; but they can't adjust to changing conditions. Even if they do thrown dynamite the Cathedral, they can't bring the whole bloomin' thing down around our ears!"

Unfortunately, Chubb had no conception of what nearly forty tons of flaming aluminium might feel like when it crashed down on his head.

CHAPTER LXXXV

The interior of the church was pandemonium. Confused people, some in uniform, were darting mindlessly through the 121-feet wide, nave and up and down the stairs.

Those running inside from the upper western portico had only vaguely heard what was going on, but rumors were rife:

An airship was dropping bombs over London.

Gunshots had been fired at the Queen.

The gunshots were the military killing the terrorists.

Victoria was dead.

Her Majesty was rolling safely back to Buckingham Palace.

Christ was descending as He had ascended, and the gunshots they had heard signified the outbreak of Armageddon.

(Ludgate Hill was a long way from Mount Olivet where Christ presumably was returning; but on that day, it made sense to Englishmen that He'd come the most cosmopolitan city in the world, rather than make His landing among the nomadic tribes of the Judean hills in the thrall of the Ottoman Empire).

Joining Chubb and Angelica, Captain Ames reporting that the Queen was safe.

However, since no one had ever bombed London from the air, it was difficult to know how precise a word "safe" was.

To Ames, Chubb explained what he and Angelica had to do, and Ames decided to stay, guarding them. His principle duty lay with Her Majesty, but his idea of preserving the Queen was broad enough to include trying to halt terrorists bombings via diplomacy.

Ames pushed through the crowd, making way for Angelica and the Inspector.

They followed Ames over the black-and-white checkerboard Cathedral floor, between massive piers, until they found a rare space clear of traffic and confusion on the south side of the great circle beneath the dome.

Angelica plopped down with her back against a stone carved with the inscription, "Blessed are the pure in heart for they shall see God."

The Cathedral's interior was welcomely cool after Angelica's active morning.

It was also dark. Candles had been lit throughout the Cathedral, but they were being knocked over and doused in the blind confusion.

Seeing they were snug where they were, Ames said, "I'm going to assist with the evacuation." Loping off on his long legs, he called, "I'll be back!"

Angelica sat cross-legged in her trouser-like cycling skirt. In the dim light filtering through the windows in the 173-feet high dome, she opened the wireless telegraph's wicker case.

Her cursory perusal of the telegraph at Herron's house paid dividends. In the gloom, her groping hand easily located the switch that sparked the telegraph to life. She slid the listening tubes up to her ears.

"Whatcha gonna say?" wondered Chubb, fanning himself with his bowler.

She didn't look up. "I'll tell them Lady Calthrop is dead. I'll identify myself as her companion Miss Trickett and say I—I saw her die."

"Don't tell 'em—" he started; and paused, uncertain of his phraseology.

Angelica knew what he meant: *Don't tell them you killed her.*

Despite her tension, she broke into a smile. "I won't. Maybe when they hear she's dead they'll turn around."

Chubb paced back and forth before her with his hands in the small of his back, his fingers waggling his hat behind him like a vestigal tail. Knowing the mind-set of terrorists, he muttered, "Not bloody likely."

"Anything's worth a—Ah! Here we go! Thank God! I have it."

Chubb nodded and continued his pacing.

Without looking up, Angelica asked, "Are you a praying man, Inspector?"

"I wasn't when I got up this mornin', but I've been at it constant since I met you. I'll slip in another word or two for you."

"Thank you." She took a deep breath, flexed her fingers and, in a most unladylike gesture, cracked her knuckles. "Here we go."

Though her heart still beat in her throat from running and biking and facing down a crowd – including thousands of armed men, Angelica felt perfectly calm now that she was sitting down to familiar work that required all her concentration.

CHAPTER LXXXVI

From Herron vantage-point in the broken windshield of the airship's car, the dome of Saint Paul's, rising to three hundred and sixty-five feet from the pavement to the top of the Cross, was London's most obvious landmark. At four hundred feet and dropping, the airship looked likely to drive right into it.

A disaster could not be averted. The bomb was due to explode at twelve precisely and they had no safe way to extract it from its ballonet – whichever one it was. Even if Stoker found a way to override the lock on the wheel, they would have to blow up *something* in London.

They had to make their own departure, soon, and Herron saw no suitable place to set down a glider in the dark canyons-like streets of eastern London.

"How far is the Cathedral?" grunted Stoker, from a crouch behind the wheel. He no longer believed he could override the lock; he suspected it was tied in with the radio control device guiding them inexorably toward their target.

"Hard to gauge distances up here, old man."

"What do you think this means?" Stoker rose, holding out two open watches, one in each palm. "Lugner's watch is set ten minutes forward of mine."

"Maybe it's on Swiss time."

"On an important mission like this, he doesn't set his watch properly?"

"More important for us, old man, is—by which time is his infernal machine set to explode, his or yours? You're sure your watch is right?"

"I set it by Big Ben at six o'clock Saturday night. It keeps perfect time, so long as it's wound. It can't have gone ten minutes wrong in sixty-six hours."

Saturday evening seemed ages ago to Herron. Had it been less than seventy hours since the haggard bird was killed?

Herron cut his eyes out the front window. "I can see the Houses of Parliament from here, but I can't read the clock. Say, what precisely is the explosive impact of all this hydrogen, and fuel, and God knows what other hellish devices?"

"The hydrogen and the petrol alone will be devastating. And *Darnley* is more than heavy enough to crush the Cathedral if we crash down with our full weight."

"Will our full weight crash down on it?"

"The ship will descend slowly at first, as hydrogen is consumed by fire. When the hydrogen is gone, our weight will smash the Cathedral to powder."

"Oh. Too bad. May I have Lugner's watch?"

"No. I want to ponder out why it's set the way it is."

Stoker pocketed both watches in different pockets in his waistcoat and disappeared again beneath the ship's wheel.

A muffled buzzing commenced from the wicker box in the corner.

From the floor, Stoker called, "What's *that*, now?"

"I don't know."

"Well, find out! We don't need any more trouble!"

Unable to pinpoint the sound at first, Herron took a three hundred and sixty degree turn around the car. At length honing in on the wireless telegraph, he started to nudge it overboard with a swift kick of his foot.

"No!" Lunging from the floor, Stoker clutched Herron's ankle with both hands. "Not that! It's the wireless telegraph!"

Herron squatted beside it, threw open the lid – and leapt back, just in case it had an explosive attached to it.

Inside was the strangest device he had ever seen – and he had seen quite a few monstrosities pass through Strangways' hallowed doorways, going both ways.

Herron would not have known a "Ruhmkorff Coil" if he saw one (or any other part of the telegraph's innards), but he noticed one quality immediately.

"It's sparking like hell! And we have a leak overhead thanks to your bullet!"

"Hydrogen rises," Stoker reminded him.

"I believe I heard once in chapel, *man is born unto trouble, as the sparks fly upward*. If these sparks fly upward—Boom!"

"You're flying upward right now! We can't close the hatch, but you just get on the roof of the car and cover that hole I made. Just to be on the safe side."

"On the roof?"

"What are you now – my echo? Go!"

Herron scaled the ladder, lodging official protests all the way.

He found no hand-holds on to on the car's roof, just slick metal sloping away from the hatch.

Since the ladder was too far for him to hold and cover the bullet-hole, he clung to like grim death to the edge of the hatchway. From there, he looked down on Stoker kneeling at the machine and putting the listening-tubes to his earholes.

"They've done an amazing job of reducing this wireless telegraphic set!" Stoker called up. "The last one I saw was huge."

"What's it saying!"

"Shhh!" With the listening tubes to his ears, Stoker winced at every pulse. The relative proximity of the machines made the pulses extremely loud.

Stoker cocked his head up. "It's from someone named Trickett—"

"Angelica!"

"Shh!"

"She knows Morse."

"Obviously! Shh!" Stoker pronounced his next words slowly, as they arrived. "*Lady Calthrop is dead stop.* Who's Lady Calthrop?"

"Never mind. That's the best present I've had since Christmas."

Another string of pulses shot up at them from below – and Stoker emitted a burst of stentorian laugher.

Having never heard Stoker laugh, Herron jumped as if the bomb had gone off. "What is it?"

"This Trickett is pleading with us to abort the mission! As if that wasn't what I've been trying to do! Who is Trickett, anyway – some sort of accomplice?"

"No, she's on our side."

While tapping out his answer, Stoker said, "Since we will shortly be bombing the Cathedral ourselves, that's hardly a recommendation."

CHAPTER LXXXVII

"It's from a . . . S-t-o-k-e-r." Angelica spelled out the unfamiliar surname as she received the letters.

Since the airship was so close, the radio signals were not the weak buzzings she had heard through Lady Calthrop's door. These pulses, heard through the listening tubes, shot through her ears and exploded together in her brain.

"Stoker!" Chubb's voice rang out and echoed in the Cathedral Ames was successfully evacuating. "He was the bloke who took Strangways from the Underground station."

Angelica clapped her hands with a squeal. "Herrie's in the airship!"

"Are they?" Chubb responded, drably.

"Herron Strangways!" She wiped her eyes. "He's in the airship with this Stoker! He's alive! Oh, thank God!" Her body began quivering and she wiped her eyes. "The silly goose is alive up there. Oh, thank God!"

"And they're still sending, Miss Trickett."

"Yes . . . yes . . ." She blinked moisture from her lashes. "Yes, they've overpowered the pilot—"

Not knowing what else to do, Chubb gave his hat a wave, like a sardonic flag.

"—but the airship is bearing down on the Cathedral—! What! Oh God! Inspector, there's a bomb set to go off at twelve but they can't find it. It's in a bag of pure *hydrogen*. The whole airship is going to explode!"

"Tell 'em to fly away! Go! Go! Go!"

CHAPTER LXXXVIII

"Shh!" said Stoker again, trying vainly to silence the excited Herron while listening to Angelica's reply. "*The conspiracy is discovered. Dap-i-fer told all.* What in hell's a Dapifer?"

"Lady Calthrop's pet gorilla."

"I don't like it."

"I do."

"It's a trick."

"Trickett," Herron gently corrected.

Stoker twisted his neck to glare up at Herron. "How do we know there is a Miss Trickett?"

"I met her. She's a peach."

"I mean, how do we know this is her on the other wireless set?"

"She wouldn't lie about a thing like that."

"If you're from Cambridge I'm sending my children, if any, to Oxford. Listen, I need the person at the other end of this wireless telegraph to prove her identity."

"Oh, I get you! Prove it's her! Right. How do you propose she does that?"

"She's your pal. Is there any secret word or phrase only the two of you know?"

Herron frowned, thinking furiously. Then,

"By jingo, there is. First, tell her you want her to establish her identity."

Stoker began sending.

Almost immediately, angry pulses were returned, so loud Stoker had to rip the listening-tubes away from his ears.

"She wants to know how she's supposed to do that over a telegraph."

"Transmit one word."

Stoker poised his finger over the key. "Ready."

CHAPTER LXXXIX

After sending Chubb's "Go-go-go" Angelica sat back, gnawing one corner of her elastic lower lip as she watched the telegraph, as if intense concentration might make a reply come faster.

Her joy at Herron's marvelous resurrection from the dead gave her an even more keen attention to duty. Though the Cathedral was cool and she was sitting against stone, she dabbed perspiration off her brow with the heel of her hand.

Chubb bent over the machine with his hands on his knees. "Ain't they home?"

Angelica shrugged.

Suddenly, the pulses recommenced.

Though he didn't understand Morse, Chubb cocked his head to hear it better.

"No!" Angelica cried. Her transmitting finger (the right middle) beat a quick, angry tattoo on the telegraph key (the angry pulses Stoker had received).

Yanking down the listening tubes, she shouted, her voice reverberating through the church, "*Damn* them! They want me to prove who I am!"

Chubb raised his eyes as if he could see the airship through the dome. "How?"

A short burst of pulses returned over the receiver. Taking up the listening-tubes, Angelica held them one ear.

... then drew them away from her head and stared at them, puzzled.

"Well?" demanded Chubb. "What did they say?"

"Just one word."

"What?"

"*Monocle.*"

"Oh, my hat!" Chubb shoot his fists in the air and kicked the wall. "What sort of rary-fied air are they breathing up there!"

Angelica repeated the word *monocle* over and over. It reminded her of—oh, something said at tea; but she couldn't finesse that ball into the hole.

"Well?" demanded Chubb. "We haven't got all morning. And we don't have any afternoon if the thing detonates at twelve."

"Shh! Please let me think."

"Oh, take all day – until noon." He started to extract his watch, then decided the better of it. He didn't want to know how much time they had remaining.

Angelica sat stark still, except for her full lips, which silently mouthed, *Monocle. Monocle? Mon*—

She froze.

"Right. Transmitting."

"What?" Chubb demanded.

"*Two* words."

"What???"

CHAPTER XC

As Angelica's message reached the airship, Stoker scratched his head through the combed-over hair. "I can't make this out."

"I thought that was your *raison d'etre*. Is the answer, *magnified insect*?"

"Yes."

"It's her. I'd trust her with my life."

"You will." Beginning another transmitting, Stoker shook his head. "Young people certainly talk differently these days than when I was courtin'."

CHAPTER XCI

Angelica did not don the listening tubes with the other machine so close. The pulses hurt her ears. Holding both ends to one ear with her left hand, with her right she brushed her hair out of her face, which was scrunched up with vexation.

"They can't control the airship – no, I don't understand why. They'll be overhead precisely at noon. The whole shebang is going to blow up and almost forty tons of blazing metal is going to come crashing straight down on top of us."

"Even if they could steer it, they probably couldn't get that gubbins of London in that time. If they're going to explode anyway, it might as well be here where there's nobody they can kill."

He glanced wryly at Captain Ames, who had just returned from his successful evacuation.

"'Cept the three of us."

Still listening acutely to the tubes pressed to one ear, Angelica waved Chubb to hush. "They're begging us to find some hidden device that's drawing them here."

"Ask 'em what! Ask 'em where!"

Angelica complied. An answer shot back. Angelica repeated the words slowly and intently as their pulses arrived, "*I-d-o-n-t-b-l-o-o-d-y-k-n-o-w.*"

Angelica, Chubb and Ames gazed all around the vast, empty interior of St Paul's Cathedral's – eighty-four thousand, three hundred and eleven square feet.

Two unspoken words occurred to them: *needle* and *haystack*.

CHAPTER XCII

Herron dared a glance over his shoulder. "Cathedral dead behind."

"There's nothing more we can do, Strangways. To the glider!"

Herron was already edging around the ladder when Stoker's resigned tone changed abruptly.

"No! Stop! Maybe there is one thing more we can do!" Stoker frantically pounded the telegraph key. "There – *that's* all we can do."

"What?" Herron called down through the hatch.

"You stay out on the keel, near that *thing*. Don't go near the glider."

"Can't we take a vote on whether to go or stay?"

"I'm breaking the tie. Go out along the keel and roost near that device. I'll join you shortly. Maybe."

"What do you want me to do?"

"Point out the device. Maybe someone on the other end can shoot it dead!"

CHAPTER XCIII

"The Golden Gallery!" shouted Angelica, receiving Stoker's message. "What's that?"

Captain Ames replied, "It's at the top of the dome."

"He wants there. *Pistol*! Yes. He wants us to shoot something. *'Then telegraph back to say it's done and run like Hell.'* Sorry, just repeating—"

"That's okay, Miss," answered Chubb. "I say that quite a lot." He turned to the Captain. "How do we get to this Golden Gallery?"

"Aren't you a native Londoner?" shot Angelica, accusingly.

"Yeah. So I'm not a bloomin' sight-seer! Where is it, Captain?"

Ames described how to get there. Then, springing ahead on his long legs, he called, "You two go on up the stairs! I have a stop to make first."

Helping her rise and carry the machine, Chubb turned quizzically to Angelica.

"Did you say shoot some*thing* or some*one* . . . ?"

CHAPTER XCIV

Facing south on the keel, Herron saw Tower Bridge drift by in the distance, the Monument, London Bridge. They were still descending.

London Bridge being the easternmost extent of the Procession route, when they passed that point the streets became black with people. They were sailing low enough for Herron to see faces turned up to them and fingers pointing, but he could not discern facial details. Herron was one of those people who, in a high place, always had a desperate urge to spit; but he was well-bred enough not to.

As they neared the Cathedral, Stoker yanked the cord on the whistle. The jet of hydrogen gas shooting through it made a high-pitched whine that nearly shattered Herron's eardrums. The terrifying whistle, like the shriek of a soul in Hell, coming from a descending flying machine, assisted the evacuation.

If they went any lower and settled directly over the lantern, Herron considered leaping down to the Golden Gallery crowning the dome. It was the only part of the Cathedral he could possibly reach without a rope (he knew from experience how impossible it would be to lower himself from the airship at the end of a rope).

He rejected the plan at once. The Golden Gallery made a small target and he might crack his shinbone on the stone. *And all those bally stairs!* he recalled.

More than five hundred steps down to street level. Not enough time remained to run down downstairs and out of the Cathedral.

As he watched the great, grey dome of Saint Paul's Cathedral floating up to him, Herron was shocked to see three tiny figures scurrying out onto the Golden Gallery. Whoever they were, they were doomed.

The breeze was stiff at that height, and the approaching airship engines added to the turbulence. One of the trio, weighted down by a wicker box just like the wireless telegraph box in the car, brushed hair from her face.

Cinderella! What in God's name is she doing up here!

He tried shouting, "Get out, this dam' balloon's gonna pop!" but they were too far away to hear. Even if Herron had been directly overhead, the drone of the engines would have drowned his shouts.

Herron lost all fear for himself in a greater fear for her. He'd remain in the airship to be reduced to a vapor, if only he knew she could get safely away.

And there she was, on top of the dome, with about ten minutes to spare before the worst man-man explosion in history erupted just a few yards over her head.

Chubb was with her. After the questioning he'd endured Sunday, Herron was glad to know the Inspector would shortly be reduced to his constituent particles. But Chubb's imminent loss to the world did not compensate for Angelica's.

Attracting Chubb's attention by waving his arms, Herron pointed out the radio control device and mimed shooting at it with thumb and forefinger.

CHAPTER XCV

Chubb took aim with the bulldog revolver.

Angelica was sick of gunfire that day, though she had been responsible most for it. Circling the lantern, she sat facing out, ready to receive and/or transmit.

Since the airship was approaching from the northeast, Angelica circled the gallery to the southwest. Fortunately for her, it was the best view.

To the northeast and northwest one typically saw only sooty roof-tops spreading out to the hazy distance. To the southwest, on this sunny day Angelica overlooked the curve of the river where it was crossed by Waterloo Bridge, near the spot on the Embankment where she spied the Cathedral. Also in eyeshot were the picturesque (if squat) neo-Gothic towers of the Palace of Westminster.

She did not look out long. From here, she also had a good view of the the clock tower of Saint Paul's, and she sedulously avoided glancing at it. Like Chubb, she didn't want to know how much time she had to left to live.

She had only just seated herself – when she jumped at an explosion. Peering around the gallery, she saw Chubb had fired a shot to get his range – then a second – then a third. Chubb hadn't been modest when he said he was no a crack shot.

Herron, on the airship's keel, ducked to one side with his hands over his head, as if his elbows would stop a wayward bullet. Chubb's shots were puncturing the envelope all around him, introducing oxygen into the ballonets.

After reloading, Chubb lowered himself to one knee and steadied his arm against the Golden Gallery's railing.

His first shot in that position struck the device dead center.

Herron looked to the door of the car. Stoker appeared, shaking his head. The Tesla Coil was undamaged. The steering gear was still locked.

Herron motioned for Chubb to fire again.

It took nine direct hits – out of two dozen rounds – but Chubb finally tore enough bullets through the metal cover to damage the device.

A message began rattling through Angelica's listening tubes. To compete with the furious noise of the approaching airship, she shoved the listening tubes into her ears and covered them with her hands.

Angelica's machine had been overworked, dragged through the streets, bumped about in a bicycle basket, and shaken up hundreds of stairs.

With the two machines so close, as Stoker tried to announce he had gained control of the ship's wheels, a tube in the maltreated machine exploded, *BANG* – with flash of light and a puff of smoke through the shattered glass.

Angelica was thrown flat on her back.

She didn't notice the pain in her cheek from a glass shard in her face, or the blood drizzling down her jaw.

Her eyes were fixed straight up. From where she lay on the Golden Gallery, the top of the Cross on Saint Paul's towered eighty-five feet over her. Higher than than the Cross, she saw the enormous underbelly of the golden airship nosing thirty yards directly overhead.

CHAPTER XCVI

Stoker's right hand vainly tryied to turn the locked ship's wheel. His eyes were fixed on his watch, which lay open in his left palm.

His minute hand was mere minutes away from XII when the Tesla Coil was sufficiently damaged for the ship's wheel to become operational.

Stoker immediately went to the wireless and tapped a message to Angelica – the one that blew a tube in her machine. Pausing to raise a satisfied thumb at Herron through the open door of the car, he tossed out the grapnel.

Herron wondered why he did that; but since Saturday, Stoker had moved in mysterious ways, his wonders to perform.

From his vantage point just north-east of the lantern, Herron did not see Angelica. He frantically waved for Chubb to scarper, believing even the Inspector had sense enough to take her with him.

Then Herron clenched his eyes as the huge ship nosed sharply upward.

CHAPTER XCVII

No time remained to charge back into the Cathedral and clatter down hundreds of steps. From where they stood, Chubb, Angelica and Ames had to descend the two hundred and eighty feet to the pavement by a quicker route.

While Chubb was shooting and Angelica operating the wireless set, Captain Ames had not been idly enjoying the view. He had been knotting ropes.

When he was satisfied as to their length, Ames secured one end of a rope to the railing around the golden gallery.

Climbing over the railing and swinging down onto the dome, Ames descended swiftly all the way to the Stone Gallery at the dome's base. His leather gauntlets protected his hands as he slid. He had two other ropes coiled on his shoulders.

Tying another rope on the stone gallery's stone rail, he mounted the Stone Gallery's rail (with difficulty), and slid down to the Cathedral roof.

The Golden Gallery was 280 feet from the pavement, and the Stone Gallery 173. And when he reached the roof he was still more than 100 feet high.

Lighting on the southern roof like a cat (even in heavy boots) Ames tight-roped along the spine and secured a final rope fast around the base of the statue directly over the south portico. Here, he dropped off his helmet and cuirass.

All this done, he ran back along the roof and climbed up the ropes – from the roof to the Stone Gallery, then up the dome to the Golden Gallery – while Chubb was still trying to find his mark.

CHAPTER XCVIII

The airship's nose shadowed Angelica's face where she lay sprawled back.

Unable to transmit any longer, she abandoned the wireless set and ran to Ames. The Captain assisted her over the rail of the Golden Gallery. Being young and tall and agile, Angelica easily topped the rail. Ames helped her grip the rope, and she descended hand-under-hand.

She had left all her lovely gloves at Park Lane, since Lady Calthrop had given them to her. And she hadn't thought to pilfer a set of Herron's.

Perhaps that was a lack of foresight on her part; but, even after all she'd been through, Angelica never expected to be slithering down ropes on the dome of Saint Paul's Cathedral before luncheon.

Without gloves, the ropes tore into her palms. She was still on the outward swell of the dome when she noticed bloodstains wherever she touched.

Edging down the ninety feet of curving lead dome along one of its ribs, the wind swept her hair over her face. She let it fly.

When she looked down, she saw nothing beneath her feet because of the dome's curvature. She could almost believe that if she lost her grip she would splatter out on the street.

Actually, if she lost her grip she'd slide down the dome to the end of the curve, accelerating all the way. At the end of the curve, she would shoot off the dome and free-fall to the stone gallery at the base of the dome, breaking both her legs and probably her back and neck.

Or, overshooting the Stone Gallery, she would plummet an additional seventy feet, smashing to instant death onto the lead roof.

She didn't look down again. Hearing an almighty *thunk*, she glanced up, almost afraid the bomb had exploded early.

The airship's car struck the Cross in the small of its back, twisting it to the south and buckling it out. Meanwhile, the airship's nose began ascending.

A humongous grapnel swung wildly beneath the rising car. One of its huge flukes snagged the lantern.

With the grapnel hooked to the heavy lantern, the rising airship was anchored in place, though—yes, both the Cross and the ball beneath were so damaged by the collision they looked likely to topple right on top of her.

That gave Angelica the strength to continue swiftly down the rope.

Before long, she rested on the lip of the lead dome, high above the Stone Gallery. She clung there panting until Captain Ame's boots came in sight. Then she slid down the Stone Gallery, searing her already damaged hands.

Instead of going down the second rope immediately, politeness dictated she wait for the others. Besides, the rail was too high for her to climb without help.

Captain Ames slid to with ten feet of the Stone Gallery. Dropping the rest of the way, he leaned back at the rail, ready to catch Chubb if he fell.

Chubb, though, was sturdier than he looked. Perhaps aided by a hefty dose of adrenaline, he was down almost as quickly as the Captain.

Ames had been leaning back over the railing and looking up at Chubb. When the Inspector landed, the Captain rushed suddenly forward, slamming Angelica and Chubb back against the Stone Gallery's wall.

The ball and Cross on top of the lantern broke loose. Chunking hard against the dome, it skidded down the lead with a terrible screech of metal against the metal – until it reached the end of the curve and tumbled free.

The ball struck the rail of the Stone Gallery, shattering part of the balustrade and showering them all with sharp chips. Then the ball and Cross slammed onto the southern roof of the Cathedral, caving in part of the spine.

Fortunately, the missing part of the stone balustrade was near where Ames had tied his rope. Ames helped Angelica step through the gap and grasp the rope.

This was a shorter distance down than the dome, but it was more precarious.

The Stone Gallery was supported by Corinthian columns, and the rope hung straight down in an empty space between two of them. Angelica's shoes vainly kicked the air for a foot-hold as she spiraled down.

Just before her foot touched down, her bleeding hands refused to hold. Losing her grip, she fell the rest of the way to the roof, smacking down bent over the spine. The wind was knocked out of her; she wondered if she'd cracked a rib.

Pushing herself up on her hands—she was dismayed to see the ball and Cross lying in the way. The roof was dented and crushed beneath it, and the slope to either side was difficult to negotiate in button-shoes.

Chubb plopped onto the roof behind Angelica, and Captain Ames brought up the rear – so close, his boots nearly clumped down on the Inspector's head.

With Captain Ames' welcome assistance, Angelica and Chubb navigated around the battered ball and Cross, fighting the dented lead slopes until they reached the statue at the end of the roof. Poking around the Cross, however, wasted precious moments.

Had Ames had tied the final rope to the balustrade, they might have rappelled all the way down to the ground; but the Captain deemed that too hazardous. The rope reached the ground but by way of the southern portico.

Slipping swiftly down the rope from the statue, Ames balanced himself on the semi-circular roof of the southern portico. The roof was arched, but the stone was terraced in rings, which afforded Ames' boots some traction.

Holding the rope taut with one hand, he extended his other arm up to steady the others when they came within reach.

Sidling around the statue under its uplifted right arm, Angelica saw the airship rising, at a forty-five degree angle, to the extent of its tether. The grapnel's rope strained between the lantern and the car.

Despite herself, she also glanced at the gold Roman numerals of the face of the clock in the Cathedral's western tower to her left. Three minutes of twelve.

Her shoulder and side aching from her fall to the roof, Angelica began a cautious descent down the rope, though Ames called for her to hurry. She wanted to hurry, but she couldn't move any faster.

Her slow descent gave her a good view of figures carved on the wall on this side of the Cathedral.

The triangular pediment over the south portico of Saint Paul's Cathedral was decorated with a rising Phoenix. The Fire Bird had a more than passing resemblance to an angry chicken spreading its wings in a conniption fit.

Beneath the explosive nest a word was carved in stone:

RESVRGAM

Gasping at the huge word stretched before her eyes, Angelica lost her grip—yards above the portico roof.

She grabbed for some stone scrollwork as she plummeted, and a stone head beneath it – a cherub, or a petulant baby. It slowed her fall; but her bloody hands could not cling on.

Ames caught her before she pounded onto the stone, and they fell together.

Rolling out of his arms on impact, Angelica bounded face-up, down the step-rings terracing the roof of the portico until her long legs kicked out over the edge.

She stopped sliding, but she teetered on the edge. Unable to hold onto anything, she was terrified of making any movement. If she tried squirming back, she might slide forward—more than fifty feet to the pavement.

For his part, Ames, landing facing forward, clutched frantically at the terraced stone with his gauntlets and his boots. Stopping his own slide, he slithered forward on his stomach and reached an arm out to her. "Grasp my hand."

The least movement on her part might send Angelica over the brink. She saw neither Ames or his hand; but, facing up, she had a good view of the enormous airship. She had just come more than two hundred feet to get away from it, and it still directly overhead.

Deciding she might as well die one way as another, she threw her arm back over her head. A gauntleted hand grasped her wrist. She slid a few inches—and stopped. If he released his grip, she'd be over.

She was no longer in danger of falling; but, for all his strength, Ames was unable to haul her up in his position. And the edge of the southern portico dug painfully into the small of her back, breaking her in two.

"Can I be of assistance?" Inspector Chubb had slithered down behind Angelica, and was leaning over them with his hands on his knees.

Instead of helping pull her up, Chubb handed her the rope.

Angelica had no time to worry about bloody palms or aching ribs. She slid. The rope passing through her shredded flesh felt like it was woven with thorns.

She struck the walk hard and, button-shoes or not, ran for all she was worth toward the river.

Crossing the street without looking, she was nearly run down by the horses of the Metropolitan Fire Brigade, screaming up to contain any blaze.

She was still exposed in the street when she heard the first explosion.

CHAPTER XCIX

Herron clung desperately to the airship's keel while the elevators lifted the airship's nose higher—higher—! The grapnel hooked in the lantern kept the airship from moving away from the Cathedral, so it nosed up at a slant. It was tossed unpleasantly to and fro by the winds, but it wasn't going anywhere.

After pushing the engines to their top speed, Stoker shot out of the hatch to the roof of the car bellowing "Go! Go! Go!"

Herron was stepping gingerly through the struts attaching the keel to the superstructure when Stoker pushed up behind him, not caring whether he shoved Herron along the keel or off it.

"Shut up," he snapped, though Herron had not spoken. "Onto the glider!"

The glider had two seats, one directly behind the other.

Straddling the seats with Stoker in front Herron asked, "How's it work?"

"You bank it by shifting your weight."

"How do I know which way to lean?"

"Just what I do. And hang on!"

Herron thought that superfluous advice, when they were exposed on a glider dozens of yards over the Cathedral roof at the tail end of an explosive airship being blown about by the wind. "Where are you going to land!"

"In the river, if I can control it through the explosions. Can you swim?"

"Oh, yes."

"I can't. I'll get you out of the air—you get me out of the water. Cast off!"

Stoker reached up and pulled a handle above their heads. The glider came loose from the ascending airship.

Herron expected to feel the glider held up by the weight of the air.

Instead, it dropped like two rocks.

CHAPTER C

The first, faint, explosion simultaneously released oxygen, from a container attached to the bomb, and fire. This caused a flame in one of the ballonets.

Glancing over her shoulder, Angelica saw a glow inside the envelope near the tail, like a giant Japanese lantern.

Immediately afterward came the first *BOOM* of exploding hydrogen.

Angelica felt the shock of the explosion quivering through the pavement – through the very air, shattering shop and house windows and littering the street with glass. The shock waves nearly bowled her over.

By now, she was even with the rear of the warehouse. Captain Ames, collecting his armor on the run, had caught her. Helmet cocked over one eye and cuirass under his arm, Ames grabbed her waist and flung her around the corner.

Chubb was right behind him. They all three flopped down with their backs against the wall. The grey bricks against Angelica's spine vibrated from sound.

Angelica peered around the corner and saw orange flames mushrooming up from the airship's fins.

Shooting through *Darnley*'s hollow interior, the flames spat out the airship's nose like they were fired from a cannon.

Since the airship was ascending at a slant, Angelica thought it redolent of a rearing dragon spewing fire in its dying moments.

Then orange blossoms of fire flowered out from various parts of the envelope as hydrogen-filled ballonets – and other explosive surprises hidden throughout the airship – detonated one by one.

Taken together, the bright orange-yellow fireballs and the noxious black smoke literally darkened the sun at noon.

The radiance hurt Angelica's eyes, but she was unable to look away.

At the first explosion, the airship had been nosing up at forty-five degrees. Moored to the lantern by the grapnel, it appeared to be straining at its leash. As the hydrogen burned and exploded away from the stern first, the airship's angle became sharper.

The stern itself was quickly reduced to a blackened skeleton, with its rubberized skin sizzling away from its bones.

For a few awful, breathless moments, the half-consumed flying ship hung motionless. Then it trembled. With hydrogen erupting in the forward ballonets, thirty-six tons of metal, some of it molten and every inch of it engulfed in burning, rubberized fabric, hammered stern-first onto the Cathedral.

The airship was longer than the Cathedral. As the airship's nose crashed down, the Cathedral bells clanged as the western towers were knocked loose on impact, and leaned out *almost* to breaking beneath the crushing weight of aluminium. The towers clung to the Cathedral at a desperate angle by a few sinews of Portland stone and mortar.

Blazing fuel, mixed with melted lead, spread and flowed like lava between the balusters around the roof, running down the walls into the street.

Just as the aluminium girders draped over the dome, a delayed explosion shook the atmosphere with another thunderous *BOOM*. The wood and metal shell of the dome burst deadly fragments out in all directions.

Angelica yanked her head back and covered it with her arms as lead fragments and bits of stone pelted down the street past them.

The vibrations and explosions ceased. Exchanging glances Angelica, Chubb and Captain Ames slid upright against the bricks.

Ames pinned Angelica against the wall with one hand while he eased his lanky frame around the corner to see if it was safe to emerge.

Chubb, walking faster with shorter steps, circled the enormous Ames into the street. Angelica ambled behind them and stood on the far end of their line.

A massive fire was breaking out in all parts of the Cathedral simultaneously from the flood of fiery petrol.

The outer dome was gone. The towers were gone. Weakened by fire, the weight of aluminium, and the violent final explosion, the brick inner dome collapsed with a furious flame-burst and a flight of sparks, with so much force a few sparks stung Angelica when they landed.

The Cathedral was burning from end to end. Had Baron Belper not acted with alacrity in summoning the Metropolitan Fire Brigade, this might indeed, as Stoker feared, have sparked a second Great Fire of London. Even now, the Fire Brigade had the hardest work of their lives containing the blaze to the Cathedral precincts.

The darkened air was permeated with the choking stench of burnt rubber. But thank God and the Coldstream Guards, and the military and the police, no whiff of human flesh was mingled in the odor.

Captain Ames excused himself and ran away behind the warehouse. His job here was done; he had to find his Queen.

No one else had ventured from cover, so Angelica and Chubb stood alone together in the middle of a street littered with bits of lead and stone and glass.

Tongues of flame licked out a broken window at the southern portico, sooting over the Phoenix and the word *RESVRGAM*.

The skies were painted black from the smoke.

A few words drifted through Angelica's mind,

And the sun was darkened, and the veil of the temple was rent in the midst.

Then she remembered—*Herron!*

In her own struggle to get away in time, she'd forgotten him. The last she'd heard from him, he was *in* that airship. He could not have escaped the holocaust.

A lump large enough to choke her rose in her throat. She fought her tears—

Until she heard sniffing at her shoulder.

Inspector Chubb was dotting his eyes with his shirt-cuff.

Remembering that he had discarded his own handkerchief at Herron's house, she rested her cheek on the crown of his bowler and let him bawl on her shoulder. In this position, neither of them noticed a huge dragonfly humming out from the inky smoke east of the Cathedral.

CHAPTER CI

Stoker's glider – little more than two gossamer wings and a tail strung together with piano wire – had never inspired Herron with confidence.

When, despite Stoker's assurances, they plummeted away from the airship, Herron fully expected the contraption would land them unceremoniously in an impenetrable tangle of arms, legs and glider parts.

To his delight, Herron felt the odd sensation of being supported from beneath by invisible hands. It made his tummy all fluttery, but it wasn't unpleasant.

The wind in his face hummed shrilly through the piano wires like tuneless music as they spiraled around the Cathedral from on high, gently as a feather on the breeze. But even feathers float *down*. The earth rose remorselessly.

Stoker banked the glider, and Herron leaned with him. London's bewildering maze of streets and steeples lurched lopsidedly beneath his feet. Herron saw the crowds on the roofs pointing up at them; and he saw millions of souls in the streets dashing away from the Cathedral in all directions.

Starting east of the Cathedral, the glider circled around the south to the west, then north, away from the river.

The lower they went, the more Herron could envision their being smeared like a squashed bug on the side of some great public building.

When the first bomb released oxygen and fire simultaneously, Herron heard a *hiss*, like an enormous gaselier being turned on very high; but they were turning west, beneath the airship's nose, and he could not see the Japanese lantern effect from that angle.

Almost immediately after the hiss came the *BOOM*, which rippled through the air around them. The sound waves rocked the glider so violently, Herron feared they would be knocked out of the air by noise alone. An airquake.

When the orange-yellow flames mushroomed up from the stern just forward of the upper rudder fin, the glider was circling around the Cathedral's western façade, actually underneath *Darnley*'s high-angled nose.

Passing over the statue of Queen Anne, they banked again and zoomed along the north side of the Cathedral. This gave Herron a good view of the blazing airship's settling stern.

Seconds after they had circled north, orange fire streamed out through the airship's nose, high to the west.

Herron gasped for breath as the fire sucked all the oxygen out of the air.

Reaching into Hawkins's pocket, he found a polka-dotted neckerchief. Dingy as it was from years of use in the rodeo, Herron covered his mouth and nose with it so – whenever he was able to inhale again – he would not suck in black smoke with the noxious stench of rubber.

Angelica had imagined the airship as a dragon spitting fire in its dying breath. Herron had a robust, but not fanciful, imagination; yet even to him, the steel cables and mooring ropes bursting free and flailing dangerously around the airship looked like the tentacles of a giant monster in its death throes.

He drew his helmet down as far as possible in case one of the steel cables lashed out at him.

Hands over his head, fingers around the spike on the pickelhaube, he watched the metal keel snap in two from one the force of an explosion. With its cables flailing free and the struts bursting loose, the back half of the keel jackknifed down like it was hinged. The weight of the aluminium shattered the lantern on top of the dome with the force of an explosion.

As the hydrogen sizzled away from rear of *Darnley* to her front, the airship dropped, stern-first, toward the Cathedral.

Detonations continued forward through the ship. The car broke free and flipped head-over-heels to the roof. As the airship's nose drifted down over it, the car tumbled wildly westward, pulverizing the statue of Saint Paul over the west façade and sailing down to the street.

Striking the ground, the car bounded up and smashed against the statue of Queen Anne, giving her a mighty blow to the spine. As Queen Anne staggered forward onto her face, the car somersaulted back to the Cathedral.

It bounced back across the churchyard where, not long before, the Prime Minister and a host of other dignitaries were waiting for Her Majesty.

Skipping up the red-carpeted steps, the car slammed into the columns in the Cathedral's west porch, sending a shiver through the entire west façade. A flight of sparks climbed up the west façade; the towers quivered and toppled out. Their crash raised a choking dust cloud.

Had the ceremony been taking place when the airship exploded, the nose, poking over the west front, would have cremated the Queen, half the government and hundreds of men in uniform. The car would have pounded the surviving choristers and band members on the steps. The towers would have crushed many dignitaries from many nations, and nearly all the government of the City.

Just *Darnley*'s mass of flaming girders draped themselves over the dome, a final explosion splintered the outer dome in a hail of metal and wood.

The glider was on level with the dome by now. Herron felt shards of lead and brick pattering against the glider and the back of his neck and head. He was grateful for Lugner's helmet and scarf.

The brick inner dome of Saint Paul's Cathedral had more tonnage than the airship; but, mortally wounded by the intense heat of burning hydrogen and fuel, the final explosion caved it in altogether.

At the same time, the fire-weakened great chain around the dome snapped. The chain slung itself savagely down into the street, where it alone might have killed and wounded dozens of survivors had there been no evacuation.

Freed from bursting containers, the surplus fuel blazed out over the roof. The Cathedral had good drainage, but fire, not water, was running down its chutes. The airship carried so much fuel, the chutes could not accommodate it all, and it ran down the walls in a lava-like mess of petrol and melted lead.

The airship would burn its way through the roof. The Cathedral interior would be utterly destroyed by fire.

But Herron saw none of that. The smoke belching up from the ruins was too thick. Had the glider passed directly over the fiery pit in its corkscrew descent, Herron and Stoker would have been asphyxiated.

It was bad enough as they soared over the Cathedral's eastern face. Passing over the stern, the glider shot through the smoke to the south, like a giant dragonfly humming toward the river. Even with Lugner's goggles, Herron's eyes were filmy and burning. And he *still* could not breathe.

Stoker leaned, banking again. Herron almost forgot to lean with him.

They made another slow turn, this time to the west, over Blackfriar's Bridge, to level out directly over the Thames. Herron had air at last.

"Hang on!" Stoker shouted. "We're splashing down!"

The Thames looked a slender target at first; then, as its breadth quickly expanded, it looked too wide for Herron to swim.

The grey water rose at them faster, faster, *faster*—

Screaming, Herron threw his arms over his head.

Stoker raised the glider's nose just before skidding into the river near the northern bank. When the undercarriage struck the water, Herron felt like they had slapped down on top of a wall – except for the fierce spray trying to drown him.

One wing snapped off the dragonfly on impact. The glider skimmed sideways a few times, heeled over, and fell apart. Its pieces were dragged under by the steel wire and metal fittings.

Herron swam the few yards to shore with Stoker in the crook of his arm.

Slopping out of the water on his hands and knees, Herron dragged Stoker onto the marshy bank. Brown with mud from Lugner's pickelhaube to Hawkins's deteriorating boots, Herron knelt, coughing and panting, on river's margin.

Click-cluck.

Herron reached up and pushed his mud-caked goggles from his eyes.

The front hole of a .303 Magazine Lee-Enfield rifle barrel, closed and cocked, was staring him squarely between the ears.

Click-cluck. Click-cluck.

The muddy river bank was becoming a rainbow of color from the varied uniforms of military units serving at all points of the British Empire, some carrying the Magazine Lee-Enfield (MLE, affectionately called "Emily"), some armed with the shorter cavalry carbines.

Click-cluck. Click-cluck. Click-cluck.

Candian Dragoons, in scarlet tunics with white collars and cockaded busbies. The khaki tan and slouch hats of the Natal Carbineers. The Cape Mounted Rifes, with their blue tunics and their bright, white pith hemets shining in the sun.

Click-cluck. Click-cluck. Click-cluck. Click-cluck.

New Zealand Mounted Rifles in slouch hats with narrow pagris, with the brims turned up to the right. The Cape Mounted Rifles in green jackets and spiked helmets. The Gold Coast Hausas Constabulary with red caps, dark blue zouave coats and red cummerbunds. Red uniforms, white uniforms, green, blue, brown and violet, from the margin of the river up the bank.

Click-cluck. Click-cluck. Click-cluck. Click-cluck. Click-cluck.

Gold buttons, gold braid, gold epaulettes, gold piping – gold badges, medals, stars and stripes. Kepis, pith helmets, bush hats, fezzes, tarbooshes, turbans. Ebony faces, ivory faces; faces of cinnamon and saffron and pinkey-white. Dressed in tunics, kurtas and kilts. Men of every nationality and language in an Empire that spanned the globe, coming together in all their glorious diversity.

Click-cluck. Click-cluck. Click-cluck. Click-cluck. Click-cluck. Click-cluck.

Thousands of rifle-barrels were lowered in an arc around Herron as he knelt in the mud on the verge of the Thames.

When all the rifles were closed and cocked, a quiet descended, save for the whispering river.

Herron offered a weak smile.

"Now for number eighty-eight, 'Shall we Gather at the River.' *AH-CHOO!*"

EPILOGUE

Angelica cycled up to the gloomy, granite gaol. Parking her bicycle just outside, she entered swinging a covered basket in the crook of her elbow.

By pre-arrangement, she met Chubb at the door. He was merrily swapping stories with City police acquaintances, but he was happy to let them see him leave in the company of a beautiful, cheerful young lady a head higher than himself.

So long as word of it didn't leak back to the dreaded "Missus."

They traveled together up the narrow steps, along galleries of cells, until they reached a cell door blocked by a phalanx of unsmiling red-coated guards in busbies, with rifles sloped on their shoulders.

The guards were slow to part even for Chubb. Only when he showed their sergeant certain official documents did they part for him.

The cell had a metal door, solid but for a sliding square aperture slightly lower than Chubb's eye level. Chubb pushed the little door aside and glanced in. With two fingers, he motioned for Angelica to bend down and take a look.

Because the City Police, who had claimed authority in the affair, considered this ruffian a particularly dangerous prisoner, the room was practically bare except for the bed-roll, which lay on the floor.

Hunching over, Angelica peered in to see Herron sitting with crossed arms on his bedding, leaning back against the far right-hand corner of the narrow cell.

After days of incarceration, when word descended from *certain quarters*, Herron had finally been allowed to see Merridew. The valet had provided Herron with a shave and decent clothes – including (Herron was adamant on this point) clean undergarments.

Merridew had also brought a few toiletries, which he left on a triangular shelf fitted into the cell's far right-hand corner, above Herron's bed-roll.

When Angelica saw him, he was dressed in tweeds and a Norfolk jacket. A Trilby hat with a red feather in the brim slouched down over his closed eyes.

He was apparently trying to sing himself to sleep in a low drone.

Angelica recognized the song, which she had heard in chapel.

> *"Free from the Law, O happy condition*
> *Jesus has bled and there is remission,*
> *Cursed by the law and bruised by the fall,*
> *Grace hath redeemed us once for all."*

Herron sang listlessly up to the chorus, when Angelica's mezzo-soprano voice joined in harmony,

> *"Once for all, O sinner, receive it,*
> *Once for all, O brother, believe it;*
> *Cling to the Cross, the burden will fall,*
> *Christ hath redeemed us once for all."*

Herron pushed up brim of his hat. "Is that an angel's voice I hear?"

Removing his hat, he stood abruptly – banging his head on the triangular shelf in the corner and rattling the toiletry bottles. Massaging the crown of his head, he approached the door until he recognized Angelica's dark-green eyes.

"It is! Cinderella."

Tenderly, Angelica's voice oozed, "If you call me that again, I'll tie a knot in your tongue. May we come in?"

"There's no knob on this side. They may be afraid I'll walk in my sleep."

Chubb came to their rescue. He had prevailed upon friends on the City police, and he flashed a bit of iron in the doorway. "I have the key, sir."

"I'll wait for you in here, then."

When Chubb opened the door, Herron bowed and beckoned them in with a respectful wave of his hat.

"Do come in, Inspector, Miss Trickett. Make yourselves at home. Pardon the dust, but we're just getting settled. As you could tell, Merridew popped by. Sometimes his blasted songs stick in my head. Since you knew that one I suppose you're Non-conformist?"

"I'm nonconformist in some ways," winked Angelica, "but being a nonconformist in every way is as boring as being an conformist. It's just saying 'no' when a conformist says 'yes.' Sometimes, I like to say 'maybe.'"

Chubb interrupted their repartee. "I'm not long on hymns, sir, but, as songs go, it's apt enough. You are free to go. From the law."

"Oh?" Herron stepped gingerly across the threshold of the cell before Chubb changed his mind. "I suppose that's a grave disappointment to you, Inspector."

"No, sir."

"That's an interesting *volte face*."

"Beg pardon?"

"You've been trying to get me jugged for days."

"Have I?"

"You didn't believe my story when I told it on Sunday."

"I'm sorry that impression came across."

"You *did* believe me?"

"No, sir."

"It must be one or the other."

Chubb demurred. "T'ain't my place to believe or disbelieve stories. I'm paid to establish facts enough to present a case to a jury. That cockamamie story of your doin's Saturday just didn't ring true."

"But it was true."

"That's what had me buggered. Most people, when they lie, they'll say, *Oh, I had to leave urgently . . . we had intended to come back . . . I was so shocked by the tragedy I didn't know what I was doin'*. They do not say they was led away by Inspectors who ain't Inspectors and crammed into a coach with blinds over the windows and took to an empty building where they told their story in private, and were brought back. That's a yarn, sir. It's the sort of thing the young lady might dream up for her fiction; but you ain't that clever."

"I say—!"

"No sir, you ain't that clever by a long chalk. You said you had given a statement. That was an obvious lie, which could be checked and proved a lie."

"But it wasn't a lie."

"You insisted that you had given a statement to a man named Stoker who was not an Inspector but who would send that statement on to the Yard. That was a stupid lie. Whatever else I might say about you, you are not that stupid."

"Inspector, that's the kindest thing you've ever said to me. I'll return a compliment some time. If I ever think of one."

Angelica, who felt she owed a debt of gratitude to Chubb for pinpointing the site of the bombing, nudged Herron with her hip and shot him a brutal glance from the corner of her eye.

"So," Chubb continued, "I wondered why you reiterated a stupid lie when I told you to your face it couldn't have happened that way."

"You didn't seem to believe my story when we went over it the first twenty times. Unfortunately, it was the only one I'd come out with that morning. I believe you doubted my veracity."

"What I believed didn't signify. I wanted to see if *you* believed it. People who lie don't insist on their lies being true when they're practically told they're wading up to their hips in bilgewater. They backpedal. *'Maybe I heard the name wrong. No, I remember, now, it wasn't Stoker, it was Llewellyn.'* They make up a slue of new 'facts' they 'only just remembered.' Or they concoct, on the spot, some new story outa whole cloth. From that point, it's easy to wind 'em up into their web of lies. We catch a lot of crooks just by lettin' 'em talk their way behind bars."

"But . . . I was a suspect?"

"Well, yes. I didn't know what to make of you. You're a man of hijinks, who has the mentality it takes to think it's funny to administer a light push to a man in front of a moving train. It's just as well Stoker did take you away that night. If they hadn't given you a ridiculous story to stick too, even though hundreds of thousands would be dead and London burnt to a crisp and the Queen and her family charred to a how-de-do, you might be in the dock for that one murder."

"Then the 'haggard bird' was murdered? It wasn't an accident?"

"He was murdered. That has been established."

"Shot?" wondered Herron

Angelica shook her head. "Poisoned."

Flummoxed, Herron yelled, "Poisoned! Ye gods, now what!"

"Please stop talking, dear. Listen to the Inspector."

"I can deny you nothing, Cin—er, Miss Trickett. Carry on, Chubby."

"Inspector Chubb, if you please, sir."

By this time they had reached the front of the prison, where Chubb had left a tacky lady's bamboo parasol. He extended the exhibit to Angelica.

"Can you identify this, Miss?"

"It's Lady Calthrop's," she answered, as if she was in the witness box.

"She had it Saturday night, the nineteenth, at the train station?"

"Yes, sir."

Standing it upright, Chubb examined the handle. A small circle, almost like a hallmark, was just visible on the crown. Taking her hand, he rubbed Angelica's index finger lightly over it. She felt a plug of some sort.

Taking a small knife from his pocket, Chubb prized the plug out and handed the parasol to Herron. When Herron held it up to the light, he and Angelica thumped their heads together trying to peer down it simultaneously. They saw a small hole running all the way through the bamboo.

"What in—?" Herron gasped.

"A blow-gun, sir. For poisoned darts. Probably from her husband's collection. Made special into a parasol, when she wanted to murder her daughter, most like. I told you, sir, most folks are like trains. They lay their tracks and run on 'em. They fall into patterns. This is true in crime, 'specially. The criminal is lazy. If he wasn't lazy, he'd get a job, like folks. He thinks, 'This plan worked once. I'll do it again.' And he don't change it much. We nab lots of criminals that way."

"I saw Lady Calthrop fiddling with this thing just before the haggard bird shoved by. And—by God! So did Jessup! *He said the haggard bird was shot because he saw who shot him.* Lady Calthrop, he meant. He said 'if the haggard bird knew what I had seen, he'd never have given half of it to her.' Meaning *you*, Miss Trickett." Herron smiled at Angelica. "He warned me against you."

"Against *me*?"

"He saw you were with Lady Calthrop. You might have been in on the plot."

"I!"

"Some of the best assassins out there are women. I can see why. You can murder me any time."

"Don't think it hasn't crossed my mind."

"But Jessup also said he didn't want to prejudice me against you, *so he didn't tell me any of this*. And there sat Lady Calthrop, waiting for me with the parasol on her lap! If I had only kept my eye on her Saturday night—! But how could I keep my eyes on a withered old harpy when she was in such charming company?"

Angelica shook her head with an indulgent smile. "Don't you ever relent?"

"I won't relent until I'm dead or married. Or both."

"I don't appreciate flattery."

"Flattery, Miss Trickett, is, by definition, untrue."

"It think you mean it has a connotation of exaggeration to mendacity?"

"Er . . . if you say so. Well, this is true as the day. You are the loveliest—"

Chubb jerked the conversation back to the matter at hand. "On a hunch, sir, I had the body of our train victim exhumed."

"Doesn't that take a long time?"

"Not when you know a good pair of grave-robbers."

Herron and Angelica gaped at him.

Chubb winked. That was *his* idea of a little joke. "He's been lying unclaimed in the morgue since Saturday night. In a day or so he'll be shelved away in an anonymous grave. I don't know if Lady Calthrop had it all thunk out, that when that 'haggard bird' of yours was stung by the dart in the backside he'd go flyin' off the platform into the path of the slowing train. Might have been what they call seren-dip-ty. Don't matter. According to our toxy-coly-gist, even if he hadn't been hit by the train he'd have been dead in seconds. We found a small hole in his upper thigh. He had a quick-actin' poison in his system. As you would have, Miss, if one of them bloody things had struck you. It's good you shot her first."

"Thank God for handguns," breathed Angelica. "And," she added, with a sly glance at Herron, "for the men who make presents of them."

Herron nodded an acknowledgment. To Chubb, "And you didn't suspect any of this when you questioned me?"

"Now, sir, who would look for a small hole in the thigh, or traces of poison in the system, of a man who had been mangled by a train? It was a sudden trip she took to the station, Miss?" asked the Inspector.

"Yes, sir."

"Did she normally behave that way?"

"No, Inspector. She liked to plan visits well in advance."

"On the Underground?"

"She hated it. She always went by carriage however clogged the streets were."

"But we know everything now," Chubb assured them, "From that butler, from what Stoker told his department, and from our obliging Herr Lugner."

"He talked?" asked Herron. So much for martyrs.

"Oh, yes, sir. As the Americans might say, he's singing like a canary."

Herron and Angelica winced. "Torture?" Herron ventured.

"Sometimes when we have a suspect, we deprive him of a cigarette. In this case, officers smoked around him until he coughed up what we wanted to know. He didn't have a heap to add. When we could get him off rants about Mister Lincoln, he told us *he* sent Lady Calthrop word of the your haggard bird's defection on his wireless telegraphic machine. Stoker had a good idea where the haggard bird was bound, *and he's the one who told Lugner.*"

"Why!" demanded Angelica. "I thought he was on our side."

Herron explained. "The haggard bird wanted to nip their plans in the bud. Stoker wanted them to go through so he could arrest Lugner in the act – or, if he couldn't arrest him then, appear as a witness against him later. By tattling, Stoker earned Lugner's trust."

Chubb nodded. "Stoker got sent to shoot him, but it was so close to the day, Lady Calthrop herself went to head the haggard bird off at the station."

"How did she recognize him?" asked Angelica. "They weren't acquainted?"

"We found files in her bedchamber, of all her employees."

"Files! Another reason to keep her bedchamber in the dark."

"It's too bad you're no Pandora," said Herron. "You would have opened all the forbidden boxes."

"And been shot by poisoned darts long ago. No, thank you."

Chubb coughed, attracting their attention. "Lady Calthrop usually received photographs of all her employees from Lugner, that butler-feller told us. But the employees didn't know her, and referred to her only as 'She who is to come.'"

"They even had a picture of *me*!" said Herron. "I never worked for her."

"You've never worked," Angelica pointed out.

"Anyhow," Chubb continued, sensing Herron was about to interrupt on another tangent of repartee with the young lady, "Them files will assist in our round-up."

"Have your people been rounding up the gang, Inspector?"

"We had some success with the telegraphers. Cutting all but certain lines meant their connections with each other were iffy. In some places there were gun battles, but by noon nearly all the revolutionists were captured – or dead."

A shiver tickled through Angelica. One of her fingers felt her clothing over the scar in her side.

"By the time we located the nest on the fens, though, the birds had flown."

Angelica demanded to know how they found out.

"I can answer that," said Herron. "They had a relay wireless transmitter between London and their compound. Probably monitored all our messages."

Chubb gave a curt nod. "Stoker thinks so, too."

Angelica frowned. "They'll reform and build another airship!"

Herron doubted it. "Not unless they find a way to get cheap and plentiful aluminium. I'm sure Hiram Maxim's company in California has instituted tighter controls by now. And Lady Calthrop is no longer bankrolling them." He turned to Chubb. "I don't suppose they had time to pack their metal in their grips?"

"No sir. But they blew up everything. Shed, the airships, metal, everything was blowed all to smash."

"Probably with the hydrogen canisters. And they stole away into the night."

"But, unless they all left England by a deserted stretch of coastline, and land in another deserted stretch of coastline in another country, we'll find 'em. Unfortunately, the butler died this morning of lead poisoning."

Herron leapt like he'd been kicked. "Lead poisoning? *Now* what!"

Angelica extended her index finger and pantomimed firing a pistol. "Bullets. I've killed two people."

"In self defense," Chubb pointed out.

"It doesn't make them any less dead."

"Would you rather it had been you?" asked Herron. "I wouldn't."

"I'm glad, Mister Strangways," she said with arch stiffness, "you didn't want me dead. I suppose even you are not interested in necrophilia?"

"I've never seen anyone in a coffin that looked half as good as you."

Angelica's lips parted. A retort to that 'compliment' hung on her lips.

Chubb stepped between them. "You may cheer up, sir, Miss. Word has come down that your name will not be mentioned in this affair."

"Will Lady Calthrop figure into any stories about the . . . the disaster?"

"Her glowing obituaries will say she died of 'injuries sustained in a fall.'"

"And Dapifer?" wondered Herron. "What are you going to say about him?"

"For public consumption, sir, when she took her fall—she fell on him."

"Since I'm being released, I assume Stoker got in touch?"

"He was released, as you know, through channels when he sent a message to 'certain persons' in Whitehall late Tuesday."

"And left me mouldering in gaol, the—!"

"This 'Stoker' had been working in the plot on for some time. As you said, sir, he did not want them terrorist blokes to change their plans, especially as he had been in-stru-ment-al in their making. He believed he could nobble 'em in the act and bring the full might of the law down on them like a ton of bricks. He'd see them plans through even if they killed the Queen, so long as he bagged his quary. Your 'haggard bird' was working for Her Majesty from a different angle; he meant to thwart their plans altogether so no one would get hurt. He escaped from their the fens and was very close to the end of his journey. Stoker, our agent provoc-u-tater, could not have their nefarious plans changed out from under him at the last moment. He did mean to kill your haggard bird, sir, and that's a fact."

"But the joke was on him, Inspector. Even Stoker didn't know everything. Once he found out he and Lugner would be alone in the airship, he thought he could seize control of *Darnley* when it was airborne. No one told him about the remote control devices. Stoker very nearly bombed the Queen himself. And half the government. So, after all, it wouldn't have been a total disaster. The less government, the better. Still, there would have been chaos!"

"Which," Angelica pointed out, "Lady Calthrop would have seized control of, by making herself a uniting figure."

"Or," the Inspector suggested, "remaining in the shadows herself, she might have ruled through puppets like Lugner simply by threatening more bombings. And who could have fought her airships? We just proved all the Queen's hosses and all the Queen's men were worthless against 'em."

"The haggard bird," said Herron, making sure he had it straight, "wanting to avoid that, fled the compound to pass that cigarette with the details on to Jessup."

"And Lady Calthrop had to make sure they kilt anybody knew about the thing," Chubb concluded. "They got your 'haggard bird' and they got his contact. And they were gunning for you two."

"Poor Jessup. He laid those rails you mentioned by appearing in my room a second time." He turned to Angelica, "Dapifer must have been eavesdropping when you and I thought we were alone. He heard me say I was meeting a man in my bedroom. Dapifer killed Jessup. And you thought 'they' killed me."

"And Lady Calthrop was coming for me with her blow-gun in the middle of the night. She'd have shot me, too, while I was in bed, then taken out the thorn out. It would have looked like I died in my sleep. My wakefulness forestalled her. I'll never curse wakefulness as a bad thing again. *All things work together for good to them that love God, to them who are the called according to his purpose.* But it doesn't say all things that happen are good in themselves."

"Anything that brought us together is good," said Herron.

"We've moved the body from your house, by the way, sir," Chubb said.

"Another anonymous corpse. But let's get to important things. How about me? Any chance of a medal for yours truly?"

"For blowin' up Saint Paul's Cathedral?"

"For saving the life of Her Majesty."

"Mister Strangways," said Chubb, leading him to the front door of the prison, "You were just lucky no bystanders was killed. As far as medals – men in Stoker's profession do not receive honors. He works under cover."

"I don't."

"You do now. We still have enough to charge you with. We found a dead man in your room. You were with the terrorists—we have thousands of witnesses, in uniform, who saw you drop from the airship and land in the river."

"Though I'll wager none of them recognized the urbane owner of Strangways' in that helmet and dungarees. I don't even sell the things in my Emporia."

"What I'm saying is, we can still charge you as a murderer and an incendiary."

"It's a frame-up!"

"*I* won't bring the charges. 'Certain persons' in Whitehall will, unless you promise to take an oath of secrecy over this matter."

"I took one," said Angelica. "It's mostly painless."

Herron saw he was beaten and knocked over his king. "'Mum' is the word. Heigh-ho. I am sorry about Jessup. I liked him for all his smug fancy-dress."

"And he got us this." Chubb showed him the marriage certificate. "He hid it by the simple expedient of sitting on it. Dapifer driv that spear-thing right through it, making sure it stayed with him. It's a certificate for the marriage for Bonny Prince Charlie's daughter to some Archbishop."

"She was shacked up with him. That would legitimize Count Roehenstart, Bonny Prince Charlie's grandson. Lady Calthrop claimed he was her father. Yes! What was that poem Lady Calthrop recited? By Burns? I wasn't listening."

"I read it to her a thousand times," said Angelica. She recited,

> "We'll daily pray, we'll nightly pray,
> On bended knees most fervently,
> That the time may come, with pipe an' drum,
> We'll welcome hame fair ALBANIE."

Herron nodded. "That's the baby. Bonnie Prince Charlie called his legally legitimized daughter the 'Duchess of Albany.' Lady Calthrop was the new lass of Albanie. So, Inspector, was Lady Calthrop the rightful heir to the throne?"

"No, sir. The marriage certificate was a forgery."

"She could not have claimed the throne, then?" asked Angelica.

"Miss, it would have been hard to argue with a Secret Society that can rain fiery death from the skies like we was the cities of the plain. If it hadn't been for you two, the airship would have come. There was no way to stop it. And Lady Calthrop would be alive to clean up the mess."

"What about the Jacobites?"

"So far as we can tell, there was no genuine Jacobite involvement in this conspiracy. It was hatched on the continent. We don't want anyone in England blamin' the Scots for it. The last thing we need right now is a rising of the clans."

"One more question, Inspector," said Herron. "I don't know how you knew 'they' meant to drop their bombs on Saint Paul's Cathedral."

Chubb asked Angelica to write out RESVRGAM on a bit of paper, which he then held up before Herron's eyes.

"I'd seen that there word hundreds of times. My eye is trained to observe them things. But I never did know what it said or how it was pronounced. How do you pronounce 'SVR'? It's only when I saw it writ out on paper that I recognized it as bein' a word carved on the south portico of the Cathedral."

"What does it mean?"

Chubb replied, "It's said when ol' Wren was in the ruins of old Saint Paul's, beginning to lay out his new Cathedral after the Great Fire, he asked a worker to get a stone to mark a certain place. The first stone the worker found was an old, flat gravestone with that word writ on it."

"*Resurgam.* 'I will rise again.'" Herron clenched his eyes.

"*For the Lord himself shall descend from heaven with a shout,*" whispered Angelica, "*with the voice of the archangel, and with the trump of God: and the dead in Christ shall rise first: then we which are alive and remain shall be caught up together with them in the clouds, to meet the Lord in the air: and so shall we ever be with the Lord.*"

"Whatever."

Chubb continued, "Wren had that there word carved on the Cathedral on what they calls the 'pediment to the south portico,' with that Phoenix-bird as a symbol of the Cathedral – and of London itself, rising from the Great Fire of 1666."

"It wasn't even a code-word! It's plain as a pikestaff for all the world to see on one of the most famous buildings in the world! But Angelica is new to London and when she went to the Cathedral as a sight-seer she probably went through the west doors and never circled round the building to the south. And I'm so used to seeing the Cathedral I never even notice it anymore. If that message had come to anyone but us, they might have cracked it with nearly a day to go. It seems the haggard bird picked the two worst people in London to deliver his message to."

Angelica drawled, "'Why don't you speak for yourself, John.'"

"Oh, here's your stick, sir. We won't be needing it after all. And the book we borrowed. Still with the same playing card marking your place."

"I don't want to finish it."

Angelica took the book. "Looks jolly interesting. May I read it?"

"Go ahead," Herron said. "I never want to see the bally thing again. I'll tell you where to return it when you're through."

"I would not recommend it, Miss," said Chubb. "I thumbed it while it was in our possession. That was the principle reason I took it. It looks quite improper."

Angelica beamed a smile. "A man once wrote, 'There is no such thing as a moral or immoral book. Books are well-written or badly written. That is all.'"

"What about Jessup's pea-shooter?" Herron asked Chubb.

"I took it apart and scattered it around the Cathedral on my descent. In case there was a problem with the ballistics. No one will ever trace it to any of us."

After returning the stick he had confiscated Sunday morning, Chubb glanced around, to make certain they could not be overheard.

"Let me tell you, sir, what the Whitehall boys told me. If it hadn't been for you and the young lady, there might have been an awful disaster."

"Do tell. Seems to me like we had one, anyway."

"Awfuller than we had, I mean, the death-toll." Chubb extended a hand between Herron and Angelica. "For what it's worth, sir, Miss – and I don't speak on behalf of the Empire, just of me – thank you both for a job well done."

Angelica accepted the proffered hand.

Herron, though not wearing his monocle, examined the hand as if scrutinizing it critically through an eyeglass. "That's all the thanks I'll get?"

"Yes, sir."

"Then, by Jove, I accept it." He, too, clasped Chubb's hand.

"By the way, sir, I was told to pass on, from unimpeachable sources, that an honor officially meant for your father will be bestowed on you next year."

Herron's eyes brightened. "What sort of honor?"

"The Royal Victorian Order. For distinguished service to Her Majesty. And on a knight grade, so you can call yourself 'Sir,' sir. Sir Herron Strangways, KCVO. The real reason for the order *must* remain a dead state secret. Most folks will think your father earned it and you just inherited it like everything else. But persons in certain quarters know what you did, and they are extremely grateful."

So! At last, he could print cards with the name *Sir Herron* . . . though he wasn't so eager for a title as he once had been. He wanted to impress only one woman. Who wasn't impressed by small titles and orders. Or moneybags.

He was gratified that, in her eyes at least, he was out from under his father's shadow. She was all in the world that mattered to him, the most beautiful woman he had ever seen. Recently.

2

Herron strolled out of prison with Angelica on his arm, pushing her bicycle along with his free hand. The book and his stick were in the wire cage on the bike. Angelica carried her covered basket.

"How does it feel to be free?"

"Oh, I'm merry as a robin that sings on a tree. Thank you for coming to visit an old gaolbird, Miss Trickett."

"*Verily, I say unto you, Inasmuch as ye have done it unto one of the least of these my brethren, ye have done it unto me.*"

"And I am the least of the brethren, I suppose?"

"*Thou sayest it.*"

Once, Saint Paul's Cathedral could be viewed from where they walked. Now, days after the fire, a hideous, burning stench hovered around the still-smoldering ruins.

Angelica averted her eyes. She kept telling herself, people are more important than monuments; but it was a grievous loss and she felt partly responsible for it.

"I still have a question about '*resurgam*.'" she said. "Or RESVRGAM, with a 'v.' I was close enough to see it quite plainly. Why was it spelled that way?"

"The Romans didn't use the letters *u* or *j*. It must have been a frightful hardship on them, with no jams or jellies. They only had 'iams' and 'iellies.' I have a feeling the haggard bird may actually have spelt that word r-e-s-v-r-g-a-m in his message – but, if you remember, I burnt the v. If I'd seen it written with a 'v' I'd have known at once it must have come from some great public building."

"Yes, but we'll never know, will we, Sir Smokes-a-lot? Your dreary habit nearly cost a lot of people their homes and lives." She perked up, trying to be more positive. "How does it feel to be 'Sir' Herron, Sir Herron?"

"I won't be able to try it on for size until next year. I'm very glad to take something away from these last few days. However, that's not all I salvaged from the wreckage."

In a demure tone, "What else did you come away with, Mister Strangways?"

Herron held out his hands, palms up, with a wide smile. "Blisters!"

She spared them no more than a cursory glance. "Oh. Your first?"

"I did some rowing on the Cam that raised a few."

"Did you."

"Yes."

"How utterly uninteresting."

"You don't understand! These little blisters came from digging my own grave. I didn't think I'd live long enough to have blisters."

"Well, Mister Strangways, do you want to see mine?"

"Oh, I'd like that." His leer was a tad too suggestive.

"My blisters. I won't show them to you, now."

"Well, then, what's in the basket, Little Red Riding Hood?"

"If I'm Red Riding Hood you must be the wolf."

"You bet!" He unloosed the latch and lifted the basket's cover.

A Skye terrier leapt out and snapped at him, nearly nipping off his fingers.

"Son-of-a—!" He slammed the lid and latched it. "What's she doing here?"

"He."

"Who can tell, under all that hair!"

"The family gave him to me."

"That family would give you the gift that keeps on taking. Nothing else?"

"Till's all empty. Lady Calthrop spent every penny she for her 'projects.' Everything she ever bought for me was purchased on her name alone! All that expensive jewelry she wore was entailed—"

Herron said, *So was the dog*, but Angelica shushed him.

"The family moved into the house, but the dog bit one of them and they gave it to me. They must be the wrong sort of people. As if this sweetie," she let the dog out of its basket far enough to rub noses with it in a way that made Herron envious, "would bite anyone who didn't deserve it."

"Do you realize if it hadn't been for that mutt, we'd have met days earlier, and maybe none of this might have happened to us?"

"I'm glad it did. I wouldn't change the way we met for anything in the world. Dressed as a maccaroni!"

Herron was perplexed. "As a pasta, you mean?"

"I'll explain it later. Besides, if we hadn't gotten involved in this, so many lives might have been lost. We must think of others."

"Oh, must we!"

"Yes, Mister Strangways."

"Herrie?"

"Her-ron, maybe. When I get to know you better."

"Do you . . . want to know me better?"

"I can only know you better, since I hardly know you now. I only set eyes on you for the first time on Saturday and we never exchanged a word until Monday afternoon. I'll stick with 'Mister Strangways' for the time being, *s'il vous plaît*."

"*J'accepte avec plaisir*. What's the mutt's name?"

"It's a purebred Skye. Its name is Charlie. You're not a dog person?"

"I'm not a that-dog person. But enough about the pooch. Say, where did you got that rope when I saw you slithering down the side of the Cathedral?"

"Captain Ames raided the bell-tower while the Inspector and I were puffing up the stairs with that heavy wireless telegraph between us."

Herron sighed. "If I'd gone to church more, I'd have seen that *RESVRGAM*."

"Let's pray that, like the Phoenix, the Cathedral rises from its ashes – just like it did three hundred years ago. Even if we had cracked all the writing in the cigarette paper, we'd never have stopped an airship sitting around a tea-table."

She glanced him over approvingly in the corner of her eye.

"Did you know, this is the first time we've ever talked when you were in presentable clothes? Your clothes were bad enough when we met, but you've been filthy and disreputable the last few days."

"Have you swum in the Thames lately?"

"You look almost handsome in nice clothes."

"Thank you." He looked her costume over. "I'm surprised you're not in mourning for Lady Calthrop."

"I feared that might be in bad taste, as I'm the one who killed her."

"Do you feel guilty?"

"Not as much as I should. I suppose I'm heartless, but she called me a 'perfect specimen.' Being called 'a specimen' makes me almost glad I shot her."

"Miss Trickett, since she was firing those hellish darts at you, I'll always be thankful you shot her good and hard. And – I've never said this to a woman before – but I don't think you're perfect."

She beamed up at him. "You don't?"

"No. You're nose is too broadish."

"Thank you."

"And that dimpled chin is not to my taste. Though I'd dearly love to taste it."

She gave his arm a snap and nearly wrenched his shoulder out of it socket. "Let's preserve the decencies of debate. But—thank God I'm not perfect!"

"Amen."

"And thank God she's out of my life. But then, so is my livelihood."

"What will become of you?"

"Thank you for asking. I've no idea. No one will hire me if they ever learn I kicked an invalid in my care down a flight of stairs. People are funny that way."

"Why not come to work for 'Strangways' Emporium'?"

"'Emporia, for you are legion.' And have you as my boss? 'Miss Trickett, there's a little thing you need to do if you want to keep your position—'"

"Horrors! I'd never do that. It's not playing the game."

She uttered a shuddering *oooooh!* "Mister Strangways, I do not play games."

"You ought to. They're fun."

"What about you? What does the released prisoner want to do on taking his first lung-full of free air?"

"I'm turning over a new leaf."

"I'm gratified to hear it."

"The first thing I intend to do is eat more meat."

"I beg your pardon?"

"Until I'm bursting with it. It's my part in striking a blow for uncollectivized individual human freedom. I don't insist that others do as I do, but I will show others I will not slavishly imitate them. Ergo, I am carnivorous."

"*Tu racontes n'importe quoi.* You are the worst purveyor of nonsense—"

"The best, I think you mean. *À l'oeuvre on reconnaît l'artisan.*"

"Yes, I suppose that is what I do mean. I hate it when you're right."

"To speak just a little sense . . . may I call upon you again, Mademoiselle?"

"*Je ne dis pas non.*"

"Will you say *oui*?"

The green eyes slipped coyly into their corners at him. "*Peut-être.*"

"What's that? Maybe?"

"I hope so. Either that or 'my aunt has lumbago.'"

"'Maybe' on the plus side, or the minus?"

"Mister Strangways, within seventy-two hours of first setting eyes on you, I witnessed a murder; lost my job; shot a woman in a wheelchair – twice – and kicked her down a curved stairway; mortally wounded a butler; discovered a dead body; disrupted a royal ceremony; barreled into an Archbishop – York, I think; kicked a choirboy (who richly deserved it); threatened dignitaries of many nations with a gun, not to mention a doorman; swore in church and defaced a Cathedral. I'm curious to learn into what further depths of depravity you'll drag me. Or are you going to take refuge in your Emporia and hide under a desk?"

"I've been thinking."

"Good first step. You should try it more often."

"I'm serious."

"I'm not?"

"During my time in stir, I wondered . . . Maybe I'll sell the old firm. Though you'll call that killing the golden goose."

"No, I'd call it killing the goose that laid the golden eggs."

"What's the difference?"

"The Golden Goose was the goose you couldn't get loose from once you touched it, unless a lonely princess laughed at you. The goose that laid the golden eggs—well, laid golden eggs."

"I'm proud to say a lonely princess did laugh at me, Saturday night. And that has set me free. But I was saying, perhaps I'll sell Strangways' and use the cash to support myself while I look for something else to do."

"You mean – work?"

"An intelligent and resourceful young man should find a niche in the world."

"Yes, but what about *you*?"

Herron's demeanor became unwontedly solemn. "Miss Trickett, I knelt at the brink of my grave while a man cocked a pistol at my skull. That moment couldn't have lasted five seconds, but, oh dear God, it felt like a lifetime. Staring up into that barrel, knowing I had reached the end of an unproductive life. I was going to be a dead man forever."

"Yes, death does have a way of lingering."

"I feel like I've been reborn. Like the Phoenix, flying up from the ashes of its dead self. *Resvrgam*. I will rise again."

"Like prices and taxes."

"I'd be buried in an unmarked grave with a bush on it, and the only life God ever gave me would be snuffed forever and I'd have done nothing of value with it. Oh, I made a lot of women happy—"

Angelica's eyes flashed at him and her lips tightened.

"—but most of the time, I've spent bored. Jessup told me so, and he was right. My God, how can one have a life and be bored in it? When I was kneeling at the gaping maw of that pit, I wondered how a man could ever be bored with life!"

"We who work all our lives for what we have don't bore so easily."

"The late Mister Jessup, whom you met in my bedroom—"

"Don't say that too loudly."

"—made a lot of sense, you know."

"What did he say?"

"He told me every day men and women live – and die – in the shadows, risking and giving their life so idlers like me can keep their freedom."

"I'm sure that's true. But what can anyone do about it?"

"My life was given back to me for a reason. Now that I'm the walking dead, perhaps I should creep into the shadows and risk my life so others may enjoy the fruits of freedom. People don't seem to understand or cherish their freedom. I mean real freedoms, those inherent in nature. The freedom to think, to speak, to travel at will – even, by hell—oops, *pardone moi.*"

"*Comme l'enfer.*"

"Even the right to disappear of your own volition, if you want, so the government can't track you with numbers. These freedoms must be cherished."

"This from a man who doesn't vote."

"You told me freedom doesn't come from a ballot box, but it can – by God! – be taken away when politics comes from the barrel of a gun. I want to venture into Stoker's territory and become a protector in the shadow war for freedom."

"Stuff and nonsense. You're not trained for that life."

"I've done pretty well so far."

"What have you done to suggest you're capable of being a shadow warrior?"

"I've shown pluck and tenacity I never knew I had. A man never really knows his character until he's tested."

"How will you contact these people if they're all tucked away in the shadows?"

"I don't know. People join the Masons. Must be the same sort of thing."

"My brother's a Mason."

"Is he?" said Herron, in a tone that deliberately expressed his sincere disinterest in ever hearing about her brother again.

"He says it's the easiest thing in the world to find a Mason and ask to join. All you have to do is look for their square-and-compass watch-fobs. I'm sure it must be much more difficult to find members of these shadow organizations."

"It's been all too easy for me. I've stumbled over them everywhere. Can't go into my bedroom for having to beat them back with a stick."

"Let's not talk about your bedroom any more, with or without bodies."

"Say – I know Stoker. I saved his life, don't you know. He owes me."

"Where is he now?"

"I don't know."

"What's his real name?"

"I don't know . . . but I'll find him and volunteer my services to my country."

"Assuming your country wants them. It's extremely dangerous work."

"Not so dangerous as *ennui*. I can do this hush-hush stuff. I'm good with my fists – and my head."

Her voice sounded slightly choked as she coughed out, "I wouldn't have anything happen to you—Herron. Don't do it, for my sake."

"Really?" His heart soared like the Phoenix, hearing his name on her lips.

"Really. Until we know each other better. Then, I might not care so much."

"You do care, right now?"

She could not look at him. Her eyes were suddenly absorbed by the fascinating pavement. "I would die for you, Herron Strangways."

"Would you live for me?"

"That's harder, isn't it? I suppose— you really have *known* lots of women?"

"Never with one who really mattered."

"Am I the first woman who really mattered?"

"Yes."

"Am I the first woman you ever told that to?"

"Oh . . . ah, give me a moment to think."

Angelica sighed. This was going to prove a difficult relationship. "Besides, Strangways' Emporia need you. You do more than sell good tea, you know."

"Do I?"

"Certainly. You sell good coffee, too."

"To change the subject, may I see you home?"

Her smile and sunny disposition returned. "You may. What do you think I came to the prison for, chucklehead?"

"Where are you living?"

"With my brother."

"Well, do you have any money?"

"Very little. Lady Calthrop saw to all my needs but never gave me a farthing. I never understood why, until I learned she didn't have two to rub together."

"Does your brother have money enough to support you both?"

"I'm not a charity case, Mister Strangways. I don't live off people."

"Nevertheless, you have no resources to call on?"

"I have a little money, at his house, wrapped in a cambric handkerchief."

"Why don't you stay at my house? I can have Merridew see to all your needs. And you can make that your base while you look for a job."

"Where will *you* be while I'm at your house?"

"I'll put up at the Club for a few days. I have all the amenities at home, don't y'know. And food. Merridew says you should eat more."

"So I'll move into your house as your kept woman? No, thank you. I'm staying with my brother until I find my feet, but only until."

"I don't see that's any better. From the descriptions I've heard, you're nothing like your brother. I can hear the neighbors now. 'Did you see that woman who moved in with Trickett? He says she's his sister, but she's tall and blonde, he's short and dark! I know what's going on between them—'"

"Just hush up and escort me there."

"Very well. May I call on you while you are there?"

Softly, "*Oui.*"

"Your brother won't object to me?"

"I'd be surprised if he didn't."

"Also," he added, "this ought to please you. I'm giving up smoking."

"Good. How about drinking to excess?"

"I wouldn't stop drinking to please a dying aunt, and I wish mine were."

"Just the man every woman dreams of in her heart of hearts: a drunken spy."

"Oh, here's Edgar." Herron waved his free arm. "Coo-ee, Edgar."

Edgar panted up to them. He was a powerfully built man, but he didn't have a frame suitable for running. "Mister Strangways! I heard they was releasin' you."

"Yes, they was. I've paid my debt to Society – though Society owes me some change. What may I do for you this fine morning?"

"Gemmy sent me to find you, for his clothes you borrowed t'other day."

"Ah. Yes. The waiter's togs. I think I'll have to recompense him for those. I can tell him exactly where they are – the spot is branded on my memory. But I doubt he'll want them back. Tell him to meet me at my home this evening, and I'll pay him for them in full, plus a gratuity almost as large. And one for yourself. And if he loses his job, tell him to show up and see me in my office at Strangways' sharp at nine on Monday."

In unision, Angelica and Edgar gasped, "*In your office!*"

"I've always had an office."

"When was the last time you were there sharp at nine on any morning?"

"I said I was turning over a new leaf. I'll start Monday. That'll give me a few days to cram in as much as I can of everything I mean to give up."

When Edgar was gone, Herron turned to Angelica. "Which way do we go?"

"South. Let's go from here." She indicated a nearby Underground station.

Herron opened the door for Angelica while she was still on his arm, and as she started to step inside—

—he yanked her back into the street.

"Let's hail a cab instead."

Breinigsville, PA USA
08 April 2010
235797BV00001B/11/P